A MOMENT *Forever*

CAT GARDINER

A LIBERTY SERIES NOVEL

WWII ROMANTIC DRAMA

A Moment Forever

Copyright © 2016 by Cat Gardiner
Publisher: Vanity & Pride Press
ISBN-13: 978-0-9973130-0-0

Cover Design: JD Smith Design, 2/10/2016
Editors: Sheryl Gordon, Kristi Rawley

For all visual inspiration for *A Moment Forever* visit
the **Pinterest board**. https://goo.gl/quTCoU
For **Chapter Blog**, Glossary, End Notes,
and song information visit: http://goo.gl/tIMCCd

Spotify Playlist: https://goo.gl/RwL0Cm
YouTube Playlist: https://goo.gl/yKZLCc

Dedicated to the Sisterhood of the Swan
Women who believe in soul mates, enduring love,
re-kindled love, and finding love a second time around.

Maps

Long Island, New York

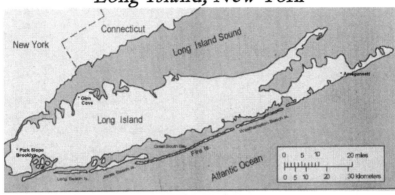

Florida

One

A String of Pearls
<u>Summer, 1992</u>

I know it looks a bit worse for the wear and needs some work, but I imagine you'll have Primrose Cottage back to her former splendor in no time," the Martel family lawyer stated from his position at the curb before 300 Bradford Road in Victorian Flatbush, Brooklyn.

Juliana Martel raised a humored, disbelieving eyebrow. The once beautiful three-story home was an absolute train wreck. "You're an optimist, Mr. Gardner."

"Four million dollars can restore a few homes, Juliana. I'll put you in touch with some contractors who are experts in historical restoration and will have it completed by the fall."

Age and neglect had taken its toll on the historied home and, unfortunately, the picturesque tree-lined neighborhood did nothing to hide the smashed flower urns, broken steps, and dirty windows. A black, wrought iron security door looked out of place, taking away from the former magnificence. The 1901 building's once peaceful Wedgwood blue color had now faded to dingy gray along with the white trim surrounding the bow windows on the second floor. The third floor looked downright spooky with its two newspaper-covered windows as though concealing the secrets of the former owner who vacated it in 1950. The saddest image of all was the sweetheart swing, hanging by a single chain on the front porch.

Standing at the curb beside the old gentleman, Juliana gazed up at her great-uncle's former residence. If it weren't for the giddy, euphoric feeling coursing through her at this moment, the hair might have stood up on her slender arms at the thought of what lurked in that attic.

"Should we go in?" she asked.

"That is why we're here, right? To get you settled."

Barely able to contain her enthusiasm, she bounced in her black converse. To say she felt awed by the residence before her was an understatement. "It's really mine, isn't it? The creepy house, the money ... the renovations?"

"All yours. Mr. Martel saw to its transfer to you alone."

"Why me? I didn't think he knew who I was."

"Trust me, he knew, and I'm positive he had his reasons for gifting you Primrose."

"Would it have gone to my father had he lived?"

"Nope. Just you."

"And my money-hungry, evil ex-mother can't get her greedy hands on it either, right?"

"That's correct. Do not worry on that account. Your great-uncle made sure that this bequest was documented after Susan's divorce from your father was finalized."

Wow. This century old home was now *hers* and hers alone. Continuing to examine the house from the curb, she thought of all the work Primrose Cottage needed. The term "fixer upper" was an understatement, but that didn't matter. She wouldn't be looking this gift horse in the mouth. The house was free and located in one of the most sought after neighborhoods in Brooklyn—and *hers* she reminded herself for the one hundredth time. The real estate market in this once affluent area was on fire and with a potential value of a million dollars, she wouldn't concern herself with the current condition. Mr. Gardner was right. Both her father and great-uncle's estates paved the way to a complete historical restoration with more money to last at least two lifetimes and six decrepit old houses.

At the recent reading of her father's will, Juliana had been surprised to learn that Primrose Cottage was given to her on her twenty-fourth birthday—four weeks earlier. She had no idea her great-uncle even knew of her existence, let alone would bequeath a house to her along with a fortune. Who knew this home had been sitting here empty for all those years?

"My great-uncle isn't going to show up some day demanding his house back, is he?"

The lawyer looked around the neighborhood. "I have no reason to believe that William Martel will be returning."

The grandniece knew only small details about her grandfather's brother. How could she know more when no one spoke of him? She was two generations removed from this man her father once mentioned had survived a German POW camp. Did she even remember what he'd said or how that had happened? No, she was never very interested in her family history, not that she had much other family to learn about. As a junior writer for *Allure* magazine, fashion and visual art were her passions. Ancestry, history and social science, not so much.

What Juliana *now* knew was that her great-uncle had been wealthy beyond belief and without question never wanted to be found because he never was. Mr. Gardner explained that on occasion, the family would receive a special birthday card or a brief note to let her grandfather know his only brother was still alive. All included the same instruction: not to sell the house, he had arranged for its conveyance. William never included a return address, and he never indicated what he was doing with his life.

What Mr. Gardner couldn't explain to her was why William had left Primrose Cottage to her without a word in the first place and, apart from morbid curiosity surrounding the specific details, she really didn't care. Although, she did wish she could thank him.

"You'll thank him for me, right?" she asked the lawyer.

His warm eyes and gentle smile met her gaze before he stammered slightly. "I, er, don't expect to hear from him."

"So he could be dead?"

"Anything is possible. He is my age, after all." He chuckled.

The petite, blonde shrugged then politely stated what any person of good upbringing would. "You're not old. In fact, you look about 50!"

She promptly turned her attention back to the house, hoping that the mystery surrounding the money, the cottage, and her great-uncle's disappearance would be forgotten. Why dwell on the unimportance of it? The man was wholly unconnected to her and her modern, day-to-day life.

Disregarding the big red "fragile" label, Juliana not-so-carefully held one of the many moving boxes from the back of her new Jeep Cherokee as she continued to bounce up and down, ready to take the walkway stairs two at a time.

A woman walking a small dog at the curb came toward them. "They say it was built by the Guggenheims as a honeymoon cottage for their daughter."

Curious, Juliana glanced over to where the stranger stood. "*The* Guggenheims, as in museum Guggenheims?"

"Yes, sad how the home fell into such a state. I never knew the previous owner."

"Neither did I." She glanced at Mr. Gardner. "But he did."

"Yes. It was once the Guggenheims. The former owner purchased the cottage from them in 1942 before leaving for the war."

In typical New York fashion, having dispensed her unsolicited information and unenthusiastic of further conversation, the woman continued on her way with both hers and the dog's business. She looked back to Gardner and Juliana, noting the moving box and reconsidered her abrupt adieu. "Welcome to Beverley Squares. Geraniums would look lovely in new flower pots."

Juliana promptly turned to the lawyer, ignoring her neighbor's passive aggression about the condition of her new home. "Well, shall we enter, Mr. Gardner?"

"Of course! I'm as curious as you are."

"Thank you for meeting me today. I really had no one to do this with. My best friend has so many responsibilities at the magazine, and Grandpa, well, you know. This is difficult for him."

"Has he said anything about your father's death?"

"Nothing. I just figured that coming here to his brother's home, might add to his grief. It's sad that they lost contact with each other."

"It is, but there is a season for everything, and just maybe, this house could be the catalyst for change."

She didn't know what he meant by that, and frankly, she couldn't see how a house could bring people together, particularly if her great-uncle was dead. "Well, thanks again."

"I'm glad to be of assistance to you."

Together they ascended the steps to the broken walkway then stepped onto the tenuous porch where she placed the moving box at her feet.

A floorboard creaked when she tried to peer through the decorative antique glass panes of the front door. The dusty curtains on the opposite side hindered her view. She took a deep breath, readying herself as though about to be carried over the threshold.

"Welcome to Primrose Cottage, your new home, Juliana Martel," the lawyer said with a smile when he handed her the key.

"Yoo hoo!" another woman waved from across the street. "You there, at Primrose Cottage. Yoo hoo! What are you doing?"

"You go ahead, Juliana. I'll attend to your inquisitive neighbor." He winked before departing down the walkway.

The key fit, the door groaned, and the cobwebs freaked her out when she entered into the dark foyer.

"Ew, ew, ew!" she screamed immediately feeling suffocated by the stale, dead air within.

Halting her dramatics, she snapped her mouth closed, standing shell shocked in wonder of her surroundings.

She gazed around feeling as though she entered into a time warp and she was a visitor from the future. With the turn of the house key, she had turned back time. Covered with thick dust and the scent of age, the furnishings and décor were that of a bygone era she knew nothing about. Up until that very second, Juliana had never given any thought to those "old timers" referred to as the Silent Generation. Primrose Cottage was a perfectly preserved, frozen narrative.

A vintage time capsule, the house had a strange appeal that might have been comforting if not for the darkness and the chill rising up her spine. It felt empty and cold, dank and musty, a place void of life and breath for forty-two years. Sadness hung in the air.

She placed the box at the foot of the staircase, then took in every detail; her wide-eyed gape traveled the length of the hallway before her. In the kitchen at the far end, she could make out a white stove, unlike any she had ever seen. It was massive and dominant yet exuded warmth and security. Three matching dishtowels, each embroidered with large, red roosters hung from the oven door.

Behind the French doors beside her was a spacious parlor. She opened the grimy glass, and her eyes fixed upon a fireplace, which still had charred wood remains on the grate; broken pieces lie scattered in the hearth. Juliana imagined it once ablaze, particularly when she noted a piece of scorched paper lying amidst the ashes beside one of the tarnished owl andirons.

A few photographs were displayed upon the mantle, their images shrouded behind an inch of soot and dirt. Across the room looked to be an antique radio and record player. She could just make out the word "Zenith" at the center of the console. Even a folded afghan lie undisturbed over the arm of the damask chair beside the cabinet. A pack of Camels sat forgotten on the end table and a half-smoked, snuffed out cigarette rested at the edge of a cut glass ashtray. Juliana imagined a thin blue trail of smoke rising from the lit end of the now extinguished existence of her great-uncle.

It was exactly how William Martel left it on that hot summer night, August 8, 1950.

Forgetting the moving box, she entered the room, strangely disregarding the drooping cobwebs hanging from the ceiling light fixture above her head and the intermittent squealing she heard behind one of the walls. She felt at once as though she intruded or trespassed on sacred ground.

Drawn like moth to flame to the four picture frames on the mantle, she crossed the room to examine the largest—a brass and black hanging stand. With the edge of her oversized sweater sleeve, Juliana wiped the dust away. Each circling smear slowly revealed the image below until finally a gorgeous, sophisticated young woman's face stared back at her. Eyes filled with laughter, long lashes, and perfectly painted lips were only small details to admire. Lush, dark waves framed her pretty face. Pearls. Juliana fell in love with the three-strand pearl choker hugging the woman's neck.

"Who are you?" she curiously asked the black and white photograph as though expecting an answer.

She picked up another vintage frame. Ornate silver surrounded the image, and again, it revealed the same woman sitting upon a park bench. Long legs crossed demurely at her ankles above white peep toe shoes. Fashionably dressed under a wide-brimmed hat, she sat waving to the camera, her radiant smile making it clear to Juliana that the woman was in love with the person taking the photograph. At the bottom of the image read in sloppy penmanship, *Lizzy—1942* in black ink.

Juliana smiled. "Hello, Lizzy. Nice to meet you."

Taking the smallest of the four into her hand, she wiped away the vestiges of over four decades, revealing the alluring brunette standing with a handsome uniformed man beside an old car. They appeared so happy, so in love. She wondered if this was her great-uncle. If it was, well then, suddenly his mystery was worth a little investigation. Suddenly, William Martel's previously disregarded obscurity had turned enigmatic and intriguing. This gorgeous, tall, soldier beside this attractive woman was worth a second look, and judging by the expression on Lizzy's face, she thought so as well.

After replacing the photograph beside the first three, Juliana noticed a Christmas greeting card, and at the edge of the mantle, a crushed service cap with its gold, spread eagle medallion rested beside another photograph. Cobwebs spanned from one to the other as though creating a connection between the two, a connection she severed with a quick swipe of her wrist over the glass and web. It revealed his military portrait. Below the image sat silver wings and a uniform patch embroidered with a stork holding a bomb instead of a baby.

"Wow. This stuff is so cool, and he was soooo handsome."

She suddenly realized that this was a shrine to the love of this couple—to this woman, Lizzy. Juliana's eyes moistened at the obvious feeling and care put into the displaying of each item and, truly, she felt an interloper in her newly acquired house.

Removing the Christmas card, she read the inscription.

December 25, 1942
My Dearest Darling,

I miss you terribly. Know that you are in my heart this Christmas and always. I love you. Please take care of yourself and come home to me soon.
Yours,
Lizzy

In the space of four minutes, her great-uncle was no longer the mysterious man she felt indifference toward. Her once morbid curiosity had now become genuine poignant interest. It didn't matter that what happened to this couple was fifty years in the past. What mattered was that something *did* happen, and she couldn't help but to feel the emotion displayed upon the mantle. She found her mind formulating a resolve—*I have to know.*

The inquisitive writer in her demanded to uncover and discover the hidden and long-forgotten truth. Oblivious to her snug fitting, drainpipe jeans, Juliana squatted before the charred remains in the fireplace and very gently picked up the scorched remnant of the letter lying in the hearth. Barely discernible, but definitely there, she read what remained upon the once elegant stationery. The letters *E.R* were embossed in a flourish at the top center of the page.

August 8, 1949
My Dearest Darling,

My hand is trembling as I write this. My heart is breaking for what I must do. My tears won't stop, yet I must .... You know that what we did ...

... I love you. I will <u>never</u> stop loving you, never. I am yours until the end of life's story.

A tear formed in Juliana's eye and trailed down her cheek as she carefully placed the letter beside Lizzy's photograph. She didn't even know the woman yet she felt the pain flowing from the slip of paper written from her heart with elegant penmanship. Her own hand resisted the urge to tremble as well.

Turning from the mantle, she once again took in the simplicity of the room and walked to the open dusty door of the record player. She was part of this room now. She was part of this *story*—*their* story—and felt compelled to see it through the eyes of her great-uncle forty-two years earlier.

"What were you listening to when you left?" Juliana asked the emptiness, so filled with tangible spirit and entity.

Picking up the 78 rpm record's paper sleeve, the word "Columbia" read back in bold letters. She noticed a black record resting upon the turntable. On a whim, she pressed the biggest button, inhaled deeply, then expelled her breath through pursed lips to dislodge the top layer of dust. She lifted the arm over, delicately lowering the needle upon the record.

As though the room suddenly cleared of its cobwebs, soot, and the foggy memories of a distant past, the record player and its Zenith emblem lit with life. Hearing the needle scratch through the powder embedded within the grooved surface, an unfamiliar voice—that of Doris Day, the sleeve had said—filled the parlor. Without realizing what she was about, Juliana sat in the armchair, took the musty-smelling afghan into her arms, and listened to the mesmerizing lyrics of "Again," sung with so much bittersweet heartbreak and love.

She glanced at the cigarettes beside her on the table, and it became clear that William had sat here, just where she did. He smoked. He listened and stared at the mantle. He remembered. He read the letter and may have even cried. Lord knows, she was tearful. Her great-uncle's presence and palpable longing filled the room.

The 1949 lyrics of yearning, reunion, and anticipation wrapped around her, taking her imagination to the significance the song must have held.

Although imagined, Juliana saw that night unfold before her eyes in the dimly lit room, where perhaps in 1950 only the light from the Zenith tuner and the dying embers of the fire had existed. Her imagination was uncannily accurate.

Having lost track of the hours that had passed in his nostalgia, William finally rose long after the song ended. The needle had remained circling endlessly upon the record in scratchy cadence, but he was oblivious to it when he walked to the fireplace where he read Lizzy's painful words once more. It was the last time he swore to himself—the last time he would think of her. His index finger brushed over the embossed initials of the woman he loved. The R—not an M—sliced and stabbed his heart again and again and again, mincing it into a million tiny pieces of barely beating flesh. There was no accurate description for the cold he felt inside. Perhaps the cold of death was most appropriate. Finally, he found the courage to toss the letter into the grate and picked up her portrait. The glass covering her smiling mouth met his lips when he said his good-bye to her memory. He turned his back on her image then turned off the record player. On his way to the front door, he grabbed the subway tokens resting on the table in the hallway and left the house—her house—for the last time.

As though walking behind his ghostly shadow, Juliana followed his footsteps into the hall. She peered up the staircase to the floor above then glanced down at the forgotten moving box lying at her feet.

Curiosity overruled all the other plans she had for the day. She slowly took the stairs one at a time and, completely oblivious to the dust, enjoyed the feel of the smooth, wooden banister below her fingers. A step creaked, but she continued until she found herself standing before the first of several doors and entered.

From below she heard the closing of the front door and Mr. Gardner calling out to her. "Juliana?"

"I'm upstairs. I'll be down in a second. Make yourself at home."

In the pretty bedroom, soft yellow walls had turned dingy and a floral satin bedspread looked never used. Upon the walnut vanity sat two photographs on either side of the sunken table. Strangely, Juliana didn't mind her new modus operandi for what she believed would be the next few weeks of discovery: she wiped the glass with her sleeve, revealing another photograph that captured Lizzy sitting on a blanket before a large hotel on the beach. Below read, "*Pink Palace, St. Pete Beach—1942.*" She looked lovely and happy and her playful spirit leaped from the image. Juliana was riveted—as riveted as she assumed William had been—captivated by this woman.

The other was the image of a beautiful white mansion situated behind large wrought iron gates. The letter *M* was forged within the intricate metalwork of the archway. A small notation in the corner of the snapshot immortalized someone's fond memory, "*May 30, 1942.*"

"What is this place and why is it so dear?" Juliana mused. "What happened on May 30, 1942?"

A singular item drew Juliana's attention away from her speculation of the black and white photograph: resting beside Lizzy's photo sat a small, royal blue velvet art deco era box.

She opened it. Nestled inside, within the pearl gray satin lining, was a cushion-cut diamond engagement ring.

"I have to know. I have to find out what happened to you."

After long minutes later of speculation, she quit the room, leaving the ring where she found it then descended the steps where Mr. Gardner stood examining a painting upon the hallway wall. His fingers traced the wooden frame, his body leaning toward the oil landscape as he fixed his eyeglass upon the bridge of his nose. At the creak of the step he said, "This is an expensive Dutch Master, Juliana. You may want to have this insured."

"I'll look into it. Hey, Mr. Gardner, do you know who Lizzy was?"

wo

Green Eyes
May 30, 1942

Affluent and opulent were two words that only touched the surface in describing Glen Cove, a small town situated on the North Shore of Long Island, New York in an area referred to as the Gold Coast.

Upon rolling hills of breathtaking vistas of the Long Island Sound, the resort locale boasted lavish mansions ranging from ostentatious castles to English country manors. It was a town where its wealthy residents were as separated and segregated as those who worked for them. Money—old blueblood, inherited wealth of Republican stock—differentiated these select denizens from every other American who survived the Crash of '29 and the depression. Names such as Vanderbilt, du Pont, and Loews lived on sprawling estates built during the Gilded Age, and now, the next generation had taken up residence within these imperious dwellings.

Far from their home in Brooklyn, two brothers, whose dear mother often called them "thick as thieves," drove up on a Saturday afternoon to the gated entrance of one of these ritzy mansions. They were about to visit the home of Mr. and Mrs. Frederick Renner for a Memorial Day lawn party.

Handsome in his Army Air Forces "green and pinks" uniform, William Martel stopped his father's 1935 Auburn Cabriolet before the towering white stone and arched wrought iron entry. He gazed up at the giant letter *M* staring back at him through the windshield while his older brother, Louie sat chuckling from behind his new Kodak's lens.

"Would you put that camera away? Do you really need a photograph of someone's grandstanding wealth?"

"Well, then drive on," Louie replied with a mischievous grin. "Don't tell me you're too chicken to hobnob with the likes of Benjamin Guggenheim and John Pratt?"

"Benjamin Guggenheim went down with the Titanic, you knucklehead."

"Whatever. You know what I meant."

Will nervously strummed his fingers against the steering wheel; the pilot gold insignia ring his parents gave him bounced up and down. "Hardly. It takes a lot more than this kind of money to intimidate me. Tell me again how you wrangled this invitation?"

Louie, the smooth-talking, charismatic charmer couldn't resist bragging to his conservative polar opposite. "I met this dish at that U.S.O Ranch Party I went to while on pass. What a honey and she's a volunteer with the American Red Cross Motor Corps."

"You're nuts! You went to Sweetwater Valley Ranch over two months ago. You mean to tell me we wasted all this gas and rubber and you might not really have an invite to this Meercrest place? We're here at this highfalutin estate, about to crash some tycoon's garden party, on the off-chance that this 'dish' remembers you?"

Louie's pearly white, shit-eating grin gave away his implication, particularly when he added, "Oh, I have *no* doubt that Miss Lillian Renner will remember me. If I do say so myself, it was quite unforgettable."

Will chuckled, shaking his head at his brother's never ending doll dizziness. "You wolf."

"Yup, and she tells me she has four single sisters, three of whom are just dying to meet a flyboy like you, which is fine by me because this devil dog is spoken for."

He adjusted his khaki service cap with meticulous pride and rightfully so. Will knew that many of those in the Marine Corps were considered the toughest men fighting this war. He was proud of his brother's enlistment and confidence.

"What's wrong with the fourth sister?"

Louie shrugged a shoulder. "Beats me. I wasn't about to ask. At the time, I had silky unmentionables on my mind."

"You're such a jarhead."

"Personally I like leatherneck, which is certainly more admired than you being called an airhead or vaporhead."

"At least I'm not a numbskull. I can't believe you're trying to fix me up. I'm leaving for Florida soon and you want me to get rationed. No way."

"Hey, you need a girl and a little I and I before you get behind one of those B-26 Widowmakers and crash and burn to death in Tampa Bay."

Will reached down and shifted the gear handle. The car slowly rolled through the open gates onto the narrow driveway. "I'll leave the intoxication and intercourse to you, Lou. I'm not looking for a girl and won't be until I return home—*if* I return home."

There. He said it. He finally admitted aloud his whole rationale for not dating—getting close meant the possible breaking of a heart. Either hers at the receiving end of a Western Union Telegram or his at the receiving end of a Dear John letter. It was bad enough he knew the B-26 bomber was considered a death sentence—but wasn't all war, in reality, a death sentence? Will didn't even want to think about what his brother was going to encounter when Louie arrived in the Pacific, let alone the possibility of not returning home.

"Better not let Mom hear you talk that way. I was joking about crashing and burning. We'll *both* return home." Louie slapped his brother's shoulder. "Now, let's focus on what's important—we have a few rich honeys to meet."

Loud honks and equally loud music from the car behind them interrupted the brothers from their banter-turned-serious talk. The incessant blaring of beep, beep combined with the swing sound of Tommy Dorsey's "Keepin' Out of Mischief Now" broke the peaceful air with its disturbing cacophony. Will looked in the rearview mirror to see the impatient noisemaker.

He noticed that the gorgeous woman in the driver's seat of a shiny, black convertible insisted on coercing the older model car out of her way with each impatient depression of the horn.

Louie turned to look out the back window. "Hot Damn! That's a convertible Lincoln Zephyr."

Obviously frustrated by the slow, uncertain speed of what she probably thought a jalopy in front of her, one of the young woman's gloved hands slammed against the horn again. The other remained gripping the steering wheel in anxious anticipation.

Beep, beep.

Will motioned with one arm out the window. "Go around," he complained with equal frustration though his eyes remained riveted on the rear view mirror at the reflection of the woman adorned in a light green headscarf and tinted eyewear. After removing his Ray-Ban aviator sunglasses, he continued staring until the Zephyr sped past the driver's side of the Cabriolet.

Taking up the entire expanse of the driveway, her luxury sports car caused Will to veer off into the ditch running parallel. He had just enough time to notice the woman's pert nose, radiant smile, and beautiful profile as she raised her arm high in the air, waving to signal her thanks for getting out of her way.

Her laugh was almost taunting when she gassed the vehicle, kicking up gravel from her tires with a burst of cloudy dust. Even over the blaring swing music, Will heard the subtle pinging of rocks against the metal of his father's car where it sat with its passenger side wheels six inches deep in mud.

The normally genteel and amiable pilot stuck his head out the window. "Thanks for burning the rubber my bomber wheels need!"

That devilish laugh of hers rang out in response.

"Holy smokes! Did you get a look at that dame? Wowza!" Louie exclaimed, obviously unconcerned that the car was now stuck. "Now, that's one high-class woman."

"Yeah, so high class she rudely ran us off the road. Her wealth obviously removes her from upholding gas and rubber ration constraints. If she keeps driving like that, her tires won't last the duration. She's not helping the war effort."

"Don't be such a hard-ass. Besides, gas ration was only put into place last week. You can't expect these people to jump to it. That attitude isn't going to win the war or get your johnson any closer to successful action either."

Will rolled his eyes and answered his brother by getting out of the car followed by a hard slam to the door. He walked to the front end of the vehicle, motioning to Louie. "C'mon, help me get the car out of this mess."

Thirty minutes later, the Cabriolet finally came to park at the *public* entrance of the estate on the opposite side of the mansion. Apparently, they had come through the *private* entrance and Will surmised it was the reason for Miss Hoity-toity's frustration. Of course, that didn't excuse her rude behavior, and he just wouldn't let that go.

The two brothers walked along the pathway, around the sixty-thousand square foot mansion, to the gardens and lawn overlooking the Long Island Sound. The salty sea air grew stronger as they stepped onto the grassy hill, taking in the panorama before them. Both men resisted their jaws slackening in awe of the massive estate where building after building was as impressive as the vista and gardens surrounding them. All of it overlooked the deep blue water where Renner's private yacht sat moored at the boat landing. Just beyond, U.S. Coast Guard Reserve patrol boats dotted the view of the water.

"Take a gander at this," Louie stated in awe followed by a whistle.

"Yeah, we're a far cry from Brooklyn."

On one side of a fountain pond, in a small section of the estate's one hundred acres, white tents billowed in the coastal breeze. Even a dance floor lay in the center of the field with lantern lights strung across it leading to a white gazebo where a band played.

Gentle strains of "I Don't Want to Set the World on Fire" traveled from the wood structure, and it seemed that many of the guests matched the slow, dragging tempo. The women of society's crème de la crème congregated on the lawn, each one wearing large hats and fashionable pale colored tea dresses. Some sat drinking tea or lemonade, as the men, clothed in summer suits, smoked or held drinks. Long tables laden with food and draped in American flag bunting sat under the tents and off to one side, a game of lawn croquet occupied some of the younger guests. The only spectators were a young woman in a high-backed, wicker wheelchair and her nurse standing at attention behind her.

Over the music, Will heard that familiar melodious—mischievous—laugh carry in the wind. It was *her*. He saw the woman in green raise her croquet mallet high in the air in victory, and it got under his skin. Irked, he looked down at his brother then his muddied trouser bottoms and once shined shoes. He clenched his jaw. "I think you and I stick out like sore thumbs—not to mention filthy ones at that. We're the only GIs here. Are you sure we're welcome?"

"Of course we're welcome. Stop being such a stick in the mud. What's really eating you—the dame in the Zephyr or your dirty uniform?"

"They're one in the same." Will sighed. "Maybe I'm more offended by the Zephyr itself. Don't these people know there's a war on?"

"Life goes on brother and when you've got it—flaunt it. Someone had to buy the few cars rolling off Ford's assembly line before they started building bombers and tanks."

Will resisted the urge to spit at the name "Ford" and it was a darn good thing he did.

Louie raised his arm, waving at a young woman. Will assumed it was the one and only Miss Lillian Renner, who approached up the small hill, wearing the standard issue American Red Cross Motor Corps blue-grey uniform. She was a looker—definitely a dish—and he now understood his brother's interest.

Blonde tresses, blue eyes, and a beaming, welcoming smile greeted them. "I knew you would come! My sister Ingrid tried to convince me otherwise, but I just knew it!"

The object of Lillian's affection was suddenly shy and uncomfortable, and Will smirked when he noticed his brother was shifting his weight from one foot to the other. It was obvious that Louie was smitten with this girl, and Will reveled in the fact that finally someone had unseated his brother's womanizing bravado.

Louie kissed Lillian's cheek. "Thank you for inviting us. It's swell to see you, Lillian. Say, this is my brother, Will. You remember I told you about the knucklehead who wants to fly bombers?"

Lillian shook his hand. "Welcome to Meercrest. I have a few sisters who will love to make your acquaintance. The youngest is an outrageous flirt, and a pilot is right up her alley, so look out."

Genuinely pleased to meet her, Will smiled broadly. "It's a pleasure to meet you, Lillian. You have a beautiful home, and the weather is just perfect to celebrate Memorial Day while enjoying the magnificence of the estate."

She chuckled sardonically. "Yes, we couldn't have arranged for better weather. Of course, mother probably found a way to pay Mother Nature for her cooperation, but the American Red Cross will be happy since I persuaded her to make this a fundraiser of sorts. Once I convinced Mother that all the women of Glen Cove and the yacht club are involved in the war effort, she suddenly had to do her bit." Lillian sniggered, enjoying every opportunity to mock her parents, their lifestyle, their opinions, and their gross affluence.

"The A.R.C. does so much for the Armed Forces. I'm glad Louie and I are here to represent two branches of service. Maybe there is someone here from the Navy?"

"Nope, just you two and boy am I happy you are. All I can say is ... keep your sense of humor. You may need it."

Again, the brothers looked to one another, curious by that comment.

"Follow me. We Renners have quite a day planned. The Robertsen family from the estate next door has called for a swim match and Father is keen on beating them this year. He's so competitive—actually all us Renners are competitive, but he's rapacious."

"Robertsen? As in Robertsen Aviation?" Louie asked.

"Yes, that Robertsen family. Our childhood friends Greta and Susanna, as well as Susanna's husband, will be swimming against my father and sisters, Ingrid and Lizzy. The Princesses Luxembourg are here as well, but they won't be joining in the match. It's reserved for the ongoing battle between our families: railroad vs. aviation. G-d help us all." Lillian rolled her eyes dramatically.

Will raised his eyebrows when his brother looked his way, exchanging that silent communication they did so well. They both felt out of their league even though they grew up within what most people considered the "nouveau riche," but *this* world—this level of affluence—was wholly unfamiliar to them. This class of gentry was their father's clientele. F. Scott Fitzgerald clearly understood the denizens of this upper crust of society that he wrote about in *The Great Gatsby*.

Unlike the affluence within the Renner circle, the Martel money was never flaunted and never spent frivolously. Moreover, it was earned and accumulated as the result of their parents' and aunt's hard work. They lived unassuming lives in Park Slope, Brooklyn, an area also referred to by Brooklynites as the Gold Coast. It was there that the Martels had survived the depression because the European interests of their family's business had flourished. Now with the outbreak of war—it was the reverse. Business was booming in America. Everyone was back to work with money to burn for luxuries not placed on the ration.

With each step down the grassy knoll, Will felt more and more out of place. Discomforted when he noticed a frown on the countenance of one particular man, insecurity caused him to straighten his uniform's tie but then he figured it was the mud on his trousers causing the disapproval. Lillian continued to chat incessantly, clearly excited by Louie's arrival. She certainly was a talker and made no bones about conveying her patriotism and commitment to the war effort.

That torturing laugh of the hotrod hellion woman grew louder, assaulting Will like a tease. He had to admit it was enchanting and would have been quite infectious if he didn't feel the need to chew her out for running him off the road. He fought the curiosity to look in her direction, afraid of exhibiting uncouth manners by shooting daggers into her with the severe mien upon his face.

"Lizzy, Ingrid! Come meet the Marine I told you about," Lillian shouted across the lawn with a wave of her arm.

"Ingrid is the blonde on the left and Lizzy is the brunette. My other sisters are beside Nurse Keller. Kitty is the one in the wheelchair and the khaki wacky one is Gloria."

Will spared a quick glance at the two other sisters, but his attention fixed upon the woman in green when she dropped her croquet mallet and approached. This "Lizzy" was the Zephyr's driver, Lillian's sister and Meercrest was her home.

He fully turned to watch her draw near. Her cascading chestnut curls, refusing to remain pinned in place, seemed to have a mind of their own. They blew in the gentle breeze along with the flowing, short sleeves of her floral print dress, its shade of green billowing like a metaphor of her affluence. He was sure that smile of hers stopped his heart, but he willed it back to life when he reminded himself that Miss Hoity-toity was responsible for his soiled uniform. His resuscitation failed to work as that vibrant red kisser of hers neared. Suddenly, whatever annoyance he felt toward this Lizzy had dissipated in the coastal breeze.

There was only one thing he could do—stare, and stare he did.

She laughed, and he knew he must look like a complete fool standing shell-shocked and spellbound by her beauty, wondering if she was laughing at him.

In stark captivating contrast, Lizzy walked between two blondes—her sister Ingrid and a man their age. It seemed everywhere Will looked, the elite fair-haired, fair-skinned *Herrenvolk* surrounded him, as though he and Louie had just stepped into a mini-Aryan world that only Hitler could appreciate. Even the young woman in the wheelchair, as well as her nurse, was blonde. Of course, all except for the servants who wore and were black, but in society such as this, the contrast only caused them to blend into the unnoticed, unseen background, dismissed because of their race.

Will chastised himself for making the Aryan race analogy, but the military's training movies had become ingrained and second nature in his thinking.

Keenly aware of Will's directed stare at Lizzy, Lillian leaned into Louie, butting shoulders with her Marine. "See, didn't I tell you?"

Will heard the whisper but begrudgingly remained captivated by the vision approaching him as though floating on Zephyr's wings. Her laughter and buoyant spirit carried her in his direction. He didn't know what made her so light and gay, but damn him, he wanted to find out.

Ingrid, looking lovely and sophisticated with rolled hair and pale colored lips, greeted the soldiers coolly; a nod of her head was the most she was willing to offer. Her haughty, disinterested demeanor made them feel neither welcome nor respected for the uniforms they wore. Her missing requisite victory red lipstick made the passive statement. Even her eyes failed to convey any warmth or zest for life. Her pert nose, the exact nose as Lizzy and Lillian's was held high in the air, literally and figuratively. No three sisters could have been more opposite in spirit.

"Welcome to Meercrest. I'm Ingrid Renner. My sister mentioned you would be attending our little lawn party. I'm sure she's very pleased you're here."

The woman's voice of affluent air wasn't melodious and certainly not pleasant. Delivered through tight lips and a thrust jaw, her accent sounded dry and flat, lacking inflection or humor when she greeted them.

Ingrid gave a pointed look to Lillian before her glance traveled down to the muddy trousers. "Why, you're positively inches deep in mud! Whatever happened?"

Will's eyes met and fixed upon Lizzy's. He watched as her perfect, cherry bomb lips twitched into an impish smirk when he said, "My brother and I had a slight car accident when we were run off the road by some wise guy on our way here. A real *pistol* behind the wheel."

"Maybe you were in the *pistol's* way and driving like a fuddy duddy. Was that old timer rumble seat slowing you down, *Flyboy?*" she retorted.

"Maybe I was protecting the rubber on my tires and didn't expect to be run off the road by such an inconsiderate driver." He raised an eyebrow. *Damn, she's perfection.*

Lizzy looked directly at him with confidence but sincere contrition. "I'm sorry about that. I was running late, and any minute longer my father would have been angry. That would have been a sight to see—one I was not eager to be on the receiving end of."

"Hmm ... then it would seem you *were* misbehaving after all. Tommy Dorsey was a fabulous ruse."

The playful laughter in her voice affected him when she said, "Ha! Me? Misbehave? Never."

For a minuscule second, Will wondered if she was flirting with him.

She smiled then held out her hand for a shake. "I'm Lizzy, by the way."

Warm hands met, and he couldn't deny the attraction when his sweaty palms caressed her soft, self-assured, firm handshake.

"Nice to meet you, Lizzy. I'm William Martel and this is my brother, Louis."

Louie shook her hand. "Please call me Louie."

"Hi, Louie." She greeted enthusiastically then turned back to face his brother. "And what can I call you? Certainly not something so formal as *William*? How about Billy or Willy?"

"You can call me Lieutenant Martel if that's more to your liking." *Perhaps Pistol may be more appropriate than Lizzy.*

"Well, you leave me no choice, Lieutenant. William it is." She playfully smirked. *I'll just settle for Fuddy Duddy.*

The young man who Ingrid had previously hooked arms with eagerly stepped forward, bearing a welcoming smile. He wasn't in uniform and, given the fact that it was six months after Pearl Harbor, that was surprising since there had been an incredible surge in enlistment in one branch of service or another. Instead, he wore white slacks and a Basque sweater, both matching the brilliance of his countenance and happy manner. The brothers simultaneously wondered if his family's wealth and War Department connections arranged for his non-service.

"I'm John Robertsen. It's swell to make your acquaintance. Lillian told me a lot about you, Louie. Lucky devil you are to be headed into the fight." He eagerly shook both men's hands. "What about you, William, are you headed to the Pacific or Europe?"

"I wish I could tell you, but for the moment I'm just headed off to B-26 bomber training in Florida."

"Uncle Sam needs men like you too, John," Louie said.

"Unfortunately, he didn't want me. They declared me 4F for no particular reason other than a little shortness of breath. It's certainly not enough to keep me from fighting. I'll be involved in this war one way or another."

"Don't be foolish, John. I'm sure your father went through great lengths to keep you out of this silly war," Ingrid stated.

"That's not true, Ingrid. Besides, it would have been for naught because I'm thinking of working at the plant out in Farmingdale where we build the P-47 Thunderbolts."

Ingrid gasped. "You can't be serious, darling!"

"Well ... maybe ... or I'll become an Air-Raid Warden."

Lizzy reached out, thoughtfully touching John's forearm. "I love the idea of you volunteering as an Air-Raid Warden. You would be especially valuable to Long Island. News of that U-boat torpedoing off the shore in January scared the daylights out of me and everyone else on the North Shore. That was too close for comfort in my opinion. Some say there are Nazi saboteurs everywhere!"

Louie pulled at his collar with his index finger. "Gee, I'm sorry about the classification. Look, even Frank Sinatra is 4F, and he's got dames falling at his feet, so don't sweat it. Lizzy's correct, there's a lot you can do on the home front. I know pilots like Will would appreciate your work in the factory."

Will nodded politely in agreement as the discussion continued, but he was oblivious to most of it, particularly the fact that Ingrid's interest had wandered to two older men standing across the lawn, two men who stood watching the assembled group of new acquaintances.

All Will noticed was the way Lizzy's pinky finger continually tucked a stray curl behind her ear every time it dislodged in the breeze. He grew fascinated by that unconscious motion as well as the joyful expression in her eyes as she listened attentively to the conversation. That sparkle of effervescence held him captive—a prisoner of her blithe spirit.

He resisted the urge to scoff at his previous words of not wanting to meet a girl because this girl, Lizzy the pistol, had a magical air about her. He was intrigued by her and thought very briefly that he just might be willing to risk heartbreak. Furthermore, she just might be strong enough to survive the dreaded War Department telegram. But, he knew she would give him the brush off if he tried to talk to her. A high-class dish like Lizzy Renner wouldn't be interested in the son of a merchant.

Three

Mr. Five by Five
May 30, 1942

F rom inside the pool house, Lizzy heard her father's latest boast through the white louvered dressing room door.

"It's Olympic-sized! Largest in the area and even larger than the pool we have in the bathing casino!" Frederick Renner declared with bombastic pride of the newly dug, outdoor swimming pool. He stood poolside, arms akimbo, with his hands resting upon his chubby hips and his thin, grey mustache twitching as he snickered. "Even larger than yours, Robertsen!"

"It might be bigger, Renner, but that doesn't mean your children will be victorious today!" Herbert Robertsen slapped his son-in-law, Lionel Hearst's shoulder. "Like this war, it's the power in the air that's going to win. The only purpose your tired railroad serves is troop transport. Big deal, so rail travel has gotten a second wind."

"Second wind? Second wind? You underestimate our strength. Railroads built this nation!"

"And flight will take it into the future!"

"Balderdash. We're transporting supplies, machinery and don't forget coal, Robertsen ... without the railroad your planes and the men who fly them aren't going anywhere. This war is the best damned thing to happen to the railroad. Don't be so sure about winning today or even this war for that matter. Renners are fueled by superiority!"

Mocking his tormentor's schoolyard style bravado, Robertsen responded with a lip flapping raspberry.

Being a braggart was something those in Renner's circle accepted about the verbose financier of FHR Worldwide Investments. His hospitality and contrived friendliness toward those neophyte attendees made them feel important, and he knew that a coveted invitation to his home falsely cemented their social climbing aspirations. He was, after all, one of the top five wealthiest men on the Gold Coast and an invitation to Meercrest represented acceptance. It was as though these newcomers imagined they were being invited into the inner sanctum of Yale's Skull and Bones secret society, that Meercrest was "The Tomb," and they were now "Bonesmen." That was hardly the case even if Renner and many others in their elite society were, in private actuality, members. Ultimately, what Renner wanted was to part these social climbers from their newfound wealth.

Although she loved him dearly, Lizzy hated this aspect of her father's personality. She never approved of his grandstanding, but like most facets of his disposition, she rationalized them away. His self-importance was considered pride in Renner achievements born out of his own father's rise as a railroad magnate. Frederick H. Renner insisted on remaining at Meercrest even when others were vacating the opulent, over-sized mansions. Lizzy admired her father's commitment to secure the Renner legacy and heritage, believing it to be the means of promoting his daughters to the best suitors as well as providing for Kitty's polio-stricken future. All but one of his five daughters believed his intentions were always the best, even if there was no true need to tell everyone that the Jamaican palms in the tropical house set him back sixty thousand dollars or that his 147 foot yacht, the *Odin*, sleeps 10.

Not everyone from the Robertsen and Renner families were nearby for the anticipated swimming competition. Lizzy's mother, Frances, remained with several guests on the lawn, discussing the latest events printed within the *Gold Coast Social Diary*. Who married who, and whom her daughters should marry. Who, due to the war, had closed up their winter retreat homes in Florida and worse yet—who had enlisted or been drafted. It was just as well that she remain at a comfortable distance, blissfully ensconced with her Gordon's martini, getting soused in the tea gazebo.

Lizzy breathed a faint sigh of relief, thinking the less her mother exposed herself to the Martel brothers, the better. Checking the fit of her blue and yellow one-piece swimsuit in the mirror, she engaged her reflected image with exasperated humor, imitating Frances's high-pitched childlike voice.

"And my Ingrid will marry John, of course, and poor Kitty will remain a spinster with those withered legs of hers. *And* Elizabeth, I just don't know what to do about that girl. Fair hair is so much more becoming, so much more suited to families of our stature and bloodline."

Her mother's opinion of her didn't matter, but her opinion of Kitty mattered a great deal to Lizzy. She, of all her sisters, was most beloved to her.

She walked through the Palladian doors into the beating sun, sensing almost every male head and too many eyes turning in her direction. She palpably felt two soldiers, a childhood friend, and her father's employee staring down her trim form—in spite of her atypical dark hair. A year ago, she might have delighted in the overt attention of several suitors, but today it strangely unnerved her—all except the stares from one—the dreamboat in the Army Air Forces uniform.

Following Ingrid's elaborate debutante ball of 1938, Lizzy's debut presentation to society at eighteen in 1940 at the Waldorf Astoria was of equal extravagance. And like Ingrid, the requisite following year to "marry well" had passed with all the various social obligations failing to produce a suitable suitor. In Lizzy's opinion, not a single man vying to win her hand was deemed exciting or intriguing enough to tempt her, and in her father's opinion, none were of the right "quality."

Born ten months after her, Lillian's debut had also passed, but she refused a coming out ball to begin with, not even a small tea dance. In her altruistic sister's opinion, the whole notion of being a debutante and having an extravagant ball analyzed and touted in the *New York Times* and the *Diary* while people were starving in Greece and Russia was repulsive. Next year would technically have been Kitty's coming out, but sadly their mother decided that girls with polio would never find a husband, nor warrant being presented to society, so why spend the money. Nineteen forty-five and the lavish expense of a ball for the youngest daughter Gloria loomed ahead, but Lillian cautioned that if the United States yet remained at war, then more and more things would be put on the ration even for those with wealth. Most likely a small tea would be more suitable. Mother's reply was ridiculing laughter. She could and would have anything she wanted and no local ration board was going to contradict that. Pfft, points and ceiling prices!

The platinum blonde siren, sunning on the diving board, sat up and waved hello in Lizzy's direction. "Yoo hoo. Lizzy, over here."

She prepared herself for Greta Robertsen and her new word, *"beguiling,"* sure to be inserted into every sentence spoken. "Oh, what a darling swimsuit. That floral print is simply beguiling. Wherever did you find it?"

As much as Lizzy had determined to go sit beside William, John, Lillian, and Louie, who seemed to be having a good time, it was obvious that Greta, who never talked with her, had ulterior motives, and the wicked creature in Lizzy couldn't resist the opportunity to toy with her. She ignored Greta's inquiry about the swimsuit because she had seen it at least four times prior and knew it was just a ploy to get her to come over.

"Hi, Greta. I didn't think you would attend the party. Johnny said you were out boating with Dickie Phipps."

"Forget Dickie. He's business, dahling. Robertsen Aviation needs his father's connection to steel and U.S Steel needs our airplanes. We're planning to announce an engagement shortly. Now, who is that GI Joe sitting beside my brother? The tall one with that beguiling wave to his hair and let's not overlook those impressive pilot wings. A girl could get lost in those strong arms."

Lizzy didn't need to look. She knew to whom her arch nemesis referred, but she turned anyway, especially upon hearing Flyboy's deep laughter at something John said. She'd embrace any and all opportunities to observe the dimples and cleft chin on the unexpected six foot two, distraction who showed up at her mother's fundraiser. Earlier, Lizzy had admired how his smile and playful teasing were delightfully expressed in his chestnut, bedroom eyes. *For once, Greta is right. Lieutenant Martel is beguiling.*

Turning to gaze at the object of Greta's inquiry, she noticed how Gloria preened as she sashayed up to William. It surprisingly affected Lizzy to witness how he graciously tolerated their unfolding conversation as well as her sister's playful donning of his service cap. While she wouldn't admit to outright jealousy, she did feel somewhat competitive toward gaining his attention ... away from her least favorite sister.

At only sixteen, Gloria acted as if she had already come out. Apparently, Miss Chapin's private school in Manhattan was having a difficult time curtailing the adolescent's salacious behavior.

Lizzy hadn't realized that she mused long enough for Greta to notice.

"Don't tell me you're interested in him, too? Who is he, dahling? He's just beguiling."

Yes he is. "Oh, him? You know I don't go with 'uniforms'. He's just one of Lillian's friends, definitely not my style nor wealthy enough to tempt me and positively not *your* type. He and his brother are from Brooklyn."

Greta's disdain-filled repeat of "Brooklyn!" drew unnoticed attention.

Lizzy grinned mischievously. "Yes, and I think their father works as a shoe shine in Grand Central Terminal, and his mother sells fruit from a push cart on Canal Street. Maybe she's a fish monger ... I can't remember ... Oh, and they're Catholics, too."

She covered the devious smile upon her lips with her fingers.

Reacting and sounding more and more like her best friend Ingrid, Greta gasped. "And your father let them pollute the shades of Meercrest? Your sister, Lillian, with her unorthodox behavior and undesirably common acquaintances is an embarrassment to the *Social Register*. Next she'll be consorting with Jews."

Lizzy knit her brows. "Jews? There's nothing wrong with Jews. You're nuts, Greta! I have associated with them on a few occasions. When I visited with the de Rothschilds in Paris, I found them to be perfectly acceptable people. Their home, Château de Ferrières was larger than yours *and* they served caviar, pate, and canapés. You never serve that." Lizzy shook her head, laughed, and rose from the edge of the diving board. She glanced over at Ingrid who sat under an oversized white hat below an umbrella. G-d forbid her lily-white complexion tanned.

The distasteful curl to her sister's pale lips accentuated the cold, deadly venom of her words as Lizzy approached. Ingrid held her cigarette aloft with an air of superiority, punctuating her statement. "She's right you know. They use the blood of Christian children for rituals. I even hear they have horns hidden under their wigs and hats."

Lizzy jutted her chin. "You're wacky, too! Bethsabee de Rothschild didn't wear a wig and certainly didn't have horns nor did she drain my blood when I was invited to tea with her during my grand tour two years ago." She rolled her eyes. "She's a cultured patron of the arts, Ingrid. You should have seen the Rembrandt and Cézanne artwork, and when Esther Frazier recommended a séance, Bethsabee was positively aghast at the idea. Rituals? Please don't make me laugh at the absurdity."

Ingrid shrugged one shoulder while looking at her fingernails. "The French Jews must be different from the German ones, but in my book the de Rothschilds are no different from the Guggenheims—Jews are Jews. You'd have to live under a rock not to see how they conduct business, selling cheap goods, undermining honest German merchants and ultimately affecting the German worker through inferior wages."

"Ingrid, you never even met Bethsabee, and this is Glen Cove not the *Fatherland* for Heaven's sake. Even though grandfather was born in Munich, I hardly feel affected or concerned by the plight of the German factory worker. What you say is completely untrue. You have been spending too much time listening to Father's lawyer, that creep, George Gebhardt."

Ingrid leaned back onto the chaise and closed her eyes. "You're so naïve, Lizzy. One day, you'll wake up from your sheltered party life and your eyes will open with a shock. Your world won't be so happy when the *Juden scheiss* take over everything our family has worked for and you're thrown into the hedgerow, forced to live in the servant's cottage with Mrs. Davis." She opened her eyes and laughed to see her sister's annoyed expression. "Wouldn't that be a conundrum—living with a Negro over a Jew? Both *Unzuverlässige Elemente*."

"You *know* I don't understand the German language, but judging from your tone, I don't think I want to. You really need to get over yourself and these vulgar opinions of ..."

Renner clapped his hands, breaking up the sisters' difference of opinion when he emerged from the pool house, wearing his ill-fitting swim trunks. Ill-fitting because even Lizzy had to admit, no man his size or age should be caught dead wearing a white swimsuit, but he was king of his castle and he could do and say whatever he wanted.

"Teams, take your places," he ordered, ready to railroad over Robertsen's inferior warbirds.

The afternoon's swim match represented titan against titan—two men whose combined net worth rivaled that of the Rothschild family's worldwide assets. Like their daughters, Lizzy and Greta, Renner and Robertsen were amicable enemies. Their estates shared an eastern property line; what separated their estates was not only the stone wall built in 1882, but also the fact that the Robertsens' wealth was not inherited. Their considerable assets were amassed rather recently, the result of honest-to-goodness hard work through the fortunate growth of the aviation business. Everything Robertsen represented, apart from his politics, annoyed Renner and with President Roosevelt's slogan "Arsenal for Democracy" on the heels of 1941's passage of the "Lend-Lease Act," the Robertsen fortune was growing right before Renner's blue-blood eyes.

A lifelong affliction of not-so insignificant asthma was a carefully guarded Robertsen family secret that kept John poolside beside Louie and Will rather than competing in the race.

Ingrid, Lizzy, Gloria, and Renner stood at the edge of the pool alternated by Robertsen, Greta, Susanna, and Hearst. The women slid their white bathing caps over their heads, a soon-to-be luxury item they were oblivious to, since the war effort had now put a moratorium on rubber. With a snap of the edge, elastic met skin, concealing their intricate hairstyles and Lizzy's obvious difference as the only dark-haired participant of the eight.

The high, hot sun wasn't the only thing warming her skin; she looked up to find William's eyes on her. When their eyes met, she smiled. He returned the gesture with his own, complete with a dimple that made her heart flutter.

Like everyone standing on the edge of the pool with their toes hanging off, Lizzy took a deep breath, readying herself for the race. She bent, anticipating her father's friend Gebhardt and his shout of "go!" In that brief moment of waiting, she was sad to see William rise from his seat and turn his back on her. He was no longer watching, and she felt a stab of disappointment at not being able to impress him with her athleticism. That was until she observed him pour a glass of lemonade and bring it to her sister Kitty sitting in the shade of the pool house's awning.

That was all she needed to see. She grinned just as Gebhardt shouted, and she pushed off the edge of the pool.

****

The martini sloshed from the rim of Frances Renner's glass when she held it high to make a toast to her husband at the other side of the opulently decorated dinner table. Her drunken baby-like voice carried across the evening air at dusk as they dined alfresco under the open tent.

"To Frederick for his recent acquishition of the Edgar Degasssh ballet danshers now hanging in the *hiccup* library. I love to dansh and would have be a great profishient worthy of a portrait, too!"

Gloria giggled at her mother's repetitive hiccups interrupting her slurred string of words. Renner's steel blue eyes bore into his drunken wife's amber ones, sparkling more from the alcohol than the lanterns swinging above their heads or the two towering candelabras between the husband and wife.

"How ever did you accomplish it, Renner?" Robertsen asked.

"Connections that even you don't have Robertsen."

"Yes, I imagine a man of your age has acquired a great many connections throughout the years."

"Age has nothing to do with it, my friend. It's experience, knowledge and a respect brought about by two generations of dealing with men of my societal circle. Something your millions have yet to attain in your relatively short time living on the Gold Coast. We have built a legacy whereas you are still a fledgling."

From across the table, Will watched as a placid smile spread across George Gebhardt's lips. He obviously enjoyed the grandstanding and animosity between the neighbors. The man got under his skin. Each time he lifted his fork to those sneering lips of his, he couldn't dismiss his growing dislike.

He glanced at Lizzy sitting beside Gebhardt, and noted how she watched the man from the corner of her eye. If his elbow crossed the space separating their table settings, she inched closer to John on her other side. However, never once did she act dismayed or affected by his obvious attempts. Gebhardt's efforts to touch her further rankled Will as he surprisingly felt attuned to her discomfort in spite of her playing it off with grace.

To some measure, Will could understand Gebhardt's subtle trespasses into Lizzy's personal space. She was, in fact, an alluring woman, and he would have no doubt found himself tempted to do the same thing if seated beside her. Her cinnamon colored, silk dinner dress complemented her dark curls and captivating, light-green eyes perfectly. The delightful lilt to her voice and playful manner was enough to drive any hot-blooded man crazy, and he could currently attest to that acutely. She was driving him dizzy.

The corner of Will's mouth twitched in a thoughtful smile when he looked across the table at her beautiful upturned face while she chewed the roast duckling. Every slow, deliberate movement of her jaw spellbound him and, at that moment, he was glad he allowed Louie's insistence to stay for dinner.

Following the swimming match, Will was determined to leave for home. Convinced that there was nothing or no one for him at Meercrest, he had pulled Louie aside and begged him to leave. He had overheard the poolside conversation between the sisters and determined that in addition to this high society affluence, hobnobbing with an anti-Semitic family wasn't where he wanted to spend his day. However, Louie refused to leave, and, well, since he was departing in three days for Norfork, how could Will object to his brother's pleas? He saw the way Louie flirted and hung on every word of Lillian's and that lightened his heart considerably.

Lillian was obviously not of the same ilk as Ingrid and now faced with the intoxicating, spirited cookie before him, he wondered what sort of girl Lizzy was at her core. What did she believe? What were her ideals and values? Was she truly ignorant about how many in the world negatively viewed Jews and others?

She caught Will's stare and playfully asked, "Are you not enjoying your meal, Lieutenant? You haven't touched your duck."

"I'm enjoying it very much. Thank you. I find my attention diverted, though."

"Hmm ... I hope toward something more to your liking." Another playful smirk appeared on those kissable lips of hers, then Lizzy popped a piece of boiled potato into her mouth.

Will looked down at his dinner plate, wondering if she could see the smile upon his face. He couldn't help it until his brother kneed him under the table, which startled him from the most pleasant thought of devouring her sugar sweet lips instead of the bland duck.

He glanced up, his gaze settling on his host, their eyes locked. A barely perceptible sneer crossed Renner's mouth, along with a cold look in his eyes.

A chill ran up Will's spine. He looked to Gloria sitting beside him, her chin resting in her palm, elbow on the table as she stared at him unabashedly.

No, this world—these people—and Miss Elizabeth Renner were only playing with him. Most likely, this society dame was just a terrible flirt like her sister, Gloria.

The rivalry between Robertsen and Renner continued to heat up at the end of the table. As expected by almost everyone, the competition hadn't ended poolside with the Renner victory. In fact, it seemed to grow and now had rolled into business cock fighting until Frances interrupted the twenty-five guests, some of whom were vastly entertained by the cordial duel of arguments and insults parried with backhanded compliments.

"So tell me, Shargeant, what type of name is Martel? *hiccup* Is it in the Shoshial Registrrr?"

"I'm a Corporal, ma'am." Louie replied. "I'm sorry, I don't understand what you mean by *type*."

Will placed his fork at the edge of his dinner plate and wiped his lips with the linen napkin. "Its origins are French, Mrs. Renner. My grandfather came to America through Castle Garden in the 1880's."

"Lizshy went to France! Didn't you, Lizshy?"

"Yes, Mother." She looked at Will and Louie to elaborate. "I went on grand tour in March of '40 just following my debut. We toured Paris, Bavaria, and London, but I never had the chance to see Italy. I regret never visiting the Sistine Chapel in Rome or skimming Venice's Grand Canal in a gondola, but after the war, I can always go back to Europe."

"That sounds like it was quite an ambitious, exciting itinerary," Louie stated.

"Oh, it was! Father felt that those countries would be good to see before the economic growth and influence of the new Germany changed them in the future." She laughed as did several others, but Louie and Will didn't.

"I'd say they changed it," Will replied coldly.

Renner raised his arm to garner everyone's attention. "You are correct, young man." He looked so authoritative and refined wearing his white dinner jacket. "One cannot deny the transformation of Germany under the Third Reich. The Great War decimated my father's homeland, breaking it apart, reparations that plunged them into poverty, unemployment, and hyperinflation of their currency. Now, they are experiencing prosperity and a sense of nationality like never before. It was a natural choice—Bolshevism or National Socialism. The people spoke overwhelmingly."

His continually raised arm in punctuation of his points looked odd to Will. "So you are saying you believe in National Socialism, sir?"

Louie elbowed his brother in the ribs when he posed the question.

"What I am saying is that I believe in Germany's strength and right to restore itself back to the nation it once was. Give back to the people a country they can be proud of, and America should keep out of it. There is no need for us to be involved in this war. Lindbergh has the right of it. 'We can have peace and security only so long as we band together to preserve that most priceless possession, our inheritance of European blood'."

"And what of the rights of its *European* citizens who do not meet the Führer's ideal? Do you think they are proud of what National Socialism is denying them under this *new* Germany?" Will took a sip of wine hoping to calm his rapid heartbeat while waiting for Renner's reply. He noted how his host's face grew red and his head shook slightly but how his smile never wavered.

"If you mean those who ally themselves with the ideals of Bolshevism, then there is no place for them in Germany. Bolshevism is against expansion and private property and dangerous to national solidarity."

Will clenched his jaw as Renner spoke.

The silence at the table was deafening. Half the guests found themselves in agreement with Renner and a handful in mute accord with the officer making a brave, challenging argument to his host.

The Army pilot was ready to throw his napkin in disgust on the table and slide back his chair to depart but the subtle gesture of his brother's clasping hand placed upon his forearm calmed his reaction. Instead, Will's reply was respectful and democratic.

"I respect that your views on Communism are valid, Mr. Renner, but what of those citizens subject to pogroms and to the Nuremberg Laws? Those whom Nazi Germany falsely accuses of the spread of Communism. Even Lindbergh acknowledged that Hitler is a fanatic, and now that the America First Committee is dissolved, he supports our involvement in the war. Surely, as a man whose family has helped to build the framework of

America, you must see that National Socialism denies democracy, liberty, human rights ... even capitalism. Do you think the people of Germany or the other nations he bullied into treaty are proud of Hitler's plans for those *particular* citizens who find themselves victims of National Socialism's radical doctrine?"

"You speak of things I know nothing about, things that have been falsely reported and are hyperbole. I am a businessman, Lieutenant, and apart from the lucrative business of war, I see that Germany acts in its own best interest. Who are we to keep them from their expansion? Every nation, like America, has their own destiny, and we should not police them. This president has been influenced by those *particular* citizens to enter this war on their behalf."

Before Will could reply to the boldfaced lie, because surely everyone knew that even New York City's Mayor LaGuardia had never ceased in his encouragement for the president to do something on behalf of the populace Renner referred to, Lizzy came to his rescue.

She rubbed the back of her neck. Her eyes darted between Lillian and their mother already properly soused at the end of the table and raising her glass in agreement with her husband's regurgitation of the America First Committee's former position on war. Embarrassed by it all, Lizzy then noticed the sardonic aspect to Ingrid's lips, which caused her to interject quickly, "And surely, there is a difference between Germany and Nazism, right? Isn't that what German-Americans here have been stating for years?"

Admittedly, she knew almost nothing of importance on the topic at hand and felt painfully inadequate before this intelligent, honorable man who was a guest in their home. Almost pleadingly, she looked to her father, begging him to end the inflammatory conversation.

He did so, dismissing both her and William when he looked to his left to strike up a conversation with Greta Robertsen whose lips currently wrapped around the end of a long, ebony cigarette holder.

Lillian rose from her chair, nearly knocking it over, and shuffled to the gazebo as quickly as her utilitarian shoes could move her. Within seconds, the band began to play "Moonlight Serenade," signaling to the servants to begin clearing the dishes and an end to conversation about war, Nazis, and National Socialism.

Gebhardt turned to face Lizzy. "Would you care to dance, Miss Renner?"

Before she could answer, Will promptly interrupted, "Forgive me, but Miss Renner has promised this dance to me."

She faltered at first then beamed that radiant smile of hers. "Yes, that's right Mr. Gebhardt. I'm sorry, but the Lieutenant here has promised to show me what a ducky shincracker he is."

Will was thankful dinner had ended because surely he had lost his appetite. No amount of roast duckling was going to appeal to him after that conversation with a man he came to determine was a Nazi sympathizer. The distraction of this attractive woman in his arms or a stiff drink (and he didn't imbibe) were the only welcome remedies to abate the bile rising in his throat.

He walked around the table then held back Lizzy's chair, escorting her to the small dance floor illuminated by soon-to-be extinguished white lights draped overhead. Darkness was falling fast as the sun faded behind them and, within an hour of sunset, the blackout along the coast would be enforced.

He took Lizzy into his arms, guiding her across the floor with soft, smooth Fox Trot glides. Their bodies fit perfectly when they rocked to the gentle swaying rhythm. Will breathed in the orange and jasmine bouquet of her perfume and closed his eyes to its pleasurable assault upon his senses. *Yes, much better.* She smelled as delicious as she looked and felt, causing him to think about his other senses, the sound of her laughter and its tickle to his ears, the allure of what her lips would taste like against his—the sweetness of her kiss, her pink tongue playing with his. He nearly groaned at the thought of what kissing her would feel like.

Lizzy gave a slight squeeze to his shoulder. "Thank you for coming to my rescue. I'm not very keen on Mr. Gebhardt and the thought of dancing with him gives me the willies."

"You came to my rescue, as well."

A gentle turn under his arm, sending Lizzy away from him, kept her from replying.

With elegant grace and the sway of her silk skirt, she seemed to float back into their close dance frame. "You're a lovely dancer, Miss Renner."

"Miss Chapin's school—both dancing and the school were the bane of my formative years. I'm more inclined to sports than dancing, but Mother was insistent on making an impression at my debut."

"Oh, I wouldn't say you lack natural ability. I think you're the perfect dance partner." *For me.*

"Thank you but had you watched the swim match, you might have a different opinion of my proficiencies and what my natural abilities are, Lieutenant."

"You seem disappointed that I didn't admire your form." He smiled in playful banter, pulling her closer to him and reveling in the feel of her small waist below his fingers.

"On the contrary, I would rather your attention be to Kitty whenever possible. I greatly appreciate your concern for her, and I'm sure she thought your conversation a welcome diversion. Kitty's confinement to her wheelchair these past four years has been a challenge to her. I know it kills her to see us participating in things she used to love to do. She and I are the competitive tomboys of the family and well, her sitting on the sidelines when it comes to swimming or croquet is very hard."

"There are many things that she can do, in spite of the chair."

"You are right! And she does. Much to my mother's abhorrence, she is learning archery from the chair."

"That's impressive and shows a strong determination to move beyond the incapacitating label of 'crippled' that everyone seems to dole out with no thought. Prejudice can be quite oppressive in itself, but Kitty, with her chin held high, seems to rise above the snide comments made by that *un*beguiling Greta Robertsen and your youngest sister Gloria."

"Yes, they are very cruel to her, and she's such a darling, bearing it all with a smile through her hurt."

"If you don't mind me asking, what is it that afflicts your sister?"

"Poliomyelitis."

Will turned Lizzy again, and she floated back into his arms as though the most natural thing. "I thought so, given her leg braces, but I wasn't sure."

"She never complains though."

"Not only is Kitty a sweet girl, but I understood her to be extremely intelligent and certainly protective of you." Will chuckled. "She thinks you drive too fast—too reckless."

"Ha! It seems to me you two are in cahoots, and you don't even know me, sir."

There it was, that humor of hers again reaching into him, eliciting a continuance of the repartee she clearly enjoyed.

"Maybe, but Kitty also thinks that you and I should be sweethearts."

Lizzy looked at him with a wry smile. "And what do you say?"

He didn't answer. Frankly, he didn't know what to answer. The woman in his arms was a dangerous enticement—one his conscience was battling with, but she was causing him to flirt and banter shamelessly. Moreover, he was enjoying her provoking flirtation.

The bandleader took to the microphone, and they continued to dance in silence wondering what the other was thinking, as the romantic lyrics spoke of love, stars, and dreams. They were caught in the whirlwind of their rapid heartbeats and tingly palms, holding onto one another while dancing and daydreaming.

The song ended and before they parted Will leaned into her. "Well?"

"Well, what?"

"Am I a ducky shincracker?" He folded his arms before his chest, grinning broadly.

He didn't miss her meaning, but his gut cautioned him strongly when she replied with a beautiful twinkle to her eye, "William, you can hold me in your arms anytime. You're a wonderful dancer."

Four

Mean to Me
June 1992

T he view of Central Park was spectacular through the windows of the dining room at the exclusive members-only Metropolitan Club, but it did nothing to divert Juliana Martel's recent preoccupation. That preoccupation had compelled her to ask for this unprecedented lunch with her estranged mother Susan.

She had loathed making the phone call and loathed even more sharing the next hour with the woman who negligently tossed her husband and daughter aside eleven years prior for her boy-toy Jazzercise instructor.

Across the table sat the former Mrs. Gordon Martel looking as poised and elitist as her new trendy image allowed given that she was a forty-three year old attempting to look twenty-three. She wore perfectly coiffed, big, blonde hair, which hid any telltale signs of her recent facelift. Her glossy manicured nails casually smoothed the clingy v-neck of her dress selected to accentuate her new breasts. Husband number four was obviously very wealthy and generous—two traits Susan required in choosing and preparing for the eventual, inevitable disposal of a husband. Nikola Markopolousolous was obviously worth the unpronounceable, six syllable, sixteen-letter last name. The previous husband's surname was Ho. Juliana had a good laugh at the dichotomy.

Glowering, she watched the woman—"mother" by DNA only—spread a translucent, barely worth the effort, sliver of butter on a warm dinner roll. The woman's delicate hand mirrored her own, causing Juliana to frown with each passing swipe of the knife. Susan's crystal-blue eyes were the same color as hers and her petite figure was almost identical—with the exception of the

34D bustline and an additional fifteen pounds. Juliana hated the fact that genetics made them look like sisters but even more so because natural youth was apparent in her whereas, her mother simply refused to allow the natural progression of aging. The younger resisted chuckling when she equated the older woman before her to the physical state of Primrose Cottage: Frozen in time.

Susan opened the conversation with her usual tone of obnoxious, deliberate haughtiness that always grated on Juliana. It seemed that her Locust Valley Lockjaw had grown even more pronounced since recently purchasing a new mansion on the North Shore of Long Island.

"It was good to hear from you, darling. I'm surprised, but delighted nonetheless. It's been what, eight, ten months?"

"It's been a year and a half. Don't you remember the last time? The meeting with my father's divorce lawyer?"

"Oh yes, that's right. I remember now—Collins that sycophant."

"What are you talking about? You slept with him, too."

Susan chuckled. "How do you think I got the Jaguar?"

The waitress delivered a small Cobb salad. "Aren't you eating anything, darling?"

Juliana looked down at her empty bread dish and played with her fork. "The crackers are enough."

"You really should eat something. You're as thin as a rail."

Fighting her knee jerk reaction to make a scene, Juliana snapped, "That's my business. When I called you to meet for lunch, I didn't think you would insist on Dad's club. Didn't your membership expire after the divorce and doesn't your new husband have his own membership somewhere—maybe in Greece?"

"Your father graciously reinstated it for me several years ago. You just know how I always disliked the Colony Club," Susan harrumphed. "I don't care what the history is or who its patrons are. The whole idea of a 'women's only' club repulses me."

Juliana couldn't suppress her annoyance from surfacing. "Gee, there's a surprise."

"Juliana, cheap, low class shots do not become you. I didn't agree to this lunch to subject myself to your vitriolic jabs. Divorce happens, darling and so does death. Both are like taxes—inevitable. The quicker you realize that, the quicker you can begin enjoying life and reaping the benefits of an expertly negotiated pre-nup."

Susan reached across the table and placed her hand upon her daughter's. The newest huge diamond solitaire nearly blinded Juliana.

"Speaking of death, how are you making out? Gordon's tragic passing was so sudden, and I'm terribly sorry for your loss. You were very close to your father, and he loved you so."

A strained smile answered Susan's unexpected sincerity.

It may not have appeared so, but the woman was genuinely sorry for her ex-husband's premature death. That's not to say she wasn't overwhelmingly jealous that her daughter's fortune now exceeded her own, especially since the girl didn't have to endure four marriages to acquire it.

"I'm fine, Susan. Dad left me with many wonderful memories."

"Not to mention money."

Ignoring her mother's passive aggressive comment, Juliana took a moment to turn back toward the expansive view of the bustling city. It was a beautiful day, although sitting across from Susan had quickly zapped that wonderful, romantic feeling she had awoken with in her dust laden new home. The room she had chosen as her bedroom had a stunning genuine Louis Comfort Tiffany semi-circular window. The priceless art glass had been installed near the ceiling within a dormered eave, allowing the morning sun to douse the room with a colorful spectrum of light.

"Susan, believe it or not, the reading of the Will is the reason I asked you to lunch today. I was given Great-uncle William's house in Brooklyn."

"Of course you were. Your grandfather Louie is in no position to inherit that big house, which makes you the logical Martel heir—you're the only family remaining. Had your father and I remained married, then I would have inherited, but I'm happy for your newly found wealth."

Screaming, *I'd rather have my father,* to her mother would have been fruitless—loveless, self-absorbed creature that Susan was. Juliana would never forgive her for her abandonment. She bit back her words of anger and retaliation and continued in her "interview." That was, after all, the only purpose of this meeting. Certainly, it wasn't to form any sort of bond with the woman. As subconsciously starved as Juliana was for a close-knit family and a place to belong, and as strange as it sounded, she would never pursue it with, of all people, her mother.

"You're wrong. You never would have *inherited* Primrose Cottage. At some point, it was left in trust to me by Great-uncle William. Whether Dad died or not, the house became mine when I turned twenty-four. Since you apparently forgot to send a card—that was last month."

"You know I'm never one for cards, darling. Well, I suppose it's just as well that I didn't get the house. I hate Brooklyn. It's almost as bad as Staten Island."

Juliana rolled her eyes, removing a pen and steno pad from her over-sized, backpack handbag. Preparing to take notes, she waited for Susan to stop carefully chewing the minuscule piece of chicken she just placed in her mouth. She mused whether the woman had trouble eating with her new porcelain veneers.

"I was wondering, what can you tell me about Great-uncle William? Do you remember hearing anything about the house or his life? Anything at all might be helpful to me. I arrived at Primrose Cottage a few days ago and it was left ... well ... left untouched and rather spooky."

"Well, I can tell you very little. The person you need to speak with is your grandfather."

"You know that's not possible. I saw him last week and he couldn't even acknowledge Dad's death." She sighed. "I think grandpa is too overcome by his grief to speak."

"Overcome? He hasn't uttered a sound in almost two years. I'm sure now that you own the majority of DeVries Diamond House (DVDH) it is your obligation to take over his remaining share of the business and move him into a nursing home. He shouldn't be living alone in a senior community. He's senile, Julie and it's about time you acknowledge that."

"He's not senile! He's healthy as a horse and I believe, after Grandma's death, he's simply chosen to remain silent as a clam. It's grief, Susan. I'm not here to discuss Grandpa or DVDH. Besides, it's not like you care. You stopped caring on April 7, 1981 at 4:11 in the afternoon."

"What happened on that date to make you believe that I don't care?"

Juliana's eyes widened and her jaw slacked. "Duh ... that's the day you abandoned Dad and me."

"Oh, poo. I do care, Julie. All of that is water under the bridge." She took another drink then continued. "Well then, is this research about Primrose Cottage for the magazine? The mystery surrounding your grandfather's brother could perhaps, make a fascinating article."

"I'm now working for that new magazine, *Allure*. I don't think they would be interested in the disappearance of a man back in 1950."

"*Allure*? Are you still an administrative assistant?" her mother asked.

She shook her head in annoyed wonderment. "No. That was over two years ago when I graduated NYU and worked for *Women's Wear Daily*. I'm a junior freelancer for the magazine—in fashion and style editorial."

"Yes, now I remember." Susan's eyes traveled the length of Juliana's flat chest and thin torso. "Maybe you should consider an article on the fashion faux pas of this messy, baggy look combined with this waif-like Kate Moss image."

"Look, if it's okay with you, I'd like to stick to the subject of our meeting, please. Do you remember anything about William? Anything that Dad or Grandpa may have said over the years?"

"Such an interesting mystery, isn't it? One that inquisitive mind of yours feels compelled to get to the bottom of, but be careful where this may take you, darling. You just may find him alive and wanting his money back."

"*Is* he alive?"

Susan shrugged a shoulder. "How should I know? Last I remember was your grandfather's distress following a letter he received. Hmm ... around 1980, as I recall. It was postmarked from Paris. I remember the year because at that time, I just had my first poodle perm and it was atrocious. Not to mention, I was annoyed because your father never took me to Paris."

Juliana stubbornly remained on point, refusing to be diverted by her mother's narcissism. "What was so disturbing about the letter? What did it say?"

"I don't know, but what I can tell you is that your grandfather never spoke of his brother. Not because he disliked him but because it hurt him too much to do so. Apparently, after your father's christening, the brothers had a falling out."

Writing furiously in her pad, she scribbled notations that, although seemingly inconsequential at the moment, could very well be integral pieces later.

"Do you know what their falling out was over?"

"No. Louis was very secretive and your grandmother even more so. For a woman with such a gift of gab, she never spoke of her family or her past."

"I can't argue there, it's as though Mimi's life began with Grandpa. I don't ever recall her even mentioning siblings or where she grew up. Was she even from New York? For all I know there could be a whole family out there."

"A family of wackos most likely. If you ask me—your whole Martel lineage is screwed up. It's a wonder you're normal, but then you are half Johnston and my family is the pinnacle of society and normalcy."

Juliana smirked, half acknowledging the joke but the other half—the serious half—grabbed this fortuitous opportunity to explain to her mother the damage she had inflicted on her then pre-teen daughter. "I think I can confidently proclaim that I am *not* normal. Is it normal at the age of twenty-four to have no "family" whatsoever and to shy away from seeking one of my own? Is it normal that because of the abandonment by my mother, I question whether I'm *worthy* of a family or love. Is it normal that my psychologist feels I might have an eating disorder as a result of my unrealistic guilt over said abandonment? I doubt the silence or eccentricity of the Martel family have anything to do with my fear of commitment or my fear of intimacy. If anything, I think those particular personality flaws were created because of one *Johnston* person in particular, someone who thinks herself the pinnacle of society and normalcy, yet her fake face, breasts, and teeth are completely *abnormal*."

Susan's body language spoke volumes to Juliana when she folded her arms across her new breasts. "I take offense," she scoffed.

"Why? It's the truth and you know it. The point is, Susan, that oftentimes secrets are held for very good reasons, not because the people holding them are strange, but because circumstances warrant it. I'm not here today to drudge up the sordid past of *our* relationship."

"But we need to discuss our relationship, darling. We need to clear the air. There should be no secrets between us. You may not accept it, but I *am* your family."

Juliana snorted at that last statement. "The word 'family' represents something more than shared DNA. The sole reason I am here is to unlock the mysteries of my new home, the man who once lived there, and why he left it to me. I don't intend on exploiting the discovery of wounds and hurts in my grandfather's brother. I intend on celebrating his life, the man he was—the love he had for a woman named Lizzy and his wartime service to this country as a pilot. Who knows, maybe I'll submit his name to some museum or something. Maybe he has medals or a Purple Heart. Maybe he did something incredibly heroic or maybe I will find out he was just like me ... a bit wounded and scarred by the events in his life. Everyone has a heartwarming story to tell—probably even *you*. And no, I'm not afraid that he's still alive and may want his money back."

Juliana didn't expect to defend the life or mysterious secrets of her great-uncle, but after having spent the last couple of nights in her new home—his home—she felt an almost kinship with the man she once thought wholly unconnected to her. She picked up her pen and resolutely continued her interview.

"Did Dad ever say anything about his uncle?"

"Julie, are you not even going to allow me the opportunity to discuss what clearly is at the core of this luncheon?"

"No, Susan. Did you ever hear the name Lizzy spoken by anyone?"

"Dear, you must understand that your father and I were very young when we married, and we only married because I was pregnant. It was a mistake, a foolish mistake during a passionate, drunken night in the back seat of his father's Buick. Certainly, we were doomed from the start."

Again, Juliana's eyes grew wide as her jaw fixed. Through clenched teeth, she seethed her response. "I was not a *mistake*, Susan."

Susan sighed then took a sip of her iced tea, resolved to the fact that this lunch was not going as she planned. She finally acquiesced to her daughter's determination with a quick, false smile. "Very well, I know very little about the man. When your father was a teenager up until we married, he maintained the property around Primrose Cottage. From about the age of twelve, his father sent him on the Q subway down to Flatbush. He'd mow the lawn and rake leaves—things like that, but when he and I moved up to the East Side after our wedding and you came along shortly thereafter, well, there wasn't much time to go back down to Brooklyn. Speaking of the East Side, have you not gone through your father's things yet? I'm sure Gordon saved a letter or two from his uncle. Although they never met, William always made it a point to remember your father's milestone birthdays. He even sent us a wedding gift and a christening gift for you."

"I haven't been to Dad's yet." Juliana swallowed hard. "It's difficult, but I know I have to pack his belongings soon, send things to St. Vincent DePaul, and eventually, I'll put his co-op up for sale. I have no interest in it ... too many memories. Strangely, I feel I can be happy at Primrose Cottage."

"I understand, Julie. There are too many bad memories for me, too. I was never happy up on 84th Street. It was too far from the Theatre District and Saks."

"Yeah, whatever. So, let's get back to William. Do you know anything of his military service?"

"No, but I do know that your grandfather fought in the Pacific and your grandmother was with the Red Cross. Maybe you can start there."

"Hmm ... maybe. Not that it'll help me in uncovering my uncle's story, but what was Grandma Mimi's maiden name?"

Susan blotted her lips with the linen napkin. "I can't say I ever knew it or actually cared enough to ask. I never liked my mother-in-law. She had this stony, correction, *iron* wall around her. Her life was Park Slope. She never left it, never talked about what was outside of it, and never expressed an interest beyond Prospect Park. As far as Gordon and I knew, there was no family to speak of. My wedding was a pitiful affair, one half of the church was practically empty! I suppose her background is just one more mystery surrounding the secretive Martel clan."

"Well, maybe the attic at Primrose Cottage can shed some light on those secrets. I was too overwhelmed upon my arrival and chose to wait to go up there. That may be a project I'm ready for this afternoon ... *after* I clean the kitchen top to bottom and arrange for an electrician to come out to upgrade the wiring and circuit breakers. Those little glass fuses kept blowing whenever I plugged in my boom box, so I spent the evening listening to old 78 rpm records."

"Oh, I remember those. My parents had tons of them for their RCA. We've come so far with these compact discs now." Susan chuckled. "I bet you'll find some of our eight track tapes among your father's belongings."

Juliana said nothing in reply, refusing to further engage her mother in any personal discourse, even if it did appear that she started it. She pushed back her chair from the table and began to pack away her things, pausing with one last thought.

"One last question ... do you know how William got his money? His wealth is unprecedented. I mean, Grandpa gave almost all the holdings of DeVries Diamond's to Dad but what of William's money? If he left in 1950, his wealth has nothing to do with the family business."

"Again, I can't help you there, Julie, but enjoy it while you have it." Susan smiled brightly.

Juliana understood the meaning behind that particular smile of her mother's. Diamonds had always been Susan's best friend, but four million in hard currency could easily become her new favorite.

****

The closed door to the attic appeared innocuous, but like the pleasant personas and expressions many people conveyed, Juliana felt it was a dead giveaway that something terrible hid behind it. She was, after all, an example of that. Her deepest wounds, she believed, were cleverly masked behind her jovial expressions and happy demeanor, but she didn't realize that the signs were evident in her near anorexic figure.

However, on this late afternoon, she felt open and liberated after surviving the luncheon with her mother. She had bared her inner feelings and animosity then came home to clean the vintage kitchen. Feeling renewed, she went to the grocer around the corner because her white Frigidaire looked as hollow as she had felt these last eleven years. Strangely, she was in the mood to cook a cheeseburger.

From the top of the staircase, Juliana could still hear the record player from the parlor. Melancholy tunes by the Ink Spots and Ella Fitzgerald filled the entire house. She hoped it would carry up into the attic, thinking the soulful music would transport her back to the era and mindset of William when he had last locked the garret.

Yes, it was locked and after an hour of searching the house high and low, she finally found the key inside a small box in one of the dresser drawers. Beside the brass skeleton key sat a gold signet ring with engraving upon the face: propellers and wings surrounded a small diamond at its center. The inscription along the inside of the band read, "With Love, Mom and Dad."

"Here it goes," Juliana said before holding her breath and nervously turning the key. She felt on the verge of a full-blown panic attack.

The door creaked like all the others in the house and her heart rate sped up as it had time and again in the course of this home's unveiling.

Once the door was fully open, she pulled the slender cord hanging against the wall, illuminating the narrow passage by the bare light bulb fixture.

Each step up the steep staircase issued a groan from the hardened planks beneath every footfall of her black Converse sneakers until she stood at the top, fiercely gripping onto the simple banister. She looked around the large, dark room before taking the final step into the unknown, mysterious, and yet-to-be-discovered past of her great-uncle. After working herself up to it for the last two days, Juliana had been expecting something ominous and frightening in the attic, yet instead she felt a sense of peace coupled with sadness. Her thoughts traveled to her father, and her emotions became even more pronounced. Her eyes welled with tears at the morose tranquility the attic emanated.

Essentially, but for a couple of trunks and a few boxes neatly placed upon a shelf, the attic was empty, having lain undisturbed and unfilled since its purchase in December of 1942.

If these walls could talk, they would tell her how William had slid his footlocker under the eave after placing the last of its contents within and how he had waited one full year before doing so. They would tell his grand-niece how he waited until the very last minute to place the newspaper over the windows. Once beige strips of masking tape were now an aged, burnished orange. The empty space staring back at the modern-day interloper represented the very reason for William's departure.

Although expecting the worst in the attic, she wasn't prepared for the emptiness. She had imagined cobwebs extending from box to box and odd pieces of furniture and tools that had long outgrown their usefulness. She thought the attic would surely be filled with scary dolls and broken strollers, perhaps a rocking chair or an eerie mirror, maybe even some Dorian Gray-type painting and faded photographs. Expecting an antique cemetery of sorts filled with memories, stories, and voices of the past residents who had once lived at 300 Bradford Road, she was surprised by the vacant space before her.

The startling emptiness of the room confirmed to her that no happy memories had ever been created in this house. The house never became a home, had never filled with children's laughter or generations of family dating back to its initial construction. No household item ever had the luxury of being used enough to justify its disregard, saving and eventual storing on the third floor. It was clear to Juliana that Primrose Cottage was only a place where William laid his head, not his heart. *True* life had never infused these walls. The attic led her to believe he had been a bachelor—never married, never had children, never sharing his life, let alone this house, with anyone. The starkness of the attic revealed the loneliness of the man at the time of his departure.

Her denim-clad legs walked to one of the windows and carefully removed the yellowed *Brooklyn Daily Eagle* newspaper dated from the morning of William's departure. The last remnants of daylight eerily filled the room as dusk cast a gloomy orange feeling to the already melancholy interior.

Below the shelf, where a box labeled "Mom's China" was stored, stood a beautifully carved claw-footed lowboy. It was deep, looking to be a blanket chest, even a hope chest. Beside it, under the eave, sat a green, military footlocker. Scuffed white lettering was stenciled across the metal top and side: LT. W.G MARTEL.

Juliana went first to the trunk, knelt before it, and carefully lifted the cover with a creak. Taped inside the lid, a collage of black and white snapshots greeted her. There were some of Lizzy, some of an older couple, one of a single older woman and one of a dirty, war-beaten man sitting beside a bombed out ditch wearing a helmet. He held a rifle in one hand and smoked with the other. The soldier looked the spitting image of her father. Carefully,

Juliana removed the snapshot, turned it over and read that it was her grandfather, "Lou—Pelileu Bloodbath—Oct. 14, '44."

"Wow, Grandpa. I never knew. You never said anything." She turned the photograph over again, gazing at his expression. Even in his weariness, he still maintained that twinkle in his eye she knew all too well. "Since you can't tell me, I'll find out your story, too. I promise." Carefully, she placed the slick image beside the footlocker.

Resisting the hurried temptation to remove the items neatly folded within the trunk, she chose to gingerly pick up the corners to glance at the contents one by one: William's uniform, his leather bomber jacket, flight manuals, pilot log, and patches that resembled the one on the mantle. Hidden at the very bottom of the military locker, beside an envelope marked "POW" and another containing many more snapshots of Lizzy, was the one thing she hoped to find—a stack of letters. There was no hesitancy in her when she dug her hand deep down to pull them from their resting place of over forty years.

Tied with a green ribbon, the stack stood at least four inches in height. The well-worn letter secured firmly at the top of the stack and the few below it were without an envelope. Juliana sat back and crossed her legs before the trunk as she faced the striking image of Lizzy tacked within. After untying the ribbon, she recognized the first light-blue, fifty year-old letter's handwriting from the one burned in the fireplace and in the dim light of the sunset, began to read.

May 31, 1942
Dear Lieutenant Martel,

I hope you will forgive my presumption in sending this letter to you, but it didn't escape my attention that you failed to ask for my address to correspond. In case it escaped yours, I was hoping you would. Perhaps it was the mud or perhaps something more—something along the lines of your treatment at Meercrest and not by me or my little ole' Zephyr this past Saturday?

Please accept my heartfelt apology for the unkind, and dare I say unpatriotic, treatment toward you and Louie not only by my elder sister but also by my parents. Unfortunately, Father makes no bones about his former involvement with the America First Committee and, as you heard, makes no apologies about Lindbergh's statement that the U.S. military won't achieve victory in the war against Germany. I believe, when those words were spoken, he truly believed they had armies stronger than our own. Isn't that correct? While you indicated that Lindbergh's opinion changed, my father still holds those beliefs. I can offer no excuse for his treatment of you other than the fact that sadly, your noble enlistment and service, represented by your uniforms, only added fuel to his fire. I am impressed by the way you graciously handled my father at dinner with neither condemnation at his inflammatory opinions nor disrespect because someone of his stature in both the Social Register and business held them. Even my mother, in her usual silliness and ignorant parroting of my father's political views, was met by your courteous understanding during the Bananas Foster. As for my sisters—Ingrid, as I am sure you noticed, is only concerned by her representation in the Gold Coast Social Diary and society pages. Moreover, her expectation of marriage to Johnny and his family's fortune causes her to be a bit ... caustic, particularly when it comes to his home front contribution. Your kindness and attention toward both Johnny and my sister Kitty touched my heart. Thank you for it all.

Now, about Gloria—well, she is admittedly a handful and your pilot wings and uniform seemed to enflame her. While I cannot condone her deplorably precocious flirtation with you, I can certainly understand it. In fact, you may well think my letter a forward flirtation in its own right. Lieutenant, you are very handsome and an extremely articulate man. How can I resist when you look so spiffy in your uniform to boot?

So what do you think of me now? Do you think I'm a scandalous, wacky girl from Long Island for writing you? Are you still angry with the mischievous driver of the Zephyr? Do you believe me indifferent to you because you are not of my social circle? I hope no on all accounts. Your coming to my rescue last evening on both the dance floor and later the dock showed you to be an honorable man and someone whose acquaintance I would like to continue. You are certainly someone I'm grateful to for fighting to keep America from falling under tyranny. I suppose it funny that I should equate that jerk Gebhardt with war, but you saved me from taking matters into my own hand. Muddy trousers would have been the least of his problems. Ha!

If you wish further association with the hotrodding daughter of a bad-mannered businessman, tipsy mother, and a hoity-toity sister, well then I'll look forward to a response letter through your brother and my sister.

Oh, and the answer is no—I am never this audacious. Brazen, impetuous, and a little free-spirited, yes—but never arrogant. I'll look forward to your correspondence. Did I mention I'm also an optimist?

Sincerely yours,

Hotrod Lizzy

Juliana barely tempered her curiosity and desire to tear into all the other letters right then and there but the attic was now dark with the only light coming up from the narrow staircase. Carefully, she re-folded the letter, retied them then closed the footlocker.

"I'll be back tomorrow with a steno pad for note taking—Lieutenant William Martel. Your secrets will soon be discovered, and I promise you, yours and Lizzy's love story will be told."

With the letters and the photograph of her grandfather in hand, she went back downstairs where she cooked and ate the first of many dinners in her vintage kitchen while devouring the first few letters from Lizzy that her great-uncle received during his service.

Five

Now is the Hour
June 2, 1942

D on't cry, Mom," Louie consoled. Taking his mother Anna's hand in his, the delicate, familiar touch comforted them both.

The brim of her hat didn't conceal the tears rolling down her cheeks as she patted them dry with a lace edged handkerchief. Her native Dutch accent still pervaded her every word and phrase, tugging at Will's heart as he covertly observed the tender scene between his older brother and petite mother.

"I can't help it. I'll cry for your *broeder*, too, when he leaves. You're both still my babies."

It seemed a funny thing for him to hear standing in the center of Pennsylvania Station, waiting for a train to take Louie and other uniformed servicemen of the Armed Forces off to war.

"*He* might be a baby, but I'm a Marine. I'll be fine." As usual, Louie gave his mother that trademark smile that caused her to laugh through tears.

"Always the jokester. Keep that humor, *Lieverd*."

Louie chuckled at the irony. "Someone else told me that recently, too."

Anna wiped her tears and her voice broke slightly. "Who, my dear?"

"That girl, Lillian, I told you about. She may write you while I'm away."

"I hope so. I'd like to know the woman my boy is in love with."

Also wearing his summer service uniform, Will stood off to the side beside their father, Julien. Both knew their time would come not only to say their good-byes to Louie but also to part ways from one another. Will didn't even want to think of what *that* scene would be like. He knew his mother would barely hold it together when her youngest son left New York for G-d knows where. First, he had to get through training down at MacDill Army Airfield in Tampa, Florida.

All around them, similar scenes were taking place. Some mothers wept, some infants prophetically cried, sweethearts hung on for dear life, yet others stoically seemed to fight back the emotion by trying to display impassive faces. Many soldiers sat waiting—alone, perched upon their suitcases against the Servicemen Information Booth or beside the gate entrance. That had to be the hardest, but he imagined some fellows wanted it that way. Some of those soldiers were still boys and perhaps that was the reason for their lack of family—they up and enlisted in secret, lying about their age.

Against the backdrop of American flags hanging from steel pillars and the large, *V* emblazoned banner suspended overhead, the entire waiting concourse was simultaneously the most patriotic and poignant moment Will had ever witnessed. When his time came to depart for combat, he wouldn't want it any other way—just his parents and him. He knew Louie would be with him in spirit wherever he went.

Anna reached up and touched Louie's cheek. "Do you have the food I packed for you? Make sure you eat something. You need your vitamins to remain strong."

"Don't worry, Mom. There's a reason the Marines are first to fight." He kissed her cheek and she grabbed him, wrapping her arms around him tightly.

Standing on her tiptoes, she whispered something in Dutch into his ear as she hugged him with all the love a mother could have for her eldest son.

Will watched them from the corner of his eye, noting how his brother nodded to appease her request then tenderly replied, "I will."

The smile and impassivity behind Louie's dark eyes confirmed to Will nothing beyond the fact that his brother always had a great poker face. He could lie like the best of them when it meant sparing someone's feelings or taking blame for something he didn't do. For all of Louie's grandstanding, mischievous behavior, and in spite of his doll dizzy ways, he really was an upstanding fellow.

Anna kissed his right cheek, left cheek, then back to the right, and Louie laughed. "Enough with the kisses!"

"Shush, that's the DeVries way. I may be a Martel, but I'm also a DeVries and you are, too. We kiss!" For his objection, he received another three from his mother, willing herself to appear as good humored as her son.

He walked to his father and brother and looked at his wristwatch. "I have to board the train. I want to get a good seat for the long ride down to Norfolk. I'm afraid if I drag this good-bye out, Mom might not let me go."

Julien put on that stoic face Will had seen displayed on so many other fathers present, but he knew what was in his heart. Like their mother, he was having a difficult time with his son's departure. He hugged Louie, surprising Will by the unprecedented public display of affection.

"I love you, Pally. I'm proud of you."

Evident in the way Louie's Adam's apple moved, it was obvious to Will that his brother felt the emotion and sentiment conveyed by their father's simple yet powerful statement, particularly because 'pal' was his father's childhood nickname for Louie.

"Thanks, Dad. I love you, too."

"Come home safely to your mother and write her often. Sleep whenever you can." He, too, whispered something into his son's ear, when he pulled him in for a last hug.

Will picked up his Marine brother's small travel case and then slung the duffle's strap over his shoulder, surmising what his parents had imparted in secret.

"C'mon, I'll walk you to the track," he said, sad to see how his parents, a good foot difference in their heights now stood arm in arm, watching their boy leave for the Pacific.

It broke their hearts knowing Louie headed to where each day's news and newsreels reported significant Naval battles as well as the devastating failure of the Battle of Bataan.

Louie gave them a slight wave before the two brothers walked side-by-side through the throng of passengers. Uniformed in different khaki colors, their garrison caps were decorated by dissimilar medallions, one bearing the Army Air Corp gold propeller wings as well as a gold bar and the other with the impressive Marine emblem. Overhead, the unusual occurrence of a woman announcer called out a train's arrival adding to the loud din in the crowded station's waiting area.

"Will you write to Mom?" Louie asked his brother.

"Of course. You know I plan to."

"Well, try to type it if you can. Your handwriting is like chicken scratch."

Will smirked. "Yes, big brother."

"And write that girl."

"Which girl?"

"You know which girl. Lizzy. In case you conveniently forgot it—I left her address beside her letter on your desk."

The brothers stopped before the arched stairwell to the track below, and Will placed Louie's suitcase at his feet. A shrill whistle carried up from the sub-level below the city, adding to the heaviness of the moment.

"I don't think I'll write back to her. It's a shame because I really like her. It's just ... her family ... ya' know."

"Yeah, I thought you'd have a problem with that. Here you're going off to Europe to fight those bastards, and they're right here in our own backyard, but Lil and Lizzy aren't like the others, and you need a girl to write to whenever you exit out of that flying coffin."

Will smiled thoughtfully. "And a pretty one at that, but there's a reason the saying goes 'fools rush in where wise men never go'."

"Wise? More like numbskull. She'd be good for you, Will. Besides, she's got great gams."

"Her letter was pretty audacious."

"Good, you don't want some dumb Dora. You like that she's a pistol and a girl who knows what she wants. If I recall the story correctly, that's how Mom caught Pop in her trap, too. Lizzy probably thinks you're a good catch—in spite of that stern countenance of yours. Don't mess this up, and don't waste too much time mulling it over or you'll miss out on a good thing. Try for once to be a little spontaneous."

"Okay, okay, I'll write her, but that's it. I'm in no mood to deal with a family of anti-Semites, not after what Aunt Estella wrote us about Amsterdam and now with things heating up in France ..."

"Well, you'll have plenty of opportunities to take out your anger, and I'll get to enact some serious payback for Pearl Harbor."

"Yeah, but it still frustrates me when I hear fellas, in their ignorance, say that we're only at war with Germany because they're allies with the Japanese."

"A lot of Americans are asleep, but that'll change." Louie held out his hand. "Be safe, Brother."

Their palms slapped together in a firm handshake, which seemed to meld into one hand for the two thick as thieves.

"Protect your men," Will advised, his tone serious. "Keep your head down and ... and wear a rubber." He suddenly grinned like a Cheshire cat trying for a little levity although his heart was clenching as he fought the urge to choke up.

Louie tugged his taller brother's hand, pulling him forward for a hug. "Love you."

"Yeah, yeah. Don't get all soppy on me. Sheesh, some hardboiled Marine you are." Will rolled his eyes and handed Louie the duffle. "Write when you get where you're going. They'll re-route your letter to me in either Florida or England or wherever they send me, maybe North Africa."

Louie turned, giving a thumbs up. The last thing Will saw was his brother's quick descent down the stairwell until he disappeared. He turned and, through the crowd, observed his mother sobbing in his father's arms.

****

Of all the places to get lost at Meercrest, the seventy-foot teahouse water tower overlooking the Sound was Lizzy's favorite place of escape, especially when her need to pout was paramount. It was the one place where she was guaranteed solitude. No one ventured up here any longer. The heyday of its usefulness had long passed with her aunt Helga and her notorious, not to mention salacious, private flapper parties held up here during the twenties. Tea was more like illegal hooch brought in from the Sound by her grandfather's many connections during the Prohibition. Back then, the North Shore was called "Rum Row," and the teahouse had become Glen Cove's speakeasy of sorts. Now twenty years later, the silver service tray, sitting beside Lizzy, held steaming hot coffee thanks to the head housekeeper Mrs. Davis and her diligent attention to the girls' addictions and luxuries. G-d help her if those rumors of putting coffee on the ration came true. Lizzy was sure she would die.

At nine-stories up, the cerulean view beyond the arched windows was spectacular, and Lizzy had a clear view to Connecticut on the opposite side of the water. With her novel tossed to the side and Kay Kyser's Orchestra "Who Wouldn't Love You" playing on the console radio behind her, she mindlessly focused on the Coast Guard Reserve ships monitoring for U-boats and mines, which seemed to be cropping up on the eastern seaboard with greater frequency every day. As much as she fought the pull to think about the war, it was everywhere, invading her practically perfect (but definitely sheltered) life. Meeting William and Louie three days prior had certainly increased her awareness that every young man's life was affected, and she now understood John's dismay over his classification. Just the other day, she overheard two debs she knew at the Glen Head Country Club, discussing someone who they considered "damaged and undesirable" because the Army declared him 4F. John was not damaged goods and it upset her to think people would be prejudiced against him for something out of his control. He wanted to fight; didn't that matter?

With a long, deep inhale of her cigarette, Lizzy's thoughts traveled to Kitty and William's comment about prejudice. Never had she met a man her age more articulate and noble than he appeared to be, and she hoped she had made her admiration clear in her letter. She felt a heaviness of regret, thinking how she should have phrased her words differently, but she had felt she needed to apologize. Perhaps she seemed too forward, too khaki wacky ... too much like Gloria. There was no going back now. The letter had been sent, and hopefully, Lieutenant William Martel had not slipped through her fingers as quickly as when she had shaken his strong grip for that first hello.

Straight away, she had thought him handsome, impressive in his uniform, and highly intelligent. Certainly more intelligent than she, and yet he appeared to *still* be enchanted by her. Maybe she had read him wrong, but she thought there was a real interest there. She lied to herself thinking that under other circumstances, she definitely would never have been so brazen to write him. At first, Lizzy thought the dreamboat was too shy to ask to write to her or go dancing or to the movies before he left for Florida to train with bombers. Lord knows, she gave him enough opportunities, enough signals, bordering on making passes to indicate her interest. The pervasive thought in her head was that her father's controversial opinions may have scared him off. But the thought that ate away at her confidence was he stayed away because of *her*.

The elevator behind her jolted to a loud stop, and she heard the wrought iron gate clanking as it slid open. Finally, she heard the groan of exertion during the occupant's last tug, pushing the metal to the side.

"Lizzy, are you here?"

Lizzy stamped out her cigarette and unfolded her crossed pant legs. She bolted toward the elevator. "Kitty! Where's Nurse Keller? What are you doing up here?"

"Oh, that battle-axe? She's disappeared again, and I didn't want to wait around for her. Lillian just left for the hospital and said you were feeling poorly. Do you want to talk?"

"You're sweet, but what's there to talk about? He didn't reply. Lillian's letter from Louie came express, and Flyboy wasn't interested. If he was then his letter would have been enclosed." She shrugged, playing off her disappointment although she felt crestfallen.

Pushing her sister's chair from behind, Lizzy rolled it toward the window and the cushioned seat where she had attempted to read but instead found herself taking in the view, smoking and daydreaming.

Kitty looked up and over her shoulder. "I liked him, and I think he liked you, Lizzy. Maybe he's just shy. He was very proper, not to mention gentlemanly."

Lizzy plopped down onto the window seat. Facing her sister, she sighed deeply expelling all the air in her lungs. "No, I don't think it was shyness. He is a gentleman to be sure, but he speaks his mind about things he feels important ... things he is passionate about: this war—and protecting the innocent. I'm afraid he may think I am too much like Gloria. Maybe he doesn't see me as a woman with any real substance, intelligence, or purpose. He doesn't want a girl who hasn't the foggiest idea about what's going on in Europe or the Philippines. Let's face it, I'm too wrapped up in the society microcosm of Glen Cove and the yacht club. A killer-diller fella like him, going off to fight, wants a girl who will participate in Victory Bond drives and join that new Women's Auxiliary Volunteer Service they're recruiting for. Someone who will knit socks to send to him in England or get a job down at the Brooklyn Navy Yard or Robertsen Aviation as one of those production workers. I don't know ... I'm just not cut out for riveting and blueprint reading, and I'm sure as heck not suited to work as a Farmerette. I'm sorry but making butter and milking cows is beyond my aptitude." She looked away, her eyes appearing to focus on another Coast Guard boat, but in fact were glazed over as she mused.

"He doesn't want someone like me whose only contribution to the war effort is ... is ... um ... well ... I drove the mandatory thirty-five miles per hour instead of my usual fifty." She looked back at her sister, nodding with a smug grin and feeling that in and of itself was a generous contribution to the war effort.

"You're not Lillian, Lizzy. Sheesh, not many are, but there are tons of things you can do if you want to. We can do them together."

Lizzy furrowed her brow, wondering what exactly the two sisters could contribute. "I want to do something." She took Kitty's cold hand in hers and rubbed her thumb against the thick callus in her palm. "I feel useless—indulged—and for the first time in my life, I feel extraneous."

Kitty looked down toward their clasped hands at her sister's pointed reference to this startling similarity. "Yes ... I know that feeling very well, everyone discounting your opinion and your abilities just because your world is so different. Will didn't make you feel that way did he? He didn't seem the type."

"No, *I* made me feel that way, and I'm sorry that you do too, dear."

Suddenly, Kitty turned her head with a bright, positive outlook. "Well, let's change that. Let's expand our world and make a contribution to not remain slackers because everyone else around us is. We can start a silk stocking salvage campaign or a refugee clothing drive. I could do the writing to our friends and acquaintances, and you can do the collecting. Maybe we can get involved with the new victory book drive I heard about on the radio. You love books. It's a natural thing for you to do your bit. Later, you can telephone Mrs. Tinsdale the head librarian to ask about volunteering opportunities."

Lizzy kissed her sister's hand. "Kitty, when I grow up, I want to be just like you and Lillian."

"That will never happen as long as you live in this house. You do know that whatever we embark on, we have to keep a secret. Father would never stand for three of his daughters involved in the war effort. He'll flip his wig and then you'll never get to date your flyboy because he'll never let you out of the house again!"

"Yes, to some degree you're right. He is getting worse. It was evident by his objections to both William and Louie. He snapped his cap in the study, claiming he 'didn't like the look of those GIs'. His disrespect and ideology is so contrary to most of those in our circle, with the exception of Ingrid, that it baffles me. I won't even repeat the disgusting things she said poolside on Saturday."

"It's that Mr. Gebhardt." Kitty adjusted her leg braces. "He has been spending too much time at Meercrest, and I see the way Ingrid is all goo-goo eyed at him. They never even notice when I'm in the room. I suppose being the cast-aside Renner has its advantages since they seem to think I'm another piece of furniture."

What could Lizzy say to that? It was true. Everyone but her, Lillian, and Mrs. Davis ignored Kitty's presence—or worse, teased her. She offered her sister a contrite smile. "Yes, I've seen the way Ingrid watches and listens to Gebhardt, too. He's too old for her, not to mention trouble. He made a pass at me the night of the lawn party. If it wasn't for the lieutenant, I'm sure I would have had to slap him, but William arrived just in time."

Kitty's hand went to her mouth in shock. "What happened?"

"Well, it was my own fault really. I never should have gone down to the boat landing in the dark, but mother was very drunk, and I knew Father would want to stop her himself before she made a real scene. As it was, she was repeating some of his gobbledygook about the purity of the Germanic bloodline and then I noticed Dorothy Whitney cringe, refuting Mother with some comment about how that *superior bloodline's* Luftwaffe was bombing the heck out of the English countryside. Kitty ... I didn't even know the extent to which England was being bombed. I swear where have I been?"

"Having a good time with all your deb friends."

"Hmm ... yes, I suppose you're right." Lizzy paused thoughtfully. "Anyway, I got to the *Odin* and of course it was dark due to the new blackout restrictions, but that didn't stop Gebhardt with his lit cigarette. I saw him standing at the bow, looking out on the Sound and I asked if Father was within the cabin. He threw his cigarette overboard and came to stand *very* close to me, said something base about how the Renner woman are all so alluring. He ran his hand down my arm and his fingers brushed against my bosom!"

"What did you do?"

"I tried to leave the dock, of course, but he grabbed my wrist. I struggled and raised my voice, saying something to the effect that I considered him a smarmy creep and to get his hands off me. I don't care if he's handsome with those piercing eyes. He's a wolf of the worse kind. Just then we both heard the lieutenant's voice bellow, causing Gebhardt to drop his hold upon me."

Kitty cooed a romantic sigh. "He was your knight in shining armor. How romantic!"

"Hardly that at the moment. He was madder than blazes and told Gebhardt if he didn't let go of me he would pop him one in the kisser!" Lizzy opened her gold cigarette case, offered her sister a Chesterfield then took one for herself. Taking a deep drag, she blew out the smoke in a long, smooth stream away from the wheelchair. "Oh, what *was* romantic was how he took my arm, rubbed my wrist where Gebhardt had violated it, then escorted me back to the house."

"And ... and ...?"

"And nothing. I thought he'd ask to take me out for a date, or at the very least to write me but he didn't. He simply thanked me for the dances and a lovely afternoon then said good-bye." She bit her lip and flicked her ashes into the crystal ashtray.

"I know you're disappointed, Lizzy, but mark my words he won't be able to stop thinking about you. He will write you."

"I hope you're right, dear, because William Martel is everything a man should be."

Over the Rainbow
June 1992

H is beloved mother often said that silence is golden, and well, after his wife Lillian's death two years ago, he decided to remain so. Seventy-three year old Louie Martel simply had very little worth saying or even the desire or wherewithal to say it. Lillian had always spoken for both of them, and when she died, his voice went with her. He didn't expect what would follow, but in her absence, left alone to his devices and thoughts, his carefully hidden and deliberate attempt to gloss over his war experience was for naught. His silence was no longer maintained by grief; post-traumatic stress had become the dominant deterrent.

Sitting on the balcony of his luxury apartment—in of all places a *senior community!*—his granddaughter basked in the sun, reading one of the many letters she brought with her. He watched Juliana's profile from inside his kitchen as, every once in a while she smiled at the words Lizzy had written to his brother so long ago. Louie remembered how Lillian's letters had the same affect on him whenever mail made it to the Pacific islands.

Gordon's daughter was the apple of his eye—a lovely, good girl, of whom he was extremely proud. It was a shame she resembled his daughter-in-law so much, but Juliana's spirit and heart were entirely different and that accounted for so much more. Her name alone—Julien and Anna—embodied her essence. She was his treasure, and he hoped to live long enough to see her become someone else's treasure. Valued and cared for like the special jewel she is, even if she doubted that.

Louie placed her steaming cup of coffee beside his ashtray on the table separating two Adirondack chairs. He took the seat beside her, facing out onto the East River and Roosevelt Island. He loved this view of the aerial cable car shuttling commuters high above the Queensboro Bridge.

"Grandpa, are you sure you have nothing to say about your brother? I mean even the tiniest remark? You could write it down. Hell, I'll even settle for a grunt—one for yes—two for no—anything. Here, let's give it a try ... do you know if Lizzy wrote him a Dear John letter?" Her eyes studied his, waiting for his grunt. "Okay, that obviously wasn't juicy enough to elicit a response." From her backpack, she removed a clear sheet protector, guarding the preserved remnant of what looked like a burned letter.

"How about this ... What did Lizzy mean when she wrote, 'You know that what we did?' Was this the reason for their break up?"

He couldn't help but to smile. Staying silent, watching her delve into Will's life with such determination was priceless. His brother would hate his privacy being invaded so, but he brought it on himself. Juliana needed this and the family did, too. Enough of his brother's foolishness! Things needed to be set right before they both died, and she was the only one to do it. In the past, he didn't have balls enough to track him down and go and get him. He should have forced his hand to make amends and heal the family, but this one—this little slip of a girl, who blossomed into a woman with purpose and a newly found voice, could do it. But, getting her to unfold it all, connect the dots and learn from the mistakes made five decades ago would have so much more impact when done on her own than if he were to find his voice to tell her. Simply put, unforgiveness left unchecked is life-changing, and she was headed in that direction with her mother.

Louie looked behind him at the large, wilting bouquet of flowers displayed in the entry hall. A similar one had arrived two years ago when Lillian died. This one arriving with the same sentiment for Gordon—with sympathy. *How did he know?*

Juliana sighed, and he could see the frustration setting in those cool blue orbs of hers when she continued to stare at him pointedly. It was obvious, she was goading him when she said, "I met with Susan the other day. She thinks you're senile, you know, and she's jealous of the money and Primrose Cottage, of course. I can tell that she's eaten up with it." Juliana chuckled wryly. "I think those contacts of hers turned green. Anyway, I told her she could stick it where the sun doesn't shine. You're not senile, and I'm never going to forgive her no matter how hard she tries to explain herself. Mistake! She actually said I was a mistake!"

Louie reached over the small space separating them and took her delicate hand in his. He toyed with the jade ring on her index finger, given to her after his wife's death. It had been a gift to Lillian when he returned home from China in late '46.

Juliana squeezed his hand, and he fought the urge to wince. Five years ago, that didn't hurt—arthritis was a bitch, but he'd never let her see his pain. It was just her nature to become overly concerned, and she had enough on her mind, skinny thing she had become thanks to that other bitch.

He hadn't noticed the opened letter sitting upon her lap. With her free hand, she picked it up and read aloud,

"June 23, 1942
Dear Will,

I arrived safely a couple of days ago. My G-d what a long, boring transport—apart from the trip through the Panama Canal. Almost three weeks of tedious drills, card playing, reading, and catching up on correspondence. Of course, I wrote my girl and Mom and Dad, quickly posting them after the 1ˢᵗ Marine's debarkation. Sorry, to get this off later to you, but I just didn't have too much to say so I waited until we arrived at camp—in the rain! You'll be in Florida by the time you receive this. Heck, I can't even be sure if you'll receive it by the time you leave for Europe. I am so far down under that it'll probably take a good two months before the mail catches up to you. Speaking of letters, I expect to hear from you in regard to Lizzy. You may fight with your logic and reason on this, but she's perfect for you and as of yet, the only cookie I've seen who can spar with you and win! Gorgeous, funny, and a real live wire—need I say more? You do know that Mom and Dad would love her, don't you? Don't be a meatball—stop thinking too much about it and write the girl.

About N.Z, the transport arrived at the docks to cold weather, cheering children, and waiting wagons loaded with fresh milk. Damn, if the last two didn't do my heart good. I stopped drinking that armored heifer after two weeks on board. Once we made our way to camp, they replaced my Springfield

with a Reising submachine gun. Now I'm ready and it's a good thing, too, because rumors say we won't be here for very long.

Well brother, take care of yourself and don't forget to write me. I'm counting on you to keep me sane and focused during our family's separation. I expect your letter to be filled with good news about you and the girl, and, I expect you to ante up after the National League loses in the All-Star Game on the 6th. Two smackers, Mr. Die Hard Dodgers fan. I've got news for you, old man, DiMaggio and Williams are gonna' win this one for the AL.
Affectionately,
Lou"

Louie sat listening to his letter. The remembrance of writing it, clear as day. He never did get those two dollars from Will. Hopefully, his jewel will help him get it with interest.

He slid his hand from her grasp when Juliana handed the letter to him.

"I found your picture, you know. The one of you at Peleliu. It was in William's footlocker."

Well, now that really got his attention. His head snapped up from his preoccupation of looking at his youthful handwriting.

"Ha! I knew there would be something to break you out of the world you're sitting in. You were very handsome. Still are, but back in the day you must have been a heartbreaker, a real dreamboat."

Clever girl, sitting there hiding her smirk behind that coffee mug. He wanted to say something to her, but he wasn't sure if he could now even if he wanted to. So, he just smiled a wicked little grin, hoping she would understand his meaning. Lillian would have had quite a story to tell, and he would have laughed, even then remaining silent as she animatedly told the tale of how he seduced her in the horse stable at that U.S.O camp in '42. Ah, 1942—when it all began—the year he gave his heart away.

"You were womanizer, weren't you?"

Louie lit up a smoke, expecting the requisite balking that always followed from his granddaughter's lips, but it didn't come today. Only the exaggerated fanning of her hand before her face, then the cough—the fake cough she made sure drove home her message. G-d, she was just like her grandmother.

Juliana withdrew a handful of snapshots from the Tiffany blue box she brought with her, offering them, one at a time for his review. "Look, here's one of you, one of you and your brother in your uniforms, look—one of Lizzy, and Lizzy again. Do you remember Lizzy, Grandpa? I think you dated her sister at one point. Here's a photo of Uncle William, also known as Fuddy Duddy, and looking so handsome beside his airplane. Lizzy had a ton of nicknames for him, Ducky being her favorite."

He burst out laughing.

Juliana jumped in a start and dropped to her knees before him. "Oh, Grandpa! Say something, anything! You laughed! That's so much better than a grunt!"

Stamping out his cigarette, he continued to chuckle, having had no idea that Lizzy nicknamed his stoic, straight-laced brother "Ducky." That girl was a pistol. His knobby knuckled hand clasped Juliana's tiny one, and he rose from the chair, pulling her up with him.

"Where are you taking me?"

Today was a good day. She made him feel twenty years younger every time she came to see him. They passed the flowers in the hall, and he snorted a laugh. *Ducky. More like Vaporhead.*

"Who sent you those?"

He shrugged in reply.

His bland bedroom looked devoid of anything special other than photographs of his Lillian and a few other special mementos. Since moving in, he didn't even consider decorating it. What was the point? Therefore, as it stood, it looked like a model home, nothing special and everything newly purchased—no memories or antiques. All of those things were at Gordon's apartment or left in Park Slope when he sealed the house following Lillian's death. Even the Sony television looked uninspiring now that his favorite shows were vanishing one after the other. He loved that MacGyver show but that, along with Johnny Carson went off the air the month prior. Thankfully, there was a ginger-haired beauty who he cared about on the fourth floor. She needed a snuggle now and again, so Johnny's role of putting him to sleep had been effectively replaced by a little slap and tickle. Thank G-d, he had enough vim in his vigor to still do *that*.

His granddaughter sat on the edge of his wasteful king-sized bed, picking up a throw pillow her grandmother had sewn. She held it close to her chest, breathing in its familiar scent as though remembering how much she was loved by the woman she affectionately called Mimi.

Yes, for herself she needed to seek out her grandmother's family. Lord knows, he wasn't getting any younger and soon Juliana would find herself alone. She needed cousins, aunts and uncles—she needed a family, and he and Lillian—G-d rest her soul—had denied her that by protecting the Martels from the Renner legacy. His treasure should never be alone.

"Grandpa, I wish I knew more about Mimi. Susan said she was with the Red Cross, but no one has ever said anything. I regret that Grandma never told me about her life before you, who she was, what her childhood and family were like. My evil mother has me thinking that Mimi was orphaned or, worse, a runaway. Someone with terrible secrets that she took to the grave."

She did run away in a sense and we vowed to never speak of her family, he thought brushing his finger down her pert nose and smiled wistfully before turning his back to her.

He reached up into his bedroom closet, moving around a few items and small boxes until he found what he searched for—a worn Florsheim shoebox. Bringing it down, he held it out to her.

"What's in it?"

He motioned with his hand and she complied, lifting the dusty lid.

Photographs, more than he remembered, lay within among many denominations of beautifully detailed Japanese Yen, occupation money, and various other pieces of ephemera pertaining to his wartime service. Also stashed away were his Marine medals, Presidential Citation, insignia patches, and the small diary he kept hidden throughout the war. A black matchbook lay on top of the contents, its design read, "Strike 'em Dead, Remember Pearl Harbor."

Staring down into the relatively small container, Louie marveled at how it held the biggest most powerful four years of his life, and there it all sat stuffed into a box that once held brown wingtips. He shook his head in amazement, uncharacteristically feeling melancholy at the thought of it. Fifty long years had passed. Maybe Will had been right—we should never forget, but Will's wartime experience hit way too close to home. Fighting in Europe and his internment for two years by the Germans had deep significance where he was concerned.

Try as Louie might, though, his own fight in the Pacific couldn't be buried forever. Over the years, he had never truly forgotten Guadalcanal, New Britain, New Guinea, Peleliu, and Okinawa, but Lillian had helped him to pack the memories away, just as he helped her conceal her own past. Together, side by side, they looked to the future and lived in the joys of the moment, certainly not the horrors of the past. It was only after her death that the horrors came back, creeping in during his sleep. Without her there to rub his back or soothe the occasional tremor, the memories of those five months on Guadalcanal came back every night. That was his first battle and by the time it was over, he was nearly a different man from the one who entered.

Suddenly, with the letter's introduction, the photographs, and now the box of mementos, it seemed important, something he had to share with Juliana. Again, he thought of his brother's running from his past and the painful memories associated with it, much like Lillian. Will's heated words from the week before Gordon's christening came back.

-You disgrace our legacy, our very history, and you dishonor the memory of Grandfather and Aunt Estella when you forget.

With ironic reflection, Louie's heart felt sad, realizing that like losing his voice, Will had done the very thing he accused him. One cannot keep memories alive and pass them to the next generation when one disappears for forty years, remaining silent and maybe alone, letting the story die with him.

Louie silently vowed, *I will move past this grief. I will find my voice again.*

Juliana broke him from the long pause, which thankfully she hadn't noticed since she was occupied with the box's contents. "This is all about you during the war. Wow. Can I keep it?" Juliana picked up a snapshot—one of him standing in a bar during his R&R. Another showed him playing cards. He wondered if any of Lillian's letters or photographs lay at the bottom of the box. If memory served, the box represented the Marines only.

She removed a deck of playing cards from the box, and a small smile developed on his lips. *Hello, my lucky fixed cards.* From her hands, he took the pack with a big *V* emblazoned on the front, planning to have some fun with the ex-Army guys at the facility over a seemingly innocent game of poker.

Next, she held up a photograph of him sitting on the USS *Wakefield*. He was young, dumb, and green upon his arrival in New Zealand, thinking he could conquer the world and kill every Jap who came into his rifle sight. The letter she had read to him was a testament to that youthfulness. Such valiant grit; that kind of tenacity won the war.

"Where is this?"

He turned over the photograph to show her the writing. He knew he didn't have it in him today to answer her barrage of questions sure to come, but he now wanted the door open, the history told—the secrets exposed. After all, his wartime service was part of his and Lillian's story, and Lillian's story—one that Juliana needed to learn—was connected to Lizzy's story, and Lizzy's story was connected to Will's. He had confidence in his granddaughter's journalistic fortitude. His jewel would find his brother, heal the family, and bring him home or at the very least back into Lizzy's arms where he belonged. Briefly, he wondered if the pistol was still alive, kicking up dust and making mischief. *Damn, she was good for Ducky. What had gone wrong so fast between them? Had they not been as close as he assumed? Why did she stop writing to him? Most likely, Will had a pickle up his ass about something trivial, and she dropped him like a hot potato in early '43. No doubt, Lil had known and kept that secret from him in that iron vault of hers, too.*

He reached into the box and removed the gold-toned pin once tacked upon his Marine Corps garrison cap all those years ago. The EGA emblem— eagle, globe, anchor. His heart swelled. To him it was a prideful sight, a small insignia that stood for such great valor in all the men. It summed up the purpose of the box. It wasn't images of war within—it was brotherhood, camaraderie, friendship, and patriotic zeal. That was worth remembering.

"What's that, Grandpa?"

Above Will's sterling silver pilot wings that she wore pinned to her denim vest, Louie placed his insignia right above it. The Marine Corps was always first. He smiled as she toyed with it, understanding without any communication what it was.

Louie left the room, knowing Juliana would follow with the box. As they neared the hallway, they both stopped when they heard a key turn the entrance knob. The door opened and a blonde woman in her early sixties, wearing a pink, fashion sweat suit, entered holding a Pyrex casserole dish.

"Oh, I'm sorry, Louie. I didn't know you had company."

Juliana looked at one then the other and raised an eyebrow when her sight settled on her grandfather and his shit-eating grin.

"Hi. I'm Juliana, his granddaughter."

"Oh, yes. I've heard about you. Not from Louie, of course, but some of the women on the floor who see you come and go. It's lovely to meet you. I'm Vera, your grandfather's ... um... friend."

Juliana cocked her brow again when her eyes met Louie's.

He smirked and shrugged an innocent shoulder.

"Nice to meet you, Vera. I better be going. Maybe I'll see you again."

"I do hope so, dear."

Minutes later, she kissed her grandfather good-bye and left with the Florsheim box in hand, trying hard not to be upset that there was obviously a new woman in his life.

Seven

It Could Happen to You
June, 1992

Juliana's stomach rolled and cramped from the onion bagel with cream cheese she had washed down with a cup of coffee before hopping the subway to Manhattan. She wondered if it was actually nerves and not the size of what she consumed. Although, she hadn't eaten like that in ages.

Slender legs paced outside her boss's office, waiting for the door to open and the administrative assistant to emerge. Inside the Tiffany blue box at the bottom of her backpack, Lizzy's letters to Uncle William, silently signaling to be revealed, ignited her enthusiasm. The wounded daughter in her hated to admit and, truth be told, it was probably the real reason for her agitation, but Susan was right. There was a story to tell about William and the woman he had loved, and the writer in her was here at the magazine to pitch her hook to her good friend, *Allure's* senior editor.

The oversized clock seemed to tick by slowly beyond the plate glass window separating the editor's office from the many small cubicles displaying the visual, creative brainchildren of the magazine's many contributing editors, layout designers, and account reps. Tacked upon the visible interior of the editor's office walls, a collage of photographs, advertisements, inspiration, and sketches, hung haphazardly behind and beside her oversized desk.

The door finally opened and a trendy young woman exited holding a stenography pad in her hand. She winked to Juliana, smiled, and motioned for her to go in.

Maxine Grant, a chubby woman in her late thirties lowered her thick black-rimmed glasses and glanced up from her photograph-strewn desk. Short, raven hair and vampy, plum lipstick severely contrasted her pale, matte skin, but Maxine's signature look was striking, almost, even if her round eyewear resembled Edith Head's. Juliana always wondered if that was the look she was going for.

Maxine smiled brightly when her junior style writer plopped herself down in the chair before the desk. She noticed immediately the change in Juliana's appearance and overall aura. First of all, she wore a suit, and that was something the editor hadn't seen her friend wear since her job interview with *Allure*.

"Well, this is certainly a surprise. I haven't seen that pretty face of yours in months, especially since you decided to send your monthly copy up by bicycle messenger," she said.

"Good to see you, too, Max. How's business? Circulation up? Growing or are we in the toilet this month?"

From under the mess upon her desk, the editor pulled out the layout of the next month's cover. "Circulation is growing and trends are cooperating. Long, straight locks are all the rage. I see you finally entered the nineties by deciding to hack that big hair you still sported a few months ago. I'm so happy you just let it go, darling. Only Samson had a reason to hang onto his hair and even he had it cut."

"Yes, well ... I admit I resisted—as did he." Juliana shuddered. "If you had a mother like mine, you'd buck trends, too, but as a contributing fashion writer it was necessary, I suppose." She shook her locks. "I'm glad you like it. It was yesterday's project, and I actually spent the money to do it right at Bumble and Bumble."

"Good girl. Now that you have it, spend it. Your father would have wanted it that way. Don't you think?"

"Yeah, he would have. He always said I was too frugal—turns out both he and my great-uncle have forced my hand by leaving me all that money, not to mention DVDH. I suppose they were intent on spoiling me even from the grave."

"Of course your father did. He was a great man. How is your grandfather? How did he take the news?"

"Silently. He's still not speaking, *and* he has a girlfriend."

"A girlfriend? How do you know?"

"She had a key and entered his apartment as I was leaving."

"He's a character, huh?"

"You have no idea. Apparently, he's the strong silent type all the women of the apartment building are chasing after. At least, that's what the Resident Liaison told me when I ran into her in the hallway. You should see his refrigerator. It's stocked with casserole dishes."

Maxine laughed. "What a stud he is! Did you always know this about him?"

"No, I'm shocked, really. He didn't need words when I asked him about his philandering. That look in his eye was pretty damning. I'm actually a little upset about it—you know, I thought he missed my grandmother."

"I'm sure he does miss her but even a man at his age has physical needs. They'll never admit it, of course, but they have emotional ones, too. He's probably not looking for romantic love, just tenderness to fill the void."

"Yeah, I guess." She shrugged a shoulder

"So, what brings you in to see me on this beautiful day?"

Juliana reached into her bag and removed the box, resting it at the edge of the desk. She noted Maxine's piqued interest focusing at what was written along the sides of the pretty blue box in black, block letters that caused her to tilt her head to read, "William and Lizzy—My Dearest Darling."

"William?"

Juliana snorted a laugh. "Yes, and he's the story I'd like to tell, but I need your help."

Maxine tapped her Sharpie marker upon the desk and the slick images of Claudia Schiffer and Cindy Crawford. "Do tell. Do tell."

"It's a World War Two love story."

The editor dropped her marker, the creative wheels in her brain turned at the possibilities. "Oh *yes*, I can see it—*in love* with the clothing ... the elegance even during the ration. Gloves, hats, half-moon manicures, no hosiery, and hand sewed garments. The return to the basics of beauty."

Ten fisted fingers burst in punctuation. "Here's your hook: How to obtain an effortless, stylish look on a shoestring budget! How to resemble an MGM starlet during the Golden Age of Hollywood and return to an era of feminine allure and mystique. Rita Hayworth, Veronica Lake, and Brooklyn's own Gene Tierney—the young bride of Oleg Cassini, fashion designer to the stars!"

Maxine's voice rose with passionate excitement at the idea. "The hair! Oh the hair! Victory Rolls! All leading up to the pinnacle of post-war change in fashion: 'The New Look' by Dior. Yes! Ushering in short hair, cinched waists, full skirts, and luxurious fabrics in a romantic French explosion of sophisticated style. Julie—you are brilliant!"

Disheartened, Juliana responded with a slight grimace of embarrassment. "No, it's not a *fashion* love story—it's a human interest love story—an honest to goodness wartime romantic relationship—sweethearts."

Maxine's reply fell flat, deflated with the wind completely knocked out of her sails. "Oh."

"I know it isn't something we normally feature, but I'm sure this piece I'm working on could very well be an excellent F.O.B. An article such as this at the front of the magazine could segue into the feature well, covering your idea. I believe in the power of this story between this young couple and ... and I intend on finding out what happened to them at the end of my research, which could very well mean a follow up feature story in another issue. Maybe during November for Veteran's Day or on the Fiftieth Anniversary of the Battle of Peleliu."

"The battle of what? Julie, we're a fashion magazine. The only battles we face are those of wrinkles and fat." Maxine chuckled. "Well, so, I guess the Battle of the Bulge may well be an appropriate topic. Perhaps, we could compromise if you're insistent on a World War Two hook." She laughed at her joke. "Get it? Battle of the Bulge?"

Juliana shrugged a shoulder. She had never heard of the Battle of the Bulge.

Maxine slid June's mock-up cover in front of her friend. "I'm sorry, hon, but see here ... 'Split-Second Beauty', 'Diet Doctor.' *Allure* offers trends, cosmetics, fashion and hair, an insider's guide to a woman's image. That's what we do. We try to make people feel good about themselves, and if they don't we tell them how to do so. The closest we get to a love story is how to have an explosive orgasm or how to strip for your man in twelve easy to follow moves."

Like her editor, Juliana simply replied, "Oh."

Maxine opened the box and pulled out the thick stack of letters. "Is this your story?"

"Only the surface. The house I was given is at the heart of it. These are the wartime letters to my great-uncle from his girlfriend and his family. I've only read a couple, and they are starting to fill in tiny blanks. I'd like to travel to some of the places written on the pages and see if I can connect the dots about this fantastic, heartbreaking love affair. It's a mystery of sorts." Juliana swallowed hard. "I'd like to concentrate on this story, Max. It's ... it's important to me."

"Why do you assume it's heartbreaking?"

"Because as far as I know, they never married, or ... worse ... she died. See why I *have* to know?"

Fanning the tied fifty-year old letters, the professional in Maxine couldn't deny the appeal to uncover a good mystery not just for her magazine but for herself, too. Not to mention everyone loved a heart-tugging story about a veteran. She gazed up at Juliana's stylish charcoal suit. "That pin you're wearing, is it authentic?"

Juliana fingered the cool edge of William's pilot wings secured below her shoulder. "Yes, they were William's." She raised an eyebrow. "Why? Are you interested? Is there something pulling you toward this story? You see it don't you?"

"Perhaps." Maxine slid a letter from the top of the stack and admired the fine penmanship. She ran her finger over the salutation. "This is lovely stationery. Expensive." She thoughtfully sighed. "I fear the day when this 'so called' electronic mail Bill Gates talks about comes along. You'll see, before long, no one will write letters or even pick up the telephone to say hello. I shudder at what we will become. Hmm ... I shudder at what will become of the memory and stories of the Silent Generation."

She held out the letter to her friend. "May I read it?"

A sly, knowing smirk appeared on Juliana's lips. "Sure, knock yourself out."

"June 8, 1942
Dear William,

What a delightful surprise it was to receive your letter, especially since I was under the impression that you did not wish an acquaintance. I was sure you interpreted my letter as too forward, even—dare I say—pushy! I have been told, on occasion, that I can be quite relentless in getting my way, but in your case, I was prepared to accept that you weren't interested. So, with a resounding YES, I would love to meet you at four o'clock, Saturday, June 13 beside the lion at the Public Library closest to 42nd Street! Just look for the girl with a beaming smile of anticipation, that'll be me.

I am so excited about attending the New York at War Parade on the arm of such a dashing pilot. Are you sure your marching will have completed by then since the parade travels such a long way up Fifth Avenue? Rest assured, I will wait with bells on until your arrival downtown. My sister will be marching with the ARC. Perhaps, we can send your brother a snapshot should we get a glimpse of her. I am so proud of her, and I imagine you are just as proud of Louie. I'm looking forward to hearing any news you have about his destination. Oh, does that fall under 'careless talk'? Never mind then.

My other sister, Kitty and I have embarked on quite the endeavor since we met you on Memorial Day. I bet you'll be surprised to learn that we have officially begun a nylon stocking drive because you know how we debs just love our hosiery! Now if I can only get them to donate then I'll really have something to boast about. However, I do think our other venture may be a bit more realistic. We have decided to volunteer for the Victory Book Campaign through our local library. These old homes around here must all have libraries filled with hundreds of unread, like-new books, and it is our hope to get our neighbors to part with them for the war effort. I plan on visiting our librarian, Mrs. Tinsdale to discuss our ideas. In a way, I feel as though it is my first real job interview, and I'm very excited!

I wonder, do you enjoy reading? I do. I find it a fantastic escape and now that the Zephyr is in the repair shop, I am thoroughly engrossed in an Agatha Christie novel. I simply adore crime, mystery, and suspense. Once, I stayed awake until the wee hours of the morning just to finish, "Murder on the Orient Express." That was one of the most suspenseful books I have read.

Well, Lieutenant Ducky Shincracker, I look forward to a swell afternoon spent in your company. Thank you for your letter and the invitation for a date. Don't worry about my travels into the city. I'll be taking

the 1:15 train from Glen Cove—see I do take public transportation! Ha! If you change your mind, which I sincerely hope you don't but am sure you won't (remember I'm an optimist,) my telephone number is ORiole-67126.
Sincerely,
Lizzy"

Maxine lowered the letter. "Ducky shincracker? Oh, I *like* her—a girl going after what she wants and she wants him. It sounds as though she's trying to impress him. Any indication of his feelings for her? By the sound of it, he wasn't too gung ho at first. Are any of his letters in this stack? It would be great if we can hear his voice."

"I haven't gone through them all. As far as I can see from the first few, they are mostly hers and placed in chronological order. I'd like to read them as such so I can experience the development of their relationship. I know how he felt about Lizzy. My uncle was head over heels in love. There is a shrine to her sitting on my fireplace mantle that I haven't had the heart to remove."

Juliana reached into the bottom of the box and pulled out a photograph she found in the footlocker. "I found this color photograph with a bunch of other snapshots in his military trunk in the attic. I think you'll understand my desire to explore all of this when you see it." After glancing at it with a gentle smile, she stretched across the desk to hand it to her friend.

"Wow. What a handsome couple. I love how she's sitting on his lap and that bathing suit she's wearing, positively an early Jantzen knit, sort of a Wedgwood blue ... fabulous fashion. He's as gorgeous as she is—a real Hollywood-type couple."

Lizzy and Will sat poolside on an armchair, both beaming for the camera. Maxine turned the photo over and read the notation. "Where is this place, Rosebriar Manor?"

"That's what I mean. I'd really like to take the time to look into these details. I don't even know her last name. As for where she lived, I guess Glen Cove, Long Island is as good a place to start as any. Maybe stop by their public library, ask a few questions, and check out their local history room if they have one. Inquire about a Mrs. Tinsdale who might lead me in the right direction to a family with five sisters from obvious affluence."

Maxine continued to admire the photograph, noting the luxury swimming pool beside William and Lizzy. "Definitely wealthy, and if she lived in Glen Cove, that's the Gold Coast. We're talking *Great Gatsby* wealth."

"Max, I understand if *Allure* won't support me on this, but I was kind of hoping that you would—if you can. Maybe over a weekend you can travel with me or you can reach out to a couple of your contacts. Do you think Andy could part with you from time to time?"

"Andy?" Maxine rolled her eyes. "Please, that man won't notice if I'm not at home. Now that summer is here and he's not teaching, he'll be spending every weekend on the golf course. I'd love to help you, if for no other reason than to spend some time with you *and* get my ass out of boring Dobbs Ferry. It'll be fun, but don't lose hope in what a magazine *can* do for this article, Julie. While it may not be appropriate for publishing in *Allure*, that doesn't necessarily mean it may not be suited for one of Conde Nast's other magazines, the *New Yorker*, for example."

She stared back down at the snapshot held in her fingers. "He's too dreamy to dismiss, and she's completely besotted with him. I adore the way her hand is resting on his chest, almost threading through that sexy patch of chest hair. I love the way his arm possessively wraps around her waist. They were so in love. I can feel it jump off this snapshot. It's tangible. Makes me want to jump in a cab and head downtown to Andy's office to shag him senseless."

"Yeah, apart from the Andy thing, I feel it, too. If only real life in the nineties produced love and men like ..." Juliana's hand flew to her mouth. She didn't mean the slip, didn't mean the insult to Maxine's brother whom she had dated for six months. "I'm sorry. That sorta just came out."

Maxine chuckled. "It's okay. You and Rob weren't meant to be. It's not your fault that women fall faster and men fall harder. Don't worry, he's gotten over his heartbreak. Took him awhile, but he's back in the swing of dating."

"Is he? I'm glad to hear that. He's a great guy, and I know I wounded him pretty bad. It's just that he wanted more than I could give at the time, emotionally. I know it sounds strange, but I really felt unworthy of all the love he wanted to give me. I might have truly fallen had I let myself." She played with the edge of the pilot wings. "I'm in therapy now—I'm working on that—I've recently confronted one of my demons over lunch the other day."

"I'm glad, darling. You deserve ..." Maxine raised and shook the photo, "... this kind of love."

Juliana humbly smiled. Touched by her friend's unusual tenderness, she got a little choked up because, in truth, she wanted that kind of love but remained skeptical that it really existed. She wanted a large family and an adoring spouse. She wanted children and laughter in her life, and she wanted to make Primrose Cottage the home it never had the chance to become. One day, forty-two years from now, she hoped her grandchild would find the attic bursting with memories made and dusty, keepsake items.

"Thanks, Max. That means a lot to me. At the moment, apart from a silent grandfather, you're the only person to actually care."

"I do care. One of the best decisions I made was hiring you, Julie. What began as a need to hire only the best for *Allure*, grew into this unexpected friendship between us. I suppose, my fixing you up with Rob and *mayybeee* pushing a bit too hard for you to make more of your relationship than you were able to, is only because of how much you mean to me ... personally."

"Thank you. And I, truly value our friendship, too." With a sincerely brilliant smile Juliana promptly changed the subject, afraid to open her heart further. Reaching into her backpack again, she retrieved the steno pad filled with the notes she had made in the attic.

"Here are the major questions I'd like to answer first. I assembled this list while going through his footlocker and a hope chest in the attic. There was also a box filled with the most beautiful Limoges china, which I brought down, arranging all the pieces in the empty dining room breakfront. Most of the items in the hope chest appeared unused. You would love the tons of French lace, antique English Battenberg, hankies with the embroidered initial, E. I know *I* fell in love with the different table linens: Scandinavian folk patterns, Belgian lace doilies, and a silk brocade table throw. There was even an old christening gown, the likes of which I have never seen. It had a matching baby pillowcase of cotton and lace. Just wonderful, antique stuff, predominately European imported textiles."

"A baby christening pillowcase? That's unusual." Maxine read aloud the first question. "So—first question: What is Lizzy's surname?"

"I know it begins with *R* because I found a burned letter with embossed initials in the fireplace."

Before removing the next letter from the top of the stack, Maxine fanned the envelopes to glance at the corner of each where only the initials *L.R* read back "Curiouser and curiouser. Let's see what else Lizzy has to say."

"June 13, 1942
Dear Ducky,

I have just arrived home and couldn't wait until the morning to write, so here I am curled up in my favorite place on the estate, my water tower. I know you noticed it when you came for Memorial Day. How could you miss it? Even though the blackout shades are drawn, it is still at least ten degrees cooler up here when the breeze blows off the coast. Given the unusual heat of today—not to mention the excitement and the crowd—it's a fine place to sleep tonight, undisturbed and left to my sweet dreams of a certain flyboy and his dimple. Don't worry, no one will miss me or become worried. I let our butler, Mr. Howard know I arrived home safely, and as far as I can see from my perch, the Odin has yet to return to dock, so my father hasn't returned home from his visit in New Jersey with my Aunt Helga, his sister.

You are such a gentleman to have seen me all the way home to Long Island on the train. You really didn't have to, you know, but I was over the moon that you did. Thank you! I hope you arrived back to Park Slope without difficulty. I had such a wonderful time today and felt honored that you would want me as your date for the remainder of the parade. Why, you're not a fuddy duddy at all! I was correct—underneath that proper exterior of yours, you really are quite the jokester and, dare I say, as mischievous as I am. Only, you're such a terrible tease and with that dry humor of yours, I could barely tell when you were joking! I haven't laughed as hard as I did in your company today. I hope you had fun, too. Thank you for such a swell time: The parade, the carousel, and the torchlight procession. The pistol in me would be remiss if I failed to mention our memorable kiss. It was all so romantic and a date like I had never had before.

Will, I am only sorry that you are leaving in a few days for Tampa, but I'm so happy we have this opportunity to get to know one another before your departure. I'm greatly looking forward to our date out on the Sound on

Tuesday! I hope the weather is perfect because I'm planning quite an afternoon for us. Don't worry, I am not so much a hotrodder in the boat!

Perhaps, you'll telephone me but if not, I hope you get this letter in time to confirm that I'll meet you at eleven in the morning at the Hempstead Harbor Yacht Club at the end of Garvies Point. Don't be late, Ducky.
Sincerely yours,
Lizzy the pistol"

Maxine lowered the letter. "He moved fast, didn't he? A kiss on their first date in 1942 was *very* forward. Obviously, he was interested." She reached over to her phone, picked up the receiver and began to dial excitedly.

Covering the mouthpiece she spoke quietly, "I have a friend who can help you. Give me a minute and I'll see if I can arrange a meeting."

Juliana nodded, and the butterflies of anticipation and excitement went crazy in her stomach, definitely not the result of the onion bagel. It was evident to her that Maxine's creative mind was immediately at work.

"Hi, Cassandra, It's Maxine Grant at *Allure* magazine. I'd like to speak with Jack if he's available." Again, Maxine covered the mouthpiece and whispered, *"Newsday."*

"Hawaii? For how long?" she asked the secretary on the other end of the receiver.

"Well, I'd like to leave a message for his return. It's rather important, a story we're working on for fall publication, and since he is from the North Shore of the Island and *Newsday's* travel writer, I need to pick his brain. My style writer and I would like to arrange a meeting with him when he gets back.

"Yes, that's right. He has both of my numbers, home and work. Let him know we may need to do a little digging in *Newsday's* archives. Thanks, Cassandra." Maxine hung up.

"*Newsday?* That's perfect, Max. What did she say? When will this Jack guy be back?"

"Not for another week, but don't worry if there are answers out there, he'll help us find them. He's a great guy. In fact ..." Maxine raised an eyebrow just as a playful smirk appeared.

"Don't say it!" Juliana laughed. "Both your track record for fixing me up and my track record for dating someone longer than six months leave a lot to be desired."

"Trust me on this one, Julie. Andy's on-again, off-again golf buddy is *perfect* for you! Perfect, absolutely, perfect!"

Juliana continued to laugh at her friend's enthusiasm. "All right, what's his name?"

"Jack Robertsen and he is gorgeous!"

Eight

Anchors Aweigh
June 13, 1942

After months of preparation and training with the Abwehr in Berlin, four men embarked on a mission expected to cripple the United States of America. It seemed the perfect, moonless night for the beginning of Operation Pastorius. Thick fog clung to the sandy coastline and dunes along the Atlantic Ocean on Long Island's South Shore, near a beach community called Amagansett.

At ten minutes past midnight the Nazi saboteurs, all of whom had previously resided in America, came ashore bearing four wooden crates containing sophisticated sabotage "gifts" they would later deliver and deploy at strategically planned locations, beginning with the Big Apple. The plan, formulated by the Nazi Intelligence project leader, a former member of the German American Bund in New York City, was to perpetrate coordinated bombing attacks over the next two years. Another group of saboteurs planned to come ashore four days later at a similar sleepy beach community in northern Florida named Ponte Vedra. The mission's expected result would deliver a blow to America's formidable war production. No target would be spared: bridges, factories, canals, Jewish-owned department stores, train depots and even railroads, but more specifically—and hopefully—American morale.

The slender, cigar-shaped Nazi U-boat still sat in wait—or so it would have appeared if anyone could see beyond the zero visibility. Stuck on a sand bar two hundred yards from the beach, it was temporarily rendered immobile until a rising tide could change its fate. That was the first sign that the operation was destined to go to hell in a hand basket as fifty men panicked inside *U202*, afraid of discovery.

Nevertheless, the saboteurs' mission was underway as they buried the trunks and changed their clothes from Kriegsmarine uniforms to civilian apparel. One hundred thousand dollars strapped to each man would cover their expenses over the course of the operation, money provided by the continued, generous financial support of friends of the Third Reich, donors whose loyalty to the Fatherland was as secret as their acts against America. Comprised of former members of the Bund as well as agents of the Reich, their lives, for many years, were deeply embedded in the fabric of American society: politicians, lawyers, businessmen and even a pastor or two. Not all were agents but many acted as such.

The group leader breathed deeply, enjoying the salty sea air. He dug his white socks into the sand and reveled in the feel of being back in New York. He had long had a taste in his mouth for a hot dog and a five-cent Coca-Cola from a Manhattan street pushcart. Proximity to the great metropolis fostered his nostalgic desire to visit Horn & Hardart for a slice of huckleberry pie. It felt good to be home.

The misty gray fog rolled in from the water evoking a Bela Lugosi movie—thick and concealing. In the far distance, the saboteurs heard only the occasional bell clang of a buoy offshore and the nearby gentle rhythmic lapping tide breaking. Even the U-Boat sat silent before stressing its diesel engines in hope of dislodging from the sand bar holding it captive. Busy at the task of burying the munitions crates, duffle bags and their uniforms, the saboteurs never heard the approach of a lone Coastguard "sand-pounder." His presence wasn't expected since the Navy and the Coastguard had yet to ramp up security along the eastern seaboard, even following the fire aboard the SS *Normandie* and all the other U-boat torpedoing activity over the past five months.

Suddenly, a blinding light broke the blackness of night. The white beam shined upon them, illuminating their crime. A thick Long Island accent rang out, "You there! What are you doing on the beach? The coastline is off limits at night."

"We are fisherman. We've run aground," one of the four said.

Immediately, the group leader, Dasch, stepped forward after one of his cohorts foolishly said something in German. All craving for New York's famed food vanished from the leader's focus. Grabbing the Coastguardsman's arm, his threat was simple. "Do you have a mother?"

"Yes."

"A father?"

"Yes."

The Nazi spy removed a rolled stack of money from his pocket and handed it to the young sentry. "I wouldn't want to kill you." He shone the flashlight at his own face. "You'll be meeting me again. Would you know me?"

Fighting would have been fruitless. The sand pounder was unarmed. "No sir, I never saw you in my life."

After long, tense minutes, more money and more threats, the twenty-one year old sand pounder took the greenbacks and hurriedly left for the lifeboat station a mile away. He was anxious to telephone his superiors that Nazis had landed on Long Island.

****

Hot was an understatement. The Big Apple boiled like a melting pot in the unusual heat, but the sweltering afternoon sun didn't stop the city's residents who turned out for the "New York at War Parade." In support of the war, they had come in droves. Men, women, and children of all ages stood in close quarters, packing body heat onto Fifth Avenue, yet they seemed unaffected by the temperature. They had traveled from every Borough to line the sixty-five blocks of the parade route, awaiting the passage of over three hundred floats.

Lizzy stood on the curb at the corner of 39th Street and Fifth Avenue, two blocks south of the New York Public Library, with her view partially blocked by one of the city's finest policemen. She knew, she would never forget this day and was thankful for the Lieutenant's invitation to be a part of it. If he hadn't asked her for the date, she never would have attended, and now she understood what a tragedy missing such an incredible opportunity to experience true patriotism would have been. Being here—standing beside

John amidst the vast crowds, in the heat of the sun, watching a float of President Roosevelt's head pass by, was forming one of the most exciting moments of her life, and that alone surprised the heck out of her.

"I've never seen so many people in one place and at one time before. How many do you think are here?"

John continued to watch the parade, admiring the lead Sherman tank slowly rolling by. "I don't know. The *New York Herald* estimated about two million to turn out."

A palette of color passed before them with an impressive procession of women volunteers from the American Red Cross, Army and Navy nurses, and trainees in the newly created WAAC. They marched along the avenue from curb to curb, some wearing capes, others military uniforms, but all wore smiles. Lizzy's heart swelled with even more pride as she looked for Lillian in the ranks of the Red Cross.

Plant workers and air-raid wardens paraded side-by-side with other Civil Defense and volunteer groups who had turned out in support of the war— five hundred thousand in all. Norwegians, Japanese, Greeks, Italians, and Germans dressed in colorful traditional apparel, advanced carrying and waving American and other national flags. Behind their ranks of loyal patriotic display, WWI Veterans marched with their VFW and American Legion Posts followed by ambulances, jeeps, and dignitaries.

Lizzy felt immense excitement in being both a New Yorker and an American. The overall sentiment among the spectators around her was palpable and as proud as the flapping dance upon the air of every Old Glory waving in the resplendent afternoon light. Upon the faces of parade goers, she could see the raw emotion and confidence in the Allies' ultimate Victory. She felt it, too, especially when that pride became steely determination with the passing of War Bond, Victory Book and other educational platforms. The grim floats depicting Hitler's maniacal treatment of European citizens and the militarization of Germany's youths served to stoke her dormant, if not ignorant, call for defeat of the Axis. She didn't know all the players in the Axis but was determined to learn.

The U.S Marine Corps Band marched next before the two childhood friends. Their patriotic performance of the "Marines' Hymn" electrified the air, mixing with the cheers of spectators as hundreds of unified soldiers brought up the rear.

Streams of white paper ticker tape snowed down upon the hot, gray concrete and the army of Marines, the Corps of the nation's treasures, when they passed in unison where Lizzy and John stood. Chills ran up her spine in tingly excitement tangibly producing euphoric confidence at the power they conveyed when marching as one with their bayoneted rifles steadied upon their shoulders. This vision, combined with her voracious reading of the newspaper these last two weeks, was the closest she came to learning what was going on beyond the shores of America, and it was all because of one man who made her desire more than her self-absorbed life in Glen Cove. Louie and William Martel were a part of these brave men, and she wanted to be more than the affluent debutante they had met. Changing for William meant changing for herself, and with every new day, she found herself welcoming any and all challenges with a firm resolve. Lizzy stood on her tiptoes, searching every face of every soldier passing by. Her head craned around the broad navy blue official in front of her. "Do you see him, Johnny?"

He laughed. "No. He's not a Marine. His brother Louie is the Marine. Your friend William is with the Army Air Forces. They'll probably be parading with one of Robertsen's warplanes. We must have missed them or they haven't come up the avenue yet."

Bag pipers and a flag-holding delegation of Western Hemisphere nations passed and Lizzy shouted out to John, "I wish Kitty were here! She would love this!"

He simply smiled, his vision locking on her jubilant countenance for a bit longer than necessary. In all the years of their close friendship, he doubted he had ever seen her so alive, so animated before. Lizzy was ordinarily a ball of fire, but today her excitement was extraordinary. It wasn't her simple, red and white polka dot dress or the stylish, crochet hairnet she wore, nor was it her vibrant, red lips smiling and cheering. John was certain that the flush to her cheeks wasn't just from the heat and humidity. It was something more, and he wondered if perhaps his dear childhood friend was in love for the first time in her twenty years.

"Maybe Hearst will take some home movies with his 8mm camera. Kitty can still see the parade as though she were here with us. I promise she can come over to Coventry's movie showing room, and we'll make it a special night just for her."

"You're always so good to her."

"Why wouldn't I be? I love you both like the sisters I was *meant* to have."

She playfully slapped his arm when he chuckled at his own joke.

Lizzy burst out, "I'm so proud!"

John laughed again at her enthusiasm. "Yeah, me too. To think, Robertsen Aviation is a part of this power and might. We're putting good men like your lieutenant in the air."

She smirked playfully. "He's not my *anything* ... yet."

"Oh, I don't know about that. He wouldn't have made a date to meet you later if he wasn't keen on you, Lizzy."

Her white-gloved hand tilted the green glass Coca-Cola bottle in her grasp as the now warm rim met her lips. She shrugged a shoulder, not quite sure if Flyboy was indeed interested. She hated being so insecure. It was highly unusual and an unfamiliar emotion, so she promptly changed the subject. "Why aren't you parading beside your father and the plant workers?"

"Why? You know the answer to that. Apparently, my father and sisters, not to mention Ingrid, don't want me to stoop to such a level. Hearst isn't marching either, and he's the Vice President of Finance. Nope, only Dad at the helm, steering the float and pretending to salute the crowds like he's Jimmy Doolittle himself."

"Who?"

"Never mind. The point is both you and I know that even though our fathers fight with one another, they agree on the business of this war as a profitable venture, nothing more. My dad's not as patriotic as he may seem. Heck, I bet he even attends some of those wacky meetings your father goes to down in New Jersey."

"Wacky meetings? Why the heck would he go to New Jersey for a meeting?"

John glanced down at Lizzy's curious expression. No, she wouldn't know about those meetings. Renner's best-kept secret was best kept from Lizzy. She would be crushed if she knew just how her father truly felt about Hitler and the Nazis. He wished he could always protect her from knowing and hoped this war would end soon enough so she would never find out that

Renner was a sympathizer and a bigot of the worst kind. "*Heil Hitler*" wasn't something Renner heard actors declare in the movies. It was something he believed as early as his affiliation began with The Friends of New Germany and later the German American Bund.

Years ago, John had become deeply curious about the Bund's Youth Camp Siegfried when Renner had sent Ingrid out to the far end of Long Island. Lizzy was just eleven then, and he an inquisitive young man of sixteen who had a crush on her beautiful older sister. Once, he even traveled out on the train to the camp to spy on Ingrid from the forest until the wee hours of the morning. John knew for sure the Bund's camp *attempted* to indoctrinate Ingrid in the Nazi ideology. Heck, the swastika flew unabashedly, but he was never able to confirm the extent of their rhetoric until the newspapers reported its dismantling in 1939.

No, he wasn't about to burst Lizzy's happy bubble and loyalty to her family even if the truths of *die familie* Renner were ugly—as ugly as the Robertsens'. John lied, realizing he had said too much, "Um, you know those American First Committee meetings."

She shrugged again. "Oh, those. I thought they disbanded."

"Say, don't you have a pilot to meet? You better get a move on."

Lizzy glanced at the Rolex she received as a coming out gift. "You're right! It's time." She reached upward, placing her hands on either side of her dear friend's fair head and kissed John's cheek. "Wish me luck."

"You don't need any luck. After today, he'll be certifiably dizzy and head over heels with that vibrant, loving spirit of yours."

"Thanks, but we'll see."

"Are you sure you don't want me to walk you? The crowd is pretty thick."

"No, I'll be all right. Stay where you are and enjoy the parade. I'll telephone you tomorrow with all the details of my date and set a time to get those books from you for the Victory drive. Thanks again, Johnny, for escorting me into the city. I didn't mean to be such a baby in not wanting to ride the train alone." She leaned into his shoulder with a push. "Don't tell Father. I think he'd be upset with me if he knew I hated riding on the railroad."

"I won't. Hey, I had fun today." He smiled again and joked, "Next patriotic parade that comes along, I'll make sure we invite Ingrid. Maybe get her to buy War Bonds. You know I've been trying to get her to use her trust fund for that 'Buy a Bomber' program."

"Oh you're a gas! That'll be the day that she ever spends her money on *that* or attend something like *this*."

With a quick kiss to his cheek again, Lizzy was gone, headed through the crowd toward what she hoped was her destiny.

****

Lizzy hadn't planned on the library's signature white stone lions being concealed below the temporary grandstand erected to accommodate the various speeches taking place throughout the day. She almost panicked, afraid that her much anticipated date with Lieutenant Dreamboat might not happen. Perhaps, they wouldn't be able to find one another in the crush of spectators.

Built upon the steps of the library, an impressive, elevated reviewing stand, back-dropped with a huge American flag, looking out onto Fifth Avenue and the passing floats. Mayor Fiorello LaGuardia surveyed the crowd from his helm position on the battleship shaped platform in all his five foot, two inch powerhouse stature. His familiar, high-pitched voice pierced the crowded avenue as he gave one of his many memorable speeches to the thousands captivated by his message. Even in Lizzy's hurried anticipation and endeavor to locate Will, she caught snippets of the "Little Flower's" speech. She liked him at once and couldn't understand why her father hated him so. The diminutive mayor spoke of equality and justice for all people. What could possibly be wrong with that?

Looking over and around the heads of spectators, surrounding the grandstand on the sidewalk, she anxiously pressed through, fighting her way within the flag-waving contingent. Many cheered a passing float, reading its message of stalwart determination—"Czechoslovakia Fights On." Lizzy stopped to admire the black and red float, carrying patriots dressed as farmers, and she knit her brow in concern. Only yesterday, she read the small article in the *New York Times* on how the entire town of Lidice had been burned to the ground.

Wearing his olive dress uniform, Will watched her from his covert position leaning against a wood barricade behind three small boys waving American flags. He smiled at the glorious vision Lizzy created. The way her gloved white hand shielded her vibrant green eyes from the sun when she turned to view the passing float, and her quizzical brow caused his heart to flutter a little bit. She was as gorgeous as he remembered her fourteen days earlier. Those perfectly tinted red lips contrasted against her ivory skin and cheerful polka dot dress. He wondered what she thought as she watched the decorated platform roll by.

She turned to him and even through the crowd of ten or so adults and children between them, their eyes met, and her serious expression transformed into a beaming smile. Will's heart fluttered again, and he redirected that intense feeling by tossing the empty peanut bag he held into the trashcan beside him.

Making his way to her, he couldn't help matching the brilliance of her grin. "Hello, Miss Renner."

Her mouth twisted in that seductive manner he remembered and liked so much.

"Hi Flyboy. Nice, spiffy uniform."

Will touched the brim of his service cap. "That's *Lieutenant* Flyboy to you and thank you. You look lovely yourself. Well, Lizzy, what do you think of the parade, so far?"

"It's wonderful!" she blurted before he could reply, "I looked for you!"

"Oh, yeah? That's nice to hear. I'm sorry you missed us. I marched up at noon with other men from the First Air Force. We marched in review behind a couple of F4F Wildcats."

Will watched as Lizzy bit the lower corner of her lip, and he realized she didn't understand what he just said. As tempted as he was to kiss that nervous tick of hers, he quelled the temptation, remembering why exactly he asked her for a date at the parade when he could have taken her anywhere else. "They're fighter planes made by Grumman."

"Right. Robertsen Aviation's competitor."

"Not during the war. We're all in it for the same cause. Even book campaigns fight for our freedom. Books are a weapon, too." He pointed to the small *V* pin Lizzy wore below her shoulder, hoping she would understand what he meant about her recent volunteering. Reading her letter about her war efforts had made him happy—hopeful.

"Yes, you're right! We don't burn books here; we send them to the soldiers. Maybe one of my Agatha Christie novels will find their way into your hands when you're over in Europe."

"And what would you write on the inside cover ... should I get it, of course?"

Lizzy clasped her hands together, jutted her chin like Ingrid and standing straight she very prim and properly proclaimed, "Dear Flyboy. Give 'em hell, keep 'em flying, and come home safe! Yours truly, Pistol Packin' Lizzy."

They laughed, and, again, Will felt the prompting tug in his heart to kiss her.

Beside them, the U.S. Army Band marched up the avenue, passing before the mayor who admired them from his perch as they played the Army's official song, "The Caisson." Overhead, as though a moving dark cloud, combat planes filled the vibrant blue Manhattan sky in salute of the men bringing up the rear behind the band. One could almost see the white stars on the side of the planes above their ball turret.

Even in the heat of the summer humidity, goose pimples formed on Will's arms. It was a sublime, breathtaking moment not only infused with patriotic pride but also the promise of a burgeoning romance that somehow he knew would develop into something more in spite of her family and their vulgar opinions. He watched Lizzy studying the sky—innocence, excitement, and effervescence transformed her face from beautiful to stunning. This time, she didn't cover her eyes with a gloved hand. She met the warmth of the sun, watching the B-24 Liberators soar above in formation. The profile of her grin was as awe inspiring as the impressive bombers themselves, and it was then he truly knew Lizzy Renner was special, different from any other woman he knew. She was a brilliant beacon of light in a dark world and an ingénue, ready and anxious for the next chapter of her life. Silently, he thanked his brother for the encouragement to pursue her against his hesitant and suspicious judgment.

As the battalions of men filed past in review, Will stood at attention, saluting not only the marching commanders but also his brothers in arms. Sure, he was a commissioned officer, but rank didn't matter to him. They deserved a salute, especially since many marched holding the colors of the nation.

Lizzy turned to him, meeting his gaze with a timid look, and that surprised him.

Taking a step closer, she took his free hand. "What song did you march up the avenue to?"

"The Army Air Corps song. You've heard it, I'm sure." He didn't know what possessed him, but he sang it. "Off we go into the wild blue yonder."

"Well, well, not only are you a good dancer but you can carry a tune as well. Be still my heart, Lieutenant."

Will looked down at their clasped hands, thinking how comfortable it felt. "You can call me Will, you know."

"*Finally.* I thought you'd never ask. Lieutenant Fuddy Duddy Ducky Shincracker is quite a mouthful."

He chortled and couldn't help his mind gravitating to how he wanted his lips and tongue to give her quite a mouthful of the most delicious kisses, but promptly chastised himself for such wolfish thoughts.

It was bad enough that his own mouth remained full of words he wanted to say, like how he wished he had invited her for a date sooner, but how happy he was that she met him on such an auspicious occasion, but he resisted. The reserved, proper man in him fought the young eager romantic held inside—held back warily until he knew Lizzy's true opinions and beliefs. "Speaking of a mouthful, would you like to get something to eat?"

"Oh, yes, I know just the place uptown. The Rainbow Room serves up a splendid late lunch. Later, maybe we can head over to the Swing Club."

"No ... I hope it's okay, but I have someplace else in mind. No hoity-toity restaurant today and no party atmosphere tonight. You're going to have a taste of Americana like the rest of us."

"That sounds swell!"

He continued to hold her hand leading her uptown through the massive crowds, seemingly marching in unison with the Army GIs beside them on Fifth Avenue.

Lizzy asked unabashedly, "Do you know what has happened in Czechoslovakia? I read something in the *Times,* but I didn't understand why the Nazis would wipe out an entire town. Why would they murder those poor people?"

"It's the same all over Europe: Hungary, Poland, Ukraine, France, and the Netherlands. Under the guise of punishment for actions against the Reich, the Gestapo has been deporting thousands to forced labor camps and sequestered ghettos, probably since '37. The boycotts began when Hitler came into power in '33. Lidice is an ideal example of the brutality I spoke of on Memorial Day."

"Boycotts? Against whom?"

He furrowed his brow, disbelieving that she truly didn't know, but then reminded himself that most Americans didn't *want* to know even if it was reported as it should be. "Why Jews, of course."

Will stopped at the corner of 43rd Street and turned to her. This was the open door where he would attempt to fan her flame of curiosity in the hopes of deconstructing her family's ideology. A marching band played behind them as he asked, "You really want to learn more, Lizzy?"

"I do. For the last hour, Johnny and I have felt more pride in our nation than we ever had and ... and, I'm embarrassed to say, actually ashamed to say, I'm ignorant as to all the reasons we are fighting."

Will couldn't help the stab of jealousy. "Oh ... I didn't realize John is here with you."

"He played the ever-attentive big brother by escorting me into the city. His father is participating in the parade, you know."

"Right, of course." He smiled thoughtfully. "Well, if you're serious about learning more, then the best place to start is to advise you not to read just the *New York Times.* If you want the full story, the stories that shouldn't be buried on page six, read all the papers through and through, and not just the front page."

"Father used to read the *America First Bulletin* but now only reads the *New Yorker Staats-Zeitung,* but I don't understand German, so I have been reading at the public library. If you don't read the *Times*, do you read the *Herald*?"

How could he tell her what he read? He just met her and wasn't about to divulge twenty-plus years of deep secrets to just anyone.

"Among other things." He brushed a loose tendril escaped from her white hairnet. "Now, c'mon, let's have fun and not think of such atrocities today—our first date. I've thought of nothing but your smile these last two weeks, and I can't stand to see that pretty face of yours frown so."

She beamed at his compliment. "You think I'm pretty?"

Will leaned down to her, breathing in the delicate jasmine and orange blossom scent that had tormented him for two weeks. He spoke shyly, as though afraid of being heard when finally voicing the words. "Yes, Lizzy. I think you're *very* pretty. In fact, you're the most beautiful girl I've ever met."

"Really? The most beautiful girl? You must not get out much, then."

"Yeah, that must be it. I just spent the last nine months surrounded by Air Cadets in Texas. Although some of those Grey Lady Red Cross girls looked worth buzzing around."

Will found that he loved teasing her and looked over to her, wiggling his eyebrows, trying to elicit just the response he hoped for. He tried not to laugh at how the smile diminished from her lips in momentary jealousy, until she playfully slapped his shoulder.

"You're a terrible tease! So, what you're saying is I'm the first girl you've seen since coming *home,* then?"

"The first one to succeed in capturing my attention is more like it. It's not every day an alluring, spirited woman rudely runs you off the road into the mud then politely tells you with a captivating twinkle in her eye and a mischievous laugh that you're the one at fault because you're a fuddy duddy!"

She burst out with that devilish sounding laugh he hadn't stopped dreaming about since first meeting her.

"Say, I hope those fancy shoes you're wearing can withstand the walk I have planned for us," he stated.

"And where *are* you taking me?"

He started to walk through the crowd, again, on their way up to their final destination at Central Park.

"You'll see. And we can stop to eat along the way."

Nine

Street of Dreams
June 13, 1942

Renner stood on the starboard side of the *Odin* anchored off the coast of Connecticut on the northern rocky shoreline of the Long Island Sound. The choppy waves colliding against the hull reflected his pensive mood.

He loved this yacht. It proved to be the perfect escape not only for his business and his pleasure, but also for discussing his "political" views and activities far from eavesdroppers. The scent of German cigar rose in the warm sea air, infiltrating the pure salty fresh aroma. On such a clear day, he could almost see the shoreline of Glen Cove across the water. Lost in thought and the enjoyment of his stogie, he never heard Gebhardt exit the cabin until the man was standing beside him, smoking his own cigar.

Gebhardt puffed, sending billowing smoke from his lips. "How did you save the *Odin* from conscription in the Coast Guard's Civilian Auxiliary?"

"How do you get anything done these days? Money, my friend. Although, sometimes I regret that decision. The *Odin* could be very effective in helping our wolf packs up and down the Atlantic Coast. Already Operation Paukenschlag has effectively sent over four hundred ships to the bottom of the sea." Renner sniggered. "America has a false sense of security, as demonstrated by cities along the coast refusing a blackout. Look at Miami. Lit up like a Roman candle every night because they think tourism will suffer. Other cities are much the same."

"Not New York."

"Ah, well, the Island is different than Manhattan and its little swine mayor. For years, he was the Director of the Office of Civilian Defense, but that didn't stop our man's work on the *Normandie*. But even still, the Navy has proven to be inept, sitting back on its laurels while *U-123* operated in shallow waters these last six months."

Renner wrapped his lips around the stogie, drawing and puffing methodically.

"Pastorious is successful so far. They made it ashore and have most likely made their way into in the city by now," Gebhardt buoyed.

"I'll breathe a sigh of relief after the others arrive in Florida on schedule and when we receive confirmation that they have all arrived safely in Cincinnati on July Fourth."

"You worry too much, Renner. I told you, Berlin has planned this for months, not a single thing could go wrong, and even if it does, you're protected. Their handler, the good Reverend in Rahway is so respected and embedded into life within the community that no one would even suspect the Reich had turned him. His financial involvement, let alone yours, would never be called into question as far as the FBI is concerned. You are nothing more than a generous benefactor to Reverend Krepper for the building of his new Lutheran church. The testimony of your sister Helga would collaborate that."

The engine of a Civil Air Patrol plane flying overhead in search of enemy submarines caused Gebhardt and Renner to look up. Renner shook his head. "Civil. Nothing to worry about. George, I don't want Helga involved, do you understand? She has no loyalty to the Fatherland. Jazz music corrupted her long ago—her *Negermusik* is as equally disturbing as her defense of the Jews. It's bad enough you shared Operation Pastorious with Ingrid." Renner glanced behind them both, his eyes searching the lounge cabin for his daughter. He lowered his voice, "I don't like it, not one bit. You put her at risk until victory is achieved."

"What are you worried about? I said I would look after your interests and that means all of them, your daughters included. Once Ingrid marries the boy, she'll be safely protected by the Robertsen name and concealed by their American patriotic zeal."

"Yes, you are right, of course, and he does come from the best bloodline."

"With her installed as wife to the heir of Robertsen Aviation, any knowledge or sabotage within the factories will be hidden behind her generous financial contributions to Bundles for Britain and the Red Cross, which all imply her personal support of the war. Just today, she has donated fifty thousand to that 'Buy a Bomber' program to build one of those Thunderbolts Robertsen Aviation manufactures." He laughed. "Did you know they'll actually paint her name on the side of the aircraft? The dedication ceremony will bring just the right amount of press."

Renner cocked a graying eyebrow. "Does she know that she's contributed to those organizations?"

Gebhardt responded with his prototypical charmingly suave smile. "Of course not, but I have seen to the details, or I should say—you have seen to the details through FHR Worldwide. As far as anyone is concerned, your daughters do not share their father's recognizable opinion on American isolationism or obscured Nazi sympathies."

"Good." Frederick tossed his cigar stub overboard and walked to the front of the boat. He stood at the prow with his hands on his broad waistline, surveying the expanse of shoreline before him with sanguine optimism. "Soon, George, soon this will all be Germany's."

George puffed his cigar. "And not a Jew in sight."

Renner looked at the sneer upon his lawyer's lips. "One step at a time, my eager friend. Have arrangements been made with that special group of investors? Among my friends, those in our circle, I want it known that Frederick Renner is a part of this solution. When the New Germany comes to America, I expect to be heralded for my financial contribution to IG Farben."

"I wonder, Renner, if you have given thought to what your other daughters will think of that? I only ask this because, take Lillian for example, you are put at risk. You can't be so naïve to believe that if your association is discovered, she would be pleased—or silent—about her father's involvement in addressing the *Gesamtloesung*. While I certainly can find no nobler cause, this is your family, and Lillian is rather similar to that sister Helga of yours."

"She is just like Helga. The moment Lillian volunteered for this war effort, she lost her father's affections and respect. Her fate is her own. When she is in residence at Meercrest, which is thankfully rare, I tolerate her presence only for the sake of my wife's nerves."

Gebhardt laughed. "Nerves?"

Renner's eyes bore into his lawyer's. "Yes, you know what causes her nerves." He looked out to the sea again. "As for the others, Kitty is in no position to voice any objection at all. She is too dependent on my benevolence, and if she were living in Germany, her usefulness would have been brought into question under the T4 Programme. It would be only my economic status to protect her. Simple-minded Gloria is too self-absorbed and indulged to bother herself, and Lizzy ... well Lizzy is as loyal to the Renner name and lineage as Ingrid. In time, she will come to understand and, with the proper indoctrination, she will agree with my collaboration. Besides, like Gloria, Lizzy enjoys the life Meercrest affords her. Our affluence alone precludes her objection. As for Frances and her *nerves*, so long as the martinis flow and she has her mink and diamonds, she remains ostensibly oblivious."

"Oblivious even to Nurse Keller."

Renner laughed, his mood changing on a dime when he slapped Gebhardt on the back. "You did well in finding her for Meercrest. Not only has she been an invaluable courier and an unexpected source of information, but she has also been a delightful diversion in the bedroom." He laughed again, feeling so self-satisfied and so pleased that after years of celibacy, now he had someone willing and sober enough to indulge him. "I don't think the *Odin* has seen so much action since I courted Frances in '15."

Gebhardt looked wistfully toward the cabin door behind them. "Yes, the *Odin* is a perfect escape for sexual liaisons. As is the boathouse ... so I have heard."

"Hmm, yes the boathouse, the tropical house and a time or two in the bathing pavilion. Water is good for a man's constitution. Greystone in the city has also proved to be a splendid location for our *Liebesaffaire*. The woman is insatiable, and I don't mind in the least bit."

A silence settled between the two men, both lost in their own thoughts of sexual liaisons and desire. One with a perpetual hard on for his daughter's nurse, and the other lusting after one Renner sister while screwing the other. Gebhardt was working on changing that situation. The closer the Party came to victory, the closer Renner came to an agreement of a union between Elizabeth and him. Marriage arrangements were looked upon as a favorable means of spreading the Nordic seed throughout the world, and his blood was the closest to the *Schutzstaffel*. He had the *Großer Ariernachweis* to prove it. Until then, Ingrid was a convenient and willing vessel.

"If you'll excuse me, Renner, I have some paperwork to attend, something requiring my focused concentration."

"Yes, of course. Thank you for your attention to detail, George. Thank you for your guidance and expertise and as usual your intercession with the Party on my behalf."

Gebhardt left Renner standing on the bow of the boat, the narrow door sealing tightly behind him when he entered the cabin. With his approach, from within Ingrid's closed stateroom door, he heard her singing to Glenn Miller's "Forever Faithful" on the radio. He opened the door to see her sitting at her vanity, brushing her fair hair in long, smooth strokes.

"Are you?" he asked, drinking in her bare back.

She spoke to him in her reflection. "Am I what?"

"Forever faithful, of course."

Ingrid placed the monogrammed silver brush onto the vanity before her and rose, sauntering toward him with the look in her eyes that he had come to know intimately. She looked beautiful wearing a blue and white skirted two-piece swimsuit. To any observer, she resembled the patriotic woman he and her father had just spoken of, but nothing could be farther from the truth. Gebhardt knew all about her. He liked that he was able to feed her ideologies, and he loved that her appetite for power was as equally voracious as his. He enjoyed that she never held back by playing coy or demure, always giving him exactly what he wanted when he wanted it. She idolized everything about him, and he used it to his will.

His eyes and mouth hungered for a taste of what headed in his direction. Her bare midriff caused him to lick his lips. "Well answer my question, Miss Renner. Are you forever faithful?"

"To whom? Adolph Hitler or George Gebhardt?"

"Both."

Ingrid's half-moon manicured hand reached for the cabin's small door, slamming it behind him. She locked it and grabbed his necktie, pulling him toward her. "Let me show you just how committed I am to the cause."

Their lips met hungrily, crashing together.

There was no need to completely undress, no need for foreplay. Neither wanted emotion or sentiment from the other. They only required a fast, pounding release. Ingrid's hand quickly sought his erection, dropping his trousers at the moment her swimsuit slithered down her leg, landing atop her bare, painted toes.

From the prow, where Renner lustfully surveyed the nearby coastline, he never heard the perfume bottles, brushes, and cosmetics crash to the floor when Gebhardt gave Ingrid exactly what she wanted on top of the vanity with her shoulders pressed firmly against the cold glass mirror.

****

Lizzy and Will fought the heated crush of the crowd along Fifth Avenue's sidewalk, hands tightly clasped as they navigated their way uptown. Maneuvering around the groups of fixed spectators, they were silent as a particularly heinous float passed their location. Boos and hisses shouted out when the papier mâché sculpture of Hitler standing atop a fearsome dragon rolled past. The caption on the side of the platform read, "Hitler—the Axis War Monster."

It seemed appropriate the couple would view that float just as they approached the Channel Gardens of Rockefeller Center bordered at the far end with proudly waving flags of thirty-three free nations. The once beautiful beds of flowers had been transformed into a victory garden where broccoli, Swiss chard, and lettuce grew on the outside of the small fountains. Making do with less for the boys of the Armed Forces, as represented by the vegetable garden, was just a small example of America and New York's local commitment to fight and win on all fronts—even in the kitchen.

They paused before a storefront window where an American propaganda poster dominated the display. Two forceful forearms and fists punctuated with determined purpose brought home the boldly printed message of "Together We Can Do It."

During the short span of four months since Lizzy had last traveled to Manhattan to shop at Bonwit Teller, the whole city had been transformed. Now, across the street at St. Patrick's Cathedral rose a growing pile of aluminum. She was in awe of the changes visible at every turn. Straining to observe the source garnering the attention of many gathered patriots toward the sunken plaza before Prometheus's fountain, she asked Will, "What's down there?"

"I don't know, maybe it's a Liberty Bond drive. See that big, red *V* stand? It's probably a Victory Booth. Well … you have a choice, Miss Renner, dinner first from that pushcart right over there and then we can view the display."

"What's my other option?"

She giggled behind her glove when his stomach growled as if on cue. "Well, that settles that. We'll eat first. I'm hungry, too."

Will grinned and wanting to see Lizzy's playful smile, he gently removed her hand from her mouth.

Reaching the hot dog vendor stand, they waited patiently for the man in front of them to be served. Quickly taking a deep draw from the bottle, it was obvious the man had much desired that thirst-quenching Coca-Cola. They both noticed, in profile, how he bit into his frank as though he had waited years to taste the uniquely flavored fare from the murky waters of a New York City food cart.

The man removed a thick roll of money from the pocket of his suit and paid the vendor. "Can you tell me where the closest Horn & Hardart is?" he asked with an accented voice, tossing a nickel in the air, catching it, and then smiled. "A piece of huckleberry pie would be a nice dessert."

Abruptly, in his distinct Brooklyn accent the vendor declared with distaste, "Dang Jerry-owned automat. Closest one is on 57th and 6th. You can 'ave a piece a pie at Woolworths' five and dime. They're the best part of the good ole' U. S. of A."

Lizzy raised her eyebrows when Will looked over at her. She was a "Jerry" and judging by the accent of the man headed toward Horn and Hardart, he was one as well but that wouldn't get in either's way of appreciating a traditional American pastime. Her uncle was Sam not Adolf.

She rose in her white peep toe shoes, whispering behind her hand into Will's ear, "Some say that the Woolworths' Winfield Mansion in Glen Cove is haunted. I knew the family."

He smiled, not giving in to any Renner grandstanding and whispered back, "I know. Do you want one hot dog or two?"

"Just one and a root beer, please." She removed her gloves, and Will handed her the frank, their fingers brushing against one another in an almost deliberate, slow movement. A traveling electrical current ignited the goose pimples on her arms, her heart rate spontaneously increasing from just that small, seemingly innocuous touch. She was sure his caress was deliberate.

Together, they sat on the concrete wall between two small pools surrounded by Swiss chard. Lizzy couldn't help smiling while she chewed her frank, feeling giddy inside as though she were a schoolgirl with a huge crush. Fascinated, she watched the small wink to his dimple as he chewed.

Wondering if he was going to say anything at all, just like the Memorial Day dinner, she caught him obviously happy in his thoughts, watching her.

Her fastidious father would surely scold her if he witnessed her speaking with a mouthful, but she didn't care. She felt comfortable with Will. She felt as though he wouldn't condemn her for anything, particularly just being herself—well, a new and improving self and she was trying. Finally, she broke their silence.

"Tell me about your family, Will. Do you have other brothers or sisters?"

"Nope, just Lou and me. He's my best friend, but whereas he's all fun and games at twenty-three, I'm his straight man at twenty-one."

"I can tell, but I think there is a wise guy hidden inside you. You're not as serious as you pretend to be. Perhaps you just need the right enticement to get into a little mischief now and again."

"And are you the right enticement, Lizzy?"

She grinned with a mouthful of hot dog, and Will reached over to wipe a dollop of mustard with his thumb from her bottom lip. Her tummy fluttered when he sucked it from his fingertip, his eyes locking with hers in flirtatious amusement as he did so. She wished it had been his lips sucking hers clean.

"Perhaps, I *am* the right woman for the job. You'll have to stick around to find out and allow me to introduce you to all sorts of trouble."

"Unfortunately, I leave for Florida in a few days. That's barely enough time to get into trouble."

Disappointed, her smile disappeared quickly, feeling a bucket of ice water attempting to douse her desire to impress him, and make him hers. "Hmm, too bad. I'll miss getting to know you further."

"I'll miss lots of things, too."

Her spirits continued to feel dashed by his pensive expression. "Lots of things? Like your family? Your home ... where is your home?"

"I live in quiet, tame, and *well behaved* Park Slope. We moved there when I was just a boy. Before that, we lived near my father's business on the Bowery."

"And, what does your father do?"

"He's not a shoeshine in Grand Central Terminal if that's what you're thinking."

He took a swig from his soda, and she noticed the way he watched her reaction. She didn't miss his implication, causing her to blush in embarrassment.

"I ... um ..."

Lizzy bit her lip, and he chuckled. "Don't worry, Lizzy, I know you were just teasing John's sister, and I'm just teasing *you*. My father works at the DeVries Diamond House in the new diamond district on 47th Street. So you see, I'm actually glad you didn't know on Memorial Day. You might have told Miss Robertsen the truth, then my holiday would surely have been ruined."

"Diamonds? Ooo, how glamorous!"

"Not really, but you can understand why someone like her would see that as an opportunity."

"Oh yes, Greta would have sunk her claws into you for sure. She's quite the gold-digger even with all her money. I only said what I did poolside to dissuade her. I was being a good hostess." She laughed, noting Will's expression. Obviously, he saw through her cheeky transparency.

"Is your father a manager at the diamond house?"

"Dad actually owns the business and runs the American branch while my Aunt Estella and grandfather ran the European branch from, well ... up until about two years ago ... Amsterdam. They're both in France now where my aunt has lived off and on for years." Will's voice trailed slightly and a shroud of darkness came over his countenance. "They live in Paris now."

"That's right, you did say you were French."

"Of French ancestry on my paternal side, but like you and your family, I'm American. My mother was born in the Netherlands, and she emigrated just prior to the outbreak of the First World War. My aunt, who never married, remained in Europe with my grandparents and focused on developing the European market."

"So your mother is Dutch?"

"Yes. Hardly speaking English, she taught herself from the newspaper and then became a citizen. She married my father before he left for the war in 1917."

"That sounds romantic, brave, and determined. Have you ever visited your mother's homeland?"

"I did, and I loved it. As a family, we traveled to both Holland and France in '34, touring some but mainly visiting with relatives. It was the first time she had been home since her arrival in America."

"How exciting! I enjoyed Paris but wouldn't want to go back. One day, I hope to travel to the places I have yet to see. Share them and experience them for the first time with someone special, someone who wouldn't mind taking Kitty so she, too, can see the world."

"It's a different Paris now than what it was before the war. Perhaps, things will set right once America joins the Allies fighting in Europe. Like you, I always desired to see Italy ...Venice and Florence. Perhaps, afterwards, your visit to Rome will be possible."

"Yeah ... after the war."

Lizzy reached across the soda bottles resting between them and played with the silver wings above his breast pocket. She was about to say something clever, probably flirtatious about seeing Rome with *him*, but was distracted by the crowd reaction to Roy Rogers and Trigger trotting by the promenade's entrance. After a minute, their attention was drawn to two passing, well-dressed women. One held the other in support as they walked by the gardens back toward Fifth Avenue.

The parade elicited various emotions, ranging from sadness and fear to determination, and for just about everyone, the war hit close to home. Lizzy had come to learn this, having reflected upon it only days earlier.

The woman sobbed something about how she missed her husband and how the baby would never know him. Lizzy couldn't help feeling choked up by the stranger's pain, feeling as though she wasn't a stranger at all because they were "all in it together." Her eyes pooled with sympathetic tears, and her hand stilled upon the pilot's wings with a strange tingling sense of foreboding.

The slight lip tremble accompanying the tears welling was the confirmation Will needed. The unchecked droplets filling her eyes showed the sensitive woman she hid behind this bold personality of hers. Sympathy for another, rather than apathy, indifference or worse—prejudice—was all he needed to see to know and *believe* that she could never share her father or sister's hateful views.

He surprised himself when his hand automatically clasped her clinging fingers, enclosing them within his grasp. He couldn't help his burgeoning admiration, as his strong fingers smoothed into gentle caresses. Gone was her flirtatious party girl persona, and in her place sat an uncharacteristically shy and demure woman who watched as the man she brazenly pursued held onto her hand, stroking her palm.

She blushed.

"Will you write to me, Lizzy? Will you tell me all about yourself and life in the city and on the Island?"

She nodded, suddenly finding herself speechless, vowing to herself that she would tell him everything, share all of herself within every letter. Whatever he needed and wanted, she would give to him in every word, prayer, thought, and deed. There was no doubt in her mind—she was undeniably crazy about this flyboy, wishing to never part from him again.

Will entwined his fingers with hers. "Will you send me your brilliant effervescence written with this delicate hand of yours?"

So happy and unable to conceal that vibrant spirit of hers, she beamed, now convinced of his interest. "I thought you'd never ask, and if you write back to me, I may be so inclined to pen you a few sonnets. Some say it is the food of love."

"Let *your* words be the poetry and the rest will fall into place if it's destined to be."

****

Foolhardy. Dangerous. Illogical. These were the three reasons why a thinking man of 21 about to depart for war objected to romance. Then again, when Will formed that opinion, he had yet to meet Elizabeth with that intoxicating smile and mischievous laugh of hers.

From the first moment she ran him off the road in her Lincoln Zephyr, the battle had ensued within him, knocking him for a loop. Then, with the introduction of those smirking, cherry-bomb lips and the green sparkle in her fine eyes, he was completely captivated. That was two weeks ago, and try as he might he couldn't fight her allure. He was a goner, officially doll dizzy, for only one doll.

Now, walking in the darkness toward Central Park with its dimmed lights, he held her hand in his tight grasp. The parade's torchlight procession was just about to begin as ragged rows of glowing amber lit the entrance to the park and Fifth Avenue. She looked over at him, beaming with her excitement that reached down into his soul, shaking it to life. There were three *new* words that any thinking man would declare following a day spent with the most fascinating woman he had ever met. Be. My. Girl.

"This is so exciting, Will! I'm so happy to be a part of it with you."

She nearly skipped from her newfound patriotic enthusiasm as he led her toward the carousel, causing him to smile like the wacky, love-struck fool he had become in the short span of four hours. The calliope music grew louder above the growing din of processioners filling the pathway.

"Where are you taking me?"

"You'll see. It's a surprise."

"I love surprises!"

He didn't. Well, not usually. But meeting her had bolted him from the blue, and darn if he didn't love the way it made him feel.

When they reached the amusement ride, she squealed, and he laughed along with her. "Have you ever been on it?" he asked.

"Never! It's positively lulu."

They stood hand-in-hand, alternating shy glances of unspoken burgeoning emotion with childlike awe of the painted horses rising up and down, circling round and round without destination. Every time Lizzy gazed up at him, he noted how the reflection of hundreds of bulbs from the merry-go-round sparkled in her eyes, and he felt a slight flutter in his heart. The carousel may have illuminated the park but it was her own effervescence that lit her countenance from within.

Children's laughter combined with the music in a delightful symphony, mixing with the intoxicating scent of the fragrance she wore. Sublime. It was all so perfect and felt so unreal as he stood proudly attired in his military dress uniform.

"C'mon, let's go for a ride, Pistol," the spontaneous pet nickname unexpectedly emerging from his mouth.

The aged attendant stood with hands on hips surveying the carousel with a keen eye. Will observed how he turned away a few other GIs and their girls who had gathered from the parade. The words, "Sorry, boys. This is the last run for the night. Gotta shut her down," pricked his ears with disappointment, and he did the most impulsive thing he'd done in years.

He whispered into Lizzy's ear, "Follow me," tugging her hand.

Her hurried footsteps followed on his heels. "Oh, Ducky are you going to do what I think you're going to do?"

"Ducky?"

"Your new nickname. Ducky as in shincracker. Now, are you being a naughty flyboy, sneaking us onto the carousel? I'm so proud of you! It may seem that you're not a fuddy duddy after all."

"What can I say? You're a bad influence on me."

"I won't say I told you so."

Yes, you did and I do believe you're right. You're exactly what I need.

They reached the wood barricade on the far side away from the attendant's view, and, with an impromptu lift, Will scooped her up into his arms, causing her to break into a fit of laughter.

"Shush... he'll catch us."

He placed her on the other side then hopped over in a swift move that made her guffaw. There was no time to puff his chest in pride of his dexterity.

He grabbed her hand with a chuckle at their monkey business, and together they jumped onto the circling carousel.

Watching her choose her mount enchanted him. It was as though each one had some special singular appeal. First, she'd touch the mane then move onto another, feeling the braided pole. It was obvious how the colors attracted her, like her own vibrant personality attracted him. Unlike other girls, she didn't acknowledge her reflection in the large mirrors that formed the decorative center panels. Instead, she admired the whimsical beauty of each horse. She chose a stallion and grinned like a schoolgirl. Lizzy's blithe spirit warmed his heart and captured his mind, transporting him to a place where war and prejudice didn't exist.

Coming to stand beside her, his arms slid around her slender shape as she rose up and down, her delicate hand encircling the metal pole. His fingers delighted in the curve of her waist and the soft feel of her dress. "Lizzy?"

Biting the corner of her lip, she gazed into his eyes. He felt the heated flush to his cheeks, uncontrollably mirroring her coy blush. The ride's calliope music cast a magical spell that prompted a memory to be forged, one he was sure would carry him through war. His heart raced in a nervous staccato.

"May I kiss you?"

Her smile bowled him over. It reached her eyes and his heart.

"I thought you'd never ask," she said.

Tentatively, his mouth inched toward hers, and he closed his eyes. Soft, warm lips met with a delicate pucker, growing deeper in sweet innocence, both unwilling to part in their discovery of the first promptings of love. He'd never tasted anything as incredible and delicious as her lips.

"Hey you two! What are you doing on there?" the attendant yelled, jolting them from the most glorious four seconds of their young lives.

They laughed and then so did he, waving at them with a dismissing hand.

"Ah, love," the man said. "I remember it well."

Ten

You Are My Sunshine
June 16, 1942

With preparations and his packing well in hand, Will's attention this morning centered on how much he loved breakfast spent with his mother and how much he would miss it. That tender thought moved quickly to how Louie loved his morning eggs and would have to keep a stiff upper lip when eating those powdered ones aboard the transport ship.

Sitting, clutching a hot cup of coffee at the table in the center of their homey kitchen, his mother stood at the stove behind him. Will supposed the Martel kitchen looked similar to most family kitchens and wondered if the Renners ever ate in theirs. Probably not. The kitchens in those ritzy mansions were reserved for staff, and the family most likely wouldn't share breakfast together in what he supposed was a lavish dining room that could seat forty or more.

His fingers traced the red and white rooster and hen salt and pepper shakers and he smiled, thinking how the Renners probably used crystal or silver at every meal. His mother loved roosters and the theme seemed to have taken over her kitchen with a cheerful invasion of red gingham and rural Americana motifs. One would assume Delft and windmills would be her choice of knick-knacks, but no, his mother was All-American. Like his father, he didn't care about the kitchen decoration. It was a place where she spent a lot of time, and the décor represented her happy demeanor. He couldn't help but speculate with sardonic humor how the Renners most likely decorated with Goebel figurines. Add another *b* and it surely summed up the patriarch's purified version of "All American."

Even the weekly newspaper, *Hadoar*, spread out before Will offered yet another example of the difference between his and Lizzy's worlds. Who would have ever thought he'd pursue a society dame and in four hours be on his second—much anticipated—date with the dangerous temptation.

"I am sorry there is no sugar for your coffee." Anna apologized to her younger son, her native accent still inherent in every word and phrase as she fried the eggs for their version of a traditional Dutch breakfast. "It is ration's fault. It is Hitler's fault, not your *mouder's*."

"It's okay, Mom. I can do without it." Fried eggs and freshly percolated coffee combined with the baking currant buns made the kitchen smell delicious. He'd rather the sugar for the buns than the coffee.

When the bread popped up from the shiny Sunbeam World's Fair toaster, Will rose to help his mother. He put his arm around her shoulders and kissed the side of her head for no reason except that he loved her and the unusual melancholy tone in her voice alerted him to her need for affection.

She leaned her head on him for a brief moment, continuing to watch the eggs before covering them to steam.

"What will I do without you and your gentleness and your brother and his humor?" She sighed heavily. "What is a *mouder* to do?"

"Pray I suppose—stay busy. We both had only been back for a few weeks. You'll go back to your old routine, right?"

"My lonely routine."

"Maybe you can go with Dad to the shop. I bet he'd love to have you, and I know he could use the help since he has his hands full fighting off the government's attempt to grab industrial diamonds from the syndicate."

"I have thought to go back, but so many years have passed. I do not like change at my age."

"Change is here whether we like it or not, but there is a lot of good change, Mom. Women are working in every position a man vacates when he goes off to fight."

"I do not know. This new location on 47th Street brings the orthodox, refugee Hasidim to do business in the district. They do not allow or associate with women at work. I would be looked upon as an outcast and the business will suffer for it."

Will kissed his mother's head again then chuckled. "Well, then it's a good thing you're not Hasidic and that everyone believes that DeVries Diamond House is owned by a *Christian*, isn't it? Stop looking for excuses to resist change. Another war forced change upon the DeVrieses and you rose to the occasion, coming to *New* Amsterdam. You can do it again."

She placed a slice of cheese followed by the egg upon the toast, handing the dish to her son. "That was by choice. My home was neutral during the first war. Hitler has given us no choice now. Your *tante* and *grootvader* have no options, no choices either now thanks to that Vichy government in France. They never should have left Amsterdam."

So that was at the heart of her feeling so glum. "No, it's good they left. Things are escalating in the Netherlands. Besides, Aunt Estella had no choice. Your sister was very wise to travel from Paris to get Grandfather and clean out all of DVDH's diamonds and assets before the Nazis seized the bourses in Amsterdam. The diamonds and money have been in safekeeping these last two years in New York, and Grandfather and she have been safer in Paris than Holland."

"But, they are not safe. I know this and so do you, there is growing intolerance by that new collaborating government."

Will could tell by the tone in her voice that there were things she wasn't saying, which was so contrary to her usual frankness. He furrowed his brow. "Have you received a letter from Paris?"

"Not from Estella but from the House's courier. He writes in Dutch. Your *grootvader* is very ill. They could not leave for Spain or Switzerland even if they wanted to. Money or diamonds cannot buy their way to safety when he is so frail."

Will sat, his heart sinking into the chair with him. His mother was right, of course, but he would not feed her fears. Silence was better than lying and certainly better than agreeing with her in this instance. Only days before he had read of even more restrictions on Jews, and not just on the foreign-born ones residing in France. The article spoke of the mandatory wearing of the yellow, six-pointed star, causing Will to become consumed with concerns for his closest remaining family in Europe.

Anna sat across from her son, watching him eat and noting his sudden silence. With a mother's loving concern, she changed the subject. "This girl, Elizabeth, must be special to spend your last day with."

"She is."

"Is she Jewish?"

Shoveling food into his mouth and not meeting his mother's inquisitive gaze, he continued to stare at the Hebrew newspaper before him. "No."

She shrugged a shoulder, raising an eyebrow.

"You did not tell her that we are, did you?"

"No, of course not."

"Good. Is she Dutch?"

"No."

Her hand reached out to Will's, stilling the fork. "Are you in love with her, *engel?*"

Will sheepishly looked up from his eggs; a tender smile formed upon his lips. "Getting there."

****

Lizzy impatiently waited at the Yacht Club, unknowingly redirecting her energetic anticipation into a makeshift dance of sorts, shifting from foot to foot. Ducky was late, and she prayed he hadn't changed his mind. With her back to the shingled Cape Cod-styled boathouse, she eagerly watched for his arrival, feeling guilty that he offered to come all this way once again. He wouldn't take no for an answer, insisting on treating her with gentlemanly protocol.

She looked down at the picnic basket Mrs. Davis filled, resting at her sandaled feet beside another square, leather case, and thought how she should have worn her boat shoes. But then they wouldn't have matched her outfit, and she wanted to look especially smart, wearing her blue and white playsuit with button skirt. A white, brimmed hat with a wrap scarf protected her from the sun's harshness even before it reached its noontime peak. Eager barely described how she felt, and she had the butterflies to prove it. They seemed to be attacking her from the inside, fluttering rapidly awaiting Will's arrival.

The barrage of nerves worsened the moment the yellow checker taxicab pulled into the dirt parking lot at the bottom of the hill, stopping beside the Zephyr. She gracefully signaled to her date, raising one hand in the air from her strategically visible position, tempering her excitement to jump on the balls of her feet and wave enthusiastically.

Will exited, looking relaxed and handsome wearing casual trousers and a ribbed slipover and shirt. He sheepishly smiled at her, and paid the taxi driver. Lizzy had yet to see him in civvies and became embarrassed when he caught her obvious appreciation as her eyes drank him in, top to toe, from that enticing wave of hair at his forehead to the rubber-soled boat shoes he wore.

In similar fashion, his own heart nearly stopped seeing her lean against the building the way she did with the drape of her skirt opening to show shapely, bare legs posed with one foot's sole against the shingles. Her risqué, bare midriff seductively displayed tanned flesh. Even from the distance of thirty feet, he could see that sparkle of excitement in her eyes held at bay behind a saucy expression.

"Beautiful day today," he said with a smile that flooded his eyes as he approached her, holding a small box.

"Yes it is, but can you hear the train?"

"Ghosts of your grandfather, come to make sure I behave?" He tilted his head to listen carefully for the sound.

She nervously chortled. "Probably to see that *I* behave. There's an old folklore on the Sound that says if you can hear the train, it's going to rain. We might be in for a storm later."

Will bent to her, and she breathed in his fresh, shaved scent that she liked so much.

"We'll have fun anyway, and if we get caught in the rain, so be it." He held out the box. "This is for you. I couldn't resist when I saw it at the flower shop beside the train station. I hope you like it."

Lizzy took the gift from his grasp and carefully opened it. Inside sat two white flowers entwined upon a hair comb. Immediately, their sweet scent wafted upward. "They're so lovely; gardenias are one of my favorites. Thank you, Will." She removed her hat. "Will you help me?"

His hand trembled slightly when he removed the flowers from the box and slid the comb into the side of her wavy locks. She couldn't help but wonder if he was as nervous as she. Already, all she wanted to do was to kiss those soft lips of his again. The thought of a day spent gazing at that killer-diller dimple and cleft chin was a delightful prospect. Add the thoughtfulness of the flowers along with the gesture of travel to see her, and she was positively over the moon. Both spoke volumes of his interest, not to mention the fact that he had asked for this second date with the words, "Will I have the pleasure of spending another day with you before my departure on the seventeenth?"

"How do I look?" she preened, tucking a stray hair behind her ear with her pinky then tilting her head from side to side to show him all angles of the ornament.

Will smoothed his thumb over her cheek, once again spellbound. "Beautiful, but not because of the flowers."

She instantly feigned the coquette, boldly batting her eyelashes. "Oh, you are a wolf, Lieutenant."

After looking right then left to make sure they were alone, he bent his head close to hers, hovering.

Lizzy raised her chin, positioning her mouth toward his and expectantly waited. Their lips held a hair's breadth from one another, his eyes locking with hers as he watched her pupils dilate and lips part. Oh, yes, she wanted to be kissed, and he wanted to give one to her. From her parted, willing lips, he could almost hear her increasing ragged breath as it tickled his mouth.

Lizzy's knees felt weak, her heart thundering in excitement. She closed her eyes in anticipation, slightly puckering her lips.

Tingles upon her flesh followed the slow grazing of the back of Will's fingers up the side of her neck. They languidly tickled the throbbing pulse running straight to her heart. She breathed in deeply in want and expectation, swooning from the sweetness of his breath when he whispered, "I'm not a wolf—*yet*, but I'm open for instruction."

She opened her eyes, meeting his impassioned ones. Resisting the urge to kiss him audaciously, Lizzy breathed a thoroughly discombobulated, "I'm … a patient teacher."

She didn't want to act like Gloria, but dang if she wasn't happy by his proclamation, even if a kiss didn't follow it. She knew that in spite of his strong and serious personality, which she felt instinctively drawn to, once his levee broke, theirs would be a whirlwind, exciting romance. But there was little precious time. He was leaving for Florida the next day.

Will smiled and reached down to pick up the wicker picnic basket as his free hand entwined with hers. They walked along the side of the boathouse making small talk about his trip out, both feeling that being together was the most natural thing in the world.

Their arrival at the long dock, once again, cast a striking light on the obvious gap in their disparate social standings exemplified by the bobbing, luxury, pleasure boat tethered to the dock.

Will smirked, looking down at her. "I thought you said we were going sailing?"

"I never said *sailing*. I don't sail. I said *boating*. Do you like her? She's number seven out of only nineteen manufactured. It's a Chris-Craft Hydroplane."

Across the stern of the boat, in gold script was the name *Flying Home*. Above it, a small—and surprising—American flag raised up from the shiny, wood hull, waving in the breeze.

"She's a beauty," Will declared in awe, admiring the sleek, barrel-shaped hull and bow. At only about sixteen or so feet, it was just small enough for her to bullet through the water at maximum velocity—and burn through fuel. "Flying Home, indeed."

"It's my favorite song." She squeezed his hand and turned, speaking with sincerity. "C'mon, let yourself go today. Forget about the war, Will. You leave tomorrow, so let's make today memorable. Don't worry about the gas ration. Mr. Billings fills the fuel, Father pays the sales invoice, and I get to fly around the Sound with my flyboy."

Yes, I am your flyboy and today is already memorable. He chortled. "What happened to all that excitement about doing your bit? You're incorrigible, you know."

"Yes, I am. I thought you figured that out already." Lizzy stepped into the boat and stood in the narrow, red upholstered cockpit. With a beaming, mischievous grin, she reached out her hand, wiggling her fingers for the picnic basket.

"What's in that case?" he asked, pointing to the latched box she had placed on the floor of the cockpit.

"You'll see. Now unhitch the boat, Lieutenant and let's fly!"

Will stood at attention, saluting her, and she laughed that wicked laugh of hers, which grew when she saw how he shook his head, smiling at her determination. It was obvious to him how she just loved to press his buttons.

Only a matter of minutes passed before Lizzy put her sunglasses on, turned the key and, with the press of a button, the throaty growl of the engine bellowed to life. She sat at the helm ready for action as though master and commander, adorned by those pristine white flowers staring back at him. It was when she turned her head with another one of those smiles of hers and patted his hand in mocking reassurance, his heart stopped for the second time in the short span of thirty minutes.

Already, it was an unforgettable day. The promise of her luscious lips upon his, combined with the warming brilliance of the sun, the crisp blue sky, and the commingling of the salty air with Lizzy's jasmine—now gardenia—infused perfume relaxed him. Several white sea gulls in flight surrounded the boat, seemingly laughing along with her infectious exuberance contributing their distinct ha-ha-ha call. He felt that liveliness, too. That energy of hers made the worries plaguing his heart and the realities of the war—bombers, the Pacific, Paris—all seem so far, far away.

"Ready?" she asked.

"My life is in your hands, Pistol."

"Good, that's just the way it should be. Do you trust me?"

He meant it when he replied, "Implicitly." For all Lizzy's wildness, he truly felt he could trust her with his heart. During those two sweet kisses the night of their first date, he felt it upon her lips, a sweetness and honesty as genuine and lasting as the emotion he put behind its delivery.

Smoothly, the boat pulled away from the dock into the Sound. "Unfortunately, we can't go out too far. Mr. Billings cautioned me about the Coast Guard trolling for mines, especially today."

"Why *especially* today?"

She felt proud, for a change, to be the one to inform him on war news, as though "in the know" on all things naval. "He told me that a steam merchant ship was torpedoed by a U-boat last night off Cape Cod, but don't worry, we can stay in the harbor close to the shore. I can still point out some of the local sights of interest and there probably won't be many boaters out today, given the prediction of rain."

"The train's prediction?"

"See, you're thinking like a boatman already." She pointed to the rocky shoreline where some local residents walked with metal buckets. "Over there, they are shell fishing mussels from the rocks. Poor things, having to resort to eating them. Blech! Muscles are hardly a delicacy, unless of course they're on bomber pilots."

He thought he saw her wiggle her eyebrows flirtatiously behind her white sunglasses.

She throttled the boat a smidgen faster. "The harbor is abundant in oysters and clams though. Sometimes Johnny takes me out to fish for mackerels just for kicks, and Mrs. Davis loves those Littlenecks we bring back for her."

"John fishes? I wouldn't think so."

"There's a lot about Johnny one wouldn't think. Behind his smile, he hides a lot. For example, he's sicker than he lets on." She looked at him, holding his gaze pensively. "He has asthma. Lately, he's been using those special cigarettes of his. Of course, everyone thinks he's smoking a Viceroy because he explains that fags smell differently than American ones. I think I'm the only one who knows about how truly ill he is and that's only because I threatened to tell Ingrid he had a crush on her the year of her debut."

"So not even Ingrid knows?"

"Well, Johnny and I have a unique friendship. He doesn't want anyone to think he's ... well, you know ... inferior in any way, and he knows it wouldn't make a difference to me."

"So his 4F is the real McCoy. That's a tough break."

"He only thinks it's a tough break because his father treats him much like my sisters treat Kitty, as though he's sickly or weak, but mainly with indifference simply due to his illness." She snorted a sarcastic laugh. "The Robertsen family has kept his asthma a deep, dark, safely guarded secret.

Brilliant beyond belief, heir to a fortune, heart of gold and his father won't let him work toward victory. It's a shame, really."

"I would imagine that with Ingrid being his girl and all, she would be concerned at the very least. If she loves him then it wouldn't make a difference if he was ill or not. Right?"

"You don't know my sister—and in truth I don't think she loves him. In fact, I think she's incapable of love. She and I don't quite get along." She turned her head and started to whistle a snappy tune, clearly changing the topic of her sister.

Will shook his head, feeling remorse about the small jealousy he held in his heart for the man with whom she spent so much time.

As he looked up at the many magnificent mansions perched in the hills above them, he imagined their expansive views of the Sound. Feeling the gentle breeze in his hair, he breathed deeply—reflectively. *Even the affluent had their troubles.* Something deep within him stirred, and a surge began, which he hadn't felt since Louie and he rode the Cyclone roller coaster at Coney Island in '36. Life was short and getting shorter. "How fast can this baby go, Pistol?"

She squealed in delight. "Glad you asked! Hold on, Ducky!"

It was as though her floodgates opened with his green light of encouragement because the hydroplane was now cruising at top speed. The bow rose, floating above the water with barely even a slap, the stern hardly leaving a wake as it skimmed the harbor with a hard spray that dissipated in the sea air behind them. The speed of the engine purred in time with the determined flap of Old Glory as Lizzy's *Flying Home* flew the coop with exhilaration.

Clearly an Ace in the cockpit, standing at the controls, Lizzy expertly handled the boat and laughed with a big "Woo hoo!" Her joyous howl was carried away in the wind along with Will's normally stoic reserve. The flowers he gave her, remarkably, remained pinned behind her ear as the other side of her hair blew wildly just like her untamed spirit. She began to sing notes from the boat's namesake. With jitterbug feet and swiveling hips to the tune, she boogied behind the steering wheel.

He knew then, he had fallen in love with her. Her live wire connected straight to his heart. She was the long awaited lightning bolt, shocking him to life.

Impulsively, Will slid closer to her and slipped his arm around her slender waist. He pulled her down beside him onto the seat. The boat slowed, dropping the bow into the water in her distraction. Turning her body to face him, he leaned her against the bulkhead, his lips poised at the ready to plunder her luscious mouth only an inch below his.

Lizzy grinned with expectation. Her cheeks were flushed waiting for the inflamed kiss of deep passion she had hoped for in her dreams the last three nights.

"I'm going to kiss you now," he said with seductive intonation while removing her sunglasses. "And we're not talking a tiny peck of admiration upon your cheek or given with any modicum of gentlemanly restraint. I'm warning you that this kiss—"

He didn't finish his sentence because her hand came around the back of his head, pulling him to her. Consuming lips and petting hands barely controlled themselves as they simultaneously gave into the escalating passion coursing through them.

Will's hand hesitantly explored her bare midriff, brushing against her heated skin, reveling in her softness.

Lizzy moaned clasping her right hand around his bicep, her other snaking through his hair, clutching him to her. His scorching lips adhered to hers and the surprise entry of his exploring tongue made her feel things she had never felt before.

He was near lying upon her and fighting the strong temptation to caress her in other places, inch his hand upward to unknot her blouse, but that would have been beyond the pale. Decorum and desire fought one another because her siren call was too great for this mere mortal man. Her lips tasted as sweet as she smelled, as heavenly as she looked, as thrilling as she felt, and as perfect as each mew sounded when she responded to him in ways he had only dreamt she would.

Their combined intensity grew but before it truly unleashed, his restraint mere degrees from snapping, he breathlessly parted from her, gazing into her eyes, now deep hunter green and dilated with hunger.

"Now, I'm a wolf," he stated, his breath ragged.

"Wow," she barely enunciated but definitely conveyed. It was more a fast expulsion of air that tickled his still hovering lips when it came out. Their heavy pants commingled, becoming one breath. "Wow," she breathed again.

His heart pounded as though twice its size against his chest wall, overwhelming him with intense emotion. Leaning only fractions away from her, admiring her thoroughly kissed lips, now swollen with passion. Words popped into his mind, *Open up your heart, and let this fool rush in.*

"Will you be ... my girl, Lizzy?"

She ran her hand through his hair and pulled him back down to her lips. "Will, I've been your girl from the moment I ran you off the road."

Eleven

Taking a Chance on Love
June 16, 1942

F *lying Home* bobbed in the gentle waves where Lizzy and Will had beach anchored it from the bow as close to the sandy shoreline as they could get. She had been correct; not many boaters or sunbathers were out on a day when rain was forecast, let alone it being a Tuesday. Now with the war on, the various ship builders that lined the harbor's coastline were open around the clock, and weekends were hard to come by. Like every other day, everyone was hard at work—everyone except this Army Air Forces pilot and his debutante sweetheart.

Will leaned back comfortably, digging his elbows into the white sand of Bar Beach, a local, summer attraction on a small peninsula near Mosquito Cove. Just beyond the boat, a diving float barely reacted to the incoming waves, but that image lost its tempting appeal soon enough. Apart from the overall splendid perfection of the beach and the brilliant sky strewn with cotton-shaped clouds, hardly anything held his attention because Lizzy garnered it all.

He watched her intently as she knelt in the sand before the no longer mysterious, square case—a Zenith battery-operated portable radio. She fiddled with the dial until a signal came in, broadcasting Glenn Miller's Chesterfield Show. The Modernaires singing, "Moonlight Cocktail" floated into the air, causing the few other beachgoers to search out the source of the disturbance. The audacious creature in Lizzy waved to them, and Will expected to hear her naughty laugh after drawing the sudden attention. Instead, she stood, digging her perfect, painted toes into the sand and with singular deliberation removed her playsuit, revealing a marine blue, two-piece bathing suit on a pin-up worthy shape.

Further thoughts beyond that kiss, which left a delicious tingle upon his lips, and the feel of her soft flesh below his fingertips ceased to exist as he watched her undress. He tried, ever so hard, to be discreet when his eyes particularly settled upon her bosom and truly felt like a wolf of the worse kind, but she did that to him.

Secretly, Lizzy hoped he was as bewitched with her figure, as she was transfixed by his when he disrobed to his navy swim trunks. Growing up on boat and beach, she had seen many men wearing a swimsuit, but none cut a figure like Will. He was all man, not boy, with broad shoulders and a patch of chest hair. Muscles that she already knew were firm to the touch showed him to be a swimmer. Solidly sculpted, powerful thighs and, she almost laughed to admit, nice feet. Not that she had made a purposeful study, but feet were curious things and, well, could ruin the lot if they were ugly. John's looked similar to eagle talons, her father's looked like little fat bratwurst sausages, and George Gebhardt's were weirdly shaped resembling an Egyptian pyramid ascending to a point! Now Will's, in her opinion, were perfectly proportioned, just like the rest of him.

"You're staring," she playfully challenged.

"It's what I do best. How can I not stare when you undress with such ... such ... enticement?"

"Are you staring or admiring then?"

"Both."

"Are you making a pass at me?"

He smirked. "Me? No—I'm an officer and a gentleman."

She playfully twisted those kissable lips of hers. "Yes, I thought the same thing in the boat twenty minutes ago when you were lying on top of me." Lizzy nimbly knelt beside him on the blanket. "Are you hungry for lunch?"

He had a particular twinkle in his brown eyes, one she was only now coming to understand following his kisses. Therefore, she wasn't surprised when he replied, "I'm starved."

"I meant for lunch, Lieutenant Gentleman."

Lizzy unpacked the picnic basket of all sorts of goodies Mrs. Davis insisted he would enjoy. Things like fried chicken and deviled eggs—two delicacies she had yet to eat. She used a bottle opener and popped the tops of the Hines Root Beer and Coca-Cola bottles kept chilled by cold towels within the basket.

Leaning over to hand him his soda, she hesitated, toying with the two steel dog tags hanging around his neck. "So, what is the notch in your dog tags for?"

"It's a toothpick."

"No fooling?"

"I'm just kidding. Rumor has it, they stick it in between your teeth when you buy the farm, but I'm not sure how legit that is."

"Oh." She couldn't help looking away, anywhere, finally settling on Tex Beneke's voice as though visible upon the radio dial.

Will's fingers reached over to lift her chin, turning her unusual forlorn expression toward him. "Don't worry. I'll be back before you know it. After all, look what I have to come home to."

"Are you afraid? I mean, do you get afraid when you're flying, afraid of crashing and not making it home?"

"Not afraid like you think. Like you, I positively love to fly. When Howard Hughes flew around the world in '38, I became captivated by the idea. Watching in the movie theatre his landing in Floyd Bennett Field in Brooklyn hit me like a thunderbolt, and I couldn't sleep for days, contemplating the possibilities as an aviator."

"I remember that! Wasn't there a ticker tape parade for him?"

He smiled, pleased that she had remembered this important piece of New York's history in aviation.

"So you're not afraid? I don't think I would be either." She beamed.

"My fear is more for those I'd leave behind to mourn me if something happened. We're a close family and I know my mother wouldn't take it well if anything happened to Lou or me. I also worry about my flight crew, the men under my command. It's my responsibility to bring them home safely. I suppose, I haven't given much thought to my *personal* inconvenience of a premature death. Perhaps, I had just been reconciled to that real possibility." He thoughtfully toyed with his dog tags. "But now that you've agreed to be my girl, it would be most inconvenient."

"Yes it would be. So don't be reconciled to anything other than coming home!"

She handed him a fine bone china, luncheon plate piled with fried chicken, which he promptly dug into, grabbing a drumstick off the top and moaning with the first bite.

After a few minutes of Will devouring and Lizzy sampling the basket contents, he asked, "Did you stop in to see the librarian about the book campaign?"

"I did, and Mrs. Tinsdale seems to think that Kitty and I can truly make a difference. My sister will write and telephone our friends, and I am going to do the gathering. I plan on setting up a collection center with the help of Mr. Billings at the club. With all his spare time, Johnny has agreed to put up a donation box in the employee break room at the plant."

As though able to smell the gastronomic goodness spread out on the checkered blanket, the seagulls on the sand inched closer. A few alerted the others by their call that dinner was served.

Will broke off a small piece of cornbread and tossed it far out toward the lapping water, enticing them away, then watching them dive bomb for it.

"So you're really excited about the campaign?"

"Oh I am!"

"What does your father say?"

Lizzy gazed out at the boat her father bought for her twentieth birthday. "We're not going to tell him. If he knew, he wouldn't be happy with us. He hasn't spoken directly to Lillian in months since she joined the ARC."

"I'm sorry to hear that. Why is he angry with her?"

"You know; you heard him on Memorial Day. He's not a supporter of the war, and her volunteering made him snap his cap, but I'm not going to let his opinion stand in my way if that's what you're wondering." *Nor will Lillian and I let his negative opinion about you and Louie stand in our way either.*

She met his gaze, drinking in the warmth in his chestnut eyes. "It's just ... just that ... looking back on the last six months since Pearl Harbor, I've been so ignorant and compared to everyone else—so *un-American*. The boat, the fuel, the Zephyr, everything ... I do see that now, and I do want to support the boys. You being the most important one. It's all thanks to you."

"Me? I didn't have anything to do with your joining the war effort. Well ... apart from chewing you out about your speeding, but I was joking. No, you did this all on your own, Lizzy, your own essential patriotic zeal and determination. Not because of *me*, but because of you—for the nation, for *you* and for the love of your sister Kitty, too, by giving her something to help validate her ability."

"It *was* you, and truthfully, I ... I want you to see that there is more to me than just a society party girl. I'm not all fun and games, you know."

"I know that. I also see you don't give yourself much credit. You're an incredible woman, who I know will change lives, *affect* lives, once you put your mind to it. Your willingness to learn, above all, is impressive. Coupled with that loving, jubilant heart of yours, you're changing *my* life and I know you will make a difference for others. Your future hasn't been written yet— you can accomplish anything with it."

"Do you truly believe that, Will?"

"Of course I do. It's *you* who is helping me to see that there is more to me than my serious ways."

She snorted a laugh. "Well, I think you're hiding behind that serious persona of yours. A true dud wouldn't neck with such 'zeal' as you do."

Will wiped his embarrassed smile with a linen napkin.

"Lizzy, this might be out of line, but about John ... um ... did you used to go steady with him? I mean, you spend a lot of time together, and I'd be lying if I didn't admit that I'm slightly jealous. He's a swell fellow with all the qualities that make him a good catch for any girl. I would understand your attraction to him." He swallowed hard, not that he had food in his mouth to warrant it.

Lizzy would have laughed at the question if not for his pensive expression. If insecurity had been a new emotion to her, well, then his sincere adulation certainly solidified the stirrings of another unfamiliar emotion in her—romantic love.

Shifting her weight, she leaned over to him and placed her hand on his smooth cheek. Cherry bomb lips slowly met his when she deposited a tender, heartfelt kiss filled with such deep ardor that he couldn't doubt her constancy.

His gaze locked on her brilliant eyes, awestruck once again by her nearness and completely taken aback but thrilled by her forward manner. "Hmm ... what was that for?"

"You silly man. Johnny is *just* a friend. Has always been my best friend since we were children, nothing more. You'll never have need to doubt my affections for you. Like the song, I'm yours. Will, don't you know how nuts I am about you?"

His hand thread upward through her wavy locks, and again their mouths met, this time sharing one heart. She tasted like sweet root beer, and their lips melded with growing passion, tongues determined to explore one another.

"You leave me dizzy, Lizzy, and I'm *crazy* for you, too."

Will kissed her a third time, fighting the urgings of white heat coursing through him to lay her down upon the sand. He wanted to forget about decorum, frowned upon public affection, the sea gulls, and the radio announcer talking about the pleasures of cigarettes. All he wanted, before leaving tomorrow for bomber training was to experience every drop of real joy in sweet romance and loving tenderness with this woman. But, his girl knew him well enough ... he was a gentleman and would respect her. These many kisses, given and taken with such intensity, were liberties he had never gone so far to take from *any* girl.

Playful Lizzy emerged from their kiss, grabbing his hand and pulling him up. "C'mon!"

Kicking up sand, he ran after her into the breaking surf, and they laughed when he tried to grab her waist to no avail. Shallow waves splashed around them as she attempted to escape his reaching arms.

"You can't outrun me!" he laughed.

"Oh yes I can!"

Once in deep enough waters, she dived in, and he promptly followed, eager to catch his girl and perhaps another kiss.

Thankful for the clear water, from below he saw her legs treading ten feet ahead. Long, bare legs bicycled in alluring fashion until he grabbed her ankle, pulling her down toward his body. Lizzy's hair floated around her, and he kissed her underwater until they both rose to the top, bodies clinging to one another.

Will's smile undid her, as rivulets ran down his cheeks, dropping from his disheveled wet hair. They panted from more than the playful exertion.

Her legs instinctively wrapped around his middle without thought, and she hung on him, feeling the strength of his hard body gripped between her thighs and pressed against her torso. She thrilled when his arms encircled her waist with one hand dangerously low near her bottom.

With only their dripping heads feeling the warmth of the air, her body trembled slightly. Lizzy wasn't sure if it was the Sound in springtime or the nearness of Will. Each kiss of his had left her breathless and, this time it wasn't her stomach where the butterflies fluttered. They fluttered elsewhere, and she wanted nothing more than to give into those urgings of awakening taking over her body and reason. His caress upon her back was doing things to her flesh and she, too, felt hungry for more—forbidden more.

He held her securely as the shifting waves around them caused their bodies to rise and fall. "You're shivering."

"I'm okay." Suddenly shy, she bit her lip and looked at him through her lashes.

Will reached up, touching where a pearly white tooth bit cooling flesh before his soft, wet lips met hers, covering, and warming them. Heated kisses sent her arms around his slick, broad shoulders and she felt a warming rush inside her when his hand cupped her backside, pulling her even closer.

Lizzy could feel his arousal and knew then that his allure was too great to stop her own body's response to his caresses. She forced herself to address that persistent voice inside her, demanding that she do things she had never done before. Begrudgingly ending their kiss, she breathlessly panted, "Are you a good swimmer, Will?"

"I guess. Why? Is that competitive Renner trait calling for a swim match?"

"Oh, you know me so well. Shall we make a wager?"

He loved her feistiness. "Sure. What did you have in mind?"

"To that diving float and back to the shore. The loser treats the other to a chocolate egg cream at the club."

He noted the dark clouds rolling in and the seagulls having a frenzied field day on their blanket. The other beach goers were frowning at the activity or was it Gene Krupa's persistent drumbeat on the radio they disliked? He dismissed the nearby distractions and provoked, "Oh, you know the way to this Brooklyn boy's heart. I warn you, get ready to part with your money, Pistol."

"Don't be so sure, Ducky." She let go of his waist and positioned her body beside him. "Ready, set ... Go!"

The first few raindrops didn't stop their competition, but once Will made it to the diving float he stopped, letting her continue to the shore line. In the rain, he sat on the wood pontoon, watching her perfect form as her arms chopped the waves and her toned legs kicked. Every few strokes, he was graced a peek at those kissable feet of hers. She reached the shore and raised from the water like Thetis the sea nymph, dripping wet with her swimsuit clinging to her. The latent wolf in him thought she looked just like a cheesecake pin up standing at the breaking surf, waiting for him.

Lizzy called out to him, "What are you doing there?"

"Watching your form; it's spectacular. You're right, Lizzy, you are quite the proficient!"

She playfully curtsied then waved him in. "We better get going, unless of course you're going to swim back to the club like the duck you are. You have an egg cream to buy me!"

That's just the way he planned it. He stood and dived in, keenly aware of how she was watching *his* form.

****

Two hours later, following an extra chocolatey egg cream at the club and the playful banter they both loved so much, Will found himself at the family entrance of Meercrest after a too brief ride in the famous Zephyr. He glanced over his shoulder for a last glimpse of the landscaped gardens and reflecting pool, surmising that the view of the grounds from the terrace above them must be spectacular. The rain seemed to make the already colorful flowerbeds come more alive. Each planting of shrubs, trees, and blooms existed in perfect accord with the marble statuary and French neoclassical style of the mansion. He reflected upon how his mother would love to spend an afternoon enjoying the harmony, either here or with a walk through the apple orchard they drove passed.

"Are you sure it's okay if I come in?"

"Don't be silly of course it is. Why wouldn't it?"

"Well, last time I was here, I let my opinions get the better of me, and I fear I wore out my welcome by voicing them."

"You're worried about that? Don't worry. Father loves debate. You're my guest, Will, and besides I can't let you get back on the train in wet clothing."

They entered into the grand marble vestibule of the fifth largest home in America. Two statues depicting classical ideals towered from recessed niches on either side of the mahogany door. Above the inlaid imported wood floor, a large Tiffany stained glass window added color and light even on the cloudy afternoon. A life-sized standing portrait of an elegant Victorian woman wearing black hung above an Egyptian Revival credenza on one side of the entrance hall.

Will compared "Madame X's" ivory beauty to Lizzy's, quickly coming to the conclusion that John Singer Sargent should have lived long enough to paint such as subject as his girl. Even half drenched, she was gorgeous.

Lizzy removed the picnic basket from his hand. "Are you sure you won't re-consider staying for dinner? I promise, Father won't be angry and Mother ... well, she probably won't be sober enough to notice."

He was surprised by her admission to her mother's drinking problem, but then again, today she had opened up about so many things. There was a deep seriousness and sensitivity about her, which was gratifying to confirm. Her frankness and heavy heart about Gloria and Ingrid's cruelty to Kitty, her father's shunning of Lillian, and her inquisitiveness and dismay about the massacre in Vilna, Lithuania of 60,000 Jews all further validated why he was falling in love with her. He had been surprised to learn about her delving into the newspapers every day, even reading Mr. Howard's *Daily News*.

Will gazed up in awe at the vaulted ceiling, admiring the ornate moldings above the living hall. He'd never been inside a home such as this but tried not to let his opinion of the magnificent décor or the over the top affluence appear too apparent. He tried to ignore the deadened stare of the taxidermy ostrich standing in front of the diamond designed glass windows.

"I can't stay, Lizzy. I leave in the morning and as inviting as spending the evening with you is, I need to be with my parents. My mother is planning a special meal and it's important to us to spend my last night together—as a family."

"I understand."

Will heard the disappointment in her voice and took her free hand. "Thank you for today. It meant a lot to me ... I had a swell time."

She smiled wistfully. "Me, too. I'll miss you, Will."

Taking a step closer to her, he bridged the small gap separating them and ignored the impropriety. The approaching sound of Kitty's cumbersome wheelchair provided background noise to the pounding of his heart in his ears.

"I'll miss you as well." He bent to kiss Lizzy sweetly, and she rose to her tiptoes, bending her leg upward when his arm came around her bare waist.

The kiss remained as chaste as he could manage given that his spirited cookie's lips were delicious.

A female throat cleared followed by a giggle, and the sweethearts separated in a start. Lizzy's hand went to her lips when Will stepped back from her, creating a wide space between them.

"Don't stop on my account," Kitty laughed. "That looked almost as good as Rhett and Scarlett's."

"Kitty!"

She giggled again. "I'm sorry to interrupt you, but Father has been asking for you for about an hour. He's been in a foul mood all afternoon and mother's well ... you know ... sleeping it off in the tropical house until dinnertime."

"I'm sorry, Will. Let me find Mr. Howard and get you some clothing." She backed away from him, keeping her eyes locked with his, resisting the urge to tear up. "I'll let Mrs. Davis know you are here and she'll bring you a soda pop."

"I'm fine, Lizzy. I'll be in good company with Kitty."

He watched her departure, once again feeling himself becoming the hungry wolf she had inspired. Unabashedly crazy about her, his eyes drank in her receding form, appreciating her slender waist and the sway of her hips in that wet, cotton skirt of hers. What a day he had, what an incredible afternoon—so much better than the Cyclone at Coney Island. Again, he thought how Louie had steered him in the right direction.

Kitty cleared her throat again, and he met her playful expression with a sheepish grin.

"So, you're in love with my sister?"

"Perhaps."

"Are you going to marry her when you come home from fighting?"

He smirked. "Perhaps."

"Will you have room in your house for a girl with a wheelchair to navigate?"

Will put his hands in his trouser pockets and walked toward where she sat at the threshold between the living hall and the south corridor. "Kitty, I expect that when I come home, you'll be walking. There's nothing you can't do in spite of what others foolishly claim. Heck, by the time I return, you may even be *married.*"

"Not likely, Will. Girls like me rarely have opportunities to meet killer-diller boys like you."

He leaned down to her ear, covered by cascading blonde curls. "Think big, Kitty. With a little encouragement from my brother, I finally did and now your *killer-diller* sister has agreed to be my girl."

As though the air was suddenly sucked from the room, Renner entered from the north corridor, bursting into the quiet conversation of hope and optimism, bringing a dark, commanding disharmony. His navy blue, double-breasted suit fit snuggly and the expression on his face looked almost choleric.

Kitty sat upright immediately, her smile disappearing in a flash, her hand instantly gripping the arm of the wicker chair tightly.

"What goes on here?"

"Father, you remember Lieutenant Martel from Memorial Day, don't you? He's visiting from Brooklyn."

Like two bulls about to ram, they both stood tall. Will towered over the stout man who repulsed him in every way but, out of respect for Lizzy, he composed his expression and walked toward her father with an outstretched hand. "Mr. Renner, it's a pleasure to see you again. You have a magnificent home."

Renner, chin raised, stared him down when their hands met almost painfully. His eyes came to rest on the gold and diamond insignia ring the flyer wore. "Of course it is. Built with railroad money, young man." Scornful gray eyes locked with inscrutable brown ones. "I remember you. You're that patriotic idealist, off to fight what you view as tyranny."

Will readily saw through the now phony smile plastered upon Renner's face. "Yes, I suppose I am a patriotic idealist."

"It is a noble position, one all sides of this war embody. Will you be leaving soon to fight, Lieutenant?"

"Yes, sir, I leave tomorrow. Your daughter, Lizzy, and I enjoyed a day out on the Sound until the rain. The hydroplane is an impressive boat."

"Nothing but the best for my Lizzy." His eyes drew to where Kitty sat, seemingly dismissing her, causing her to leave the room. The departing squeak of the chair's wheels filled the hall as Renner boasted, "One day, my daughter will marry someone from our *elite* society and that little Chris-Craft boat of hers will be but a small pittance in her holdings."

"And what if she chooses to marry a patriotic idealist with very little wealth but enough love to make her happy?"

Renner took a step forward, leaning in toward Will, his tone grave yet confident, the smile gone. "That will never happen so long as I live."

Will smirked, thankful his brother wasn't there to elbow him in the ribs or kick him under the table. "Well, perhaps, you won't live long enough to see it happen when it does."

"Oh, I assure you I will." Hubris infused his self-satisfied chortle throughout the hallway as Lizzy approached. "It would appear that with you headed to Europe, *your* odds of survival are a lot *smaller* than mine."

Lizzy's melodious voice rang out when her effervescent breath of fresh air entered the living hall. "Father, you remember Will, right?"

She knew it was a stupid question but it was the only one she could think of given the serious expression upon her flyboy's face as she came upon the uncomfortable scene.

Renner smiled, pretending to be imperturbable. "How can I forget? We were just re-acquainting ourselves and discussing who will be the victor ... in the war of course."

Holding a bundle of clothing, Lizzy stood between the two men in her life she loved. Her father—the first and most influential man—owned her heart from the beginning of life in this affluent society. But this humble flyboy was opening a whole new world to her, encouraging her in ways that gave her optimistic hope and determination for the future. Proud, yet guilt ridden, she was coming to feel that Will's opinions meant more to her than her father's. His were becoming a great disappointment.

"Why, America will win, of course!" she exclaimed.

Will watched as Renner controlled the shielded scowl behind the contrived smile, even as his eyes narrowed ever so slightly when he took in his daughter's flush cheeks and still swollen lips.

Lizzy handed the neatly folded pile to Will. "I'll show you to the powder room where you can change. Mr. Howard is about your physique. Excuse us Father, Will has a train to catch back to the city."

Once again, Will extended his hand, ending their standoff with both clearly understanding the position of the other. "Mr. Renner."

"Lieutenant Martel. I wish you good luck. You're going to need it."

"Thank you, sir." He turned his focused gaze toward Lizzy's quizzical brow. "I have all the luck I need. Lizzy's my good luck charm."

They left Renner standing with furious, tight lips beside the antique parlor suite, his rigid hand gripping the frame of the sofa.

$\mathscr{T}$welve

How Little We Know
June 1992

"Wat do you mean you can't go with me, Max?" Juliana groaned into the telephone receiver craned between her shoulder and her chin as she folded the letter she held.

"I'm sorry, Julie. All of a sudden, Andy's become a little too clingy. He's decided to forego golfing Saturday, instead wanting to take me away to Cape Cod for an extended weekend."

"You're joking, right? You're sending me into this meeting with *Newsday* all by myself? You know, I knew, just knew, you would back out, you sneaky girl you."

Maxine laughed. "You'll do fine. Remember, you're the girl who ambushed Donna Karan into an interview at New York Fashion Week last year, so a meeting with Jack Robertsen should be a walk in the park. He's harmless, hon, a real pussycat and he's offered to get access to the archives going back to the inception of the newspaper in 1940. Who knows, you might find all the answers, maybe even get a date out of it."

Juliana lightly traced her fingertips over her great-grandmother's handwriting on the envelope she was examining. "Doubtful. He'll probably run for the hills when he gets one look at me. Say, do you know what *ik mis je* means?"

"Excuse me?"

"*Ik mis je.* My great-grandmother signed off a letter to William with that phrase. It's Dutch. She was Dutch."

"No, I don't know, but take the letter with you. Maybe Jack can ask one of their foreign writers. He may even know since he travels the world for the paper."

"Oh, I intend on taking all the letters. After spending three hours, making a list of the contents of the footlocker, I have even more questions than when I began. Fifteen letters into the stack and so far, I've been able to discover that the *M* in the photograph stands for Meercrest, Lizzy's home on Long Island and that Rosebriar Manor was also her home in Sarasota, Florida. And they had a townhouse in the city—name yet to be disclosed."

"Mansion in the city? That makes sense. Many of those affluent Gold Coasters had winter retreats in Florida and townhouses in Manhattan. Long Island was technically their summer retreat, but many lived there year round. Finding her family should be easy for Jack now that you know the estate name."

"Great! I also have discovered that William and Lizzy's first magical kiss was on the carousel in Central Park after they sneaked on just before closing. Other letters describe her volunteering for the Victory Book Campaign, collecting books and sorting them into piles to send them overseas to the GIs. I never even knew about that amazing stuff. She writes him about driving the library's bookmobile to keep people from wasting rubber and gas, stuff like that."

"So she's still trying to impress him."

"No, it's more than that. Her letters tell him of life at home and what she is doing. I can really feel her love of volunteering—not so much to impress him, but because she's taking pride in it. Every one of her letters is upbeat and clearly expresses how much she likes him. Reading them gives me a real sense of her spirit and voice. She was a wild one."

Juliana opened a particular letter. "Here, listen to this. It's her first letter about the bookmobile."

"June 30, 1942
My Dear Will,

I was so happy to receive your long letter this morning, but it made me sad to read about your friend who crashed last week. That poor fella. I'm truly sorry and wish I could be there to comfort you. Please, take care when training, or I just may need to come down there and wrap you in padding. I'd do it, too, you know. As much as I'm not too keen on train travel, I would do it!

Now, try not to laugh too hard—Mrs. Tinsdale asked me to drive the bookmobile around Glen Cove, even allowing me to go into Suffolk County! Isn't that a gas? Well, after the first day of driving the <u>painfully slow</u> Victory Speed of 35, I was ready to burst unable to adhere to the forced speed limit. Needless to say, I grew impatient. You can imagine the speed in which I <u>now</u> accomplish my route. True, it's not my Zephyr but it does make great time since I discovered I can take the speedometer up to 50 with barely a shake to the steering column. Ha! I only did it once, so try not to let your fuddy-duddy self rear its ugly head when you chew me out for burning rubber your bomber wheels need. Well, maybe it was more like a few times—<u>but,</u> I promise you, I have not run anyone over or caused anyone to crash into the mud ... yet. Although ... there was an incident with a squirrel, but it was not my fault at all. I am sure, it was an incognito Nazi saboteur because the bookmobile became stuck alongside Elm Avenue, and I couldn't deliver the books I had picked up from Mrs. Whitney for the victory campaign. But don't you worry, speeding isn't something I've done consistently, but several of the Merchant Marine radio operators do cheer me on when my library on wheels kicks up the dust at Oheka Castle. Don't be jealous, those fellas are working hard while stationed there, but the books are a welcome diversion for them, and I'm glad that Mrs. Tinsdale lets me drive all the way out to Huntington just for them. I did have one MM ask if I had a girlie magazine on the shelves of the truck! I'll have to work on that. You know—it's all for the boys! I wouldn't even know where to begin to look for that kind of magazine. Maybe Johnny will know—but hopefully, you don't!

Mrs. Tinsdale also suggested a uniform. Now that is positively lulu! I hope it's green, so I can look official and match you.

Speaking of books, I have yet to go through Father's library at Meercrest. Kitty and I have to time it strategically when he is away from home for an extended period and, if we can, we hope to also do our sorting when Nurse Keller is out on one of her many errands. I have my suspicions that she tells Father everything, so we must remain covert. They're just books for goodness sake, and going to such a noble cause, but better to be safe than sorry. Kitty and I are having a swell time, and we would hate for him to put the kibosh on the successful progress we are making. Given that the bookmobile is considered "essential to the war effort," I get a whole eight gallons of gasoline a week using a B ration coupon. Where else can I be permitted to get behind the wheel and drive like a hotrod? Are you shocked that I even know what a B ration coupon is? I even know what blue food stamps are!

Did you read the newspaper this morning? I was shocked to read about the Nazi saboteurs who came ashore in Amagansett on the south fork of the island. It positively frightens the dickens out of me—Nazis here in America! Funny thing, though, the paper mentioned that all those men were part of something called the German-American Bund. I can't be sure, but I vaguely remember Ingrid attending a summer camp and she always referred to herself as a Bundist. Perhaps, that's a common term for campers? I'll have to look into that, maybe ask Johnny. Lately, my sister seems more sympathetic to the German plight than the Allies fighting and winning the war, and like my mother, parrots my father on many of his beliefs. Is this something I need to be concerned about or have I been reading too many novels and spending too much time at the movies?

No, I have not had another run in with GG, but if I did, I would have no qualms about running <u>him</u> over. Vile man! And since reading Agatha Christie's "N or M", I wouldn't doubt if he were a Nazi spy and the squirrel his cohort! See there I go again—too many novels.

I'm off to the Cove movie theater tonight with some of my girlfriends. Dreamy Tyrone Power is set to romance Joan Fontaine in "This Above All." I'll let you know all about it after I determine if his kisses were as romantic as yours.

Now, when you write me back, please, please, please practice your penmanship or sit at a typewriter! You are making me whacky. It took me nearly thirty minutes to figure out that the curls on my head make you dizzy and not frizzy! Sheesh, some way to woo a girl! Ha Ha. Make sure you tell me all about the places you have visited in Tampa. You absolutely must visit the Colonnade for lunch and enjoy a juicy burger and an olive in your Coca-Cola! My next letter will tell you all about Rosebriar Manor, our winter home in Sarasota.

Yours,
PPL (Pistol Packin' Lizzy)"

Smiling, Juliana carefully folded the letter after reading the contents. Apart from the Nazi reference, it was a happy letter and made her feel giddy. She laughed when Maxine said,

"She's positively lulu!"

"Well he is a *ducky shincracker dreamboat*, so I can understand her being so *keen* on him."

"You have a lot of good leads in that letter alone, so go forth, darling, and I'll look forward to reading this article when it wraps up. If you need anything, I have my beeper on, so don't hesitate. Good luck today."

"Thanks for the meeting, Max. I'll let you know if I think Jack is *swell* or not."

"Did people really talk like that? Remind me to ask my dad about some of his slang."

****

Although she could have driven her Jeep, the city girl in Juliana had always felt more comfortable on subways and trains. The Long Island Railroad followed by a taxi brought her to *Newsday's* headquarters in the county seat of Mineola.

At precisely nine in the morning, she sat in the waiting room, looking professional and stylish wearing a cream-colored pantsuit and high heels. Apart from Maxine's description of Jack being a gorgeous hunk, she didn't know anything about him and given Juliana's petite, five feet, two inch frame, she figured the extra height couldn't hurt. Sitting with her legs crossed, she nervously bounced her foot in the air, waiting and listening to the receptionist answer telephone call after telephone call with a nasal Long Island accent, "*Newsday*, please hold. *Newsday*, please hold."

A new, even larger Tiffany box of letters and photographs sat concealed in the accountant-sized briefcase Juliana oftentimes took with her on assignment, and she resisted the urge to read the next letter in the stack calling to her. Although her pursuit began out of curiosity, it had unexpectedly morphed into so much more. There was no doubt in her mind—she was obsessed with this story. So obsessed that the questions lingering out there unanswered felt heavy, yet she didn't want to rush the process, feeling the innate need to draw closer to Lizzy and William so to better understand their relationship and the depth of their love. It was difficult for her to put their full wartime romance together from only one-sided communication, but she hoped, with Jack's help, she might find some of Lizzy's sisters and interview them.

A tanned man, she figured in his thirties, approached with a wide smile. Like his above average height, nothing about him was average. Light brown hair, trim, fit, and handsome with chiseled features made his bright blue eyes even more alluring. When he stopped before her, there was definitely an appealing look in those sparkling eyes.

"Are you Juliana Mart?"

She stood abruptly, chuckling and jutting out her hand to shake. "Yes, I mean, no ... Martel not Mart."

His warm hand met her cool, delicate one, and their eyes locked in immediate attraction. "Oh, I'm sorry. I guess Cassandra, my secretary ... um ... Welcome to *Newsday*. I'm Jack Robertsen."

"It's great to meet you, Mr. Rob," she teased. "Or shall I call you by your first name?"

"Rob or Jack—I'll answer to it all. Just don't call me by my middle name."

Juliana cocked an eyebrow. "Oh, do tell."

"Herbert," he laughed.

"Yeah, shortening that would make you sound either seasonable, smokable, or drinkable. So Jack it is, which is certainly edible. Tell me, are you Monterrey or Pepper?"

"I do love California and have a keen addiction to cheese. So, I'll go with Monterrey."

She openly returned his smile back at the silly joke. "Thanks for taking the time out of your busy schedule, *Jack*. I'm sure you have tons to catch up on, or are you planning your next trip?"

"I'm happy to assist, and I can't think of anything I'd rather do than help you with your project until my trip next month."

"Are you off to somewhere exciting?"

"Paris, over July 17th weekend." He leaned into her, lowering his voice. "... with my grandmother."

"Aw, that sounds very sweet and memorable."

"Oh, it will be." Jack bent down and picked up her briefcase.

Already he had made an impression on her. Cute humor, dressed in his preppy style, acting in a thoughtful manner, world traveler with his grandmother, and his willingness to help her all spoke volumes of the type of man he was. Not that it all mattered, she was here on personal business, and most likely, this stud had a string of girls lined up to capture him.

"Follow me. I set aside a conference room where we can dig into some newspapers and talk about the Gold Coast."

Juliana followed him through a busy newsroom lined with rows of occupied desks and filled with the low hum and ding of IBM Selectric typewriters as well as the tap, tap, taps of fingers meeting newly installed word processing keyboards. Phones rung, reporters chatted, and secretaries filed, took notes, and scanned microfiche. It was a busy hive of exciting activity, something she had experienced and enjoyed on a smaller scale during her first foray into the world of reporting, working for *Women's Wear Daily*.

They arrived at a large, glass-enclosed room that could easily seat thirty. Displayed before them on the conference table were Danishes, bagels, and cream cheese as well as coffee, juice, and pitcher of water.

Jack could tell by the way she surveyed the table offerings that she must be hungry. "Yeah, I'm famished, too. After your train ride, I thought you might need something to kick-start our research. Shall we dig in?"

This new and continually improving Juliana did just as he suggested— she dug in, delighting in the vegetable cream cheese smear on top an everything bagel.

They sat with their breakfast on paper plates, catty-cornered from one another at the end of the long table, and in between chewing and sipping, Jack inquired about the article she was writing. He seemed genuinely interested, even prepared to take notes.

"So, Maxine tells me this couple you're researching is related to you and you're trying to unlock the mysterious disappearance of the former owner of your house. Is that right?"

"Yes, he was my great-uncle, William Martel, an Army bomber pilot with the 9th Air Force, who was completely in love with a beautiful, spirited woman from Glen Cove. They had a whirlwind romance of only seven months, until their correspondence abruptly ended at the end of December 1942. That was when he received the last letter from her, a Christmas card, only he never stopped loving her. I need to know so many things and have so little to go on, really. He disappeared in 1950, although I really can't be sure if he died. Strangely, I feel he may be still alive. I don't know why—maybe it's wishful thinking on my part—but if he *is* alive, I'd like to find him and find her for sure. She, though, may be dead."

The name "Martel" continued to sound familiar to Jack. "Glen Cove, you say. Wow, I grew up in Mill Neck, right next door. Small world. I love a good mystery, and the Gold Coast is rife with them. Fortunes made and lost. For example, the Woolworth fortune—a billion dollars totally wasted and spent by the granddaughter heiress Barbara Hutton and her seven husbands. Some of those homes were incredible with fascinating stories and histories. The Woolworth mansion is said to be haunted."

"Barbara Hutton sounds like someone I know. So you say—*were* incredible?"

"Yeah, many of them have been torn down. We're talking estates once owned by J.P. Morgan and Vanderbilt. The heirs of these great treasures demolished many of them when usefulness outweighed size and especially when the tax burden became too heavy. When they were built during the Gilded Age, there wasn't an income tax as we know it today and it was at a time when economic growth had increased exponentially, so money was aplenty."

"I saw the movie *The Great Gatsby*. Was it really like that? All that pretentious wealth and high living?"

"Absolutely, but the movie was filmed in Newport, Rhode Island. Those two social circles still run very close together. They all do, actually, Newport; Chestnut Hill, Philadelphia; and Palm Beach, Florida—they're all the same. Speaking of movies, *Sabrina* with Audrey Hepburn was filmed in and around Glen Cove."

"Using one of the mansions? How exciting."

"Yes, a Pratt mansion and a Guggenheim one, I think. Today, some of the estates are utilized as museums or catering halls. Some are schools, one is even a planetarium, but most are just sitting unoccupied, left in disrepair for as long as twenty or more years. My dad is an active member of the Society for the Preservation of Long Island Antiquities, a committee to help save and restore some of the estates."

With a mouthful of bagel Juliana reflected, "Sort of how I found Primrose Cottage, the house my great-uncle gave me. It's a time capsule and what started me on this quest. I'm thankful it's restorable."

Jack couldn't help staring at her, consuming her bagel with gusto, and when a tiny piece of cream cheese-laden carrot ended up on her chin, he instinctively reached out but stopped himself short. "You have ... um ... on your chin."

Juliana giggled, wiping it away with a napkin. "Oh my G-d. I'm so embarrassed."

He stuck his finger into the cream cheese tub, put some on his own chin, and smiled. "Don't be. We'll play with our food together."

Already, she felt at ease. He was just as Maxine had indicated, an absolutely gorgeous, genuine guy with a pussycat, mild manner. She reached over with her paper napkin and wiped the offending green pepper from his face.

Jack smiled, wondering if he should mention about the solitary poppy seed wedged between two of her pearly white teeth. "I hope it's okay, but I've set aside some time today to drive you up to the North Shore. If the mansion you're looking for is still standing, maybe we can arrange for a tour, and if not, you can get a general feel for the luxurious lifestyle of some of the residents along the Long Island Sound. I've always loved the area."

"Do you live there now?"

"No, I live not far from here. I hate it—too far from the water. I spent many years with my grandparents, learning to sail at the Hempstead Harbor Club in Glen Cove. Apart from New Zealand, it's my all-time favorite place to spend on the water. The Sound is so tranquil when it wants to be and from there I can sail to Connecticut or Block Island. Do you sail?"

"Me? G-d no! I'm terrified of the water. In fact, even a bathtub makes me uneasy. Drive me across a bridge and I'm a veritable nervous wreck."

"Well, maybe we can find a way, on another day, to take you out on the water. I assure you, it's very safe, and I'm an excellent waterman."

He flashed a flirtatious smile and suddenly Lizzy's word "lulu" popped into her mind. "That would be nice. It seems as though this year is exposing me to all sorts of adventures, discoveries, and even a few resolutions, so I might consider getting up the nerve."

Excitedly, he clapped his hands together. "Good. I'm pumped already! So tell me a little about your research thus far."

Juliana reached into her briefcase, removing the blue box. "These are the letters received by my uncle from his girlfriend during World War Two. Totally romantic stuff, but her letters don't paint the full picture." She withdrew the photograph on top of the stack and slid it toward him. "This is the estate's entrance where she grew up with her four sisters, one of whom was wheelchair bound."

Jack froze, staring down at the entrance to a mansion he knew well. He felt the blood rush from his brain from the shock of seeing the *M* staring back at him. Forcibly trying to control any and all expression—giving away nothing of what he knew of Meercrest or its loathsome secrets bulldozed to the ground in 1975—he remained expressionless, feeling as though he was about to pass out.

His eyes shifted away from the snapshot, unwilling to look at Juliana, and he deliberately picked up his Mont Blanc. Pretending to be at the ready to write, his mind raced a mile a minute for discernment.

"Do ... do you know the name of the estate?" he barely managed without an obvious stammer, his smile waning ever so slightly.

"Meercrest," hung heavily in the airspace between them as if she had spoken the poisonous exclamation, *"Heil Hitler."*

Jack closed his eyes, the smile wiped from his lips, panic rising within him like an ominous sea wall readying for mass destruction. His heart seized in his chest, yet his pen remained stilled, and his eyes continued to stare at the legal-sized pad before him.

"Meercrest, you said? Are you sure?"

"Yeah, Lizzy wrote about it in her letters. Do you know it?"

He fought the pull to search her expression for fear that she would read his own. He looked to the door as his mind silently scrambled for an answer, his heart rate increasing expeditiously. *Lizzy. She just said "Lizzy."* He hadn't heard that moniker since he was a boy.

Internal panic rose like a tidal wave, and a clammy, cold sweat spread over his body from head to toe. Terrified, yet curious about what Juliana knew, he finally peered up to meet her expressive, blue eyes. A half-truth formed on his lips as he attempted to maintain their amicability, if not his own composure.

"No. Um ... I mean, the mansion is gone now, razed to make way for a senior home for veterans."

Jack could see the disappointment upon her face fall like a shadow, but there was no way in hell he was going to expose the dark secrets of Meercrest to a woman writing an article for a magazine with over one million readers no matter how attracted he was to her. He'd die with the Renner family secrets tightly locked within his heart and mind. The legacy of *those* people had been replaced with new, honorable legacies. The past was dead, and he'd see that it remained so, despising himself for the necessity of the sidestepping and lies he knew he'd be forced to employ.

"I'm sorry, Juliana. I could still drive you out there to look around, but I think only the boathouse and a water tower remain, maybe this archway, too. It's probably all overrun with weeds."

"Oh, I see. Do you know who owned the estate?"

His smile had now disappeared altogether. "Nope. Haven't a clue."

"Do you think your father may know?"

He continued to lie, his expression remaining impassive. "Doubtful. It was demolished long before he became active with the Society."

"Maxine mentioned that the archives of the newspaper may shed some light. Any chance we can check them out?"

"Sure, but we only have papers onsite beginning in 1976."

That was a definite blockade, or rather a lie, on his part. All fifty-two years' worth were in the room down the hall, but he wasn't about to let her see anything pertaining to the Renner scandal or Meercrest, knowing unequivocally that she would find the sensational news coverage splashed across the front pages in 1945 and 1947.

Jack tapped his pen upon the pad and still unable to meet Juliana's gaze looked away. "Besides, *Newsday* probably didn't cover the local happenings in a sleepy coastal town such as Glen Cove."

When he finally chanced a glance at her, she looked crestfallen. Internally, his shame struggled with righteous duplicity when she dejectedly surmised, "I guess I misunderstood Maxine when she indicated you would show me the archives going back to 1940. That's disappointing."

"Juliana, I hate to bring this up because truly I can see how important this is to you, but have you given any thought to the fact that maybe ... just maybe ... Lizzy or William don't want to be found. Maybe the past is better left in the past, and we should just look to the future. Let sleeping dogs lie and all that."

"I've thought about that, but I disagree with you. My uncle's military service shouldn't be forgotten simply because it happened two generations ago, and this girl Lizzy was a part of that time in his life. I imagine that her story during the war years is as worth telling as my uncle's. I realize now how important it is to share someone's legacy, especially how it relates to such a period of time as historically important as the Second World War. While I admit, I've been clueless about the war, its effects may have shaped the dynamics of my family." She snorted a laugh. "My dysfunctional family. So, if love is there—in the midst of despair and heartache—I need to find it."

Jack hated to stonewall, hated not being able to truly help this intriguing woman in her quest for her great-uncle's story, but that story, according to her, was inexplicably tied to Lizzy's.

Juliana removed a stack of photographs of varying shapes and sizes from the box; most depicted Lizzy and the man he assumed was William. His heart lurched. They were a handsome couple, and Lizzy was stunning in her youth, as legendary a beauty as his grandfather had often claimed her to be. Her spirit leaped from the images, and Jack smiled thoughtfully.

"Jack, to be frank, Lizzy and William represent so much more than a historical romance—they give me hope for the here and now. Up until last week, the love you see in these snapshots seemed unreal to me, especially in 1992 when divorce is rampant and a respectful, loving relationship seems nearly impossible to attain. Yet it *was* real. Romantic love such as theirs intrigues me. My own history in the romance department, not to mention the example set by my parents have left me with ... how should I say, a large measure of skepticism. But then, these two come along and well ... whammo! I want to hold onto what they shared, feel it as they did, cherish it for a lifetime and spread it to my children."

"Do you think your readers *want* to read about a wartime romance that was probably nothing more than a summer fling between a couple, actually more like two *kids,* fifty years ago?"

"Not just any couple. *This* couple." She pointed to the photographs.

He scanned through the snapshots as though dealing playing cards until he held up a photograph of another man standing with a familiar woman. The familiarity of the surname Martel was now confirmed, his shock barely contained. A woman he knew by the name "Lillian Renner," whose story he knew by heart, stared back at him, smiling. Through the years, he heard it time and again, remembered and retold with pride. Heck, her photograph currently hung with honor in the Long Island Holocaust Museum in Glen Cove. Lillian was a local heroine—in spite of her birth into the disgraced family.

Stunned that Juliana would have her image, he held up the snapshot, again feigning ignorance with impassivity. "Who are these people?"

"Oh! Those are my grandparents. Louis and Lillian Martel. He was a Marine in the Pacific, and she was a volunteer with the Red Cross, I'm told. I guess I got their photo mixed in with the pile by accident after my grandfather gave me a box full of his war memorabilia. William was his brother."

And Lillian was Lizzy's sister! In all of his travels and his experience in dealing with people all over the world, Jack Robertsen had never been as blown away as he was at that very moment. The coincidence astounded him, and this unsuspecting, young woman delivered it with an innocent smile, rendering him speechless. His boat began to capsize—this squall was too great to navigate unaffected.

"The American Red Cross?"

She shrugged. "I guess. I think so."

Her *grandmother,* Lillian Renner was so much more than "a volunteer with the Red Cross." She was the incredibly brave woman responsible for rescuing his three-year-old father from the jaws of the Nazis and starvation when she found him and other children living alone in the French countryside. It was because of Lillian Renner that his father became a Robertsen through adoption.

Jack was amazed that Juliana was clueless about her grandmother's connection to Lizzy, but then the sobering reality of her Renner family relations came back. No, no one would admit to being a part of *that* family—not even Lizzy. Apart from Kitty who lived in the town over, Lizzy never even spoke of her other sisters. Jack knew telling Juliana of Lillian's bravery meant opening the door to the stories and secrets of the other Renners and he was unwilling to do that. Others would disagree with him, but he felt strongly—nothing good ever came from fanning long extinguished ashes which could damage and engulf people in renewed flames of anger.

He hoped to G-d she couldn't see through his façade of a beaming smile and enthusiastic proposition. "You know, Juliana, maybe we're going about this in the wrong way. Let's take another route. You want to know about your great-uncle, so why don't we start with him. I have a couple of contacts down at the National Archives and the National Personnel Records Center who might be able to locate something from William's military service records. It might be tough since so many of the records were burned in 1973, but we can try. At least we can get his social security number."

"Well, I do know a few facts about his military history. He kept some of his things from his POW internment in Stalag Luft I, as well as a flight mission record over Holland."

"That's great! I can take a look at our databases here and reach out to Veterans Affairs for any services he may have needed or receipt of Medicare benefits. We can play detective and see if, in fact, he did die. Perhaps he is still alive and we can track him down. Would that work?"

He watched as her face transformed from downtrodden to outright jubilant. "That would be wonderful! In the meantime, can I take you up on that offer to drive to Glen Cove? If for no other reason, I'd like to see the water tower. Lizzy loved the water tower."

Jack thought wryly, *I know.* "Sure, we can certainly do that much."

Juliana slid a letter out of the bundle. "Here, just to give you an idea as to why I'm so keen on finding them, and why their story gives me a glimmer of hope."

July 2, 1942

My Dear Ducky,

After three hours at the movie theater, I have come to determine that Tyrone Power may have been handsome on screen, but he and Joan Fontaine had very little chemistry. Isn't romance about the chemistry between two people? Don't you agree? For example, I would say we have chemistry. Wouldn't you? I felt it from the start when I noticed you sticking your head out of your father's jalopy window on Memorial Day. You may claim it was my mischievous laugh that left you spellbound, but it was your shout about my speeding that did it for me. Oh so commanding and hardboiled. And how can I have not felt the chemistry when we danced to "Moonlight Serenade" and then later to "Stardust"? Just the feel of your hand resting against my back gave me goose flesh—I mean, duck flesh. You flirted almost as shamelessly as I did!

In the movie, Tyrone Power failed to deliver in his kiss to Joan Fontaine that overwhelming feeling which causes bobbysoxers to swoon as they do with Frank Sinatra. You, on the other hand, had me swooning when we circled round and round on the carousel. That magical sound from the calliope playing as a backdrop as you held my hand between our bobbing horses made me outright dizzy. Our first kiss left me breathless and I must confess—it was the most romantic kiss I have ever received!——ooo ... the chemistry, made all the more so by the way you made love to me in that deep voice of yours. And I could not fail to mention the kisses you gave me in the boat and on the beach. All positively creamy and made my knees go weak! Yes, William Martel, you and I have chemistry.

Are you blushing yet, Flyboy? C'mon, you cannot deny the chemistry, no matter how chicken you are. Why, you're positively as smitten with me as I am with you. It's okay, go ahead and admit to me again how crazy you are for me. I'll never tire of hearing it, and I assure you I won't blush.

Now, let's get serious about something. How are you? Have they been training you too hard? Feeding you well? Giving you enough passes for recreation? You wrote that the airfield has an officer's club? Do the base nurses attend the dinners as well? I am sure they would appreciate the opportunity for some air conditioning and a dance with some of the boys. Some—not all.

Have you heard from Louie yet? Has he arrived at his destination? It's been quite a long time since his departure last month, but Mrs. Frazier, three estates over, tells me it can take weeks to get to the Pacific Theater. I did read in the newspaper how the first of the Marines arrived in the Pacific, but I'm not sure if it was him. I do so hope he is safe.

Stay safe, Will. Next letter I promise to tell you about Rosebriar in case you get a pass and want to take the train or bus to Sarasota. I can tell you where we hide the key. I miss you.
Your girl,
PPL

With his heart clenching hidden behind a warm smile, Jack handed Juliana the letter. It near killed him to read just how much Lizzy Renner loved William Martel. But that was fifty years ago, things happened, people changed and life carried on after the war.

He spoke as though unaffected because, in truth, he wanted to help Juliana find her great-uncle if he was still alive. Of course, there was his *personal* desire to help her. "PPL?"

"Her nickname. It stands for Pistol Packin' Lizzy."

"Pistol and Ducky. Well, she seemed in love with him. Now, what do you say to giving me fifteen minutes to make a few phone calls, and then we'll take a drive to that water tower of hers?"

Juliana beamed, boldly asking, "Can I buy you lunch as a thank you?"

"Sounds like a plan."

Thirteen

Sentimental Journey
June 1992

Sitting within the close leather confines of his new Alfa Romeo Spider, Jack and Juliana drove languidly through the hills of the northwest shore of the island. It was a splendid day for touring, especially with the convertible top down and U2's "Mysterious Ways" playing on the radio. This newspaper reporter was by no means a speeder, and it seemed to Juliana that he was comfortable taking life slow, enjoying the sights and sounds of the area he called home.

The road they traveled was narrow and tree-lined, sparsely dotted with vast estates hidden behind impressive wrought iron metal gates or imposing gatehouses. They passed a few newly developed family neighborhoods that seemed incongruent to the unapproachable, old money mansions and surrounding quaint villages. Like a carefully applied veneer, the area's blue-blooded affluence, obvious with each passing Bentley, Mercedes, and Jaguar, concealed the many secrets of prior generations. Juliana briefly mused that these neighborhoods could be a metaphor of her own life.

The Alfa Romeo eventually turned down a charming lane named Rosebud, offering a fine view of the water on their left. Juliana lifted her chin to the vibrant blue sky, deeply inhaling the salty sea air.

"What an incredible day," she remarked. "Thank you for taking me out here."

"Thank you for coming with me. It's not every day I have the opportunity to travel anywhere with company, let alone such pretty company. My life is rather solitary."

"Do you like traveling so much—seeing the world and writing about it for others to experience?"

"I do, but it's getting tiresome. I'm thirty-one, and I can't be a fly-by-the-seat-of-my-pants guy forever. There's got to be more than jet setting and having a blast in every city in every country I travel to. What started as a lark, has taken over my life."

"A lark?"

"Yeah. I did it for my grandmother, actually. After World War Two, she had refused to travel outside the Tri-State Area, so when I graduated Columbia with a degree in journalism—which she paid for—she asked if I would show her the world through my eyes, young eyes with a young soul, she said. And she encouraged me to use my writing ability to share what I saw with others as well as with her."

"She sounds like a true romantic."

"Oh, she is." He looked to his right, his eyes locking with hers. "So are you, even if you're fighting it."

Juliana smirked, "Oh, so you think I'm fighting my innate inclinations?"

"I think ... we are all hiding or fighting something to some degree."

"Perhaps you're right." Crossing her arms in front of her, she promptly changed the subject. "So how is it that you convinced your grandmother to go to Paris with you next month if she doesn't like to travel?"

She noted how he paused in his response, furrowing his brow thoughtfully.

"Well, it's ... um, the commemorative ceremony for the fiftieth anniversary of the Paris roundup of Jews during the Shoah. For that she's willing to travel—and well, as much as I don't see the need to go—it's important to her. *She* convinced *me* and she's rather tenacious at getting her way."

"I'm not familiar with the Parisian arrest of Jews. I'm sorry. Admittedly, my knowledge of the Holocaust is meager at best. I mean, I know about the Nazis and recently read about the Warsaw Uprising but nothing about Paris."

"No worries, not many are familiar with it. It's referred to as the Rafle Vél d'Hiv, but we'll be visiting the Drancy Internment Camp as well."

Without realizing her impertinence, heedlessly she blurted out, "Are you Jewish?"

"I am. Does that matter?"

Juliana shrugged a shoulder then shifted in the seat to look directly at him. "No. Not in the least."

"Are you?"

"I'm what you'd call, born Lutheran raised Agnostic."

As they neared Meercrest, Jack slid a compact disk into the player on his dash. Glenn Miller's "Tuxedo Junction" lifted in the air, and he watched as a grin appeared on Juliana's shapely lips. "Just to get you in the mood."

"Well, then 'In the Mood' might be a better selection."

"You know your swing."

"I like Big Band music—Benny Goodman, Glenn Miller, Tommy Dorsey. Lately, since I moved into Primrose Cottage, it's all I listen to."

He smiled. "I keep it handy for when my grandmother wants to go for a ride through the hills."

"She sounds like a trip."

"Oh she is. She's not your ordinary grandmother. She'd kill me if she knew I told anyone but she begs me shamelessly to get behind the wheel. There is no way I will ever let her drive this baby. She drives like friggin' Mario Andretti."

Juliana laughed. "How old is she?"

"Far younger than her seventy years. For her birthday, I took her skydiving. Again, something *she* insisted upon—not me. Apparently, it's been something she has wanted to do for over forty years."

Juliana guffawed.

Jack laughed, too. "Are any of your grandparents living?"

"My paternal grandfather. He's seventy-three, currently acting like a hormonal teenager and determined to remain mute since my grandmother's death."

Surprised, he looked over at her.

"Don't ask. Grandpa Louie is quite a character."

The sports car stopped in front of Meercrest's broken, crumbling archway. "Well, this is it."

Juliana removed the old snapshot of the gate from the purse stowed beside her feet, then glanced up at the half-remaining stone pillar. The wrought iron was gone and the forsaken crumbling relic sat shrouded in ivy and weeds. "Sad. I can't believe this is it, the same place—Meercrest."

"Do you want to get out or shall I drive through?"

"Let's drive through. I'd really love to see Lizzy's water tower. It's a piece of her life's history she wrote about affectionately."

Jack watched her as best he could while driving on the old familiar dirt road now littered by deep potholes and weeds, encroached by overgrown bushes. They passed the few remaining utility outbuildings along the way. Barely discernible was a small footbridge hidden by brush, a forgotten remnant where Lizzy had received her first kiss from Henry Sturgis Morgan, Jr. —so she had once told him.

Briefly paralleling a bend of the rippling brook, he wondered if the waterfall and cave had been filled and demolished. It always made for a wonderful hiding place during "hide and seek" with his cousins. Try as Jack might, he couldn't resist the lure of Meercrest or the pull prompting him to help Juliana. As riddled with scandal as the estate was, it still held a magical air about it, eliciting fond childhood memories each time he visited.

Ahead, like the tower of Pisa, stood the slightly tilted water tower. Once painted a vibrant yellow and now sadly worn through to gray by the elements over these many years of neglect, it was still an impressive sight. He watched as Juliana's nervous palms tapped her thighs in excitement with each turn of the tires. Clearly, she felt transported back to a time she had been living through the letters.

She leaned forward grabbing the dashboard. "Oh my G-d! That's it, isn't it?"

"Yeah, let's take a look around. I see a few of the smaller structures remain." He pointed ahead to the left. "There's the tea gazebo. The bathing pavilion's foundation still remains down that incline there. We can't go into the tower, but we can scout around the grounds."

"Is that okay? Will anyone discover us?"

"No, no one will care. The owners are still waiting for variances and permits, not expecting to break ground on the senior home for another six months to a year."

Juliana shut the car door and quirked a playful eyebrow, noting the familiarity in which he spoke about the estate. "So you do know more about this place than you alluded to, Mr. Robertsen."

He smirked. "Perhaps a little more, but not much. I may have come here a time or two when I was a child."

Jack kept the music playing when he exited the car, stretched, and surveyed the overgrown surroundings. He took a prolonged minute to breathe deeply, filling his lungs with the welcome sea air. He focused his senses on the shore off in the distance and the lapping tide. The Sound was prophetically choppy today.

Juliana walked around the entire edifice, regarding the seventy feet, easily envisioning Lizzy in her tower like Rapunzel waiting for her flyboy to soar by in his B-26 bomber. She looked back toward Jack to unexpectedly catch sight of him crouching beside the sports car, picking up a handful of dirt and smelling it before casually dropping it to the ground. He brushed his hands together, closing his eyes for a moment, and that was when she knew—he knew this place, its owners, its story, and its history. She was sure of it— Jack Robertsen was part of Lizzy and William's story, too.

Feeling brazen and bold, as if Lizzy herself had jumped into her body, Juliana walked over until she was standing within inches of his squatting form. She felt as impetuous as she did with her mother over lunch days ago.

His lowered gaze first caught her trendy pumps and the billowing cuffed hems of her slacks. Slowly his eyes scanned up her petite, slender form as she stood blocking the sun. Her blonde hair literally glowed in the sunlight, forming a resplendent golden-white halo around her angelic face.

Her hands gripped her hips and she jutted her chin. "In the words of Lizzy the Pistol, go ahead, you can tell me. Don't be a chicken."

Jack stood up toe-to-toe, looking down into her eyes flashing in challenge, suddenly desiring to kiss those smirking lips of hers. "I'm not chicken if you tell me what you want to hear."

"Tell me your history with this place. You know everything about it don't you?"

He ran his hand through his hair then looked away, up at Lizzy's perch in the water tower. He needed a moment, gathering his thoughts so as not to say too much. A deep breath preceded his gaze to Juliana's attentive expression.

"It's not my story to tell, Juliana. I'm sorry. It's just ... there are things about Meercrest, that if dredged up, can hurt a lot of people. Some of the family members who lived here brought about terrible tragedies, even death to millions, and telling you everything, for the purposes of satisfying your curiosity or worse ..." He looked back at the water tower before continuing. "... for a fluff-piece article for publication, would reverse all the steps taken to atone for those actions. Forty-five years have been spent attempting to right a horrific injustice that can never be righted, years of seeking forgiveness when none will ever be given by those who were the victims. Don't insist on me telling you, because I won't. I'll die protecting those who still live with the scars and the memories."

"I'm not asking you to share what they did, I'm just asking for a name. I'll do the rest of the research at the Glen Cove Library after our lunch. I can take the train back to the city from there."

He bowed his head, taking her hand in his. "I know you don't know me, and you don't owe me anything, but I'm asking from the bottom of my heart. Don't go there. Please don't investigate this family. I'm begging you."

She looked down at their clasped hands. The best she could promise him was not to print anything she found out. "Jack, I don't know your connection to Lizzy, but I promise you, I would never tarnish her legacy. You have my word that whatever I discover I will protect her and those she loved, because of the love my great-uncle had for her. But, know this—I will be researching everything in spite of your stonewalling."

It was fruitless. This intoxicating woman was as headstrong and determined as Lizzy, equally undeterred and stubborn. *Of course she is—it's the German-American in her.*

****

Standing in front of the library, Juliana leaned over the passenger door of the Alfa Romeo and removed her briefcase from the small space behind the seat. "Thanks, Jack. Are you sure you don't want to come in with me?"

"No, I'll leave you to your research. Whatever you discover, I only ask that you use your intellect's best discernment *and* tap into that romantic heart of yours." He removed from his wallet a business card. "Call me if you ... well, just call me. It's my cellular phone number. The ball's in your court."

The sun streamed down upon her, but it was her smile that cast its brilliance when she said, "It was really nice meeting you. You still have my word. I won't publish a thing." She reached into her jacket pocket, removing her business card. "*You* can call me. It's not a cellular phone, and I hereby, give the ball back to you."

His fingers brushed hers when he took the card. "There's one last thing I'd like for you to answer honestly. Is there another reason you're so persistent in finding these people? Something you may not be telling me?"

"Yes, there is. You spoke of atonement. My grandfather can't go back to the forties, but it was a time when he and his brother shared everything. Finding my uncle could enable the possibility of healing a forty-year rift between them and that I know would make my grandfather happy. After seeing him last week, I feel as though he's just buying time. No one should die having never been forgiven or without having the opportunity to ask for forgiveness."

Jack nodded, thinking he should do a little covert investigating on his end as well. Something else must have happened, something other than the Renner scandal. His mind rapid fired of all the possibilities that could have separated two close-knit brothers, and he wondered if Lizzy, Kitty, or Lillian were at the heart of it. *Maybe Ingrid.* He shuddered at the thought.

Juliana looked behind her at the brick, municipal building. "I better go in. Thanks again for everything. I really appreciate your time and generosity."

"No thanks necessary. I enjoyed myself and meeting you. Thanks for a great lunch." Jack started the car and put it in gear. He abruptly stopped, turned around, and placed his arm on the headrest of the passenger seat.

"Hey, Juliana? You wouldn't have any objection to loaning me a photograph of Lizzy and William until the next time I see you?"

"You're serious?"

He nodded, and she squatted beside her briefcase, removing a snapshot that she had tucked inside her notepad. It was a particular favorite and she kept it with her at all times to remind her that great romance is truly possible.

She handed it to him, suddenly intrigued by his eagerness. "What's your plan?"

"I don't know yet." He glanced down at the image, then broke out into a fit of laughter looking up at Juliana then back down at the snapshot. "You've got to be kidding?"

She laughed, too. "I told you it was her nickname."

Lizzy and her sweetheart beamed into the sun, posing beside his B-26 at an airfield. He wore his pilot flight uniform, and she wore a light-colored, print dress, gloves, and hat. Together they stood arm in arm at the plexiglass nose turret of his plane below its clever, significant nose art: the spitting image of Ducky's girl wearing a two-piece, white bathing suit, flowing chestnut locks with a flower tucked in one side. Lizzy's sexy gams seductively dangled from the side of the bomb on which she sat. Beside the vibrant image, the aircraft's name, "Pistol Packin' Lizzy" was proudly identified in white paint.

"I'll be in touch," he said driving away, laughing, and waving.

****

It was already late in the afternoon when Juliana entered the library greeted by a bespectacled librarian standing behind the circulation desk. Her smile did nothing to quell the heaviness of Jack's ominous implications of what Lizzy's family had done. Juliana took a deep breath, just as she had done before entering the attic of Primrose Cottage. Were the actions of this family what caused William and Lizzy's breakup? She thought the worst but was in too deep to turn back now. She owed it to herself to find out.

"Hi. I'm looking for a Mrs. Tinsdale."

"Mrs. Tinsdale? Oh, honey you're about twenty years too late. She retired in 1973. Is there something I can help you with?"

Juliana rested her briefcase before the desk. "I hope so. My name is Juliana Martel, and I'm writing an article for *The New Yorker* magazine. I'm trying to track down any living descendants of the family who resided at Meercrest on Rosebud Lane during the 1940s."

The woman immediately redirected her attention to her task, clearly avoiding Juliana's questioning gaze. She made no reply and her hand continued to stamp "Property of Glen Cove Public Library" inside the cover of each book stacked beside her. The heavy thump of the vintage metal stamper filled the sudden frigid silence from the librarian.

Again, the *M* gate snapshot slid across wood. It was becoming a familiar action with this photograph. Juliana continued with persistence, "Meercrest? One of the mansions? Wealthy family of five sisters? It was demolished in 1975 and will be the location of a nursing home for veterans?"

Again, silence and an obvious head turn to facilitate the avoidance of eye contact met Juliana's smile. The woman's hand continued to depress the large stamper in assembly line fashion. It seemed apparent that the librarian's activity was a wee bit more vehement than it should be.

"Okay, I get it. You don't want to talk about that family and the scandal surrounding Meercrest. Would it help if I were to tell you the article is more about the library's bookmobile and the Victory Book Campaign that took place here during World War Two? That's why I was looking for Mrs. Tinsdale."

The librarian looked up to meet Juliana's smile. "Oh, well *now* I can help you. We have a whole section devoted to the campaign in our Local History and Genealogy Room. The campaign was sponsored by the American Library Association beginning January 12, 1942. However, the bookmobile was Mrs. Tinsdale's idea and highly successful. In-house circulation may have been down due to the gas rations but that didn't keep residents or war workers from reading. I'd say it was one of her greatest achievements."

Apparently, this woman was a non-stop, veritable treasure trove of interesting, yet extraneous information when one hit on the *right* subject, or rather, one she was *willing* to discuss.

"Great, I can see I came to the right place. Can you tell me, did any of the local residents volunteer for the book campaign? Collections and sorting?"

"I imagine so. We couldn't have done it without the generosity of the women from the Yacht Club. I do believe that the *Gold Coast Social Diary* published several articles about the girls who set up collection centers throughout town. Follow me."

After one final stamp into a pristine copy of Jane Austen's *Sense and Sensibility*, the two women moved toward the quiet back of the library to a small, unoccupied room at the end of a hallway.

File cabinets lined the perimeter facing five, tall shelving units, surrounding three microfiche, two microfilm machines, and one word processor. The obligatory and necessary Dewey Decimal System, wooden, card catalog sat beside the door. Posters tacked above the metal cabinets invited readers to "Donate Good Books" and "READ." Maps of the North Shore hung beside local family genealogy trees as guides for the novice.

"Well, Miss Martel. This section here is where you will find *almost* everything pertaining to the war years, and this section here contains every *Social Diary* dating back to 1922. Good luck in your research. If you need anything, my name is Barbara, just come and get me."

"Thank you, Barbara."

"Oh, and we close in twenty minutes."

Juliana placed her briefcase on the long table and removed its precious contents, placing them neatly beside her yellow legal pad and pen. Left alone in the relative silence, all she heard was the air conditioning forcefully blowing through the ceiling vents, as she pondered where to begin. This was it—the treasure trove of information, all tucked away in file cabinets.

Her vision raked over several metal cabinets where little identifying labels read: 1921 U.S Census, 1911 U.S. Census, 1925 NYS Census. *Yes!*

Juliana was sure that searching through rolls of microfilm without a last name would only leave her arms and eyes tired and frustrated. Searching the census records could take days before finding who lived at Meercrest on Rosebud. Without a last name, she couldn't even translate it to a Soundex code to use the index. She sighed heavily, resigned to go the gamut if necessary but, for now, she'd start small utilizing the World War Two files.

The first drawer she slid out was the obvious place to begin "Victory Book Campaign 1942—1944." Filed amidst papers and thin ledgers, listing every book donor and book title along with the book's ultimate disposition, Juliana saw the booty: hundreds of eight by ten glossy photographs.

One after another, she sorted through until she found one image of Lizzy tacking a poster to the side of a building. She wore a beret and a smile, and swung a hammer. Juliana's giddiness surfaced; an elated chortle escaped her jubilant lips, breaking the library's stoic silence. *Could it be any easier?* Juliana wondered when she flipped the photograph over and it read, "Elizabeth Renner 1942."

The words caused her to spring from her seat, jumping up and down excitedly in her pumps. Aloud, she proclaimed in victory, "Renner!"

She kept flipping through the photographs and found another image of Lizzy standing beside a handsome, fair-haired man. His joyful exuberance matched hers as they stood beside a large collection box formed into the shape of a book with a depository slit on the side. The structure read, "Victory. Be a Book Buddy." Turning the glossy photograph over, written in fine penmanship were the names, "John Robertsen and Elizabeth Renner— 1942," staring back at her.

"You dirty dog, Jack. You do know Lizzy. Is this your grandfather or uncle? Is Lizzy your aunt or just a friend of the family? Oh. My. G-d, no wonder you didn't want me to research her."

Juliana rose up from the floor, grabbed her purse, and hurriedly returned to the library's main entry to find Barbara.

The librarian still stood positioned behind the circulation desk, stamping books with rhythmic dedication. She smiled as Juliana drew near with assertive steps practically announcing success.

"Excuse me, Barbara. Do you have a copy machine?"

"Of course, dear, twenty cents a copy. Did you find something helpful?"

She held up the two photos. "Paydirt. I need front and back copies, please."

Barbara took the photographs and furrowed her brow when she read the back. "You're very skilled as an investigative reporter aren't you?"

"It's what I do. I'm sorry. I didn't mean to mislead you. It's just that this is personal, not really an article, and with your imminent closing and my scheduled departure on the 6:10 back to the city, time is of the essence."

"I see. So you would consider this genealogical work, then?" The librarian raised an eyebrow.

"Yes, I guess I would. Do you know the Robertsen family?"

"The Robertsens? Well, now *that's* a family I have no problem discussing. Generations of well-respected pillars in our community, benefactors and patrons of the new Long Island Holocaust Museum here in Glen Cove. They live in Mill Neck where they continue to do good works, not just for the community but also for the world through The Phoenix Foundation, their private charity. Their roots on the Gold Coast date back to 1910, known then as Robertsen Aviation, which, of course, today is called Zephyr Avionics."

"And the John Robertsen in the photograph?"

"A kind, sickly man most of his adult life. But in spite of his illness, he built Zephyr as one of the leading avionics companies in America, following his father's death in the late sixties. Unfortunately, he died in 1985. His loss will be greatly felt here on the Gold Coast for many more years."

"How sad, and do you know Jack?"

"His grandson? Not as much as I know his parents. I think he travels quite a bit, works for a newspaper or something."

His grandson. "Yes, he works for *Newsday*. Do you know his affiliation with Elizabeth Renner?"

The question was met by silence, again. The only thing missing was the stamper in Barbara's hand.

"Please?"

Barbara looked at her watch. "We're closing in five minutes. I'll make these copies for you, but then I have to lock up. Might I suggest that if you care to find out more about the Robertsens or the *other* family you may take a ride down to Our Savior's Lutheran Church in Glen Head. If she's willing to talk, their organist might be of assistance to you."

Juliana laid her hand upon the librarian's with a begging plea, "Is there anything you can tell me about the Renners and Meercrest? Anything at all?"

It seemed strange to Juliana that Barbara would cautiously look to her left then to her right since they were the only two remaining in the library.

Until she whispered, "They were Nazis."

Fourteen

It's a Blue World
July 16, 1942

Pictorial gold leaf covers, leather bounds, florid gilt edges, and rare first editions lined the walls in the built-in bookcases of the Renner two-story, sixty-foot wide library. Lingering in the air was the unmistakable scent of old books mixed with Lizzy's cigarette, as she sat on one of the wrought iron spiral steps leading upward to the balcony. Impressive ornate bronze balusters, elaborate hand-carved corbels, and old world crown moldings encompassed the stateliness of the mahogany room. However, it was the Pellegrini ceiling fresco of The Chariot of Aurora that Lizzy loved the most. Sometimes, she just lay upon the chaise lounge, staring upward lost in the clouds among the angels, a disregarded book lying open upon her chest.

The silence in the room at that moment reflected the peaceful companionship she always felt in the presence of Kitty or Lillian. Today was one of those days with her sister Kitty. Both missed Lillian's chatty presence, even a whirlwind at times, though there were moments when the sisters enjoyed each other's company without words. But these days, Lillian rarely visited Meercrest. Her volunteering kept her busy and after her argument with their father regarding the GIs she had invited to the Memorial Day lawn party, she had moved out and in with a fellow ARC volunteer.

Lizzy thumbed through one of the many like-new volumes of the ten thousand that made up her second favorite location on the estate. Breaking the silence of her activity, she spoke to her sister sitting beside the globe. She, too, busily removed and examined books from the wall for the Victory

Book Campaign. "Are you sure Nurse Keller has gone to the market? If not, we really should move this endeavor to my bedroom."

"Don't worry, she won't be back for a couple of hours."

Lizzy paused from her inspection of *Dante's Inferno* and inhaled from her Chesterfield. Her eyes drifted toward the back of Kitty's wheelchair as she watched her push herself to their grandfather's horn phonograph, reach over to place the arm down upon the Tommy Dorsey record, and turn the crank. Frank Sinatra, singing "Careless," broke the library's normally requisite silence.

"Have you seen Ingrid today, Kitty?"

"No and I'm not keen on doing so either. Have you?"

Lizzy frowned. "She's with Johnny this afternoon. They went sailing. I think he's getting ready to ask for her hand. He's a fool, but he's been in love with her since we were kids. I just don't know what he sees in her. Honestly, all it would take is one word from me on how she treats you and I think he'd break it off with her."

"You promised, Lizzy. You promised to never tell a soul what she did last week."

"I did, and I'll take that to the grave. You're just lucky to be alive is all I have to say."

From aloft, Lizzy noted how Kitty's lip trembled when she said, "Maybe she didn't mean to push the chair toward the stairs. Maybe she didn't do it and it was a problem with the wheels. I mean, she's my sister ... I can't imagine that she'd try to hurt me. Right?"

Lizzy descended the spiral steps, coming to kneel beside her sister, taking Kitty's hand in both of her own. "I know you don't believe that, and I know you're afraid, but I'm here. I'll protect you. If only Will and I were married, then I could take you away from Meercrest so you could live with us."

"I am afraid, Lizzy. I don't trust her."

"Won't you consider going to Aunt Helga's?"

"I won't leave you, especially now that Will has left for Florida, and particularly since we've embarked on this great campaign. I'm having so much fun, sissy, please don't make me go. I know I can take care of myself, truly."

Lizzy's smile must have looked pained because that was how she felt. It certainly didn't come from her heart nor reach her eyes. She wished she could take her sister far, far away. "I am having a gas, too, but I'm afraid for you. I'm spending so much time in the bookmobile and manning the campaign collection centers at The Polish Hall and St. Rocco's Chapel, I just can't be here. I should quit ... I'll quit."

"Please don't. You only just began, and you're so happy. I just need to watch my back and be more careful not to be alone with her. What you're doing for the war effort and the community is important. The workers who have come from all around the country to Jakobson's Shipyard really enjoy the books from your library on wheels."

Concerned, Lizzy squeezed her sister's hand, rubbing her thumb against the callus in Kitty's palm. "You didn't go into detail, but won't you please tell me *exactly* what transpired on the landing?"

"I can't be sure. One minute I was wheeling past Ingrid, and the next minute, the chair was rolling of its own accord—quickly—headed toward the entrance hall stairwell. I grabbed the balustrade just in time and called out to Ingrid to help, but she was gone, the elevator door had just closed."

Lizzy sighed. "And where was Nurse Keller? She should have been with you!"

"I don't know. She's gone a lot, Lizzy. Like today, why does she need to go to the market? We have everything she needs at Meercrest. Mrs. Davis gives her access to the kitchen even with the ration and all."

"I don't like her but, for no other reason, her presence may deter future *accidents* or acts of suspect behavior." Lizzy rose, walking to one of her favorite bookcases where American literature novels were catalogued. "Enough of this disturbing conversation about Ingrid, let's not give her a second thought. Let's find books for the boys!"

With Frank Sinatra's Bel Canto voice behind her, she slid one of her favorite books from the shelf. Its familiar, green spine caused her heart to swell with patriotic pride for one of America's great pieces of literature. She was sure this book was perfect for some lonely soldier to get lost in as an escape from battle. Calling to mind her first reading of it, she smiled and smoothed her red fingernail over the green and gold cover, making small circles over the embossed image of Mark Twain's hero. Yes, *The Adventures of Huckleberry Finn* was the perfect novel to send to the boys. She began to examine the book, making sure that no dog-ears marred the edges.

Out dropped a pamphlet, which floated to the Persian rug.

The book seemed an odd place to tuck a leaflet for posterity or keepsake, and uncharacteristic of her father. *She* certainly hadn't put it there, but sure that she was the only person in the Renner household to have read any Mark Twain.

What stared up from the floor caused Lizzy to gasp aloud. A shocking, unmistakable image on the thin flyer alarmed her: the Nazi swastika and a few unfamiliar German words, although one word she had recently heard Ingrid use in disdain—*Jude.*

At Lizzy's left, Kitty's casual conversation went unheard; she froze, riveted in somber awareness of what had invaded her sheltered world. She picked up the handout, attempting to read a language she did not know. The image and the large black writing instantly repulsed her, and a chill ran down her spine; the six-pointed star with the word *Jude* frightened her. Not that she understood what it read, but it was clear to her this was Nazi anti-Semitic propaganda. *Is this Father's or is it Ingrid's? Why is this terrible literature at Meercrest?*

Quickly setting the book aside, she shoved the pamphlet into her pant pocket determined to analyze it in private.

Scanning the volumes before her, Lizzy removed another American novel, *The Grapes of Wrath.* The moment she slid it from the shelf, she noticed a slight break in the foot edge. The book automatically opened to its foreign—and contrary—contents.

Tucked within the pages rested a thin booklet. The cover read: *Amerikadeutscher Volksbund.* Although she couldn't translate it verbatim, she clearly understood *"Amerika" "Deutsch"* and *"Bund."* Horrified, she recalled Operation Pastorius and the organization the saboteurs belonged to, as reported in the newspapers. There was that word again—*Bund.* There was that disturbing image again—*Swastika.*

Lizzy's heart pounded, she felt a sudden flush overtake her and braced her hand against the bookshelf. *Whose was this? Why was it in the Renner library essentially hidden from view, concealed within All-American novels?*

Her breath labored against panic as she attempted to gather even a modicum of self-restraint so as not to alarm Kitty, so sure her sister could hear the rampant beating of her heart.

Lizzy fanned through the pages of the booklet, unable to discern what it was. Within the contents, a loose slip of printed propaganda poked out from the corner. It read in English, *"Menace of the Jews. There is a great danger in the United States of America; this great danger is the Jew ... "*

Though it did not seem possible, her heart began to beat even faster as the reality of what she held in her hands dawned. She didn't have the courage to continue to read the two-sided leaflet. She lowered the distressing literature, and stared blankly at the book-filled shelves before her, her mind racing and processing. Closing her eyes to hold back unexpected tears, she rationalized: *It couldn't be Fathers, could it? No, not my father. In spite of his inflammatory opinions about the war and Germany's eventual victory, in no means did it imply he was an anti-Semite, did it? The propaganda indicates that Benjamin Franklin stated this—can that be true?*

"Lizzy, did you hear what I just said?"

"Hmm ... yes, of course I did."

"What do you have there?"

"Nothing important." *Something important, dreadfully important.*

Again, she pocketed the slip of paper after carefully replacing the booklet back where she found it. She resolved in her mind that George Gebhardt must have given her father this material and throwing them in the trash would have led the servants to believe he was a bigot and a Nazi sympathizer. *Yes, that must be it. That is the only acceptable explanation for their presence in Meercrest. The only one.*

No longer searching for books for the campaign, her curiosity, and determination to disprove the harping voice in the recesses of her mind took over. Following the pattern emerging for the culprit's manner of filing, she removed the brown, embossed first edition of *Moby-Dick* from the bottom shelf.

Disbelief fought agony. Logic and reason fought the incriminating evidence before her. The loyal daughter she had always believed herself to be couldn't fathom that this literature was her father's. Resting in her hands, tucked within chapter twelve, was another political pamphlet, printed in

German. The cover image portrayed an airplane; the words clear: *Hitler über Deutschland*.

No, no, no! You are reading too many spy novels, Lizzy. You are jumping to wrong conclusions! Father is not a Nazi sympathizer. A former member of the American First Committee, yes, but not a Nazi sympathizer.

****

The sun wasn't even up yet, but the DeVrieses were wide-awake, sitting in the pre-dawn darkness silently eating breakfast. Neither father nor daughter could sleep and eating always seemed the best remedy.

Fifty-one year-old Estella's hazel eyes held her father's gaze when she reached across the table, sliding her hand between the bread and the cheese. She patted his frail hand and spoke in Dutch, "Do not worry so, Papa. I have telephoned my friend at the Dutch Consulate. He promised to help if the rumors I have heard are true. Have faith, they will not come to our home."

Willem simply nodded, so untrusting, so sure that her friend's efforts would be for naught, as useless as running and hiding would be for *him*. "You trust too much and must go while there is still time. You have some money and diamonds to bribe the Gendarmes who are not Vichy loyal. They would not deport you."

"No. I will not leave you alone and that is my final word on the matter. Please, Papa. Even if we are arrested, we will return. No one will deport us anywhere. He has given me his word."

He sighed, toying with the jewelers loop hanging from a chain around his neck, a habit he had performed for as long as she could remember. "I do not believe that. I am old, Estella. Go now while you can. Save yourself. Find passage to America, and tell my grandsons what you have seen, what you have heard. Bear witness."

"France will prove these rumors unfounded. They will not let it happen."

Estella rose, walking to the window. Silently, she moved the delicate, linen kitchen curtain to the side and stared down out at the still dark, narrow street. Dawn was barely breaking, casting a faint red-tinged hue to the sky. The old buildings lining Rue des Rosiers were a testament to the long history of the Le Marais district where Jews have lived and flourished under the protection of the Republic of France for two hundred years. This little section of the Pletzl on the Right Bank of the Seine was filled with the rich tapestry of their faith, and nothing, not even the bombing of the Pavée Synagogue on Yom Kippur the year prior, would annihilate the history of their people. She believed that with every fiber of her being.

"The boys know what is happening in Europe. My letter to William when I sent him all of your assets and the family heirlooms, explained everything." She glanced at her father's blue sweater hanging from the back of the kitchen chair. The yellow star caused her eyes to well with tears, and her chin trembled ever so slightly. Determined, she said as brightly as she could muster, "Anna tells me both he and Louis are in love with sisters."

"Sisters? I once thought your mother's sister very beautiful, but my dear Carolien was a far better match. We were much better suited—she cooked—I ate—together we laughed. Her sister never cooked, so your Uncle Jozef never ate and they hardly spoke." He snorted a laugh. "That is why he was secretly in love with your mother. It was her bolus. Aahh ... I can still smell them."

Estella wrung her hands together. "Anna cooks but with two grown sons, she has no choice. She tells me her Julien loves her Dutch cooking."

"He is a good and righteous man my Christian son who has grown and protected our family's business, my baby daughter, and my grandsons. When I die, I will be at peace knowing that."

"Stop that. No one is dying—not today."

With heavy hearts and equally heavy minds, father and daughter could hear a commotion in the narrow street below: the unwilling shuffling of feet upon the ancient stone pavement below their window, the fisted banging upon the door of the townhouse opposite theirs, and the muffled voices of their Jewish neighbors. It was all enough to silence them, but in their silence, they prayed like the dark night of the first Passover.

Their eyes locked before Estella left the kitchen to her bedroom at the far end of the hall, promptly returning with two snapshots. "See Papa, how they look wearing their uniforms. I am so proud of my nephews. They fight for freedom."

Louie and Will's grandfather took the two photographs from her hand as she leaned over his shoulder to view them with him. She admired the boys, now men, as only an aunt would. "Louis looks like you. Anna writes me he has arrived in New Zealand, and William is training in Florida to fly bomber planes. I know one day, he will help liberate France and the Netherlands."

Willem ran his crooked index finger down one smooth, paper cheek then the other.

A fist pounding at their door sounded and father and daughter froze, one looking up at the other, eyes meeting in the understanding that her friend had failed. Estella smoothed her father's gray hair, and he whispered with intense insistence, "Hide, Estella. Do not answer it."

She smiled wistfully, ignoring his plea and left him sitting in the kitchen. In the dark, she walked slowly down the black and white, mosaic floor. Her heart hammered thunderously when the fist pounded against the wood door, again.

"Who is it?"

"It is the police, open up."

Estella opened the door to see a French Gendarme, standing beside a man in a dark suit and fedora hat. Both men were eerily backlit by the rising sun. Their silhouettes looked ominous and sinister, as they should and as she expected they would.

The plain-clothes official spoke, "You are Estella DeVries?"

She stood tall, raising her chin and bravely pulling her shoulders back. Her strength in her calmness was apparent. "I am. What is this about?"

"You and Willem DeVries are to come with us."

"And where are you taking us?"

He ignored her question, his attention garnered by her father who stood frail, hunched over and leaning upon his cane at the kitchen door. "You are both to bring three days clothing and food. Let me see your identity papers."

Shaken, Estella walked to her father, then slid their papers from the small table in the hallway. She held them out as the official entered the corridor of their elegant townhouse. "Sir, my father is ill. Can he not stay here?"

He looked over his shoulder to the police officer who still stood at the door, looking away shamefaced. Walking to the gold framed painting on the wall, he admired it. "This is an original Hendrick Avercamp, no?"

"Yes. One of a pair of paintings. They have been in our family for five generations." She paused, thinking quickly. "If you pass by this house and remove our names from your list, it is yours."

He snickered, removed a small spiral pad and pencil from his suit jacket pocket and made a notation then snapped it closed. "You are both to come with us."

Fifteen

Contrasts
August 4-8, 1942

G reystone Mansion resembled many other Manhattan town-houses built during the Gilded Age, comprising nearly fifty rooms within the five-storied structure, spanning an entire quarter of a city block. Renner had inherited the mansion, like many of his contemporaries who had done the same, but he refused to sell as they had. Even directly next door, J.P. Morgan had razed his father's impressive mansion to build a library and exhibition room, a building now called The Annex.

The Renner Beaux Arts mansion had become his personal sanctuary located on Madison Avenue in Murray Hill. It was his escape, so to speak, and there was no way he would part with it. Although designed for his mother's sensibilities, the ceiling murals, gold latticework, and painted panels were comforting to him whenever he traversed even a fraction of the palatial mansion. The opulent ballroom, art gallery, and concert hall were superfluous to him, but they were each standard requirements within a residence of this magnitude at his level of society.

Fine works of art had never held any sensorial appeal to him beyond an investment value and as such, testimony of the Renner affluence and greatness. It was only now with the gifts of gratitude from the Reich that art was becoming a new fascination. He understood the Führer's desire for his museum in Linz, Austria. Germans were culturally superior and the magnificence of the *Führermuseum* would be an indisputable declaration to the world. Surely, the Degas and the Monet would have been fine additions, yet they had been given to *him*. Acquisition by the Reich was assured—

superior blood deserved such works, and he concurred. The newly acquired paintings represented a significant badge of honor when the head of the Wehrmacht, Hermann Göring arranged for their delivery to Meercrest.

Artwork aside, Greystone's basement parking garage, accessible through an automobile elevator, was his particular favorite feature of the edifice. Autos and boats were lifelong personal passions, only reduced to distant second standing by his dedication to the Third Reich, which consumed him these seven years. Nevertheless, Greystone was his home, not his wife's. Neither she nor the children ventured to 37th Street without explicit invitation.

He sat at his desk, a massive piece dominating the space with its ornamentation and antiquity, his rigid back addressing the floor to ceiling Tiffany stained glass window behind him. Papers lay strewn, and a cigar burned slowly in the ashtray on the desktop, a ribbon of sweet tobacco swirling upward. An empty rocks glass rested beside one tightly fisted hand as the other signed his name.

Frustrated and angry, he ran his fingers through his thinning hair after laying down the fountain pen. Apologies weren't something he was used to giving, but the chief of the Abwehr was demanding an explanation. Failure was unacceptable, especially since the Führer's declaration, "The greatest activity will be necessary in America."

Renner hoped that his favor wasn't fleeting. Ursula was expecting a piece of artwork as well, and then there was his Elizabeth, who, when she understood and had taken up her role as Mrs. George Gebhardt in the New Germany, should be gifted with a Renoir or a Rembrandt. Had she not voiced her admiration of those works following her insolent visit with the De Rothschild Jews?

The grandfather clock chimed on the hour heralding the execution of the saboteurs by electric chair in a D.C. jailhouse, and Renner sighed. Still unsure what had gone wrong with Operation Pastorious, he couldn't dismiss the tremor of insecurity bubbling below his cool, calm, and ostensibly affable exterior. *Someone talked, but who? Who else knew of the plan? How did the FBI get wind of the two landing parties?* He, himself had firsthand knowledge that America's coastline wasn't impregnable and knew most of the men specifically selected for the mission. Former members of the German-

American Bund would never have betrayed this vital Operation set to dismantle the American war machine.

He had just sealed the letter when Ursula entered the study holding the newest issue of the Nazi Party's women's magazine *Frauen-Warte*. "Frederick, will we be leaving for the Stork Club at eight?"

"After you deliver this letter to Yorkville." His hungry eyes took in her appearance. The silky drape to her dress, adhered with an ornate broach upon her hip accentuated her full curves. She was a magnificent looking, zaftig woman with blonde curls and hazel eyes and lips that did things he had only dreamed about.

She sauntered to him, aware of how Renner undressed her with his gaze. She dropped the publication upon his messy desk then dragged her manicured hand along its edge to his outstretched arm, up to his shoulder. She moved seductively around the desk, until she came to stand behind him. Strong fingers massaged his shoulders, attempting to offer him relief through his dress shirt.

"You're tense, *Liebelein*." She leaned forward and flicked the top of his ear with the taut tip of her tongue. "I can do something about that."

He smirked. "I know you can, but this letter is of the utmost importance. Berlin awaits answers for the failure of Operation Pastorius."

"But our time together is so limited, my dear. I am expected back at Meercrest in the morning to care for your *dear* daughter."

The sarcasm was evident in her voice. He knew, given the go ahead, she willingly, if not eagerly, would do whatever he asked of her when it came to Kitty, but even he wouldn't go that far.

Renner wrapped his chubby fingers around the cigar and took a rapid series of puffs. "I'll be back on the Island in a few days, and we'll have all the time you desire. Frances will be visiting the Astors in Newport for the rest of the summer and, as for Kitty, my Elizabeth is considering taking her to my sister's. She tells me that Kitty feels she doesn't need a nurse any longer."

"She's an invalid. Of course, she needs a nurse."

"If it keeps you in residence, well then, yes she does. Otherwise, I would shut her in an asylum far from the Renner estate, away from my circle and name. For the time being, I will keep her at Meercrest, if only to keep you beside me."

Ursula sat upon the edge of the desk and crossed her legs baring her knees when her skirt hiked. "And what of Elizabeth's situation?"

"I cannot be sure. The boy's family owns one of the largest diamond houses in the city. Diamonds and Jews are almost synonymous ... but this Martel family is Christian. It could be a ruse; have we not seen this throughout all of Eastern Europe? Have you heard anything discussed between my daughters?"

She shook her head, reverently stroking the spine of a book she knew well, *International Jew* written for the *Dearborn Independent* by Henry Ford, a man she, as well as Hitler, greatly admired. "What do you plan to do about the soldiers?"

"The war will be their demise before I feel the need to have Gebhardt address the situation. He is, however, compiling an in-depth dossier on the family, reaching out to some of our European friends. I am curious to learn his findings. Suffice it to say, no daughter of mine, especially Elizabeth will associate with *Juden*. She's promised to Gebhardt."

"Does she know?"

Renner pulled Ursula from the desk, landing onto his ready lap. "Of course not. I have yet to discuss with her the obligations and loyalties of propagating the *Volksgemeinschaft*. Perhaps, soon though, before she becomes attached to this boy."

****

Floating heat hovered over the concrete runways and hangar line of MacDill Airfield as Will, finally tolerant to the tropical climate, walked through the hive of ground crew maintenance activity toward the Officer's Club. B-26 bombers taxied in the distance, practicing the fine art of takeoff and landing this difficult plane. More Marauders soared above him, returning in tandem from anti-submarine patrol duty over the Gulf of Mexico.

Already tanned from an unexpected pass spent at the beach three days prior, Will walked across the base with a spring in his step.

Summer dress khakis, garrison cap, and aviator sunglasses painted the perfect image of virility to one Miss Ida Flores, a civilian switchboard operator assigned to the Signal Company. Exiting the Base Intelligence building, she watched the lieutenant's long, lean strides and couldn't help but stop and stare. Handsome was an understatement. Taller than most of the men of the 322nd Bombardment Group, he had a commanding presence and that cleft chin of his drove her wacky every time she found herself in his company.

He passed her by, reading a letter and she fidgeted playing with the artificial flower pinned upon her dress. "Good afternoon, Lieutenant Martel."

He looked to her and smiled. "Miss Flores. Lovely afternoon isn't it?"

"Yes, sir, another perfect day in sunny Florida. You look happy. Is there good news in that letter you're holding?"

"Yes there is. It's always good to hear from family. My brother's with the Marines." He grinned with pride, giving a slight shake to the V-Mail in his hand then continued toward his destination.

Ida sighed at his passing form, giving his back a once over. The dreamboat was always polite, but never interested, perpetually on the move, never stopping to chat. *Lucky girl whoever she was to have captured that flyboy's heart because he never flirted like most of the other GIs.*

Apart from the occasional salute to a superior officer, his footsteps remained apace with only an intermittent upward glance, his mind stayed focused on his brother's letter from New Zealand.

July 10, 1942
Dear Will,

You owe me two dollars, old man. Bet you didn't count on me hearing about the All-Star Game all the way down under, and what a game! According to my C.O., we handed your National League their hats and Rizzuto didn't even have to play. What was Doucher thinking playing all twenty-two of his men? Poor strategy. Well, the boys over here were glad to hear that in spite of the delay and blackout restrictions, they raised quite a bit of dough for us fighting men. All for the cause, right?

Where are you now? Still in Florida? Any word on when you'll be flying over to ETO? Is that ship you're flying still giving you problems? Damn if that isn't FUBAR. Take care there.

I received a letter from my girl. She's moved out of that ritzy family mansion and is sharing an apartment with one of her ARC friends. Turns out, her father has a pickle up his ass about you and me. Tread lightly there, brother. He definitely has it in for us. Of course, my girl doesn't care about her father's opinions, and I'm sure your pistol doesn't either, but be careful what you write in those love letters you send Lizzy. The poker player in me can't resist cautioning you to play your cards close to your chest.

How is Lizzy? In love with you yet or have you convinced her that a wartime romance is foolish? Better yet, have you fallen in love and are trying to convince yourself that she ain't the one for you?

Unfortunately, there's no time to check out the local recreation here in N.Z. Ah, it's just as well, you know I've sworn off dames for the duration. I might enjoy a little "action" now and again, but my girl and I have sort of agreed to remain steady even in our separation. No I and I for this Leatherneck. Besides, the rain hasn't really let up, so it's been me and my lucky cards making a few bucks off some of the guys in between muddy drills.

Even though we just arrived, we're breaking camp soon. Don't know where we're headed but it'll be to the fight, that's for sure. Twenty-three days at sea nearly killed me, but I'll gladly get back in that tin can if it means killing a few Japs. You make sure you do some damage to those Jerrys. Be safe, Brother and write soon. I have a feeling I'm gonna need it.
Affectionately,
Lou

Will tucked the letter into his uniform trouser pocket beside Lizzy's latest and shook off the bad feeling attempting to take over his happiness. He clung to the fact that his brother may have been a jokester, but he was one tough, determined Marine. He'd be fine and probably find humor somewhere—anywhere. Suddenly, his feeling of dog tiredness from training in the Link flight simulator at two in the morning seemed inconsequential when compared to what lie ahead for Louie.

His brother's letter readily brought to mind good times and the usual baseball competitiveness that the two of them bantered about, spurring his recollection. He had a ballgame to listen to this afternoon and nothing was going to get in his way of the Brooklyn Dodger versus New York Giants round two faceoff. G-d, he wished he could be there in the stands of the Polo Grounds for another twilight game. He wanted to at least witness hearing his team win again after last night's abbreviated victory, just to ensure that the sour grapes being thrown around today were squashed. The Giants had rallied in the bottom of the ninth inning, staging a promising comeback and then, suddenly, darkness. Exactly one hour after sunset—wham—the lights in the ball field went out and the game was called early before the Giants had a chance for last licks, all because of the new black out restrictions. Tonight was the Giants' chance for revenge, and based on the boos and hisses in the club and from the stands, everyone's radio would be set to the game. He wondered if even Louie might hear about the game somewhere in the Pacific on the Armed Forces Radio Service. Probably not, since it wasn't the All-Star Game or the World Series.

For at least the sixth time that day, Will slapped the side of his neck. Since his arrival to Tampa, the mosquitoes were killing him yet he couldn't help to chuckle at Lizzy's comment when he wrote her of his plight. He could almost hear her laughter on the paper, mocking him when she wrote, *"Poor baby, that's what you get for being as sweet as candy."* He loved when she teased him, and he gave it right back in his next letter when he told her about all the pretty Cuban nurses at the base hospital who attended to his insect bites with alcohol or insecticide powder. Her next letter laughed at him again, stating she didn't believe him and it wouldn't matter anyway because he was officially rationed now, and she had no intention of sharing him with anyone, not even the mosquitoes! Yes, he was rationed and he wouldn't have it any other way. What had he been thinking by wanting to deny himself this experience? He wasn't thinking and then he met her and that kissable, twisting mouth of hers and he was a goner.

Only separated for three weeks, he missed her like the dickens and had a long list of things to write her about: his crew, his visit to the Colonnade, and the beauty of St. Pete Beach. New York's Jones Beach or Rockaway couldn't hold a candle to the sparkling white sand of Florida. Of course, in his next letter he would say nothing of what Louie's letter implied. Renner could kiss his ass in Macy's window and so could his brethren in the Fatherland when he got his chance to drop bomb loads over Germany and the Axis targets.

Will entered The Bayshore Club where "MacDill Manny" stood behind the bar pouring drinks, greeting officers, and making small talk with a few of the men with the Third Air Force. The radio beside the cash register was tuned to a local station playing "Rhumboogie." Even the Andrews Sisters' song was celebrating in Cuban spirit.

Signs hung at eye level behind the simple wooden bar with explicit edicts not to discuss military matters, most prominently displayed amongst the not-so subtle suggestions to Buy Defense Bonds. Overhead, two emblems adorned the wall: the Air Corps' propeller wings insignia and the standard mantra of encouragement "Keep 'Em Flying." On the far wall hung the requisite photograph of President Roosevelt, as though the man himself was ever-present, offering his personal encouragement of the missions before them.

Jimmy McCarthy, Will's co-pilot, a New Jersey boy, sat at a table by the window reading the base's newspaper *Flyleaf*. It seemed those in the club were mostly men from the New York area and there for the game.

"Whatya' have, Lieutenant?" asked Manny.

Will placed his nickel on the bar. "Just a Pepsi. Thanks, Manny."

McCarthy rose to get another beer from the bartender and walked to Will, slapping him upon the shoulder in his usual fashion. "So when are we back up in the air in the Baltimore Whore?"

"We're scheduled for a practice flight tomorrow, but who knows, Command has cancelled training due to that accident over at Avon Airfield. Seems like we're going for a crash record this month."

"Damn if I don't hate that Widowmaker. She scares the shit out of me every time we take off. I keep waiting for the engine to stall but you, you lift her up as smoothly as a dame's skirt."

"That's because *like a woman* she needs tenderness, you big oaf. Those ships just require exactitude; every movement should be precise. When you're ready for takeoff, you've got to be both rapid and smooth. Her flaps need to be milked up slowly at 145 then climb at 160 until you reach 1000 feet, no more, no less until you get to know her. Her rudders are sensitive. When you approach for landing, it's important to keep up the speed or she'll choke, but she'll give you a shudder before she does. Her landing needs to slide down at an angle and approach at 140, flare out between 115 and 120 depending upon your load."

"Damn, she sure sounds like a dame. Someone I know, actually."

Will snorted. Of course, he didn't mean to make the sexual innuendo out of his flying technique. "Some women, but not all." There was nothing exacting or slow about Lizzy and the latter part—the landing—he had yet to discover. Hell, he hadn't even gone beyond passionate kisses.

"And your girl, the one whose snapshot you keep taped above the altimeter?"

Will grinned in much the same manner as his brother. "I cannot tell a lie, my pistol loves to fly."

"Pistol?"

"Oh yeah, Pistol. Full of fire, spirit, and wired for maximum damage to a man's heart."

"Sounds like you've already picked your ship's name."

"I hadn't thought about that. Well, if you're assigned to my crew when we get to Drane Field how does 'Pistol Packin' Lizzy' sound to you?"

"I'll do the artwork."

Will grinned mischievously, thinking Lizzy would either be proud to have her image on the side of the ship or be madder than blazes. Either way, if only he could see the spark in her green eyes upon seeing it. Maybe he'd send her a snapshot.

****

Louie snapped his small, black notebook closed after writing in it, *Sunrise, Friday, August 7, 1942 Operation Watchtower, Guadalcanal Solomon Islands.* He shoved it into a pocket of his utility pants, figuring he'd fill in the details tonight. Who knew what the hell was going to happen when they landed at Red Beach, and he wanted to detail every memorable moment.

The 5th Marine Regiment was part of the first wave of the first offensive, and the men around him seemed confident—if just a bit clueless. It was six fifty in the morning and he'd just climbed down the Navy transport's cargo nets into the overloaded Higgins boat, squished like sardines as they headed toward the war's first land battle. Although the water was calm, an eerie mist had settled on the Pacific, one Louie was sure the top brass were thankful for. A B-17 flew overhead and the USS *Quincy* commenced hammering the beaches with its .55 caliber guns.

"Take that you filthy, Nips," Lance Corporal Price proclaimed with youthful bravado.

"They have no fuckin' idea what's gonna hit 'em when we get ashore," another voiced with valiant confidence.

Louie said nothing, just lit a Lucky Strike and continued to think of Lillian as he looked out at the convoy of ships to their rear and the fourteen other transports beside theirs. A warm spray of water coated his face and the cigarette but he didn't care, something was changing in him already. His humor had been replaced with something else.

"Hey Price, bet I get the first Jap," he finally said.

"Oh yeah, what's on the table?" the young cocky Marine from Omaha challenged.

Louie shrugged. "Your cigarette ration."

"Deal."

Time drew closer, the remaining moon cast shadows upon Florida Island and Louie buoyed himself for the fight, but truth be told, at that moment he felt scared. Actually, he was shitting a brick, but he'd take that admission to the grave, vowing never to tell a single human being, not even Lillian if he survived this. He pushed the feeling down and thought of his brave brother. He thought of his brave girl and his brave aunt and grandfather in Paris. With fondness, he thought of his loving family as he attached the bayonet to his new rifle when the boat slowed. It was precisely nine o'clock in the morning and at that moment, he determined to draw on the things most important to him. That was what would make him fearless. He'd fight for them and the men who didn't have the chance to fight at Pearl Harbor. He knew his brother would fight for the persecuted in Europe. Yes, today was going to be a fine day in the Solomon Islands.

Sixteen

Accentuate the Positive
June 1992

I f she's willing to talk" echoed once again from the back of Juliana's mind as the taxicab traveled the distance between her hotel in Glen Cove to the neighboring hamlet of Glen Head where the librarian indicated this organist would be. It was a gamble whether the woman would even be present at the Lutheran church, but when Juliana had called this morning, she was informed that Mrs. Katherine Landry practiced on Saturday afternoons for Sunday Services. A flutter of relief made her sleepless night inconsequential. She hadn't expected to stay overnight in Glen Cove, but the temptation to uncover Elizabeth's story was too great. So what if she still wore the same underwear, let alone clothing, from the day before? What was truly disturbing her was that all her necessary cosmetics still sat on the art deco vanity in the yellow room at Primrose Cottage. In Juliana's opinion, she looked a fright.

From the back seat, she surveyed the pleasant passing landscape. Two lane, tree-lined winding roadways, old strip malls, and quaint farmhouses mixed with the new and the restored in small towns of historical significance, idyllically shielding secrets too dark to speak of. She couldn't help but respect the townsfolk's silence concerning the Renner family. They were, she recognized, protecting the innocent as well as the obvious smirch upon their esteemed Gold Coast heritage. Ashamed that they had not recognized what was going on right under their noses—or maybe they did—they concealed the truth, continuing to hide the dirty secret. After all, who would want to live in a town known to have harbored Nazis? That alone piqued Juliana's curiosity. Who knew, what did they know, and how did they find out if no one ever spoke of it?

She had approached the concierge desk earlier, with dual intentions. Needing to arrange for a taxi to Glen Head, she realized that this hotel employee might be familiar with the local history. When one task was dispensed, Juliana commented on the beauty of the hotel. With a satisfied smile, the concierge responded that the luxury accommodation had formerly been one of the Gold Coast's more opulent mansions owned by Standard Oil's John Pratt. The woman gave a brief history lesson to her willing audience on the Pratt family business and residences. Encouraged by the interest, the concierge expounded that the gentleman's wife, Ruth Pratt had been New York State's first Republican Congresswoman.

Absorbing this information, Juliana cautiously inquired about the Renner family of Meercrest. The open smile and the wealth of knowledge vanished. The concierge replied flatly that she had never heard of the Renner family as a pile of papers on the counter drew her immediate attention. The discourse ended abruptly with a polite reminder that the taxi would be out front momentarily and a rote, requisite thank you for being a guest at the hotel.

Perhaps the response was truthful—perhaps not. Thus far, her research (limited as it was) had revealed much, and she was sure Jack had all the other answers. Heck, everyone had the answers, but since the town wiped out any and all existence of the story, it was proving difficult to uncover. She wondered exactly what this Mrs. Landry would be able to offer, let alone why she would be willing to divulge what others had not.

"This is it, Miss," the taxi driver said, pulling up to a white clapboard house and church surrounded by colorful annuals and pink azalea bushes. A crisp, white spire rose above two open doors, welcoming visitors.

Even from the curb, as she paid the fare, she could hear the organ music within and smiled, thankful that her unexpected visit was well timed.

Appreciating the beautiful music, Juliana walked languidly, gently swinging the wieldy briefcase. A bevy of birds chirped in the tree canopy overhead as she approached. It would have been a sublime scene of tranquility when a squirrel scampered nearby and she heard children's laughter from the churchyard playground, but a portent of ugliness hidden behind the placid and unassuming façade invaded. She wondered if anything was as it seemed. Would it be the house and attic all over again?

She entered into the narthex of the church, a small vestibule, which lead into the nave through an inner set of doors, currently propped open allowing the afternoon sunlight to stream in and the music to float out. The gathering place was large with wood beams, arching above the pews lining both sides of the aisle's red carpeting. At the far end, steps led to the altar.

Juliana took a seat in the middle, listening to the organist play with such passion at the side of the sanctuary. Only her white hair could be seen above the top of the electronic organ.

The worship space felt comfortable and peaceful. This was her faith, the religion of her father, and the religion of her grandparents, yet the last time she had come to a Lutheran church was for her own christening as a baby. With the sun shining through the inspirational stained glass, Juliana stared up at the wood cross above the altar, thinking how it couldn't hurt to pray. It wasn't as though she abhorred prayer, it was just unfamiliar, but pray she did. She prayed she would find the answers in this search she had embarked on. Sitting here, in this house of worship, she couldn't help considering that some higher power had intervened her singular path, setting her on this quest. She'd have faith that this wild goose chase to find love, romance, and the two people who embodied it wouldn't be for naught.

After about ten minutes, Mrs. Landry stopped playing and rose. A pretty woman in her sixties, wearing a cobalt blue suit and a pink scarf stood beside the organ's bench. Obviously pleased someone had been listening to her play, she offered Juliana a pleasant, surprised expression that quickly became a warm smile.

It took Juliana aback when the organist grabbed two hand crutches and adeptly made her way down the red carpet toward her. With body shifting and feet carefully landing, she swung her weight and made her way forward with only slight exertion. Apparently, the affliction wasn't new. Juliana unconsciously stared, eyes fixed with curiosity on the woman's legs. She wondered if there were braces concealed beneath the trousers, what her handicap was and ultimately, marveling at this woman's ability to manage the pedals of the organ in spite of it.

"Hello," the woman said, stopping at the end of the pew, tilting her head slightly to make eye contact.

"Hi." Juliana fidgeted because she knew she had been obvious in her staring. "You play beautifully. What were you playing?"

"I'm so happy you enjoyed it. Pachelbel's 'Ciacona' is one of my favorites. It felt appropriate for such a gorgeous day."

"Yes, it is. Are you Katherine Landry?"

"I am. How can I assist you? Are you getting married and at that stage of planning your nuptial music?"

"No. I ... um ... would you care to sit?"

"No, I'm fine, dear. I've been playing for an hour straight so sitting right now has very little appeal. I need to stretch a bit."

"I understand. I'm sorry to intrude on your time, but Barbara at the Glen Cove Public Library suggested that you might be of help to me. I was wondering if you have a few moments to answer some questions I have about the area."

"Of course. You're interested in Glen Head and Glenwood Landing?"

Fastening her full attention on Mrs. Landry's face, which seemed familiar, she fudged, "Actually ... the Gold Coast."

"Well, except for a several years in Minneapolis, I spent my entire life here, so I can tell you just about anything. Let's take a walk to the business office. It's empty and the pastor won't be arriving for another hour or so. We can talk about the area over a cup of coffee. Would you like that?"

"That sounds great."

The organist shifted her weight, readying herself to lead the way, when Juliana gently rested her own palm upon the woman's hand grasping the back of the pew. "Forgive me, but do I know you Mrs. Landry. Have we met before?"

Her blue eyes examined Juliana's face. "I don't think so. What is your name?"

"Juliana Martel. I'm from Manhattan."

Over the course of Katherine's sixty-six years, facial control was something she had mastered early on, and today—more than any other—she was thankful for that mastery. She remained frozen in expression and form, legs and mouth unmoving.

Forcing herself she slowly spoke, "Martel, you say?"

"Yes, ma'am. Are you familiar with the family name?"

"Somewhat." *Good G-d, This is Lillian's granddaughter. How did she find us?* "Let's talk in the office, okay?"

"Super!"

Juliana gripped her briefcase, trailing behind Katherine slowly. Resisting her innate New Yorker frustration at the reduced pace, she instead admired how the woman traveled down the long aisle with noble competence.

Katherine glanced over her shoulder, noticing Juliana's intent observation. "I'm sorry to take so long. These old bones aren't used to dealing with crutches and braces after so many years without them."

"No worries, take your time. Truly, I'm not in any rush today."

"Did you come out on the train?"

"Yes, yesterday. Although I had only planned a day trip, my plans changed so that I could meet with you. I was able to get a room for the night at the Glen Cove Mansion Hotel and have nothing pressing to get back to the city for. I ... I have all afternoon."

"They have maintained the gardens and property beautifully at The Manor. What a treat to stay there."

"The Manor?"

"Yes, that was the name of the Pratt home when I knew it before the matriarch Ruth died in 1965. Well, here we are."

They stood at the threshold of an office that looked more like a prayer room with a desk. Religious paintings and kitschy plaques with spiritual sayings and bible quotes decorated the walls and surfaces. Two comfortable chairs sat beside one another on the left.

"Take a seat and make yourself comfortable, Juliana, while I put up a pot of coffee."

"I can do it if you like."

Katherine smiled. "No that's okay. I can handle it." With her back turned to the young woman, her hand scooped the teaspoonfuls into the paper coffee filter. She had to be very careful—not about spilling the grounds—but about how she posed her questions and answers to Lillian's granddaughter. Too much was at stake; the exposure of all the well-concealed secrets that spanned over fifty years were now placed at her feet. How she handled it and what she divulged could affect so many lives, especially her own. She began her subtle inquiry, "So, what can I tell you about this area of Long Island?"

From behind her back, she heard the unlatching of the briefcase, a shuffling of papers, and discerned the opening of a box, its cover falling to the bare floor.

"Well, I'm interested in learning about Glen Cove, one of the mansions in particular."

The organist sat beside her, eyes settling on the slight tremble to Juliana's hand. "You don't need to be afraid of me. Honesty is the best policy, truly. What is this about?"

"To be honest, what started as a simple quest for love and life has morphed into something else entirely, so I'm not sure what it is about. Both Barbara and my friend Jack alluded to a couple of things, but I can tell you for *whom* I am searching: the Renner family or more specifically, Elizabeth Renner."

There they were, the words Katherine feared hung in the air. Further, this young woman had met Jack. She didn't know how to proceed. Juliana should learn about her family, the family Lillian had denied her. "Jack?"

"Jack Robertsen, the travel reporter at *Newsday*."

"Ah, and did he know this Elizabeth Renner?"

"I believe so, although he was rather tight-lipped about how. It was the same way with Barbara."

"And why do you need to find her?"

"It's silly really. My great-uncle William was in love with her, and I was deeded his house, which really was left as a shrine to her. Beyond her wartime letters and snapshots found in his footlocker, I'd like to learn their complete love story. It's sad because I found her engagement ring sitting in a bedroom beside a photograph. Theirs seemed a romance like none other, and I suppose I'm captivated by it." She removed a letter from the box. "Yesterday, I shared one of Lizzy's letters with Jack and it helped to convince him to assist me in finding my uncle and drive me up to Meercrest's former location."

Juliana's mention of letters strangled the air around Katherine, dangling like an expectant noose on judgment day. Fifty-year old guilt rose like bile, twisting the flesh at her neck. *An engagement ring. I didn't know. How could I have known? Oh, William …*

Oblivious to the pain of the woman beside her, Juliana enthusiastically began to read aloud.

"November 7, 1942
My Dearest Darling,

You spoke your sonnet at Lake Mirror in the words "I love you, Lizzy", and they are now deeply embedded within my heart and soul to carry me forward when you depart for Europe soon. I cannot fathom how I will adjust to periods of possible little communication from you. I have grown so accustomed to having you visit my home twice a week! Every letter, every word you write remains with me. I think of you night and day—day and night—the memory of your kisses and caresses, the lingering sound of your deep laughter, your intelligent conversation, and your goodness. These five months have been the happiest of my life, Will. Before you, everything, even the old Lizzy has become a blur. I never imagined that I would thank the war for bringing us together.

I am so happy that you have this time with your mother and father before your departure. With your ground crew's leaving of Drane, your parents' arrival to Florida could not have been any better timed. Do you think you will be flying to your embarkation airfield within the week? Please repeat my insistence that your parents could stay at Rosebriar for as long as they need or desire. The Renners will be remaining north, so there is nothing to worry about.

I love you, William Martel, but then you know that already. Thank you for not being such a chicken and finally confessing your feelings for me. Words cannot convey the depth of my understanding and gratitude in your confiding in me, and together although apart, we will pray for the safety of your family. Now that you have given me your heart and trust, I promise to guard it and protect it, always—until my dying breath. Be safe, my love. Come back to me. I'll be waiting.
Yours,
Lizzy"

"Can you see why I'm so intrigued by them and need to find out what happened to separate them?"

Katherine knew the truth, but she had expected to die with that secret, determined never to cause unnecessary pain to Lizzy.

Juliana handed her a snapshot of them together at a U.S.O Dance at Drane Air Field in Lakeland, Florida. "See how captivating they were together? She was from Glen Cove and he was from Park Slope. This one here is the photograph of the home where she lived, Meercrest. Jack took me there yesterday to see Lizzy's water tower."

As though the calendar had reversed, instantaneously wiping away decades, it was now the fearful, seventeen year old hand of Kitty Renner that trembled when she took the two offered photographs. Yes, they were a beautiful couple. She had always thought so, and her heart clenched seeing them together after all this time. She had truly liked the lieutenant, and Lizzy had loved him like no other. Her heart broke; her guilt overwhelming. Time had not "chalked it up as a result of the war," as she had once thought it would. "So, you say you would like to find him. Do you believe your great-uncle is still alive?"

"I don't know. He left his home in 1950, only sending greeting cards now and again on momentous occasions. But as far as I can tell, it's been many years of no contact."

Kitty closed her eyes for a moment, taking a cleansing breath. Lizzy had confided in her what had happened in 1949 when she and Will unexpectedly met after seven long, painful years of separation. Further, Lillian had alluded to, never truly divulging, what Lizzy assumed was his devastation when he left New York the following year after his own father's death.

A radiant glow spontaneously lit the face of the young woman, Lillian's granddaughter, when Kitty stated, "I did know Lizzy. In fact, I knew all the sisters. No five girls could have been more different in every way possible. Two, the second and fourth were especially close and still are, and two, the oldest and youngest were especially ... self-absorbed, manipulative creatures. The middle daughter was highly independent and sought refuge and peace in the joy of building her own new family with a beloved husband, son, and granddaughter. She never, ever, came back to the Island to see her sisters, not that she didn't love them, but Glen Cove ceased being a home to her in 1942. In fact, with the exception of her two beloved sisters, she ceased being a Renner."

The automatic drip coffee pot gave up its final push, and Juliana jumped up to pour two cups. "And their parents?"

Kitty sighed. "Why ... I hardly knew them at all. Does one really know a person?"

Juliana met her comment with silence, feeling extremely at ease with this woman she had never met before. The tone of her voice was strangely anodyne and uncannily familiar. She surmised it was because Kitty knew Lizzy and somehow, Juliana felt as if she knew Lizzy in a way. After a long minute spent preparing the coffees, Juliana looked over her shoulder. "Were the Renners, um, the Nazis that Barbara mentioned?"

"Well, that's a story for another time, okay?"

The hair stood on Kitty's neck, fighting against those suppressed painful memories. She leaned back in her chair, continuing this unexpected but long overdue autobiography of five sisters as Juliana placed two plastic creamer containers and sugar packets before her.

"The youngest daughter, Gloria was as wild as wild can be. Untamed and unchecked at fifteen, she was, during the forties, what folks referred to as a Victory-Girl, or V-Girl as they were called, only the family never knew it. Taking the train with her girlfriends into the city at all hours and picking up soldiers in Times Square or Grand Central Station, offering them sex in exchange for a night out on the town and receiving venereal disease in addition to a good time. It was a terrible scandal on the Renner family, even making its way into the *Social Diary*. Disowned, Gloria's father sent her to New Jersey to his sister Helga in '44. Years later at the ripe age of nineteen, she moved to California where she depleted her trust fund. Sadly, no longer a child of the affluent, society lifestyle ... well, I'm not entirely sure how she lived her life, but she died from a drug overdose in the mid-sixties."

As much as Kitty disliked her cruel younger sister, even after all these years, she paused in sad reflection. Thankful for Juliana's following comment, in silence she offered up a prayer for the soul of her wayward sister.

"I've never heard of a V-Girl." Juliana wrote furiously on her pad. Not that this Gloria mattered, but it was an interesting follow-up piece about wartime promiscuity that could definitely be featured in *Allure* at a later date.

"Now, the oldest sister, Ingrid, currently lives in the former Renner family winter retreat home, Rosebriar Manor in Sarasota, Florida. After their mother's death in the seventies, Lizzy and the other two sisters traded Rosebriar for Ingrid's share of the Renner estate inheritance. She forfeited her rights to Meercrest and anything else beyond Rosebriar. Upon her death, the Sarasota property and all its holdings revert to the Renner sisters. You see, back in the forties, the sisters had a terrible, irreparable falling out, so the loss of her sisterly 'affection' was negligible. I imagine she still lives there in her miserable world. The latest gossip was that she was on her fifth husband."

With obvious disdain and a curled lip, Juliana repined, "She sounds like my mother."

"I assure you, no matter how bad you think your mother is, there is no one as ruthless or repugnant as Ingrid Renner. Her beauty and vanity made her ugly of heart, thinking herself superior. She openly expressed her despicable beliefs in eugenics. She is the sister who is never referenced, her name considered even a further taint upon the family's already destroyed legacy—of which you alluded to earlier."

And for that last reason alone, Ingrid would receive no prayers from the former Kitty Renner, the daughter whose own father and sister considered her to be counted as an undesirable—unfit for life due to her polio. She paused, taking a sip of her coffee.

"Did she also abandon a child?"

Kitty furrowed her brow, placing the cup down on the desk. "No. Thankfully, she never wanted children."

"And the others? Are Kitty and Lizzy still alive?"

"I can see how eager you are, but humor me as I get to that. Yes, Lizzy is still alive, Juliana, but her story is her own where it relates to your great-uncle. I can't share those things with you but what I can tell you is what an incredible woman Lizzy is and how the person she became during the war changed the fate of so many people, specifically the life of the sister she is closest to. Now, *hers* is a story that I can *intimately* share with you." Her eyes filled with tears, searching for the right words to describe Lizzy, as she struggled to retain this detached second person narrative.

Juliana placed her coffee cup on the desk and sat forward, giving the organist all her attention. She reached out and touched the woman's hand, offering encouragement to continue. At the touch of their hands a shiver ran up her spine. That strange niggle in the back of her mind had now become more pronounced and she knew instinctively that Mrs. Katherine Landry was part of Lizzy's story, too, and ... maybe part of her great-uncle's story.

Kitty smiled apologetically for her tears. "The fourth daughter, Kitty, contracted polio at the age of thirteen, and it devastated her. She had dreams of dancing and continuing to study the piano, boys and sailing, tennis and swimming, and if not for Lizzy, her spirits would have been dashed when faced with a life without those things. Essentially, because of her sudden 'inferiority', Kitty was abandoned by her parents—maybe not physically but without a doubt emotionally."

She swallowed and fought the urge to burst into tears.

"At the time, it was difficult to be considered a cripple, but it was Lizzy who offered hope and encouragement to reach beyond the confines of a wheelchair. Buoyed by her sister's optimism and her own innate perseverance, Kitty learned to function and adapt to the expectation that she would never walk again, remaining determined to prove everyone wrong about her uselessness. She insisted on doing everything herself—and still does now that post-polio syndrome has caught up with her." Again, her eyes filled with tears. A smile gradually graced her lips.

"Unexpected events changed the young woman's life, and it was Lizzy who emphatically took the reins of her care—of her protection, sheltering her from the fallout of those events in more ways than most would understand." Kitty took another dramatic pause, a deep breath, rubbing her thigh in reflection before she continued, her smile broadening.

"In the spring of 1943, *my sister Lizzy* removed me from Meercrest and traveled with me to Minneapolis aboard the *20th Century Limited* train. When we arrived, she placed me in the care of an Australian nurse, Sister Elizabeth Kenny, at her new polio institute. It was there, with Sister Kenny's unconventional treatment of physical therapy, that I rehabilitated, removed my braces, re-educated my legs and learned to walk. I returned home to Long Island, a whole, happily married woman with a baby in 1952. I learned to play the organ, volunteered, and traveled. Because of Lizzy, I have lived a life I never dreamed I would. I am married to my sweetheart James for forty-four years and have two sons, a daughter, and two grandchildren. She saved me. I owe my sister my life."

Juliana expelled the long breath held during Kitty's explanation. *I knew it!*

"*You're* Kitty... book campaign Kitty? Wow." She squeezed the elderly woman's hand.

Kitty laughed, wiping away a remnant tear then tapping her faintly lined forehead in the sudden recollection. "Good Lord, I had forgotten all about that wartime drive! Oh, that was so much fun. Lizzy and I squirreled away so many of those books from the big estates. Even with his ten thousand-volume library, Father's collection had nothing even remotely similar to some of those mansions' books. I'm almost embarrassed to tell you how the two of us learned all about the varied 'ins and outs' of sex—from a copy of the *Kama Sutra* donated from the Frick's library!"

"You stole the books you collected and from the Fricks no less?"

"No, we *borrowed* them, devoured them without bending the spines, and *then* donated them. Lizzy is still a voracious reader, ever insistent on being informed about everything going on in the world and everyone's opinion about it."

"I can't believe this! *You're* Kitty! I have so many questions, a list, actually." She opened up her steno pad, prepared to ask them one by one in journalistic fashion. With photographs at the ready and the scrap of the mysterious letter found in the fireplace, she asked the first, "So, you're still close to Lizzy?"

Unwilling yet to answer the questions she was sure to come, Kitty felt undeterred in addressing something Juliana *needed* to know. Her full smile now beamed. "I am *very* close to Lizzy, and although we didn't see much of the sister separating us in age, we were close with her as well. That sister was, actually, called an Irish twin to Lizzy—only ten months apart in age. She passed on a couple of years ago, but her legacy lives on in the lives she touched."

She took a long sip from her coffee cup, watching the thin, young woman over the rim of the brown ceramic mug that read 'Faith' in white letters. Juliana had Lillian's pert nose and demonstrated a familiar expression her sister employed when curious. The young woman looked around the room, eyes finally settling on a replica of Rembrandt's *The Storm on the Sea of Galilee.*

"Juliana, before I tell you about the remaining sister, tell me about yourself and your family."

Juliana shrugged a shoulder, subconsciously toying with her grandfather's Marine Corps insignia pinned upon the right pocket of her blazer. "There's not much to tell, really. I grew up on the Upper East Side, my parents divorced in 1981 when my mother—who just recently informed me that I was considered by her to be a mistake—decided that playing housewife for a man she didn't love was burdensome. When he died three months ago, my world sort of crashed. He and I were extremely close. Apart from said bitchy mother who abandoned me, my grandfather Louie is my only living family. He's a trip and I spend every Wednesday and Sunday with him. Let's see ... I'm a junior fashion writer for *Allure* magazine, single and probably so because ... well, I have commitment issues. Maybe someday some guy will ride in and sweep me off my feet. That's it really, apart from getting the job at *Allure*, the bequest of my uncle's house and estate has been the most exciting thing to happen to me."

"Oh dear, I'm sorry for your loss. Your father must have been a young man."

"He was 44. Sudden heart attack. My grandfather didn't take it well. Following my grandmother's death two years ago, he's been silent. The Resident Liaison at his senior community explained that he's going through Post Traumatic Stress Disorder brought on by Mimi's death and his wartime experience in the Pacific is coming back. Dad's death contributed to it, I'm sure, but he does seem to be involved in his retirement community considering he has quite a harem that come and go with casserole dishes. I think that keeps him young at heart even if his heart and mind are aching."

"I'm truly sorry to hear about your grandfather's trauma." She paused before taking a deep breath. Her gaze held Juliana's for long seconds. "Juliana, do you believe in fate?"

"I never gave it much thought. Why?"

"Well, I believe that you were led here. Name it what you will, but I believe there are no coincidences in life, only G-d-incidences—or perhaps the angels, one in particular guiding us. I knew your grandfather, Louie, you know."

"You did? How? Oh! Yes, that's right, he dated one of your sisters during the war. I read that in some of Lizzy's letters to William." *Hmm … I forgot about that …*

Kitty smiled in agreement, nodding her head. "Yes, he did date one of my sisters. He dated *Lillian* … then he *married* her in 1947, and they had a son named Gordon, and a granddaughter … named Juliana."

She paused, waiting for what she had said to register.

When Juliana's smile grew along with her eyes, her growing suspicion was finally confirmed when Kitty said, "You, Juliana Martel, are my grandniece, dear. And Lizzy's, too."

Seventeen

Arm in Arm
June 1992

"Can you repeat that?" Juliana's mouth agape. "Did you just say that your sister, Lillian was *my* Mimi and that you and Lizzy are my great-aunts?"

Kitty leaned forward, taking hold of Juliana's delicate hands. "I did. So you see, your grandfather is not your *only* living relative. You have aunts, uncles, and cousins and some wonderful legacies established by my sisters to pass on to the next generation."

Not normally prone to tears, Juliana couldn't stop the unexpected trickle rolling down her cheeks, dropping from her chin onto their clasped hands. "Family?"

"Oh, baby, don't cry."

The two women hugged across the small space between them; Kitty's heart broke as she felt the palpable protrusion of bones forming her niece's back. Grandmotherly instinct kicked in, desiring to feed and fatten this precious young waif of a woman with home cooked meals, surrounded by her long denied family.

Juliana sniffled, "That's why you look familiar. You remind me of my grandmother."

"If only I could attain a smidgen of her goodness and humility, but I'm trying. I venture to guess, since you didn't know about the Renners then you don't know anything of your grandmother's history?"

"No, she never talked about her past. She always said she wasn't a past person; she was a present person and my grandfather consistently echoed her sentiment. Mimi loved to tell stories about the two of them completely captivating me, so animated when she did, but she *never* talked about her life *before* marrying Grandpa."

"Ah, well that's a story that, I believe, requires a trip."

"Huh?"

With strong hands placed on Juliana's slight shoulders, Kitty settled her back into the deep seat and removed a handkerchief from her jacket pocket. Then leaning forward to close the distance between them, she tenderly wiped her niece's tears. "Would you care to take a ride with me? I have something very special to show you."

"Of course. Will you be taking me to see *Aunt* Lizzy?"

"Not just yet. I'll need some time to talk to my sister before you meet with her. She won't be prepared for your questions and for reasons that are not mine to divulge, she needs time to process your curiosity regarding her relationship with Ducky. It's been many years since she has spoken of him, and I'm not sure how she will react or respond."

"You call him Ducky?"

"Oh, yes. It all began with a small comment about his being a ducky shincracker—a good dancer. Some nights during the summer of '42, Lizzy and I would hide away for hours in the water tower, and he was all she would talk about. Ducky this ... Ducky that. He changed her life, inspiring her to be more than a spoiled Gold Coast debutante. She truly grew up that summer and everything she is today is because he gave her motivation and confidence. Your great-uncle was an incredible man, a man who inspired greatness in others."

"Can I ask you something?"

Kitty nodded with a thoughtful smile.

"Was it just a summer wartime romance?"

"Oh no, my dear. It was so much more. What they shared was deep, respectful, abiding love."

"I thought so, but did she marry someone else?"

"She did, but she never stopped loving William. To this day, everything she has done in her life has been in honor of him and his family—your family."

"But her husband?"

"He's deceased now, but he always knew how she carried another man's sonnet in her heart."

"Then why?"

Kitty brushed Juliana's golden locks from her face. "I can't tell you that, but if she wants to—she will. All I can tell you is that it was the hardest decision she ever made, but it was a different world then. It was on fire and with a father who believed in a terrible ideology with unspeakable opinions and horrific actions, and in a society such as ours, Lizzy had no choice. She thought William was dead."

****

Jack's Alpha Romeo passed through another grand entry he also knew well. Once known as Welwyn, the former Henry Pratt Estate was now the newly dedicated Long Island Holocaust Museum situated within the extensive Welwyn Preserve County Park. His eyes scanned across the green, perfectly manicured lawn and came to rest upon the 1906 brick mansion. Stately, yet welcoming, the structure screened extensive gardens designed for reflection and peaceful remembrance. It was one of the finest museums in the county, offering both permanent and traveling exhibits as well as boasting education programs. He could see many visitors headed toward the front door. That did his heart good.

He hoped to have a long, reflective walk along one of the many trails leading to the dock on the Sound. Spending the night at his family home, Evermore in Mill Neck, only made him feel worse about his meeting with Juliana. His usual jovial personality had become somewhat taciturn after they had parted, so he chose to withdraw into his comfort zone, spending the previous night in his former suite, secluded at the far end of his childhood home.

Today was Saturday, and he knew his paternal aunt would be here in the garden. Meeting with Juliana, delightful and intoxicating as she was, left him unsettled for a myriad of reasons. Although enamored by her vivacious inquisitiveness, when directed toward the Robertsen and Renner families she had put him at a loss on how to proceed. Before speaking to the woman she referred to so affectionately, almost intimately, as Lizzy, he thought it best to seek a second opinion.

He parked his car at the far end of the public lot and took one of the paths below the towering pergola, passing alongside the Children's Memorial Garden. Its design was lovingly created in remembrance of the 1.5 million children who perished in the Shoah as well as the other children who died in the war. On this day, children of all ages sat on the concrete edge of what was once Mrs. Pratt's reflecting pool; now empty, the round pool was seen as a symbolic reminder of life, as well as a practical location for lectures. Today one of the museum's volunteers stood in the center of the former water feature, sharing the history of the museum and its inspiration to attentive listeners. This garden had special significance for the Robertsen family who were major contributors to its recent campaign.

Following the stone pavers, Jack made his way through to the flower gardens where butterflies floated above the many blossomed plants specifically chosen by his grandmother to symbolize the child victims of the Holocaust.

Even wearing gardening clothes and cloaked beneath a large-brimmed hat, his aunt's refinement and loveliness was evident. With gloved hands happily brandishing her pruning shears, she waved as he approached. "Jackie! What a surprise. What are you doing here?"

He kissed her dimpled cheek. "Well that's a fine hello, Aunt Annette."

"Oh, darling, you know I'm always happy to see you. It's just that you don't come to the center often and well, it being a Saturday, I expect you would want to be out on the Sound rather than seeking out your aunt." She shielded her eyes, looking up to the cloudless sky. "It's a beautiful day and with a lovely breeze to boot."

He resisted his innate urge to beat around the bush. "Tempting as it is, I needed to talk with you about something."

"Well, now you have my attention. This sounds serious. The last time you sought me out for advice, rather than my brother, was when you wanted to resign from the Board after the opening of the center."

She placed the rose cutters into the pouch at her waist, removed her hat letting it hang from its cord at her nape, and shook out her chestnut curls. "Shall we walk?"

He shoved his hands into the pockets of his well-worn jeans. "Yeah, maybe we can sit on one of the benches further down along the brick path."

Annette tucked her arm into his and squeezed him close. "Ooo, it's so good to see you, Jackie! I miss you when you travel, and I know your cousins miss you, too. You really need to come for dinner before the divorce is settled and I have to vacate the house. I'll invite the boys."

"I will. I promise. I miss you all as well. Grandmother has been stealing most of my available time planning this upcoming trip of hers. I've never seen her so determined before. I'm sure she's ready to blow a gasket at the French Culture Minister."

"Ah, well, you know my mother. She'll never let grass grow under her feet when she can be accomplishing something good or getting into mischief. This painting acquisition by the foundation is too important to her. I don't know why but it is. Now, tell me. What is troubling that handsome face and happy heart of yours?"

"I met a girl."

She stopped dead in her tracks and turned to her nephew. "You met a girl? This is great news! Stop the presses news! How serious is it?"

He replaced her arm in the crook of his, continuing to walk. "It's not like that. I mean ... I'd like it to be, but that's another issue. This girl is a friend of a friend who needed some help researching a family member of hers—a great-uncle who left his house to her. My friend thought my working for *Newsday* could open up avenues, you know, archives and contacts. So, I blindly offered to help."

"That's very nice of you and let me guess—you met her and it was love at first sight."

"Juliana definitely got my attention. I'd be lying if I didn't admit that I'm attracted to her and want to get to know her better. She's nice-looking and intelligent, sincere and honest. At times, she has this dynamic spark about her that reminds me of you in some ways. Other times, she's reserved and thoughtful."

"So, in other words, she's brilliant!"

He chuckled at the twinkling brown sparkle in her eyes and the effervescence of her voice. "Yes, a bit younger than I usually go for. My mother would have something to say because she's not Jewish, but neither obstacle is the issue at hand."

Aunt and nephew sat upon a stone bench, facing a small pond surrounded by the wafting scent of lilacs in full bloom. A family of ducks etched spiraling patterns on the water's surface and apart from the occasional Blue Jay call, it was perfectly serene until he quietly, but clearly pronounced, "She's investigating the former *Lizzy Renner*."

"Oh, dear."

"*Oh dear* is right. Further, she's a journalist, and in the coincidence of all coincidences—to prove what a small world it really is—she claims to be Lillian Renner's *granddaughter*. We now have the perfect storm whipping up our calm sea."

"Lillian had a granddaughter? Are you sure? This is unexpected to say the least."

Stunned, Annette paused in thought, rubbing her neck. "I suppose I shouldn't be too shocked. According to your grandmother, Lillian completely disavowed her Renner lineage. Of course, now we celebrate her *as* a Renner for her actions. Wow ... all these years and someone shows up asking questions, and she's Lillian's granddaughter no less."

"That's what I thought, too. I wasn't sure at first when she gave her name. It sounded familiar, but we only, always, refer to Lillian as a Renner around here since her acts of righteousness were *as* a Renner. Then I saw a photograph of Lillian and her husband, and I recognized her from the exhibit—the surname clicked."

"Does this girl have siblings? Are there any other members of her family that we don't know of?"

"No, it's just her, and I get the feeling she's starved for a family. We can take solace that Juliana knows absolutely nothing about her grandmother's Renner family, but she's determined to find out about them—if she hasn't already. I tried to put her off as best as I could, offering to help her find her uncle if he was still alive, but she was as persistent as grandmother when it comes to getting to the bottom of things. I'm afraid this is one can of worms Juliana will regret opening."

Annette raised her hand to her cheek, shaking her head side to side with concern. "Oh, dear. Do you think she'll publish her findings about Frederick's actions?"

"I can't be sure. I tried to explain to her without going into detail that pursuing it would have terrible results, but I don't believe she truly understood what was at the heart of it. Can you just imagine the field day the press would have dredging up his role in the saboteurs, the final solution, the investigation into his treason, and the way he died—let alone Lizzy's role in the matter? Add to the mix an alcoholic mother and a sister who touted her earnest belief in the benefit of eugenics. Well, that'll just blacken and besmirch the museum, and especially the foundation, let alone the effect on our family."

"Why is she looking for her? Did she say? Surely, there is no reason to seek Lizzy out. How did she even find us?"

"Apparently—and I've seen the photographs and read a letter to attest to it—this great-uncle was a wartime sweetheart of hers. Juliana just might be searching for a romantic hook for her story, intrigued by their youthful love story and most likely hoping to find them both alive followed by a happy ever after into the sunset. I gotta tell ya, it upset me a little to read that letter. Sappy stuff about chemistry, Tyrone Power, and kisses, but that was fifty years ago. Let it lie."

Annette smiled. "Happily ever afters are what every girl dreams about, whether they are twenty-something and single, forty-nine year old aunts recovering from a bitter divorce, or seventy-year-old widows who listen to big band music while cooking dinner for one. We live and love, Jackie. It's what we do—we cling to the romantic past and look to the future in hope that it finds us even once or if we're really fortunate, again."

Jack took her hand in his. "Yeah, but. Let the past lie."

"No 'yeah buts'. Look around you. Look at this museum. In every sense, it is looking to the future with hope by teaching the past. The reason you quit the board was because you never understood the purpose of education or looking at this particular history. Let's face facts—you were great at finding benefactors and dealing with the press and all the other behind-the-scenes stuff, but when the museum door opened, you left."

Annette swept her arm out in the direction of the pond and gardens. "This place exemplifies the foundation of your life and what your father survived. Should we not remember that?"

"You know I don't believe in looking back. I'm a person who looks forward and, honestly, I can see no reason to readdress or invite others to revisit the horrors—*or* even the romances—of fifty years ago. Moving on, not living in the past is what will change people. I don't understand why you think it pertains to this particular situation we find ourselves in."

"Well, look at that elm tree. It's the last of its kind from the estate's construction in 1906. All the others died from Dutch elm disease, but this one survived, growing stronger because it had deep roots that were anchored on a firm foundation. Almost one hundred years later, it stands as a legacy and testimony to the Pratts' love of nature. This lone elm is now a splendid symbolic focal point in the memorial garden at this museum. It represents a family tree."

"But none of that has any bearing on this Juliana girl. She—"

Annette held her hand up, stopping his refute. "Hear me out; let me finish explaining why it *is* significant to her story."

"Everything our Phoenix Foundation and others did to make this center a reality has been to preserve your roots and give testimony to the power of tolerance and acceptance. As the child of a survivor, your adamant refusal to remember the atrocities weakens your foundation. You fail to allow your roots to deepen, your tree to branch and, more importantly, you fail to honor the victims' memory."

She watched as he leaned forward, resting his elbows on his knees and grasped his hands thoughtfully. "And yet you're still wondering how this relates," she said.

He nodded, the sun catching his fair locks.

"What I'm saying is to let this unfold. As a family, we have run from the Renner legacy for too long. Perhaps the time is right to celebrate how from the ashes a phoenix of reparation and atonement was born. We are a single family who has raised our children within two different faiths. Allow the press their articles, showing how three Renner women *changed* lives—not out of guilt, but out of love. *Their* foundation, their roots inspired the personal legacies they will leave behind for the next generation. The next generation, Jack—*your* children."

"Maybe you're right, but I can't help how I have always felt."

"It's part of your generation to think that way, not mine and my brothers', and that's why the museum is so important. It's why stories such as Lillian Renner's should be told, why Juliana and the world should be educated and reminded. Look, Jack. Don't you think this girl would want to know that although her great-grandfather was a member of the Third Reich, her grandmother—one of his children—*saved* victim children, your father being one of them, hiding them in her clubmobile, bringing them to safety and then utilizing her wealth and connections to find them homes as displaced orphans? Those are *Juliana's* roots, *her* foundation, which most likely make up the person she was raised to be. She has a *right* to know."

"I suppose, but how do you tell someone that?"

"Honestly and with compassion, but these secrets must be told. I'd be pretty p.o'd if things were kept from me, that's for sure. In hindsight, if Lillian could do it all over again, I think she would have told her granddaughter about her family history."

Jack rose, pacing a few feet back and forth and running his hand through his hair. "What about *"Lizzy?"* Will she be all right with this?"

"Probably, but I'd bring her a new gardenia shrub just in case. G-d love her. For as long as I can remember, her green thumb just doesn't extend to gardenias. The harder she tries, the quicker they die. I keep telling her she just needs to give up the effort, but her reply is always the same, 'Shoot me for being an optimist'."

"And, you'll be all right with me talking to her about this William guy?"

"Sure, she's a single woman. Who knows what might happen. Is he alive? Married? Single?"

"Who knows? I made a few calls." Jack reached into his back pocket, withdrawing the photograph Juliana gave him. "I was thinking of showing her this."

Annette took the snapshot from him and had the same reaction as he. She blurted out a very unladylike laugh. "Oh my! Look at them—look at that plane! Jeez, my father was right, she was *insane*. Pistol Packin' Lizzy? Is she sitting astride a bomb?"

"Looks that way."

"And you thought skydiving was the craziest thing she's ever done. She was WWII nose art, wearing a bikini! And this guy, oh my G-d, he was gorgeous."

Together they howled in laughter, making joke after joke at Lizzy's expense until finally Jack grew serious. "Will you come with me into the museum? I think it's time I take another look at the exhibit in honor of the American Red Cross and Lillian's bravery."

"Of course. You know I never tire of watching that video of your father." They rose and once again she tucked her hand tightly around her nephew's arm as they continued to chuckle over the photograph.

"So you really like her—this Juliana?"

"I do, and I want to help her find her uncle."

She looked at the snapshot again. Her eyes narrowing as she examined it closely, tilting her head curiously. "He certainly was a hunk. You never know, darling, we might get two happily ever afters out of this. This girl could just be what *everyone* in our Robertsen family needs right now."

****

Jack and Annette entered the back of the museum from the garden terrace door. Walking past a conference room, they could hear the meeting's facilitator leading one of the museum's many teacher training seminars. Throughout each hall and gallery they were greeted by volunteers, some survivors others second generation like himself. Many stopped to shake Jack's hand, genuinely pleased to see him after so many months. He felt the power of his aunt's words about the roots and the tree.

That last surviving elm did truly represent a family tree. Everyone who came to this place of sanctuary, remembrance, and education were part of the same family—whether they were Jewish or not. Each branch represented their narrative and each leaf and offshoot represented their descendants. His aunt and uncle were examples of that—Christians whose brother, as though their own flesh and blood, was a miraculous survivor. His grandparents had accomplished that by raising them all with the richness of both faiths, and his cousins were the continuation of tolerance and acceptance in a world still mired with antisemitism and racism.

They walked through the main exhibit hall where disturbing images lined the freestanding walls. The testimonial videos on continuous loop and the accompanying sound effects were delineated and framed by boldly quoted written words that jumped out at him, almost crushing him with the weight of what they conveyed. Powerful reflections inscribed in both Hebrew and English added to the account, although words were superfluous. There could never be words. For Jack, photographs were enough.

Upon reaching the hallway beyond the multimedia exhibits, he held his aunt back when he noticed Juliana standing at the entrance to one of the gallery rooms set aside for special exhibits. He watched as the blonde beauty stood rooted in place, holding onto the doorframe as though bracing herself. She spoke to someone within the gallery.

Jack resisted the urge to point his finger. "That's her!"

"That's who?"

"Juliana, and she's standing at Lillian's Story of Courage."

"Oh, she's a beauty, Jackie. Tiny little thing, but absolutely gorgeous. Look how she's holding back. I think she's afraid to go in. Should we say something and get this perfect storm blowing?"

"Very funny. Who do you think brought her here?"

"How about we go find out?" Annette suggested just as Juliana entered the gallery.

Remaining rigidly in place, Jack admitted, "No, I'd rather wait. She'll know everything soon enough and I don't want to have a confrontation about my deception here."

Amazingly akin to her experience standing on Bradford Road in front of Primrose Cottage for the first time, shock and awe hardly seemed expressive enough for Juliana. Words failed as eyes grew wide, fixed upon the large photograph of her grandmother dressed for a formal American Red Cross portrait. Smiling for the camera, the woman known as Lillian Renner left her granddaughter spellbound.

Kitty took her niece's hand in hers, holding it tightly, shifting her weight onto the one hand crutch. "This is the grandmother you never knew. She was more than an American Red Cross volunteer, Juliana."

Utilizing their grasped hands, in a broad arch she indicated to Juliana to turn from one side of the exhibit room to the other, explaining with a quiet pride, "They were *all* more than 'just volunteers'. Where the boys were concerned they were probably the greatest of morale boosters, representing that connection to home they missed so much. These brave women gave hope and solace to the weary soldiers."

Kitty chuckled wryly. "Sometimes all it took were cigarettes, doughnuts, and a cup of coffee. Other times, it was a full-fledged sob on a shoulder, but a simple, warm smile from the clubmobile hostess was always most needed."

"This is incredible. Why did Mimi never say anything? I would have loved to hear her stories about this." She ran her free hand over the smaller images surrounding the portrait, immortalized snapshots of the volunteers at the doughnut truck, dancing with the soldiers, and making coffee on the front lines in Europe and North Africa. Some images showed the volunteers beside worn down fliers at airfields in England. "She did this?"

"She did more than this."

"But, why did she never tell *me*?" For the second time that day, Juliana's eyes filled with tears. "I never knew. My grandparents never said."

Kitty continued to hold tightly to her great niece's hand. "Listen, darling, she and I talked often about why she never told you or even Gordon for that matter. She was adamant on closing the door to her Renner past when she left for England in 1942, and she saw her war effort as a part of that past in a way. Our father did horrible, unspeakable things, and apart from keeping in touch with Lizzy and me, Lillian chose to never look back, never acknowledge, or admit that she was an offspring of a man who allied his beliefs with the Nazis. What she gave, what she did, was from her patriotic, loving heart. She never wanted to brag or bandy about this as though it were some heroic sacrifice. That is why the exhibit's coordinator, out of respect for your grandmother's wishes, waited to give honor to her until after her passing."

"The coordinator knew when Mimi died?"

"Yes, she read the obituary. She was overcome with grief. Thankfully, we have personal testimony of a life she changed—a survivor and he tells his story in this video."

"I wish Grandpa could see this. Maybe that would get him to talk. He'd be so proud."

"Yes, he would. Perhaps we can bring him out here, although I'm sure he knows every detail of her experience in Europe. When Pearl Harbor was attacked, your grandmother joined the local chapter of ARC as part of the Motor Corps, driving an ambulance, learning to fix trucks and cars, but then toward the end of 1942 she wanted to do more. She always wanted to do more for the boys. It was her nature and coupled with life at home becoming more combative, she transferred to England when the ARC created the clubmobile, servicing the airfields. I'll never forget how she promised Lizzy that she would look for Ducky wherever she went. Like me, she was very fond of him and, of course, he was Louie's baby brother. After the invasion on D-Day, Lillian volunteered to go to the continent, attached to the 36th Infantry Division."

"D-Day? Mimi went to France, too?"

"Yes. Back then, the boys called the volunteers Doughgirls and Rover girls, later during the Korean and Vietnam Wars they called them Donut Dollies. I don't know about the other wars, but back then, your grandmother slept in her truck and worked in the mud. The girls wore helmets, boots, and coveralls and when they were attached to artillery units, they didn't have earplugs. She would write to Lizzy and me how whenever their truck made its way to a camp, they would be greeted with 'Hey, an American woman!' by throngs of cold and hungry men. Oftentimes, she would write how she hoped the ARC was in the Pacific, helping your grandfather.

"Something miraculous happened, in the winter of 1944. Your grandmother volunteered to become, what they called, a 'Donut Dugout Ranger'. She traveled the backwoods to find a suitable location to set up shop so to speak, a service club in a village or town, because wherever the troops went, the Red Cross followed, no matter how small the unit. In the northern Alsace her mission changed."

Kitty pressed the button on the video monitor below the portrait of Lillian. "This man's name is Henri Robertsen. He's Jack's father, and I imagine, one of the reasons behind his stonewalling you in regard to the Renner family. Jack is very protective of those he loves." The frozen image of a handsome, well-dressed man in his late forties came alive to tell his tale.

"I was three years old when she found me and four others. Later, I was told we had been alone for about four months in that farmhouse outside of Brumath, near Hauenau, France a Nazi stronghold until March of '45. All I can remember really is the cold and the hunger. The couple who hid us disappeared one day, leaving us to fend for ourselves. I still wonder their fate. The oldest in hiding, maybe ten years of age was a girl named Giselle. She took on the role of our mother, telling us stories and finding food for us in the forest, all the while evading capture. Truly, it was a gift from G-d that the Nazis never came upon the shack where we hid below the floorboards in the root cellar.

It was December and snowing when miraculously, Lillian Renner, an American Red Cross Clubmobile volunteer drove down a snowy path and saw Giselle in the forest attempting to catch a rabbit or something. Years later, after I came to America, my adoptive mother explained to me that the yellow, Jewish star on Giselle's sweater caused Lillian to react quickly. How we never were caught before was truly a miracle. I remember the five of us, huddling together in the back of the Red Cross truck under blankets and boxes during a long, bumpy ride. We could hear gunfire until it finally grew more distant. We arrived at the main camp where the clubmobile and the other volunteers were gathered. They fawned and fussed over us." He laughed. *"I remember the doughnuts, and even though I wanted to stuff them into my mouth whole, Lillian helped me to eat slowly. All I wanted to do was eat and hold her. It felt like forever since someone loved me. Funny, the things you remember—all but three years old, filthy, hungry, and cold and I remember how she smelled like strawberries in the dead of winter."*

The speaker on the screen, Henri, paused his recitation, obviously becoming emotional. *"She remained with the five of us as we were shuttled and handed off from American zone to American zone, and eventually put on a Red Cross hospital ship, crossing the Channel to England where we remained for a time with a British foster family as displaced refugees. Lillian stayed in Europe, but from afar, utilizing her affluence, connections, and society, she wired B'nai B'rith, the Women's Committee of the American Jewish Congress, and friends in the Social Register. She cut through red tape, arranged for identity papers, visas and found each of us foster homes until permanent families were located. Our new American families—two in Philadelphia and three on Long Island, eventually adopted us. I was adopted by the Robertsen family, Gold Coast residents who also had an infant daughter of their own.*

"Many years later, I learned that through the tireless efforts of the United States Committee for the Care of European Children, 1387 orphans came to America via President Truman's 'Directive of Displaced Persons' in 1946. Thankfully, we didn't have to wait that long. I can still remember that one cold day in February of '45 I stood all bundled up, holding Giselle's hand, with the three other children and some official woman at an active London airfield where the RAF planes flew in and out around us. A beautiful woman, dressed in fur, descended the stairway from a private plane. I was fascinated, even at that tender age, watching her hat flap in the breeze, and her gloved hand grab it before it flew away. When she and the smiling man, beside her walked right to us, she squatted, and, speaking in French, her green eyes sparkled when she said, "Hello, how would you children like to fly to America in that swell airplane with me?" She took hold of my tiny hand and that was when I fell in love with my new mother."

Eighteen

Don't Cry
<u>October 5, 1942</u>

I t was late in the evening and the majority of the residents of Meercrest had long retired. Immediately following dinner, Frances bid the girls a hasty goodnight, seeking the solace of her nightcaps in the privacy of her own suite. Even Kitty sought solitude this evening after a violent argument with Gloria at the dinner table. Mrs. Davis, having turned down Lizzy's bed last, had retreated to the servants' cottage for the night. The patriarch had business in the city.

Lizzy sat at her ornate vanity, her dark curls set free from their usual pinning, clearly just brushed out and shining, they swept over her shoulder. Her head tilted slightly, long locks reaching the surface her forearms rested upon as she wrote a letter, lost in dreamy remembrances of Will.

October 6, 1942

My Dearest Darling,

Sweetheart, I received your letter dated September 29 and wish I knew all the right words to say to ease your worry. Is it possible that your grandfather and aunt are traveling to the south of France or the Riviera? I read Monaco is neutral in this war and a visit to Monte Carlo would be a perfect holiday. I suppose anyone living in Paris would tire of seeing swastikas at every turn, so maybe they decided on a getaway far from those terrible Nazis! Is it unusual that you have not heard from your auntie in three months? Perhaps the war has delayed postal delivery?

As I promised you, let us talk of happy things. I am sure you won't believe me when I tell you that I listened to the last game of the World Series on the radio yesterday. Yes, even a society girl enjoys baseball. Given my love of sports, I am quite keen on it. I have Johnny to thank for that! I knew that if you were not training, you and the boys would be assembled in the officer's club. I wanted to be with you even if through the airwaves. I closed my eyes imagining that you and I were seated beside one another in Yankee Stadium listening to the crack of Phil Rizzuto's bat in the first inning when he hit that home run. The weather was divine and I imagined the smell of the hot dog we shared and the cotton candy available in spite of the sugar ration. I even imagined our sugary, sticky lips stuck together when you kissed me afterward. Oh daddy, what a kiss you gave!! On our date, I wore a navy skirt, a smart white blouse with little red stars. I didn't wear a hat, but instead rolled my hair just right to show off another darling flower. Can you see it? I felt so patriotic sitting in the grandstands with my flyboy as you taught me what a center fielder does and what an RBI means (even though I knew already.) Later, we shared a box of Cracker Jacks and I found two prizes! One horseshoe charm for you and a ring for me! Gosh, I had a swell time on our date! Even though the Yankees didn't win, it didn't matter. You and I were together in New York City and nothing could have been more lulu than that! Soon this war will be over and you and I will share baseball for real. After this game, though, I just may have to become a St. Louis Cardinals fan, and what will your ever-loving Dodger spirit have to say about that? Worse yet, what would my Giants say? How would I ever be able to show my face at the Polo Grounds when I have turned traitor—first getting stuck on a Dodger's fan and second rooting for the Cardinals?

So you're saying good-bye to Tampa? It hardly seems fair that the Army is relocating you to a smaller airfield next week. You were just settling in. There is nothing in Lakeland that even remotely resembles nightlife. Well, apart from the Sorosis Club, but I have never been. Central Florida is mostly citrus groves, I think. However, Winter Park is not far and many of those who live in Glen Cove have seasonal homes there ...

Lost in her letter writing, Lizzy was oblivious to the soft music surrounding her from the record player in the corner of the room and unaware that Lillian, still in her uniform, stood smiling at her from the doorway.

Lillian noted how her spirited sister looked almost ethereal, wearing delicate nightclothes in the dimly lit room accented by the soft yellow walls papered with tiny roses. In Lillian's opinion, Lizzy was one of the lovliest women she knew, and now in the ambient lighting, the rosy hue to her cheeks made her even lovelier.

Silently standing there, she observed Lizzy's crooked little smile, sure that the Martel family religious secrets had yet to be divulged. Otherwise her sister's thoughts would have been troubled rather than pleasant. Will was more cautious than Louie, much more protective of his family history, particularly having ascertained *some* of the Renners' political opinions. But those were Will's secrets to share with Lizzy. Besides, as far as she knew, her sister's relationship with him hadn't progressed beyond letter writing.

To evade being seen by the family, Lillian had sneaked in through the servants entrance determined to avoid Ingrid's newest admonishments, vehemently expressed when they recently crossed paths in town.

She whispered from across the room, "Hi, sissy."

Lizzy startled. "Lil! What are you doing here?"

"I sneaked in. Father's not at home, is he?"

"No, he's in the city, staying at Greystone."

"Good, I need to talk with you."

Lizzy rose and walked to her sister, the silk dressing gown she wore draped loosely over a sage-colored nightgown. She kissed her sister's cheek and promptly tugged her into the bedroom then poked her head out the door, looking right then left, before closing it.

Hard rain assaulted the leaded casement windows, and Lizzy's attention drew to the closed brocade draperies where flashes of lightning penetrated the edges. It was an eerie night, and she was surprised Lillian would venture out in the stormy weather. Wet, sensible shoes had left a slight mud trail on the carpet, but Lizzy didn't care. Her sister removed her damp cap; the small red cross above the brim looked so important and official. A sudden chill ran up her spine when Lillian sat on the tufted bench at the foot of the bed.

"Your hair looks darling. When did you get up the nerve to cut it?" she asked.

Lillian's expression lacked enthusiasm and the tone of her voice sounded flat. "Just this morning before my shift."

"Is something troubling you? Is it Louie?"

Lillian sighed. "No, I'm sure Louie is safe. I received a letter from him yesterday. It was dated three weeks ago. He's fighting somewhere in the Solomon Islands."

"The movie newsreels showed footage from the Pacific." Lizzy knelt at Lillian's feet, resting her head on her sister's knees. "Oh, Lil you must be so worried."

"He'll be fine. He has to be. We're promised to one another." She petted Lizzy's soft hair. "Don't worry, dear heart, Will is going to be fine as well."

"I hope so. I'm so afraid for when he leaves for Europe. As it is, he writes how tired he is from class after class, flight simulation at ungodly hours, and patrol missions. He's worried over Louie and their family in France, but there's more, which he won't share. I just don't know how to help him."

Lillian soothingly continued to pet her sister's hair in long strokes.

"Where is he now, still at MacDill Airfield?"

"For the moment. Next week, his bomb group will be transferring to another airfield in Lakeland for unit training and mission practice."

Lillian swallowed hard, hating to add to her sister's worry, but she needed to tell her what she came to say.

"Lizzy ... I'm leaving."

Lizzy's head jerked upward. "What do you mean?"

"I've transferred from the Motor Corps to the new clubmobiles, and I leave for six weeks training in Washington D.C. I won't be returning to Glen Cove ... ever."

"What? Why? This can't be true!"

The pained look upon Lillian's face confirmed the truth of her words. "I'm sorry, Lizzy, but I have to go. My life isn't here in high society with our parents any longer. Their beliefs are so very different from mine—and from yours and Kitty's for that matter. If I can give one GI a sliver of humanity in this ugly world then I will. My Louie is out there fighting and very soon, your flyboy will be, too. England may bring me into contact with Will as I travel from airbase to airbase in the truck."

"What truck? I don't understand?"

"The doughnuts, remember?"

"Yes. I do remember, but you're too young. You told me yourself that you had to be twenty-five to go overseas. I don't understand."

"When my superior saw that I attended Finch, finishing a year of college, he made an exception. You know that since December, they have been turning a blind eye to my age." She snorted. "First time ever I allowed our family name to open a door. They need volunteers on the front lines, and I want to go."

Lizzy rose from the floor and began to pace back and forth until she walked to her nightstand and lit a Chesterfield. A deep drag and a lengthy, smooth exhale preceded her repeat of Lillian's words almost as though trying to convince herself. "You're leaving. You're leaving us."

"I'm sorry, Lizzy, but I feel I need to be doing more for the war effort. In going abroad, I hope I can make even a small difference. The clubmobiles are new and so important for the boys. Your role is here on the home front with the book drive and with Kitty—helping her."

"But, we need you. Lillian ... I need you, and you're ditching me."

Lillian rose, looking so official in her black tie and insignia pins. Placing her warm hands upon her sister's shoulders, she spoke with steadfast authority. "You've been managing fine without me these many months and you will continue to do so when I'm gone. I'm so proud of you, truly. You're more intelligent and stronger than you give yourself credit and certainly not a spoiled socialite any longer. You're a maturing woman who has a mind of her own, a hefty trust fund and a means in which to *not* remain tethered to Meercrest.

Although Lizzy was heartbroken to hear of her sister's departure, she couldn't help but to saucily reply. "I was *never* spoiled. Happy in my partying, yes, but never spoiled."

Lillian snorted. "That's a load of gobbledygook. Besides, you don't need me. What do you really rely on me for anyway?"

"Everything, especially emotional support." She sighed deeply. "I'll miss you."

The rainstorm outside seemed to turn more violent. A sonorous reverberation of thunder circumscribed the conversation, bringing the sisters back to a place where dismay and insecurity of one protested the bravery and independence of the other. Lizzy stepped away, leaving Lillian standing, back to the window and the unseen raindrops that were pelting the hidden panes behind her like wretched tears.

"Can I change your mind? I'm afraid for you going into war. I read the newspapers and listen to the President's fireside chats and the *CBS World News* at night. I know what is going on over there now."

"Don't be afraid for me. Where's that Lizzy Renner optimism?"

"Fleeting these days. Now that I'm in the know, I'm not so sappy any longer."

Lillian shook her head. "You can't change my mind. It's already done. I passed the physical and secured my place. Like Will and Louie, I want to do this and I'm not afraid."

Panic rose inside Lizzy. Resolved that she'd do anything to keep a most beloved sister from entering a battle zone, in desperation, she broke her promise to Kitty, blurting, "I don't think I can keep protecting Kitty from Ingrid."

"What do you mean?"

Lizzy snuffed her cigarette out in the ashtray. "I think, she ... she tries to hurt her. There was an incident on the landing and afterwards I found Nazi literature in a hat box in Ingrid's wardrobe about preserving German racial purity, and I think ... I mean ... it might be remotely conceivable that, that ... Ingrid is a believer in sterilization and euthanasia of those who the Nazis deem unfit, that whole master race absurdity."

"You've found other Nazi propaganda here at Meercrest?"

"Yes, I've been, well ... searching."

Lizzy knelt beside her bed, sliding out a Bonwit Teller hatbox and lifted the lid. Inside laid several pamphlets and flyers, some in English but most in German. "A few of these I found in Father's library in the American literature section. Two were tucked in a book from some eugenics organization located here in Cold Spring Harbor. The research they do there is supported by the Carnegies, Rockefellers, and Father's railroad associates, the Harrimans. I never even knew this Eugenics Record Office existed only ten miles from here."

Lillian remained expressionless, staring first at the box and then to her sister, torn between truth telling or lying about what she suspected for some time. "My G-d. You need to burn those, Lizzy, right away."

With the romantic music long over, Lizzy's happy letter to Will had been set aside and replaced by this speculation of heinous acts. She couldn't even fathom that here in America people advocated this.

"I know it sounds crazy, but do you think Ingrid sees Kitty as unfit because her polio has left her wheelchair confined? That she considers Kitty an invalid even though she wasn't born that way?" Lizzy removed a leaflet in German depicting a deformed child, her hand trembling when she passed the paper to her sister. "Look at how horrible this is. It advocates sterilization! Most of these do. Others are horrifically bigoted. I spent some time translating them from an old dictionary I found in the library."

"I don't know for sure about Ingrid, but I do know that Mr. Gebhardt has influence over her and his opinions are sympathetic to Nazism. She's his lover, you know," Lillian stated.

Lizzy sat on her bed beside the round box. Not as shocked as Lillian expected, her sister hesitantly voiced her question, seeking confirmation of what she most-likely suspected already. "His lover? What about Johnny?"

"What about him? I'm sure she still intends on marrying him for his family's wealth and prestige. And, as far as I know, Father's lawyer isn't listed in the *Social Register*. Her attraction to that creep is physical not financial. In that regard, she's not too dissimilar from Gloria. I overheard him having his way with her in the boathouse when I stopped by last week to pick up some of the spare life preservers for donation. I could hear the two of them upstairs in the loft moaning. It was disgusting."

"Poor Johnny! I must tell him. What if he ends up marrying her?" *It's not as if she won't find out about his asthma and think* he's *inferior!*

Lillian slid beside her sister and rustled through the box, shaking her head. She removed a disturbing leaflet. "Did Kitty see this literature?"

Lizzy gasped. "No. G-d, no!"

"Good. I wouldn't say anything to John. Don't get involved in his relationship with Ingrid, especially after what you suspect about her violent streak and now with this material ... but if you have proof that either she or Gebhardt are dangerous, well *then* you need to either turn to John or leave the estate."

"You know I can't leave. You know the gossip and the scandal that would ensue. I'm not as brave as you. I'll just have to be here more and shelter Kitty as best as I can. I can't leave her here alone, you know. Mother is useless, drunk all the time, and Father is never here. I'll talk with Mrs. Davis, Mr. Howard, and Jamison."

"And Nurse Keller."

"No, I don't trust her. When she smokes her cigarettes she always has an ugly downturn to her mouth."

Lizzy's disturbed thoughts brought her vision to rest upon the photograph sitting beside her bed. Will looked so handsome in his uniform, his dimple winking back at her. All she wanted to do was to run into his arms, far away from Meercrest and the niggling, distressing thoughts and discoveries she had made since that fateful day back in July in the library. Part of her wanted only to go back to living as that uninformed party girl, existing with her head in the sand—and the clouds. Knowledge was proving painful.

"Lil, what do you know about the Degas Mother just moved from the library to the front entryway?"

Her sister shrugged. "Nothing really, apart from its beauty. I often imagine Kitty as one of the ballerinas. Why do you ask?"

"I guess I wouldn't ask if Ingrid hadn't recently boasted about the Monet that's now hanging in her room. Aren't you the least bit curious about the Degas? I mean, Father isn't normally an art collector. Even Madam X wasn't his acquisition but was Grandmother's."

"What are you implying?"

"I'm not really implying anything, but I am curious. Maybe I'm just looking to find things that aren't there." She shrugged a shoulder attempting to dismiss her own sinister speculations. "Too many novels and movies. These pamphlets have me thinking the worst, even of Father. Though nothing points to him holding these beliefs."

"Be careful with all these conclusions you are jumping to. It'll come to no good for either you, Kitty, nor Ingrid."

Summoning as much joy as she could find in her heart, Lizzy reached over to Lillian and took her hand. Although she was unhappy with her sister's news and the discoveries within the hatbox, the brave ARC volunteer needed much more than talk of Nazis and eugenics. She needed support and love.

"You're right. It's just my overactive imagination. Now ... tell me more about the clubmobile, sissy. I'm so proud of you."

****

Apart from shopping for a birthday gift for Will, Lizzy's excursion into the city was oddly unfulfilling. On this sunny weekday, following her worrisome visit with Lillian two nights before, she found herself on the first floor aimlessly meandering through the accessory department after scanning the ladies' department in much the same fashion. For a change, Saks Fifth Avenue offered nothing of interest except for a pair of black suede gloves to match the fashion platform shoes she wore. The luxury store was crowded, even with the apparent shortage of Paris's finest designs. However, upstairs in the Salon Moderne, Sophie Gimbel's couture designs were a suitable substitute. The American designer's close-fitting, tailored ensembles for the new Fall season were called "liquid" and even met the War Production Board's yardage criteria. Still, Lizzy felt uninspired and dispassionate.

She strolled through the aisles of gloves, scarves, and belts, raised an item only to immediately put it down. The glass display counter filled with perfectly laid out handkerchiefs of imported lace had no appeal. She mindlessly picked through the display of crocodile handbags and brushed past the new arrivals in the millinery department; of all her fashion addictions, hats were her number one weakness. Even now the brown, felt picture hat staring back at her had no allure. Frivolous shopping felt flat and superficial. Apart from shopping for Will, it all felt so meaningless.

On the opposite side of the first floor, she noted the patriotic War Bond and Stamp booth. At least that had meaning as she passed through the fragrance department toward it. Yes. Purchasing War Bonds would help train Will or supply him with necessary equipment. This she believed in.

The purchase of three Series E Bonds in one hundred dollar increments was only half of her monthly allowance from her trust fund, but was a small amount of money in her estimation when faced with the call for all Americans to contribute to the Treasury so that we can build, fight, and win.

After an hour, still without purchasing a suitable gift for him, she exited the store but felt proud in taking, yet another step in becoming the woman Will believed her to be.

A double-decker bus passed by and Old Glory flapped above her. A newsstand displayed all the latest editions. Dreamy John Wayne smiled from *Look* magazine, gorgeous Lana Turner beckoned to passing men from the cover of *Modern Screen*, and Captain America fought the Human Torch on a comic book. She reminded herself to ask John to purchase a girlie magazine for the Merchant Marines in training at Oheka Castle. Will had written her that the magazines were kept on a low shelf inside the stand and had to be asked for by name. *Eyeful*, or was it *Legful*? She couldn't tell. His handwriting was especially difficult to decipher in his last letter. Lizzy chuckled at her train of thought, but wondered if he had purchased said magazine. She hoped he didn't feel the need to look at a pin up since meeting her.

She stood with her back to the department store's famed windows and breathed in the crisp autumn air. The weather had turned too cool, too quickly in the season, and she was thankful she thought to wear her fur-trimmed coat, especially since she chose to take the railroad into the city. An unexpected decision on her part, but she was learning—Will needed the fuel and rubber that Jenkins would have to burn driving Father's Packard limousine into Manhattan.

Amid the passing pedestrians of shoppers, businessmen, working women, and the myriad of tourists on leave from the armed forces, she heard her name break through the hustle and bustle.

A female French accent rose, snapping her from thoughts of war, pin ups, Will, and the annoying, innate temptation to go back into Saks to purchase that darling wine-colored fedora on the mannequin.

"Lizzy? Lizzy Renner is that you, *mon ami?*"

The woman in her late twenties approached, and Lizzy recognized her immediately from two years earlier during her Grand Tour. Never one to flaunt her wealth or live ostentatiously, Bethsabee de Rothschild was dressed in a conservatively collegiate autumn box coat, beret, and plain oxford shoes.

They gently embraced and air kissed on both cheeks.

"Bethsabee! It is wonderful to see you."

"Lizzy, you look so lovely, so sophisticated."

"Thank you, and you ... look at you—*très Américain!* What are you doing in New York?"

"I am attending Columbia University to study biochemistry."

"Oh? I thought you completed your studies at the Sorbonne. Well, you simply must come for tea at Meercrest!" Lizzy regretted the words as they flew from her lips. Her conversations with Ingrid and Greta on Memorial Day came back in a flash, and she wouldn't want her friend to feel insulted by their predictable slight. She was ashamed that her eyes momentarily settled upon the brown waves flowing from the bottom of the beret. Darn if she didn't hate Ingrid at that moment for suggesting Bethsabee wore a wig.

"You are kind, but I leave shortly for London to meet with my brother. You remember, Guy, no?"

"How could I forget? Handsome, intelligent and, unfortunately, married. I do believe Esther had her designs on him. Are your parents here in New York with you?"

"*Oui*, we fled not long after your visit to Paris and just before the German invasion. Guy has since left the French Army and met us here. He now sees to family business abroad." Bethsabee leaned closer to Lizzy. "The Vichy government has stripped our family of our nationality, removed us from the register of the *Légion d'honneur*, and the Nazis have taken *everything*. Their *Einsatzstab Reichsleiter* Rosenberg has confiscated all the artwork from Château de Ferrières and hundreds of Father's thoroughbred race horses at Haras de Meautry. They have seized our bank."

"Oh my! How terrible. Does that mean you can never go back to your home?"

"Not now, not while it is unsafe for Jews. I will go back to fight with the Free French under De Gaulle with my brother. We are otherwise, like many at Columbia, refugees. When I can, I try to help bring others escaping the Nazi persecution into America."

Lizzy subconsciously gripped her purse tightly. "They stole your family's artwork and everything your family held for a century?"

"Not everything, dear Lizzy. We are alive. But gone are my favorite works of art, among them Vermeer's *Astronomer*, Pater's *La Cueillette des Roses* and *Le Musician*. They even looted sculpture, furniture—all gone, forever."

Images of Ingrid's Monet and Mother's Degas instantly flashed in Lizzy's mind's eye. She suddenly felt colder, her voice quaking slightly. "I ... had no idea, Bethsabee. I'm so sorry that everything you loved has been stolen from you and your family."

Bethsabee removed a pamphlet distributed by Columbia's Maison Français from her purse and pressed it into Lizzy's hand. "Will you consider becoming a benefactor and making a donation? The France Quand-Même office is just across the street at 30 Rockefeller Center. You can help us."

Lizzy took the pamphlet and read the title, her brain still grappling with what had happened to this sweet woman's family. *Forever France.*

"I will read it and consider donating." She distractedly thumbed through the literature, thinking it couldn't hurt to inquire about Will's family in Paris. "Bethsabee ... my sweetheart, who is a pilot in the Army, has family in Paris. He's been worried because their correspondence has ceased. Are things so bad that mail is delayed from France?"

"What is their family name?"

"DeVries. They operate a diamond business."

She shook her head, knowingly. "They are Jewish."

"No, Will is Christian. Protestant, I think."

"I know the DeVries family. They have supplied diamonds to the de Rothschilds for twenty years or more. Dutch Jews, Estella DeVries. They are most likely in hiding."

Bethsabee breathed deeply, looking out onto Fifth Avenue before turning back to her sheltered, young friend. Her hands wrenched together, fingers twisting tightly. "Or ... they have been deported to ... to ... I do not know, but some say to death camps. My cousin has written that Pétain had rounded up the Jews from Paris in July."

An unseen vice around Lizzy's throat choked her words as she shook her head. "N ... no ... that's {swallow} not them. No, they are Christian. The newspapers said nothing about Paris."

"It is true. I am sorry, my friend. July 16 at dawn, they were taken. Days later the French Gendarmes deported men, women, and children in cattle cars."

Lizzy's fingers flew to her mouth, her eyes immediately welling with tears at the horrors: death camp, cattle cars, children, DeVries. Her heart felt crushing pain, and her world suddenly spun where she stood on that busy sidewalk. *This* was Will's secret. *This* was why he knew so much about the Nazis. *This* was the cause of his anxiety. *He is Jewish.*

"Good G-d, no! That was when Will's family stopped writing." Lizzy reached out, her gloved hand gripping tightly around her friend's bicep. Panicked words flew from her mouth in a barrage, oblivious to the turning heads of passersby. "Are you sure? Are you sure, Bethsabee?! This can't be true!"

"I am sure."

"Why would they take them? Maybe Will's family is a different DeVries family."

Bethsabee gripped her friend's hand in hers. "*Peut-être*. When I arrive to London, I will make inquiries for you. Will you now consider becoming a benefactor? There are Jewish refugees in every nation, not just France." She squeezed her hand and covered it with her other one. "Sweet Lizzy, they were taken ... for the simple fact that they are Jewish."

Lizzy's lips formed a thin, tight line to keep them from trembling. *Oh the horror!* She nodded to her friend. "I will donate. I'll go now!"

"And I will write you at Meercrest if I find any information about the DeVries family, although, you may not welcome my news."

"Whatever it is, I must know."

Bethsabee squeezed Lizzy's hand once again. "You have grown so from that new debutante of 1940. It is good to see your concern, your maturity. This man, your sweetheart, you say he is not Jewish but a Christian?"

"I have *believed* him to be Christian but we never spoke of it."

"It is possible his family hides their faith. Many do. Even in America, there are those all around us who wish to persecute."

"Yes ... I am coming to learn that. Thank you, please take care of yourself, and please correspond if you can. If only just to tell me that you are safe." They kissed good-bye on each cheek, this time their lips making contact to flesh. Bethsabee departed with a wistful glance back to Lizzy.

****

Slowly, with enforced calm, Lizzy filled her lungs with the moist salted air as she walked the remaining three hundred feet approaching the *Odin*, docked in its slip on the Sound. Pulling the cashmere wool of her coat more tightly to her as the piercing morning sea breeze whipped across the knoll, blowing back her hair, she remained determined in her mission.

Due to its size, the yacht sat motionless, seemingly unaffected by blustery weather or the choppy water. Impressive and stately with its shiny hull and gleaming nameplate, Lizzy pondered the origins of its name. No matter how large the vessel, a boatman always named it after someone or something he loved. She reflected on how, as a little girl, her governess had read the Norse myths from the book *Children of Odin*—the dwarfs, the rainbow bridge, the great Thor and his All-Father Odin drinking from the Well of Wisdom. Now, as an adult, she saw the name as something quite different. With startling clarity, she realized that the reference to Odin, the chief god of Germanic tribes served as a testimony to her father's ego and hubris, proclaiming his own affluence and ancestry, a confirmation of his bombastic gobbledygook. That Odin was considered the god of war also conveyed her father's belief that he would win any conquest at all costs.

She approached the yacht as though a Valkyrie, determined to not be the one ending in a death of words and will. Lizzy blamed him for her sister running off to Europe as part of this clubmobile experiment, but she was determined to not allow her anger to rule this meeting.

Prepared to enter battle, she pulled her shoulders back, head held high. Unfortunately, as the myths explain, Valkyries take their battle dead to Valhalla, the hall of the slain ruled over by Odin, but she was a pistol and would win this forthcoming battle.

Running into Bethsabee the day before had made her stronger and more determined than she ever expected. Her only concern was seeing Will.

The teak gangplank shifted ever so slightly when she stepped aboard, and her eyes scanned the deck, then peered into the enclosed salon interior before her. Her father was seated at the table, enjoying a cigar and drinking his morning coffee; the *Staats* newspaper was spread out on the table before him, and the morning newscast was broadcast from the radio nearby. It was obvious to her how much he loved spending time on his yacht. It seemed, no matter the hour he was either here or at Greystone, rarely home spending time with her mother or, even less so, Gloria, who was running amok of late. Void of discipline, she was acting the juvie, saying wacky things—and the reports from Miss Chapin's school grew more severe with each passing month.

Renner glanced up and smiled when Lizzy stepped into the cabin through the watertight door left ajar. "Elizabeth! What a wonderful surprise. I was just thinking of you."

She laughed. "Oh, that sounds ominous."

"Not at all. I was just reflecting on how you have matured this year. You have blossomed into a lovely young woman. That unbridled spirit has tempered some. I'm proud of you."

"Oh? I rather think I am still the same Lizzy you have always loved." She twisted her lips. "I'm still as mischievous as always."

"Sit. Join me. I was just listening to the *CBS News of the World* and its propaganda. Such lies to rally the people behind this warmongering President."

"Propaganda?"

"Yes, misleading hyperbole." He rested the cigar in the ashtray on the table and leaned forward, giving her his full attention with a smile. "Anyway, tell me what brings you onto the *Odin* this morning. Your visit is quite unprecedented."

"I was wondering if you would like for me to go to Rosebriar Manor and close up the house for the year? Mother has mentioned that we won't be traveling south to winter retreat, and I know how busy you are. With Mr. Beck having been conscripted, no one is there to oversee the details."

She noted how her father examined her every movement and expression over the rim of his china cup and in response she promptly flattened her hands upon her knees to keep from fidgeting.

"Frankly, the weather has cooled too quickly for me and I'd like to warm a bit in the Florida sun. May I go, Father?"

"And how will you travel?"

"I was hoping that you could secure a private sleeping compartment, or at the very least a berth for me, aboard the *Orange Blossom Special*. I know it's last minute, but I'd like to leave as soon as possible, within the week."

"I don't believe the *Special* will begin running their all-Pullman accommodations for the winter season now that they have been pressed into troop transport. However, if that is your wish ... well, then, I am only too happy to please you. I shall telephone their president this afternoon to see if he can accommodate both legs of your trip to Sarasota."

Lizzy beamed, resisting the urge to clap her hands with childlike glee. "Really? Thank you, Father! Thank you."

He tilted his head, examining her as though she were a curious creature. "I'm impressed by your desire to embrace household affairs. It does my heart good to see your understanding of a woman's role."

"I'm keen to do it," she lied, choosing not to be baited into that discussion.

Puffing his chest slightly as though Odin himself he said, "On one condition."

The smile slowly receded from her face. "Yes?"

Renner stood and moved to turn the radio off. "I have had a request for your hand in marriage, and I would like for you to consider it during your holiday."

"Marriage? To whom?"

"George Gebhardt. I believe he would make an excellent husband to you, and he has the means to keep you in the lap of luxury you are accustomed to. His future is bright, and he hopes for a large family." With eyes narrowed, he seemed to stare her down. "Will you think on it?"

Her need to see Will outweighed the lie as it left her lips. "Yes."

She would no more consider having George Gebhardt's children (let alone marrying such a smarmy wolf) than she would a Nazi, and, in her opinion, they had merged to become one in the same.

Renner reached into his vest pocket, pulling his gold watch into his fleshy palm. Flipping open the engraved lid, he checked the time, its accuracy assured. A railroad man lived by his watch, though most couldn't boast of solid gold heirlooms. Another quick click signaled to Lizzy it was time for her to leave. Acknowledging her dismissal, she stood then dutifully presented her cheek for his kiss.

"Thank you, Daughter."

Understanding acutely his game of "you scratch my back and I'll scratch yours," she nodded then pivoted back before leaving. "May I also ask—with your and Aunt Helga's approval—if Kitty could holiday with her while I am gone? She could use a change of scenery, too. I promise not to burden anyone with the details. I will work it all out myself. Lillian has already agreed to an ambulance transport and a full time nurse from the ARC."

He waved his hand dismissively. "Yes, that all sounds fine. Finally, my disappointing daughter is making good use of her foolishness." He tsked. "Lillian should have thought more carefully on her decision to join the war effort ..."

Lizzy cut his train of thought off with a hasty, "Thank you again, Father." She opened the cabin door and exited into the cold, accidentally barreling into George Gebhardt on the opposite side of the threshold. He grabbed her upper arm to keep her from falling.

"Good Morning, Miss Renner."

"I ... um ... good morning."

"George! Come in," Renner cheerfully greeted.

She extricated herself from the man's grasp before the deliberate brush of his thumb grew bolder. "Excuse me, Mr. Gebhardt."

Nineteen

Ridin' High
October 10, 1942

T he *Orange Blossom Special* to Florida was high-class transportation, almost as luxurious as the world-renowned *20ʰ Century Limited* Pullman train to Chicago. Since 1925, the exclusive seasonal train had traveled between New York and Miami transporting affluent snowbirds to their winter retreat homes. On this trip, however, it was crowded with GIs, and in Lizzy's opinion these current passengers were even more worthy of the white glove treatment. Although the manicurists, barbers, maids, and valets were superfluous, the fine china, porters, and air-conditioned, berthed cars were all very much appreciated by the boys.

Three days prior, her father's acquiescence to telephone the President of the Seaboard Air Line Railroad had paid off. As usual, Frederick Renner's charm and railroad influence had successfully secured a Pullman private, sleeper compartments for both routes of his daughter's travel to Sarasota, Florida. Her last minute timing could not have been better since the deluxe accommodations were about to be suspended until the war ended. Officially pressed into service as troop transport before the season's southern run, this "special" accommodation was to be the *Orange Blossom*'s final first-class trip. From here on in, it was going to be used exclusively by the Office of Defense Transportation. Her return trip to Pennsylvania Station in three weeks was to be on board the *Silver Meteor*'s all-coach class.

Lizzy cringed at the thought. Train travel was her abhorrence, yet here she sat. Since meeting Ducky, she was doing a lot of things she never expected to do.

The sleek, citrus-colored, locomotive train bulleted ahead of schedule to surpass its own twenty-six hour record to the Sunshine State. Comfortably seated in the elegantly appointed Club Car, Lizzy stared out the window at the passing landscape, lost in her thoughts. Her decision to see Will had been impetuous and unplanned, but faced with Lillian's announcement and the distressing meeting with Bethsabee, she could think of nothing else but running to him. Thankfully, Aunt Helga came to the rescue allowing for Kitty's visit and Lillian had, indeed, made the arrangement for the ambulance that transported her. She could have kissed her sister when she found a nurse to stay with Kitty in New Jersey for the duration of her stay. Father was, begrudgingly, pleased with the news, but not enough to make amends with his "disappointing" ARC daughter.

It seemed as though Lizzy had only left minutes ago on the 12:50, but time, like the train had flown by during her daydreaming.

The conductor called out "Richmond, Virginia. Next stop Richmond."

Lizzy's hand pressed against her tummy to calm the wacky feeling within. Just the mere thought of seeing Ducky in a few days elicited an excitement that nothing ever had or ever could compare. She imagined his look of surprise upon her arrival at Drane Airfield then envisioned their kiss hello. That thought brought a full grin to her lips. The outfit she chose for the occasion, she hoped, would leave him awestruck.

First things first though; she would keep her promise to her father and see that everything was in good order at Rosebriar. She needed to discuss with the caretaker about readying the house to be closed for season since neither Father nor Mother would be traveling south this winter. Next order of business was to visit the OPA's local ration board to secure a B-3 gas ration card for 53 gallons of gas in order to make the long drive to Lakeland from Sarasota. Hopefully, she would be able to accomplish this near impossible feat having learned a thing or two since she began volunteering for the bookmobile. Not that she'd fib *why* she needed so much fuel, as boosting troop morale was truly essential war business, but she just might consider bandying the Renner name to get what she wanted. She'd think about Will's expected fuddy duddy objections another time.

As the train slowed, Lizzy craned her neck to see beyond the curtains. She noticed volunteers of all ages with the American Women's Volunteer

Service local canteen, waiting on the platform to greet the soldiers on board with beverages and sandwiches. She had seen this happen at other stops along the Pennsylvania Railroad: Trenton, NJ and Wilmington, DE. Not even a kiss of gratitude was spared to those boys who hung out the windows or briefly exited the train to stretch obviously more than their legs. Here, beside the Richmond information window, a four-piece band played something sounding like a patriotic march in welcome. Waving flags and bunting festooned the clapboard station house. Lizzy smiled wistfully thinking how she wished she could have seen Will off at the train station on the day of his departure at Grand Central in New York City.

The *Orange Blossom* slowed to a heaving stop and more soldiers boarded into the coach class, more women cried, and more fathers shook hands. For a brief moment, she felt guilty sitting in this luxury railcar, smelling the sweet bouquet of fresh cut flowers and baking corn bread. Families were being torn apart as men were sent off to fight in terrible conditions while she sat in her exclusive Pullman reserved for people of her society. Observing from her window she felt the paradox, removed yet connected, in more ways than most of her station would acknowledge.

Resisting the temptation to read once again the literature she acquired from the Free French office, she instead removed from her purse the letter received from Will the day just before her departure.

October 5, 1942
Dear Lizzy,

It's two or so in the morning and I couldn't sleep. I have you on my mind and well ... wanted to spend the night with you. I felt the sudden urge to talk with you and this is the closest I can get. In case I didn't tell you in my last couple of letters—I miss you, but you expected I would, didn't you? Every letter of yours brings such a smile to my heart and lips that I wish to G-d I was there in New York to hold you and laugh. I'd take you to Prospect Park or to Jones Beach, even to the movies where I could sneak a kiss up in the balcony. How does that sound? Where would you like me to take you on our third date? It's hard to believe that we've only been on two dates!

How are the bookmobile and the Victory book collection going? I am so proud of you, Lizzy. You have no idea what a difference you are making. If you can, please send me a couple of books because there isn't a library at our new location. MacDill had a swell set up, even going so far as a bowling alley and movie theatre, but not here at Drane. Rustic is hardly the word for our base life, and darn if these Floridian mosquitoes aren't even more sinister inland than by Tampa Bay. There's even a tortuous insect the locals call a "no-see-em". That's for sure! They're like invisible Kamikaze bugs and you don't know what's bit you until it's too late. It's dry, hot, and flat here, but I make it a point to fly to the base any chance I can. There's not even running water and I won't tell you about the latrine situation—crummy. Suffice it to say, I will be getting some serious payback on those Nazi fellows!

Try not to gloat too much that I am away from MacDill and its dishy nurses up at the field hospital. I am sure that the pistol in you can't help laughing at my expense. Well, you'll just have to come down here and attend to all my bug bites yourself. I may not be able to take you out in a Runabout, but my men do call me "Skipper" and I do fly something we refer to as a "ship." See, I am a boatsman after all. Didn't you say you love to fly? With the right enticement, I might be able to sneak you onboard! Oh, Pistol, you are even a bad influence to me all the way from Long Island! See what you do to me. You make me dizzy, Lizzy.

How are things at home, baby? Is your father talking to Lillian yet and what exactly are you implying about the literature you found in Ingrid's closet? I understand your new found commitment to the war effort and not wanting "Loose Lips to Sink Ships," but forgive me for not being able to read between your lines. If I can, on my next flight to MacDill, I'll try to telephone you so we can discuss this.

Hopefully, this afternoon my crew and I will be able to listen to the World Series in the mess hall. There's an old radio in there that seems to get pretty swell reception. Of course, I'm disappointed that the Dodgers aren't playing, but I'll have to settle for the Bronx Bombers. My navigator Rocco is a Bronxite, so he's pretty gassed and hoping the Yankees can turn this around tonight. You and I have never discussed baseball and given your love of sports, I wonder if you listen to the game at all. I would love to take you to Ebbets Field in Brooklyn!

I received a letter from Louie. He's heavily engaged in fighting, and I hardly recognized his handwriting. Although he did make a joke about how it *compared to mine, so at least I know he's trying to hold onto his humor. He misses home and Lillian, even mentioning her four or five times in his short letter. He writes me they plan on getting hitched when the war is over. I'm happy for them, and I think that if the love they share and the promise of the future keeps him going through the rough times, well ... that's the way it should be. Which reminds me ... one of the snapshots you sent me is tacked on my bomber's dashboard above the altimeter (determines altitude) and, baby, I'm flying on cloud nine when you're staring back at me. You're my good luck charm.*

Well, I better sign off and try to get some sleep before Reveille. That's only about an hour from now and then I'm back up in my Marauder for practice missions.
With love,
Will

Lizzy didn't hear the train's whistle blow, or the conductor's announcement of "All Aboard," and before she realized, the *Orange Blossom* was underway again. She folded the letter and placed it in the Agatha Christie novel beside her, nearly bursting in anticipation of seeing Will. As fast as the train traveled, it wasn't fast enough! With every letter, she discovered something new to love about him. Baseball! Not to mention his unspoken love for her made her near giddy like a schoolgirl. *Oh, yes, Ducky, you are in love with me and I know it.* At that moment, she chose not to think of all the unpleasantries: his omission of news about his family in Paris, Bethsabee's supposition about them, her father's suggestion of a marriage between her and Gebhardt, and Ingrid's propaganda literature. The purpose of this trip was to escape the distress of the war and life at Meercrest and fly into the arms of love.

The sound of the railcar's passenger door opening with a tight whoosh caused her to look up. Two GIs entered the First Class Pullman. Around her, several businessmen and a well-dressed middle aged woman stared aghast from their tables. A waiter asked the men to exit back into the accommodations reserved for troop transport.

"That's okay. The soldiers are my guests," Lizzy said with blatant mischief sparkling in her eyes. She twisted her mouth when she stared back at the onlookers then cocked a sculptured eyebrow waiting for the challenge that surprisingly didn't come.

Lizzy turned her attention to the soldiers. She didn't recognize the insignia patch below their shoulders. Not that it mattered—she was all too happy to spoil them and pointed to the soft club chairs beside her. "Won't you gentlemen join me?"

"Holy Mackerel! Yeah, sure."

They took the vacant seats and removed their garrison caps, introducing themselves with appreciation not only for the opportunity to enjoy a drink in such luxury but also with a leggy dame.

One of the soldiers lit a cigarette followed quickly by the waiter's arrival to the table for admonishment, but Lizzy's deliberate charming smile kept him from asking the young man to smoke in the domed observation car. She almost wanted to laugh aloud, unsure whom she was more similar to—her father with his manipulative charm or Lillian in her outspoken non-conformity. Together those disparate personality traits made a splendid combination when a woman set herself on a path of defiance.

"Miss Renner, what are you and your guests drinking from the bar this afternoon?" the white-jacketed waiter asked.

She shrugged. "I don't know. What do you say to three Coca-Colas, boys?"

"Sounds great," agreed Private Archibald Snipes from Kansas.

Lizzy lit a cigarette as well. "Where are you fellows headed? Bomber training?"

"No, Miss. Hank and I are headed to train with the 82nd Airborne in North Carolina. We're All Americans."

"How exciting. Do you fly planes?"

"Some do, but they're glider planes. We're not with the Air Corps. We're infantry paratroopers." Archie, the younger of the two, beamed with obvious excitement. "We jump *from* planes!"

She leaned forward, intrigued beyond measure. "Really? You *jump* from planes? Are you scared?"

Hank laughed. "Not at all. I love getting up there, listening to the drone of the plane then just letting myself go above the drop zone."

She clapped with excitement. "I positively love to fly! I own a Zephyr and a Hydroplane Runabout, and I just love to feel the wind blow, the speed, the feeling of soaring uninhibited. Oh, I'm so envious that you can jump from an airplane. What type of plane? How high up are you? Does it hurt when you land? It sounds positively lulu!"

"Ah, the details ... can't tell ya' Miss, but it is definitely ... *lulu.*"

Lizzy pointed to Hank's garrison cap insignia. "That's a parachute, isn't it?"

"A hard earned Parachutist Badge."

Upon the white collar of her dress, Lizzy toyed with Will's cadet pilot pin, given to him in flight school but since replaced by his silver wings. She could still vividly remember his gentle kiss that followed his bestowing that special gift to her before their separation at the Glen Cove train station in July.

"My sweetheart flies in a B-26 Marauder. I'm headed to see him."

Her pride was evident, and both men looked at each other. That ship was getting quite a reputation, which spread like wildfire through the Army.

"What was that look for?" she asked, the smile slowly receding from her face, a bad feeling suddenly shrouding her.

Hank fiddled with his crystal glass. "Nothing really ... it's just there's a saying. 'One a day into Tampa Bay.' They can't keep those Widowma ... um ... planes in the sky and no one wants to fly them. Given a choice of bombers, everyone is opting for the Fortress or the B-25 rolling off the line after that Doolittle Raid over Tokyo." Clearing his throat, he looked to his friend beside him before speaking again. "So, your fellow is a pilot?"

"Yes." A different type of anticipation filled her. Dread and fear eclipsed joyful exuberance. Her voice sounded distracted as she continued to rub the propeller wings between her index finger and thumb uneasily. "He loves to fly, too."

Archie smiled thoughtfully and elbowed his friend. "Don't worry, Miss Renner. I'm sure he'll be just swell. We never should have said anything."

"No, I'm glad you did. I suppose he just didn't want to worry me. He's considerate like that."

"I'm sure of it. Heck, my mother thinks I'm part of a ground crew refueling transport planes. There's no way I'm going to tell her I'm a paratrooper. She would get on the next train from Wichita to box my ears."

When Lizzy turned to look out the window, Hank promptly changed the topic to something he felt sure would bring back that effervescence in her fine eyes and a smile upon those quite alluring lips of hers. He was rewarded with both when he said, "Let me tell you what I feel up in the air. The minute I hear from the Jump Master, 'Stand up' and I hook myself to the static line ..."

****

Lizzy swore she would never forget October 14, 1942 because everything about the day became an extraordinary experience from the moment she left the picturesque beauty of Rosebriar Manor along Sarasota Bay. Like the North Shore of Long Island, this area was also referred to as the Gold Coast, and it held its appeal for winter vacationers as well as year-round residents. From ostentatious, Spanish-style and Mediterranean revival homes to the lavish golf and country club, like Palm Beach and Winter Park, Sarasota was the place to be seen and enjoy society life.

Having departed Rosebriar in the early morning for the seventy-mile drive north to Drane Airfield in Lakeland, every stop she made in her father's 1938 convertible Horch was a new adventure. She had never taken such a long drive before, particularly in his 855 Spezial Roadster, as it was garaged year round at Rosebriar. What a car! What a grand tour she was on!

In her excitement to see Will, she could have sped through every sleepy agriculture town along the rural routes of State Roads 62 and 37. They all held fascination for her and, several times, she couldn't help pulling over to the side of the road and breathe in the sweet country air, which smelled so different from the sea. During one stop, she unfolded the large Florida state map on the hood of the car, looked around, walked back to the cockpit of the car, and snapped off the radio—just so she could enjoy the peaceful silence of Central Florida. Spanish moss clung to the trees and hung over the dirt road; morning sun shone through the branches and she tilted her head up to catch the beams of light on her face. She chuckled at how she must look, sticking out like a sore thumb in the cattle ranching, farming, and active phosphorous mining communities along Bone Valley and the Peace River.

She had never seen a mining town before, but it was clear that the war had caused an increase in activity necessitating a complex series of detours through far-flung back roads of dry, flat land. Security had been ramped up around the vital mines and railroad transport after the widely reported news of saboteurs in America. It seemed as though the landings of those Bundist saboteurs at Ponte Vedra and Amagansett beaches had certainly shaken America awake.

Small, quiet towns, such as Pierce welcomed her when she pulled into the filling station for gasoline. The blue-overalled attendant didn't even bat an eye when she procured her hard-won B-3 gas ration booklet from her purse, but he certainly raised the brim of his cap when she slid out of the automobile to stretch her legs.

The man outright stared, and she wondered if her stylish apparel had caught his eye. His gaze was almost as intense as Will's had been that day at Bar Beach. Feeling confident that she had chosen just the right outfit for Will's appreciation, she smiled as she removed a Hires Root Beer from the red soda cooler. Her sweetheart was going to go lulu over the dress.

"Need a hand with that, Miss?"

"No thank you." She adeptly popped the top at the bottle opener attached to the gas pump shelter.

The station attendant watched her perfectly lined, red lips surround the bottle mouth as she took a long cooling draft. He couldn't help but to stare with each pass of his squeegee across the windshield. "Hot one today, ain't it?"

Lizzy stood just beyond the two gas pumps, looking past the Horch at the empty field on the other side of the road. She pressed the cold bottle against the pulse in her neck. "It feels nice. The weather has turned so cool up north, so this is a swell escape. Why I hardly feel the heat at all."

She recognized the sound of the cicadas in the pine trees behind her. It seemed strange since summer was long gone and cicadas were only seasonal insects in New York.

"At least the humidity is gone. Where up north are you from?"

"Long Island? Do you know of it?"

"Can't says I do. I got a cousin in Philadelphia, though. Went up there to work in the Navy Yard, building ships."

A tiny bug bit her, and she glanced down at her arm. The culprit was gone. It must have been one of those invisible Kamikazes Will mentioned. "I get to Philadelphia on occasion. The Vesper Boat Club organizes the most incredible sculling regattas along Boathouse Row. Why, they even boast an Olympian!"

He didn't seem impressed, and she chastised herself for that Renner magniloquence, which so easily surfaced with her boating enthusiasm. She figured the man didn't know what sculling was.

"Where ya' headin'?" he asked.

"Drane Airfield."

He plunged the squeegee back into the tin bucket beside the pump. "That's only eighteen or so more miles. Follow this road up to old Ewell's farm in Mulberry then make a left onto the dirt road. You'll see the phosphorous dump, maybe even a watermelon stand and if not, you can't miss those noisy bombers comin' and goin'."

Lizzy beamed. "That sounds like the place." She walked around the vehicle as he removed the gas nozzle from the Roadster.

"Lucky fellow."

"How did you know?"

"Miss, we don't see many high-class cookies like you in this here parts now that Mulberry's own Frances Langford left for Tinseltown. She's with that Bob Hope, doin' her bit for the boys with the U.S.O. Although I hear she's back in town."

"She's the one on the *Pepsodent Show* and in that new James Cagney movie, right?"

"Yuppers. Apart from her and the workers at the mine, not much comes through here. There's one reason, and one reason only, that you're headed to the airfield and that's to see your sweetheart. Am I right?"

"You're right, sir. I just hope he's happy to see me."

Lizzy inserted the key and pushed another button, bringing the smooth, yet powerful German eight-cylinder engine to life. The purr barely sounded, but Charlie Barnett's "Skyliner" from the radio disturbed the quiet, rural air.

"Well if he ain't happy to see you, you just come back down here, 'cause you're a sight for these ole cracker's eyes."

She smiled kindly. "How much for the gas?"

The attendant took out his rag and polished the sleek grill of the car. "That'll be $3.18. No charge for the root beer. Say, you better remember to blackout your headlights."

"Oh, I will! Don't you worry."

Lizzy paid the man and just before she put the car in gear, he ran his hand over the long hood. "What kind an automobile is this? I ain't seen nothing like it. Never heard of no Horch."

"It's ... German." As the nationality came out of her mouth, she realized her error and with a start remembered how her father had made special arrangements during her Grand Tour for its delivery back to New York. One of only five manufactured, he had boasted it was specially commissioned for its previous owner, a "government official." A chill went up Lizzy's spine at that recollection. Vaguely, she remembered his declaration that the government official was with or was the *Jagdfliegerführer*. She'd have to ask Will what the *Jagdfliegerführer* was. He'd know.

She realized her own expression had turned pensive as, simultaneously, the smile died upon Mr. Southern Hospitality's lips when he heard the word "German."

"Have a nice day, Miss," was all he replied with a rather curt wave.

Twenty

Pistol Packin' Mama
October 14, 1942

A sudden rush of nerves flared as the Horch Spezial Roadster pulled up beside the small, windowed guardhouse. With music blaring, she read the large sign hanging above her: Lakeland Army Airfield, #2 Drane Field.

Lizzy turned down the distracting volume on the radio and removed her sunglasses, taking in the lone uniformed guard with an imposing black MP armband wrapped prominently around his bicep. She smiled nervously at the Military Policeman standing sentry as the gate security. He greeted her with a wary appraisal that, she thought, contained something akin to a hint of recognition.

A thunderous roar in the near distance garnered her attention from the approaching GI, and with hands clutched to the top of the convertible's windshield, she rose slightly in her seat. Her line of vision followed a bomber's take off upward into the clear blue sky, rising like an American eagle, and her limbs reacted accordingly, even in the scorching sun— transforming to duck flesh.

"Can I help you, Miss?" _Wowza!_

"Yes, sir. I'm here to visit Lieutenant William Martel. He's a pilot with the 322nd Bombardment Group."

"This is a restricted military base, Miss. Only authorized personnel allowed. I'm sorry."

She begged audaciously, grasping the top edge of the door and leaning forward. "Oh, please. I've come so far. I've driven all morning, and shame-lessly used more gas then I have since the ration began."

Sergeant O'Malley frowned during closer inspection of that pert nose and captivating smile. "Er ... do *I* know you?" *And if I don't I would love to.*

"No, I've never met any of William's Air Corps buddies, but you seem very nice, very ... kind. The type of man who would be sympathetic to a girl's plight." She gave him a coy smile, tilting her head flirtatiously, looking up through her lashes and the brim of her hat.

"Wait here, Miss. Who shall I say is visiting?"

"Lizzy Renner."

Oh yeah, he recognized her, but he took a double take anyway. "Lizzy you said?"

She nodded, and he promptly stepped into the guard house, picking up the telephone to call his CO.

Lizzy couldn't overhear the conversation, but she couldn't help noticing how the MP continually glanced back to her while talking in hushed tones into the receiver. Impatiently, she gripped the steering wheel trying to look as calm and alluring as she could. She so wanted to surprise Will.

"Yes, sir, I'm not mistaken, No, sir. Hot dang! ... Sorry, sir. ... Yes, it's Lizzy. Should I send her through? ... What? You'll meet her personally? ... Yes, sir. I'll tell her, and I'll get the Tower Officer on the horn to find out Lieutenant Martel's ETA ... Yes, sir."

Lizzy heard the phone settle on the cradle before he came out the door with a clipboard and a visitor identification pass. "You'll have to wear this, but I wouldn't want you to ruin your pretty dress, Miss. The lieutenant will be happy to see you I bet. Heck, I think all the men will."

She beamed. "So, I can go in? Thank you!"

He leaned toward her, pointing his finger with an outstretched arm. "Just take this road down to the base's Service Member Club. You can't miss it. It's the only building completed at this time. After you park at the club, Captain Carter of the 451st Bomb Squadron will meet you there and escort you to the flight line to await the lieutenant's landing."

"The flight line?"

"Yeah, I know, it's quite unprecedented, but you're somewhat of a celebrity around here."

"How can I be a celebrity? I've never been here before and my family is in railroads, not aviation."

The sergeant playfully smiled. "Oh, you've been here ... and affiliated with aviation ... trust me." He laughed, shook his head and waved her on

Lizzy raised her arm in the air then suddenly gassed the Horch, kicking up dirt in her wake. The sudden gust of wind blew the brim of her hat, but thankfully, it was secured in place by her hatpins. She laughed that devilish laugh of hers, unknowingly elevating him in rank. "Thank you, Officer! Woo hoo!"

The MP watched her departure and shook his head again with a grin. *Yes, she is quite a pistol.* "Martel, you're one lucky bastard."

Lizzy parked the sports car beside the building where a uniformed man stood waving and smiling to her as though greeting an old friend. Above him, a large sign hung flapping in the breeze above the doors. U.S.O Dance Tonight.

Hmm ... restricted ... only authorized personnel, huh? My eye!

She couldn't help notice how the officer seemed awestruck watching her exit the sports car, yet his enthused greeting with an unexpected, affable handshake implied a familiarity. For a second, she expected him to kiss her gloved hand, and briefly wondered if he had seen one of the bathing suit snapshots she had sent to Will.

"Miss Renner, welcome to Drane. I'm Captain Jim Carter, and I'll be escorting you to the hanger area to await the lieutenant's arrival at the flight line."

"It's nice to meet you, Captain." She almost squealed in delight. "I'm so excited to be here. Thank you for taking the time."

He stared at her, locking his brown eyes with hers. "Miss, it's really swell to finally meet Lieutenant Martel's girl."

Three GIs passed by giving her the once over accompanied by approving wolf whistles as though they hadn't seen a girl in months. One of the young men, dressed in coveralls and a ball cap styled hat, elbowed another and all three stared even harder. She thought she heard "pistol" mentioned but was sure she was mistaken, chalking it up to her anxiety at seeing Ducky after these many weeks apart.

"I have to admit, I'm really quite surprised by the reception, Captain. The soldier at the guard house mentioned that for some strange reason you boys consider me a celebrity around here." She gave him a sideways glance and a flirtatious smile. "Why is that?"

Carter chuckled. "You *are* a celebrity Miss Renner, but loose lips sink ships, they say. Shall we climb into Willy the jeep over there and take a spin to greet your flier in that ship of his?" A finger pointed to a green utility vehicle on the other side of the building.

"That sounds just swell! Will the lieutenant be away very long?"

"He's out on a practice mission right now with an ETA of 13:25—almost one thirty, in ten minutes."

Together, they walked to the ubiquitous transport. It's big, five-point star upon the hood made her smile. Apparently, here she would look like an even bigger fish out of water. Dressed to the sophisticated nines, she wore a white, yellow, and green floral dress with a matching purse of the same fabric, and she was about to imminently surprise Will, enthroned upon a military vehicle. A year ago, she might have frowned, but not today, and probably not ever again. The whole experience was simply creamy!

With a smirk, the captain kept looking over to her as she climbed into the jeep and settled in, his eyes raking up her stocking-clad legs. "Will you be staying in the area, Miss Renner?"

"Yes, for the next two nights I'll be staying at the Hotel Lakeland Terrace then head on back down to Sarasota where my family has a winter home."

"The Lakeland Terrace is some swanky digs."

"It's not the Breakers in Palm Beach or the Don CeSar Hotel on St. Pete Beach, but it'll do."

"Well, you couldn't have stayed at the Pink Palace even if you wanted to. The Army has conscripted it for convalescent rehabilitation for the AAF. Plenty of sun and sand, but I doubt any dancing for those fellas. Perhaps you'll be attending tonight's festivities? We have a whole bunch of boys sorely in need of dancing."

"If I'm invited by William then I wouldn't miss it for the world."

The vehicle sped down the unpaved roads passing makeshift, tarpaper roofed barracks, and a couple of fire trucks parked at the side. Two GIs waved to her as though they, too, knew her. She waved back, wondering, once again, if Will had shared her picture with the boys. As "Willy" drew closer to the tower, the roar of bomber planes grew louder. Lizzy leaned forward, gripping the top edge of the windshield since it was apparent that the captain loved to hotrod around the base with the same speed that she did on Long Island in her Zephyr. She highly approved, grinning widely at the rush as the butterflies beat eight to the bar in boogie rhythm inside her. Will was only minutes away.

They arrived onto a large airfield bordering a narrow taxiing path and landing strip where waves of heat seemed to cling to the surface of the reinforced concrete. Two arched hangers, various military maintenance vehicles, and at least six of the bombers Will wrote her about comprised a hive of activity. Marauders sat parked wing-to-wing, powerful and impressive, as ground crew echelon of technicians and maintenance repaired, refueled, and rechecked every component of these crafts destined to carry men into war. Beside it all, an air control tower, the nerve center of directives and radio communication, overlooked the airfield.

Welcome and unexpected as a gentle breeze, a zephyr in and of herself, Lizzy blew into the sea of army olive-drab with her vibrant light and bright spirit, shining like the sun. In awe of her surroundings, all she could say was "Wow!" at the dedicated industry of the Army Air Forces and the knowledge that her dreamboat was a part of it. Yes, Herbert Robertsen was correct— the power in the air was going to win this war.

"Impressive, isn't it? Once farmers, clerks, or students, now they're bombardiers, navigators, and mechanics. They've been transformed into a cohesive fighting unit. The B-26 is a magnificent bird now that we know how to fly her properly, but she takes muscle and skill." He stopped the jeep parallel to where he anticipated the lieutenant's plane to park in its apron. "And Lieutenant Martel is one of the Marauder Men's finest pilots, seamlessly adapting to that twin engine immediately. Why, he makes that baby purr."

The captain chuckled, now fully understanding why Martel's *particular* aircraft responded in the way she did to his every touch. Yes, if command lets him, that baby will go with Lucky Bastard Martel to Europe and see him through this war. Unless of course, he gets shot down by this gorgeous dame first.

The scent of hot metal and high-octane fuel hung in the air, and Lizzy's eyes scanned the imposing bomber parked beside her. "The B-26's nickname 'Widowmaker'... is that why they say 'one a day into Tampa Bay'?"

"Well ... yes, but don't let that worry you. Martel is quite the Mustard in the cockpit and his aircraft goes by another name."

Her eyes drew upward where she spotted approaching planes flying in formation in the distance.

When she climbed out of the jeep one leg after the other, it seemed every man around her froze in place, several whistled, but most just stopped and stared, blatantly distracted from the vital business of inspections and readying their assigned Marauders for flight.

She chortled when she observed, "Say, you boys don't see many women around here, do you?"

Carter looked to the sky as the bombers took their landing positions, the first in line making its rapid descent. "Here's the lieutenant now."

Lizzy shielded the sun from her eyes as she watched Will drawing nearer by the second. She was no longer frightened by the alarming appellation everyone seemed to have given these bombers. Confidence in him abounded in her, admiration escalating as she watched how her flyboy landed his ship, appeared to drop from the cloudless sky at a fast yet controlled, steep angle. The only nerves she felt were those of anticipation, excitement, and the sudden insecurity that he might not be happy with her surprise arrival. Although, she simply adored surprises she hadn't considered that his characteristic reticence might hold his excitement at bay, the kind of excitement *she herself* had always felt whenever bolted from the blue.

When his front wheel finally touched down, she was near bubbling over, almost bouncing in her green platform shoes. She was so proud! It wasn't the Florida sun beating down on her causing the flush to her cheeks or the moisture building on her palms inside her cotton gloves, it was the mere fact that love was a spectacular, heated feeling, and it washed over her.

On the runway, Will sighed in relief at the smooth landing. It seemed as though he always held his breath even though he knew his ship like the back of his hand. He supposed that once he was in the thick of it, getting pounded by flak, his apprehension at every landing would subside.

"Tower says to taxi directly to the flight line," McCarthy directed. "Seems you have a ... a *surprise* waiting at the apron."

He had an impish grin upon his face, one Will had grown accustomed to observing these three months but still couldn't discern the mischief behind. The second lieutenant was quite a rabble-rouser.

Will tried to read his co-pilot's expression. "Did I mention how much I hate surprises? It better not be the major telling me we're going out for anti-submarine patrol tonight."

"No, I don't think so. We've got that U.S.O dance, and I'm hoping for a kiss from that Hollywood cookie, Frances Langford."

"No, *you* have that U.S.O dance to attend. Not me."

"Yeah, that's right, You have a letter to write to your sweetheart. Doubt you'll be doin' that."

"Oh yes I will. Lucky Bastard Martel, isn't that what the Squadron calls me?"

As the Marauder's tricycle wheels eased into a turn, taxiing at a slow five miles per hour, Will had a clear line of vision down to his aircraft's apron at the end of the six bombers sitting screwdriver ready for their next flight. Vivid, amidst the olive-clad bodies crowding the flight line, an ethereal white dress billowed brightly in the light breeze. The plane rolled closer, and she came into detail, right down to those gorgeous gams of hers.

Will's heart hammered against his chest with the dawning awareness. "Ho—ly—Shit!"

McCarthy grinned. "It's her isn't it? Lizzy?"

The bombardier in the nose stuck his head up the tunnel between the copilot's legs. "Is that who I think it is at the hangar line?" He whistled. "Yowza! Come to daddy!"

Rocco the navigator unlatched his seat belts to come forward from his compartment. He climbed into the tight cockpit, looking out the window between his skipper and co-pilot. "Pistol's here? Where? I gotta see her!" With his hands, he traced the outline of her curves and whistled, too.

Will elbowed him in the gut. "Calm down and hands off."

The dorsal turret gunner spoke over the radio. "Hot damn, that *is* Lizzy. I'd know those legs anywhere!"

Finally, the last crew member craned his head to see her from his position at the waist gun window, practically howling through the ship's radio, "Martel, you lucky bastard. She's a dish!"

Suddenly, all the radio chatter stopped and six men sat mesmerized by the vision grinning mischievously, waiting for one man only.

Will wanted to laugh aloud, but he was utterly blown over, completely shell shocked. Lizzy was breathtaking—and here—for him. No doubt, he was the envy of the entire squadron.

The aircraft stopped just short of its destination, and he engaged the parking brake. What seemed like forever was only the necessary two minutes when he was finally able to cut the engine and shut off all the switches on the dash. The ground crew rushed forward, and the propellers drew to a slow wind down.

He slid his pilot window open and stared down at his girl through Ray Bans, removing his radio headgear. The stirrings of pure love created the smile he gave her as she held his admiring gaze, biting her lip to keep from grinning. He could tell that his ball of fire was ready to explode—and so was he. With her, he was a different man altogether; she did that to him.

She placed a hand beside her mouth and called up above the slowing hum of the propellers, "What's cookin', Lieutenant?"

He chuckled. "Chicken. Do you wanna neck?"

McCarthy slapped his shoulder. "Go get her, you wolf."

The second the propellers came to a complete halt, Will anxiously unhooked his seat belts, disregarded all his post-flight protocols, and quickly descended the stairs of the nose wheel well.

When he re-appeared through the bottom of the Marauder, the impressive image of him wearing his flight uniform leather jacket and life preserver caused her hand to rest upon her heart until he took a step toward her, all dimples.

Everyone watched as the lieutenant's girl ran into his arms with a squeal and laughter that had each and every hot-blooded male wishing *he* was *her* guy.

She crashed into Will, and he swept her into his arms, lifting her at the waist and spinning her around. Holding onto her tightly, he ignored the rubber Mae West draped around his neck. Lizzy's fresh, captivating jasmine scent and the passionate, soft feel of his girl pressed against him replaced the surreal surroundings of war, steel, and the smell of aviation fuel. Her presence consumed every single one of his senses.

Overcome with emotion, he ignored the whistles and hoots of the men around them and stopped his spinning. He was dizzy already by just her presence. Lizzy's feet dropped to the makeshift tarmac, and she gazed into his eyes with that green sparkle of energy he missed so much. Her breath was as ragged as his, her smile as glorious.

Soft lips met her eager, plump ones in a kiss that tenderly lingered with sweet pliable caresses. Their mouths came together, taking and tasting in their reunion. Decorum, modesty, and the on-looking 451st Bomb Squadron were completely obliterated.

Lizzy reveled in the smoothness of his cheek brushing against hers and nearly swooned from the intoxicating sensation of his lips and the waft of his clean Barbasol fragrance.

Suddenly, every care they both felt burdened with had washed away in their embrace. Both felt safe, understood, and protected by something so pure that it could conquer all their demons. True destined love did that.

When their lips separated, she was breathless and slightly unsteady on her feet but firmly held in place by his arm around her waist. "Hi Ducky."

"Hi Pistol."

"Are you happy I'm here?"

He kissed her again, a small whisper upon her mouth to keep her from biting her bottom lip. "Isn't it obvious? I'm over the moon, baby."

He looked over her shoulder as though eagerly searching for something in particular. "Did you bring me a book in your library on wheels?"

"Oh, you!"

Lizzy finally noticed all the men watching their reunion, and she giggled with uncharacteristic embarrassment. "You're far from the fuddy duddy who left Brooklyn."

"Don't be so sure. It's only when I'm around you that I get wacky, even wolfish. G-d, I missed you."

"I couldn't stay away. I missed you, too and with your birthday in a few weeks ..."

Will kissed her again, deeper this time unable to control the swell in his chest.

She smoothed her white glove up his shoulder to his cheek and their lips parted reluctantly. With a suspicious grin she asked, "Will, why do all the men seem to know me? Did you show everyone that snapshot of me you placed above the altimeter?"

Taking her hand in his, he thread their fingers tightly together so that one couldn't discern an iota of separation between the two—they were one. The smirk upon his mouth was almost on par with Louie's shit-eating grin. It certainly was as naughty.

He led her to the opposite side of his bird where his aircrew stood assembled awaiting her arrival and the eagerly anticipated introduction to themselves and her much admired namesake.

The proud skipper pointed to the nose of the plane, "Lizzy Renner meet your larger, faster ship—my beautiful good luck charm."

"Oh. My. Goodness!" She playfully swatted his arm at the sight before her.

Painted upon the grey steel was her image from Bar Beach: two-piece, white swimsuit, flower in hair, and long legs draped over the side of a bomb. Beside her shoulder read, "Pistol Packin' Lizzy."

She jumped into his arms with glee. "You made me famous! I love it!"

Twenty-One

Melody of Love
October 14, 1942

Lizzy had packed her midnight blue taffeta dress, envisioning an intimate dinner at Don Quixote's Restaurant followed by romantic dancing on its rooftop. Pearls and the lustrous silk seemed just the ticket, but when Ducky invited her to the U.S.O. dance at the Service Member's Club featuring Frances Langford, how could she resist accepting? With no time to shop, the dress would have to do. He was inviting her into his world and that made her so proud.

She stole several stealthy peeks of Will, enjoying how he looked at her with that adorable grin of his. It was clear how happy he was that she was here. Since arriving at the hotel lobby to escort her, his compliments hadn't ceased, and she couldn't help delighting that he loved the dress. Such a simple thing but one she had felt a tinge insecure about, wanting to have worn a more vibrant color of silk satin or crepe de chine. However, when he moved his hand from behind his back to give her another white gardenia, all insecurity vanished. It was the perfect complement, just the touch her dress required and she promptly swept it into her hair.

On his arm, her wide eyes took in the dance hall as they entered and she couldn't help being impressed. In her newly infused patriotic zeal, the overall splendor was as wondrous as her high society debut ball at the Waldorf Astoria two years prior. Being there with Will made her giddy inside and she audibly chuckled, thinking how her mother's high-pitch, infantile voice would state it unrefined, then hiccup before going on about how a Renner's lips should never touch anything but crystal, silver, and Meissen porcelain.

The stark, utilitarian building on the airfield had been transformed by an explosion of patriotic bunting and flags. Twinkling lights hung over the dance floor providing a canopy of glittering, magical romance. The stage was decorated with a huge American flag backdrop behind the musicians' stands, each emblazoned with the letter *S*. The Skyliners were the "in-house" twelve-piece band of the 322nd.

The local Lakeland U.S.O. had done a wonderful job seeing to the décor and amenities for the 200 boys. Only half as many girls, accompanied by several individual or group chaperones, arrived via shuttle buses. Female members of the local Kiwanis Club also turned out for the event, as did many young ladies in their senior year from Miss Langford's alma mater, Lakeland High School. The Hollywood starlet's U.S.O. performance was a highlight for almost all, but not Lizzy—that highlight was spending precious time with her flyboy before he would be leaving for Europe.

Already in full swing when they arrived, the band jumped and jived to "American Patrol," the floor crowded with olive-clad servicemen, some even dancing with each other. She took in the energized scene, then met Will's gaze, and she fought against the overpowering urge to kiss him. This place, this moment with this man was the best, most perfect moment of her entire life. It seemed that since meeting him, she had several of those. Each and every moment with him had been "the most" perfect until surpassed by the next: their first dance at Meercrest, the war parade, their first kiss on the carousel, and their second date on the Sound.

Will leaned down to her as they walked toward the dance floor. He looked so handsome in his dress uniform and smelled so good.

"Would you like to dance or would you like a drink first?" he asked.

"Can we sit and just talk for a little while? We've hardly had any time together, and I'm keen on telling you all about my trip down. I have so much to share."

"My thoughts exactly. Why don't you grab that table over there, and I'll get us a couple of drinks."

She nodded, and he boldly ran his index finger down her cheek.

A cozy deuce table beckoned her in the corner of the hall, and with Will hardly gone to the bar for mere minutes, two of the PPL's ground crew seized the opportunity to approach its namesake. "Lizzy, is that you?"

She beamed and giggled now that she was in on the joke. "It is, boys. Are you glad to see me in person?"

Suave in manner, the blond soldier slid out the chair reserved for Will and took her hand in his across the table. "Pistol, I feel like I've known you for years. I work on your body every day and spend every night beneath your magnificent fuselage."

"Well, *Joe* ... as charming as you are, there is only one man allowed to call me Pistol, but you can call me Lizzy."

"Lucky Bas ... um ... Martel is one lucky devil, but since he's over there and I'm over here, how about a dance—or I'll settle for a kiss from those pretty, red lips of yours."

She saucily addressed the other uniformed young man. "Is he always such a wolf?"

"Worse. He's tame tonight. Either that or trying to make an impression."

"Oh, he's making an impression all right."

Lizzy patted the forward GI's hand. "Although you appear to be quite a swell hoofer, I have to decline. Sorry, Wolfie, but thank you. You see, all my dances are reserved for the lieutenant, as are every single one of my kisses. Of course, *he's* such a gentleman he would never make such overt passes at me."

From the bar, Will watched as the PPL's mechanics tried to work his girl in his absence. He was amused by everyone's eagerness to meet her and acknowledged that he had only himself to blame for it, but damn if he wasn't so proud. As proud as he felt when McCarthy finished painting her likeness on the side of their war bird. In fact, at the time, he felt so uncharacteristically brazen he thought to borrow Rocco's Kodak and take a snapshot to send to Lizzy's old man, Herr Renner, with a note: "Tell your buddies in the Luftwaffe they're shooting at *your* daughter, *my* lucky charm. Oh, and by the way, *vater*, you can kiss my ass. *Mazel Tov!*"

Will navigated the crowded room with two cups of punch until finally he stood before the two corporals.

"Beat it, fellas."

"Sorry, Lieutenant, but rules of the U.S.O. are that no girl can sit out when there are soldiers just itchin' for a dance. She's outnumbered and I'm itchin'," Wolfie grinned mischievously.

"That kind of itching is gonna keep you stateside in the infirmary." Will puffed his chest slightly and looked down at Lizzy's twisting mouth. He smirked seeing how she was enjoying this, testing his jealousy and challenging him in playful response to his teasing about the nurses. "How about you give us a little time together first, then if Miss Renner is willing, you can step all over her feet. I warn you though, she's likely to make you look like a dud out there. She's quite a *ducky shincracker*."

He winked at her and she beamed, nodding in agreement at his affectionate usage of the slang that began it all.

One of the men exclaimed, "Hot damn!" and the other quickly vacated Will's seat with a sweeping flourish to his arm. The band changed their tune and both men took to the dance floor partnered with each other for a fast Lindy Hop.

"So where were we, beautiful?" Will asked, taking the empty seat and sliding it closer to her, breathing in the intoxicating scent of the gardenia in her hair.

"You were just about to tell me how your mosquito bites are doing."

"In need of care." He picked up her hand and examined the red bite upon her forearm. "As are you."

"Darned Kamikaze. It happened in a little town called Pierce. Who knew the Japanese would find such a podunk place."

Will deposited a tiny kiss to the offending welt.

"My, my, Ducky. You have become terribly sentimental since your arrival to Florida, all this public affection. What will your C.Os say?"

"They're jealous, and I'm only sappy today because my girl used gallons of vital fuel and most likely sped, like the hellion she is behind the wheel, to see me. I'm flattered by the total disregard of your newfound patriotism. Tell me, did you wipe out any armadillos in your wake?"

"Ha. Ha. I'll have you know that I took a *leisurely* drive through Central Florida and my fuel gauge barely budged a bit after I re-filled it.

He chuckled. "And where was that?"

"Eighteen miles from the airfield in that podunk town."

"Pistol, Pistol, Pistol. You're a naughty girl."

"I know. It's what you love most about me."

He tapped her nose. "Who said love? I didn't say love. Loose lips sink ships, you know."

Lizzy leaned into him, speaking low and seductively for his ears only. "You didn't need to say it. I know you're in love with me, and I couldn't be happier about it because I'm head over heels in love with you."

Her ruby kisser was mere inches from his and he had to contain himself from taking her into his arms. "Love already?"

She whispered again, and he experienced a surge of sensation from the feel of her warm breath upon his ear, like a puff of her heated essence.

Gone was the joking intonation but in its stead was heartfelt sincerity. "Yes, Will. I love you."

"You better be careful, I might not give your heart back once you give it to me."

"Too late, daddy. It's yours. Like the song—I'm *all* yours. After all, I am painted on the side of your Marauder. It's the highest compliment when a skipper names his ship after his sweetheart. It means true love. Forever love that will endure the high seas and rough waters side-by-side even when distance separates us—me and you."

This was dangerous territory he found himself in. Yes, he loved her in a forever kind of way, without a doubt, but something held him back. He'd thought about it time and again. Was it her father or was it still that fear that he might not make it back in one piece? Telling her he loved her without sharing the secrets he held in his heart seemed disingenuous. Love meant being honest about everything, but here and now was neither the place nor time to have a serious discussion with her about religion—but he would, without fail before she went back home or he left for the ETO, whichever came first.

Center stage, the blonde beauty, Frances Langford, sashayed to the silver microphone, and the crowd went wild. Her beaded champagne golden gown glittered and clung in all the right places. "As Time Goes By" brought the wolfish corporal back to Lizzy and Will's table.

"Lizzy, may I *now* have this dance?"

She looked to Will for his approval, and he nodded with a reluctant smirk. *Damn, too soon!*

"Well, since you asked so gentlemanly, yes." She kissed Will's cheek and joined the crush of dancers.

Two minutes later, he watched the PPL's bombardier tap Lizzy's dance partner's shoulder and Stevens took her further away from his line of vision.

Will played with the plastic swizzle stick in his punch and popped the maraschino cherry into his mouth. He tapped his fingers against the tablecloth and strained to find her within the crowd. It was the longest three minutes ever, and the wait for her return filled him with longing. Finally, a glimpse of her effervescence emerged from the crowd, heading in his direction with a delightful grin of mischievous exuberance.

"Did you miss me?"

"Every minute. Did you enjoy yourself?"

"You sound jealous. You shouldn't be you know. It's you who started this."

Will turned his chair to face her. "I'm not jealous. I'm proud, Lizzy. You don't realize what your presence does for the men when they're stuck here in no man's land, what a boost to their morale it is to dance with a pretty girl with a personality such as yours. We don't know when we'll be shipped out, so any opportunity for a bit of harmless carousing is welcome."

She raised an eyebrow. "So you're *not* jealous?"

"Of these fellas? Nah. In truth, there's only one man I'm jealous of and that's only because he gets to see you every day, hear your laughter, and gaze upon your smile. I suppose that's to be expected since he's your neighbor."

Gone was her playful smile. "You're still jealous of Johnny? Oh, Will, don't be. Truly, it's not like that between us, and he knows my heart is yours. Besides, he's been in love with Ingrid forever. Not that that makes a difference because Johnny isn't and could never be you. You're my soul mate." She placed her hand upon his, resting on the table. "I'm so sorry if I led you to feel otherwise. That was never my intention."

Soul mate. At that word, he felt so much better about the petty envy he continued to have for the man she often referred to in her letters. He smiled thoughtfully, rotating his hand to hold hers within his grasp, his thumb caressing her soft inner palm.

Nearly upon them, Captain Carter cleared his throat when a hellzapoppin' song sent the dancers into a tailspin on the dance floor. "Miss Renner, may I have the pleasure of this dance?"

Will wasn't about to deny the privilege to his C.O. and off Lizzy went with a sheepish grin.

Damn, can we never finish a conversation? He downed his drink at her parting and watched her dance up a storm, Lindying and laughing. Apart from her impromptu dancing in the Chris Craft, he'd never seen her move like this, and he admired each spin, kick, and syncopated swivel of her hips. *My G-d, she's a fantastic dancer!* Her ardent spectator thoroughly enjoyed the teasing looks she sent him while dancing with another, and he laughed from the sidelines whenever she winked at him. Tempted as he was to break in, he'd wait for the slow dance, the next one where he could hold her in his arms and whisper sweet nothings in her ear.

Another flier jumped into her dance, pulling her from Carter, but Lizzy didn't miss a beat. She kept on dancing like a feminine whirlwind, her smile never ceasing, her feet never stopping. At that moment, she was more than a zephyr, she was a full-blown gale! Miss Chapin would be proud—or not, because Lizzy's dancing was doing indecorous things to him as he watched.

The song finally ended and Miss Langford once again approached the microphone to sing one of her signature songs, "I'm in the Mood for Love." Will rose quickly and gently pushed through the crowded dance floor before another made any stake to dance with his girl. He tapped his C.O. on the shoulder

"May I cut in?"

"If you insist, although I must ask—what took you so long?"

Will smiled and took Lizzy in his arms. He could feel the heat radiate from her body and each warm breath from her exertion felt like a tickling kiss upon his chin. She clung to him in the tight space of their dance frame, and he bent down to her ear as they moved together.

"Do you remember our first dance?" He asked.

"How can I forget? You bowled me over with your form."

"That was the plan. Although at the time, I was pretty hard pressed to admit it." He swallowed hard. "This is the best birthday gift you could have sent me, baby. You and I, here, dancing like this."

"Oh, Will, *I'm* not your birthday gift. That's not expected for another two weeks and believe me, it'll be a swell surprise."

"I don't like surprises."

"Yes you do. You just haven't had many worth getting, and I assure you that it's a surprise you'll go wacky over."

He turned her under his arm away from him. "Is it something better than this? Because I don't think that's quite possible. Your arrival was the best surprise a weary pilot could get."

She came back into his comforting embrace. "Significantly better, but I'll never tell. As for surprises ... if I got on a train and *almost* liked it, well then you, too, can enjoy a surprise or two now and again and maybe, just maybe, cast aside those fuddy duddy barricades of yours."

"I'm learning."

"And I see my patient tutelage is paying off."

He swayed with her to the romantic words, imprinting the feel of her body against his. With lips against the soft wave of her hair, Will sang quietly. As if together they alone occupied the crowded hall, he whispered the lyrics, "Our hearts together ... we are one."

Lizzy tightened her grip on him, resting her head on his strong shoulder.

****

Downtown Lakeland was deserted, and all but the lights surrounding Lake Mirror at the end of Lemon Street were extinguished at this late hour. Though the city was asleep, two visitors were wide awake.

It was after midnight when Will pulled the sedan staff car beside the Hotel Lakeland Terrace. Although appreciative for the loaner conveyance, he hated that his high-society girl was transported in such purely serviceable, drab metal. Lizzy didn't seem to care even if it was a far cry from her luxury German sports car with its mahogany dashboard and leather upholstery. Nevertheless, *he* cared, further hating that it was a Ford. Nothing like a little war profiteering from that anti-Semitic, Nazi-loving Henry Ford. The mere thought of it rankled his nerves, which of course, always seemed to bring his thoughts back to Herr Renner. He quickly replaced the disturbing intrusion with the vision of Lizzy's innocent coyness conveyed from the other side of the front seat.

She sat observing him through long eyelashes as she removed her gloves.

He put the sedan in park, engaging the brake then cut the engine. "Shall we go in?"

Reaching out, her fingers wrapped around his, still grasping the ignition key. Her voice was laced with romantic optimism. "Not just yet."

"I was hoping you'd say that. The evening flew by, and it seems we hardly had any time together. You were very popular."

Lizzy giggled. "I had such a swell time tonight. Thank you for making me feel so special."

He turned to face her, removed his cap, then placed it upon the dashboard. "You *are* special, Lizzy."

Her captivating siren call caused him to move toward her, closing the small gap between them in spite of the large steering wheel and the belt of his officer's coat. A malleable caressed down her cheek as their eyes locked. "May I kiss you?"

Even in the darkness of the car, he could see how she bit her lower lip when she nodded. He leaned down to her, recognizing anticipation emanating from within her heated flesh. "Why are you biting your lip? Are you nervous or afraid of me?"

"No, I could never be afraid of you. I'm afraid of *me* and how I feel—how you make me feel. When I'm near you, I feel things I've never felt before. Kiss me, Will."

The softness of her plump lips tasted like cherries jubilee, and he couldn't help devouring them almost immediately. What he thought would be a chaste goodnight kiss instantly turned delicious and heated, and her slight whimper only served to enflame him all the more.

His arm wrapped around her waist, pulling her closer to him as their tongues explored with a new intensity, passionately breaching propriety without concern. The thundering in his chest matched the uncontrolled throbbing in his loins and the need to do things neither had done before.

He knew this was ungentlemanly, yet he couldn't stop, couldn't hold back. All he wanted to do was taste and caress, explore and claim.

Slowly, his hand slid up from her narrow waist, and his girl arched her back, as though encouraging his bold touch. At least, that was how he interpreted her movement. The curve of her bosom in his hand felt sublime, as his fingers gently caressed and fondled her with gentle cupping squeezes.

Sweet blissful moans left her lips when his mouth descended the delicate bend of her chin in tandem with the brushing of his thumb against her aroused nipple.

"Stop me, Lizzy, because I'm spellbound ... enthralled ... bewitched." He panted between kisses to her neck.

"No, don't stop."

Her breast filled his eager hand, as he leaned her back against the seat. His body responded to her palm sliding up his shoulder, fingers threading through his hair, making love to each lock with her touch.

He was near lying upon her as they had in the boat and he reveled in the erotic feel of his arousal pressed hard against her thigh. Hot, heavy pants filled the car, defining their exploration and the release of their pent up, taboo desires. He couldn't stop the intensity of their petting or of his frenzied kisses ravishing those succulent lips of hers.

Lord knows how he wanted to tell her he loved her, but he knew that would seem a fabricated ruse at this moment. Getting into her unmentionables wasn't the goal, and he'd hate for Lizzy to interpret his words as such. Instead, with labored breath, he gazed into her dilated emerald eyes, his heart full of the unspoken declarations. "I ... I ... we have to stop, baby."

Strong yet gentle fingers fanned through her chestnut waves, his expression as tender as he felt. "If we don't stop now, we'll go too far."

Lizzy kissed his lips with barely a whisper, swollen skin against skin, her words equally as earnest and soft. "I *want* to go too far. Does that make me as audacious as you've always thought?"

"No, because I know what's in your heart. It's in my heart, too." He swallowed hard, as though there was a thick knot of "I love you" stuck within, struggling to be unleashed. "But, it shouldn't be like this in the front seat of an Army vehicle. It should be special, as beautiful as you are, as romantic as you deserve, not rushed and certainly not on a street corner."

Lizzy nodded. "You're right. We'll wait."

Will fixed the strap to her dress then rose from her supine body, helping her to sit up with him. "Let's go for a walk and cool down, before I change my mind."

"Or before *I* change my mind." She leaned against him, resting her head upon his shoulder. "You do that to me. It was love at first sight for me, Will."

The only reply his lips would allow to escape was a kiss to her forehead, and he surreptitiously watched as a knowing smile graced her lips. He wanted at that moment to throw caution to the wind with an *"It was for me, too,"* but his reticence held him captive.

She smoothed her hand down the buttons of his coat. "Let's walk down to the lake. It's such a lovely night, and I'm not quite ready to part from my flyboy."

Will exited the vehicle and walked around to the passenger side, guiding her out onto the sidewalk.

She tucked her arm into the crook of his, and together they strolled in shy silence, passing the entrance of her hotel at the end of the street. Ahead, Lake Mirror glimmered as though a million sparks of electric light danced upon its surface from the moonlight and the dimly lit globed lampposts that surrounded the seawall's promenade walk. The ornate banisters, pillars, and the seawall itself looked just like *National Geographic* magazine had reported—replicating the entrance to a Venetian Palace, only here two American flags waved.

Lizzy felt overcome. It was all so romantic, and she couldn't help squeezing Will's arm, bringing her body closer to his as they walked through the small park to the overlook banister. "I imagine Italy looks similar. Romantic Venice and my dream of floating in a gondola."

"Under the Bridge of Sighs?"

"Yes, for a kiss of eternal love."

Will clasped her hand, resting them together as one, upon the stone wall. The tips of her fingers felt the coolness of his gold pilot insignia ring. He looked down at her with an auspicious smile.

"I'll take you there when the war is over, baby. I promise."

She couldn't help raising a teasing eyebrow. "Truly? You know what that vow means, Will?"

"I do."

"You also know I'll hold you to it."

"I do."

Her breath hitched.

"And you're willing to commit to that even though I'm impetuous, incorrigible, and utterly irresponsible?"

"I am." He took a deep breath. *Say it, fool! Tell her what's in your heart! Say it!* "Those are all the reasons I'm in love with you."

Her eyes welled with unexpected tears. Searching his eyes she grinned overjoyed that his tongue had finally became unhinged. "You *love* ..."

Will raised their entwined hands to his lips and kissed her knuckles. All his reservations for telling her had faded away in that simple avowal. "Yes. I *love* you, Lizzy."

She teasingly smiled through her tears. "I knew that."

His low laugh was filled with mirth. "Of course you did."

She couldn't resist rising to her tiptoes to kiss him under the stars. Not another person was in sight but to their left a group of the local Mute swans laid nestled in sleep at the grassy shoreline. Two others swam together in unison, in the moonlight.

Lizzy breathed in, holding Will's gaze, resting a hand upon his cheek. "I love you so much."

He draped his arm over her shoulders, and she turned, nuzzling into him. Gazing out onto the lake and its mirrored reflection of the sky above he observed quietly, "Swans mate for life."

"They do and so will I ... 'Unwearied still, lover by lover, they paddle in the cold, companionable streams or climb the air. Their hearts have not grown old. Passion or conquest wander where they will, attend upon them still'," she recited.

"You know Yeats?"

"Of course. Not every book for the victory drive is a novel, you know."

She delighted when he finished the poem she had become enamored with from a donated book by the Fricks.

"'But now they drift on the still water, mysterious, beautiful. Among what rushes will they build, by what lake's edge or pool'."

He kissed her sweetly before declaring. "I'll mate for life, too, because I know I'll never love another like I love you."

The smile that graced her visage was, without a doubt, the happiest expression to ever grow from her heart to her eyes as it blossomed upward. Elated by his confession, she was bowled over by his overwhelming romantic nature, and it filled her heart with something she had never felt before— absolute trust and contentment, as though her twenty years had brought her to this moment. She was sure he would propose now that he declared his heart and intentions for their future.

"Let's walk around the lake, shall we?" he suggested.

They strolled along the promenade, holding hands, swinging their arms between them from time to time with the shy smiles of innocent, young love. They passed the swans on one side and lily pads floating on the other. The dimly lit lamps cast a romantic hue to the midnight stroll while the lake beside them rippled beneath the lunar light, offering up an unforgettable moonglade to admire.

"So now that you are here, what are your plans? When do you return to New York?"

"Well, Father is expecting me home on November 2nd and since my Aunt Helga will be flying to Rio, Kitty will be returning in three weeks' time, too. So, I must be at Meercrest for her. Besides, I have responsibilities to the book collection and the book mobile."

"Will you stay in Lakeland longer than tonight?"

She chortled thinking naughty thoughts of her luxurious hotel room and her flyboy. "I'll be returning to Rosebriar Manor day after tomorrow. I have to prepare the guesthouse for visitors at the end of the month and see to Rosebriar's final closure for the season. Hardly anyone from the *Social Register* is coming south as long as we are at war. As it is many of the servants at the house have left for the shipyards in Tampa and Jacksonville."

"I'll try to see if I can get a weekend pass to visit with you in Sarasota, and maybe you can meet me in that hot rod of yours up at MacDill next time I fly over. I'd like to take you out to St. Pete Beach."

"Oh, that sounds creamy. Can we visit the Don CeSar—the Pink Palace? Captain Carter tells me that it's a convalescent hospital for the Air Corps, and I'd like to stop by, spread some cheer, and bring the boys some cigarettes, maybe even a few girlie magazines if you can spare a few."

"You're serious?"

"Yes, I'm serious. They are someone's sons and sweethearts, and I would hope that wherever you go, someone would be there to bring some cheer to you, not girlie magazines, of course. I see that's why Lillian is going to England in December."

He grinned, obviously delighted in her war effort, and she felt proud having come so far from the girl he met only five months ago. Finally, she didn't feel like a useless bauble of American aristocratic life.

"For your information, Pistol, I don't look at girlie magazines. Why would I? I have my own pin up tacked upon the PPL's instrument dash—and in my arms tonight. But you're right, like tonight's dance, these things are important for morale. I commend Lillian and you for seeing that."

"Thank you for saying so. It feels wonderful to be so involved, and feels even more so now that I have your seal of approval."

They stopped on the opposite side of the lake from where they began. Being of the same, remarkably, similar train of thought, they sheepishly looked at one another and headed directly toward the gazebo. Concealed from moonlight, it sat shrouded by the trees overhead. Lizzy giggled when he tugged her hand, pulling her into the shadow.

"You want to neck, chicken?" She laughingly teased.

"You bet I do. You're making me positively wacky." With her back pressed against the stone pillar, he kissed her, sucking her lips in playful nibbles. "I can't ... stop ... kissing you."

Each time his mouth touched her flesh, she tingled and fluttered, feeling and fighting the need to touch him, to explore as he had done in the car. The moment his thumb had brushed against her straining bosom, currents of indescribable desire shot straight to her womanhood, and now, with his lips attacking hers, she felt it again.

So occupied in their ardor, his service cap fell backward to the ground but neither paid any mind. A low moan escaped her lips when his hand stroked her neck, sliding to her décolletage with a tentative tuck of his fingers below the neckline. In response, she forwarded her own daring exploration, gently grinding her hip into him to once again feel him against her. The sensation of which, the first time, was like none other. He met her action with a low guttural moan, and she knew this could be dangerous. She was well aware, even in the moment, that propriety required she tamp down her rising passion; nonetheless, she chose to blatantly ignore her conscience.

Their kisses grew to a fever pitch and her hand slid between their bodies, touching him, feeling the confined evidence of his desire for her. Solid and hard, stiff yet sensual, his erection caused the fluttering within her to grow, the need building like a tightly wound cord.

He spoke her name before his lips suckled the heated flesh of her shoulder when the strap to her dress dropped, and she smoothed her palm over his straining arousal, molding around its girth. Both moaned and breathed heavily in the moonlight.

Suddenly, Will removed her hand, clasping it in his and giving her one final tender kiss to her lips. "You're dangerous, my love." He whispered. "For both our sakes, let me escort you back to the hotel lobby, okay?"

He was smart to do so, and she nodded regretfully, but darned if she didn't want to continue.

Twenty-Two

Begin the Beguine
June 1992

M axine stood at the top of the stairs on the second floor of Primrose Cottage in Brooklyn. Leaning over the wood banister, her ears caught the sound of Juliana in the kitchen singing along to the record playing in the parlor at the far end of the hallway. Happy for her friend was an understatement. After Juliana's visit to Long Island three days prior, her young friend had returned feeling elated by the unexpected revelations about her grandmother and her own connections to the mysterious Lizzy. Meeting her great-aunt Kitty, learning she had family who welcomed her and whom she would see again, had filled Julie with renewed spirit. Then there was the matter of Jack; Maxine hoped he would be calling for a date. Lord knows, as much as Juliana resisted, she was interested even if he had been evasive about his affiliation to the Renner family.

The pleasant aroma of percolating coffee overtook the lingering remnant scent of the recently baked chicken. It was the best damned roast Maxine ever ate, succulent inside and golden brown outside, and she made a mental note to look into vintage Roper stoves when she and Andy remodeled their kitchen.

She called down from the top step, "I love what you did with the bedrooms, Julie."

Juliana poked her head out the open doorway into the hall. "I didn't do anything apart from cleaning. The house's interior is just as I found it. Although, I did update the electricity and have someone install the ceiling fans. Did you check out the herringbone floor pattern in the master bedroom?"

"Old world crafted parquet floors like those in the library were reserved for the wealthy. Your uncle certainly spared no expense."

"It was actually built in 1901 during the Gilded Age, but he must have paid a fortune for the house in 1942."

Despite the lack of central air conditioning, Maxine had fallen in love with Primrose Cottage. The house felt light and bright, even in the evening hours. Pale colored walls had been washed, and the ambient lighting cast homey shadows from the now squeaky-clean, glass fixtures. This house was nothing as Juliana had described it—death didn't lurk here—life did. There was nothing remotely eerie about how the vintage knickknacks gleamed, the music floated, or the floors shined. The pervading aura felt like love dwelled here, not dead secrets of a silent generation or an aged couple, just their romantic enchantment. Time capsule, yes, but alive in the here and now. She had felt it even as she drove up, parking her Volvo in the driveway that ran beside the bow window of the library. Every single light burned brightly in the three-story residence when Benny Goodman greeted Maxine with a song her father always loved, "I Thought About You." There was something magical about Primrose.

She wandered from the master bedroom into the adjoining sitting room where a large bay window offered a clear view into the neighbor's modernized bathroom. "Julie, you'd better get some window treatments up before you and Jack knock boots in this sitting room."

"What!"

Maxine laughed. "You heard me."

"That is *so* not going to happen. I still stand by my earlier assertion; true love in 1992 just doesn't exist. I'll stick with reading letters from 1942, thankyouverymuch."

Flipping off the light switch controlling the upstairs hall fixture, Maxine made for the stairwell, enjoying the smooth feel of the polished wood banister as she descended. At the end of the stairs, she stopped to admire what looked to be a replica Hendrick Avercamp painting hanging upon the long wall leading toward the kitchen. "Do you know anything about this painting? It's so detailed."

Juliana leaned against the frame of the kitchen door, wiping her hands with a rooster dishtowel. "I don't. Mr. Gardner said that it's painted by a Dutch Master. I've been meaning to look into it, but haven't had a chance. It's interesting isn't it?" She walked closer, black converse sneakers squeaking on the recently waxed wood floor. "The frame alone must be worth a mint."

Maxine bent toward the painting, adjusting her black-rimmed eyeglasses to examine closely the detail of the antique frame. She pointed to the decorative edge, its intricate carving illuminated by the crystal ceiling fixture.

"See this ornate molding, certainly indicative of Victorian era plaster, or possibly gesso over hand carved poplar, making it much earlier and even more valuable. If I look at the back, I might be able to date it more accurately by examining the mitering on the corners."

Juliana nodded at the suggestion, but both were perplexed when the painting did not lift from a hook and wire. Instead, the painting had been affixed to the wall by hinges, causing its movement to open outward, as though a door—and a door it was, concealing a niche in the wall, measuring about eighteen inches square. A velvet curtain, as if in a sanctuary, protected the contents within the hidden space.

"What the …?"

Their interest in the painting was forgotten when both women looked at one another until Juliana elbowed her friend, prompting her. "You go first. I'm afraid of what's behind the curtain. It's the attic door all over again. Damn, if this doesn't seem to be a growing theme lately."

"Chicken. This isn't *Let's Make a Deal*, and I'm not Monty Hall. You get to keep whatever is behind this curtain, good or bad."

Juliana twisted the dishtowel and, consequently, the rooster's neck when Maxine pulled the curtain back as though drum rolls should be playing. Cobwebs spanned from one side to the other, draping eerily over several tall and short items deliberately hidden within the lath and plaster walled cubicle.

"What are they?" she asked with wide eyes, gaping at two items covered with velvet and two others placed alongside, wrapped in silver grey felt.

Maxine removed the smaller of two pouches made from the same burgundy velvet as the curtain. Gold thread embroidered the top as well as the fringed bottom edge. "I don't know what it is, but this writing is Hebrew."

She handed it to Juliana who gingerly wiped the offending spider remnants with the dishtowel. Carefully untying the drawstring, she peered in, unfamiliar with the black, leather straps and small boxes nestled against the linen lining within.

The second pouch revealed more elaborate, gold embroidery with the year 1934 stitched below a six pointed Star of David.

Inside the purse-sized bag was a folded, fringed white and blue striped piece of silk fabric. Juliana withdrew a hand crocheted, small yarmulke, and she admired the handiwork and yellowed silk lining. It appeared heirloom.

"Was your uncle Jewish?"

Juliana rested the velvet pouches on the nearby console table. "No. That would mean that my grandfather is Jewish, and I know he's not. Maybe these were left here by the first owners who built Primrose Cottage. They were Jewish."

Maxine removed the tall felt bag, untying the ribbon around the center. They both heard a subtle ping and ding when she removed the heavy contents: two ornate sterling candlesticks. The final felt bag revealed an ornate sterling silver goblet. The antique pieces had been protected from the air and kept from tarnishing by their individual soft wool felt wrappings encased within the wall these many years.

"Well, *someone* was Jewish in 1934. This goblet, I think is a prayer cup—and that christening pillow you found in the attic?—I asked around, it sounds like it's a bris pillow used for circumcision."

"Wow. It's all so beautiful and ... and antique. Why hide it in a wall?"

Maxine pointed to an envelope at the bottom of the nearly empty cubby. Its white paper, now turned beige, bore delicate handwriting. "Julie, look ..."

Juliana withdrew it, holding it with reverence, recognizing the writing as her great-grandmother's from the letters she had written William during the war. The still sealed envelope read, "Elizabeth."

"Well there goes your previous owner theory. Open it!"

"No. I can't, not now, not knowing that Lizzy is alive. This is written to her from my great-grandmother and not meant for me."

Another record dropped from the automatic orthophonics and its upbeat tempo broke the seriousness of the moment. Artie Shaw's "Temptation" seemed prophetic because certainly holding that letter in her hand *was* tempting to open. It very well could be the answer to what happened to them, what put an end to their romance, but knowing that Lizzy was out there somewhere meant that this letter, no matter how many years later, should be delivered to her.

Maxine nodded, placing the goblet back in the cubby. "I suppose you're right. Will Kitty introduce you?"

"She said she would; I'll be patient. Until then ..."

Outside the open wood door, just beyond the front porch, the sudden introduction of ramped up contemporary music invaded their 1940s world, colliding with the snappy big band tune inside. Juliana walked to the ugly, modern security door and peered out the screen. In the darkness, the streetlight illuminated one very fine looking man wearing a polo shirt, sitting in the driver seat of a red convertible Alpha Romeo. In that quick glance down the front steps toward the street, she observed Jack tapping on the steering wheel to "Life is a Highway," and she panicked.

"Oh. My. G-d. It's Jack!"

Impulse and nerves caused her to panic into an immediate retreat, running into the parlor, pressing her back against the wall beside the open French door so as not to be seen.

"Jack, Jack?"

The music and engine cut off, the driver door slammed, and his continuing whistle drew nearer.

Juliana whispered, "Yes, Jack and he's headed this way. Why is he here?"

"Duh? Looks like you may christen that room after all."

He stood at the opened door, holding a pie, sheepishly grinning at Maxine on the other side of the mesh and wrought iron. "Maxine! I didn't expect you here?"

She unlocked the door and swung it wide to bid him entrance. "Of course you didn't, darling. You brought a pie, oh you charmer."

"I ... um ... it's homemade cherry ... from the Island."

"A peace offering of apology?"

"Yes."

Maxine's tease did little to ease his nerves, and he faltered where he stood until Juliana peeked her head around the French door.

Juliana could feel the flush expanding, growing hotter on her cheeks by the second and hated that her heartbeat was now doing some funky dance at the sight of his windblown hair and sincere smile. Her eyes made a quick up and down scan from the piqué Nautica polo to brown Sperry boat shoes, and she liked what she saw.

She stepped hesitantly back into the entry hall. "Hi, Jack."

Suddenly shy and feeling uncomfortable Jack simply replied, "Hi."

An awkward silence ensued between them until he jutted out the pie in her direction. "Er, this is for you. My aunt made it from the cherry tree harvest at Evermore, my grandmother's estate."

She couldn't help the accusing remark that sprang from her lips, having yet to release her displeasure at his previous stonewalling. Her visit to Glen Cove could have been so much easier had he only told her the truth. She took the pie from his hands, their fingers brushing when she did so, sending sparks up her double crossing arms. "Your Robertsen grandmother? The one who probably knew Lizzy."

"I'm sorry, Juliana."

"Cherry tree ... I cannot tell a lie. Clever, though not very applicable to you."

Maxine clapped her hands together, disrupting the suddenly caustic atmosphere. "Well, kids, this is where I bid you goodnight and take my leave." She walked to the console table, grabbed her purse, then kissed both her friends' cheeks. "Thanks for a wonderful evening, Julie. Dinner was excellent." Her eyes bore into cool blue ones. "Now play nice and I'll call you next week."

"But ... but, Max, you're supposed to be going with me to the National Archives by Battery Park the day after tomorrow."

"Nope." Her eyes met Jack's. "I think you have another research buddy now."

Juliana sighed. "Fine. I'll call you. Thanks for driving down to Brooklyn."

More awkward silence ensued after the screen door slammed behind Maxine. Juliana noted how Jack's eyes were drawn to the opened painting, and he furrowed his brow.

"Won't you come in? I'm sorry about the heat, but I haven't gotten estimates for the central air conditioning yet."

She watched how he took in every detail of the hallway, from the antique bronze, converted gas chandelier, the hand tooled crown molding, the inlaid star design in the wood flooring, to the magnificent fireplace in the parlor. He seemed to take it all in with wonder and awe. And she loved his spontaneous appreciation.

"This house is incredible. I feel something here."

"Now do you understand? Come, why don't we sit in the kitchen and have some pie." She tilted her head to catch his eyes wandering into the parlor.

It was clear to her that he was resisting the pull to enter the room where William's Artie Shaw record continued to play. "Yes, that mantel is the shrine to Lizzy that I told you about. I have added some other items I found over the last two weeks. In fact, Maxine and I just discovered some other things right before you arrived."

"I ... um ... hope I didn't come at an inconvenient time then. I'm sorry to have run Maxine off."

"It's okay. I am glad you came. I think we have some things to discuss."

"We do, and I hope you're not too mad at me to understand how difficult a position I found myself in. The coincidence was a total shock to the ticker."

She smiled warmly. "I don't completely understand your subterfuge, but, like my Aunt Kitty explained, I have to have faith in fate and let the truth come to light in due time, with patience. As you once said, everyone has things to hide." *G-d, it feels good to say Aunt Kitty!*

Juliana closed the painting back against the wall, and again his eyes were drawn to the details of it. The ice skating, the windmill, and the community scene were the signature subject depictions by the well-known Dutch artist Hendrick Avercamp.

Together they walked down the hall into the white and red kitchen, where little, vintage rooster details caused him to smile, not to mention the appealing shape of Juliana's backside in those denim shorts that made him feel downright excited.

In the kitchen, still warm despite large open casement windows above the porcelain sink that allowed the delightful, summer evening breeze in, the lingering scent of a home-cooked meal welcomed him.

Juliana stood on tiptoes to remove two cups and saucers from an upper cabinet, and he couldn't resist his eyes once again fixating and scanning up and down her trim form. Deliberately attempting to distract the direction of his stare, Jack pointed to the Frigidaire refrigerator.

"Does that work?"

"It all works. None of it was hardly used. I figure my uncle probably lived here for four years at the most. Four bedrooms, an empty basement, and an empty attic—hardly a house that was 'lived in'. I learned from the Brooklyn Historical Society that Primrose Cottage was a honeymoon residence built for a Guggenheim daughter in 1901. I'm guessing it was barely used by them as well."

"Hmm ... the Guggenheims. My grandmother knew the family. They had a few houses on the Gold Coast. In fact, the late Harry Guggenheim, whose Falaise mansion is on the Gold Coast, founded *Newsday*."

She placed two distinctly Delft dessert plates upon the kitchen table pressed against the wall beneath another set of open windows. The details of the Palladian stained glass arch above them and the overgrown rosebush outside were both obscured by the darkness.

"So many Guggenheim connections. Would this be your cherry-tree-owning, sky-diving, seventy-year-old-who-adopted-your-father-as-a-toddler grandmother?"

When he chuckled, she knew that he knew she was fishing for any other connection. Damn, if that smile of his wasn't warm, self-effacing, and so perfect.

"Yes, she's the one."

Juliana poured their coffee and sat catty-cornered from him, cutting into the pie, which was still slightly warm. "Your aunt made this? It looks delicious. Please thank her for me."

"I will. I spoke to her about you. The day after you and I met, I went to visit her at the museum to discuss your curiosity over the Renners and the secrets, many of which I think you may know by now. We saw you that day with Kitty, and I knew she was sharing with you the story of your grandmother and how it relates to my dad."

Juliana closed her eyes at the sublime first taste of cherry pie in years. "You could have told me."

"No. I couldn't then, but I will now. I don't know how much Kitty explained but I know I owe you reasons for my evasion and my silence. Do you want to hear them? Is it too late to offer my explanation and tell you what I failed to do on Friday?"

"I'm not afraid of the truth, Jack. Kitty alluded to many things, and she did tell me that Lizzy is still alive—and I still feel the same way about protecting her. Mostly we talked about my grandmother's courage, and frankly, at that moment that was more important to me then learning about her and Lizzy's parents."

"Rightfully so and astute of Kitty to see that. Lillian was an extraordinary woman in her youth and without her, I have to admit, I would not be here today. Hopefully, after my explanation you will understand more clearly why Lizzy, Kitty, and Lillian remained silent about their past."

He uncomfortably cleared his throat. "This might come as a shock to you, but your grandmother's father was a virulent Nazi who orchestrated and financed enemy saboteurs to come ashore in America. Frederick Renner worked with Nazi Intelligence and their Marines in coordinating the placement of mines along the Atlantic seaboard, some even here in New York Harbor."

Flushed ivory skin from the warmth of the kitchen turned ashen, as her eyes grew wide, and her mouth fell slack. Forcibly swallowing, she responded, "My G-d. No wonder no one wanted to admit the Renners even existed. I would deny my family too. Who ... how did they find out?"

Jack played with his fork for several long moments waiting for the constriction in his throat to subside, until finally he said, "Lizzy made an anonymous tip to the FBI."

Juliana gasped. "You're kidding?"

"I don't kid about this and under *any* other circumstance than this ... I don't talk about it either.

"You might think that's the worst of it, but it isn't. His most heinous crime was that he funneled money to companies who had a hand in Hitler's final solution. IG Farben being the worst of them. Along with every explosive and synthetic gasoline made by this company for purposeful use by the Wehrmacht, they created Zyklon-B, which was used to gas millions of Jews in concentration camps as well as those others the Nazis considered unfit—people like Kitty or the mentally challenged."

Nauseated, Juliana dropped her fork and pushed the pie plate away from her. She stood and walked to the stove, pacing until turning to face him. She leaned her back against the counter, and folded her arms across her chest. "*My* great-grandfather did this?"

Jack felt a semblance of guilt, his forthright explanation having caused the shocked expression on her pretty face.

"Yes, *your great*-grandfather. Hardly an appropriate adjective for the man, wouldn't you say? I'm sorry, I'm truly sorry, but my aunt explained to me why she believes you needed to know. I can't understand what good it does but perhaps it helps to put your grandmother's silence into perspective. Kitty's testimony of her mistreatment and fears for her life gives even more credence to Lillian's reasoning for hiding the truth about their father, mother, and eldest sister."

"As horrific as this is, I agree with your aunt. I do need to hear this. From what I've surmised already, and if for no other reason, I truly want to better understand how his evil activities changed the lives of three of his daughters, my family, for the good."

He nodded. "In 1946, our government stated that 'without IG Farben the Second World War would simply not have been possible'. After Farben's liquidation following their trial, one of their four chemical companies survived, a well-known aspirin brand today, even though they had actively engaged in drug experimentation on Auschwitz prisoners."

He watched as Juliana opened the pantry door, removed a bottle of aspirin, then, assuming it was the brand of which he spoke, vehemently tossed it into the trash with a curled lip. Her expression was unlike any he had seen on her in their brief acquaintance, but it didn't stop his explanation. He had come this far. At her prompting with a wave as though saying, "Bring it on. I need to hear it all," he would finish.

"Later, the family learned that his payment from the Reich was a rare manufactured automobile as well as a few paintings, considered to be masterpieces that the Nazis had looted from homes and private collections of European Jews deported to ghettos and death camps."

"What happened to that evil scumbag? I hope they fried his ass in the electric chair."

"They never had the chance. He committed suicide before his arrest, but his lawyer was arrested and executed in 1947."

"What happened to Lizzy?"

"Years later, Lizzy and Kitty, with the agreement of Lillian, created The Phoenix Foundation through which every dollar of the Renner fortune has been spent making personal restitution for the acts committed by their father. Since 1945, Lizzy has dedicated her life to atonement for his acts against humanity. Currently, she is dealing with the French Culture Minister to return two paintings to the families of the original owners and she's also negotiating to recoup a painting currently held by the French government. I think she's trying to see to its return to its rightful family. For years, she has obsessively tried to determine the origin and owners of the two paintings— a Monet and Degas—which hung in Meercrest. The foundation will also be erecting a veteran's home in Glen Cove.

"On Meercrest's property?" Juliana asked recalling the sign on the estate grounds.

"Yes. They also constructed the museum this past year, and the donation of the Renner family's Manhattan mansion, Greystone, to the Polish Consulate in 1976 are some other projects. She sold her father's yacht, the *Odin*, for almost a million dollars, splitting the money in donations to several organizations responsible for relocation of displaced survivors as late as 1957. A team within the foundation works diligently to keep the Renner name removed from any and all reference that might appear, especially, as a benevolent gesture. It's all done as anonymously as possible, and even after fifty years, there is still a significant amount of money that she pours into education, remembrance, and restoration."

Juliana sat back down in her chair, clasping her hands tightly before her. "Now I understand why you didn't want me to print an article. The press could slander and misconstrue the efforts of the foundation and the Renner sisters, exploiting the fact that everything was done using Nazi money. I suppose critics would fail to report the irony that Nazi booty was restoring lives not taking them."

"Yes, particularly since we are leaving for Paris in three weeks to take part in the memorial as well as a restitution ceremony for the paintings."

Jack reached his hand out to hers and grasped over her fingers. "Juliana ... Lizzy's first act of reparation was to adopt my father. Lizzy is my *grandmother*. Your great-uncle was in love with my grandmother."

She sighed; all the pieces were falling into place as to why Jack hadn't been forthcoming. "Your grandfather was the John Robertsen in the photograph I found at the library, a man she married while William was still at war." *The letter ... the* R *on the letter in the fireplace stood for Robertsen not Renner. Did she and William have an affair in '49?* She thought of the letter's words she had memorized. *"You know that what we did ..."*

"Yes, John Robertsen was my grandfather."

"Did they ... um ... have other children?"

"My Aunt Annette, born I think in '43, and my Uncle Dan born maybe around '48."

His thumb brushed hers, and their eyes locked, both feeling contrite for their earlier discourse, both feeling an intimate connection of something deeper. In spite of the darkness of the secrets shared over pie and coffee, the magic of Primrose Cottage, as it was always intended, began to cast its spell upon them, and both felt it acutely.

Reading his expression and the intent written all over his face, Juliana withdrew her hands from his. "Jack ... I hate to state the obvious but you *are* my cousin. Our grandmothers were sisters." She chortled. "I can't believe I just said that ... *I* have family!"

"You do, you absolutely do. Seven first cousins, but I'm only related to you by adoption, not blood, and we are second cousins."

She wondered if she was looking for any excuse to pull back, but when the music ended down the hall, it seemed to amplify the sound of the beat of her heart against her chest wall. When Jack took her hand again, she bit her lip unsure of herself and the warning bells going off in her head.

He had unexpectedly been honest, and she wondered if she should be as well. A battle within her ensued on whether to share the contents of the letter she found in the fire grate. No, the only thing that letter proved was that her great-uncle and his grandmother *communicated* in 1949. Nothing more, nothing less, and whatever was meant wasn't anyone else's business. She agreed with Jack that this noble woman should never have her reputation tarnished—even if, especially if, it concerned an affair of the heart. It was clear that the man beside her idolized Lizzy, so Juliana swore to herself she would protect her, too. Lizzy was her great-aunt and someone she felt she had come to know intimately. She was a woman whose life story deserved protection. Now she fully understood Jack's discretion. No, if there had been an affair, she'd keep that a secret.

His thumb brushed against the pad of her hand. "Will you show me the mantel? Because I have something to share with you."

"Sure, of course." Their eyes remained engaged as they exited the kitchen.

Nearing the parlor, Jack stopped at the console table in the hall. The velvet pouches still sat where Juliana had placed them, and he picked up the smaller of the two, his index finger lightly stroking over the raised embroidered Hebrew lettering.

"We found those along with candlesticks and a goblet behind that painting. Do you know what it reads?" she asked.

He smiled thoughtfully trying to remember where he had placed his own twenty years earlier. "For the life of me, I can't remember my Hebrew, but I can tell you *what* it is. I received mine at my Bar Mitzvah, every young man does. They're called Tefillin and verses from the Torah, written on parchment, are placed inside the leather boxes. They're used for prayer. I imagine the other is the Tallit, the fringed, silk, prayer shawl. The embroidered date is most likely the date of your great-uncle's Bar Mitzvah."

"And the goblet?"

"Ah, well if it is sterling, it's one that might be used during the Shabbat for the Kiddush prayer. The candlesticks would be intended for the woman of the house to light the candles and recite the blessing every Friday night."

"But, my uncle wasn't Jewish."

He made a speculative noise from the side of his mouth, "Maybe he was, and maybe that was why he never married my grandmother. Think about it. Nazi father, Jewish boyfriend, maybe one or the other backed out—or worse yet—was made to. Maybe others had a hand in their separation."

"How sad. I don't think he broke it off. I found an engagement ring beside her photograph in what was supposed to be the master bedroom. Was she ... happy with your grandfather?"

"They seemed happy, sort of like the best of friends. He spoiled her to no end, and she took such good care of him."

"Hmm ..." As though a thought burst into the forefront of her mind, she dashed to the painting, swinging it outward and removing the letter. "This is to Lizzy. I found it with the other items in the wall. Will you see that she gets it?"

He sighed. "Oh, Juliana, what have we stumbled upon?"

"I don't know, but in spite of the revelations about my great-grandfather, it's damn exciting, and I suspect you're coming around to understanding my intrigue."

Jack placed the Tefillin bag back on the table and walked to the mantle in the silent front room, admiring his grandmother's image and the snapshots of her and this man she obviously loved. The grandfather clock in the corner chimed ten, while Juliana busied herself turning the record over to the second side. He wondered how on earth he was going to bring up the subject of Juliana with Lizzy. Would she welcome this living, breathing, tangible reminder of her romantic past? Would she deny this romance, or worse yet would it open a door that *he himself* wasn't yet prepared for her to enter?

Artie Shaw's "Stardust" broke into the quiet when the trumpet began the romantic piece. Their eyes slowly drifted toward one another across the space of the room as the music wrapped them in the magic of Primrose Cottage. In that moment, there were only two people in that room; gone were the specters and speculations surrounding Lizzy and William of fifty years ago.

Jack couldn't deny Juliana's allure, every smile and giggle; each furrowed brow and determined set of her jaw enchanted him. Those clear, blue eyes of hers were a sea of tranquility—and boy did he love the sea.

As though prompted by an unseen force, he walked to her, holding out his arm. "Will you dance with me?"

"Here? Now?"

"Yes, Juliana. Here and now."

"But I don't know how."

"Please."

Tentatively she took his hand, stepping into his embrace. He hoped his hand splayed firmly against her back would relax her apparent hesitance. Certainly, just the nearness of her caused him to calm and muse that romance was possible.

The persistent tugging in Jack's heart and a shiver in his soul made him imagine the chiming of the clock had transported them both to an era of romance and innocence. He was Juliana's GI and she was his sweetheart and, suddenly, it was 1942.

They swayed closely to the romantic tune because neither knew the proper dance steps. The fox trot was something he had only heard about or seen done in old black and white films; but this house made him brave, made him feel unusually romantic, and this woman was opening his heart to possibilities, even if she was afraid.

As the clarinet played, Jack surprisingly envisioned his grandmother dancing in William's arms in this very parlor, maybe to this very song, and he felt guilty over the thought that it wasn't his own Granpops he imagined holding her.

He breathed deeply, lightly resting his cheek against Juliana's soft, golden locks. She smelled like sweet citrus blossoms on a sunny morning. The overwhelming combination of intoxicating music, the feel of her against him and the scent of her hair caused a bead of perspiration to form upon his temple. It wasn't the hot summer night—it was the woman in his arms whose delicate hand was currently clasped around his bare bicep.

For a playboy bachelor, this experience with Juliana was new. This intense emotion and connection was driving his impulse and desire rather than impulse and desire driving his libido.

When his hand left her back, his index finger caressed her delicate neck, moving forward to tilt her chin upward. Their eyes locked, their lips parted, and he felt the tickle of her cherry-infused breath upon his mouth. She was so close, and all he desired was a taste of her then to consume her body and soul.

Slowly his lips descended to her waiting ones, and he closed his eyes in sweet anticipation, but it was not to be. Unfulfilled, disappointed lips met the soft flesh of her cheek when Juliana abruptly turned her face from his, left his embrace, retreating toward the fireplace.

"I'm sorry, Jack. I just ..."

"It's okay, Juliana. I'm the one who should be sorry ... I didn't mean to rush you. You're a attractive woman, and I just couldn't help myself."

She smiled shyly. "It's the house."

He walked toward her and took her hand. "No, it's Juliana."

Slowly, she slid her hand from his and took a step backward. "What did you want to tell me earlier?"

Shaking off the disappointment for the moment, he refocused. "Well, I have good news. I heard from one of my contacts, and it turns out that your great-uncle is alive."

"I knew it!"

"He's living in Sitka."

Shocked, her eyes widened with incredulity. "As in Alaska?"

"That's the place."

"Wow ... well, I've never been to Alaska before."

"You're kidding right? You're not really considering going to get him, are you?"

"Oh, I'm dead serious. Is there any chance that you might know of a good hotel?" She grinned and raised her eyebrows in expectation, nodding optimistically. "Maybe you can hook me up with some travel deals?"

The song changed to an upbeat "Begin the Beguine," and Jack held out his hand again, mischievously grinning. "Only if you dance with me one more time. Maybe we can try to swing dance."

"Are you bribing me, Mr. Robertsen?"

"Absolutely."

"I expect Michelin, five-star rated."

"Not in Sitka. But will you settle for a nice bed and breakfast with a view of Mt. Edgecumbe, amicable hosts and the best damn smoked salmon you've ever had?"

Juliana stepped into his embrace. "Deal."

Twenty-Three

Memories of You
June 1992

W illiam Martel loved the crisp morning air of Sitka at daybreak. Rising early with the sun had become the norm for him, and as he aged, he found deep sleep less and less necessary. The long summer days in Alaska spanned upwards of eighteen hours, and he always made the most of the natural light, particularly on this day. He had been up since five and hadn't stopped going for four straight hours. Several roof shingles needed tending, and he'd be damned if he was going to hire some thirty year old to do a job he easily could manage at seventy-one.

Sitting atop the gentle slope of the A-frame's roof, he rested from his repair work and clutched the plastic cup of the coffee thermos. Admiring the view of Sitka Sound, his mind traveled to a decision he needed to make, a difficult one that had been laid at his feet the night before. Decision? No, more like a gentle ultimatum. He hoped the splendid, clear vista of the snow-kissed peak of Mount Edgecumbe in the distance would afford him greater clarity.

Fifty-degree weather felt refreshing and that, too, he expected would clear his confused mind and obstinate heart. He never tired of the breathtaking view, and manual labor always helped when he faced difficult decisions. Like three years ago, when deciding whether or not to adopt a dog from the local pound. Pondering that matter allowed him to finish building the addition to the cabin.

Then there had been the question of taking the job at First Response Air Med utilizing his Cessna. Providing emergency medical transportation to the lower 48 was something he had done for years, but not in conjunction with a company. That decision pushed him to restore, rivet by rivet, a 1938 Grumman Goose amphibious plane and sell it for a mint. With the cash, he outfitted the Cessna for air ambulance service of organ transplant recipients. The biggest internal struggle he faced was whether to retire from First Response and go back to independent charters for charity only. It took six months to finish the kitchen remodel before he made that decision.

Now busier than ever, he was flying the uninsured and poverty stricken all over the world for treatment and hardly finding the time to enjoy said kitchen. His particular devotion still remained his weekly trips north to Anchorage, shuttling vets to the VA Hospital.

On this day, faced with his lady friend's ultimatum, the cedar shake roof was conveniently in need of refurbishing after these fifteen years of his residence below it. Nope, he wouldn't be making any impulsive decision, particularly about love. He did that once in his life and that taught him never to do it again. Thinking things through in a thoughtful, methodical, and thorough manner was the best course of action.

Will heard the deck door open and close, and the brief sound of the morning news assaulted his respite of quiet rumination. His lady friend, Ginny's voice carried up to him. "Will, are you all right?"

"Yeah, why?"

"You stopped hammering, and I became worried."

"Thanks, Gin. I'm fine, just taking a break is all. Sorry if I woke you."

"Oh, hon, you didn't wake me. I'm used to your productive early risings by now. I left your vitamins and baby aspirin on the counter."

It's not like he didn't appreciate her concern—he truly did, but he hated that she treated him as a man much older than his mental and physical abilities. He felt fifty and, hell, looked fifty, too. Seventy-one was only a number, not a death sentence or the requisite trip to an old age home.

"Be careful you don't throw your back out with all that pounding and hammering."

"Yes, nurse."

She laughed.

He and Ginny had known each other for five years and been romantically involved for two or three (he couldn't quite remember), and it had taken every one of those five years for him to grow accustomed to her laugh: a bit too loud, a bit too guttural, and a bit too snorty. But Ginny was a good woman and together they had shared many laughs, quite a few bottles of wine, and an enjoyment of the outdoors. They'd hike together and snowmobile, even fish. He was a far cry from the city boy he once was, and she was a far cry from the southern, teenaged war widow and young mother she had become in 1952. Apart from the fact that she hated baseball and had no desire to travel for pleasure, they did have quite a few things in common. Overlooking the twelve-year age gap had been easy until she started to care for him as though he was ninety-five.

"Do you want more coffee?" She called up, her voice cheerful and bright.

Will shook his head. "Is that your way of asking me to come down?"

"You know me so well."

He looked down at her probing expression. *What is she expecting, an immediate answer? These things take time. This roof is in need of a lot of repair.*

He knew he didn't have time. She'd be leaving permanently in two weeks to live with her daughter in Kentucky unless he stopped her—or rather— made her an offer she couldn't refuse. Damn, he hated pressure to make impulsive decisions that required a commitment, and damn it he didn't like committing to anything unless it was on *his* terms. Moreover, he had been really comfortable not *having* terms with Ginny these many years. Even as the nurse on the Cessna, Ginny did her thing and he did his, and they got together when they wanted to share whatever "thing" they needed to share with one another. Life was good and he was happy with this arrangement.

"I'm not done up here yet. Perhaps we can talk tonight over dinner?" He raised his brows hoping she got the point.

"That's fine. I'm headed into town then since you're avoiding confrontation. G-d, it's not as though I've asked you to give me a kidney or anything, but I know you need time. Well, we'll talk." She blew a kiss up to him. "I'll see you at my place at eight?"

Will took a deep gulp of cold coffee then smiled tightly. His heart really wasn't into talking let alone making any commitments beyond fixing the loose shingle currently below his ass. "Sounds good. Drive safely."

Her pretty smile beamed up, and it comforted him to know that she knew him so well and understood his nature. They were two of a kind, actually. Only now, she wanted something neither had previously desired in their relationship—a long-term commitment that began and ended with "I do." It was certainly more than he felt he could give her but faced with her leaving Alaska, he'd give it serious thought. He owed her that much.

"Love ya', hon. Be careful up there," she said with a wave, then opened the door to go back into the house. The news channel had turned to music programming and a brief snippet of Vera Lynn's "Yours" escaped from inside, floating up to him on a gentle breeze. For four seconds, heaven swirled, embracing a memory.

"Hey, Ginny? Can you turn off the radio?"

"Sure. I'll see you later."

Two doors slammed—the one on the deck and the one to that deep recess in his soul. Why was it that a simple, melodious song had the power to eviscerate a man no matter how virile and masculine he felt? Five fuckin' decades and that song *still* affected him. Thank goodness, its effect had lessened over time to only a tolerable annoyance, and he rarely allowed himself the painful memories that ushered in more than a modicum of emotion. He wasn't that man any longer and he'd lived about four of five lives in as many decades since then.

Ginny had already left the house, and he could hear her pick-up truck crunch over the gravel driveway when he said regretfully, "See ya' later, Gin."

To his ears, it sounded almost prophetic. He didn't love her (not the way she wanted anyway), and his heart was telling him to let her go. He wasn't the marrying type—not at this age. He tried it once in the seventies when he lived in Israel, but it didn't work. After a year and a half spent deciding whether he was happy or not, he and Sandra divorced in '77. She stayed in Tel Aviv, and he flew himself to Alaska, replacing sand for snow where he finally dug roots. Fifteen years was the longest commitment he'd ever made. He thanked his former Army co-pilot, McCarthy, for that, having settled in Sitka from New Jersey in the late sixties.

As the temperature rose slightly with the sun, Will stood up fully on the roof. Peeling off his sweatshirt to the white t-shirt below, he offered his well worked muscles a long stretch in the fresh Alaskan air. An eagle's call in the towering Sitka Spruces surrounding the cabin added to the serenity of the moment, and he allowed his thoughts to meander once he resumed the task of fixing the roof. His hammering seemed to reverberate in the peaceful rhythm of the morning like the echo of the Vera Lynn song, which had affected him more deeply than he thought it would. He was dismayed that it pulled him from the debate that was *supposed* to be his priority about Ginny and the prospect of marrying her. Instead, his mind swept to another woman.

"Fifty years. I wonder what she's doing? I should ask if she's still alive. He's kept an eye on everyone and everything for me, except the one person ..."

The hammer smashed down upon his thumb. "Damn!" he cursed, promptly sucking it. With the action of finger to mouth, a flash of memory rudely intruded without invitation. Sitting in Channel Gardens of Rockefeller Center during the 1942 war parade up Fifth Avenue.

-And are you the right enticement, Lizzy?

Looking so adorable, she grinned with a mouthful of hot dog, and he couldn't resist the temptation before him. With his thumb, he reached over to wipe a dollop of mustard from her bottom lip and sucked his finger clean. It was the closest to a kiss as he had gotten.

-Perhaps, I am the right woman for the job. You'll have to stick around to find out and allow me to introduce you to all sorts of trouble.

Will continued to suck the tip of his thumb even though the throbbing was negligible. He wondered why a man's first love wasn't so easily forgotten and silently acknowledged that Lizzy Renner wasn't just *any* first love. She was the first, the last, and the always. When they had courted in their youth, her mellifluous laughter, her smile, warmth, and sincerity had branded *his* soul forever. The way she had made him feel, and the way she responded to him could never be replicated by any other woman who had come and gone in his life.

Lizzy had ruined him for all others; even her cruel desertion of him after he left for England was not enough for him to forget her. To see her seven years later and married nearly destroyed him. To learn she had thought him dead was a shocking blow, but one they never had a chance to discuss. He made love to her that one magical night, August 8, 1949, to show her that no other man could make her feel the same way as he did, not even her husband. Theirs was a love that would never be duplicated, nor would it ever die. But it turns out their night together was just a one-night stand reprieve from her housewife boredom.

He sighed. "But she was right; she had a family by then, obligations that kept her from leaving him for you. I bet she has grandchildren now."

The hammer skittered down the side of the roof and crashed onto the deck below. He chuckled wryly. She even ruined his efforts to fix the damn roof. Smiling, Will sat back upon the eave and stared out at the placid Sound and the beauty before him. He hated that he could recall every detail of Lizzy with such ease after all this time, yet he reveled in one memory that his mind's eye conjured. Could anything be more magnificent than making love for the first time with a woman who consumed every fiber of a man's being?

> *She trembled in his arms as he held her, their nude bodies lying side by side, their kisses caressing as his hand smoothed over each slope and curve of her supple skin.*
> *-I love you so much, Lizzy.*
> *-And, I love you. I'll always love you.*
> *-Are you sure you want to do this?*
> *His girl bit her lip when she nodded.*

No, a man who truly loved would never forget that moment even five decades later.

The sudden vibration from the beeper at his hip saved his heart from the indulged memory, and he responded without haste by tossing out the remainder of his coffee cup with a quick snap to his wrist. He sealed the thermos, packed up his tools, and climbed down from the roof. It was time to do some good for the infirm, and that was the only way he knew how to keep loving her from afar.

Will entered the cabin to the lingering scent of brewed coffee but passed by the stove. With calm but measured urgency, he picked up the phone to call his friend, Jimmy McCarthy, who was reaching out to him in need.

"Jim! Good to hear from you. Is everything all right?"

"Been better. Well ... apart from that stint we did for two years as Kriegies in Germany."

He sat at the kitchen bar, looking out beyond the deck. Anxious fingers ran through his salt and pepper hair. "Talk to me. Is it the cancer?"

"Yeah, and I need to get up to Anchorage for surgery. I hate to ask again, but ... you know how it is. I don't think I can manage flying the floatplane."

"When do you need to get up there by?"

"They want me up on Thursday for Friday surgery. It's in the lungs, Will."

"Oh man. I'm sorry. I'm here for you. Whatever you want or need, it's no problem. Do you need money for a place for Margie to stay while you convalesce?"

"I hate to ask."

"You didn't ask. I offered. After all these years, you know I love you like a brother."

"Thanks. Speaking of brothers ..."

Will rose from the stool and began to pace. "I'd rather not."

"Look, my days are pretty much up. I've run the course, but a year ago I had the opportunity to get my shit in order when they diagnosed me."

"Stop that! I won't have you talking like you're about to drop dead from this. You've beat worse odds."

"No, this is it. I can feel it in my bones. What I'm saying is not to let grass grow under your feet any longer. We're not getting any younger and you really should patch things up with your only living relative before either of you buys the farm. You gotta forgive, old man. Mend the fences with everyone who has done you wrong or you'll die bitter."

"I'll think about it."

"And how long will that take? What'll you have to do—restore that fishing cabin of yours on Blue Lake before you decide to call him?"

"Jim, are you trying to piss me off?"

"No, just trying to knock some sense into that vaporhead of yours after all these years."

Will smiled thoughtfully. "That's what Louie used to call me when I joined the Corps as a cadet. So, I'll be downtown tomorrow at ten to pick you and Margie up. How's that sound?"

"Sounds like a smooth skirting of the issue at hand, Skipper. Fine. I'll see you tomorrow ... vaporhead. Thanks again."

"Sure, glad to be of help. You saw me through some rough times in the war when I crashed, both from and in the PPL. Your friendship is a gift, Jim. I'll see you both tomorrow."

Will hung up the phone, devastated to hear the news. It seemed those non-filtered Camels finally caught up with his friend. He poured himself a cup of coffee, warming it in the microwave and feeling an unusual surge of outright melancholy. No, he was in no mood for dinner at Ginny's tonight. Making a snap decision about marrying her wasn't fair to her and, at that moment, wasn't first and foremost in his mind. That in and of itself told him something right there. He didn't love her enough to fight for her. Fixing the cedar shakes wasn't necessary—he knew the answer before he even mulled over the possibilities. Letting her go so she might find true love, something he was unable—actually unwilling—to give her, was the best thing he could do for her.

The house seemed eerily quiet. Nothing but his rapid pulse sounded in his ears when he looked at the telephone again. It taunted him, and he stretched his arm out to the black receiver only to retract it until finally reaching over. He wondered if he felt ready to do the first spontaneous thing in a long, long time.

He glanced at his father's wristwatch. It was one thirty in New York, and his lawyer and former Kriegie buddy was most likely eating a pastrami sandwich at his desk. With a slight, unusual tremble to his hand, he grabbed the old telephone, pulled it onto his lap, and rotated the dial.

Alan Gardner unexpectedly answered the phone himself.

"Al, it's me Martel ... I'm doin' great. Sitka's fine, fishing's great. McCarthy? Well, he's in need of prayer ... Yeah. I'll tell him. How's the family? ... Good, good, glad to hear it. ... Oh, really? ... That's wonderful. Congratulations ... No, retirement has been keeping me busy ... Listen, did Louie get the flowers? ... And he's healthy, still kicking and shagging his way through Exeter? ... Good. ... Yeah, I know. Maybe I'll do that, but you know it's been some time since I came east. ... And his granddaughter? Has she moved into Primrose Cottage? ... I'm glad, glad that house could be used as it should. Thanks for handling the details. Listen, I have a favor to ask. Can you find out about a Mrs. Elizabeth Robertsen?"

Twenty-Four

Let's Do It
October 30, 1942

B y true Floridian standards, the last week of October wasn't quite the season for swimming, but given Lizzy's love of the water and the way she cannonballed into the deep end without a bathing cap, there was no stopping her. It was obvious that it gave her an audacious opportunity to show off her form in front of Will. Not that he minded in the least.

On a two-day weekend pass in celebration of his twenty-second birthday he had flown the PPL Marauder to MacDill Airfield where Pistol met him as though she was Marlene Dietrich greeting her personal fan club at the Third Air Force. Again, every Marauder man had treated her with fawning admiration and wolfish dizziness. Will loved how she had laughed at the commotion as he patiently guided her through the throng, back toward her father's car. The frenzied escape from the exuberant crowd was followed by a two-hour drive south to Rosebriar Manor in the Horch at a relaxing but restrained Victory Speed.

There was a slight crispness to the air and a clear blue sky this Saturday afternoon, providing a delightful day that found them unwinding and anticipating what they both knew would happen over the weekend.

He lounged poolside, enjoying a tequila sunrise, briefly experiencing a fragment of this society world of hers, but he could never be a part of it, nor did he want to. It seemed that since he and his girl were last together in New York, its appeal had diminished to her as well, and *that* was truly impressive.

The *Sarasota Herald-Tribune* lie open before him, his feet resting relaxed and crisscrossed on the lounge chair opposite him. An article regarding a missing bomber and the ensuing search for the flight crew over the Everglades and Gulf of Mexico engrossed and distressed him, but he tried to shake it off. Today was a splendid day, marring it with thoughts of the war was unwelcome, especially when he heard her giggle behind him.

From the corner of his eye, he could see Lizzy watching him from inside the pool where she clung to the edge, but he remained silent continuing to read, waiting for her to voice whatever was swirling in that mind of hers. He could tell that she was up to something, something mischievous. Another giggle emanated.

He wrapped his hand around the crystal highball glass, just bringing it to his mouth when she spoke with that particularly devilish voice of hers.

"You have nice feet, Ducky."

He almost sprayed his cocktail. "I what?"

"Your feet, they look like a perfect stairway climbing upward to those strong legs of yours. Each toe is symmetrical with the same amount of space between. No fooling, some people have a second toe that extends beyond the first and that's truly cock-eyed, but not yours—they're in perfect alignment."

Will removed his dog tags, laying them on the table and stood. He walked to the edge of the pool, letting his toes hang over the colorful Spanish tiling. "Is that so?"

Towering above her, he folded his arms, tanned and feeling very masculine like Johnny Weissmuller in *Tarzan*. He laughed, as her eyes raked upward in a long appraising sweep from his apparently fine feet to his own appreciative smile.

Lizzy grinned impishly, stretching her legs out behind her, kicking underwater. His naughty girl knew he would watch each exertion and muscle flex of her perfect bottom. The smile now turned to a full-blown grin, his roguish response at her obvious attempt to unhinge him; it was working. With the first few sips of his tequila sunrise and the sight of her shapely body, the fuddy duddy in him was officially vanquished.

Saucily she replied, "Yes, I'll have you know, I've made a keen study of toes, and yours by far are the most killer-diller. Just like the rest of you."

His eyes drank in each slow kick she performed, water against flesh, resistance against movement. That alone was bringing about a reaction to him. Of course, he knew she planned it that way.

"You're not so bad yourself, Pistol. I have noted your own feet looking especially ..." He smirked, leaving her to finish his sentence.

"Especially?"

Diving over her into the pool, he promptly came up from the bottom with her foot captured in his hand. Pistol giggled from his tickles and squirmed to extract herself from his grasp. "Es—pecially," she barely sputtered out between laughing gasps.

"Suckable." He covered her wet toes with his lips.

She howled with mirth, squealing as his mouth sucked and licked her toes until he released her big toe with a pop. Both laughed raucously, and he grabbed her waist, pulling her toward him.

He stood in the center of the pool with Lizzy clinging to him, her arms circling his neck as his hands cupped her bottom to keep her buoyant. "So, I'm killer-diller, huh?"

"Yes, Ducky. You are utterly charming, simply irresistible."

"Are you going to tell me about my birthday surprise tomorrow or am I going to have to tickle you further until I can extract the information."

"Is that a war tactic? Something akin to a torture technique?"

"Tickle the enemy? Now there's an idea. 'Surrender or I will tickle a confession out of you.' Never mind my bomb load; my digits are deadly weapons."

She wiggled in his arms, splashing and laughing as his fingers traveled over her body. "Yes ... they are! Okay, okay, uncle. I'll tell you, but first I get a kiss."

"Oh, so you have a ransom demand? Will you hold back your information unless I comply with your command? I don't think any enemy soldier will be offering me a kiss after I torture them."

Wrapping her legs around his waist, she beamed. "I'm not the enemy."

"No, you definitely are not. Deadly yes, but certainly *not* hostile." His playfulness sobered to passionate expression as wet lips caressed hers in a slow, heart-stopping kiss. Even the cool water couldn't contain his body's reaction. "You're perfect, Lizzy."

She pressed against him tighter, titillating him with the pressure of her hips against the hardness tenting his swim trunks. His girl said nothing, just smiled, then dropped her legs to the bottom of the pool. Taking his hand, she led him to the stairs, gaining two steps above him.

Lizzy turned her head, glancing over her glistening shoulder and whispered, "Follow me, daddy."

Dripping, they emerged, walking hand in hand to the open French doors of the bedroom that she and Lillian had always shared.

Will stopped suddenly, rigidly, before entering. His hand tightened around hers, forcing her to halt her eager gait and turn to face him full on. He released her delicate hand in the next moment.

Lizzy furrowed her brow, focusing her eyes directly up at him. "What's the matter?"

"It's ... I have to tell you something, something about me. I know it's an inopportune time but, it wouldn't be right to ... you know ... if I wasn't completely honest with you."

"There's nothing you could say that would make a difference. I love you, Will."

He released a shallow breath then smiled pensively. "I should have told you sooner, but the time never seemed right, and I hope it doesn't make a difference. I mean ... um ... Lizzy, I'm Jewish. My mother's family, which means that my brother and I are Jews."

She rested her hand upon his cheek, smiled, then whispered. "I know. Now let's make whoopee."

His Pistol cracked him up, and he laughed, amazed when she took his hand again, leading him through the doors. He felt better for his honesty, but *how* she *already* knew left him perplexed. Of course, not long enough to dwell on it at that moment. She didn't care. She accepted him, and right now, that was all he needed or wanted to know.

Although there were no servants in the house, Lizzy switched the radio on anyway. In unison with his thundering heart, Anne Shelton's voice floated in the yellow room of elegant tropical furnishings. Without a doubt, he was nervous, his heartbeat increasing its cadence deep within his chest with every forward step he took. A large part of him, his ingrained sense of character, integrity, and propriety, thought they should wait until his return, until they were husband and wife. Call him traditional, or even a dud, but she deserved that respect.

Lizzy walked into his embrace and it felt perfectly natural when they began slow rhythmic swaying to "Only Forever." Her sparkling green eyes dilated to a deep hunter as she met his gaze, both gently held within one another's arms. He kissed her, drawing his fingers through her wet locks.

"Are you sure, Lizzy?"

She nodded, kissing him back.

Trying to alleviate the battling desires within, he couldn't help joking. "Is this my birthday, present?"

"No, silly. I'll tell you about that afterward. You promised me a kiss."

"And then some." He captured her lips again, his tongue exploring and playing with hers as their bodies slowly merged into harmonious attunement.

His hand slid down her bare back exposed by the swimsuit, feeling the soft heated flesh that, in her passion, defied the cool water from which they had emerged only minutes before. Long fingers tucked below the elastic waistband of her bottoms where the cleft of that shapely backside taunted him until he withdrew his hand, entwining it with hers. Hand in hand, they walked to the foot of her narrow bed. She turned, smoothed her fingers down his bare chest, stopping over his taut nipple.

Will couldn't help emitting a guttural moan at the pleasurable assault, kissing her in reply and encouragement.

Eager and aroused, he slid a strap to her swimsuit top down with one hand and pulled the tie behind her with the other, dropping the brassiere-like top to the floor. Intoxicating and radiant with the afternoon sun streaming through the doors upon her, those voluptuous breasts were nearly his undoing.

He fought the urgent impulse that demanded a hurried, frantic coupling with the woman of his dreams, but he wanted more from this first time. He wanted her to have more. This was his opportunity to show her the violence of his love and the fervor of his pounding heart. This was the moment he could prove, through every thrilling, rushing pulse surging within, that she brought him to life. In that instant, with those glorious twisting lips playfully taunting him and her pink, pebbled nipples tempting him, he understood why she needed him now, not in a year or two, but *now*.

Eyes remained locked as they nervously removed their bottoms before one another in slow, awkward apprehension. He felt a little embarrassed, noting how her eyes reacted in wonderment and startling awareness when his swim trunks dropped to his feet, springing his arousal free. Her youthful innocence didn't quell her immediate curious touch to his manhood. The feel of her soft hand stroking his swollen tip felt like nothing he had ever experienced. Sublime rapture met his normal reticent discomfiture, which faded as quickly as it came, leaving only the blissful feel of paradise as the woman he loved caressed him. Her thumb slowly gliding up the bulging vein of his shaft to the escaped droplet at his tip, nearly caused him to burst in her hand.

She marveled, whispering in awe, "It's so big. Bigger than I imagined it would be."

He couldn't help smiling at his girl's innocence, confirming the ethereal image she posed before him, unfazed by her nakedness and unaware of just how enticing she was. Soft and shapely, her narrow waist and creamy curves delighted his flesh when his hand glided over her damp body. Mind, touch, and sight memorized every inch of her perfection. He'd never forget this moment. Lizzy was an angelic, seductress, enchantress and vixen all in one. He was spellbound by the powerful hold she had upon his entire being and the gentle hold she had on his manhood.

Her quizzical hand continued to explore, feeling every part of his arousal, eager fingers following the same circuit as his when they brushed through her pubis. When Lizzy's mellifluous voice moaned with rasps at his brazen touch to her sex, he guided her down to the satin-covered bed where his hand continued to explore and tenderly bring about sultry mews and shallow pants, her evident gratified confirmation of his inexperienced lovemaking.

Their kisses grew, her touch becoming emboldened when she caressed his scrotum, causing his heart almost to explode in parity with his erection.

"Oh G-d, Lizzy. Wait, wait, baby. Slow down."

"I can't." She draped her leg over his hip, opening herself up to him. "I can't wait. I need you so. I feel this urgency coursing through me. It's making me wacky, the fluttering, the intensity from your touch is driving me toward bursting. I ... I can't slow down. I *need* it—I need you."

Lizzy trembled in his arms, their bodies lying side by side, as he brushed the plane of her cheek with his thumb. "I feel it, too. I love you so much."

"I feel the same. I'll *always* love you."

From cheek to neck, his hand traveled downward, savoring each silken slope of her body, smoothing down around the curving fullness of her breast, sliding over the indentation of her waist up onto her hip. He asked her a second time, "Are you sure you want to do this, baby?"

His girl nodded with certainty.

Dropping suckling kisses to her neck, his mouth branded the flesh his hand vacated. Wandering suckles tasted her décolletage until his lips surrounded a swollen nipple, enveloping her arousal, the capture of this tantalizing pinnacle an added aphrodisiac to him. It was an effort to keep from spilling on her hip when flicks of his tongue teased her tautness, setting her to writhing below him. Circling swirls around her delectable berry encouraged hungry suckles and nibbles, her pants deepening in response, her cries escalating.

His long finger gingerly entered her tight virgin passage where wetness confirmed just how ready Lizzy was for him. Slow, smooth glides in and out reveled in the slickness, as his mouth and tongue plundered hers in unison. Their consuming lips never separating for more than split seconds.

Small whimpers of ecstasy escaped when the arching of Lizzy's back met every gentle plunge of his finger until she cried out in frenzied writhing, spreading her legs wider for him.

"Will ... please."

He felt it, too, that need to be in her, joining them as one, claiming her as his forever. Settling atop her eager body, their hands entwined as he positioned himself. A bead of perspiration formed on his brow in nervous anxiety, wanting her so badly, hoping he could please her, yet fearful of hurting her. His tip brushed against her apex, beckoning him by the feel of her slick heat.

Bestowing tender kisses to her swollen lips, Lizzy became his as he entered her slowly, feeling her body stiffen beneath his. Only part way inside the most perfect place he'd ever find himself, heaven clenched tightly around his shaft. Momentarily motionless, he consumed the pained grimace from her mouth with his own.

Their rapid breaths commingled in heated puffs of passion when he said, "Do you want me to stop? Does it hurt?"

Her whisper against his lips, "Don't stop," was all he needed to hear. Filling her completely, he broke her maidenhood with a piercing thrust, their cries overpowering the radio until, as one, their stillness grew to gentle movements, building in intensity.

Lizzy never spoke of the pain of his penetration, instead she moaned in pleasured reward with every delving descent he made until her body trembled and quivered below him and her sheath tightened around him. That was a feeling he'd never forget. Her soft, yielding warmth enveloping and clenching around his hot, rigid flesh for the very first time was pure ecstasy, and he knew it was because she loved him as fiercely as he loved her.

His rhythm and pace grew with her meeting each thunderous thrust until stars collided. Scorching, white heat sent them both shooting through the heavens into a shuddering, blissful climax. Will burst, both crying out the other's name as he gave his forever girl all of himself—his love, his seed, and his soul.

Collapsing upon her, Will's spent body clung to her, and she wrapped him in her long legs. He buried his face in her neck, depositing kiss after kiss, his heart slamming against hers, their breaths labored. The feeling of her hand threading through his wet locks where she played with the short strands, calmed the frenetic pace.

"When ... when can we do it again?" She panted with labored breath.

He was lost in her sparkling eyes, so filled with passion and happiness. She grinned naughtily, wiggling her eyebrows.

Will chuckled, sliding from her, rolling to his side. Unwilling to sever their connection, he couldn't keep from caressing her as his hand traveled over her flat tummy up to her bosom. His fingers began their second pleasurable assault on her aroused peaks, his shaft already growing in response.

"Did I hurt you?"

"Yes, but I read in a book that it's to be expected, along with some blood." She looked at his johnson, as did he, and she flippantly stated, "I guess the book was correct."

"Book? I thought Yeats was your preference and here I discover you're reading about sex. That is some library on wheels you've collected."

Lizzy rolled to her side, her hand caressing his slick, swelling tip as she spoke.

"Oh, yes it is. You'd be surprised by some of the books I get, none of which are suitable for you GIs. Did you know there are something like sixty-four different ways we can do this? I saw pictures in another book."

He kissed her grinning lips. "You're incorrigible."

"I know." She draped a leg on his hip again, her hand now sliding up and down his already throbbing erection. "Do you think we'll be able to try all the positions before I leave on Monday?"

"I don't know, but I'll give it my best shot."

The salacious thought of loving Lizzy again made his pulse race, his manhood strain stiff with immediate need to be entrenched in her hot softness again. He didn't realize that it could happen that quickly, but then again, this was Lizzy. Yes, sex with his Pistol was heaven on earth. Gone were the thoughts of waiting for marriage, summarily replaced by how perfect this was, at this time, with the only girl he'd be with for the rest of his life.

This time she rolled him on his back with a lingering, deep kiss, shocking him when she straddled his torso. She leaned down to continue the kiss with her hair falling in disarray around them.

Coming up for air, Will asked with a teasing raised eyebrow as she slid down on his erection. "What's the name of this book? I think I may need to read it."

"The *Kama Sutra*."

****

Their afternoon of loving one another as husband and wife was followed by domestic tranquility when Will cooked dinner for Lizzy in Rosebriar's impressive kitchen. Three times the size of his mother's domestic haven of Dutch warmth and productivity, this kitchen embodied the cold sterility of an operating room—or a German assembly line, and there was no evidence of the ration here.

The radio played in the background as he stood at the stove, wearing the seasonal housekeeper's frilly apron over his uniform trousers and white tank undershirt. The entire scene felt natural and perfect, a feeling he wanted to hold onto forever. He decided then and there over a frying pan of eggs that he would ask for Lizzy's hand as soon as he returned home from the war.

From her perch in the breakfast nook, she bit her lip, attempting but unable to suppress her devilish grin.

After lowering the flame below the eggs, Will turned and folded his arms across his chest, leaning against the tile countertop. "I'm going to break you of that habit, you know."

"Which habit is that? The one in which I can't stop admiring my flyboy or the one that wants to 'do it' morning, noon, and night?"

"Neither. The one where you bite that beautiful lip of yours."

"And how are you going to do that?"

"With kisses. As many as it takes. What's going through that mind of yours?"

"I was just thinking of the surprise you're going to get tomorrow on your birthday."

He approached her in the breakfast nook and smoothed the wavy tendrils framing her face. She looked so lovely wearing a pale peach dressing gown even if it was only seven in the evening. "Ah ... that's right. You never did tell me. I suppose my tactics failed in the end."

"Oh Ducky, I assure you, your tactics were very effective. Do you really want to know your birthday surprise?

As if an overeager youth, he nodded before bolting back to the stove to turn off the eggs. Lizzy rose and came to stand behind him, wrapping her arms around his middle. She toyed with the ruffle on the apron as he assembled the traditional Dutch breakfast his mother made every morning.

She kissed his back. "Where do you go after Drane?"

"Hmm, well I'm not sure, but the air echelon will fly to a stateside airbase for our aerial embarkation to either Africa or Europe. My guess is that we'll be back at MacDill. We could be there anywhere from a few weeks to a couple of months. What does that have to do with my birthday gift?"

"I invited your parents to stay at Rosebriar until your departure. They arrive tomorrow afternoon on the Silver Meteor. I purchased their sleeper berth tickets for them and ..."

Will turned his head with a sudden snap of disbelief. "My parents? Here?" He beamed.

"Yes, that's swell right?"

He scooped her into his embrace, laughing almost giddy, feeling as though this day couldn't get any better. "That is more than swell! Thank you!" Elated, his kiss was strong and purposeful against that luscious, pliable mouth he loved so much. He loved every single thing that came from it.

"G-d, you're incredible, Lizzy. You did that for me? I'm the happiest man alive."

"Of course. I know how close you are with them and what it would mean to you to have them see you off and well, in truth, I did it for me, too. I wanted to know your family and I knew with you leaving soon, there wouldn't be another opportunity until your return."

"I wish you could stay longer. Spend more time with us as a family than just having tomorrow."

"Me, too, but I made a promise to my father. Kitty will be returning home in a few days, and I need to be there for her. I just hope you can spend some special memorable time with your mother and father."

"I'll see if I can get myself a few passes so I can." He removed the apron and handed her a fine china dish filled with toast, fried eggs, and cheese. They sat across from one another at the marble top table.

"Thank you for bringing them to Florida and inviting them to stay at Rosebriar."

She smirked with a pleased "You're welcome," before popping a piece of toast in her mouth, chewing in a rather self-satisfied fashion with her chin held high.

"Are you going to tell me how you came to know about my Judaism? Was it Lillian?"

"Lillian? G-d no. She keeps secrets like an iron vault. She'd never tell another's business. I just know, that's all." Shrugging a shoulder, clearly unwilling to discuss it with him, she dug into her eggs with sidestepping gusto. "This is good. I should give Mrs. Davis the recipe. It would be great with a piece of ham."

"The traditional Dutch dish calls for ham, but Jews don't eat dairy and meat together, let alone pork of any kind, but that aside, Lizzy, you're avoiding my question. You don't want to discuss how you came to know my faith, because..."

"Because, I'm happy and so are you and it's not a discussion for this perfect moment. I'm not keen on ruining this time we have together with thoughts of war and what's going on in Europe. I'm tired of hearing from everyone's lips, 'There is a war on'. Not this weekend, not after what we shared and how we feel right now."

"We can't escape it. What's going on in Europe and the Pacific can and will come here. Even President Roosevelt warned us of the Fifth Column. The saboteurs in California, New York, and Florida are prime examples. If we turn a blind eye to the atrocities going on elsewhere, then we're doomed to the same fate. Pearl Harbor was an ideal example of that. Look at what the Japanese have done to the Chinese."

"Will, I don't know anything about that. Nor do I want to. I'm tired of it all." She reached across the cold marble and took his hand in hers. "Can't we, please, just pretend, just for the weekend? Pretend that you don't fly a bomber they call the Widowmaker, and that I won't be going home to a sister who, I think, just may be a Nazi sympathizer or a fascist who believes in the horrid ideology of eugenics."

"Ah, so that's what you meant in your letters, and why you've been so unwilling to discuss it these three weeks." He sighed. "As much as I wish we could—we can't pretend. My family and others like us pretend to be something we are not. Mother has done so since 1914, living as a Christian, hiding her true faith in fear of being victimized by vicious government pogroms and antisemitism. What's the point?—they'll find us anyway and here we have denied ourselves living our religion proudly and openly. Further, it is no way to honor those who have—and are currently—dying for that same faith all over the world."

Lizzy stared blankly down at her eggs.

"Lizzy?"

"Very well, if you insist. I know because I met Bethsabee de Rothschild in the city two days before I traveled on the *Orange Blossom*. She told me what happened in Paris, and I inquired about your family and why you hadn't heard from them since July."

He sat back in his chair, his expression turning dour. "And what did she say? What has happened in Paris?"

She turned her head and folded her arms across her chest, looking out the window at the colorful rose garden. "It's such a wonderful evening. Please, Will, don't make me talk of such things and ruin the swell memories we have made."

"It's okay to tell me. I have my suspicions, anyway."

Her lip trembled when she reached over to take his hand again. "I can't."

The pleading yet stern expression he offered said everything.

"She said that ... that ... your family has sold diamonds to the de Rothschilds for years. That's when she told me that the DeVrieses are Jewish."

"Yes, that's true but you're avoiding my other question. You know what I mean."

With sudden sobering maturity, she spoke as quietly as possible. "This is so hard. She explained that in July the French police rounded up Jews for deportation and that your family may either be in hiding or sent ... to ... to a camp. People were put on cattle cars. That can't be true!"

His heart clenched. Not as intrepid as he thought, he hung his head, expelling a deep breath and squeezing Lizzy's hand in his. He fought the tears welling in his eyes then slowly withdrew his hand to wipe his face, covering it for long seconds of silent agony.

"G-d no. Good G-d no." Finally, he looked away from her and stared blankly out the window, covering his mouth with spread fingers, a cold perspiration forming upon his brow. "My G-d; it *is* true."

Lizzy rose from her seat and knelt beside him, reaching round to hold him as best she could. "I'm so sorry, Will. I'm so sorry to tell you this. She promised to write me of news and try to find out about your aunt and grandfather. Perhaps they are safe in hiding. Perhaps they left Paris beforehand. Maybe there is a letter with good news awaiting my arrival home."

His heart broke, and his ears hurt upon hearing the word "deportation". He shut pained eyes for a few seconds, then looked at Lizzy with a hard swallow, as he pushed down the misery, summoning the hardboiled Army flier he had become to fly the B-26. "How will I tell my mother? *What* will I tell my family?"

She reacted, rising upward with an immediate, strengthened embrace, his cheek pressed against hers. "You won't tell them anything. You can't. You would strip them of hope that they are alive and feed the fear that those Nazis could come here."

"My mother already fears that." He sat back and with somber declaration cupped his sensitive girl's cheek, locking his eyes with her, hoping she would fully construe his intimations. "They *are* here and closer than you might even think. There is only a fractional difference between believing as a sympathizer and participating as a collaborator. It takes only the smallest of deeds to facilitate evil. You need to be mindful and look for those actions and words from both your sister *and* father that may point to the latter."

Will could tell that a chill ran up Lizzy's spine by the way she seemed to recoil from his words, but he had written to her that they needed to talk about the things she discovered in the Meercrest library and Ingrid's bedroom. They just hadn't had the opportunity until now, but it was clear she had already considered these same notions—at least concerning her bigoted sister.

Reaching for her hand, he pulled her upon his lap. They hugged one another, and he rested his head against her shoulder as she kissed his head.

"Hold me, baby. Just hold me," he said in just a whisper.

Twenty-Five

The Sheik of Araby
November 2, 1942

U nlike the speedy *Orange Blossom*, the *Advanced Silver Meteor* streamliner train arrived at Pennsylvania Station behind schedule from Florida. This delay was almost expected since the Office of Defense Transportation began moving over one million men a month. The institution of the East Coast's ration on gas and rubber put usage of public transportation at an all-time high, causing every "chair-car" coach seat to be coveted and filled. Between Lizzy's disdain of train travel, coupled with leaving her heart at Drane Field, the delays only made the thirty hour trek north all the more unbearable.

She hated to leave so early but that was the deal she made with both her father and Aunt Helga. Lizzy Renner might seem flighty or flippant to some, but her word was her word. She would never break her promise to anyone especially when it involved Kitty's care. Moreover, with the arrival of Will's parents at Rosebriar the day prior to her departure, she acknowledged that the time he spent with his family was more important for his morale than anything else. He needed their supportive, loving send off, and as much as she wished she could visit with them as part of the Martel family, she had made promises to her own family to stay away no longer than three weeks.

There were tears though at her farewell. She couldn't help sobbing like a baby knowing this was the last time she would see Will before his departure. They spoke tender promises, both vowing with certainty that after the war, they would be together. Their romantic rendezvous, whenever he could steal away with a pass, had left her confident that unbounded love, uniting them on so many levels, would follow him into battle. She held no regrets whatsoever for going all the way and giving herself to him completely. The time together and that act had sealed their commitment to one another. Like the swans on Lake Mirror, they had mated for life and what a mating it was—all three times. Yowza.

Walking below the great arched glass roof of the station's grand concourse, she glanced upward noting the diminished daylight beyond. Hovering storm clouds in the late afternoon sky were promising winter rain on the Big Apple. Lizzy's thoughts traveled to the social season calendar and the many Gold Coasters who would not be traveling to Florida. With a wry smile, she mused how infuriated her father would be to know that the Martels were vacationing in Rosebriar's guesthouse until Will's imminent embarkation for who knew where. People of the day-to-day working class were not and never would be welcome in any capacity other than as servants at any Renner home. Keeping her word was one thing, but no one ever said she wasn't proficient at subterfuge and willful disobedience. Ingrid, in particular, would have quite a lot to say given her obvious antisemitism. Now that Will had confided his religion, Lizzy was sure that, if divulged, quite a bit would be said about that. All of it was of no consequence, however. She would remain steadfast and true to Will. No one would know and certainly not from her lips. Repeating her usual mantra in the back of her head, *I'll take that secret to the grave,* she nodded distinctly, confirming to herself the resolute commitment.

Gripping her small suitcase, she navigated through the crowds of servicemen, many of whom had arrived most likely for rest and recreation or for their embarkation following their stay at Last Stop U.S.A. A few of them could very well be with the 322nd Bomb Group's ground echelon now that they had left Florida. She tried not to pay attention to the wolfish whistles and stares, remaining focused on the stairwell ahead leading up to 33rd Street, intent on hailing a checkered cab to take her across town. She was just another weary traveler in the city that never slept in spite of the new dim out restrictions. A wrinkled mess and ready to dim out herself, her unscheduled destination was Greystone Mansion in Murray Hill, a hot bubble bath, and a snifter of her father's cognac. It was too late to travel back to the Island and, frankly, another train ride would be the death of her. Hopefully, the aged head housekeeper, Mrs. Albrecht, would still be at the townhouse to see to her needs.

Through the center archway, Lizzy exited out onto the darkened street where the tops of skyscrapers disappeared into the cloud cover. A long row of parked taxicabs sat at the curb waiting for fares, and Lizzy felt drawn to the colorful green cab catching her eye in contrast to the bland looking others. Her lips curled into a pleasant smile at the surprise of a woman exiting from the driver's side to take her suitcase.

"Where ya' headed?" The cabbie asked, smacking her chewing gum in hardboiled fashion, as though attempting to conceal her gender. She wore uniform trousers and a pea coat. Her hair was buried under a black cap, but Lizzy could still tell she was a woman, and thought it pretty swell that she had braved to enter into this man's world.

"Can you take me to Murray Hill? 233 Madison Avenue."

"That's Greystone Mansion, right?"

"How did you know?"

"Toots, I know this city like the back of my hand. Why, this summer I had a guaranteed fare to that ritzy place twice a week."

Lizzy climbed into the taxi and removed her gloves, warming her hands against one another in a fast rub. She furrowed her brow, wondering who on earth would visit Greystone from Pennsylvania Station. Immediately, she recalled Will's encouragement to "dig deeper" into his suspicions about her father's *supposed* actions.

"Twice a week you say?"

The taxi eased into the busy thoroughfare, and the cabbie spoke while navigating the crush. "Like pennies from heaven ... up until three weeks ago. I had it down to a science, sitting here waiting every Wednesday and Friday at nine-fifteen in the morning for my fare to exit from the station."

"Really? Always the same person? Is it a short, chubby man with grey hair and a mustache?"

"No, Miss. Some highfalutin' dame: blonde, tall, and dressed to the nines. Like you, dripping with greenbacks. I figure, she was meeting up with her sugar daddy."

Lizzy started to cough and promptly removed a handkerchief from her purse to cover her mouth. That last remark was unexpected. She didn't think she dressed so hoity-toity, and at once touched the fur collar surrounding her neck. *Perhaps it was Mother who hired this cab?* That speculation was promptly dismissed acknowledging that she would never take the railroad into Manhattan. Never with a capital *N* and certainly not twice a week. Where would she keep her Gordon's gin?

"I'm sorry, Miss, I didn't mean to imply ..."

Horns blared from the congested traffic on Seventh Avenue and Herald Square. Lizzy watched Macy's department store become shrouded in darkness as one after the next, each display window light dimmed.

"That's all right. Can you tell me anything more about this woman?"

"She never smiles. In my book, that just ain't right, but I suppose everyone has someone shippin' out these days and that's enough to make any woman melancholy."

"Hmm, yes. I suppose so." Lizzy continued to stare deep in thought out the cab window. Sudden raindrops splattered the glass in long streaks, blurring her vision. Her musing drifted to her Agatha Christie novels and how they always inspired her to play detective—even if the discoveries of late had produced horrific incriminating evidence where her sister was concerned. *Perhaps it's Ingrid traveling to Greystone? No, she wouldn't be caught dead in a taxicab. Greta? No, why would she need to see her father? Well, she is a golddigger. Maybe it was Mrs. Robertsen en route to one of those "slenderizing salons" she spoke of at the Memorial Day lawn party. No, No. I'm too tired to think of this, not tonight.*

Long minutes of speculation had passed when the cab pulled up to the curb directly in front of Greystone. It looked dark and menacing as it always did to Lizzy's happy spirit. Its five-story, stone edifice reminded her of an old world castle, a place she never liked to stay, even with its magnificent artwork and décor. Nothing like Meercrest with its palatial grounds of gardens, fountains, and the view of the Sound, she hardly came here.

"That'll be one dollar, Miss."

With thanks, Lizzy paid the woman, making sure to give her a generous tip. She grasped the handle of the suitcase and exited the taxi.

She stood in the drizzling rain, unperturbed by the precipitation, protected by the brim of her Stetson. In fact, she was more disturbed by the conversation about the frequent visitor—a possible mistress, she considered.

From her position on the curb, no interior light was visible from the dark grey exterior of the mansion, and she wondered if her father was on the Island, which would be fine by her—a relaxing bath in a house without the ever-present Mr. Gebhardt was surely more appealing than the alternative. Father's absence would also put off the inevitable conversation about said creep that she was sure would be forthcoming.

The front door opened without a sound into the darkened grand foyer and judging from the narrow beam of light casting into the hallway from behind the stairwell, she assumed that Mrs. Albrecht was still preparing the house for the evening. A glowing sliver of orange light breached the narrow aperture of her father's study door, ajar only a mere inch or two. A woman's low laughter assaulted her through the crack—and it wasn't followed by the usual hiccup at its end. Lizzy resisted calling out. Instead, she silently removed her coat, draping it over the end of the stair's handrail. Prompted by the fiction-inspired detective in her, she followed the light with tiptoeing footsteps. From behind the door, she heard muffled voices of non-discernible conversation. Some she thought to be German. The woman cooed in a familiar tone, sounds of passion and ecstasy, sounds she had recently made herself when in Will's arms.

This recognition caused the hair on her neck to stand, not from goose flesh but rather, alarm and revulsion. As though a curious child, she pressed her eye to the crack, immediately seeing the roaring orange blaze within the granite fireplace. She strained her neck to scan the room with a wide eye.

Horrified, from her limited view, she observed her father bent over an unrecognizable woman, a blonde, lying with her back upon his desk. Her stocking-clad legs spread, revealing her garters, as they wrapped around the girth at his waist. His hidden face was nuzzled at her neck and her hands grasped the back of his head, holding him to her.

Lizzy's palm flew to her lips. She ran from the door, appalled and repulsed from the image now forever burned upon her brain. Grabbing her coat, she shoved her arms within and barreled to the entrance, opened it, then with deliberate intensity, slammed it. Remaining inside at the threshold, she heard nothing and waited for what felt like minutes of catching her breath, attempting to calm her heart rate. She called out, "Hello? Father? Mrs. Albrecht? It's me, Lizzy. Is anyone here?"

Renner exited the study with an imperturbable smile, smoothing his hair. "Elizabeth, dear. What a pleasant surprise. I didn't expect your arrival at Greystone."

She kissed his cheek trying not to remember that the woman in the study had just done the same. "Hello, Father. You look flushed, is everything okay?"

"Just surprised. Let me help you from your coat."

She shirked her arms from the wool, and he draped it over the banister just as she had moments before. Her mind was scrambling, her heart breaking, and her expression struggling to remain placid

"Is Mrs. Albrecht here? I sure could use a hot bath and a cognac after my long trip. I'd like to go directly upstairs." She trained her ears upon the study door, now fully closed, but heard nothing.

"She has left for the evening. I'm afraid I'm the only one in residence. Come into the study and we'll have that cognac together."

"Your ... your study?"

"Yes, I have a fire going and since it is such a rainy, cold evening, you can warm yourself while we chat a bit. You can tell me all the news of Rosebriar and your trip south. I've missed you, Daughter."

"Thank you. It's swell to be back in New York." *Not really.*

Her father opened the door, and Lizzy's eyes frantically scanned every space of the massive room. Apart from the fire and the taxidermy owl staring back at her, it was empty. She knew what she saw. She unequivocally knew that a woman was here and felt confident that the fatigue of travel and her salacious thoughts of Will hadn't caused her to imagine things—imagine *that*. Only the lingering perfume in the air gave testimony to her sanity.

She sat with crossed legs, removing her hat and resting it upon the red velvet settee as her father poured two snifters of amber liquor. Lizzy could hardly look at him, so diverted by her searching she was, so disappointed in him. "Have ... you eaten, Father?"

"Yes. Have you?"

"I ate aboard the train. Although nothing like the southbound *Orange Blossom*, it was sufficient enough."

He handed her the nightcap with an unusual shake to his hand. "The War Department is certainly changing the face of rail travel, especially with the introduction of innovative streamliners and diesel locomotives. Although, I must admit Seaboard is reporting profits like never before. Gone are the days of the depression's diminished revenue and steam engine travel. I am quite enjoying these OPA restrictions on gas and rubber. Along with the modern technology, we rail investors are benefitting greatly."

"I had the pleasure of witnessing troop transportation on both my trips. The men were certainly appreciative of their treatment on board the *Orange Blossom*. With the exception of not allowing them into the Pullmans, Seaboard spared no expense."

"That'll eat into their profit margin significantly. I'll have to discuss that with SAL's Board."

Sitting in the armchair opposite, her father crossed his stubby legs as he lit a cigar.

She hated the sudden realization that he never seemed to care about her disdain of the putrid stench. Crinkling her nose would be fruitless. He made several consecutive puffs to start the embers, and she, in deliberate defiance, lit a Chesterfield. Normally, she smoked privately behind closed doors, but it pleased her to see him raise an eyebrow at her boldness.

"How is Mother?" she quickly asked a bit louder than her natural dulcet tone.

"Traveling as usual, visiting Blanchette Rockefeller at their retreat in Westchester. She's expected home to Meercrest the day before Thanksgiving."

"Oh, that's nice to hear. Have you heard that the President has changed the date of Thanksgiving again? It's so confusing."

Renner made an annoyed sound with his lips. "More propaganda."

"And Gloria? How is she?"

"In residence at Miss Chapin's. I have instructed Jamison that he's not to drive her anywhere. She needs to be under supervision. Now, tell me about Rosebriar? Did you have an enjoyable visit? Good weather?"

Still covertly searching the room, unconsciously, she smiled warmly. "It was much needed and the weather was simply sublime. The humidity was gone, and I was still able to swim up until my departure for home. Everything went smoothly with sealing up the house."

He looked to the fireplace as though lost in thought for a moment.

Lizzy followed his line of vision and furrowed her brow. "And Ingrid? How is she? Gotten herself engaged to John yet?"

Renner's lips pursed into a thin line. "Not yet. That boy is dragging his feet, and I've about had my fill of his indecisiveness. I expect both my daughters to be married by spring, and he seems to be in need of a push or two in that direction. It's no wonder his father doesn't give him any responsibility in Robertsen Aviation. John must be blind not to see what an opportunity it is to marry into the Renner family."

She delighted in the fact that no engagement had happened in her absence, but ignored his insult to John, choosing instead to take the bait for the subject she had feared. In light of his evening liaison, she felt emboldened. "Both your daughters?"

Renner placed his cigar in the crystal ashtray before him and leaned forward, tenting his fingers. "Yes, Elizabeth, *both* daughters. It's time. In my day, a young woman of your age would at the very least be courting with serious intentions for marriage."

"Then it is a good thing we have entered the modern age—diesels and streamlining and all that. Why should relationships or the roles of women not evolve as well, especially now with the war on? Women are working in factories, driving taxicabs, changing the future. The traditional roles are over. Lillian is an example of that."

"And your wayward sister will end up a spinster. What she does with her future is of no concern to me. I no longer consider her a member of this Renner family. She is a disappointment to me in every way. The Renner women of this family clearly understand that a female's role is at home, attending to her husband and many children."

She guffawed. "That's bonkers! Mother is rarely home and nineteen or twenty are hardly ages verging on spinsterhood. I have no intention of marrying just anyone for the sake of marrying, particularly someone to whom I feel such repulsion."

Her father stood, and she noted how he attempted to reel in his displeasure. He smiled down upon her as she brought the cognac to her lips with as much equanimity as she could muster. She was no longer that naïve, misguided debutante with her head stuck in the sand. The last three weeks had fully opened her eyes, and the lens in which she now saw her father was no longer rosy hued. In fact, in light of tonight's glimpse into his extramarital affairs, she had serious reservations about the man she once thought him to be.

"It is my wish, Elizabeth, and it is your duty. Gebhardt is a man of power and means and has expressed his interest in you repeatedly. A marriage into *his* affluent, racially pure German family is an opportunity any young woman of our circle would kill for. Have you not given this serious consideration as we discussed before your departure? You gave me your word."

And there it was, the second unavoidable fact she feared in the depth of her soul. Spoken by her father—*"racially pure German"* hung in the air as clear as *Heil Hitler.*

"I have, Father, and I do not believe that in 1942 there is a place in society for arranged marriages, no matter one's ancestry. I'm sorry, but my answer is no. I do not love him nor will I, ever."

He placed his hands upon his hips. "It's that soldier. The Jew."

She rose, standing eye to eye with him, the coffee table separating them as the raging blood raced through the pulse points of her neck. *Oh, G-d. How did he know?*

"The what?!"

"You understood me. You're consorting with a Jew!"

"I am not! My answer is final on the subject. I find George Gebhardt a creep of the highest order. His opinions and assumptions are as vulgar as his slimy touch upon my flesh. His blatant bigotry is abhorrent to me, and if you make me marry him, I'll jump from the Brooklyn Bridge to my death."

"Don't be ridiculous, Elizabeth! This is your future we're talking about here."

"Exactly. *My* future, Father. Not yours."

He stared at her for a long moment. "You've changed, Elizabeth."

"Perhaps, so."

Bending, she snuffed out her cigarette in the ashtray beside her father's freshly abandoned stogie, its robust streaming smoke attacking her senses as her hand trembled. She couldn't control the sneer or the condemnation with her words. "Besides, marrying Gebhardt runs the risk of offending your precious, perfect Ingrid—the *other* bigot."

"Ingrid? What does she have to do with this?"

"Because she's been sleeping with him for months. My sister is a whore."
He slapped her.

Stunned, Lizzy's hand flew to her stinging cheek. A long second passed as she stood shell shocked by his violence until fleeing the room with him calling out after her.

"Elizabeth ... Lizzy ... I'm sorry. Come back. Let's discuss this rationally."

"Dammit!" he finally exclaimed a minute later into the silent room as a decorative wall panel flanking the fireplace quietly popped open.

Ursula whispered. "Is she gone?"

He motioned with his hand for her silence and nodded. This night had not gone as planned. His daughter's arrival here at Greystone was totally unexpected. Her newfound self-awareness and the confidence she exhibited were utterly baffling. Three weeks in Florida, and she had returned an entirely different woman, one that might prove difficult to indoctrinate into the expectations of the people's community. She simply must be educated that her primary role as a woman within National Socialism was for the purpose of pure Aryan propagation.

Certain that Lizzy had retired to her bedroom, confirmed by the reverberating slam to the door two flights above, he closed the study door. "What do you know of Ingrid and Gebhardt?"

Ursula shrugged an apathetic shoulder. "Nothing worth worrying you over. It's a simple dalliance on her part. A young woman's first love should be with someone powerful and virile, and Gebhardt has proven to be very effective in educating her in the ways of the Party. She idolizes him and while she may have bedded him, she has done so willingly. I would think you proud that she is consorting with one as pureblooded as he, not upset."

"Why did you not tell me this? I do not approve. He has deceived me and my generosity."

"*Liebchen*, with any luck he will impregnate Ingrid, and you will have the bloodline we wish for. His and Ingrid's racial purity would make for the perfect Lebensborn, no?"

"Without access to Robertsen Aviation? No, Robertsen's Scandinavian genes represent the ancestral home of every German. He alone is for my Ingrid. Without his realization, he represents the Lebensborn Initiative even more than Gebhardt does. Only their child will not be adopted or brought to Germany. You forget my position in society, Ursula. A pregnant, unmarried woman of superior blood in Germany may be acceptable and encouraged under the initiative, but not here among my circle in America— not until we have victory. No, Ingrid will marry Robertsen and Elizabeth will marry Gebhardt, and that is my final word."

****

Shocked but refusing to give into her tears, Lizzy leaned against her closed bedroom door, breathing heavily with her hand still adhered to her cheek. She had never been struck before by anyone. Pigtails pulled by Henry Morgan in the Japanese garden, yes, but that was what happened during childhood crushes.

"He hit me. My father hit me. He knows about Will."

Suddenly Will's words of caution came back to her in a flash that if, in fact, her father was a member of the Nazi party, and she demonstrated any signs of dissension, he could become violent. Their cultish ideology was unwavering. Their cause was not receptive to diplomacy, no matter who tendered the appeal, beloved daughter or not.

She closed her eyes, regretful for having pushed him, but he had spurred her on by his inflammatory bigoted opinions and despicable unfaithfulness to her mother. Drunk as she always is, infidelity was wrong, wrong, wrong.

Lizzy locked her bedroom door, then dragged the carved mahogany chair from the writing desk over to it, wedging the top firmly beneath the crystal doorknob. She couldn't believe that she was resorting to this in fear of her father. Withdrawing to the private adjoining bath, she pulled the light fixture cord, and promptly turned on the water to fill the claw-footed tub. The hot steam soon rose, warming the white marble, but not her.

After long minutes of distracted undressing, she finally slid into the bath, allowing the warmth and bubbles to soothe her chilled flesh and trembling nerves. She imagined Will's arms surrounding and comforting her. In her despair, she wept, knowing that beginning tomorrow her focus must be turned to discovering her father's possible hidden actions and affiliations. She needed to find evidence.

Twenty-Six

Confess
June 21, 1992

On the Sunday following Jack's visit to Primrose Cottage, Juliana arrived earlier than usual at the Exeter Senior Apartments. Along with a barrage of questions, she brought with her two things she should have considered earlier to get her grandfather's lips flapping: onion bialys and lox. Bribery she hoped would be just the ticket, after all it worked with Jack four nights earlier regarding Alaska and now she had a first class plane ticket and a week's lodging secured at Sea Otter Bed & Breakfast in Sitka.

She stepped into the elevator and pressed the button with anxious determination. Torn between the need to lambaste her grandfather for keeping important secrets from her and her hope to coax him from his silent world, she vacillated in her anger. Not that she wasn't pissed off—oh, she was—but she was determined to reach deep down into herself to find diplomacy. Awakened by a nightmare of Mimi laughing at her, she felt emboldened in her pursuit of answers as well as an apology from him.

The elevator slid open onto the sixth floor, and Juliana observed Mr. Wooten leaving Mrs. Brighton's apartment, holding a small overnight bag. The sheepish look upon his face when she greeted him with a polite, "Boy you're up early, Mr. W," caused her to remember Vera's unannounced entrance into her grandfather's apartment last week. This only seemed to reinforce her dismay at his past and present behavior. This senior home seemed a veritable brothel, and she couldn't help wondering if it was the reason he had insisted upon this particular place.

Even still, she didn't expect that anything untoward would be going on inside at this hour. She slammed the door a bit harder than usual.

"Grandpa, are you still asleep?"

She could hear the shower running inside his master bath. "Grandpa. It's only me. I'll put up some coffee. We need to talk."

To her surprise, it wasn't Vera who came through the bedroom door but another woman wearing a beige towel wrapped around her torso. Ginger-haired, buxom, attractive and in her sixties, she greeted Juliana's shocked expression with a pleasant smile.

"Oh, hello. You must be Lou's granddaughter, Julie. I've heard so much about you. Everyone has told me what a beauty you are. Why, you're as cute as a button."

The offending stranger squeezed Juliana's cheek just as Mimi used to do. Unable, unwilling to welcome the woman with even a cordial acknowledgment or smile, she stammered.

"Um, er ... and you are?

"I'm Louise but everyone calls me Lou. Your grandfather is in the shower at the moment."

Lou and Lou, oh isn't that just too cute. Not.

"Can you please let my grandfather know that I'll be in the kitchen preparing breakfast for me and him?"

"Of course. Make yourself comfortable, dear."

Fuming, Juliana walked to the galley kitchen.

How could he? What happened to Vera? And who the hell does this stranger think she is telling me *to make myself comfortable!*

Already the morning was off to a bad start. Her anger was about to explode to the surface, but she shamefully had to admit that this Louise person, unfortunately, found herself in the line of fire. Perhaps if the woman had answered the door wearing actual clothing that might have helped, but the thought of her grandfather in some shag fest with a sixty-year-old was too much to handle. *Pinching my cheek! Only Mimi gets to pinch my cheek! Oh, that's right ... Mimi's dead and this one obviously thinks she can fill her shoes!*

The coup de grâce was pulling open the refrigerator door and finding two different Pyrex designs and four different Corning Ware patterns, all dating between the 1960s and 80s, none of which he actually owned.

Apparently these were the modern day, senior citizen equivalent to a calling card. Perhaps the pattern names suggested some subliminal message to the recipient from the giver, potentially a physical trait or a promise of dessert to come: Cornflower, Balloons, Floral Bouquet, Country Festival, Autumn Harvest, and the ever-present Spice O Life that seemed to sum up his playboy behavior toward them all! She wondered if Louise had brought Strawberry Sunday.

She harrumphed. "Six casserole dishes, all different designs. My seventy-three year old grandfather is a total Don Juan!"

Apparently, the two of them had been up for some time—coffee was made and there were those pink Sweet-n-Low packets on the counter. He didn't use a sugar substitute. So they must be *hers*, Juliana assumed with a curled lip. Her irritation was growing by the minute, fueled by the unexpected presence of this presumptuous woman.

She poured a mug of coffee, grabbed her blue Tiffany box, and walked to the balcony to wait for her grandfather's expected shit-eating grin to arrive. Today, she would find it neither cute nor endearing.

Even on a Sunday, the tram soared above the East River, and she sat back, cradling the warm mug in both hands. She forced her thoughts to Jack and the good vibe she had felt on Wednesday night, their near kiss, and her growing affection for him. In fact, she had thought about that night frequently, and how he really was a "ducky shincracker." All the horrific revelations of "*die familie*" seemed to pale when stacked against the beating of her heart when he held her.

She wouldn't admit it then, but she'd admit it to herself now: she was feeling pretty darned happy about their growing relationship. Maybe romance and a good man—a man worth putting her heart out there for— did exist. Jack Robertsen was the first guy to make her feel something meaningful, and she actually found herself excited, even hopeful. When he phoned her the following morning to tell her how he hadn't stop thinking about her, she could no longer rationalize her insecure excuse that only Primrose's magical spell was the likely cause for his romantic interest. He left her with no doubt that it was her.

The apartment door closed and Juliana heard the glass carafe slide back into the drip coffee maker, followed by the slider to the balcony, scraping along the track. She took in her grandfather's appearance. His hair was still wet and slicked back, a whiff of Fahrenheit aftershave overpowered her. He also wore the anticipated mischievous gleam in his eyes that spoke volumes to her. In her opinion, he looked twenty years younger, wearing blue jeans and a polo shirt, but that didn't stop her anger from flowing and the subsequent verbal assault. The unveiling of too many secrets—by others— all strangers—had set her on this warpath.

"You really need to start talking. How was I to know you were knocking boots with some fourth floor floozy? You should sign up for that TTY service the deaf use through New York Telephone and call me to let me know when you're otherwise occupied."

Louie knit his brows and sat next to her. She was surprised when he glared at her, then pinched her arm—hard. It was clear to her that he was disciplining her smart mouth, something she was not prone to do.

"I brought you bialys. Do you want one, or did *Lou* give you breakfast all ready? Seems like she skipped breakfast and went straight to dessert." She knew that was a low blow, but couldn't help herself in spite of the pinch and, as expected, he pinched her again for her smart ass comment.

"I just didn't expect to see someone half naked in your apartment."

He sipped his coffee and watched the tram; suddenly remorse replaced anger, and Juliana was unable to withhold her compassion for her grandpa. She couldn't help speculating on the loneliness he must feel since the love of his life passed away. After forty-four years, he had suddenly found himself alone, single and most likely feeling the effects of aging. He was still overwhelmed by grief at losing both his wife and son within the course of two years and missed them terribly.

Juliana reached out and smoothed his hand, realizing that apart from her, touch was absent from his life and most likely his lady friend's, too. Everyone needed touch, a caress, something to say, "I care."

She was surprised when his hand slid from hers. "I'm sorry, Grandpa. I never intended to be so angry or judgmental, but I *am* angry with you, only not for the reasons you think. Please believe me. I guess, I just miss Mimi, too, and it's hard for me to accept that other ladies may enter your life. I mean, it's not as though you're looking to fall in love or anything. That kind of love only happens once in a lifetime."

He shook his head and pursed his lips, and she wasn't sure if he was disagreeing with that statement or just plain disagreeing because he was pissed off at her for being rude to Louise and a brat to him. *Damn, I'm messing this up.*

She tilted her head to garner his attention away from the view and his coffee. "Please forgive me?"

He smiled forgiving her as only a beloved grandfather would.

"Thank you. I came by early today to talk to you about a few things." Wringing her hands together, she paused briefly, and he searched her face.

"I'm really angry with you and Mimi. I just don't know how to begin to talk with you about it. So, let me just start by telling you that I met a great guy, Grandpa. I really like him and think that maybe ... I could let myself, I don't know, *really* fall for him."

Louie grinned from ear to ear.

"He's Lizzy's grandson." She reached into the Tiffany box before acknowledging his shock, oblivious to how he gripped the edge of the chair with his free hand.

Juliana removed a letter from the box. "I'll get to that in a minute, but first there's this letter in Uncle's pile that I'd like to read to you if it's okay."

"December 19, 1942

My Dear Boy,

I know you have not had time to write since, I am sure, you are settling into life at the airbase where you will fly to Europe from, but just a word of your arrival will do my heart good.

How wonderful it was for your vader and me to see you off in Florida, how proud we are of you. I still cry when I think of what your sweet Elizabeth had done for us. When we received her telegram with all the arrangements, we could hardly believe it.

I know that I cried as shamelessly as I did when your broeder left, but you are my baby. As though it was yesterday, I remember holding you in my arms for the first time. How chubby you were. One day after you're married, I will look forward to the blessing of your own children and holding yours and Elizabeth's babies in my arms.

G-d will guide you and watch over you. He will keep you safe. Remember to pray, remember this: "Be strong and take heart, and have no fear of them: for it is the YHVH your G-d who is going with you; he will not take away his help from you."

I wrote this to your broeder, too, but now he writes how beautiful the Pacific Islands are when I know he does so for my benefit. Perhaps I should write him a verse or two about lying. It is not as though your vader and I do not read the newspapers or go to the cinema. I know my zoon's handwriting, and he shakes. He feels he must keep his thoughts and experiences a secret. Keep him in your prayers. He needs your letters.

We were surprised you would make such a sudden request but, rest assured, your vader and I have already found a suitable house for when you return home and propose to Elizabeth. He is currently negotiating with the Guggenheim family for its purchase in <u>Dutch</u> Flatbush. What a beautiful home and what a project you have laid at our feet, my zoon! In my busyness, I will nary have time to bite my nails in worry over my boys, and will be so engrossed in making a suitable home for you and your girl that I may hardly have time to write you. I am just kidding, of course. She will be so surprised and I promise to make it very special for her. We are both happy that you decided to spend some of the money your tante sent from France. Estella would want it that way. It is your money to do as you wish. Do not worry so about your broeder. He will have your vader's share of the business.

We live in wait for word. Your vader and I pray together, and we remain hopeful that your tante and grootvader are safe. We have gone to the French Consulate on Fifth Avenue, but they are of no help and there is no word even from the neighbor whom I wrote to.
Be safe my zoon. We love you and miss you,
Your moeder

Juliana folded the letter and watched as a tight smile formed upon her grandfather's lips. Finally, she reached into the box again and removed an item she found last night, waiting for discovery in a small box within the hope chest. She unwrapped the blue velvet, uncovering the item to reveal an antique, sterling silver mezuzah. "Lizzy's grandson is Jewish. Just like Uncle William."

He took the mezuzah from her hand, rubbing his thumb against the Hebrew lettering with affectionate tenderness.

"I started out today with a bazillion things I wanted to admonish you about, but somehow they've all faded. I'm mad at you, but seeing this expression on your face now, seems to lessen my anger. I was prepared to yell at you about not telling me that I have a huge family out there or about Mimi's brave American Red Cross history, or her finding the children in the forest. I'm shocked and saddened that you both chose to keep from me the horrific history of her Renner family. It makes my skin crawl to know that I'm related to a Nazi, someone who had a role in the murder of millions, but hanging onto my anger over that doesn't do me any good. It was fifty years in the past, and I suppose it was Frederick Renner's actions that caused such heroism in Mimi. That's how I'm going to look at it."

She held his gaze, their eyes locked, his smile still tight as he nodded in agreement. "If it weren't for my grandmother then Lizzy never would have adopted Henri, one of the children, and Jack, the guy I like, wouldn't have been born, nor would have the descendants of the other four children she saved."

Louie furrowed his brow, confused by her last statement.

"Did you not know about Lizzy adopting one of the children in 1945? Did you know that there is a tribute paid to Mimi in the Long Island Holocaust Museum in Glen Cove?"

He shook his head and brought the mezuzah to his heart, holding it in place.

"But all that doesn't take away the fact that my own father and grandparents chose to keep all of it a secret from me. I found out from strangers, Grandpa."

Louie reached out his hand, taking hers into his grasp. He bowed his head contritely.

Her heart clenched at the image he presented. "Lizzy's alive, you know, and Kitty is going to arrange for me to meet her. Kitty also took me to the museum to tell me about Mimi."

She observed how her grandfather swallowed hard, without a doubt affected by the news. "Anyway, that religious article in your hands?—I found yesterday, but on Wednesday I discovered a bunch of other things hidden in a wall behind a painting. Did William convert to Judaism when he came back from the war?"

Louie looked out at the tram, lost in his thoughts for a long moment until he raised his hand to his throat and smoothed down the ligature. He forced himself to cough and struggled to form a sound, finally croaking out in a weary, unsure voice. "N ... o ..." He coughed harder.

"Oh my G-d!" Juliana dropped from the chair beside him, throwing herself at his feet, handing him his coffee to drink. "Drink, Grandpa, drink. Take it slowly."

He guzzled the lukewarm coffee then finally after clearing his throat said, "We ... hid it."

"I can't believe you're speaking! What did you hide?"

"Our Jud ... aism."

"You're Jewish? The Martels are Jewish?"

"Just ..." he paused, gripping the mug, trying to speak. "Just me, Will, and our mother."

"Why ever would you hide your religion? Why deny your family your faith? I don't understand."

Louie brushed Juliana's hair from her face. No, his treasure wouldn't understand, never having walked in those shoes, never facing or fearing bigotry, having never seen or read about Pogroms or experienced being hated or shunned strictly because of her religious beliefs. He remembered distinctly, even in high school, how the Jewish students were sent to sit in the back of the classroom.

"My mother was a Dutch Jewess."

He coughed and drank again, but was determined to speak a truth long overdue, one that his brother had admonished him over all those many years ago after the war.

"She came to American in 1914 outwardly {swallow} pretending to be a Christian, but remained a Jew, raising us ... as Jews with the agreement of my father who was Protestant. To the public, we were ... a Christian family, but in private ... we kept Sabbath and even received our Bar Mitzvahs in a synagogue in Paris in 1934. We learned Hebrew."

He paused, drinking again as Juliana sat back on her heels, rubbing his shin up and down in concern. She remained patient, watching how he took his time from the exertion of speaking again. His arthritic hand clung to the mug, trembling when he held it to his lips.

Louie's chest expanded in a deep breath. "G-d, it feels good to speak, if only just to tell you that I didn't appreciate your disrespect to Louise or me earlier."

Juliana rose up and hugged her grandfather. "You're right. I'm so sorry I was mean. Yell at me if you need to. I just want to hear you speak. I've missed you so much. I love you."

"And I love you, my jewel. There's more to tell you, so let me speak it all because when I am gone the story dies with me." He rose from the chair and walked to the railing of the balcony, looking out at the tram. This was hard. He never thought he'd share this history with anyone, but from the start had hoped that Juliana would discover it on her own. "Our family business, the DeVries Diamond House was established by my mother's father, Willem in Amsterdam. Upon my parents' betrothal, he asked my father to run the business as his own—as a Christian business to further its growth, as well as to protect its assets."

He looked over his shoulder to where Juliana had taken a seat, making sure she was attentive to this part especially. She sat ramrod in her chair, listening.

"You see, some Jews concealed their true faith expecting that history might one day repeat itself and persecution would come again."

He paused at her nod of understanding and recouped his labored breath, resting his sore throat. She waited patiently until he began again.

"It did come again, in Russia and then the Second War. Just before the Nazis invaded the Netherlands, my aunt sent all our European assets by courier to my brother: diamonds, money, jewelry and treasured heirlooms to protect our family's wealth from being plundered by invading armies or confiscated by Nazi officials. *That* is the money he gave to you. His share of the diamond business. And when I am gone you will have mine, too, and you will give it to your children and grandchildren in honor of the DeVrieses."

"But you never said anything about the faith of your family, or the details of the family business."

"You were wrong about your father keeping this all from you. He never knew—I never told him. After the war, religion of any sort seemed so pointless to me, but it was important to your grandmother that we christen Gordon in her faith. That was one of several reasons for my falling out with Will." His voice was weakening and he stopped speaking abruptly, cleared his throat, and rubbed his neck. When he began his voice had grown raspy. "At the time of your father's christening in 1949, my brother and I suspected that our aunt and grandfather had been deported and had most likely perished during the occupation of France. The roundups in July of '42 ..." his voice trailed off. "In 1980, your great-uncle traveled to Paris, demanding answers from the government in regard to our family's whereabouts. He discovered that they were sent to Auschwitz."

Juliana gasped. "Oh G-d! That's terrible. You're speaking of the The Vel d'Hiv, Grandpa! Lizzy is making Jack take her to the fiftieth commemoration next month."

Louie was astonished. "Really? Why would she do that?"

"There is so much to tell you about Lizzy. I just don't know where to begin." She rose from the chair and walked to him. "I guess the best place to begin is to tell you that I'm leaving for Alaska on Friday to bring your brother home."

"He's in Alaska?" Louie snorted a laugh. "Only a vaporhead would think he could escape his past and memories by moving to Alaska. What a jackass. When you see him, tell him he owes me two bucks with fifty years of interest."

"I will. I promise. Now, please tell me all about your aunt and grandfather. I want to know everything about them."

Louie clutched her hand in his. Yes, it felt good to speak again.

****

Apart from his forty-eight foot sailboat, *Liberty*, Jack's grandparents' home, Evermore, was one of the happiest places on earth for him. Although he had traveled the world these last ten years, no destination had offered such perfect harmony and beauty than the estate in Mill Neck, Long Island. Peaceful views of Mill Neck Creek lent to the appeal of meticulously manicured grounds and expansive English gardens.

It almost seemed sacrilegious to disturb the tranquility surrounding the estate when his black, Kawasaki motorcycle arrived, bringing its cacophony of noise toward the house. But today was a perfect day for a bike ride. In fact, he needed this ride for what lay ahead of him—a visit with his grandmother.

With the white mansion in sight, Jack rode his bike up the drive. The sweet aroma of the blooming honeysuckle penetrated his helmet, and the picturesque water to his left provided a sudden calm. The happy image of his grandfather fishing at the shoreline popped into his mind's eye. They had never been able to catch a thing because laughter was part of every moment spent with his dad and Grandpop John. The three of them were sure to scare off more fish with their raucous hilarity than could ever be caught.

The motorcycle's wheels crunched the white gravel of the long driveway, and he stopped before the entrance, dismounted, and removed his helmet. Similar to his actions at Meercrest, Jack breathed in the intoxicating fragrance of flowers, herbs, and the sea, a distinct bouquet he could never replace or even fully define. It seemed particular to old Long Island, which, to him, represented the scent of home. He vowed to move back to the North Shore as soon as he retired; work and travel no longer had any appeal. It's not as if he needed the money, he rationalized.

It was still early morning, and he knew where his grandmother would be—in her secret tea garden. For as long as he could remember it was her particular escape every Sunday morning with the *New York Times*, *Wall Street Journal* and, since its first publication, the *Weekly World News* just for fun. If one thing could be said about Elizabeth Robertsen, it was that she dearly loved to laugh, and the *Weekly World News* was like the comics for her.

He followed a path leading to the back of the house where it wound through lush, green hedges and around a couple of small ponds until he reached the footbridge of a third pond surrounded by colorful ornamentals. On the far side towered a splendid, long arbor, vibrant with blooming yellow roses. As he crossed the bridge, he could see his grandmother in the distance sitting at her tea table in a clearing surrounded by a colorful spectrum of blooms. The morning sunlight streamed down upon her. She was a vision and he saw her fifty years younger at that moment. Her brown hair was pulled back into a ponytail, and she wore a teal, one-piece swimsuit from her daily swim. One to always take great care in keeping herself trim and in shape, Jack couldn't help but to admire her long toned legs void of all the preconceived expected features of a seventy year old: no spider or varicose veins, no age spots nor any flab.

Her mischievous laugh rang out as she held onto the ridiculous, supermarket rag of tabloid reporting. "Good Lord! ... Oh my ... he's ... a bat boy!"

Jack couldn't help laughing along with her. It was infectious, devious, and downright sinister at times—one of the happiest sounds in the world. At that moment, he realized that "Lizzy" was her essence. She was and always would be the pistol that William had fallen in love with. She could never change that part of herself, just hide it, but sometimes it showed itself. "Elizabeth" embodied the Robertsen she had to become and the woman she needed to be to manage the Phoenix Foundation with such diligence and grace.

When she heard his approach through the hedgerow, she peered up and lowered the tabloid. "Jackie! What a surprise!"

"Hi, Grandma." He kissed her warm cheek. "You're looking especially beautiful this morning."

She furrowed her brow. "Am I? Go figure. And here I was just thinking how sometimes I must look like this bat boy." She threw the paper on the table. "Such trash, but it's funnier than the funnies, which aren't even funny any longer. Why I remember when Mayor La Guardia read the funnies over the radio in '45. Now *that* was a hoot!"

"You hardly look like this 'bat boy'. More like a Hollywood starlet."

There was that laugh again, her eyes sparkling with humor. "Oh, do go on. I haven't heard such sweet nothings in years!"

Jack took a seat across from her and filled her coffee mug, thinking nothing of stealing it for himself. Already, his heart was pounding in anxiety. He had to take this slowly.

"So, what brings you home today? Tired of that closet of yours in Garden City or have you just missed me?"

"Good day for a bike ride, *and* ... I missed you." He dipped a strawberry into a bowl of sugar and popped it into his mouth.

"Well, you wouldn't miss me if you would just move back home, dear. You know this house is yours when I'm gone. My children don't want it, and you are the oldest of my grandchildren. So you should start to make arrangements. Would you be so scandalized to move in with your grandmother or are you waiting to find the perfect apartment in the Big Apple?"

"The Big Apple? No one calls it the Big Apple anymore."

"It used to be a song ... and a dance ... and I'll have you know the origin of the term is sketchy at best. I never knew a single Gold Coaster who sold apples in the city to make ends meet!" She snorted a laugh. "Well ... anything is believable, huh? For cryin' out loud, I still waterski!"

"You loved growing up here, didn't you?"

A contented smile spread across Lizzy's lips. "I love the Island. I loved Meercrest, but there's something special about Evermore. I feel the most peace here, especially this garden."

"I took a drive over to Meercrest the other day. The water tower looks to be leaning a little. Sort of like the leaning Tower of Pisa, and I noted that the gazebo was damaged from the ice storm in January. The roof is caving."

"Ah, my water tower. If only I could move it here. I'll have to look into that. As for the tea gazebo, I think we should have a bonfire." She shuddered. "My mother's personal tavern."

Lizzy watched as her grandson leaned back in his chair, folding his arms across his Izod insignia. He tilted his head up to the sun, warming his already tanned face. His visit was unexpected and—his talk of Meercrest and visit there—unusual. She wondered what he was about coming to Evermore this early on a Sunday morning. To share in her Sunday morning ritual? She didn't think so, but she'd be patient. Jack's mind was like an onion. She needed to allow the layers to peel back. He'd get to the point when he was ready.

The first peel she figured was his question, "Are you still up to go to that Mets-Giants game at the end of August with me?"

"Of course! Why wouldn't I? The Giants are my team even if they abandoned us New Yorkers in '58"

"I could get tickets to see the Dodgers game the week before."

"Why ever would I want to see the Dodgers? They're another traitorous team. Abandoning Brooklyn like they did. You're a dear to ask, but no thanks."

The second layer fell away when he stared in distraction at the vibrant pink and white Sweet Williams at the border edge of the garden. "I was wondering? Have you ever been to Victoria Flatbush?"

She couldn't meet his eyes when she answered, her focus traveling instead to what held his attention. The flowers named "First Love" caused a small, thoughtful smile upon her lips. "Flatbush, Brooklyn? Maybe. I can't recall. I once visited your great-aunt, Lillian, in Park Slope when she christened her son. Gosh that was ... hmm ..." She shrugged. "Gordon, yes, that's his name."

It was Jack's sudden fidgeting that alerted her to his inner struggle. He rested his hand on the leather fanny pack clipped around his waist and began to play with the zipper. She waited for the third layer to fall away. While waiting, she dipped a strawberry into the sugar bowl. G-d, she loved the sweet, succulent taste of fresh berries.

"When was that?" he asked. "The christening?"

No, she wouldn't allow this conversation to go any further. Definitely not.

"Darling, after your overnight visit last week, you never mentioned that you'd be back so soon. Not that I'm not happy to see you and enjoying this delightful little tête-à-tête, but it's clear to me that you're making small talk in your attempt to procrastinate." Her voice grew concerned. "You can tell me anything, you know. Your secrets I'll take to the grave. I'm very good at keeping secrets."

"You know I don't keep secrets."

"I have not seen you this distracted since you broke up with that ... that ... what was her name?"

"Amy?"

"No, not her, the other one."

"Lisa?"

"No, she was evil incarnate. I mean the one with the ... you know." She held her hands far from her chest.

He raised his eyebrows. "Ohhh ... Cindy."

"Yes! Going so long without those probably knocked you for a loop." She laughed, trying to divert his line of curious questions. "Is a girl involved? Or perhaps, there is no girl and that's the problem. A man's unfulfilled needs can certainly feel like the end of the world."

"What? Getting girls is *not* a problem, Grandma." He rolled his eyes. "Sheesh, the places your mind goes."

"Then what *is* the problem?"

He took a long drink from the coffee mug, and Lizzy lowered her eyeglasses to the very tip of her nose. She raised an eyebrow, her locked gaze calling him out. Getting him to talk was like pulling teeth.

Jack put the mug down and now began to play with the roses in the center of the table. "Well ... this *is* about a girl, but I'll get to that in a minute. First, I have a question about the painting."

Another beating around the bush question, another peel. She sighed. "Which painting?"

"The one you are fighting with the French Culture Minister over."

Lizzy grit her teeth. "Oh that man is infuriating! He's dragging his feet on this when he knows damn well that the painting doesn't belong to the French government. He's as bad as some of these museums I read about— claiming ignorance over the many paintings in their possession. I know for a fact that the Hendrick Avercamp was plundered by either the Vichy government or Nazis! They need a Commission to make this process easier. The French government owes the Jews millions!"

"I agree, but why is *this* particular painting so important to you?"

She furrowed her brow. "I'm not sure what you mean."

"Well, I understand about the Monet and the Degas and your eagerness to return those paintings to their rightful owners, but I never did learn how you knew about the ownership of the Dutch Master that the French have in their possession. Whose is it and why are you playing proxy for them?"

"I didn't think you cared to know, Mr. I Prefer Not To Get Involved." She drank from the coffee mug, watching her grandson from over the rim.

"Do you think you'll be successful in acquiring it?"

"I am ... as usual ... optimistic in my endeavor. I'm sure that when I meet with that insufferable little putz and hand over the two other Masters, he'll have no choice. If you must know, I'll share this with you because you have asked and it is obviously bothering you, but the painting belongs to the family Lillian married into. It was taken from them upon their deportation during the Paris Roundup. If he's still living, I hope to have the foundation deliver it to Lillian's husband Louis. His grandfather and aunt were murdered in Auschwitz."

"But, how did *you* know the history of that painting?"

"Their name, DeVries, was listed in a Nazi document of reported stolen works of art during the Roundup. I knew this family had been deported. What's at the heart of these questions, Jack?"

"I saw an almost identical painting Wednesday night and ... and well ... that's where the girl comes in."

Fear bubbled within her at his statement, and she watched as Jack unzipped his fanny pack and withdrew an old photograph, its decorative edges scalloped, its back slightly yellowed with the passage of time. She wondered what the snapshot had to do with the painting, let alone his sudden interest in it—and involving a girl no less.

He slid the photograph across the metal table toward her, and she froze when it stopped at her outstretched fingers.

Her left hand flew to her heart and she gasped in intense, stunning shock. Eyes blinked with disbelieving snaps as she beheld herself fifty years younger beside the man who still owned her heart, now beating a fierce litany.

She could barely control the shake to her hand when she lifted the image from the table. *William. My love. Oh G-d, Will.*

Lizzy physically felt a fracture form in her usual cool composure as though split by a scalpel to her heart's wall. She focused solely on that incredible, sensitive man whom she wounded so many years ago. With her trembling index finger, she traced his image, remembering that day when she surprised him at Drane Airfield. How handsome he had looked in his flight gear, how in love they were.

Faced with his image, she pushed down the usual fight that always began with the emergence of such memories. Instead, she welcomed the rush of them. She closed her eyes and raised the edge of the photograph to her bottom lip where she smoothed it against the curve of plump flesh. After thoughtful seconds, the image lowered, caressing her chin, sliding down the sensual slope of her neck. Soft skin met the now warm photo as it glided over her bare chest, finally coming to rest upon her pounding heart as though pretending to hold Will within the rhythmic cadence of its beat.

Lost in memories and clutching the snapshot to her body, another crack in her retaining wall appeared, a deeper fissure this time. Her lips trembled as she held back the tears, vividly remembering their pledge to one another.

-Please wait for me, Lizzy. I love you so much it feels like my heart is going to explode.

-I promise, I'll be waiting. I'll always be your girl. After all, I was born to be yours.

She could still feel the lingering tingle of his gentle, soft kiss against her lips after her declaration at the train station when she left him in Florida.

A lone tear streamed down her cheek.

"Grandma? Are you all right?"

Brought out of that place in her heart where sheltered memories of her sweetheart dwelled waiting for her dam to break, Lizzy wiped the moisture from her cheek, opened her eyes, and smiled in wistful remembrance.

Once again, she looked to the image and whispered in a voice that sounded so young, so contrite, "Where did you get this?"

Jack sighed, reaching out his hand to her, which she took. "This is why I didn't want to do this. Looking back is never happy."

"You're wrong. He made me so happy."

It was then that she realized the buried secrets of five decades were unavoidably being exhumed. Her grandson had given her this photograph; he knew of William. The barrier holding all the secrets and emotions back split even further. "Where did you get this, Jack?"

"The girl is William's great-niece Juliana. I met her last week when she came to the paper looking for information ... about you. She told me about your wartime romance. She knows about Lillian, Kitty and the *whole* Renner history."

"His niece. Lillian's granddaughter?"

"Yes. She met Kitty who took her to the museum. Grandma, she desperately wants to meet you. Would that be okay?"

Lizzy was stunned, her words exiting as her mind raced ahead at the ramifications of this girl knowing part of her history with William. "She wants to meet us? Oh that Lillian could be here. Yes, I would love to meet Juliana."

"Good, she'll be so happy. You see, she inherited William's home in Brooklyn where the painting is ... and she found all your letters in a footlocker filled with snapshots and his war memorabilia."

The splintering fissure spread into a thousand leaking cracks, and she couldn't stop her dam from shattering with a powerful burst. Her heart seized, and she clung to the snapshot even tighter. "In-in-inherited? Primrose Cottage? Is William ... did he? Please G-d, no!" She cried out, panicked from the depths of her soul. "Tell me, please!"

Jack rose from his chair and knelt in the grass beside her, taking her hand in his. "Please don't cry. He's not dead. Please don't cry. I meant to say that he *gave* her the house. He's alive. She's flying out in a few days to find him. Would you like to see him again?"

She bowed her head, allowing the flood of tears to roll unabashedly unchecked, her head shaking with raw emotion flowing through her. Closing her eyes again, she whispered, "I have never wanted anything more in my entire life. To see him again is ..." Her voice trailed off with unspoken words concealed in the privacy of her heart.

Although relief washed over her, and joy soared through her, she knew judgment and atonement for her past actions would be at hand. She knew the one secret she concealed for forty-nine years would need to finally be told.

Lizzy smoothed Jack's askew hair. "But, he may not come. I hurt him so terribly—twice, betraying him in every way he thought possible. After your grandfather's death, I was too afraid to find him ... too afraid to face his condemnation and anger. He will never forgive me, but there are things he must be told."

"If he loves you, he'll forgive whatever you did."

"He won't. He won't come, and I am sure his love for me has long extinguished."

"That's not very optimistic of you." Jack took a deep breath. "Grandma ... if he does come, does he still own your heart, as you once said—until the end of life's story?"

She looked down at the snapshot again. "He does. He always has. I established the Phoenix Foundation in honor of him."

Lizzy crumbled, falling onto her grandson and sobbing with deep, wracking emotion as his arms came around her, comforting her in his embrace.

Twenty-Seven

Trade Winds
June 25, 1992

After check-in at JFK Airport's Delta Airlines ticket counter, Juliana stood by the gate, waiting to board the first of her flights to Sitka, Alaska. High above the tarmac, she looked out the huge terminal window, watching planes taxi down runways, maintenance crews scurrying to keep on schedule, and the ever-present baggage trolleys pulling cargo and luggage. Lost in thought, she ignored the hive of gate activity behind her, vaguely registering the garbled overhead announcements. Sporadic glances toward the closed door of Gate 39 indicated that departure would be some time yet. She sipped her black coffee, continuing to observe the men below her work on the nearest wide-body jet awaiting its next journey.

Expending nervous energy, she tapped the fingers of her free hand against the glass. She was anxious, not because of the air travel, but of what she'd find at the other end of the eleven hour trip across the country. Jack hadn't indicated details, just that William was alive, and he had provided her with an address where the man had lived for the last fifteen years. Questions weighed heavily upon her shoulders. Was her great-uncle married? Did he have children? Was he healthy? Where had he been all these years and, more importantly, would he be willing to come east to see her grandfather—or Lizzy, for that matter?

She was no longer concerned about all those questions she had at the beginning of this mysterious journey, the ones that asked, "Why did you give *me* the house and the money?" "How did you even know about me?" "What happened in the war and your being a POW for two years?"

Again, her mind found its way to Jack and his phone call about his meeting with Lizzy this past Sunday. He hadn't expected his grandmother's tears, and it upset him to know she'd never stopped loving William after all these years. Juliana felt a kinship with him when he expressed his dismay in questions such as "What about my grandfather?" "I feel so bad for him." "Did she love him?"

Yes, she understood completely because it had been unnerving when her grandfather shared that he had feelings for Louise. Talk about being blown away. It took two days for her to come to terms with the fact that he needed companionship and that it didn't stop him from loving and missing Mimi. That would never change. Louise would never replace his wife of forty-three years, but she could add joy and laughter to his otherwise lonely life.

Juliana thought of the last of her uncle's letters that made reference to Lizzy. Correspondence received from her grandfather indicated the brokenhearted man on the receiving end of the V-Mail.

March 16, 1943
Dear Brother,

    Training, training, and more training but at least the 1ˢᵗ Marines are out of the thick of it. We'll be back better and stronger with our next engagement, but for the time being, Down Under is having summer, while you're freezing your backside off. Though like you, I'd much prefer to be freezing back home in the Big Apple. What I wouldn't do for an egg cream or a knish.

    Take me to task if you will, but you need to get it into that vaporhead of yours that for whatever reason Lizzy called it quits, your relationship wasn't meant to be. I know you fell in love with her, but maybe now wasn't the time for you both. You had fun while it lasted and that's a good thing. You're in war, old man, and you need to focus on the job at hand any way. Would you rather have received a letter kicking your ass to the curb? I don't think so. I've seen firsthand what that kind of demoralization can do to a man. One of my buddies received his with mail call at the arrival of the Army on Guadalcanal. After what we went through, that letter near sent him over the edge. What I'm saying, Will, is to accept it as a casualty of war and move on. Your focus should be survival in that tin can of yours. You've done all you can, trying everything in the hopes to get a letter through past her father, even writing to Kitty upon different stationery. Truly, if it was old man Renner standing between you and her, either Mother's letters or the ones you sent to Kitty would have reached her. So stop worrying that he's the one keeping you from her. In the interim, I'll write Lil and hopefully she'll have heard from Lizzy and can shed some light on what has happened back on Long Island. I warn you though it may be months until you hear from me about this. She's traipsing all over England in that doughnut truck of hers.

Now, the best thing for a broken heart is to go find yourself one of those British birds and have a good time. Oh, and in the words of my very wise brother—Wear a Rubber!

Affectionately,

Lou

Juliana rose up and down in her Converse sneakers, flexing her ankles with mindless action as she contemplated love and heartbreak, surrounded by the hustle and bustle of the frenetic New York airport. Lizzy and William's love had spanned fifty years! Her grandparents' love remained true and faithful until death separated them, and, possibly, love of a different type had come to her grandfather again. These were hopeful examples to her skeptical mind. Then there was Jack ...

"Excuse me, is this the gate for departure to Seattle?"

A slow grin spread across her lips when she saw Jack's brilliant smile reflecting in the window before her, setting her heart into a thunderous beat. She turned. "Why yes. Are you going my way?"

He looked down at the paper ticket and seat assignment clutched in his hand. "Seat two C on the aisle."

"Gee, isn't that a coincidence. I'm at the window in seat two D. Looks as though we'll be traveling together."

"Well then, this promises to be the best trip I've taken in years." He set down his camera bag and walked toward her, removed the tepid coffee cup from her hands, and boldly drank from the opened lip.

She raised a brow at his familiarity but acknowledged to herself how right it felt. "Are you always in the habit of drinking other people's coffee?"

"Only people I feel comfortable with. Is it okay that I'm joining you on this trip?"

"Why not? You're as much a part of this story as I am. It's hard to extract yourself from this love affair as much as you may want to, isn't it?" She bit her lip, thinking he would assume she meant *their* not-quite, burgeoning love affair.

"You have no idea. I'm in too deep now to get out even if I wanted to. Julie, she cried for hours, convinced he'd never forgive her of something she did all those years ago. In my thirty-three years, I've never seen such expressive emotion from my grandmother. It was as though her dam broke and a flood of memories and regret came flowing out."

"Regret for marrying your grandfather?"

"No, something else, but I don't know what. When I left her last night, she was resolved to write William a letter if he refused to come east. I told her, essentially, that she was full of shit because if I know her, she'd just get on the next plane and fly out to see him. I refused to give her his address until I know more. Hence, my joining you."

Juliana couldn't help feeling a slight sting of disappointment. "Oh, so that's the only reason you're going."

"No. That's not the only reason. I'm actually worried about you making a trip alone, so far away. I know the area and the people and it's truly magnificent this time of year. I'd like to show you around, spend some more time with you. And ... if I can keep my wild grandmother from flying out there on, what could be a fool's errand, then all the better."

"What if she does? What about Paris?"

"She'll be there, but has it in her head that if *he* could be in Paris, everything would change. It must be about the painting in your hallway."

"The Dutch one?"

"Yeah, the Avercamp. There is a sister painting that matches yours and is currently held by the French government. My grandmother explained that she's trying to obtain it to give to your grandfather. Apparently, it was looted from your family during the Paris Roundup and no effort had been made to locate surviving family."

Juliana took Jack's hand and led him to two blue seats against the window. "Jack, you were right and your grandmother's claim confirms it. My grandfather and great-uncle are Jews. That means that I'm part Jewish in my blood. I never knew—they hid their faith. Grandpa's aunt and grandfather perished in Auschwitz. They were sent to Drancy in Paris and then onward."

He looked down at their still entwined hands. "I'm so sorry to hear that."

Suddenly it dawned on him. "She truly loves him, Julie. All of it ... the creation of the Phoenix Foundation, the veteran's home, the Vel d'Hiv commemoration, securing the painting ... all of it was to honor him and his family ... your family. Not just restitution to millions, but specifically restitution to *him* because of her love for him and the overwhelming guilt for what her father did—and maybe what she did."

Juliana's eyes filled with tears as she listened to the tender tone of Jack's voice.

"For whatever her reasons for marrying my grandfather, it seems as though the foundation took on a physical form of William for her. She was able to continue to love him *through* the foundation while simultaneously giving my grandfather a happy marriage that lasted four decades."

"William and Lizzy had a true romantic love. Aunt Kitty said it was deep, respectful, and abiding, not a summer fling as you thought, but something that should have been everlasting. I bet that in some form or another, he has held a torch for her, too, these five decades. When someone touches your heart so deeply, it's impossible to remove them. Jack, let's see if we can bring them together in Paris. I've never been to France, and I have a passport just waiting to go somewhere."

He chuckled deeply. "You are so mischievous."

"I know. I'm learning from my aunt Lizzy."

"Ladies and Gentlemen, we will begin boarding Delta Flight 675 to Seattle..."

Juliana grinned, "So my partner in crime, where are you staying when we get to Sitka?"

"In the room next to yours."

She stood before him, slung her backpack over one shoulder and clutched her hip with her hand. "What's your plan? Late night dancing to Glenn Miller?"

Jack took her hand in his. "How did you know?"

"Just wishful thinking on my part."

****

Louie loved his 1967 Eldorado Coupe Cadillac and hated that for two years it had been collecting dust in the locked garage behind his house in Park Slope. On this day, he was setting out on a mission and needed his wheels for this important journey.

While the area's Revolutionary War historical significance was commemorated with parks and monuments, the actual neighborhood of Park Slope was founded only one hundred years and three generations ago. This cozy, friendly section of the Big Apple, once a neighbor to Ebbets Field, home of the former Brooklyn Dodgers, had seen many changes come its way in the span of the Twentieth Century. The stadium itself had been torn down, replaced by an apartment complex attesting to the encroachment of time and modernization.

Always a busy intersection, Ninth Street and Seventh Avenue was located in a section of Brooklyn known as the South Slope. Lined by local businesses and townhouses of limestone, brick, or brown stone, it was easily distinguishable from the now-coined Historic District, formerly known as the North Slope, with its opulent mansions built from old money. In its heyday, before a neighborhood decline precipitated by the Great Depression, South Slope represented working class and new money, whereas North Slope represented old affluence. The Martels had lived in the south.

What began as a "trip to get the car" seemed to have morphed into something altogether different. Having taken the F Train down to Ninth Street for the first time since Lillian's death, Louie was soon ascending the steps of their three-story townhouse. Once his childhood home, this was the place where, on emergency furlough in '43, he sat Shiva to mourn for his mother. Her death had been brought on by the War Department's letter notifying her that Will was shot down, Missing in Action. And seven years later that he mourned his father in this house. But the sad memories also accompanied the joyful because it was here that he raised Gordon beside the love of his life.

Since that first amphibious transport to Guadalcanal and later his arrival at Peleliu, this was the first time in a long time he felt fear. By giving into the moment, and that prodding voice in his head that demanded, "Go on, go in." His palms began to sweat when he turned the key. He stepped inside even though he wasn't quite prepared to face the pain of doing so.

He surprised himself at how the fear immediately dissipated when crossing the threshold through the heavy front door. An enveloping wash of comfort surrounded by the familiar and the love that this house had held for the Martel family for seventy years came over him. He felt extraordinarily attuned to it. Like the neighborhood in which the house dwelt, revitalization came and went. Now in his sunset, the Slope was revitalizing once again, and just like the introduction of Louise and the possibility of seeing his brother again, as well as Juliana meeting a fellow, he seemed to be getting a second wind, too. Maybe this old house has more life in it yet. Maybe, one day, Juliana will come back to the Martel home and raise her family. Perhaps Primrose Cottage was only meant to be the beginning for her. He'd have to think on that.

The home's dry air hung thick and unmoving reminiscent of the death it had represented following Lillian's death. It was then that he left for the Exeter, to be closer to Gordon before his own sudden passing.

His eyes welled with tears upon smelling a faint trace of Lillian's Shalimar perfume still lingering in the living room. Unconsciously, he rubbed his furiously beating heart. The memories were crushing yet sweet. He almost thought he heard Gordon's laughter as a boy but knew it was his imagination. The pains of life ran a bittersweet course beside the joys of living and here, in Park Slope, he was reminded of them all. Suddenly finding himself a "past person," he felt aptly sentimental as he ran his aged hand over the white sheet tossed over his mother's dining table.

"We had a beautiful life here, didn't we, Lil? I can still remember you coming home with me after our bare-bones civil ceremony by the Justice of the Peace. You brought life to this house and my dad who was still grieving."

Louie slowly climbed the stairs, that loose floorboard on the fifth step creaking like it always had, but he never had time to fix. He walked straight into his and Lillian's former bedroom, which smelled sweet, like roses and honeysuckle. Catholics would probably refer to it as the "odour of sanctity," he mused. Lillian, after all, had been angelic, heroic, and *almost* saintly, and she had died in this room—in his arms while they slept. His girl had slipped away with nary a warning, leaving a heavenly fragrance in her place.

Sitting upon their sheet-covered full-sized bed, he thought how he loved cuddling close to her. She'd hate his California king bed now and would give him an earful about it.

"Well, sweetie, our granddaughter is going to heal this family once and for all. I suppose you and Gordon put those wheels in motion from where you are. She's headed to Alaska to bring that vaporhead brother of mine home, and she's met your sisters, too. Our treasure has even fallen for Lizzy's grandson. Hard to fathom after all your Renner subterfuge, isn't it? I'm so proud of her, and I know you are, too."

Speaking may have been new, but talking to Lillian from his heart wasn't. It was the most natural thing in the world and he'd been doing it every day for the past 762 days to be exact. Not hearing her lengthy replies was the unnatural part. "I love you—I miss you." He swallowed hard then, shaking his head, smiled wryly. "Even though you kept secrets from me. Yes, I know, you never broke confidences pertaining to your sisters, but it wouldn't have done any harm to tell me about the Phoenix Foundation or the orphaned Jewish boy she adopted. I have my suspicions why, but I'll leave that for Juliana to bring to light."

He sighed, working up his courage to discuss inviting Louise into his life, but chickened out instead choosing to purge his guilt to Lillian's spirit, which he felt was infused in their room. Rubbing his brow his confession flowed, "Both you and I know we did wrong by Will and, hopefully, I'll have an opportunity to atone. The shock on his face at seeing Lizzy for the first time after all those years in '49 is an image I wish I could purge from my brain. Her marrying the very man he was insanely jealous over and their arrival with two small children beside them, I'm sure broke him. During the war, he always feared a Dear John, but she just stopped writing and that was proof why.

"After you gave birth, and she came to the hospital with her husband, I should have told Will that she had married. But you should have told me why or, at the very least, that she was coming to Gordon's christening. Not that I expected Will to attend, but I could have prepared him, could have finally been honest with him. It would have broken my heart to do so, but I would have done it to try to lessen his shock. Instead, I wounded him, just as your sister did. What did he ever do to warrant her treatment of him? He was at war for G-d sake! Of course, you probably knew everything but kept that a secret from me as well. *Our* silence delivered the final blow and for that I'll never forgive myself."

Louie rose and walked to the window, opening the wood shutters to look out at her overgrown garden at the back of the house. He spoke under his breath more to himself, "What happened to them? Why did she marry John? I suppose it's irrelevant after all these years."

A quiet overtook him for many minutes as he just stared out the window, his eyes fixated on the rose bushes growing wild now against the rare privately owned garage in Park Slope. Finally, he choked without tears. "I miss Will, Lil, especially now with both you and Gordon gone. Our Juliana and I have been having a difficult time." He ran his hand across his face, wiping invisible tears.

"Anyway, baby, I just wanted to thank you for sending Louise to me for these last years I have left. She's not you, nor will she ever be since ninety-nine percent of my heart is still yours, but she's a good woman and good company. She's also a terrible gin rummy player, and it gives me a great sense of satisfaction to finally win at a game you kicked my ass at for four decades." He snorted. "And let's face it, doughnuts were the only thing you knew how to cook well. Louise makes a mean beef brisket. I ... I hope this is okay. I hope you're not mad at me for feeling more than just a friendship with her.

"I'm headed off to Long Island today to see your photograph in that museum. It's about time the world knows of your bravery. If I have the nerve maybe I'll seek out one of your sisters to thank them."

Standing there, looking out the window, he smiled, feeling buoyed and at peace about so many things. Going home did that and the realization gave him pause to think that there was another home to visit, too.

He walked toward the empty cedar closet at the far end of the room and opened the door, summoning the same courage he had finally found on the morning he stormed Peleliu with thousands of Japanese soldiers lying in wait in caves. Thoughts swirled in his mind like little ripples growing into larger wakes: home, peace, sanctuary, forgiveness.

Inside the walk-in closet hung three short shelves and below them a bench. With the remaining strength in his arthritic hands, he yanked the cedar plank of the bench upward until its old nails gave up their grip. With a groan and a final heave to the wood, the top of the seat popped off.

Louie bent forward and reached in, ignoring the cobwebs. His hand searched in the darkness of the cavernous space until it touched softness. He grinned. They were just where he hid them almost sixty years prior. Covered in dust, he withdrew the soft, blue velvet pouches: his Tefillin and Tallit.

Lovingly, he wiped the remnants of age and neglect away, shaking his head as he removed from a third pouch—the mezuzah his mother brought with her from Amsterdam. Set aside by her, she had always meant for it to be placed at the threshold of her family home when it was safe to declare, "We are under G-d's watchful care. We are Jews, and we will keep his commandments." She always hoped the day would come when a utopian world of harmony vanquished prejudice and antisemitism.

"You were right, Will. Too many secrets for far too long," he declared crossing the room, holding the long forgotten religious items, now considered priceless treasure.

Stopping at the open door of the bedroom, he turned and blew a kiss back to the room. "Give a special kiss to our son, sweetheart. You're a lucky girl to have him all to yourself now. Take care of him until we are all together again. I love you."

He left the room, descended the stairs, and then exited the house. It no longer felt as though held in a death grip. It now felt at rest and at peace. Just as he did.

****

Forty minutes later the still pristine black Cadillac navigated the winding hills of Glen Cove, drawing attention from passing drivers. One young fella even gave him a thumbs-up at a stop sign on the corner of Landing and Crescent Beach Roads as he neared his destination. This car made him feel young and virile. That was the purpose when he purchased it at the height of his midlife crisis. Thank G-d all it took was a car to help him over that hump. Together, he and Lillian made many good memories in the generous backseat. He chortled at the remembrance.

For kicks and curiosity, he deliberately drove past the remains of Meercrest's crumbling archway. Only having visited on the solitary occasion of Memorial Day in '42, he was surprised how easily he found Rosebud Lane. That now-famous snapshot of the entrance to the estate, the one he took on that long ago day, Juliana had been passing around like a marijuana cigarette to anyone who might want to participate in her detective work. That brought about a laugh, too. Today was turning out to be one of the best days he had in a long time. He felt rejuvenated having purged his feelings over his and Lillian's role in adding to Will's pain. He felt open to the possibilities before him.

Picturesque and peaceful, the former Pratt estate, now turned museum, greeted Louie. His gaze immediately drew to the towering Elm tree surrounded by gardens at the far right of the grounds.

"You did good, Pistol," he said following a long whistle and nod of admiration. "He'd be proud of you even if you broke his heart. Hell, I'm proud of you and I know Lillian is, too."

Very few cars sat in the parking lot on this Friday, but he was pleased to see an empty school bus, obviously waiting at the ready for its class of visiting students. Like the bright yellow against the serene green of the trees, Louie's recollection of teaching Gordon about the Holocaust burst into his mind's eye. His sensitive son had cried. His memory quickly turned toward another serious parenting moment. Lillian had garnered a completely different reaction when she attempted to explain to their young son about the birds and the bees. For a minute or two she thought he would cry, but then she outright suffered to keep a straight face when he finally, simply but loudly, proclaimed, "Yuck." Yes, the sweet and the sorrow always went hand in hand.

He parked the Caddy, paid his admission, and held tightly to the map and welcome pamphlet. Straining eyes took in a history he had long pushed further and further to the recesses of his mind. Images lined the walls, reminding him that the DeVrieses had a testimony in this tale, one that went beyond Lillian's story. If it weren't for his jewel, well then, he might not have ever felt the call to "go home," back to his roots and history—the joyful and the horror-filled.

Subconsciously, he ran his index finger around his shirt collar, an uncomfortable, anxious sweat breaking upon his brow.

The carefree, innocent laughter of children running down the hall toward the door of an exhibit room stopped him, giving him pause. The sign against the wall at their destination read: *The Diary of Anne Frank*.

Even over the chatter and the beating of his heart in his ears, he could hear the multi-media sounds of war and personal stories at the end of the hall. Of their own accord, his tassel-loafered feet remained glued to the hardwood floor below him, vacillating whether or not he could go on. It had been so long since he faced the truths of his ancestry.

A woman's pleasant voice breached his sudden wary inertia. "Can I direct you, sir?"

He turned to meet a gentle, concerned smile, one he always thought was reserved for the elderly.

She pointed to the brochure. "Are you looking for a particular exhibit or would you care to start at the beginning?"

The middle-aged woman was striking with long, brown, curly hair, and a thoughtful expression that seemed so familiar. Tall, slender and obviously a woman who took care of her appearance, she wore a simple beige blouse and a camel colored skirt that almost reached her sandals.

"I ... um ... yes, I appear to be lost. I'm looking for the American Red Cross exhibit. My granddaughter mentioned that there is a Story of Courage to Lillian Renner."

Louie didn't know what possessed the woman, but she hooked her arm within his. Of course, he completely didn't mind. She was quite a dish and the latent wolf in him couldn't help accepting the attention. He may be officially off the market and seventy-three, but he wasn't dead.

"Well, I'll take you there myself. That is a story worth hearing." She chortled and that too seemed familiar. "Actually, they are all worth hearing, but I have a particular love for Lillian Renner."

Now that got his attention. "Oh? Why is that?"

Arm in arm, they walked slowly down the corridor. "Well, she was a remarkable woman, quite an inspiration. One of the thousands of pioneers who ushered in the feminist movement during the World War Two era. She had a mind of her own to break free from the constraints and expectations of the affluent society into which she was born, instead choosing to volunteer with hard work, sacrifice, and dedication for the war relief."

"That's unusual of debs back then," he interrupted, holding back a smile.

"It was! Before the WAC, the WAVES and even the WASP came into existence, Lillian joined the American Red Cross—the ARC, even being younger than the official age requirements and was determined to make a difference. She changed the narrative of marrying young, remaining barefoot and pregnant."

"She sounds like quite a woman," Louie said, his heart swelling.

"Oh she was! Lillian was brave on so many levels. In a sense, she's my hero. I know for a fact that she was my mother's hero, and her Story of Courage introduces her to many young women who arrive through these doors eager to learn, teaching them that they, too, can make a difference and change lives by exhibiting pride without prejudice. They can be and do anything they want."

Louie was choked up just hearing how this woman praised his girl. Sure, he had been proud of Lillian, loved her beyond measure, and knew of her unabashed spirit of idealism, but he had no idea that others, too, thought the same way. They stopped at the door to the exhibit.

"Well, here we are, sir."

He peered in, afraid of the sappy feelings about to bring him to tears in this public place beside this stranger—as kind as she was.

"Don't you want to go in?"

He wiped his brow. "I do." He paused, turning to look into the woman's fine eyes. "What's your name?"

"Annette Churchill. It's a pleasure to meet you." She held out her hand for a shake. "And what's your name?"

"I'm Lillian's husband, Louie Martel."

When she gave him a full-blown grin, he knew there was more to this Annette Churchill than had initially met the eye. He was staring right back into his brother's dimpled smile. Suddenly it was all clear. She was the reason Lizzy married John in Will's absence.

Louie didn't relinquish her hand, continuing to hold onto her as he smiled his most mischievous grin. "You're Lizzy's daughter, aren't you?"

"Yes. Yes, I am!"

Twenty-Eight

Sisters
December 17, 1942

O ver six weeks had passed since that horrible night with her father at Greystone townhouse, a night Lizzy had tried to forget, but to no avail. Diligently attentive to his comings and goings, she could not find anything that pointed to him being a true Nazi sympathizer or worse— collaborator. There was no evidence that the items of propaganda in Meercrest's library were his and there was nothing otherwise untoward to be found. Even his flagrant infidelity with the willing blonde, undisputed by her own observation, seemed carefully hidden. For that, she was thankful because, as disappointing a mother as Frances was, she still didn't deserve a philandering husband.

No, his only crimes were an unquestionable, pompous, Germanic arrogance and the clear fact that he had shown himself to be as anti-Semitic as Ingrid. Bigotry and excessive pride were character flaws to be sure, ones that diminished her daughterly affection for him significantly, but in no way did they verify that her father was what Will believed him to be. She was determined to prove that estimation wrong. However, the one thing that truly troubled her was how on earth her father had discovered that Will's mother's family were Jews. Will explained that was a secret tightly held by his family for almost forty years.

Lizzy walked past the Aeolin pipe organ prominently situated by the base of the entrance steps where Mr. Howard and one of the maids, unceasingly worked entwining evergreen into the banister of the public hall.

Thanksgiving had come and gone, and now Christmas decorations showcased the full splendor of Meercrest. Decorated fir trees stood elegant in every room and each fireplace mantle was adorned with pine as plenteous swags and boughs hung lavishly throughout the mansion. The decorations were early by some standards, but not for those in the *Social Registry*. The upcoming weekend launched a series of balls and festivities until concluding on Twelfth Night, but it all commenced at their estate.

Mrs. Davis had stocked the pantry with the girls' favorite holiday treats, acquiring sugar, and now coffee, through illegal black market channels. Beef, even though in short supply, was purchased from whatever dubious contacts could be contrived. Frances didn't care where these expected commodities came from so long as they were available. She, herself, rarely drank coffee, only occasionally partaking in the new craze of Irish Coffee, but she hated the Irish—Catholics as they all were.

The overpowering scent of pine turned Lizzy's stomach nauseous as she made her way through the grand marble foyer, passing the Degas painting her mother, just the day before, had Mr. Howard re-install above the ornate Eighteenth Century gilded console. Outgoing mail sat upon the silver tray awaiting the afternoon visit of the letter carrier, Mr. Murphy. She hoped Will would receive her Christmas greeting card in time. After all, this was the postal service's busiest season, particularly during wartime, and she was late in mailing it. If only she hadn't been so tired and had purchased one sooner. With less than two weeks for it to get to England—or wherever he was—she was sure it wouldn't arrive in time but she hoped her last letter, filled with all the right sentiments, would.

Ingrid strolled past her in the west hallway, having just come through the family entrance. As usual, she looked gorgeous, right down to those perfectly sculpted eyebrows and that fake beauty mark above her lip. "You're looking positively ghastly, Lizzy."

"Gee thanks, you look stunning as well. Love the dead animal draped over your shoulder. Looks like something I saw flattened on the side of the road."

"Don't be so droll. Red fox stoles are all the rage. You could use a little color to brighten up that peaked complexion of yours, perhaps a little rouge. Are you ill?"

Lizzy's false smile matched the sarcastic tone in her voice. She was in no mood for this challenge from her sister, not today. "No. I'm not sick, just disgusted by your obvious penchant toward death."

"You'd better not be ill. Mother will have a fit. The Society's Christmas Ball is in two days, and you *are* expected to be at your best as her co-hostess. Many of Father's most influential business associates will be in attendance, and I plan to make an announcement with John. I cannot be expected to act as hostess since *I* am the guest of honor."

"You can't be serious?"

"Oh, I am serious." She held her chin higher with an air of superiority. "Father has assured me that my offered dowry will guarantee the engagement. It's a natural match. Robertsen Aviation with Renner Railways. It'll be the talk of the society pages."

Lizzy chortled. "So, you've had to pay off Johnny. That's a gas! He'd be a fool to agree to marry you otherwise."

"He hasn't quite said yes yet, but rest assured he will. He's been in love with me forever."

"I wonder, Ingrid, what will George Gebhardt have to say about your announcement?"

Ingrid took a step closer to her, eyes narrowing to mean slits of cold blue ice. "What's that supposed to mean?"

"Nothing. I'm just curious that's all. Whose bed will you share once you're married? After all, you are a share crop."

Ingrid's hand was swift but not as swift as Lizzy's quick step backward, barely avoiding the malicious slap aimed at her cheek.

"Be careful with that sharp tongue of yours, sister dear. Between you and Kitty, I just don't know who should receive the majority of my attention," Ingrid threatened.

Lizzy's voice lowered an octave, all traces of its melody or her customary effervescence were vanquished from her steely words. "Stay away from Kitty."

"Or what? What will you do? You're as worthless as she is. Just like Lillian, you're not fit to bear the Renner name now that you've fraternized with a Jew, even if he is dreamy looking."

"And what makes you assume that?"

"Oh, I have my ways. Tell me, Lizzy ... is he circumcised?"

Now it was Lizzy whose hand was swift, achieving firm contact. The slap was in defense of Will; the words following the strike were for Kitty. "If you go anywhere near Kitty, you will have to answer to me, and I assure you, I'm not as docile as you think. As for Johnny, you better ditch him and this conniving plan of yours, or I'll flap my lips to the society pages about what a bigot and whore you really are. Then we'll see who'll want to marry Miss Ingrid Renner! Money won't save your tarnished reputation."

Ingrid laughed, showing no effect to the sting on her cheek. "Why, *Elizabeth*, I should think you would want me to marry John. Then I wouldn't have to look at those shriveled legs of Kitty's every day. I'd be taking up residence at the Robertsens' estate Evermore in Mill Neck."

"Yes, that's right. You would be miles from harming her, far from pushing her down the stairs." She raised a challenging eyebrow.

"You're such a naïve fool, Lizzy. Distance won't stop me. You'll see. It won't be long before New York State finally mandates compulsory sterilization." Turning her back, she walked away, not even glancing over a shoulder to bid her sister adieu. "We'll see whose threats hold more weight. Your *Juden scheiss* isn't here to protect you or your deformed sister."

"Such Christmas spirit, Ingrid. Peace on earth and goodwill toward *all* men. Not only have you become a shameless harlot, but you're a barbaric zealot, too. You make me positively sick to my stomach."

Lizzy watched the confident sway exaggerating her sister's hips with each departing step she took. When she flung the poor red creature around her neck over her shoulder, the accompanying malevolent cackle echoed through the paneled walls of the stoic hallway. A chill shot up Lizzy's spine until the distracting, welcome squeak of Kitty's wheelchair in the entrance foyer alerted her that the postman had come and gone.

Her favorite sister loved to get the mail. It seemed to be the one task she looked upon as her contribution to the Renner family, validating her and providing her with an opportunity to not appear so ... so useless. Twice a day, she greeted Mr. Murphy, handing him the outgoing mail, carefully sorting the incoming post into piles, then personally delivering all of Lizzy's correspondence from Will.

Lizzy's false smile couldn't hide her tumultuous feelings over Ingrid, or the fact that she was indeed ill for the past two weeks straight and, additionally, now felt a head cold coming on.

"Kitty, you shouldn't be at that door. It's below freezing out there."

"I know. Just doing my bit. There's no mail from Ducky this afternoon."

"He's probably overwhelmed with training or the squadron's departure for England. I haven't received a letter in a few days, but I know he'll write when he can. He told me that there may be a delay." Having reached her sister, she pushed the wheelchair from behind, giving a quick glance to the silver tray to ensure Will's Christmas card was now en route.

"How are you feeling, sissy?" Lizzy asked. "Is your cold any better today? Maybe you should have stayed in bed."

Kitty blew her nose, congestion distorting her speech. "I feel like you look. What is wrong with you?"

Lizzy met the query with silence.

"Lizzy?"

They headed down the east hall, wheels squeaking and soft footfalls patterning in unison to the beating of Lizzy's thundering heart. "I'm keen on visiting the solarium today. How about you? It's a sunny day and it'll be nice and toasty in there. Perhaps some quiet time for you and me is just what the doctor ordered."

"I think that's better than that disgusting cod liver oil Nurse Keller makes me take. I swear, I think she enjoys giving me that stuff."

In companionable silence, they passed through a long corridor lined with statuary and massive family portraits peering down on them with disapproval. Even those were ceremoniously draped with evergreen, leaving no wonder to an imaginative mind as to why they frowned so. Several open anteroom doors revealed maids hard at work, dusting every nook and curio, busily preparing for the upcoming ball, *the* event of the social holiday season and one Lizzy had once looked forward to with gleeful anticipation. Inevitably the belle of the ball, dancing and flirting with society's most sought after bachelors had always been a gay time. Not this year. In fact, following the wonderful visit with Will, she had entirely forgotten about it until her arrival home.

The sisters passed by their father's study as well as three sets of double doors opened wide to display the grand ballroom in all its finest Christmas décor. The massive tree, reaching to the frescoed ceilings stood twenty feet tall and was fully festooned in opulent gold and red.

"You're very quiet lately, Lizzy, ever since your arrival home from Florida. Is everything okay?"

"Sure, everything is fine. The book collection is still going strong. Even the milkmen are involved in the collecting now, and the VBC is preparing for a nationwide campaign next month. There is even going to be an event held on the steps of the New York Public Library. Mrs. Tinsdale says that Merle Oberon and Danny Kaye will be there."

"Oh yes, I read about it. I wish I could go, too. If only to see Gypsy Rose Lee. She's a campaign volunteer just like us! That would be such a kick!"

Lizzy laughed. "The burlesque star? You're nuts!"

"I am not. She's not trampy, Lizzy. It's art what she does, and she won't be doing it on the steps of the library with her feathers and fans, at least not in the dead of winter. I read in the newspaper that she actually wrote a mystery book for the boys. Something about a G-string murder."

"Do you even know what a G-string is?"

Kitty glanced upward over the tall back of the chair, and she giggled. "Maybe. I'm not sure."

"Mrs. Davis tells me that the Woolworth heiress is attending the ball here with her new husband." Lizzy smirked knowing how her sister enjoyed reading *Modern Screen* magazine for all the latest Hollywood gossip.

"The dreamy Cary Grant is coming here?" Kitty squealed, clasping her hands.

"That's what she said."

"Hot dog!"

They turned down another hallway lined with potted palm trees, towering upward toward another frescoed cathedral ceiling. Lizzy loved this wing of the mansion. Tranquil and exotic, it reminded her of warm nights beside Sarasota Bay and that midnight skinny dip she and her flyboy had taken. Her eyes welled with tears, as they seemed to do with great frequency lately. She thought of his tender kiss when he carried her nude body up the stairs from the swimming pool.

The warmth and quiet of the solarium greeted the sisters with streaming winter sun from the arched glass above. The delicate scent of crisp tropical greenery and non-seasonal flowers filled the peaceful sanctuary. It had yet to be turned into a Christmas explosion for the ball, but she was sure that her mother had dictated specific instructions for its transformation by the following day.

A trickling stream moved around the intricately embellished, white gazebo that connected to a footbridge just wide enough for Kitty's chair. "Shall we sit in the gazebo? I need to talk with you about something important," Lizzy said.

"I knew it! You had that look about you. Apart from your unusual fatigue, I could tell something was eating you."

A tender instinct unconsciously caused Lizzy's hand to smooth over her tummy at her sister's words. If her suspicions were correct, it wouldn't be long before the new John James dress she wore wouldn't fit properly, but she was torn between feelings of elation and fear.

The chair rolled over the bridge, and she looked down at the ornamental Koi swimming below, colorful and content, the Japanese carp clustered as a family. "Aside from the water tower, I think this place is my favorite. It reminds me of Rosebriar in a way."

"I'm keen on it, too. You can almost guarantee that neither Gloria nor Ingrid will ever come here and mother says the heat frizzes her hair," Kitty stated.

"Yeah, well, there are many reasons her hair frizzes. She's still using tonic from the 1910s, swearing it will grow her hair."

"Then I'm surprised she doesn't drink it!"

Lizzy shot Kitty a humored, wry smile, took a seat on the bench facing her dearest sister, and reached across to clasp their hands together. "What I have to tell you, you have to promise to take to the grave."

"Sure, you know me. I'm great at keeping secrets, not as great as Lillian, but still good. Like the time you and Henry broke Father's model of the *Odin*. I never told a soul."

"This is different, Kitty, and I need your advice."

Tears welled and she bit her lip to keep it from trembling.

"You're worrying me, Lizzy. Please tell me. I promise to help you any way that I can. Whatever it is we'll find a solution ... together."

Lizzy looked out beyond their small shelter, her eyes locking on the amaryllis at the far corner of the room. "At Rosebriar, Will and I ... um ... remember the book you and I read?"

Kitty furrowed her brow.

"You know the one ... with sixty-four positions."

"You didn't! What was it like? How did it feel? Did it hurt?"

"Yes, wonderful, incredible, and yes it hurt but only for a little while ... and ... I um, think I might be in the family way."

Freeing one hand, she covered her eyes and sobbed, feeling the relief of telling someone what she suspected after missing her menstrual cycle two weeks earlier. Tears wracked her body as Kitty's hand squeezed hers tightly.

"Oh, Lizzy. Could you be mistaken?"

The sobs continued to come as Lizzy bent forward, resting her forehead upon their hands. "I don't know. I don't know."

"Oh G-d, I wish Lillian were here. She'd know what to do and say."

Lizzy nodded, but was sure that this was one secret she would never share with Lillian. "I have an appointment with a doctor in the city on Saturday morning."

"But that's the day of the Christmas ball!"

"It was the best I could do. I'll have to think of some reason to go to the Bronx, maybe for last minute shoes or a purse, maybe to run an errand for Mrs. Davis."

"You can't use shoes as an excuse; they're on the ration now."

Anguished, Lizzy snapped, "Whatever, Kitty! I don't know. This doctor has assured confidentiality." She lowered her voice to a whisper. "If I am *expecting*, I need it confirmed as soon as possible."

Her sister sighed deeply, then focused her worried gaze intently upon her. "What will you do if you are preggers? Father will disown you!"

Lizzy sniffled, removed the handkerchief from her pocket, then wiped her tears. "I don't know. As soon as I'm certain, I'll write Will and together we'll decide. He'll know what to do. Until then, I'll pray the war will end before the year is out. There is talk of that, you know."

"And what if he doesn't come home? Think about this clearly, Lizzy. Father will send you away, take away your Trust, abandon you. Girls of our society *do not* become unwed mothers!"

"Don't be so negative. You're not helping the situation."

"I'm not negative. I'm a realist."

"There's a difference between being a realist and a pessimist. I'm an optimist. Will is going to be home soon, mark my words, and as soon as he is, we'll marry. No one will be the wiser."

Yes, she'd convinced herself of that over the last two days. There was no way she could leave this house—and Kitty—under any circumstances other than a marriage where she could bring her sister *with* her. Ingrid had just confirmed the necessity of that, less than fifteen minutes ago.

"What could Will possibly tell you, Lizzy? He's most likely in England by now and not coming back any time soon. If you are preggers and unmarried, then they'll take your baby away!"

Frantic fear shot through Lizzy. "Stop it. I can't hear that. The war will be over by Christmas. He will come home."

Kitty reached over, clasping hands with her. "You have to listen. We have to have a plan."

Standing abruptly, breaking their joined grip, Lizzy paced the small confines of the gazebo, passing left and right before Kitty's blanket-covered legs. She wrung her suddenly freed hands, attempting to literally hold herself together, already feeling nauseous for the sixth time today.

"One step at a time. First, I'll see what the doctor says. Maybe I'm just late. Perhaps, a solution will present itself beforehand. I have to believe that. Leaving you here alone with Ingrid is not an option and never will be."

"Maybe you should take Father up on his ultimatum to marry Mr. Gebhardt."

Aghast, Lizzy's hands instantly flew to protect her tummy. She gasped. "Never! This is Will's baby—*I* am Will's. I would never consider accepting Gebhardt's hand in marriage even if he was the last man on earth."

"But if it meant giving your child a name—legitimacy—then it seems a swell option. No one would know the baby wasn't his, and I'd never tell. I could go to live with you both."

With a bleak expression, Lizzy sat once again before her sister. How could she tell her of the suspicions she had about where Ingrid came to believe such hatred and evil ideas? How could she elaborate about the pamphlets and National Socialism's views of the "unfit"? How could she tell

Kitty that she had already, firmly surmised Ingrid and Gebhardt were both fascists and that raising this child in any family other than Will's was unacceptable?

"Kitty, I know my imagination can run wild, but I fear that Gebhardt ... um ... may be a Nazi sympathizer and ... and ..." She whispered into her sister's ear. "Not only would it be dangerous for *you*, but Will is Jewish and so is this baby."

Now it was Kitty who gasped.

Twenty-Nine

I'm Beginning to See the Light
December 19, 1942

Having arrived home from her doctor's appointment on the Grand Concourse in the Bronx with little time to prepare for the ball, Lizzy had retired immediately to her suite. She forewent the usual stop into Kitty's bedroom, instead choosing a warm bath with a relaxing cigarette to soothe her nerves. The brief respite brought forth tears, which didn't abate until the hot water turned tepid. As her mood vacillated, the pent up emotions of joy and fear commingled, one alternately displacing the other. In that soothing liquid cocoon, something happened, as though a baptism of a sort, whereby, sloughing off the impetuous debutante, she emerged from the water as a matured young woman.

Now sitting at her vanity readying for the Glen Cove Society Christmas ball, her mind still whirled from the doctor's visit. He had stated in a thick Eastern European accent, "Most likely with child, but we'll await the results of the urine test." She was to telephone on Tuesday for the results which he was sure would confirm her in a family way.

A tender smile graced her lips. *What would their baby look like? Would it be a boy or a girl? Will Ducky be happy?* But the persistent question determined to undermine her happiness: What on earth was she going to do? She sighed, rubbing in awe the flat plane of her tummy for the one hundredth time that day.

She gazed at her forlorn expression in the mirror. *There is no possible way you could look beautiful tonight.* Distressed from the recent weeks of never-ending sickness that plagued her and this long day's travel, Lizzy chastised herself for not having driven her Zephyr, but she reconciled her decision that fuel was at an all-time low with shortages along the entire East Coast.

An unwelcome knock upon her door snapped her from the distracting thoughts. "Come in," she said mustering as much effervescence as she could, her wine-colored lips fabricating a false smile. Her heart was uncharacteristically disconcerted for the evening ahead.

Dripping in diamonds and stuffed like a knockwurst sausage into a light grey, satin Paquin gown, Mother stood in the doorway, resembling holiday tinsel bursting from its package. Great-grandmother Elisabeth's Austrian crystal tiara was perched within her overly elaborate blonde coiffure. As the namesake of the great Austrian Baroness, that tiara was to be hers one day, and in time it would be her daughter's. *Hers and Will's daughter*. Now that thought brought a genuine smile.

Not yet outwardly inebriated, Frances spoke in her high pitched whining voice that went straight through Lizzy, grating whatever nerve remained. "It's time, my dear. The Morgans and Phippses have already arrived and Mr. Gebhardt is eagerly asking for you. We must take our places within the ballroom to properly greet the arrivals. You must hurry. Your sister is ready to make her grand entrance."

Rising from the vanity stool, Lizzy was a picture of elegance and refinement. Wearing an exorbitant haute couture gown, a three-strand diamond and garnet necklace, and a fresh, floral hair adornment to remind her of Will and the ones he had given her. She smoothed her merlot colored chiffon skirt, adjusting the subtle train. Normally, the crisp rustling sound of the sumptuous fabric did something exciting to her, but not tonight. It was an unwelcome reminder that Ingrid would be making an announcement with John in a matter of hours. Her heart felt heavy for her friend and the precarious direction of his future, as uncertain as her own. She couldn't help feeling fraught by the responsibilities suddenly laid at her feet, nor by the sudden maturity forced upon her: unintended pregnancy, motherhood, unmarried and alone without Will, and lest she not forget the worst of it— a possible forced marriage to a man she despised or the baby being taken away for adoption.

With those thoughts fleeting through her mind, she struggled to force an amicable smile. "Yes, I'm ready, Mother."

"You look lovely. I'm sure you will have an announcement to make shortly, too." Tapping her daughter's chin, she examined her countenance on this rare occasion with clear, motherly eyes. "Smile, darling. This is a big night for your sister. Envy does not become you."

Lizzy didn't argue. What was the point of it? Actually, she felt compelled to laugh because Ingrid was so sure that she and John were the "perfect" match. However, only she, his close friend, really knew that he was terribly infirm, a fact that would make him, by Ingrid's so-called impeccable standards, an *unacceptable* mate for her sister, an *unacceptable* husband and father, and an unacceptable *individual*. It broke her heart that if ever discovered, Ingrid would make him pay for it. No, that wasn't funny in the least. Envious? Definitely not. One could never be envious of such a malevolent creature.

Frances hooked arms with her and together they proceeded out the door. Seeking strength and comfort, she glanced back over a shoulder, eyes settling upon the nightstand drawer where she had, once again, placed Will's framed portrait for safekeeping.

In the long corridor of the second floor west wing, Gloria ran past them, hiking the skirt of her immodestly draped, clinging velvet gown to allow for fast movement. She squealed in excitement, "Ogden Phipps has arrived!"

"Gloria, he's married!" Lizzy chastised, choosing not to recall all the times she had felt the same when Henry Sturgis Morgan, Jr. arrived at Meercrest.

Her sister stopped and turned, placing her hand over her heart. "I don't care. He's a dreamboat in that Naval uniform of his! Positively creamy and I'm lulu over him."

Frances giggled like Baby Snooks. "That's my baby, always eager to show herself before all these useless men of the Armed Forces. I thought Miss Chapin's would have corrected her of that habit. Renners do not mix with soldiers. Ah, but your sister never does as told. La!"

The cheeky deb in Lizzy couldn't help to smirk. *Will is a commissioned officer, a pilot, not a mere "soldier." Would that make a difference, Mother?*

Lizzy ignored the remark. It was simply another example of her mother's stupid comments. As vehemently opposed as her father was about those who supported or assisted in the war effort—they were, in fact, in attendance "mixing" with the Renners tonight. To exclude them at the ball would be a slight on the *beau monde* of the Social Club and the Yacht Club. Never mind that denouncing his own *daughter* Lillian for doing her bit wasn't a concern to him. She took a deep breath. What did any of it matter, least of all her mother's rude opinion? In another hour, her mother would be quite soused and making a spectacle of herself by saying all sorts of wacky things.

They lingered at the top of the two-level marble staircase, prepared to make their descent toward the entry foyer below. Lizzy straightened her back, tightly clasping her hands at her waist when her mother said, "Your sister will be here any minute. She insists on making her grand entrance, as the honoree of tonight's celebration, before us."

"Yes, of course she does."

Above the escalating din in the entry rotunda filled with arriving guests dressed in their finest evening gowns, furs, and tuxedos, Lizzy could hear the quartet playing Mendelssohn's *Weinhacten* from the living hall. The music orchestrating the arrivals felt more like a dirge than a joyous Christmas musical selection, but it was German and a better choice than Wagner whose works she disliked even more. When in residence, it was her father's choice of classical music.

Her mother leaned into her ear, giggling, and it was then that Lizzy smelled the gin on her breath. "Look how they admire that Degas. Your father's friends in the German government have been very generous indeed! I'll be the talk of the Gold Coast."

Lizzy's head snapped to take in her mother's pleased expression and the startling admission inadvertently made about where that painting had come from. Disguised beneath heavily applied mascara, her still somewhat reddened eyes flashed, bulging with shock, but she said nothing. She thought of the Horch Roadster. *Was that another gift and why?*

From her perch, she watched the assembled crowd below, some pointing to the painting, others preening while admiring their friends, and she couldn't help but notice how many of these society crème de la crème barely acknowledged that a war had been on for one full year now. Some placed themselves above it until one of their own were sent overseas. They most likely didn't even notice—or care—that tonight's Christmas ball wasn't dedicated to raise money for Liberty Bonds or the American Red Cross.

More than likely, the discussions among them revolved around the recent marriage or engagement announcements listed in the society pages or the fact that they were inconvenienced by the fuel shortage. Men dying in Africa and the Pacific or the deportation of innocent European Jewish families to camps posed no significance in their elite lives. Already Lizzy felt as though she didn't belong here among these people any more than Lillian did.

Her eyes scanned the assembly. The Guggenheims were conspicuously absent and she had to wonder about that. Apparently, it was more acceptable *to* include members of the Armed Forces than it was to include a philanthropic Jewish family whose old-money wealth and prominence in the *Social Register* were greater than the Renners or many of these families in attendance tonight.

The whoosh of Ingrid's lace and golden silk shantung gown rustled as she approached mother and sister standing in wait for her. She looked statuesque and regal, her piled hair was adorned by a diamond encrusted tiara nestled within.

Frances nearly squealed at the vision her eldest daughter presented. "Divine, simply divine. Your photograph will be splashed all over the *Diary*, my darling."

"Yes, it will." Ingrid smugly replied, smoothing gloved hands down the fitted lace bodice of the gown. "This Parisian Alençon is terribly coveted these days. I will be the envy, for sure."

Lizzy smiled impertinently, maintaining her silence.

Ingrid held herself with an air of superiority, clearly feeling every bit the distinguished guest of honor, however, in Lizzy's opinion, she looked like a garish, gilded holiday bauble. Her eyes met her elder sister's and they bore into one another, no words were spoken. There was no need following their conversation two days ago. The line had been drawn in the sand and both women knew where the other stood. Their hatred of one another would have been palpable to their mother if she had been sharp enough (or less self-absorbed) at that moment. The self-important sneer upon Ingrid's lips reviled Lizzy.

Her sister gazed down at the gay circle of attendees eagerly awaiting her arrival. Her eyes locked on George Gebhardt, standing in the center of the group, his hands in his pockets striking his trademark stance, and a roguish smirk upon his lips. John stood beside him, unknowingly the fool, having been played for years by Ingrid's machinations.

Ingrid raised her chin and descended the staircase at a slow, imperial pace, allowing for the proper adulation she was sure to elicit. In all of Lizzy's years with the woman, she had never fully recognized her sister for the monster that was; tonight she saw her clearly. Pure evil.

From the balcony, Lizzy's eyes drew to Greta Robertsen in the crowd, looking gorgeous in sleek, emerald metallic lamé. Her nemesis held a flute of champagne in one gloved hand, the other hand tucked possessively inside Dickie Phipps's arm as he talked with Junius Morgan. Greta looked annoyed and glanced upward, meeting her gaze. Their eyes locked, and the color she wore seemed too fitting as a pinched expression of jealousy passed over the Robertsen debutante even though she had successfully nabbed one of the most attractive, eligible bachelors of their circle. It was rumored that her dowry was close to two million dollars. Lizzy reflected upon how like many of the marriages assembled in the foyer, theirs was not a love match, but a match of finance and industry.

Once again, her novel thought served to recall Will and how much they loved one another. Her love was the dowry, his gift their baby.

From behind, she watched Ingrid's descent, the rigid, proper posture and how her hand slid along the banister. Each graceful step downward encouraged whispers from the elite gathering below, and vastly differing smiles upon the faces of two particular tuxedoed men admiring her form. The arrogance dripping from her sister's every pore, served to illuminate the further distinction between the young woman Lizzy had once been and the woman she had become with the introduction of her flyboy and the shocking revelation of pregnancy.

Those four little, yet powerful, words—"in a family way"—had changed her life and how she saw *this* world. Will had helped her to see beyond it, but their baby now caused her to take a hard look at it.

Frances preened the blonde curls at her nape. "Shall we go play hostess, now? You have one particular suitor awaiting you, and I have a dry martini awaiting me."

Lizzy smiled as best she could, and placing one platform sole in front of the other, she descended with deliberate, tortuous, poised elegance.

Mother's excessive jewels were competing with the imported Austrian crystal chandelier above. The woman's gross affluence dripped with Germanic pride filled with bombastic haughtiness and drunken silliness. Her own normally youthful exuberance was tempered by the overt pompous vanity and the sobering realities of the society she was descending into. It was as though the blindfold of youth, society, and material comfort had been pulled from her eyes. Behind Lizzy's skilled debutante smile, she felt sick and miserable, just wanting to get through the night unscathed by her sister, her father, and Mr. Gebhardt's vulgar intentions.

She noticed Kitty sitting ignored, cast off, and overlooked in her wheelchair at the side of the entrance rotunda. Virtually hidden beside the glorious, towering Christmas tree, she still did not escape Lizzy's watchful eye, and her heart clenched at how her dear sister was considered an outcast among this society who felt above everyone. Kitty looked so pretty, so festive in red velvet and holiday plaid, and Lizzy felt proud at what a lovely young woman she had become. They smiled at one another. *No, you can never leave her here alone to languish, to be victimized.*

She suddenly realized that Kitty was all the connection she had to this family and visa versa. Five sisters reduced to two, both needing the other.

Mrs. Davis, invisibly attired in black and demoted to the role of food server, expertly navigated the rotunda, offering canapés and pate. She, like Kitty, was ignored for her perceived inferiority, not just social class but also her color.

The hair at the back of Lizzy's neck stood on end when her vision fell upon Gebhardt standing at the bottom of the long staircase, leaning against the finely carved newel post, posturing there as though he were the dashing Rhett Butler awaiting Scarlett. He gazed up at her with a hungry look in his eye and a wicked smirk taunting upon his lips. Although devastatingly handsome, he repulsed her in every way.

She noted how Ingrid, now center stage in the rotunda, surreptitiously watched Gebhardt, while her arm possessively draped through John's. *Poor Johnny.* A chill traveled up Lizzy's spine, and she felt slightly woozy, gripping the handrail tightly to steady herself. She was careful not to alert her mother whose arm was tucked around her other bent elbow.

Upon their arrival down to the foyer assemblage, Gebhardt greeted her with slick intonation, "Miss Elizabeth." He took her hand, bent, and kissed the satin glove. "You are a dazzling vision. Your eyes sparkle like emeralds tonight."

His obvious disregard of proper decorum accentuated his pompous air of superiority, ignorantly circumventing Best Society's standards of proper etiquette. He was not so familiar with her to initially compliment a woman in such fashion.

"Thank you, Mr. Gebhardt."

She promptly attempted to withdraw her hand, but he held fast a moment longer, leaning toward her. "I hope to have a word with you this evening. There is something special I would like to ask you."

She cringed, nearly gagging from the scent of his cologne, an odd mixture of cigar and shaving lotion and its combined effect with her already unstable stomach.

The impudent debutante in her resisted the ingrained reaction to play coy when posed with such a statement. *His* advances were unwelcome, not worthy of her perfectly honed skills of flirtation through joie de vive and playful laughter.

While she hesitated for a moment to consider her most prudent response, Kitty's wheelchair banged his calf muscle.

"Oh! I'm so sorry, Mr. Gebhardt. This wacky chair has a mind of its own."

He brushed his leg, scowled in a most menacing fashion, and abruptly left the women without a further word.

Lizzy bit her lip to keep from laughing raucously. She whispered, entirely too pleased with her sister's actions, "You are so devilish! Thank you!"

"It was the least I could do. You looked ready to vomit on him Why didn't you come to my room when you came home? I've been on pins and needles all day."

"I'm sorry, sweetie. I was just exhausted. I'll tell you everything tomorrow, after we get through this charade."

"Charade? But you always loved this ball, Lizzy."

"Yes, I used to, but tonight I feel like Lillian ... disillusioned. I wish Will were here. I can't imagine dancing with anyone other than him, particularly you know who." She looked over her shoulder to see Gebhardt talking with Barbara Hutton and her dashing, Hollywood husband, Cary Grant.

"I'm sorry," Kitty said.

"Don't be. You didn't send Ducky to war—Tojo did that when he bombed Pearl Harbor a year ago."

Kitty frowned. "Father was looking for you this afternoon. I had to lie. I said you were shopping for an engagement gift for Ingrid."

"Thank you. Have you seen him tonight? Do you know where he is?"

"Last I saw of him, he went with several gentlemen into his study and closed the door."

"And where is Nurse Keller?"

"Father told her that she could attend the ball as a guest and not as my nurse. She went to her room to change into evening attire, and I'm on my own." She rolled her eyes. "I thought she'd never get lost. Finally, I can have a good time without her looking over my shoulder and dogging me for everything I do."

Lizzy forced an optimistic grin, determined not to succumb to the uncharacteristic melancholy she felt. Today was getting the best of her with every trip to the bathroom and the thought that Gebhardt and her father just may well force her hand with a marriage proposal tonight. If Kitty was happy, then so should she be. "Well, then let's try to have a swell time, sissy. Mother has arranged for Guy Lombardo's Orchestra, and I know how you enjoy "When You Wish Upon a Star.""

Leaning closer to her seated sister, she noticed a reddened shadow upon Kitty's left cheek. Placing her gloved palm against the darkening skin tone, Lizzy inquired, "Kitty, what happened to your cheek? It seems a bit brighter than the other."

Kitty turned away from Lizzy's concerned expression. "Oh that. It's nothing. I guess I was sitting too close to the fireplace waiting for everyone to arrive. It'll fade in an hour. I'm sure.

"Say Lizzy, did you see Cary Grant over there?"

"I did ... he's very handsome. Some say he married her for her money."

"I don't believe it; they look so in love."

"Yes, well, looks can be deceiving. After all, just look at Johnny and Ingrid."

Thirty

All or Nothing at All
December 19, 1942, con't

T he sit down dinner for sixty had been its usual presentation of extravagance in Meercrest's lavish three thousand square foot dining room. Seven courses ranging from Guinea hen, pheasant casserole and stuffed lobster tail to extravagant desserts made without regard to the sugar ration were all served with tantalizing elegance and fine wines. Excessive praise to the host and hostess was profuse. This holiday and most likely for the duration of the war, there would be no such thing as a meatless Christmas in this house, which was further proof to Lizzy that her place was beside Will and his humble life in Park Slope.

It was an evening of opulent Christmas indulgence at a time when the nation was turned upon its head. Women in the workforce, families separated, more and more goods showing up on the ration, nationwide restrictions, and the ever growing fearful threat that war could come to America's shores after Pearl Harbor all contributed to the new norm of daily life, but not here—and certainly not tonight.

Lizzy felt strangely defiant sitting at the table beside some unknown middle-aged man. She thought she knew most of her family's friends in the *Social Register* and wondered if perhaps he was visiting a relative for the holiday season. His perfected New York City English grated upon her withering nerves, particularly when he spoke pompously of his travels to Eastern Europe before the war and how "It was a jolly, swell time in Krakow."

Petulantly, and not because he really deserved it but because she had enough of this evening and this exalted company in general, she asked, "Tell me, Mr. Dittmar, did you read last week in the *New York Times*—page eleven in fact—how the Polish government has begged for the Allies to put a stop to Hitler's mass extermination of their Jewish population?" She bulldozed right past the stupefied shock upon his face with nary a heartbeat. "Already one-third of its three million citizens have been murdered by the Nazis and the *Times* buries it deep within the paper while we sit back on our laurels, having a *jolly, swell time.*"

"I ... well ..."

Her statement caused a few scowls and several forks to rest upon the fine china with audible landings. As she had deviously hoped for, conversation then ensued about the war with the introduction of political discourse inaugurated by a well-informed Roosevelt supporter. Lizzy couldn't help feeling proud of her steering of the conversation so effectively until her father cleared his throat, smiled in that manner of his, and declared that the orchestra was getting restless for dancers, thereby putting an end to all conversation about the war.

Renner fumed inside at his daughter's insolence. As it was, he was unsure of the political opinions of many in attendance on this festive night. Although his affiliation with the American First Committee was only meant as a cover to his true reasoning for America's "isolationism," conversation about the war could prove dangerous, thereby opening up scrutiny to his sympathies and those of his collaborating, industrialist allies seated at the table.

His facial demeanor, understood perfectly by his daughters and wife, caused Ingrid and Frances to rise, ushering in a night of dancing and gaiety.

The rustle of skirts, gossiping tittle tattle, and hiccups left the dining hall for the ballroom, but Lizzy was halted in her departure by her father's hand upon her wrist. "Just a moment, Elizabeth. I'd like to have a word with you in my study."

"But the first dance, Father ..." she protested, expecting to be called on the carpet for her instigation or something other. It didn't escape her observation that Gebhardt stood about ten feet away, by the nearest set of double doors, with his hands in his pockets. He looked dashing and disgusting all at once. She could feel his eyes undressing her and was reminded of his fingers brushing her bosom on Memorial Day.

"Your sister and John Robertsen will be opening the evening with the first dance." Her father offered her the crook of his arm. "Shall we?"

"Yes, of course."

"Did I mention earlier, how stunning you look this evening? You make me proud."

"Thank you. It is a lovely gown. Mother tells me it was made in Paris especially for tonight."

"Yes, I have friends."

She didn't ask. She didn't need to; her mother's comment earlier intimated as much. Half of France was now occupied by the German army, and Paris had fallen two years earlier. He had friends whom she didn't want to learn about but of whom Will insisted she become informed.

Arm-in-arm they walked through the east wing with Gebhardt trailing behind them, still by a good ten-foot length. Occasionally, Lizzy glanced over her shoulder, noting the smug, expectant look upon his face. She wanted to cry out, "You can't have me!"

They entered the massive study, a room entirely different from the one at Greystone. This one was welcoming and reminded her of sitting upon her grandfather's knee as a little girl. It seemed sad that the memory would be supplanted by the events about to unfold. She sat on that same maroon settee Grandfather Heinrich always had, her gown blending into the color of the brocade. She folded her hands delicately upon her lap in wait. In her mind, she clearly heard Will's words,

-I'll mate for life, too, because I know I'll never love another like I love you.

Lizzy noticed Ingrid's gold cigarette case on the table beside her and wanted to light up a Chesterfield, but she thought better of it. In an attempt to tamp down and hide her anxiety, she clasped her hands together. Resolved, she lifted her chin, realizing that the worst moment in her life was telling Will about his aunt and grandfather. Facing her father and Mr. Gebhardt's expected offer of marriage was nothing in comparison to the gut wrenching, pain-inflicting pronouncement that the DeVrieses had most likely been deported.

The Renner patriarch nodded to Gebhardt. He came forward with a smile like none she had seen before. A cross between smug confidence and an attempt at humility. Her father stood directly to her left with hands upon his hips, his eyes burning expectantly down into her. He was so sure he had convinced her of his wishes, nay demands.

"Miss Elizabeth," Gebhardt began, fluidly dropping to one knee at her feet, taking her hands into his. Through her gloves, she imagined his palms and fingers to be cold, as numb as she felt, and she immediately broke out in a cold sweat in response. She could smell his breath from a foot away. The scent of tobacco caused her stomach to roll, her baby as repulsed as she, willfully protesting. Lizzy fought back her nausea.

"I am sure that your father has made my desires known to you. I am further assured that he has made his own wishes known to you as well. It would please me most to know that they are your desires, too. Will you marry me, Elizabeth? Together, we will be sustainers of the Germanic race. You will be the spiritual caregiver to our many children, a queen of our superior people. Will you be my bride?"

Lizzy closed her eyes in revolt when he kissed her fingers, and if not for the thought that he would have misconstrued her meaning as one of sublime rapture, she promptly snapped them open, realizing what he was saying. She gagged. "No. I'm sorry, Mr. Gebhardt, but my answer is no." She gagged again.

"Elizabeth!" Her father reprimanded. "Your answer is yes!"

Clutching her hand tighter, almost constricting, causing her pain. "It is my wish," Gebhardt insisted, his voice dropping a menacing octave.

"Be that as it may, it is not *my* wish. My answer is no. I do not love you!" She wrenched her hand from his grasp.

"Love is inconsequential! It is your duty!" He rose, violently agitated and turned to Renner, raising his voice. "You assured me, Renner!"

Her father came to stand before her as she looked down at her hands, once again, tightly clasped together, a tear dropping as she had never felt so alone in that moment. Miraculously, in that moment, the image of Will's smile played before her mind's eye, comforting her.

Renner clasped both his hands upon her shoulders and shook, loosening the flower in her hair. "Look at me, you insolent child! You *will* marry him!"

It was then that the bile rose in her throat, the burning feeling of ascending vomit ready to be purged from her like the affluent debutante she had been groomed to be. Her right hand flew to her mouth and she suddenly stood, knocking her stout father backward. His protestations went unheard. Gebhardt's frustrated anger went ignored. All she heard was the slamming of a book upon the mahogany desk as her left hand grabbed the fabric of her skirt and her hasty feet ran for the study door to avoid retching upon the antique Persian rug.

Lizzy navigated through the crowd assembled in the hall outside the ballroom quickly reaching the door of the lavatory, not a moment too soon. Heavy retches into the commode spasmed her body as it bent forward. Her hand clutched her abdomen with each agonizing heave until the floating foie gras disgustingly stared back at her. She lurched again, her muscles contracting. All she wished for at that moment was Will's support and comfort, for him to be there with her, to hold her head and stroke her back with his strong, warm hands.

Ashen, sweating, and dry heaving, she hadn't yet felt this ill in her morning sickness. The small bathroom was stifling and now, quite rank. Desperate for relief, the cold snap of winter air was all she could think of when she finally exited back into the hallway where the fast tempo of Latin music riddled the air from the festivities just across the way. With lipstick in place, eyes dabbed dry, and her posture seemingly unaffected, she was determined to leave the house with this night behind her. Her eyes focused on the end of the hall, ignoring all the merrymakers between her and her escape route.

"Lizzy, are you okay?" John asked when she squeezed passed by the ballroom doors where he stood at the threshold with Ingrid, her visage, a haughty combination of disdain and unconcern. She tugged at John's tuxedo sleeve.

Determined to escape Meercrest without a scene, Lizzy tried to dismiss him. "I'm fine, Johnny. Please, excuse me."

"No, wait. What is it? You've been crying and you look ill. Can I help you?"

"Please. No. Just leave me be." She looked over her shoulder to see if she was followed by Gebhardt or her father. "I have to ..." Her eyes began welling with tears again, as she hurriedly attempted to leave, but the assembly was crushing.

"John, leave her!" Ingrid snapped, pulling him back into the ballroom as his eyes followed after Lizzy pushing her way through the crowd.

"Stop, Ingrid!" He tugged his arm from her grasp. "Something's terribly wrong with your sister."

"No, *you* stop. This is our night. *My* night, and she will not steal it from me."

John shook his head disbelieving her utter disregard for anyone other than herself. "You can't be serious? Something is upsetting Lizzy and all you care about is yourself. Fine, have *your* night, but you'll have it alone. I won't turn my back on her, especially if she's ill."

"She's probably caught something vile from that *Judensau*."

"What's that supposed to mean?"

Ingrid's fingers gripped his bicep, and she leaned into him, speaking through grit teeth. "She's a pig, an insignificant Jew-lover, and I will *not* have her get in the way of our announcement."

John scowled. "I hardly know who you've become, Ingrid." Disgusted, he removed her hand from his person. "There is no announcement. You can keep your million-dollar dowry. Find another stooge to marry."

She looked shell shocked as he ran after Lizzy, leaving her standing alone at the threshold of the ballroom with the band aptly playing, "Perfidia" in the background.

Mr. Howard stood at the public entrance door, ignoring the blackout restrictions by opening it wide for Lizzy as she bolted through without a coat, the train of her gown whooshing and trailing behind her.

John quickly grabbed any coat from the cloakroom and followed her into the midnight, freezing air. She stood in the forecourt behind the barren Japanese fountain, breathing deeply as tears fell unchecked down her cheeks, her arms crossing round, holding her waist.

He came up behind her covering her shoulders with a man's woolen topcoat. "Lizzy, what is it? Talk to me."

She turned her body into him, allowing the sobs to fall upon his shoulder. He wrapped her within his arms and rubbed her back. "It's okay. Everything will be okay. I'm here when you need to talk."

John had never seen Lizzy cry so, and it pained him to witness her so distraught. Over what, he had no clue, but their friendship was such that no matter what it was, he would help her. In typical Lizzy fashion, she lifted her head and forced a smile.

"Lizzy?"

She nodded resolutely and wiped her face with her gloved hand, her warm breath puffing into cold air when she spoke. "Don't worry about me, Johnny. Tonight's a special night for you; don't let me ruin it."

He buzzed pursed lips in mocking disregard. "We need to talk."

"Yes ... we do."

He was surprised when she thread her fingers with his and led him around the mansion, past the tea gazebo and down the darkened pathway, which led toward the now silent waterfall. "Where are you taking me?"

Below the top coat, her free hand gripped at her skirt, attempting to keep it from tearing or becoming soiled. "Sshh."

Their hands remained clasped as they neared the entrance of the grotto that was usually hidden behind falling water from spring to autumn. It was a place where they had played together as children and whenever Lizzy needed to escape, it was to either here or the water tower with a book. No one, most of all Ingrid, would dare enter the dark cave, but Lizzy had that daring nature about her and in her thirteenth year had requested of Mr. Abernathy, the groundskeeper, to make her a wooden bench and table for within.

They entered into the silent, eerie space. It had been years since he'd been there. A teacup and several stacked books sat upon the table. They were most likely moldy, discolored from the cave's moisture, exposure to dirt and to the elements. John held onto Lizzy's waist tightly so that she wouldn't slip on the stone.

"Gosh, it's been five or six years since I've been in here," he said, thankful for the fragrance of her perfume trailing her, covering the dank smell of the cave.

"I think it's been a year since I've been in here, too, but I need to talk with you in private and I don't want anyone to overhear what I have to say." She moaned. "Oh G-d, this has been one of the worst days of my life."

Lizzy sat on the bench, her skirt bunching around her. She removed the flower from her hair and stared down at it as John sat beside her.

"How can I help make it better, Lizzy?"

"You can't. All you can do is listen to me and be a comfort to me because with Will not here ... I feel so alone." Her eyes filled with tears and her voice cracked. "So ... terribly alone." She brought the flower to her lips.

"Tell me."

"I'm pregnant."

John tried to keep a passive face, but it was difficult. Shocked by her admission, he barely whispered, "Pregnant? Goodness. Does William know?"

She shook her head. "I only found out today and the doctor will have confirmation on Tuesday when I telephone. Oh, Johnny, I don't know what to do. I don't know where to turn. What if he doesn't survive the war?" Lizzy's hand flew to her eyes and she wept. His only thought was to comfort her, giving her his shoulder his arm came around her shoulders, bringing her body closer to his for support.

Long minutes of gentle weeping within the cavernous space echoed upon the stone until she stifled herself, sniffling through her voiced concerns. "There's more, so much more ... I cannot have his baby here at Meercrest and I cannot leave here either. Kitty needs me and my protection, but this baby needs the same. I'm damned if I do and I'm damned if I don't!"

He furrowed his brow. "Protection? Why does Kitty need protection? I mean, I understand not wanting to be an unwed mother and the censure that would be brought upon you and your baby but staying at Meercrest until Will's return would be foolhardy. The baby would be considered, well um ... a *bastard* and your reputation ruined. You have to leave, go to your aunt in New Jersey."

"I can't leave Kitty. It's Ingrid ... threats she's made, attempts to hurt her ... I found propaganda about euthanasia and sterilization of the unfit and disabled in her room."

John blanched, his heart nearly seizing. The woman he considered marrying had indeed become indoctrinated to Nazism's truest ideology. No wonder he hardly knew her this past year. "You're sure about the literature?"

Their eyes locked and he could see the fear in hers. His heart broke when Lizzy said, "Yes, I'm sure of what I read. She—and Father—are virulent anti-Semites, and they both know that Will is Jewish. Our baby is half Jewish, Johnny. I cannot raise it anywhere near here."

"Good Lord, Lizzy. I had no idea that Ingrid's opinions had grown to such zealous hatred until I heard her voice ugly words tonight. Suspected her leanings, yes, but I had not confirmed it—not until you ran past us. Does your fella know about Ingrid?"

"Yes, and he thinks Father is a Nazi collaborator, although I disagree about that, even though Gebhardt certainly conveyed his own sympathies tonight when he proposed."

John paused, his mind whirling from all this information. His breath grew short and he forcibly calmed himself to keep from having to light an asthma cigarette. Finally, he ran his hand through his sandy blond hair. "Lizzy, William may be right."

"I can't think of that right now. I said no to Gebhardt, and both Father and he became very angry."

"And that was why you fled?"

"Yes, I could never marry him. I also became ill. I've been very sick."

"Would you not consider marrying him if it meant giving the baby a home, a name?"

She gasped, and he regretted the words as soon as they had come out of his mouth. He saw the truth of it, she couldn't marry that creep especially given the fact that she knew where his sympathies lay.

"I'm sorry. Of course you can't marry him." His hand brushed against her head as it continued to rest upon his shoulder. "Has William professed his intentions to marry you when he returns? I mean ... he didn't take advantage of you, did he?"

Lizzy's head snapped up to look at him in the dark. "G-d no, Johnny! It was mutual. We love one another deeply, and we spoke of the future together, leaving Long Island and maybe moving to Brooklyn. He didn't officially ask but he gave me his heart when I was in Florida." She looked away, biting her lip to keep it from trembling, inadvertently drawing blood. "He gave me this baby ... unintentionally, but it is his love."

"Forgive me, I didn't mean to imply him so dishonorable to get a girl knocked up before he left for Europe. What I really mean to ask is ... do you think he'll be *happy* ... about the baby ... that is?"

She shrugged. "I don't know, but I'll only have a small window to find out until I begin to show and then any decision will be too late."

"Then write to Will and see what he advises. Maybe you can fly to England and get hitched in London or something. I could see about getting you on a supply flight along the South Atlantic Air Ferry Route. Your flyer will tell you what to do or if that's even possible."

"I don't know if he's left for England yet. I haven't received a letter in a week or so."

A deafening silence settled between the long-time friends, until before he knew what he was about, he turned to face her, taking her hands in his, fingers brushing upon the flower she still held. She looked so beautiful, so innocent and all he wanted to do was to protect her if her sweetheart couldn't. "Lizzy ... I ... I obviously don't know your fella like you do, but if he's *not* happy about the baby, or if he doesn't have the answers or worse ... if something happens to him, will you consider me as a last resort?"

"What do you mean?"

His heart pounded thunderously, but he had never felt more sure about anything in his life. "Marry me, Lizzy. I'll raise the baby as if it's my own. I'll protect it and you and take Kitty to live with us at Evermore or send her for the therapy she really needs, maybe inquiring about that nurse who treats the President. It would be my honor to do this."

"But what about Ingrid? You love her ... you've loved her since we were children."

"I loved the kind and generous Ingrid, the girl who loved her sisters, the sweet girl who visited old Mrs. Pratt up at Killenworth house when she was ailing. That's the Ingrid I fell in love with, not the cold calculating woman she became and certainly not the prejudiced ideologue we both believe her to be."

"I wanted to tell you about Ingrid, truly I did, but Lillian cautioned me not to. I thought you loved her, wanting to marry her, and I didn't want to hurt you. In the end, I fear I hurt you more by not telling you about that heart of stone of hers."

"I don't love Ingrid, and I could no more marry her than I could turn my back on you. I'm at fault for not listening to my gut feeling sooner."

"Does she know this? She's expecting to announce your engagement tonight."

John snickered. "I just told her. Look, if you'll have me—you would be doing me as much a favor as I you. Life with Ingrid would be a half-life and remaining a bachelor in my family home would be worse. Father will never see me as the man I am. You're the only one who knows of my health issues, and now I'm the only one who knows of yours."

"Kitty knows about the baby. She suggested that I marry Gebhardt as well."

"So between the three of us, we can protect each other. Will you consider it? Will you consider marrying me ... becoming Mrs. John Robertsen and raising William's baby as a Robertsen?"

Tears streamed down Lizzy's face, and he knew she would consider it.

"I'll deal with Ingrid when the time is right. Until then, write to your flyer and see what he wants you to do. Do we have a deal that if all else fails, you'll consider my offer?"

Lizzy nodded. "I will consider it, but only as a last resort. Not that I don't care for you, but you understand—I could never love another like I do Will. It would be very hard for me to marry anyone other than him."

"I understand. I'd expect no less from that passionate heart of yours. In the interim remain optimistic and hope for your heart's desire."

"Thank you but are you sure this is what *you* truly want. I don't want you to do this out of misguided loyalty to me as your friend."

"There is nothing misguided about my friendship with you. I love you, but not like that ... not like you love William, but I love you enough to protect you and your baby. For the service your fella gives to our nation, it would be an honor."

"And you wouldn't care that his child is Jewish?"

"Why would I care about that? The babe that you carry is an innocent child of G-d."

"Thank you. Thank you so much, Johnny."

They hugged and she held onto him tightly for a long time, both lost in their thoughts, her tears flowing upon his shoulder. *Ducky will tell me what to do. The war will end soon.*

Thirty-One

That's Sabotage
January 25, 1943

With every straining, circling push, the wheelchair groaned and clicked against the inlaid wood floor as Kitty made her way toward the main entrance hall of Meercrest.

Squeak, squeak, squeak was the only sound within the empty corridor. The annoying din from the chair's wheels reverberated against the marble pillars, seeming to grow louder with her every pounding heartbeat.

She halted her progress when she heard the melodious voice of her most beloved sister enter the foyer around the corner. As tired and sick as Lizzy had been with unceasing morning sickness, Kitty knew she was doing her best to convey the normal effervescence her family expected. Her voice pierced the chilly winter air of the wide hallways, breaking through the stone cold silence with her warm spirit.

"I'll be right there," she called out as she walked past the silver mail tray, obviously looking to see if Mr. Murphy had come and gone.

Kitty bent forward and peeked her head around the pillar, watching Lizzy examine her image in the long, pier mirror. She smoothed her skirt and, turning from side to side, looked at her figure in the reflection. Her usual radiance had grown wane. Peaked and drawn, she pinched her cheeks, hoping to add a rosiness to what others assumed was winter pallor. Although fear plagued her sister's heart, Kitty knew that optimism and deep love for Ducky was her sustenance. Yes, she would do whatever she could to protect Lizzy and his baby.

As quickly as her sister had burst on the scene in hopefulness, she was gone again.

Kitty had to act fast; well, as fast as the debilitating confines of leg braces and the wood and metal chair would allow. Midway through the foyer, her blonde head stole a furtive glance over a shoulder then up and above the tall wicker back of her prison. She cautiously looked around for any further interruptions to the crime about to unfold. It's not as though her arrival at the mail twice daily was unusual, but the act she was about to commit was. An act she abhorred doing, but one that was necessary.

Mr. Howard and Mrs. Davis were nowhere in sight and, thankfully, Nurse Keller had once again disappeared. That was fine by her. The woman had become cruel and verbally abusive since the end of December, and when she attempted to discuss it with her mother, shamefully begging to visit Aunt Helga, she was met by a scornful expression and a series of hiccups. She should have known that turning to her mother was pointless. The abrupt slap she received just before the Christmas ball when she had spoken ill of Ingrid, had proved that even her own mother cared nothing for her well-being. Lizzy was all she had but she knew that Lizzy had enough worries, and sharing her own daily fears would only add to those of her dearest sister.

The blackout shade over the Louis Comfort Tiffany stained glass window had been raised, allowing winter sunlight to shine into the foyer. A beaming spotlight illuminated Kitty's straining body, calling incriminating attention to her, *"Look! She's doing it again!"* But the warning went unheeded—unnoticed by anyone.

Her anxiety and guilt conspired in tandem with the ever present grinding screech of the wheelchair, calling attention to the deceitful, albeit well-intentioned, act about to transpire.

This wasn't the first time she had committed it. One would think her conscience was now reconciled, but it wasn't. Kitty laid awake guilt ridden every night questioning her duplicity, resolving that absolute fear and adoring love drove people to do things they never imagined they would. She had been acting for five weeks in this uncharacteristic manner for Lizzy's safety, the baby's safety—and for her own. She'd be fooling herself if she denied that last fact. She rationalized, her sister would never know what she did and, in time, it would be negligible, chalked up to a tragic result of the war. Everything was the war's fault, especially the reason she was moved to such lengths of protection. No, there was no other way. Lizzy must believe Will dead or indifferent to her plight in order for her to marry John before the baby started to show.

Her face felt hot and flushed, but her hands remained chilled with each turn of the metal wheels. As she rolled by the large oil portrait of her grandfather, she couldn't help but acknowledge his painted frown of disapproval. The stern countenance glowering down upon her every pass convinced her that he was a man with an abhorrence to any deceit. She stiffened her resolve by believing if he only knew *why* she lied, he would most likely thank her in the end.

She briefly glanced to the other side of the rotunda, pausing just long enough to admire the lovely Degas painting. Lizzy had questions about that painting, but she didn't look any deeper into its arrival at Meercrest. She loved its beauty and, on this morning, the movement and lightness of the ballet dancers was made all the more resplendent when bathed in the subdued winter sunbeams. It was this image of innocence and spirit that buoyed her to continue. Maybe Lizzy would have a little girl and one day Aunt Kitty would see her dance in a ballet.

With each turn, she drew closer to her destination—the door. The postman, her unknowing accomplice in this crime of the heart, would be arriving at the appointed time of his route to drop off Father's important mail and bring the family any correspondence. He was always so kind to arrive at precisely ten in the morning and five in the afternoon, knowing how she waited for the family post—some of it to steal.

Her heart had clenched each time she placed letters from Ducky and the Martels in the box she kept secreted away in her bedroom, along with Lizzy's outgoing letters that were entrusted to her for mailing, but too much was at stake to let one slip through. Even Lizzy's letters to the Martel family in Brooklyn found their way into the box. They might have welcomed William's sweetheart into their home, but they certainly wouldn't want the responsibility of a "poor crippled girl," too.

Poor? Definitely not. She didn't need any National Society for Crippled Children handouts. Crippled? That was a matter of opinion—and one she strongly objected to. After all, no one referred to the President of the United States as "that poor crippled FDR." He was her hero. As far as she was concerned Ingrid and her opinions could go to Hades. If only she would. Her eldest sister was pure evil and she was petrified to be alone with her.

With great difficulty, she bent forward and turned the gold doorknob, pulling it open. The winter wind whipped through the two-foot aperture, causing her to pull the lap blanket draped up to her waist. She hated the winter; it was when she felt her worst. Like the inert fountain standing in the center of the Japanese garden, she felt all the harshness of winter in her bones.

Precisely on time, Mr. Murphy rode up the gravel road on his bicycle, turning to circle the forecourt toward the mansion steps. The sight of his familiar bulky, wool scarf wrapped around his neck and chin caused her to smile despite her nerves and the frigid wind that entered through the open door. In his usual cheery manner, he waved.

"I'm sorry," she whispered in a heart-felt apology to the letter from William that she was sure Mr. Murphy carried intending to deliver to Lizzy. "It's for the best, Will. It's going to hurt, but it's for the best. I promise, if you return, you'll find another sweetheart. Lizzy has to marry Johnny—*now,* not when the war is over—*if* you even return, and she won't leave me here either. Johnny can protect all of us. It's the only logical solution for the three of us."

"It's a lovely morning!" the postman greeted, removing a stack of letters from the leather bag draped over his chest while ascending the marble steps. "Better get yourself inside, Kitty or you'll get a chill."

She hoped that her fake smile conveyed sweetness and blamelessness. "I know, Mr. Murphy. Thank you for your concern. It's a shame you have to deliver the mail on your bicycle in this cold."

"Just doing my bit for the boys." His eyes fixed briefly upon her covered legs, quickly diverting his glance not to stare like he did every day when she greeted him. "Did you read in the newspaper how we're beating back those Tojos on Guadalcanal? We're finally winning the battle and sending them running."

He handed her the short stack of bittersweet treasure she awaited, the top two envelopes clearly V-mail, small in size with the big red "V-Mail" emblazoned above the address. William's distinct sloppy handwriting first taunted her then immediately filled her with remorse.

"That's swell! Last we heard was that Lillian's sweetheart was on the Solomon Islands. I bet she'll be relieved to hear that victory is assured."

"Brave girl, that sister of yours. She makes us all proud."

"She's in England now, driving a clubmobile somewhere across the countryside. Thank you, Mr. Murphy."

"Is there any mail to post this morning?"

She couldn't help how her lips suddenly tightened. "Nope. Nothing at all. Not a one."

He touched the brim of his blue hat, got back on his bicycle and rode off back down the gravel road.

Kitty tucked both V-mail letters under the blanket. "It's for the best, Ducky. You'll thank me in the end for protecting Lizzy and the baby. If she waits for your return, terrible things may happen," she repeated the rationalization in her mind yet again, more for her own edification.

After organizing the few arriving letters into neat piles on the tray, she headed back from whence she came. The wheelchair rolled across the barren wood floor as now trembling hands slid upon the metal, turning the wheels. The repetitious squeak echoed in the cavernous foyer, a sudden ominous feeling overtaking her, but there was no turning back. The damage had already been done.

The commanding sound of heavy footsteps invaded the chilled airspace a moment before her father suddenly appeared.

Her body grew rigid and she sat straight up, clasping her hands on her lap.

His dominant presence filled the large entry hall when he placed his hands upon his broad hips in trademark fashion. "Did Murphy bring the morning post?"

"Yes, Father. I placed all of yours on the tray in its usual place."

"Good. There wasn't anything from that soldier was there?"

"No, Father. Nothing at all."

"You tell your sister, she can't avoid me forever. She will be marrying Gebhardt at the end of March come hell or high water."

"I will, Father, but don't worry, he's stopped writing to her. It's been some time now, and I know she stopped writing to him, too. They're no longer sweethearts."

"That better be true. No daughter of mine is going to be mixed up with a Jew." He brusquely patted Kitty's blonde head without thought or warmth. As he turned to depart, he queried, "Where's Nurse Keller? She's supposed to be assisting you."

"She's around some ..."

He had already left the hall with his anticipated mail before she could answer. A chill ran up her spine. The sound reasoning for her act of deception had just been confirmed by her father's cruel anti-Semitic hatred and his firm intention of marrying Lizzy off to that creep.

Thirty-Two

Say It
June 25, 1992

T hough the long trip to Sitka Airport was physically tiring, particularly
following a change of planes in Seattle, Juliana didn't feel it to be
tedious. In fact, she and Jack had a great time traveling first class together,
getting to know one another, and laughing. It was a luxury they hadn't
enjoyed yet since their acquaintance was born out of the search for her great-
uncle then later somewhat solidified over cherry pie at Primrose Cottage.
Although, they had discussed the family secrets in the kitchen and
afterwards, dancing to Artie Shaw in the parlor, a deeper personal exploration
of what made the other tick hadn't been pursued. Not because he had been
unwilling—on the contrary—but because she had been afraid. However,
when Jack held her hand to and through the Delta boarding gate at Kennedy
Airport, she was pretty convinced that she wanted to pursue the personal.
He was everything she thought a man should be. Witty, laid back, free
spirited, responsible, and with the kindest heart of any man she had ever
known. Like her, he had always looked to the future and only now felt
himself compelled to look at the past.

No topic seemed unapproachable. Heck, they'd even discussed her
relationship with Susan and why she felt relationships were just a set up for
abandonment and more disappointment. It felt like the best therapy session
she'd ever had. He had actually listened more attentively than her
psychologist. And in return, he opened up about his hope to settle down
now after so many years of travel, even sharing with her his recent epiphany
to get involved in the museum once again.

Sitting in the small shared sunroom that connected their rooms at the bed and breakfast, Juliana watched in awe as the sun set behind the dormant Mount Edgecumbe volcano, on Kruzov Island. It was hard to believe that at ten at night the sun was just setting. In theory, she should be exhausted, but she was too wound up for what tomorrow would bring. Only mere hours away, she was to be meeting her great-uncle and, hopefully, having a myriad of questions answered. She couldn't help the unsettling feeling that perhaps, he might not be happy to meet her, but she tempered that fear with the resolve at least to thank him for his gift. Four million dollars and a house were worth the long travel day to Alaska.

Lizzy's last letter to William from the stack found in the attic lay opened upon her lap. Once again, she was reminded that true love—the kind that's meant to last forever, the soul mate type that moves worlds and mountains—was possible. After reading all her great-aunt's letters to her flyer, Juliana was sure that something or someone had separated them outside of their control, because those two would never have willingly parted. She admired Lizzy's elegant penmanship then began to read.

December 15, 1942
My Dearest Darling,

I spent an hour or more today daydreaming. It hardly seemed that time had passed because I was so wrapped up in my memories of you and me and the time we shared together in Sarasota. My thoughts drifted to our visit to St. Pete Beach and what a perfect day it was. Anyone watching me as I doodled on the paper before me—completely oblivious to Mrs. Tinsdale's reminder that scrap paper is rationed—would have thought me wacky for sure. I couldn't help but to grin in swell remembrance of our visit to the Don CeSar to see the boys, bringing them some good cheer, books, and saltwater taffy. Six weeks ago seems like yesterday, and I hope that time flies just as quickly to bring us to the end of the war and your return. I miss you more than you could ever know. I need you more than I ever thought possible. You are my light and my life, Ducky. Please come home safe to me. If you have arrived in England, please wear that flak jacket you were telling me about. I'd rather you uncomfortably draped in steel than the alternative.

Holiday decorations are starting to transform Meercrest in anticipation of the Glen Cove Society Christmas Ball on the 19th. It's all so beautiful and with the cold weather and promise of snow, it feels magical already. The only thing missing is you and an end to this stomach bug I seemed to have picked up, but don't worry about me. I'll be back to my swell self in no time.

Well, your last letter didn't tell me if you have "officially" left for England. If you have, I want to hear all about it! Is the countryside as stunning as they say? I had only traveled to London on my Grand Tour and that was spectacular. Don't you dare tell me that the women are more beautiful than those at MacDill Air Field because I would surely find a way to come to you and slap you silly. There are no bugs in England in December that would warrant a visit to the infirmary, so get that notion out of your noggin. You are rationed, sir, off the market and belong to only one woman for the rest of your life! Ducky and Pistol—and you fly a bomber with my image to prove it! How is the Pistol Packin' Lizzy? Am I a hit with all the RAF fellas?

In regard to our serious discussions about Father, I have not found anything out of the norm, apart from that situation I mentioned to you in my letter last week—which is still quite a mystery to me. I know you'll think I am wacky, but the more I think on it, that woman's hair was similar to Kitty's nurse! How's that for reading too many Agatha Christie novels? Ha Ha Ha. Still ... there was a similarity from behind.

I still have not received a letter from Bethsabee, but I will continue to believe that no news is good news. I can only continue to pray for her safety as well as that of your family. We must believe that they are protected somewhere. As soon as I hear something, I will send you word, and I promise to be honest and not sugar coat it should it contain news that may be upsetting. The optimist in me doesn't believe it will, but I gave you my word not to hide from these realities ...

Juliana propped her sneakers up on the hassock and took in the view. Vibrant orange bursting behind the snow-capped mountain was mixing with the purple clinging fog surrounding the distant wonder. She sipped her Coke from a can designed for the upcoming Summer Olympics in Barcelona. The letter, the view, and the crisp soda made it a perfect moment. Feeling comfortable, she burped then giggled. It wasn't such a perfect moment when she realized that Jack stood behind her laughing.

"Oh my G-d. I'm mortified! Why didn't you tell me you were there?"

He had a playful smile upon his face when he replied, "I was taking in the view."

"It is a gorgeous sunset isn't it?"

"I was taking in the *full* view and yes, it is gorgeous."

She blushed and he came to sit on the worn recliner beside her then pulled the tab of his Coke, releasing that familiar pop. His sandy hair was tousled, and he had changed into sweatpants, after the day of cross-country flights. "Do you like the place?" he asked.

"It's amazing and the owners are so friendly, so accommodating and trusting to give us run of their house. They're definitely not from New York City." She snorted, continuing to make small talk even though she was having a tough time doing so. Perhaps it was the caffeine in the soda—or something else. He looked damned incredible and smelled so freshly clean that she was having difficulty fighting her desires just seeing his blue eyes alit with excitement.

As she felt that flutter below, searching for a safe topic Juliana nervously blurted out, "Mr. Crenshaw is a Toronto Blue Jays fan. He hates the Yankees."

"So does my grandmother. She's a huge Giants fan."

"Really? But the Giants are in San Francisco. That seems almost traitorous of her. What self-respecting New Yorker doesn't like the Yankees or the Mets?"

"Ah, well the Giants used to be in New York as were the Los Angeles Dodgers. Back in the day they were terrible rivals."

"What about you? Do you like baseball? I think that's the only thing we didn't talk about on the plane." She looked coyly at him, imagining them attending a game together when they got back to New York. Sharing a hot dog or splitting an ice cream cup—the vanilla half would be hers and the chocolate half for him. Apparently, not even her "safe" topic could contain her burgeoning urges.

"I enjoy baseball. I'm not as fanatical about it as my grandmother is, but she and I attend a few games together. Perhaps when we go again in August, you can come with us," he said.

Juliana grinned. "I'd like that. Maybe my grandfather can come with Louise, too. Who knows, maybe William will be on Long Island and we can go as one big family. Rent a box or something."

"That's certainly something to look forward to. I'm game if you are."

She nodded with an optimistic grin. "I am."

"So it sounds like you're resolving to the fact about your grandfather and his lady friend."

"I finally decided to take a chill pill about the whole thing. If it makes him happy, then it makes me happy. Mimi would have wanted it that way. Anyway, the more I thought about it, his relationship with Louise doesn't take away or diminish the memory or love he shared with my grandmother. How about you and the issue of William being the first and maybe even the most powerful, influential love of your grandmother's life? Are you reconciling with the fact that Lizzy might renew their romance if given the opportunity?"

"I think so. In hindsight, I see that what she had with my grandfather, special as it may have been, wasn't that kind of consuming passion we all secretly desire. Your great-uncle may have been that to her, but maybe your great-grandfather separated them."

"We *all* secretly desire?"

"Yes, *all* of us. Recently, I've come to learn that true love can come when people least expect it, and a guy can't help to feel that tugging of his heartstrings no matter how hard he tries to fight against it." He raised an eyebrow and she deliberately looked away, taking another swig of her soda.

"What's that on your lap?"

She picked up the letter. "It's her last letter to my uncle before Christmas in 1942. She tells him that he is her light and her life. Isn't that romantic? To be loved so much, to be thought of so highly that someone proclaims you are their life?"

"It is, but that's what true love does, I think."

"Not in 1992, and who are you kidding, you don't really believe in everlasting love in today's society any more than I do."

"You're wrong, Julie. I believe in love and so do you. You're just gun shy, as was I up until about a week ago."

"Perhaps." Avoiding his heated gaze, she faced back toward the mountain and took another sip of her Coke.

Jack smiled knowingly, reflecting on how hours before when their small plane to Sitka hit a rough patch of turbulence, she had jumped into his arms. If she was truly immune to her feelings or what was developing between them, then she wouldn't have remained in his embrace with her back against his chest afterwards, while reading a *People* magazine. His arm had stayed firmly wrapped in place around her small waist.

Silence settled between them on the porch until Jack rose and stood before her, blocking the view of the setting sun. Juliana quizzically furrowed her brow when he removed the soda from her hand, placing it on the table.

"What are you up to?" She asked, laying the letter beside the can.

He took her hand in his and with one swift pull, tugged her up from her seat, her slight body crashing into his hard chest. Their faces were mere inches from each other as she gazed into his hooded eyes. His hand smoothed down her spine until his palm rested at the small of her back, and he gently pulled her against him. She smiled in knowing anticipation and her heart skipped a beat when he smiled back teasingly, raising his eyebrows. His nearness felt so good, close but not crushing. It had been way too long since she allowed herself this rush of feeling for any man, the anxious prospect of their first kiss surging her already rapid pulse. Her breath hitched when he lowered his lips to hover above hers, his warm, spearmint aroma mixing with her sweet soda pop scent.

He whispered, "Don't fight it, Julie. Kiss me."

She did. Her lips touched his with soft tenderness. There were no tongues, wild sucking or out of control, raging impetuous passion. There was only the undeniable acceleration of her heart beat from the sweetest of kisses. Sparks collided, then traveled the length of her body. This was, without a doubt, the best and purest kiss she ever had given or received.

When their lips parted, he said, "Thank you. May I have another?"

Feeling strangely unfettered, Juliana chuckled and ran her hand up his chest.

The sun had just set leaving the sky aflame with deep orange and purple casting an erotic feel to the night. There was no denying her attraction to him and she couldn't fight it any longer even if she wanted to. With their second kiss, she banished some of her fears, giving in to what she really wanted. Exploring with tentative tongues, they breached their united flesh, searching and playing in delicious unison as their mouths claimed one another.

Covering her one hand upon his chest, Jack entwined his fingers with her other at their side, holding her fast. She moaned under the pleasant assault of his molding lips and she pressed against him even further, reveling in the securing connection. His intention had taken on a physical form, that they were now a couple, inseparable not just in this journey but also for the unknown journeys ahead, their lives intertwining.

After a few minutes, their passionate kiss was growing too intense. A battle of opposing wills erupted within her, reason and logic fought with her body further warring with the promptings of her heart, each having its own agenda. She wasn't quite psychologically ready for what her body wanted to do. Two kisses weren't enough to vanquish eleven years of emotional insecurity, and a roll in the sack would only complicate things, confusing her even more. She pulled away.

"That was lovely," she murmured across the short distance she had made between them, their hands still connected.

He suddenly became worried. "Too much? Too soon? Did I scare you?"

"No, the kiss was just right." She leaned in, closing the space between them again and rested her head upon his shoulder. "I'm just afraid of what comes next. Right now my heart and head are conflicted and well ... you know."

"I understand." Jack tilted her chin upward to gaze into her eyes. "Do you know why I've become a romantic?"

Juliana shook her head.

"It's because of you. This crazy, hopeful search of yours for something so beautiful and everlasting has opened my eyes. Your romantic heart has opened mine."

"Me? Romantic? You've got the wrong girl."

"I don't have the wrong girl. Julie, I'm falling for you. I *have* fallen for you. Before you, I'd never met a woman with your purity of heart, someone willing to search for the most important truth in life—to love and to be loved. I know you are worthy of that kind of happiness because you are as gorgeous inside as you are out."

Wow ... what could she say to that proclamation?

"I want to believe that because ... because I'm falling for you, too. Can we just take this slow?"

"As slow as you need or want. I've got all the time in the world to show you how special and worthy of love you are. You have my word—I'll never hurt you or abandon you. I intend on proving to you that a romance like Ducky and Pistol's can happen in 1992, too."

****

Will arrived back at the cabin late Sunday night after flying McCarthy up to Anchorage. Even the sun had finally set and by Sitka time, it was well after eleven when he closed the door behind him, glad to be in his peaceful sanctuary. Coming home was always a pleasant, comfortable feeling. Alaska was honest and pure living for him, without pretense or outlandish affluence. Sitka, in particular, with its rich cultural heritage and broad tolerance was void of societal or religious expectations. Even attendance at Shul was in a makeshift building on Friday nights, and he liked that for the times when he couldn't make it up to Anchorage for the more traditional services.

The bad news of McCarthy's unsuccessful surgery and the physician's declaration of "two, three months at the most," had left Will bone tired and emotionally spent. Resting his overnight bag by the door, he gave the narrow hall table, and the stacked mail upon it, a quick dismissing glance as he tossed his keys into the hulled wood bowl. Ginny was always so careful to organize his mail for him. She had learned early on that, for reasons he avoided explaining, his mail was important to him. Tonight, it would wait though. His heart felt heavy and his eyes even heavier. He just needed to unwind a bit before going to sleep.

The spacious open plan of the main floor was dark, allowing a clear view of the Sound beyond the floor to ceiling windows, the full moon illuminating the calm sparkling water. Mount Edgecumbe looked to be barely a shadow on the horizon. An empty wine glass and a dish of half-eaten quiche still sat on the coffee table and a balled wool blanket lay at the edge of the sofa. He frowned thinking Ginny obviously didn't expect him to arrive home tonight. She often came to house sit in his absence, but her mess—at least tonight— was an unwelcome sight.

He heard her classical radio station one flight above in the loft. "Gin? I'm back."

She peeked her head over the balcony. "Oh! Hi Will. I didn't expect you until tomorrow. How did everything go?"

"I'll be up in a few to tell you."

"Do you want me to come down?"

"No, I'll be up soon. I need to unwind first. It was a rough flight, and you know how that unnerves me. Thanks for staying at the house while I was away."

"Sure. I look for any chance to get out of that flat of mine."

He walked into the kitchen with her plate and glass, placing them in the dishwasher with strains of Chopin drifting down from the upper floor around him. Silence was preferred, but at least it was soothing to his inner disharmony. The rawness he felt tonight would require more than a beer to assist his mental decompression. He poured himself a much needed double shot of scotch.

Drink in hand, he eased open the sliding door to the deck, then stepped out into moonlight. He stood on the deck listening to an unseen owl hooting from the forested acreage behind him until stone silence fell. Ruminating, the events of the last two days occupied his mind until he heard nothing else, not even Chopin.

"Life is short," he spoke aloud, remembering McCarthy and Margie's tears and the way their hands remained clasped on the way home.

His mind drifted, as it had all too often over the last couple of days, but tonight, his buried recollections took form. The desperation that Margie felt when all hope seemed lost brought forward dreadful memories from January of '43. He vividly remembered waiting for mail call at Rougham Air Field in England, when that panicked feeling overtook him, that Pistol had done the unthinkable—moved on. That same blistering anxiety was germinating again tonight, anticipating Alan's packet to arrive any day.

Penetrating winds whipping the dreary cold rain of Suffolk couldn't release him from waiting for the sergeant to call out his name. The boys of the 322nd stood beside a metal nissen hut, seemingly unperturbed by the weather or the wait as they anticipated letters from home. Hell, he'd wait at attention for hours if it meant receiving one small letter containing even one brief line from Lizzy. "I'm safe. I love you. I miss you." That was all he wanted, just reassurance but none had come for four weeks now. He knew that it wasn't the military's fault, knowing that mail hadn't been misdirected. Rocco, the PPL's navigator from the Bronx, had received a letter from his sister, replied, and had already gotten back a response. So what was Lizzy's excuse? He couldn't help fearing the worse. She either had bad news about his family in Paris and was avoiding telling him or she had dumped him. Maybe her father even had his hand in their separation, all three possibilities causing a fear in him disrupting his core stoicism, obsessively tormenting him.

Searching his mind for fortitude, he referenced the 322nd's motto "I fear none in doing right," but the words were an empty platitude as he stood there waiting. He needed to hear from his sweetheart, to know that his girl was safe and still his.

The last letter in the stack was called by the sergeant, and the recipient wasn't "Martel." The disappointment was immense and he wanted to hang his head and cry, but shook it off when McCarthy slapped his back in his familiar fashion.

-C'mon. Let's go make a record.

-A record? What'a you talking about?

-Yeah, there's this dishy British bird over at the Red Cross Club at Rattlesden and she suggested we stop by to record one of those Letter on a Records. You can send one to Pistol and by the tone of your sappy voice, she'll be writing you in no time.

-We have a practice mission at 16:00 hours.

McCarthy winked. -Stick with me, Skipper. I'll have us back in no time.

An hour later at the nearby RAF airfield, Will was approaching the "dishy" blonde whose pleasant smile did nothing to quell the pain in his heart.

The woman stood beside the entrance to a small booth. -Go ahead, Lieutenant. It's very simple, really. When I close the door you should begin speaking into that microphone so that your voice will be cut into the record.

He looked at her dubiously. -Into a 78 rpm? Me?

-Yes, you. Your girl back home will love you for it. It'll be like you're there with her, and don't you worry about a thing. I won't be listening.

Will ran his finger under his collar, afraid that he might say the wrong thing. If Lizzy was mad at him for unknown reasons, he didn't want her to snap her cap at something he said in a wrong way but, by G-d, he was resolute to say what he should have said in October. The woman closed the door and motioned to him through the glass to begin speaking. He was tentative at first, holding back, then finally, removed his service cap and placed it on the small counter before him. He leaned toward the silver microphone.

-Um ... Hi Lizzy. It's me Will. I bet it's a shock to the ticker to hear me on this 78 but the Red Cross volunteer said that it would sound just like I was home. It's probably as scratchy as that old Ink Spots record we listened to at Rosebriar.

He broke out into a sweat and wiped his brow, watching the black lacquered record go round and round below the needle.

-I'm recording this from England where I've been for four weeks now. The weather hasn't been too good, but thankfully, my squadron is still in training. The Marauders have yet to show off what we can do.

-I miss you, and I hope you miss me, too. The thing is, Pistol ... I've been writing you and haven't heard back since before I left Christmas week. I know there was a delay in my getting a letter out to you, but it took some time to embark, paper work and all that, then flying out and the whole process upon our arrival into the Eighth Air Force. The last thing I received from Glen Cove was your Christmas card and the letter the week earlier letting me know you had the stomach flu. I hope you're feeling better and that everything is okay on Long Island.

Tilting his head, he surreptitiously looked to see where the Gray Lady was now seated at a small desk, then he moved closer to the microphone.

-Lizzy, I'm desperate, baby. I've tried everything to get to you, even writing my parents and Louie asking them to write to you. It's not going into battle I'm afraid of, it's that something has happened to you. I'm terrified that ... that we're through ... that you've found another fella and given me the heave ho. Say it ain't so, because I don't think I could survive it. I love you. I know I should have asked you before I left, but I was chicken. I wanted to get everything in order for you, for a life with you.

He took a deep breath, looked out the glass again, and dropped to his knee in the small booth. -Will you marry me as soon as I come home? Will you be Mrs. Martel forever, till the end of life's story?

He rose and gripped the arm of the microphone, the hardboiled Army pilot now reduced almost to tears.

-Please write me. Just two words, Pistol. The only two words I hope to hear from you: I will.

It was many more long minutes in the dark with his scotch before he stepped back inside to look at the mail, something niggling in the back of his mind, gnawing at him.

As Will drew nearer, he could see the edge of the large white envelope taunting him. The bold blue *F* of FedEx stuck out like a sore thumb. With a tentative hand, he slid it from the bottom of the pile. It was from Alan Gardner. Although thick and tempting, he hesitated. *He obviously found her. Now what are you going to do? Can you really go back in time? Do you really want to?*

Standing in front of the native Tlingit carving on the wall, he ran his finger along the edge of the envelope, flicking the paper tab back and forth. *Pull it. No, don't pull it. Not tonight.* No, he'd wait, of course he would. The phone call was too impetuous, too spontaneous. He had to think of the road ahead if he pulled the cord to the envelope. This was one packet that needed all his attention. Besides, he still had to talk to Ginny and it was best that he gave her his answer before reading the contents of his lawyer's findings.

He carried the envelope out onto the deck with him, settled back into the Adirondack chair, and nursing his scotch, stared up at the millions of stars. Most were simple pinpoints of distant light but there were just a few that twinkled brightly. They always called to mind a pair of sparkling green eyes and from there, those twisting lips of cherry bomb sweetness. Denial was fruitless. After fifty years, he was still in love with her and over the last two days, she was all he could think of. When McCarthy got the news that the cancer had spread everywhere, his mind had gravitated to life and death, and how he didn't want to leave this world without seeing her—or loving her—just one last time.

His fingers tapped the strip seal of the FedEx envelope, and he spoke to himself. "What if she's dead? Can you deal with that? What if she's alive and still married? Can you deal with *that*? You're not twenty-one any longer, even if you feel like it. What if she doesn't like who you have become?" He looked down at the dark shadow of his floatplane docked at the pier. It was in need of a tune-up. That should take him a good two days to accomplish while he mulled over the ramifications of opening the packet. Tossing the envelope onto the table beside him, he said, "Foolish whim. This'll come back and bite you in the ass. Just like seeing her in '49 did. Loving her that one last time nearly did you in."

"Did you say something, Will?" Ginny asked appearing on the deck, disturbing his privacy.

He turned to see her all bundled up in one of his sweaters, and he smiled thoughtfully. She was a pretty woman with a wonderful heart and a great sense of humor, but she wasn't Lizzy. She could never be his Pistol.

"Hey, Gin. Listen ... we have to talk."

Thirty-Three

One O'clock Jump
June, 29 1992

The Antelope Tavern overlooked Sitka's Crescent Bay Harbor, conveniently located down the street from the premier attraction of St. Michael's Russian Orthodox Church. The cruise ship business had brought welcome tourists to the small town and the tavern, however, on this day, it was unusually quiet during the normal lunchtime rush of travelers.

Will sat at the rustic bar, chowing down on an authentic New York-style Reuben sandwich that Grace, the barmaid and owner made sure was available at one o'clock every Monday for her favorite regular customer. CNN silently broadcast images of the recently assassinated president of Algeria from the small TV mounted above the booze bottles, neatly tucked beside the obligatory taxidermy antelope head.

Against the far wall a 1970s silver and black jukebox currently filled the bucolic space with Brooks and Dunn's "Neon Moon." Nearby, a couple of teenagers were playing a game of pool.

Will drew a much needed long quaff from his pilsner glass as he watched a young couple enter the almost empty restaurant. Based on the young woman's trendy black apparel and her New York Yankees baseball cap, she was obviously a tourist, most likely having just stepped off the Holland America ship that arrived this morning. He couldn't help reflecting on the irony of his corned beef sandwich and the symbol of the Bronx Bombers, Louie's favorite ball club, colliding here in Alaska. He immediately chastised himself for al-lowing something as innocuous as a cap to call his brother to mind so readily.

"Take a seat wherever you like. Menus are on the table." Grace called out in her native Tlingit accent to the newcomers.

The young woman's eyes locked with Will's as she entered and walked toward him, causing him to think she was coming to talk, but instead she and her companion, a fair-haired male, sat at the table behind him.

Will continued to eat with gusto, lost in the images on the black and white television and those also being simulcast within his mind's eye. That impulsive, unopened FedEx envelope still taunted him from his nightstand back at the house. He hadn't even made headway on tuning up the floatplane this morning, having walked down the dock to stare at it for an hour without doing a blessed thing. Shit, he'd even mulled over renaming it, but thought better of it given his past experience and luck in naming airplanes. Agitated and annoyed at himself for letting Pistol get under his skin after all these years, he was in a foul mood, particularly since, after having been banished twenty years earlier, her photograph was ceremoniously reinserted within his wallet at five a.m. this morning. Further, he couldn't escape the guilt at delivering the disappointing blow to Ginny the night before. He hadn't expected her to cry, but she did.

Not even the corned beef was doing the trick to find his good humor, only serving to remind him of that little corner delicatessen beside the RKO Prospect theatre in Park Slope. Everything haunted him: Brooklyn, her beautiful face, their song, and now his brother and those damned conceited Yankees. Although, in that, at least, there was a tinge of satisfaction when recalling how they were having a shit season.

The country music was failing miserably to take his mind away from all things New York.

Will glanced over his shoulder at the couple again and her blue eyes met his. Even this sweet-looking tourist plagued him! Fighting a grimace, he gave her a half-hearted "leave me the fuck alone" smile, then turned back to his sandwich.

Juliana thought her heart would stop when she immediately recognized her great-uncle sitting at the bar. He hadn't changed a bit from the photographs she committed to memory. Older, yes, but in a good way. William was devastatingly handsome, fit and, my G-d, she was sure that Lizzy would go lulu for him all over again. Heck, if he weren't a senior citizen and her own relative, she could easily crush on him.

At that moment, it seemed voyeuristic that she knew almost verbatim the words Lizzy had penned to him five decades prior. Each tender memory they had shared, each declaration of love and teasing playfulness she had read was as though having written them herself. She felt like a trespasser. Her great-uncle was no longer a missing person or a one-dimensional flat image in a snapshot. He wasn't a trinket in a military footlocker or a name written in ink on fine stationery. Her grandfather's brother and her great-aunt's sweetheart was real and right there—only feet from her.

After she and Jack had failed in their attempts at connecting with him over the weekend, she hadn't expected that finding him in town would be so easy. As it turned out, it was uncannily fortuitous that their Alaskan host, Mr. Crenshaw, shot pool with William every Wednesday night at the Antelope and informed them about his ritual Monday lunch. Sure enough, he sat at the bar dressed in blue jeans and a long sleeved Henley. Wavy salt and pepper hair reached to his collar. Unfortunately, the most expressive eyes she had ever seen immediately told her that he was annoyed.

Grace came to stand on the opposite side of the bar in front of Will, wiping down the counter area surrounding his plate of piled high French fries. "This is unlike you to eat greasy stuff," she said pointing to the curly potatoes.

He grunted and shrugged a shoulder.

"Boy you're a grouch today. What happened, did Ginny give you the boot after all these years?"

"Sort of. She gave me an ultimatum and I don't deal with those well. My ex-wife gave me one too many back in '77. Two ultimatums was my threshold and as I get older my tolerance is even less. Sorry, Grace. I don't mean to take it out on you. It's been ... a bad week."

"Oh, darlin', at your age you should understand women by now. We only give ultimatums because we want you to hang around not run you off. Don't you know that by now?"

He sniggered. "Based on my history with women, I can unequivocally state that I know *nothing* about them and will never understand them for as long as I live. At 71, I am no more educated in the ways of women than I was at 21."

"Now, that sounds like a bitter heart. Who knew you even had it in you? You need to read that new book, *Men are From Mars, Women are From Venus.*"

"No thank you. I don't need some psycho-babble book to tell me that most women are alien creatures—present company excluded of course—and Ginny, too. She's not really responsible for my piss poor attitude."

"*Of course* I'm the exception. I make a mean Rueben."

He smiled as he chewed, "Yes you do. Now if you could just learn to make an egg cream, I'll consider you a goddess."

Will heard the insistent whispers behind him, the man encouraging the Yankee fan to "don't be frightened, just do it. He won't bite."

Grace called out over Will's shoulder. "What are you folks drinking?"

The man replied in a northeastern accent, "Two Alaskan Ambers."

Well, now that got Will's attention. That wasn't a beer easily attained in the Lower 48.

The owner was also surprised that the patron knew of the relatively new Alaskan Brewing Company specialty beer. "You're not a sourdough. How do you know about ABC?"

"I've been out here a few times, covering the cruise line business and Denali National Park. I'm a travel reporter for *New York Newsday* newspaper."

Will let out a deep sigh and almost hung his head in defeat. Damn. This couple was either from the City or the Island. Was everything determined to undermine the peace he found these last fifteen years of escape and seclusion? Finally, with beer in hand, he swiveled on the barstool to face the New Yorkers, his legs firmly planted before him.

"Where in New York are you from?" he asked. The young woman stared at him as though a deer caught in headlights. Actually, she looked similar to that antelope on the wall, flaxen haired and wide-eyed, and he wanted to chortle at her expression.

The young fella said, "I'm from Mill Neck, Long Island, just outside of Glen Cove and she's from ..."

He looked at the girl, elbowing her arm resting upon the table until she blurted, "Victorian Flatbush, Brooklyn."

Glen Cove and Flatbush. You've got to be kidding? Will was further shocked when the five-foot two beauty rose from her chair, smiled at him with Louie's shit eating, mischievous grin and declared, "300 Bradford Road—Primrose Cottage—to be precise."

The beer glass slid from his fingers, falling between his legs and smashing to the wood floor. Damn he hated surprises.

He hardly paid the glass shards or the splattered beer any notice. His jaw went slack before he croaked, "Juliana? What are you doing here?"

Bolting him from the blue, she ran to him and hugged him tightly. He didn't know what to do with his arms and chose the logical thing: he hugged her back when she cried, "Uncle William!"

Neither Will nor Juliana noticed when Jack rose from his seat and politely exited the tavern with the intent of leaving them alone. They had much to discuss and, at this time, his presence would only be an intrusion. This was her journey, and when and if the opportunity presented itself then, and only then, he would introduce himself as Lizzy's grandson.

"I can't believe I found you!" she beamed, drawing back from their embrace as Grace came around the bar with a broom and dustpan.

"Um ... I can't believe you found me either."

She looked at him shyly. "I'm sorry ... I'm so sorry if I'm not welcome or am intruding. I just wanted to thank you."

"Why don't we take a seat outside on the deck? We can talk over that beer of yours. How does that sound?" he offered, confused and still whirling from the complete shock of her appearance into his world.

He didn't know what compelled him but he took her hand in his and laughed. "You flew almost three thousand miles to *thank* me? A simple card would have sufficed."

"I guess a card would have been enough if that was all I had to say, but it's not."

Will signaled to Grace to bring the beers outside, mouthing the words, "I'm sorry," as they walked out the door into brilliant sunlight.

Juliana bit her lip, and damn, if that quirky habit wasn't further testimony to what a shitty week this was; the reminder was almost painful. "Don't bite your lip. There's no need to be fearful of me."

"Right. Of course. I know that." Her heart beat rapidly and she could almost hear her pulse pounding in her ears. However, when her uncle pulled out her chair, she felt so much more at ease. He was the gentleman, Ducky, she had come to know.

The vista surrounding them was breathtaking. One hundred and eighty degrees of mountains with low lying clouds reflected in the still water. Niece and uncle sat facing one another at a small, somewhat rickety table, both feeling incredibly awkward by their meeting and unsure how to begin conversation as strangers. Will couldn't help his eyes drawing to the pair of silver wings she wore and he wondered if they were his.

Juliana wrung her hands together and breathed in the salty sea air. "You look just as I thought you would."

"And I had no idea how you would look, but it's very nice to finally meet you."

"I ... um ... installed ceiling fans in the house and hope to have central air conditioning put in during the spring."

"That's good to hear. Has it been terribly warm in New York this summer?"

She nodded. "Barely tolerable, but the fans help. The stove generates a ton of heat."

"I'm glad it's so efficient. I had that oven special ordered when I purchased the house."

Grace placed two beers on the table and gave Juliana a wink before quickly departing.

"Well, Juliana, I'm sure you didn't come all this way to give me an update to *This Old House* or to talk about the weather in Brooklyn. I admit, I'm a bit shocked, but I am curious. As far as I knew, no one knew my whereabouts." He raised an eyebrow.

"You're right, no one knew where you were, but Jack, the guy I'm with, had connections and was able to locate you."

"That's a lot of trouble to find me. It must be important. It's not Lou is it?"

"No, Grandpa is fine. It's ... well, you see ... I'm here because I wanted to ask you face to face why you gave me Primrose Cottage when I didn't even know of your existence. You left way before I was born and, now with my father gone, no one ever spoke of you or why you left. I found the house just as you left it in 1950 and it troubled me. Strangely, I felt your pain and thought something terrible must have happened in your life. It made me sad, and I wanted to know your story. Grandpa stopped speaking when Mimi died, so really, I didn't have anyone to explain to me how you knew about me. How did you?"

Will leaned back in his chair and held her gaze. She was so innocent to have sought him out, to have cared so about him was unprecedented.

Frowning, he rubbed his chin. "I've kept tabs on New York through my lawyer, Alan Gardner."

"I know him!"

"I'm sure you do. He'd been our family lawyer for forty years before his son took over the practice, but Al still keeps me informed of the important stuff. I'm sorry about your father and Lillian's death. I only knew Gordon as a baby, but I knew your grandmother. She was a good woman, and I'm sure my brother is heartbroken. As for Primrose Cottage, it's a special house—enchanted even. I left it to you because I hoped that by the time you were ready to fall in love and pursue a relationship it would be the home for you that I had envisioned it would be for me. I hoped that enough years would have passed for that kind of love to be appreciated and maybe in style again. The forties were a great—and foolish—time to be in love."

"Yes, I gathered that. Was it a great time to be in love with someone like Lizzy?"

He furrowed his brow.

"I found your footlocker in the attic and read the letters and looked at the snapshots. Her letters are what led me to look for you."

"Hmm ..."

"She was very beautiful."

"Yes, extremely." He sighed deeply and looked away from her inquisitive stare. Clearly, she was looking for more than his acknowledgement of Lizzy in his life during the war, but he didn't know the girl sitting before him enough to share with her anything about himself or the loss his heart felt when he allowed it.

"Pistol is alive," she said, causing him to snap his head to attention. She grinned impishly.

A wry smile developed as Will tapped his fingers against the side of the beer bottle. "So, you know about my wartime sweetheart." He sighed. "She broke my heart—twice, but I survived. The first time by the skin of my teeth and the grace of G-d when I crashed the bomber named after her over Holland."

"Was that when you were taken as a prisoner of war?"

Will laughed. "What is this, an interview? Sheesh. Yes, I was so overcome with grief that I put my entire crew in jeopardy. Thank G-d we all survived."

Juliana leaned forward. "If you don't mind me asking, what happened between you two? I mean—why did it end? Was it because of her Nazi father?"

"I don't know. Her letters stopped right after Christmas of '42. I kept writing, but I never heard from her again. After my plane was shot down in May of '43, there wasn't any means she could have reached me by anyway. I had two years to realize that she had moved on. When I finally saw her a few years later at your father's christening, I knew I had been correct. She had completely moved on thinking I was dead. Apparently, no one in my family saw fit to apprise me of her marriage or her of my survival. Based on the age of her children, she had obviously gotten a better offer to marry into that high society world of hers right after I flew overseas."

Saw her again ... '49 ... the affair, the letter.

"Well, from everything I read, heard, and discovered it seems more like the world moved on, but I don't believe her heart moved with it."

He laughed sardonically. "That's doubtful. I don't know what else I can tell you, Juliana. It's very personal and something I don't share easily. I'm sorry, but I'd rather not say more on the subject. At the time it hurt too much, and I've kept it bottled up for too many years now to begin rehashing the past."

"I understand about hurts and not wanting to face them. Truly I do, but I'm coming to learn that everyone needs a chance at forgiveness." *Even my mother.* Her eyes unexpectedly welled with tears. "This way healing can take place in ourselves. My grandfather needs that opportunity. I want him to see his brother again and make amends for whatever happened between you two." She wiped her eyes. "He misses you so much, and I want what's left of his future to be happy."

Damn, now she was getting him all sappy. He couldn't help the prick of tear in his own eyes. He missed Louie, too. Missed what they had shared, missed being a family. "When you walked in with that ball cap of yours, I remembered that I owe him two dollars from the '42 All-Star game. Lucky bastard that he always was."

"He said it's time to ante up with interest." Juliana raised her eyebrows hopefully.

"That knucklehead knew you were coming out here to see me?"

"Yes. It's been about two years now without a single word spoken due to grief and post-traumatic stress from the war but last week when I told him about the things I discovered in the wall of Primrose Cottage he found his voice to tell me the truth about your growing up Jewish. He also explained to me what happened to your grandfather and aunt."

Will nodded, saying nothing just slightly pursing his lips.

"When I told him that I was coming to see you, he said something to the effect that only a vaporhead would try to hide from his past in Alaska. He wants you to come home, as do I. We want to be a family."

"You found the items behind the painting?"

"Yes, Jack explained to me what they are. He's Jewish, and that's when I surmised that you were, too."

He simply nodded, neither confirming nor denying his faith, but happy that she discovered what his brother had denied Gordon and her—their ancestry.

"Why did you leave? Was it because of something Grandpa did?"

"In part, and also because of Lizzy, and then my father died the summer of 1950 and I couldn't stay. I had to get out of New York and everything that reminded me of that incredible seven months of my life. There was nothing worth staying in New York for, and I thought I could make a different life for myself."

"You bought Primrose Cottage for her didn't you? Staying would have reminded you of her every day. I saw the shrine; I put the pieces together, and I went in search of her out on Long Island."

"Why would you do that? Truly, it couldn't have been only to learn what happened to some old man you didn't even know."

"Because ..." She rubbed her slender arms as if chilled. "Because I needed to know that true love, apart from what my grandparents had, existed out there. I want what you had with Lizzy and to find you both would prove to me that it was real—more than just snapshots and emotions on paper. Was it real?"

He let out a deep sigh of resignation. Clearly his niece wasn't going to let this conversation about Lizzy go. She was forcing him to admit the truths he didn't want to verbalize. "In fifty years, I have never found anything that came close to it or her. I can't say I even looked or tried very hard. She still owns every heartbeat, and your grandfather is right—my moving to Holland in 1950 then Israel in '52, then Sitka in '77 still couldn't take her out of my blood. Everywhere I went and every morning I woke, she haunted me. Still to this day, I can see her eyes dancing, but she's another man's wife."

"I knew it. Your love gives me hope, makes me believe that romance can happen with the person that's meant just for me. Fairytales can come true."

"What about this fella you're with? Are you going steady? Do you have feelings for him?"

She shrugged. "I'm sorting that out. He's not my boyfriend if that's what you mean, but I think I want him to be. I care for him more than I've allowed myself to care for anyone before."

"Let me give you some advice. If you care about him, fight for him. If there's even the slightest chance you could lose him, hold tight because love—love like mine and Lizzy's—only comes once in a lifetime, and regret is the worst thing to follow you through life."

"So you didn't fight for her when you found out that she married John Robertsen?"

He smiled wryly. "Boy, you think you know it all don't you?"

Grinning like a Cheshire cat she said, "I do, and I also know that she's no longer married to Mr. Robertsen. She's a widow and according to her grandson still pining for you with tears."

Now this was a surprise he could be happy about.

The Antelope's door swung open, slamming behind Jack who held a beer and was walking toward them tentatively. He smiled sheepishly.

Will stood, offering an outstretched hand. "Hi, we didn't meet. I'm Will Martel but you know that already."

"Great to finally meet you. I'm Jack Robertsen."

"He's Lizzy's grandson, Uncle Will."

What a fuckin' day.

Jack pulled over a chair from another table and took a seat, attempting not to stare at the shocked look upon his grandmother's sweetheart's face. "I hope I'm not intruding."

"No not at all. I was just giving my niece some lovelorn advice." He smirked at her embarrassed expression.

Juliana cleared her throat. "That beer went right through me. You men will have to excuse me." She gave Jack a covert eye roll and a head nod in her uncle's direction and departed toward the restaurant.

An uncomfortable silence hung heavily between the two men in the blissful setting where water, sky, and mountain united. Jack shifted his weight then leaned forward clasping his hands before him on the table. "I realize that we've taken you by surprise, maybe even shock. I'm really sorry about that, but Julie was tenacious, and well ... I like her ... a lot and want to make her happy."

"That's good to hear. I often wondered what she was like. She's a sweet girl and has her grandmother Lillian's spirit."

"My great-aunt."

"Right. Your great-aunt. Lizzy's sister. That makes my great-niece your cousin, doesn't it?"

"Yes, but not by blood. My father was adopted by the Robertsens in '45. He was a Jewish war orphan who managed to avoid a death camp by hiding in the forest. My grandparents traveled to London to bring him to America. He was just three years old when Lillian Renner ... I mean, Martel ... found him in the Alsace, contacted her sister, then the rest was history."

Will's eyes nearly widened. He had no idea. *Lizzy did that?*

Jack took a swig of his beer then placed it down before him with deliberate ease. "Can I be frank—sort of man to man?"

"Please do. You traveled a long way, and I suppose this must be just as difficult for you as it is for me. I'm sure it can't be easy to meet the man who preceded your grandfather."

"I admit, at first it wasn't easy, but I'm reconciled with the fact that he's passed on and she's here vibrant with, G-d willing, a lot of years ahead of her. I loved my grandfather, but I can't deny—in hindsight—that what my grandparents felt for one another didn't even come close to what you and Lizzy apparently felt."

Several fast blinks to Will's eyes alerted Jack to his astounded disbelief about his grandparents' relationship. "It's true. They didn't have that passion. Fact is, Mr. Martel—I envy you. You weren't afraid to fall in love with a girl whose father was a member of the Nazi party as the world was on fire around you, especially as a Jew. You were going off to war and its uncertainty, yet you pursued a girl and found something that most of us only dream about. You took a chance and opened your heart in spite of the many obstacles."

Will chuckled in fond remembrance. "It took some convincing on my brother's part but when I finally jumped, I fell hard, but your grandmother was..." He cleared his throat. "An exceptional girl. A zephyr."

"She still is, although that part of her is deeply hidden. Even still, you *did* jump. That's something I was never able to do, not even during the best of times. I was never a romantic and never imagined that kind of love existed, so I never looked—then I met Juliana and I learned of your past. After that, I held my weeping grandmother in my arms when I told her you were alive somewhere."

He ignored the weeping comment, torn between being sympathetic, elated, or pleased for her pain. "So you credit me for opening your heart to my niece?"

"I do. In a way, you brought us together when she coincidentally showed up at my office for assistance, wanting to find Meercrest." Jack leaned back in his chair. "I gotta tell ya', I'm not a past person and hated to look back at that place, facing the unspeakable things that happened there during the thirties and forties. Things, as a family, we swore never to speak about after Meercrest was bulldozed. Nevertheless, in my looking back, I learned about a love that never died in spite of those horrifying acts. In looking to the past, I see how those heinous actions and your deep love for one another changed the future. After reading some of my grandmother's letters to you, I'm certain that she is who she is today *because* of you."

"It did die. Our love died when she married your grandfather soon after I left for England. She didn't even have the decency to send a 'Dear John' letter. Lizzy destroyed what we could have had. But that was long ago, Jack. Five decades and any number of things could have made her the woman she is today, not some love-struck, idealistic fella she met as a young woman."

"Again, I know for a fact that's not true. It may be fifty years in the past, but she never stopped loving you. I know this not because she told me but because of how she lived her life, the specific things she did with her life. Your idealism shaped her future. Mr. Martel, your influence in my grandmother's life acted like a pebble tossed into a pond, creating ripples and waves throughout two generations. Trust me when I tell you that you shaped and changed lives *together* even though you were separated."

"You're very kind, Jack, but I'm sure the girl I once loved chose to live a different life than the one I thought or hoped she would."

"Don't be so sure. Further, it's obvious that you never stopped loving her, and it's possible that you've been holding onto an unforgiving torment all these years. Am I correct?"

Will didn't reply. In part because he didn't like being lectured by Lizzy's grandson, but also because he didn't want to give voice to the truth.

"As you gave Julie advice, allow me to give you some. Stop looking at the pain of the past and what happened to separate you and look at the happiness that awaits you in the future with the one person who would make you feel whole again. Someone very wise has recently told me to only think on the past as its remembrance gives you pleasure."

Will lied, "I feel whole, Jack, and I don't often look to the past. What's the point?"

"You're in denial. I used to think that way, too."

Juliana approached the table with a wide grin and a skip in her steps. "Well, how are you two getting along?"

"You found a keeper, Juliana. I might have to like a Robertsen male after all. You'd do well to take my advice," Will said.

"Did you tell him, Jack?"

"Not yet."

"What good are you? Sheesh. I leave you to do one thing."

He joked, "Nag, nag, nag."

All three laughed and Juliana took her seat. "What he was supposed to tell you was that we're going to Paris from July 13ᵗʰ to the 20ᵗʰ and you should come, too. We're staying at the Turenne."

"In the Marais district?" Will asked, knitting his brow.

"Yes, near the Pletzl," she stated fully aware of why he asked.

"Why would I want to go to Paris?"

Jack toyed with his empty beer bottle. "Because, I think you need to be there. It's important; there's something you need to be a part of."

"Nah. Paris, *especially* during that week, isn't for me. Been there, done that in 1980. I'm happy here fishing. The salmon are spawning you know."

Will watched as Jack removed a snapshot from the pocket of his denim jacket then slid it across the table to him.

It was Lizzy, and the remembrance of that sunny day in Florida gave him so much pleasure that he smiled wistfully when he picked it up. There they stood in front of his B-26. Ducky and Pistol with his girl's image painted on the side of the Pistol Packin' Lizzy. He gazed at it thoughtfully for a couple of minutes then held it out to return to Jack.

"Keep it," Jack said.

"But it's yours."

"No, Mr. Martel it's yours. It always has been and so has she."

Juliana removed his pilot wings from the outside of her black corduroy jacket. "This is yours, too. After all, you are Lizzy's flyboy."

He picked it up from the table, running his thumb over the engraved details, looking at it remembering the day it was pinned to his chest.

"Oh, and this is yours, too." She said, placing the engagement ring box in front of him. "I'm sure its intended recipient would like to receive it, even after all these years."

Thirty-Four

Body and Soul
<u>August 8, 1949</u>

T wo nightmarish years of imprisonment as a guest of the Luftwaffe in Stalag Luft I did not inflict the crushing pain Will felt physically at this moment. His head was still reeling from the myriad of revelations that bombarded him in a single afternoon, one that was intended to be a joyful celebration for his brother. With the day long over, he sat alone in the library of Primrose Cottage, nursing a scotch, swirling the liquor at the bottom of the glass, eyes fixed upon the rotation hoping it would hypnotize him, take him away into another mindset than the one he was in. Barefoot and still in his dress shirt, now wrinkled and pulled from his trousers, he slouched in the armchair. He looked over at the matching chair beside it, ever empty, awaiting its always intended occupant. Not a single lamp in Primrose Cottage was lit, and thick rain clouds hovering outside darkened the house all the more. The antique grandfather clock in the corner of the room chimed twelve thirty in the morning. Its singular clang echoed in his ears.

A violent thunderclap startled him from inertia; he shifted in his chair, then mechanically lit a cigarette with the metal flick, whoosh, and click of his Army-issue Zippo. In the darkened room, he could still easily recognize the small details he had arranged at the end of '42 in optimistic, impulsive anticipation of Lizzy's residence as Mrs. William Martel upon his return from the war. The empty bookshelf he had planned to fill with her favorites, the globe to choose the places they would travel to together, and the Victor Victrola for the 78 rpm records of the music she loved—once awaiting her arrival, now gathering dust.

The torrential downpour of rain beat against the windowpane, leaving long streaks of tears upon the glass, succinctly reflecting his emotions, taunting him into deeper depressive reflection.

"Damn!" he finally expelled.

He'd had no intention of attending Gordon's christening today because it was something he felt his brother was foolishly acquiescing to for Lillian's headstrong sake. In fact, he had flatly refused Louie's invitation, which was followed by a bitter argument. In truth, though, Louie was never overly religious, and it was Jewish custom to raise a child in his mother's faith. Will didn't have it in his heart to argue his case or disrespect his older brother or new nephew by not going to the ceremony at Trinity Lutheran Church. Even though his father helped sway him into attending, he knew it would be difficult to witness, but had no idea just how much and for an entirely different reason. He attended—probably the last spontaneous act he would ever do—and regretted that decision with every fiber of his being.

Seven years had passed since he'd gazed upon Lizzy Renner and when she entered the back of the church with her young, beautiful family, he could hardly breathe at the lovely, loving image she presented. No one had told him she would be there, and he immediately surmised no one had had the courage to tell him she had married, of all men, John—the very man for whom he'd always questioned her affection. Two children clung to her sides and an infant, he learned, was home with a nurse. His heart clenched, squeezing the blood from it at the sight of picture-perfect domesticity. She was breathtaking, and he was spellbound watching her and that tender motherly smile emerge upon her lips as she removed the hat from her daughter. An angelic looking child with curls just like her mother's, and in spite of her five or six years, she seemed too mature, too serious for one so young, so small.

He knew he would never forget the shocked expression upon Lizzy's face when she rose from tending the little girl and saw him at the front of the church, holding the infant, Gordon, beside his aging father. It was as though she thought him a ghost. Even John's expression was somewhat contorted at the realization that he was there, in the flesh, and not some vanquished apparition come to rattle their chains. He wondered about that. Had it been wishful thinking on their part, wishful enough so that their deceit and malice toward him could be hidden forever? He had trusted Lizzy in every way and given his heart to her unequivocally, yet she had cast him aside for the heir of Robertsen Aviation without even a Dear John letter.

The hatred that flared when she and her husband walked toward the front of the church didn't last, and now he hated himself for that. Hating her wasn't something he had ever accomplished, in spite of her breaking his heart into a million pieces. His love had been too deep—still was—but his wounds were real and still bleeding.

Will sighed heavily, remembering how gorgeous Lizzy looked this afternoon. She had cut her hair and appeared very fashionable in a black and white dress, but he wondered if it was his jealousy that observed how wrong she looked beside John. For over an hour, he studied them, looking for signs that their marriage and relationship was even a modicum of what *they* had together; it wasn't there. John appeared to care deeply for the babies and her, yet something was missing between them as a couple. Perhaps Lizzy had been reserved, even embarrassed, because of his unexpected presence. He couldn't be sure.

Over the pastor's blessing of Gordon, Will's eyes had locked with hers and something passed between them—unspoken words, but after all these years apart he couldn't decipher the look she gave him. Her magnificent, green eyes filled with tears, and she bit her lip, a habit she still retained. He wanted nothing more than to go to her and take her into his arms. For a small second, in the space of that halting of time, she was his again. It was only Ducky and Pistol in that church.

Suddenly John's hand came to rest upon Elizabeth Robertsen's shoulder, snapping them from their unspoken mourning. The pain in his chest suffocated him: he couldn't touch her; she was another man's wife for all eternity; she was the mother of his three children.

Seeing her and remaining in her presence for the sixty-minute ceremony was the most difficult thing he had ever done, even more difficult than safely landing the PPL with a burning engine in Nazi-controlled Belgium. He couldn't bring himself to stay for the luncheon afterward, and he hoped his brother, sister-in-law, and father understood why. Retreat was warranted, even if it appeared that he was fleeing to lick his wounds. Taking his brother to task for lying, concealing, and making light of Lizzy's appearance as Mrs. Robertsen would come soon enough.

A knock upon the front door sounded rapidly, bringing Will out of his deep thoughts. He listened through the teeming rain and heard it again. Rising, he walked to the hallway and flicked on the chandelier above the entryway.

He opened the door to the most tantalizing image of Lizzy he had ever seen—wet and standing alone at the threshold, her hair dripping from the deluge outside. His chest hammered in shock, but he controlled his expression, attempting to appear vacant and emotionless.

"May I come in?"

Saying nothing, Will stepped back and held the door wide for her to enter. He seized that moment to breathe in her unmistakable Indiscret perfume. Having never forgotten the scent of sweet orange and jasmine, the memory of their evening on the carousel flooded his brain. Even after being caught in the rain, a trace of that delicious essence remained, the memory of their innocent love vivid.

She wore a different dress from the afternoon, more demure, yet just as flattering to her newly curved figure. Maturity and three children had given her an enticing swell to her bosom and an alluring, slight fullness to her hips. He couldn't help his outright stare of appreciation in spite of the pain and impact of seeing her at his doorstep.

He closed the door, promptly crossing his arms over his chest as the two stood facing one another. Still, he couldn't bring himself to say anything, not even to address her wet disarray.

Nervously, she quickly scanned her darkened surroundings, heart thundering as she silently took herself to task for acting the brazen Lizzy she had banished these long seven years. Her voice trembled slightly. "I'm sorry to intrude. You ... you have a lovely home."

Will shifted his weight, nodding with pursed lips. That one observation gutted him.

"I ... um." Lizzy took a step toward him, her eyes pooling with tears. "I had to see you. Please say something, Will. Say anything."

He tipped his head back, closing his eyes to keep her from seeing the pain they held. "Please go, Lizzy. Just go."

When she took another step toward him, he was sure that she was there to torment him deliberately. He thought he'd die from her nearness.

"I can't go. Not just yet. Please. I can't believe you're here."

His pulse pounded in his ears, his blood rushing throughout him at the response to her body heat, mere inches away from him. It was as though hot, summer steam radiated from her. He looked down into her pleading eyes, and her hand reached out to rest upon his forearm folded inadvertently, protectively across his heart.

With barely a whisper, she held him prisoner.

"Don't make me leave, Will. I need you ..."

Impulse without thought and the feel of her gentle touch against his flesh caused his immediate reaction.

He swept her into his needy arms. She was *his* in that moment and he would remind her how it felt to be together, would show her the mistake she made in marrying another and not waiting for him—he who loved her more than life itself. He who would die loving her.

She let out an indiscernible cry of release before their lips crashed with combustive heat, each consuming the other's breath. No further words spoken, their mouths and hearts were fully engaged in a communication so long ago forsaken.

The taste and feel of her supple mouth was just as he remembered, her response to him the same as it ever was, and he reveled in that. She pressed her body against him and his came alive. She clutched at him with starving hands of reunion and his soul reacted.

Gone were the images of the family he had witness this morning. His only actionable thoughts at that moment were how much he needed her and how she had come to him feeling that same need. He would consume her soul and haunt her memory just as she had imprinted herself into him so long ago.

With frantic, anxious hands, Lizzy popped all the buttons of his shirt, pulling it off him in passionate frenzy. This was not why she came, but this was how it always had been between them. Passion that had never, could never, be tempered. She shoved reason and logic to that ordered domain where Elizabeth Robertsen lived. In this moment, she was Lizzy Renner, Will's wild, impetuous Pistol, flying half-cocked into her flyboy's arms.

Will resisted tearing at her dress, instead scooping her up into his arms, their lips still taking everything they could draw from the other.

He ascended the stairs with her captured in his fierce embrace against his chest. Her arms encircled his neck, her fingers thread through his hair, her lips tasting and savoring his. Long legs hastily climbed steps two at a time as Lizzy clung to him. His heart soared, remembering with righteous familiarity how perfectly her body felt against his. He was going to love her with every atom and molecule that formed him, for tomorrow was promised to neither of them.

Storming rain, thunder, and lightning collided simultaneously, seeming to shake Primrose Cottage as they reached the top of the stairwell.

Against the doorframe of the room he had once chosen as *their bedroom*, he let go of her legs and kissed her violently, moaning into the dark at the feel of her wet skin against his lips. He couldn't stop his hands as they moved over her with passionate purpose, remembering how her body felt under his hands. After all these years, he recalled every slope, every curve, and he wanted to retrace the same path, caressing her as his mouth lay siege to her neck, her blood pulsing violently below his ravenous suckling assault.

With reluctance, she released her hold round his neck and slid one hand downward toward his face as she hitched her stocking clad leg upon his hip. He could barely hold back his arousal's need.

Their lips separated, remaining a mere inch from one another. Deep, heavy pants commingled, and eyes remained locked as his heart released his truest smile.

Lizzy touched his dimple then tenderly kissed it. He took her hand in his, threading their fingers as they so often did years ago, and led her into their bedroom.

In the dark, Will unbuttoned her dress with tenuous fingers. Enraptured, he was about to say, "I love you. I never stopped loving you," but she silenced his lips with her finger replacing it with her mouth when the dress dropped to the floor.

His trousers pooled at his feet, exposing him. Her slip rose above her head and floated to the floor at the foot of the bed. It only took seconds before they stood facing one another, heartbeats pounding, bared in both body and soul, stripped to only emotion and desire. She was a vision of mature perfection, her breath ragged and filled with longing against his neck when she stepped into his heated, pulsing body. Her lips began a tantalizing trail across his chest.

Will's hands circled her soft waist and he couldn't help crying out, "Oh G-d, Lizzy," when her tongue flicked his hard nipple and her hand encircled his arousal. The wolf in him had been unleashed, and he guided her back toward the bed.

He made love to her heart, renewing his claim upon her soul with his tongue, fingers, and lips until her pants grew so labored that he knew neither could go further without bursting, without consummating their reunion. When she finally spoke the words he longed to hear, "I love you so much," he entered her, both with tears streaming down their faces and cries of absolute convergence. They loved one another as they had never loved before. She was his and always would be—he knew that unequivocally. With each thrust and writhe, long lick and deep suckle, and every shudder and moan of passion, Will knew that he'd never be able to get over her for his entire life. What was meant to brand *her*, had done so to him.

Their passionate lovemaking was unbridled and her continued calling of his name drove him mad. He rolled, laying her upon him.

She rode him with unabashed vigor, rocking and rising with his hands cupping her full breasts, his manhood filling her deeply as though reaching for her heart.

Their ardor escalated to a feverish pitch of cries and need for release. As if liquid hot magma, it built to an explosive level until he suddenly lifted her, withdrawing from her just in time. Both shuddered and crashed in a red blinding eruption, crying out, "I love you," in their climax as he spilled upon himself.

Will pulled her down to his chest and held her tightly against him, feeling her tremble in his arms. Reaching to the nightstand, he grabbed a handkerchief to wipe her of his seed, wishing for an entirely different outcome to their lovemaking if she had been his wife.

Stroking her back and dark locks, he clutched her, reveling in the heat of her flesh. He could feel the power of her heartbeat against his ribcage and never felt so fulfilled, so complete as he did at that moment. "I've missed you so much, Lizzy."

She kissed his shoulder, continuing to lay her head upon him. "I've missed you, more than you can ever know."

"You couldn't have missed me. You married someone else."

Depositing a tender kiss to his glistening chest, she spoke softly as though in a daze. "I thought you were dead."

Will sighed deeply. "The record, didn't you play the record I sent you from England?"

With a lift of her chin, their eyes locked, each searching the other's for answers. "I never received a record."

She never received it. She doesn't know I proposed to her. He groaned. "I felt dead when I lost you."

Her lips sought his with sweet emotion, traveling to his cheeks where they felt the telltale wetness of the broken man he had become. "You never truly lost me, Will. I love you more with each passing day. I've never stopped loving you. Ever."

"But why ..."

"Sshh ... let's not talk of the past. Not now. Not at this moment of perfection. As fleeting as this halt of time is, we'll have it forever, darling. Let's not taint it with 'should haves' and 'whys' or talk of our fears and disappointments these seven years apart. It happened and can't be changed."

He nodded, and they shifted their weight to lay side-by-side, gazing at one another in disbelief until he brushed the hair from her face. "G-d, you're so beautiful. Is this a dream?"

"No, silly. This couldn't be a dream because in my dreams I never get to hold you. My dreams are nightmares, but just knowing that you're alive is a dream come true."

Silence and captivated study ensued as the storm tapered to drizzles of tears down the stained glass window. He wanted to beg her not to leave him again. He was a step away from pleading with her to run away with him, but he knew that she wouldn't. She would be gone come dawn. His logical mind told him that this would never happen again, but his heart vehemently disagreed. "Baby, just answer me this—are you happy? Does he treat you well?"

She closed her eyes and nodded; a tear dropped from her cheek, and he reached to gather it. "He's not you, if that's what you mean. No one could ever be you. Hold me, Will. Just hold me. If this is a dream, then I don't want to wake up."

"I'm here, sweetheart, and I'm wherever you are, in your dreams, in your heart, and in your arms, forever, just like we dreamed."

They fell asleep like that wrapped in one another's embrace with legs entwined and hearts calming to a peaceful silent unison, both finding their home once again beside the other. Will slept as he hadn't slept in years, and Lizzy dozed until her guilt surfaced, consuming her—she had a husband to face in a few hours. She, too, had questions and things to say to Will—such as if he was alive all this time, why had he not written her, and what record was she supposed to have received? Did he receive her letters? She had written him for three straight months, sometimes two letters a day, just to be sure if one got lost, he might get the other.

The tears rolled down her cheeks as she held onto him in the dark, watching the rise and fall to his strong chest as the vacating storm still illuminated the sky with flashes of lightening in the distance. Whatever happened was in the past now, no sense in reliving it. The damage was done. She was Mrs. Robertsen, another man's wife and mother to his children.

This unforgettable night was not how it was meant to go. Her sole purpose was to hold Will's hand and tell him that he had a child—they had a perfect daughter together. The words formed upon her lips, ready to wake him with her confession, but they died before spoken, knowing that in the light of day one man would be devastated—the sickly man who saved her and their baby: John, a good man, her best friend and faithful husband. He loved his little princess, Annette, raising her as if she were his own. It would kill him if he knew that she was even here.

At three in the morning, she quietly rose from the comfort and security of her lover's firm embrace and sat at the edge of the bed, gazing at him for over thirty minutes. She tried to imprint his peaceful, contented expression upon her heart so that when life became too difficult, she would always remember this moment. He was beautiful and virile and still as sensitive and gentle as the young man who courted her years earlier. Moreover, he was alive and still loved her and that would see her through life's challenges and provide a lifetime of sweet dreams. Hopefully, he knew just how much she loved him.

Scooping up her clothes and stockings, she padded barefoot down the stairs and dressed in the sitting room while staring at her image on the mantle. Yes, he still loved her. For many minutes, she looked fixedly at the framed snapshots above the fireplace and her tears flowed. Her heart clenched and she had to cover her mouth to keep from crying out in anguish.

She walked to the table nearest the console radio to borrow a pen. From her dress pocket, she removed the folded piece of stationary she had brought with her from Evermore after she and John had returned home following the christening. Initially, if her resolve to speak with Will failed, she planned to sit in the car and write to him, then slide the letter under the front door. Not only was that plan cowardice, but it was for naught because when faced with the temptation that he was only on the other side of that door, she couldn't make herself write it. He was only a knock away. The letter she now wrote was not the one she originally intended.

August 8, 1949

My Dearest Darling,

My hand is trembling as I write this. My heart is breaking for what I must do. My tears won't stop, yet I must swallow the anguish as I leave you, apparently, yet again. You know that what we did tonight should never have happened, but I will carry it in my heart forever, never forgetting your touch or your declarations. I will never forget how you bring me to life. My coming to see you was not to hurt you, but I don't know, I needed to hold you in my arms and feel once again how it was between us. You are alive and my heart soars!

I know you have questions and so do I but that is in the past, a past we can never get back—the damage is long done. Let us not dwell on the forces that separated us so many years ago, but let us remember those few glorious months we spent loving one another in our youth. Let us remember this moment our souls shared together, reaffirming what we have always known— the depth of our love.

Loving you, Will, was the best part of my life, but my life is different now. I am no longer that pistol you fell in love with. I have responsibilities to the children and to John now. And I have obligations to clean up the mess, dishonor, and horrors my father left behind, and I must do so with dignity.

You once told me that I could do anything I put my mind to, and I vow that to you. I will make right the wounds he inflicted upon your family and so many others. An impetuous one night of lovemaking could only lead to your and my disgrace, and I refuse to tarnish the beautiful memory of our romance.

I love you. I will <u>never</u> stop loving you. Never. But know, my love, you will remain in my heart and in my dreams until the end of life's story.

Forever yours,

Lizzy

Her tears lay spent in droplets upon a letter to the man she should have married—remained optimistic for—no matter what the circumstance she had found herself in. Lizzy folded the letter, wrote "Will" across the face, and kissed his name. She left Primrose Cottage like a thief in the black night, having unknowingly stolen the last shred of love from his romantic heart.

Daybreak saw Will's rising with a muddled scratch to his head. If not for his naked state and her lingering redolence upon the bed linen, he would have sworn it was all a dream. He ran his hand over the cool sheet beside him and closed his eyes in recollection of the unforgettable night before.

She had repeatedly spoken her daughter's name in her sleep; he knew that looking or calling for Lizzy would prove fruitless. His girl was long gone and she took what remained of his heart with her—back to her husband and children.

He laid back down on the bed breathing in her scent and drew the linen over his head. Long gone was the stoic Army Marauder Man. He wept.

Thirty-Five

I Think of You
June 29, 1992

The telephone continued its incessant ringing from the kitchen. Surrounded by the current mayhem of her bedroom, one flight up at Evermore, Lizzy deliberately chose to ignore it. Old empty suitcases, retrieved from storage compartments concealed behind walls, sat gaping open. Standing within the open archway that divided her normally pristine master bedroom from the adjoining dressing room, she took a deep breath. Her spacious walk-in closet was in utter disarray from its usual fastidious condition. As the ringing ceased, she sat in the armchair surveying the sleeping area of her all-white suite. Contents of hatboxes lay strewn across the carpeting at the foot of her bed and piles of purses had been unceremoniously dumped upon it. She shook her head in frustration at the absolute mess she had made.

"Where is it? Think, Lizzy, think? It's *only* been twenty-eight years. Sheesh, your memory isn't gone yet!"

Searching for something, put away somewhere, so long ago and meant not to be found, was like looking for a needle in a haystack. She had been living in this house since her marriage in 1943 and, needless to say, she and John had accumulated a ton of stuff along the way. Who knew he was such a pack rat? Well, there was a lot she didn't know about him when they married, but that was to be expected. Back then, and at the time, his penchant for saving every single thing was the least of her problems.

Scanning the tornado-like result of her crusade, her attention was drawn to the unopened letter that lay upon the coffee table. Facing emotional pain infused with her guilt and regret, was something she naturally abhorred, but she chastised herself for putting off the inevitable. Jack had delivered the letter to her three days prior, unknowingly dumping all those emotions right in her lap. She was still spinning from the potential ramifications.

"The truth is always brought to light, isn't it, Lizzy? What did you think—you'd just die with these secrets? Will should have been told why you married John. You should have told him when you found out he was alive."

Shamelessly, she had cried in Jack's arms for hours as he patiently handed her Kleenex and blew her nose as if she were a five year old. He never pushed or prodded, although she could tell he was dying to know the real reasons for the flood of tears.

She picked up the envelope, knowing full well who had written it and the guilt became oppressive.

The phone began to ring again, snapping her from her recollection of the wonderful woman she had only met once, in Florida the fall of '42.

The ringing below went ignored when she rose and resumed her search through the closet. She pulled open lingerie and scarf drawers, removing their contents until finally dropping to her knees to attack shoeboxes with ferocity, sorting through them then summarily tossing them from the closet and dressing room. Chanel, John Jourdan, Ferragamo, and even those jelly pool shoes Annette convinced her to purchase soared through the air, meeting their demise when they landed in a heap on the floor of the bedroom.

With a huff of frustration, she sat back on her bare heels and looked up to the top shelf of the closet as though looking for direction from heaven. It was then she noticed the colorful Lilly Pulitzer beach tote peeking out from the far corner of the shelf. Bingo!

Agile and deft, she climbed the cubbyholes of the closet and snapped the bag out from its hiding place, making sure that she held onto the handle tightly. "I knew you were never far from me! The Pistol lives! Ha!"

Lizzy retrieved the bag and held it as though it was a precious treasure; to her, it was. She carefully removed its solitary item, a velvet glove box, and placed it beside the letter upon the coffee table. She toyed with its key and sat staring at the locked Victorian glove box, her eyes switching from letter to velvet container, heart racing. She suddenly felt apprehensive about opening it, her personal Pandora's Box, knowing it held the physical memories of a love that had never died. It had only been opened twice before: once in 1949 and later in 1964 when Lilly gave her the tote bag where the keepsake box found its home until its reemergence today.

She couldn't cease the slight tremble to her hand, knowing the contents by heart. Carefully, she placed the key beside it then left the room.

"Laundry. Yes, I think I need to do a load of dark wash ... chicken." A flash of dialogue emerged from its dungeon in the recesses of her mind.

-What's cookin', Lieutenant?
-Chicken. Wanna' neck?

She immediately fled from the glove box as though it were a casket.

If there was one thing that could be said about Elizabeth Robertsen it was that she was not a procrastinator, by any means. If she had been, the Phoenix Foundation would have never gotten off the ground and Zephyr Avionics would never have reached to its present level of global expansion. Side by side, she and John had seen to both achievements, both were stalwart and committed to making the other's venture as successful as possible, both understanding their reasons and need for doing so. However, today she couldn't help feeding that insecure Lizzy Renner who lingered deep within her heart. She was petrified to face her past and her ever present optimism had seemingly abandoned her.

She walked through the empty, lonely house toward her record player in the corner of the den. It was the same record player that had kept her company in the water tower so many years ago. Repaired time and again, it refused, like her, to give up. A particular record rarely made an unscheduled appearance on the turntable, reserved for its annual emergence on the morning of July 21. It was a rare indulgence of longing. However, on this day, she would make an exception to the rule. Yes, there was a rule—a self-imposed one. Ducky could only meet her in her dreams when she slept or visit with her in the tea garden every Sunday, but dancing with her was reserved for July 21 only. During her day-to-day life, memories of him were kept at bay, blocked from surfacing. She was John's wife, and he had deserved her loyalty

Anne Shelton's "Only Forever" filled the room as the suddenly twenty-year-old Lizzy Renner danced alone in the open space. She swayed, lost in the memory of the day she and Will made love for the first time, both innocent, both nervous, but both consumed by the passion of their intense love for one another. Her palm slowly smoothed over her bare bicep, the delicate tickle caused her flesh to respond as it always did. Duck pimples of recollection rose. She closed her eyes remembering his kiss to her shoulder and how his lips traveled along the heated, wet skin of her décolletage.

As happened most years, her memories only had the opportunity to progress as far as the dropping of her bathing suit strap before the three-minute song ended too quickly for the weight of emotion it elicited. In her dancing, bare feet had instinctively taken her toward the stairs, back in the direction of the box waiting for her a flight above, but the battle ensuing within her took her back to the laundry room.

The phone rang a third time and this time Lizzy was thankful for the intrusion.

"Hello?"

"Dahling, where have you been? I've been calling for hours."

"Oh, hi Greta. Sorry I couldn't get to the telephone—I'm a bit constipated." She smirked mischievously, unable to resist teasing John's sister.

"Don't be vulgar. Really, Elizabeth, I have no desire to discuss your bodily functions."

"Then why did you call?"

"Because I visited a friend in Sarasota this past weekend, and while shopping on St. Armand's Circle, I ran into Ingrid's husband, Eduardo."

A shiver ran up Lizzy's spine. It had been at least three years since last hearing her sister's name.

"Eduardo? What happened to Victor?"

"Pfft, that was years ago. Eduardo was her Cuban refugee masseuse and Victor her Russian diplomat before this last one. Don't you remember me telling you he died of a heart attack in Rosebriar's swimming pool?"

Lizzy opened the refrigerator door for no apparent reason. She eyed the contents, looking for a diversion from the pointless conversation about a woman she hated. There was nothing of import or significant interest that

Greta could impart about Ingrid. "Hmm. I vaguely remember that he wasn't a diplomat but rather newly displaced KGB. Shame, I have such good memories about that pool. What's this about, Greta? You know that I don't keep abreast of the goings on in her life, and you also know how irrelevant she is to me."

"Tsk, tsk. You really should have gotten over your anger at Ingrid by now. I'm sure she didn't mean all those silly things she professed so long ago. It was a fad of her youth, as were my own ill-formed opinions. Fifty years, Elizabeth. Holding grudges will give you angina in addition to your constipation, Dahling."

"*Dahling*, she tried to kill my sister. Why on earth would I ever forgive her evil, eugenics-supporting, anti-Semitic, Hitler-loving Nazism? You, I can forgive. You were just plain stupid and ignorant. No, that woman could drop dead for all I care."

"Well, that's why I'm calling. Haven't you been contacted by your lawyer?"

"No, why?"

"Ingrid's dead, and now her Cuban husband remains in residence in the Renner home."

Of all the things Lizzy expected to hear, "dead" wasn't one of them. Unthinkingly, she smoothed her hand across her forehead and down her cheek, fingers settling upon her lips as she processed what that meant, not only to her, but to the family, and the secrets they had run from for so long.

"Did you hear me, Elizabeth?"

"When? When did it happen?"

"About a week and a half ago. Are you upset? I know it must be quite a shock and I'm so sorry to be the one to telephone you, but you needed to know."

A tear pricked Lizzy's eyes as she pursed her lips. *Closure,* she thought. *One step closer to fully burying the demons of the past. One step closer to finishing what I began in 1945.* In addition to the paintings, Ingrid had remained a piece of unresolved Renner history, a bitter reminder of the constant stain upon her family. So long as she had lived, they could never truly move on from their family's association with Nazism.

"I'm not upset, Greta. I'm relieved. Her death is reason to rejoice, one more deep breath of life into The Phoenix Foundation's mission."

"Aren't you even going to bat an eye about Ingrid's demise? She was your sister after all."

"No, she ceased being my sister when she voiced her malevolent opinions about Kitty and her polio. The repercussions of that woman's existence in the Renner family, as well as the Robertsens by association, mind you, have echoed for fifty years, and we can finally have peace."

"Well, I certainly didn't expect this kind of response. Frankly, I'm appalled."

"What would you rather—sarcasm and flippancy at such a pivotal moment in my life's commitment? How's this?" Her voice changed to one Greta could better understand. "You say Eduardo is already out shopping? Sounds like true love."

Greta responded in kind, as only someone as unaware of her own shallowness could, "And driving your Father's Horch with a Barbie doll sitting beside him."

"That stranger is entitled to nothing pertaining to Rosebriar or its assets. I will be selling the estate as well as that miserable car on the auction block at Christie's, and the American Red Cross will be receiving that money."

"Will you telephone Kitty to tell her the news, or shall I?"

"I think I'll wait until she and I can properly celebrate together, maybe with a bottle of Dom Perignon."

"You are terrible, Elizabeth!"

Lizzy looked over her shoulder in the direction of the RCA, recognizing the next song on the record. It wasn't the song that garnered her attention but the mere fact that she knew she was deliberately prolonging this conversation in avoidance of the letter and the box she'd left upstairs. She was finding herself angry that a conversation about Ingrid had replaced a perfectly sublime moment of memories of Will.

"Lizzy ... you can call me Lizzy."

"You're seventy and you want me to call you a name from your childhood? Is there some dementia you need to let me know about?"

"Very funny, Greta. Listen, thanks for calling, dear. I have to go; laundry beckons. Will I see you next week?"

"For your annual Fourth of July party? I don't think so. There's much to do here."

"Well, you'll be missed. I'll try to come out to Fisher's Island for a visit before the summer ends. Would you like that?"

"Will you bring my favorite great-nephew? The season will be over before you know it, and I'll hardly have the opportunity to introduce him to some lovely, appropriate, young women at the Club."

"No. Jack left for Alaska for a few days, and then we have the party followed almost immediately by our trip to Paris. I think your matchmaking days for our dear boy are over since there is a new, special girl in his life."

"Why ever would he write about Alaska? Anyone who is anyone knows those cruise line trips are so droll. No one from the *Social Register* goes to Alaska!"

Lizzy rolled her eyes. "He's not there on business ... it's pleasure, of a sort."

"He's just like your sister Lillian was—unconventional."

"I know. It's one of the things I love most about him. Gotta go, dear. Thanks for the call."

Lizzy hung up the phone and with steely determination exited the kitchen. Walking through the den, she passed the now silenced RCA, then barreled up the stairs to her bedroom. Standing at the threshold of the room, her breath puffed raggedly and her heart fluttered anxiously, but she was resolved now.

Her eyes fixed upon the table, ignoring the mess. The silver key lay next to the box, shining in the streaming sunlight. "You're being silly, Lizzy. It's just a box—it's just a letter."

She spoke convincingly to herself with a head nod to punctuate her statements. "You thought Will was dead, and you made your decision. There should be no guilt; you did what you had to do in both 1943 and in 1949. Open the damn letter, chicken."

She walked to the table, swept up the yellowed envelope, and settled on her divan beside the picture window. A carefully twisted fingernail easily separated the decades-old glue.

December 20, 1942

Dearest Elizabeth,

Words cannot express a moeder's appreciation to you for all you have done for us. The most important of which is loving and accepting my zoon whose heart is so sensitive and forthright. Your love for him is obvious and for you to have arranged for our visit and stay in your beautiful home in Sarasota before his departure to Europe, I will never forget. The short time that Julien and I spent with you before your return home to Long Island filled my heart with such joy at seeing you and my boy as affectionate as husband and wife. You already feel like the daughter I never had and I can see why William loves you so. It is evident, and I must confess, I have never seen him so happy. You bring to him the joyful spirit his serious nature so craves but his reserve holds him back from embracing. I can see that together, you and he bring to one another that which you both need. Elizabeth, you are a remarkable young woman with a heart of pure gold.

Within our Sabbath prayers at Rosebriar Manor, we prayed that one day when this war is over, we will all be together as a family. I wish you both all that a moeder's love can hope for her zoon. May your love and marriage be as blessed as mine and as I hope Louis and Lillian's will be.

This home that my William has purchased for you and named Primrose Cottage in honor of your beloved home in Sarasota, he has taken great care in every detail for your happiness and comfort. He has spared no expense, which proves his devotion to you. The china was my moeder's which I brought with me from Holland, and the hope chest at the foot of your bed is filled with many things from the old country and some new ones, too, that I am making for you. There is, of course, the painting, which I explained to you the history during our too brief visit. It is now the time to pass my Avercamp to William for his future bride and one day he will give it to his firstborn. I pray that my sister Estella will have the opportunity, with warm hands, to give her matching Avercamp to Louis as it was meant to be since the boys' infancy. Two sisters—two paintings, two brothers—two paintings. These masterpieces, passed from generation to generation, will bind our family, yours and Lillian's family and future DeVries descendants.

Within the house, you will see small details that I personally arranged as are evident by these items found alongside this letter. William will explain them to you, along with the bris pillow and baby dress found in the hope chest. I know you are not of our faith, but I have hope that in time you will embrace the tenants that have formed such men as my children. I pray that one day the world will be a safe enough place to feel the freedom in openly declaring we are Jews. As evident by the horrors in Europe, one can live in hope that evil will once and for all be vanquished.

I do not need to ask you to be kind to my boy since I know you will be. I only ask that you protect and safeguard that which we all hold dear. Life, Elizabeth. Above all things, life. …

Lizzy's eyes filled with tears, and the words on the stationery became blurry. Never knowing that Primrose Cottage had been for her, she lowered the letter before finishing. Each line tore at her heart, the last ones profoundly resonating with her. She bit her lip to keep it from trembling, tears gently dropping, rolling to her chin.

She looked over at the red velvet treasure box where she'd left it sitting. Yes, it was time and if necessary, she would fly to wherever he was with that box, contrite tail between her legs.

She moved back to the coffee table, sat on the sofa before it, and took a deep breath, her heart pounded. The key fit, the lid lifted, and she stared down at the contents, each a precious fragment representing the sweetest and best part of her life. Inside letters and photographs of Will and her rested neatly organized. A long forgotten pocket-sized edition of WB Yeats' poetry concealed a pressed Gardenia on page 25—*The Wild Swans of Coole*. Trembling hands removed his gold and silver pilot cadet pin, and she promptly affixed it to the collar of her blouse. Tucked below the book were two postcards from her stay at the Hotel Lakeland Terrace, one bearing the swans. However, her eyes continually drew to the one item she treasured the most a pink baby bracelet, its glass beads spelled, *A. Robertsen*. Lizzy toyed with it, then picked up the illustrated baby announcement the hospital had presented to her, running her finger over Annette's inked newborn footprints upon the parchment dated July 21, 1943. With heart wrenching clarity, she remembered holding her newborn for the first time and weeping like a baby herself. Tinier than the average child, Annette passed as premature. Wrapped tightly in a white, cotton cocoon of swaddling, she whispered into the ear of her and Will's daughter.

-Your daddy loves you as much as I do, but he watches you from heaven, little one. You're safe, and together we'll be Robertsens and make Daddy proud from above. Every day we'll give thanks to your papa John.

Lizzy picked up Annette's sterling silver bib clip—Ducks. Everything in her nursery had been ducks.

****

The doorbell rang but Lizzy failed to acknowledge it, too lost in her memories. Although she knew, word for word, Will's last letter to her before he had gone missing in December of '42, she was about to read it again. She was reminded of her shock at seeing him at Gordon's christening, and how, with emotions spinning out of control, she blamed Lillian for not telling her. How could she have concealed such a thing from her? But her sister's reasoning of "what would have been the point in your knowing?" was oppressively logical. Apart from her obvious relief, the damage (or rather path) had already been set. John was her husband and father to her three children and that was that. What good would have come from learning that the father of her first born, a child everyone knew to be John's, had returned from the grave? No one but John and Kitty knew of Annette's true parentage and all three vowed to keep it that way. Rationalize as she might though, she knew she had been wrong for keeping it from Will. That guilt had followed her all these many years.

Incessant chiming sounded from the front door. Lizzy shut the box, wiped her eyes, and descended the steps. Following a quick fix to her hair in the foyer mirror, she opened the door to see Kitty standing there. She stood awkwardly; a large shopping bag barely containing a bulky white box was gripped in one hand as the other hand retreated from pressing the doorbell button yet again.

"Sissy, what a wonderful surprise," she greeted Kitty, aware that the forced cheer sounded a bit false, even to her own ears. "Come in!"

They kissed and hugged. Kitty smiled meekly. "I'm sorry to spring in on you, hon, but ... but ... can you put up some coffee?"

"You came for coffee? Oh, that sounds heavenly. I could use a good strong cup and am so in need of my baby sister."

Lizzy attempted to remove the bag from her sister's grip but Kitty grasped it tighter. "No that's okay, I've got it."

"Of course you do. No crutches today?"

"I feel pretty good actually. It helps to have a son who's a physical therapist. It's truly helping."

"What's in the bag? That box looks pretty old, from B. Altman's, isn't it?"

"Something long overdue for discussion between you and me."

Lizzy sighed. "It's been one of those days. So I'm not surprised by anything. Coffee and chocolate sound like just the thing."

One sister followed the other into the kitchen and Kitty took a seat in the breakfast nook overlooking Lizzy's herb garden. "Do you have anywhere to go today?" Kitty asked.

"No."

"Good because what I have to discuss with you is really important." Kitty pulled the oversized box from the bag, tracing the burgundy B.A cursive insignia design on the lid with her finger nervously. Her eyes fixed upon the cadet pin that her sister had once worn as a young woman, surprisingly adorning her collar.

Lizzy stopped scooping the coffee into the filter. "Does this have to do with Lillian's granddaughter? Don't look so surprised. Jack beat you to it. Oh, and by the way Ingrid's dead."

"Really? So ... finally. Well, you must be *devastated*."

"Relieved actually."

Kitty sobered. "Is that why your eyes are red and your irises vibrant green? Were you crying over Ingrid?"

"I admit to shedding a tear, but not out of grief. I'm just more cognizant of the reality that someone so evil has left us as we still continue to try to do good in direct response to that evil."

"I'm cold to her death. I know that's wrong of me, but I have no feeling or emotion to your news."

Lizzy pressed the button on the automatic drip coffeemaker. "I can understand that. Truly, I can."

Kitty shifted in the seat, looking over her shoulder at her older sister, attempting to read her for any sign of anger or regret. "How do you feel about this Juliana discovery?"

"I feel unsettled. This whole situation has brought back a flood of memories about Ducky that have me completely ..." She sat down across from Kitty who took her sister's hand in hers over the glass top.

"Tell me ... what you are feeling."

"Confused. Guilt-ridden, of course. Joyful to know I could see him again and fearful that so many, many years have passed that we'll hardly recognize, let alone, know one another."

"You are very different now than you were at twenty, Lizzy."

"Yes, and I'm sure he's very different from the deeply introspective, tender man I knew in my youth. I'm sure he's still angry with me for having left him the way I did in '49."

"I'm sure if you do see him after all these years that spark will be just as powerful as you explained it was that night."

"Please ... For the last three days, I have spent literally every minute remembering that day and the shock of seeing him alive. Yes, it was as though seven years apart hadn't separated us at all. We spoke briefly at the christening, but always with the children nearby and John never far from earshot. It was strained and awkward, and I could see the pain and anger in his eyes, but I had no idea *why* he would be angry with *me*. It was *he* who never responded to my desperate letters, ignoring my pleas for help. To know that he had been alive and never acknowledged my pregnancy was devastating, yet I couldn't resist going to him, forgiving him, and unwilling to discuss the disappointments we both felt."

"You never said, but did you ask him about the letters? About his not replying to you?"

"No. We didn't discuss much. That night ... that night was passionate and combustive, but so very foolish and unguarded. I should never have gone to him so impetuously, so ... so Lizzy like, but my initial intent of telling him about Annette was cast aside the moment I saw him. I just had to hold him as though we were one again."

Kitty patted Lizzy's hand, the pain twisting in her heart and enveloping her conscience to an even darker degree of remorse. But she knew she had to hear this as her own punishment for her acts. "Lillian mentioned he left in 1950 after his father passed away. Do you think he expected you to leave John after learning he was alive?"

"I'm sure not. Will was a moral man, and I could never have left John, not after everything he did for me. He was too sick for me to abandon him. You know. You saw how I grew to love my husband—not like I loved Will, but with a respect and friendship that gave us a meaningful marriage and a child of our own who was only six months old when I found out Will was alive."

Lizzy looked away from her sister's intense gaze, feeling as though Kitty was trying to dissect her innermost thoughts with her eyes.

"My chickens have come home to roost, and I have to tell Will about Annette and why I married John."

"He'll understand."

She sighed. "Will he? Further, will Annette understand?"

"Yes, when you explain how it was back then. Love and forgiveness go hand in hand, Lizzy. Sometimes, out of love ... and fear ... we do things we think are for best. Sometimes, we make mistakes that come back to bite us. Sometimes, we can't know the ramifications of the road chosen until it's too late, but it's part of human nature to err, just as nature spurs our human heart to know that forgiveness is divine. You married John *because* you loved William. You'd thought him dead and wanted to protect your baby from censure as an unwed mother—or worse yet, marrying and raising her as a Gebhardt. You remember how Father was relentless in that pursuit and John ostensibly saved you from that hell."

"Yes, both are true. I was also afraid they would take her away from me. Further, at that time in our family, the baby needed the protection of a Christian father, and John needed a safe haven and a strong partner to see him through life."

Kitty looked down, swallowing hard and slumping her shoulders. "Yes, I felt that way, too. I ... *I* wanted to protect your baby from death."

"I know."

Kitty closed her eyes tightly, vividly remembering each time she wheeled her way to the silver mail tray beside the door of Meercrest. Entrusted with the delivery of all of Lizzy's incoming and outgoing mail, she had done the unspeakable—perhaps even the unforgiveable. The sound of her wheelchair screeching through the cavernous hall remained with her for fifty years. It echoed in her psyche symbolically reviving the repercussions of her actions through time, affecting the lives of those she loved.

Kitty's lip trembled and her tired eyes pooled with unshed tears. "I failed you. In my young, immature mind, I made the decision to do the unthinkable in order to protect you."

Lizzy slid her hand away, her brow furrowing, the tone of her voice emitting the measured question, "*Kitty?* What are you saying?"

Shame-faced, her sister shook her head, biting her lip.

"What did you do?! What was unthinkable?"

"I knew William *wasn't* dead because I took his letters, and yours, too. I also took your letters to and from the Martel family, everything up until we left for Sister Kenny's on the train. But by that time, they had stopped coming."

Kitty stared at the box, unable to witness the expected shock and anger on her sister's face.

Dumbfounded, Lizzy's voice trembled. "You *stole* ... our letters? *You?*"

"I did. I am so, so sorry to have separated you and William." She hung her head and stared at her clasp hands before her.

Lizzy abruptly stood, towering over Kitty. "*You? You!*"

Shocked, she yelled, "*You* were the reason I never heard from him? You mean to tell me that all of the letters I entrusted to you, you *stole?*"

As though seventeen again, Kitty fearfully looked away.

"Look at me!"

"No. I can't." Her voice cracked and her eyes brimmed over with tears.

Lizzy's hand flew to her heart and she gasped, her own tears releasing, her vehement words a cry of dismay. "Why would you do that to us? You *broke* his heart! Because of you he must have believed I dumped him! Why would you deliberately separate us? You of all people *knew* just how much we loved each other?"

"Why? Why do you think? Father, Gebhardt, and Ingrid knew William was Jewish, and here you were pregnant with his baby! Even at seventeen, I could see what would happen if you had waited for William's return, no matter what his letters said?"

"That was for me ... for me and Will to decide—not you! You took away our choices!"

"You had *no* choices, Lizzy. John was your only option, and you dragged your feet in taking his offer of marriage up to the very last minute, optimistically holding out for some miraculous end to the war and a happy ever after! Even if you had decided to wait for William, you *still* would have been unwed and pregnant with no guarantee of his survival in the war! No marriage and no husband's surname to give to your baby! You were already starting to show, foolishly believing that stupid maternity girdle concealed you. Did you think Ingrid would let a Jewish baby live as a Renner? I knew what she was capable of—remember? Don't pretend as though you didn't know just how anti-Semitic she and Father were! Annette could have been killed!"

"How dare you! Don't you think I knew what Frederick and Ingrid were capable of? I was the one to telephone the FBI after making sure *you* were safe, far away from their reach!"

"Lizzy, I was afraid! A scared teenager who looked over her shoulder at every trapped turn, afraid of everyone and everything!"

Lizzy grabbed the box from the table, clutching it against her chest, yelling as the tears streamed down her cheeks, "Are these our letters?"

"Yes."

"I can't believe you did this! I protected you. I was your greatest champion! I did everything for you and this is how you repaid me—by keeping me from the only man I have ever truly loved, ever felt I belonged with, ..." Her voice cracked and she blubbered," ... felt whole with, felt one with? You let me believe he was dead! I cried for months! I secretly cried for years!"

Astonished she added, "And you just sat by and watched."

"If I *hadn't* misled you, then both you and Annette could never have survived at Meercrest! *I* could never have survived!"

Still clutching the sizeable box, Lizzy paced as though a tigress before Kitty. "This was about *you*! You pushed me to marry John so that I could remove you from Meercrest and take you here or send you to Sister Kenny."

"No! This was about your unborn child!"

"Don't give me that shit. Had you given me the opportunity, I might have gone to Will's parents for help after writing them, but that would have left poor crippled Kitty Renner stuck in her wheelchair without her sister to protect her from the big bad Nazi wolves!"

"Don't be cruel, Lizzy. It's not like you!"

"And I thought it wasn't like you to hurt me as you did. To not trust that I would have protected you above all things breaks my heart! To not have trusted the Martels to take us both in! Leading me to believe that Will was killed and that his family wanted nothing to do with me *left* me with only one choice. You took away his parentage!"

"No, *you* took away his parentage. You yourself admitted that you chickened out in telling him about Annette the night of your affair. That was your doing, not mine!"

Turning her back to Kitty, Lizzy sighed. Her sister was right on that issue. No amount of rationalizing could take away her own reproach, especially not upon hearing that Will hadn't been indifferent to her plight—he was ignorant of it. "*That* is none of your business. Don't put this back on me when you know that I could never have betrayed John!"

"But it was all right to betray him by *sleeping* with Will!"

"Shut up!"

"Why were you not this angry with Lillian for not telling you that he was alive?"

"Because Lillian didn't steal my letters! And I *was* mad at her. But don't bring her into this. She is not alive to defend herself. Her silence wasn't outright deceit, just her insane need to shelter her beloved family from the evils in ours! She didn't put the wheels in motion that separated two young lovers for fifty years! Unlike *only* you—she had no concept of the depth of Will's and my love. To her, we were just a wartime couple who dated and corresponded. In her opinion, there was no reason to tell me—I was a married woman with children by the time she returned from Europe."

Kitty rose from her chair, attempting to walk around the table. *"Please forgive me."*

"No. I don't think I can. You ruined my life—my dreams. I sacrificed everything, including him, for everyone and I—we—can never get it back."

"I'm sorry. I am so sorry, Lizzy. Please try to forgive me. I was scared for all of us. I was so young. I was only seventeen for G-d's sake, isolated in that house for years by then, and did what I saw as the only feasible option, but I was wrong, so, so wrong."

Lizzy stood face to face with her sister, as the tears poured forth. Her arms circled the white box tightly. Nostrils flared and her lips sneered when she stated with icy calm, "Feel free to enjoy your coffee then let yourself out. I don't care to remain in your presence."

She left Kitty standing beside the breakfast table and ran upstairs, clutching the box to her heart.

Thirty-Six

Tears in My Heart
February 16 & 18, 1943

B itter winter cold, unabated morning sickness, and a subway ride south from her doctor's visit in the Bronx was an unwelcome combination for Lizzy. Tired and dismayed, overjoyed and terrified, she arrived at the Greystone townhouse in Murray Hill for a warming cup of tea before taking the railroad back to Glen Cove. She knew that she would have time to kill before the 2:15 train. Returning to the scene of her father's infidelity four months prior was unnerving, but she had given herself an important mission to accomplish.

Entering the mansion, she was greeted by the usual stoicism of Mr. Krauss the butler and the cloyingly sweet scent of fresh baking cookies that almost immediately turned her stomach.

"Miss Elizabeth," he said, taking her coat, hat, and leather gloves. "It is a pleasure to see you."

"Thank you, Mr. Krauss. Is Father in residence this afternoon?"

"No, Miss."

Maintaining the requisite air of indifference toward the help, her low-heeled spectator pumps crossed the rotunda as she glanced up at the daunting spiraling staircase to the five flights above. Her fingers unconsciously toyed with Will's cadet wings upon her sweater, pinned above a terribly heavy heart. Her effervescent spirit had finally evaporated with the reality of what she had to face—Will had not written her, had not replied to a single letter, nor had his mother or brother. She had no choice but to accept John's offer of marriage. Her baby needed a father—someone other than Gebhardt. Her sister needed a safe shelter and a future.

"Is Mrs. Albrecht in the kitchen?"

"Yes, Miss."

"Please tell her that I'd like a cup of tea. I'll wait in my father's study. Can you arrange for a fire, please?"

"Yes, of course."

"Do you know when Father is expected to return?"

"Not until Monday, Miss Elizabeth."

Krauss gave an ingrained formal nod, maintaining his position until Lizzy pushed open the study door. The scene before her sat in stilled silence, the sun streaming through the vibrant colors of the stained glass creating glorious rays of light. A strange chill ran up her spine when she immediately recalled her father hovering over the unknown woman, a visual image that surfaced frequently throughout these past months.

In truth, she could have chosen any room in which to unwind with her tea. In this townhouse she disliked so much, the library or the music room had, at times, both provided peaceful refuge from the hustle and bustle of the city. Though she hadn't really spent much time here, not long ago she had thrived on the energy and excitement of New York City. But there was a worldwide war on, and now she knew there was more to life than the society debutante girl she had embodied. Being schooled at the College of William Martel had helped her to see that.

Lizzy chose this room for the specific purpose of examining her father's desk in his absence. Her mother's inadvertent admission the night of the Christmas ball and the wording of Gebhardt's proposal had resulted in a persistent tug to continue fact-finding into her father's activities. All hope in his innocence was not entirely lost, but before she left Greystone she needed to be sure. She sincerely wanted to find him above suspicion of un-American acts!

She took a seat on the divan in the corner of the room as one of the housemaids entered to start the fire. Polite conversation lasted until the amenable entrance of Mrs. Albrecht bearing a plate of Frankfurter Brenten marzipan cookies and a "Köppke Tea," as she referred to the East Friesian beverage, all lay upon a silver tray. The housekeeper's grandmotherly manner and caring nature was a warm welcome as she handed over the cup of tea and gingerly placed the lap blanket across her chilled legs. It was as if the woman knew something was amiss.

Finally left alone, Lizzy's eyes scanned the study looking for anything she may have missed that terrible, rainy night when she sat before her father, listening to his demands for her to marry George Gebhardt. That demand had continued in its repetition and pressured inevitability over the last eight weeks following the Christmas ball since that man's unwelcome marriage proposal.

Tired eyes glanced beyond the stack of newspapers on the footstool beside her to the old issues of *Social Justice* by Father Coughlin piled neatly on the end table that held absolutely no interest to her. At that moment, she only had sleep in mind—where uncomplicated imaginings of Will's and her baby could dwell untroubled. It wasn't long before the fireplace glowed and warmed, hypnotizing her with each crackle of the embers and dance of the flames. The soothing tea had worked its magic, quelling her nausea.

A sudden unusual flutter in her womb caused her palm to rest upon the constraining girdle she wore to conceal her thickening middle. Her fingers couldn't feel anything, but the tickle was there, as if butterflies beat feather light wings within. Elated, she giggled. It was the first time she had felt her baby's life. The doctor had said that a quickening would signal hello any day now.

She whispered, "Hello, little duckling. Mommy's here."

G-d how she wished Will could be here at this incredible moment. Her eyes welled with tears at the thought that he would never know his child. *Please let there be a letter from him when I get home. Please, G-d. Please may he be alive and safe.* But she knew in her heart that there would be no letter forthcoming. She briefly thought of Lillian, now in England, who had not seen him or the 322nd Bombardment Group at any of the airfields she traveled to in her clubmobile.

With both hands cupping her barely noticeable belly, she rested her head against the plush back of the sofa, displacing a few of the bobby pins holding her victory rolls. A tear rolled onto the brocade, and she closed her eyes in weariness and grief, thinking of Will and the many other children they would never have together. Believing him dead was not something she could resolve, but she had no choice.

The comfort of familiarity in this room, where as a child she had played underfoot with Lillian when their father worked on important business matters, reached into her untapped memory. Her mind quieted as images and events long forgotten stirred in her cognitive recesses, wrested awake by the emotional upheaval of the day and the recollection of the events that transpired when she was last here.

Swirling words came to the forefront of her conscience: Baby, marriage, Will, John, "consorting with a Jew," pure bloodline. Somewhere beneath all those tumultuous thoughts emerged the question of where did the woman from that night go? She was sure she saw what she saw, but the woman had mysteriously vanished.

In Lizzy's dreamlike state, a snippet of memory played. She and Lillian, no more than four and five sat in the center of this study, playing together with their new Steiff teddy bears. Father entered the room from a hidden passageway beside the fireplace.

Lizzy's eyes flew open with a start, and she tossed back the coverlet, immediately looking from the roaring fire and its ornately carved wooden mantelpiece, to the decorative wall panel beside it. Rising, she moved swiftly to stand before it, feeling the heated blaze against her stocking-clad legs. She touched the surrounding frame with searching hands, looking for entrance, eventually knocking upon the center of the carved mahogany panel. Not that she knew what she was doing, but when the hollow sound echoed back to her, she recalled vividly that it was from behind this particular panel her father had emerged, that day long ago.

She stood before a closed, secret door to a hidden space, unsure how to enter and beating back the anxiety she felt about entering. What would she find? And, further, what did she want to find? She was no longer naïve to what was going on in the world but, in some measure, she wished to remain ignorant of her father's true political leanings, if, in fact, they were different from his (hopefully) innocuous affiliation with the America First Committee. Absolving him of wrongdoing was her mission—not convicting him before she had the facts. But the truth of the matter was that her heart and instinct told her otherwise.

On impulse, she stroked her hand over the gilt-bronze lion's mask at the corner of the mantelpiece then tugged at the gold ring from its nose. The narrow panel popped open.

Immediately, she was assaulted by a musty smell of antique books, cigars, and old stone. Different from the cherished scent of antique volumes within Meercrest's library, this wafting vulgarity was dank and putrid, as vile as her father's filthy stogies. She gagged.

The interior before her was pitch dark, and she hesitated, unsure and feeling unsteady with queasiness from the stench. Her hand covered her mouth to keep from vomiting and her thoughts flew to Will for his strength to proceed. She recalled their few conversations about the propaganda papers she had found as well as his opinion based on her father's own affirmations the night of the Memorial Day party. He had explained how every word her father used was code for his anti-Semitic beliefs.

There was no turning back now. The impetus of her actions resided within her womb. Resisting hesitation, her feet moved forward, eyes scanning into the darkness. For a moment, she feared that her heart might stop, but inside her chest, its deafening beat rapidly increased.

Lizzy turned sideways, crossing the threshold through the panel's narrow opening. In the pitch-dark, her hand smoothed against the stone, feeling its strange coolness considering the close proximity to the fire just beyond. Trembling fingers brushed against a cord dangling upon the wall and she pulled, dimly illuminating the stone hallway where a bronze sconce cast an eerie aura. Her cautious footsteps traversed the damp and slippery, descending incline. To keep steady, she braced herself by dragging a splayed hand against the wall, which alternated in texture from stone to plaster. It seemed illogical that her chubby father could walk through this passageway; she couldn't help but to reflect how its narrowness was akin to his bigotry.

The tight ingress ended at a wood door. She knocked and when no reply was forthcoming, she entered, promptly closing the door behind her.

A flip of the electrical wall switch beside her illuminated the converted gas fixture hanging low above a desk, casting a green tint from its crystal globes. Dark wood paneled walls and recessed bookcases filled with mementos, volumes, and other varied objects lined the perimeter of the small room. Papers and books lay scattered and the heavy smell of his cigars permeated the confined space. A crystal ashtray sat filled with remnants of the habit.

All her senses were acutely alive. Her vision, though, was the most affected—and horror-struck—when it immediately settled upon the flag of Nazi Germany proudly hanging to her left.

She gasped, her hand flying to her mouth in fright as the blood red background, white circle, and evil black swastika hung as proof of what she feared.

Through spread fingers over trembling lips she croaked, "Oh, G-d! No. Lord, G-d this cannot be."

Tears instantaneously filled her eyes and, reviled, she backed away, pressing against the wall behind her where a large map of the United States marked with red circles hung. She looked upward over her shoulder, fearful of what she would see, and it was in that mille-second that any remaining hope was crushed. Confirmation, attestation, and loyalty to the Third Reich were proclaimed in her father's fine penmanship. The handwritten title above New York read: *Operation Paukenschlag/Drumbeat—Success; Operation Pastorius—Failure.*

"Oh, Father, what have you done? Who are you?"

Lizzy bit her trembling lip, the tears now rolling freely as anger and repulsion did battle with the daughterly love that had once been in her heart. All hope for her once esteemed father had been replaced by rightful condemnation against a man she hardly knew after all. Her vision flew to the painting behind his desk—Adolf Hitler.

Eyes scanned the room frantically, as she walked toward the bookcase: *Mein Kampf, The International Jew, The Myth of the Twentieth Century, The Protocols of the Elders of Zion* and other volumes, their titles printed in German that she did not understand. Abruptly she turned, her vision riveted upon the strewn folders covering his messy desk, each cover stamped with the Parteiadler, the eagle emblem of the party.

Panicked, her heart beat furiously as she shuffled through them, many written in her father's hand with words or names she didn't understand, until she understood one very clearly. She picked it up. In the upper corner it read—Martel *Familie.* The nausea came again as though her baby knew what she held, and her hand shook as she opened it. The thin, grey paper wavered, as did her entire body. The word "*Juden*" was stamped diagonally in vicious black letters across the first page. Inside read Will's complete, accurate family history, including the details of his grandfather and aunt's arrest and detention at Drancy Internment Camp in Paris followed by their deportation to a concentration camp, Auschwitz, in July by the Gestapo.

An indiscernible, anguished cry escaped her lips, echoing against the walls. Her knees buckled. She dropped the folder and held onto the side of the desk to keep from falling to the stone below her. Her hand protectively flew to her womb, covering it as she sobbed violently, wracking in agony, her struggling breaths constricted.

Lizzy's eyes locked upon another file lying before her. Facing up it read, John Robertsen. She flipped open the folder as blurred, tear-filled eyes scanned furiously, and it was then that she knew she had made the right decision. The contents of the dossier confirmed it. Apparently he, too, was of *superior* blood and the one specifically chosen for her deleterious sister. Ingrid's claws were determined to dig into the heir of an aviation fortune, poised for sabotage and eventual control by New Germany's Luftwaffe in America.

****

Forty-eight hours later, foregoing the pre-marital blood test, Lizzy slathered rose scented cream upon her hands before donning her new wedding gloves. Wringing fingers together to spread the lotion, she stared down feeling as if she were Lady Macbeth, wanting to cry "Out, damned spot." With painful realization, she recognized the truth that it wasn't an outward stain that could be washed away. It was the stain below her skin—her "pure Germanic blood" tainting and defiling Will's baby repulsed her. A pure innocent conceived out of their love was receiving her life's blood, which was poisoned by such malevolent genes.

Although not visible, the outward corruption to her flesh after touching those files upon her father's desk was too much to bear. She twisted her fingers, nearly pinching her flesh, feeling unclean—even violated as she recalled moving her grasp to the Hitler statue used as a paperweight. There was no overriding of the feeling of pollution upon her hands and eyes. Finally, she donned her gloves.

Lizzy looked at her image in the mirror, losing herself in thought. The reflection staring back was dispirited and vacant and if not for the life developing within her, there would be no way she could marry anyone other than William Martel. A hand smoothed the hair at her forehead of its own mindless accord. For the baby's sake, she had to move forward, even if into a future void of blissful passion and romance, into a life knowing that she came so close to complete happiness. The worst of it was the knowledge that the life of one noble, extraordinary man, who was exemplary above all other men, was cut short, along with members of his family, due in some part, perhaps entirely, to the collaboration of her own father. The loss she felt superseded grief. It now ventured into the abysmal—a black void that would never be filled. The guilt by such close association tore at her heart. She vowed to spend her future atoning for the lives ruined by this war born from evil, by saving and restoring whatever or whoever could be made whole again.

Lizzy sighed in defeat and despair as she removed Will's cadet pin from her dress, instead pinning it to the label within her glove, hidden, yet resting against the pulse of her wrist. The cool, gold propeller wings dug into her flesh uncomfortably, but she welcomed the feeling. It proved that she wasn't dead after all.

The small Bakelite clock on her vanity informed her that it was time to leave, time to face the future by becoming Mrs. Elizabeth Robertsen, wife to John, the heir to Robertsen Aviation. They were scheduled to meet at the yacht club and drive south to Elkton, Maryland for a quickie wedding where only a brief waiting period for the marriage license was required. Elopement was the only answer, and they would deal with the fallout afterward, neither looking forward to what they anticipated from both sides of the stone wall separating their family estates.

Ingrid had been tenacious this past month, attempting to trap John, each attempt narrowly avoided but not without arguments and conflict. Even Greta pushed, pressuring John to acquiesce in marrying Ingrid, convinced that with a Renner as her sister, she would rise to even higher acceptance in the *Social Register*, thereby wiping away the stain of "new money."

As for her father and Gebhardt, the two had already chosen a wedding date in five weeks. A seamstress was scheduled to arrive at Meercrest the coming week to take measurements for a wedding gown that Lizzy was adamant she would never wear.

She stood before the mirror, examining the simple dress she wore. Winter white by an unknown designer, and purchased off the rack at Singer's Department Store, it hid her pregnancy girdle well. Adjusting her hat, the mother of pearl hatpin slid through the fabric below the feather. She smoothed her hand down the tiny bump and attempted a smile at her reflection. All she felt were the stays of the girdle from the outside and she desperately wished, at that moment, to feel the baby flutter again. Sighing, she wished Kitty would knock to wish her well or to bring her a miraculous letter from Will demanding a halt to the wedding or inform her of a radio news report that the war was over. She hoped even for a happy letter from Lillian about all the things she was doing and seeing, but there was nothing. Of course, there wouldn't be. Lillian knew nothing of the events leading up to this desperate, spontaneous decision. Today she was on her own; not even Kitty knew where the Zephyr was bound.

Her eyes filled with tears for the umpteenth time as she walked lifelessly to Will's photograph, holding it reverently in her hands with tears dropping one after another onto the glass. Her body lurched as she contorted to hold back the noisy sobs that begged to emerge. Only a garbled whisper left her lips, "Good-bye, Ducky. ... Good-bye, Pistol."

With a sadness the likes of which she had never known, she deposited a tender kiss upon the glass above his lips, leaving a remnant of her love in an imprint of ruby lipstick. Her gloved hand shook when she pretended to smooth an errant lock of hair below his uniform hat. Not only was she sure that her sweetheart was dead, but as the wife of another man, she would no longer be able to gaze upon Will's face every morning. Frame in hand, she walked to her hope chest and lovingly folded this most treasured photograph within the blankets, closing the cover to what was once the future of her dreams.

With finality and resolve, she straightened her posture and wiped her tears with a maturity brought about by heart wrenching events. "Are you ready, Elizabeth?"

Thirty-Seven

Yesterday's Gardenias
June 25, 1992

With her back braced against the bed, Lizzy sat on the floor, surrounded by their letters. The ones that she'd opened, consumed, and digested were now carefully stacked. Others were tearstained and scattered wherever her agony left them. Each word from Will was progressively more desperate, visibly evident as his messy penmanship worsened; each word of hers clung to hope until there was none left. Many of the missives remained unopened. There were many, too many to count in her haste to devour every word Will had written, bled, upon the paper. To her left lay a protective cardboard sleeve stamped "Do Not Fold": the U.S.O. Club Letter on a Record he had spoken of in '49, sent to her from Suffolk. She resisted the urge to immediately run down the stairs and play it. Lord knew, she could barely get through reading his pain. Hearing that pain in his voice after all these years would be too much to bear. Beside her, in a pile of their own, lay letters to and from Anna Martel and one from Louie. Clearly, Kitty had been very thorough; no related correspondence had escaped her crime of interception.

Dammit, she wanted a cigarette!—a habit long ago banished on the advice of her doctor back before Danny was born. She handled her stress in a different way now. Yoga breathing techniques usually calmed her, but not today. Who gave a damn about yoga? Once again, her world was crashing around her. Escaping the fallout was not in the cards, dealing with it head on was. Although, she never imagined *this*—and from Kitty, no less.

Dabbing at her streaming eyes with yet another saturated, balled Kleenex clutched between her fingertips, Lizzy gazed about at the strewn letters. Her heart clenched, and there seemed to be no stopping the tears. Words erupted from the pages, tormenting her mind, proclaiming the truth that the great love she and Will shared had been wrenched from them by the actions of one person. Around two fingers, their daughter's beaded baby bracelet was encircled, the tangible binding ring of the profound connection between them.

I hope this letter reaches you, Will. I have to talk with you about something important, please write me. I miss you so much – and I missed something else as well.

Lizzy, baby. You don't know how worried I am about you. Please write me soon. There are rumors that the air echelon will begin leaving for the ETO in just days, and I need your love to send me into the unknown. Please, sweetheart, write to me. Have you forgotten me already?

Will, I know you are busy and have many things on your mind, but I pray you have not forgotten me. We have much to discuss. News, good news. Well, news that makes me happy but I don't know what to do about it in your absence. Please, please send me even a short note with your new A.P.O address if that is the reason my letters are going unanswered. Have you left for England? Is that the delay in the post?

I know the bookmobile is keeping you busy, and I'm so proud that it is, but I cannot imagine that it has consumed all your attention. I have written you my new A.P.O address, so I cannot imagine what the delay is.

Ducky, I'm trying to be an optimist, truly I am, but it has been nearly six weeks and still no letter from you. There are important decisions we have to make. What we did during our time "together" has resulted in something that I am so over the moon about and I know you will be too! I miss you more than you can know, and it feels more so because of your silence. I'm worried beyond measure for you AND for me. I love you and I need your advice!

Are you not at Meercrest or have my letters fallen into another's hands in an attempt to separate us? Could your father be at the heart of my not having received letters from you in over seven weeks? I cannot imagine that Army mail, even with a change of airbase to England, is this slow. Although I just arrived, I have been told that the Eighth Air Force receives mail with frequency, yet I wait and hope to receive something from you. Nothing has come since I received your Christmas card! I'm worried. I'm frustrated and I'm not focusing on what I need to focus on. I miss you so much, baby. Every day, I see these B-17 bombers come back to the airfield battered and beaten. And although we Marauder Men have not yet gone for our first mission, there is a need for your brilliant effervescence that is missing with every mail call. Please, if only just to tell me that you are safe – WRITE TO ME!

Will, please don't abandon me. Please don't leave me. I fear the worst every night when I lie awake with my hand resting upon my tummy. You must be alive. You must come home. We're having a baby. You promised we would be together forever!!

I can't bear this pain. Was it all a game to you? You got what you wanted—a roll in the hay with a "Flyboy." You've ditched me without so much as an explanation. I truly did not think you capable of this, but I suppose that in the end you just proved your kind. High society, hoity-toity girl who loves a good time without consideration of the feelings of another. I can't believe that I wasted my time on you!

What should I do? I have waited for word, even writing your mother to inquire of your safety, but have heard nothing. My heart is breaking thinking the worst—that she is so grief stricken she cannot bear to tell me. I thought of going to Brooklyn directly, but I have been so ill, morning, noon, and night I cannot travel. So, I will write her again. Please tell me you are safe. My whole life is you, Will. We had dreams of seeing Rome and Venice, of sharing our love under the stars, and of a family to raise together. You can't be dead. You must be safe. You must see your child grow! I love you!!!

I have loved you with every fiber of my being. I have carried your laughter in my heart to propel me forward. I have given you everything a man deeply in love can give to a woman. I proposed to you all the way from England on a record and hoped to raise a family with you. I purchased a home for us to spend the rest of our lives together. The ring is being specially made. I gave you my trust and heart!! But you have cast all my dreams and me aside. I had foolishly thought they were your dreams, too. We burned bright, hot, and fast—but you never intended to share my future, did you? I hope you are satisfied, Lizzy Renner, that you have broken my heart, shattering it into a million tiny pieces of shrapnel. I hate that it may take me time to forget you, but rest assured that in time I will. I hope that if I return and I see you one day on the street or at the future home of your sister and my brother, that I can look upon you with indifference. -William Martel

Will, I love you and I love our baby. I am overjoyed to bring our child into the world, but I must keep it safe. To be unwed and in this particular house, given the knowledge that my father and sister have of your faith and his confirmed "interests," I must make a decision. I need to hear from you. I have waited and waited and now our child shows itself. Johnny has asked for my hand, pledging his protection of the baby. He wants to do this and he can provide for us the only hope I can see. I shudder to think that you have been killed. G-d No! My love, this is truly the only option for me because I can never love another as I love you. You are my every breath taken, and our baby is the embodiment of what we share for all eternity—even in death. I can't stop crying. Life without you just won't be a life at all, but it'll be our baby that will keep me from joining you where we could marry in heaven.

She picked up one of the letters she had just read. This time she blubbered, fresh tears uncontrollably flowing. Unable to control the pain, she cried out, "He had proposed!—my G-d, he proposed! Oh ... my ... G-d!"

Now, realizing fully the agonizing hurt she had unknowingly inflicted on that impetuous night in '49, the emotional words tore her wound open again. Their liaison must have been all the more painful for him when she left like a thief before the dawn while he still slept. Seemingly abandoning him for the second time in his life, breaking his heart, and leaving him with only renewed memories that tormented her, too.

After many painful minutes, clutching a letter to her heart, her tears finally ceased. Laying it aside, she rose from her cross-legged position, and then stepped over the scattered missives to the velvet glove box still open on the coffee table. The aging postcard of the swans in Lake Mirror brought back her promise to him. Yet she couldn't stop her thoughts from traveling to Kitty and her deceit. She dearly loved her sister. They had come through so much together. When all hope seemed lost, Kitty had emerged from the ashes as Katherine who could walk again and live life as she had dreamed. Lizzy, too, had been reborn as Elizabeth—mother, dutiful wife, and philanthropist.

For four hours, her tears had flowed. Bloodshot eyes and a rubbed-raw nose were now joined by a growling stomach. Lizzy looked over at the letters again. The only thing she could think of was a glass of wine—several glasses, in fact, and, perhaps for medicinal purposes, that box of Whitman chocolates stashed in the pantry. She was numb and all cried out.

After carefully replacing the precious postcard in its treasure vault, she emerged from the safety of her bedroom and descended the dark stairwell. The house was quiet, with only a thin slice of light from the kitchen seeping into the den and breaching the entry hallway. Kitty must have left it on before her tear-filled dismissal. Lizzy sighed, torn between raging anger and confused compassion.

She stopped abruptly at the kitchen threshold, startled by her sister's presence at the table scattered with used tissues. Her eyes were equally bloodshot. It was apparent that for the entire four hours past, she, too, had embarked on a pity party. Lizzy resisted the urge to voice her opinion but "*good*" was on the tip of her tongue.

Bitterly, with the frost of barest civility, instead, she said, "I thought I told you to leave."

"You did, and I ignored you. You're not the only obstinate one. We can't leave things unsaid between us."

Lizzy sauntered toward the kitchen cupboard, head held high, purposefully aloof. "We didn't leave anything unsaid, at least I didn't. I'll repeat it if you didn't hear me earlier: You ruined my life, and I gave you yours. You're sorry, and I'm livid. What more can we say to one another besides don't let the door hit you in the ass?"

"You're right. Of course you're right, and I stayed because I am expecting you to kick me out of your life after reading the letters, then certainly your condemnation. Although knowing what may come torments me, it is deserved. It would have been too easy for me to leave you to deal with the fallout and the suffering, just as I did in '43 when you took me to Minnesota. Leaving after giving you the letters would only demonstrate, once again, my inherent proclivity to protect myself, and it's time for me to face the consequences of my actions. If for no other reason than to atone, I need to help find a way to make this right between you and William."

Lizzy removed two wine glasses from the center shelf. Beaten and fatigued she stated, "You can't give back the fifty years you took from us. There's nothing you can do or say that would change that."

A large photo album lay open on the table and Kitty slid it away from her. "Then I'll go if that's what you want, but not before I apologize for earlier, handling this so poorly by further wounding you with accusations. It was wrong of me and none of my business. None of it was. I was at fault for keeping Annette from her real father; the fault rests solely upon my shoulders."

Lizzy sighed, closing her eyes before barely breathing a whispered, "Don't go."

As though relief washed over Kitty, she burst into tears the likes of which Lizzy had never seen. The palms of her hands flying to her face, her head dropping to their concealing shelter as her body bobbed. Sobs poured forth, mixing with words.

"I can never forgive myself for having hurt you. You were right, there was no excuse ... no excuse for having never told you all these years. I'm so sorry."

Lizzy walked to the refrigerator and removed a bottle of Chardonnay. She uncorked it with painstaking precision, allowing her sister's reprobation and self-loathing to thicken and hover while she remained stoic, ignoring her instinct to comfort. In her mind, she questioned whether she could ever forgive such a heinous act perpetrated by the one person she was sure would never hurt her. Feeling devastated by Kitty's betrayal was an understatement.

She glanced over her shoulder at her sister's silvered white head moving up and down, face covered with delicate fingers adorned only with a slender gold wedding band. Lizzy recognized the opened photo album chronicling Annette's first year, as well as, noticing the not so well hidden, half-empty box of chocolates beside Kitty's arm.

A signature raised eyebrow accompanied Lizzy's requisite snarky comment about the half-eaten box of Whitman's. "You can add the theft of my chocolates to your dastardly list of sins."

Kitty looked up and their eyes met. A tinge of humor graced Lizzy's voice, and Kitty responded in kind, in spite of the oppressive tension between them. "Then you should have hid them better."

"Hmm, well, just like my letters they weren't meant to be taken." Lizzy stood over Kitty, placing two filled wine glasses upon the table. She glanced down at the album and smiled thoughtfully at the images, unable to maintain cold aloofness when faced with the joyful purity and innocence depicted in Will's adorable daughter.

She reflected with a tender smile, "I haven't looked at these pictures in years."

Kitty's heart clenched, as she studied the album, viewing the events she had missed, both joyful and sad. She wasn't there for Lizzy's postpartum depression, nor when Annette had suffered with the croup and the only family Lizzy could turn to were the Robertsens. She missed the adoption of Henri, the birth of Danny, all the skinned knees, all the ballet lessons, even the foundation's launch. Her sister had given everyone life—sacrificing everything—because of her. Furthermore, Will had missed all of it, too. That fact was the most contemptible. Fresh tears of contrition rolled down her cheeks.

Still angered, Lizzy ignored the newest deluge of tears, instead commenting on the snapshots in the book. "G-d, Annette loved that damn birthday cake. Like a sugar fiend, she shoved the icing in her mouth with both hands, absolutely gleeful. Unfortunately, right after that photo was taken, Mother dropped her rocks glass smack into the cake and became madder than blazes. The woman went ballistic at her own clumsy drunken loss of gin. She actually, somehow blamed Annette, who cried for thirty minutes straight. John had to physically remove our dear drunken mother from the house."

"I never told you, but she hit me once," Kitty confessed, wringing her hands.

"Annette?"

"No. Mother did. It was just before the Christmas Ball of '42. You had gone to the doctor and Ingrid had said something terrible to me. I can't remember the exact words, but it was along the lines of how I would never be announcing an engagement—that I should never procreate. I told mother that John was better off dead than marrying her."

"You never told me!"

"She slapped my face. And no, I did not tell you. I was terrified."

Silence fell between the sisters as they slowly continued to turn each page, the old photos producing the only shred of joyfulness that either woman could cling to in the awkward air. Without realizing it, they chortled simultaneously at John's silly face as he played puppeteer with that lopsided Daffy Duck hand puppet his mother had made.

"John loved Annette so much," Kitty reflected.

"He did. They had a special relationship. She was his daughter and even when Henri and Danny came along, she remained his little duckling."

"I wish I could have been here to celebrate these milestones with you."

Lizzy took a seat beside Kitty but kept an unwavering distance. "You were. Both you and Will were never far from me even in your absence, but thank G-d for John because I don't think I would have survived my depression after she was born."

"But you looked so happy here."

"Oh, I was, but my heart hadn't healed and I certainly still grieved Will's death." She smoothed her index finger over Annette's image then sighed. "Kitty, you have *no* idea what your actions precipitated. You have *no* *conception* of the depth of my heartache, and I imagine, Will's as well, especially after some of his letters I've read just now. John knew how I suffered, and he never said anything, just cared for her and me with such kindness."

"That was his way."

Kitty's hand stilled upon hers, but Lizzy withdrew. She was seething yet trying so hard to feel forgiveness, but it was too raw. Perhaps it would always be raw, and most likely they would never have the same relationship as before. With her own tears spent, she felt cold and exposed. She couldn't forgive Kitty—not now.

Her sister's face was pleading and ashamed. "Can you ever find it in your heart to forgive me for what I've done?"

"No. I'm not sure if I can—I don't know. Not yet. I need time to digest what you did to us, but if Will forgives you, then maybe I can. I do remember how frightened you were. If I hadn't felt your fears were warranted, hadn't seen for myself the need to get you far away from Ingrid, Frederick, and that *nurse* he had hanging around, I might not have taken you to Sister Kenny as soon as I did. As pregnant and sick as I was, your safety was my first concern. For you not to have trusted me, hurts so deeply. And I'm sure Will felt the pain just as acutely from actions he assumed were mine, but were actually *yours*."

Kitty felt seventeen again, chastised and riddled with deserved shame, but she strangely welcomed it. There was no explanation or argument to defend, only honest penitence. What she felt was deeper than remorse and sadness, and her heart broke for hurting Lizzy.

"I disappointed you, I know. I disappointed me and have never been able to reconcile the guilt. It was my punishment and I've carried it every day as my torment. I loved Lillian, but you were my only family, really. You were the only one to care for me, and, by my selfishness, I hurt the one person who I loved the most in this world."

"Well, that's an understatement," Lizzy replied wishing she had more strength in her to give her another set down. "And if it were only selfish and immature—if that was all I considered it, I might be able to say that I forgive you right now. Kitty, you *betrayed* me—you betrayed Will, and that's something ... something altogether different."

Lizzy sipped her wine, observing her sister's reaction from over the rim. As expected, another tear fell.

Placing the glass down, she continued. "I can't help thinking that if you had only been honest with me, even after I had married I would have written to Will, at least to let him know that I married and why I did so. I know I would have written him about Annette. When I felt up to it, then I could have gone to his parents, to let them see their grandchild. He proposed on that record but when he never received anything from me, he thought I had dumped him and he stopped writing. Your actions, *not mine*, broke his heart, and I don't think I can ever forgive you, *especially* for that. All these years ... all this time ... and you never said, not even after John's death."

"There was so much time, but never the right time. With each passing year, it just got harder to say anything, and you seemed happy, truly content in your life when I returned to New York. The last thing I wanted to do was confuse you or throw mayhem into your family." Renewed tears flowed, and she picked up one of the used tissues. "Oh! If only we could go back in time! With the maturity and knowledge of these five decades, I would have done things differently, Lizzy."

"No, I don't think you would have. Neither of us would have. We were young, so damn young and naïve about everything." She shook her head, recalling her own headstrong, oftentimes, immature optimism. "But in truth, what if Will *had* been killed, even after months of correspondence and knowing about the baby? I still would have been an unwed mother. You and I were scared and desperate. If I had gone to his parents, we still would have been a burden at their time of extreme stress and, eventually, their knowledge of Frederick's actions might have made them hate us."

"I pray I can help make this right, Lizzy."

Lizzy released a deep sigh. "Me, too."

Kitty nodded, truly understanding that her misguided actions were irrevocable.

"This family has kept too many secrets, each one of us," Lizzy finally voiced after long minutes of contemplative silence between them.

"Time, Kitty. Just give me some time. I admit that I had culpability in keeping Will from his child, but you put the wheels in motion, and now I have to seek my own forgiveness from him."

Kitty blubbered, her ruddy cheeks full wet. Lizzy shook her head and took in a deep breath, seeking to shift the atmosphere that had occupied the kitchen. She slid the seat closer to her sister, finally allowing the physical divide between them to be breached. They hugged. "I love you. I'm so sorry."

"I love you, too, but that's not the issue, and ..." she turned her head, eyeing the box with its empty brown wrappers scattered. "And ... your eating half my chocolates only further pisses me off."

Kitty's gaze followed her sister's and they both chuckled. The ice melted ever so slightly.

They continued to turn pages, pointing and laughing until Lizzy said, "I'm glad I was obsessed with taking these photographs. I can give them to Will now, along with the photos of his grandchildren.

"What will you do? Will you go to see him ... where he lives?"

"If need be, I will. I know it seems strange but part of me still feels like that twenty-year old. After reading our letters, so much has come back to me. I feel butterflies, thinking about the moment that I can see him again. The thing is ... I love him still as much as I did all those years ago, and it's not as if I'm in love with just a memory. I have always loved him as his soul mate, but we've been separated by time. I love him differently than I did John. I love him like the long lost piece of my soul has returned to mate with mine until my last breath. I just pray to G-d he won't hate me when I tell him about Annette. And let's hope he's not married!"

Lizzy took a long draw from her glass, closing her eyes to the refreshing taste of the crisp white wine. She thought of John and the content of the letters.

"I know it may seem strange to you, Kitty. But I feel ... released. John and I had a rich, caring marriage born out of convenience. It wasn't the kind of love I had with Will. Very few ever have *that* kind of love. I feel blessed that *now* can be my time with Ducky—if he'll have me. Maybe we can begin again and get to know one another as adults with experiences that shaped who we've both become."

The front door slammed and the foyer light flipped on. "Mom? Are you home?"

The two sister's eyes locked. "In here, darling."

Annette walked into the kitchen, her smile turning to a frown when she noted the red eyes of her mother and aunt and the crumpled debris of Kleenex tissues upon the table. "What happened? Did someone die?"

Both sisters sniggered before Kitty said, "Your aunt Ingrid died, but we're sure as hell not crying over *that*. Your mother and I were just reminiscing. You were such an adorable baby, such a little duckling."

Annette pulled out a chair and sat facing them. Sliding the photo album across the table toward her with one hand, her other dove into the open chocolate box. "Gosh, you haven't called me a duckling in forever. Wherever did that come from?"

Thirty-Eight

Haunted Heart
July 1, 1992

W ill's visit with Juliana and Jack extended well beyond a couple of beers over lunch. They had spent the next day together for a flight in his floatplane over the Inside Passage.

They hardly spoke of Lizzy, and he was thankful; instead, they spent the time learning about one another and it killed him to like Jack more and more. The young man's personality made him a perfect fishing buddy. He had shared his worldwide travels, and Will especially delighted in conversation about Jack's trip to Amsterdam the year prior. Together, the three of them also spoke of Louie and what he'd been going through since Lillian's death. It hurt Will's heart to hear of his brother's sorrow and PTSD. Upon Louie's return from China in late '46, he never spoke of his experience in the Pacific just as Will never spoke of his experience in captivity, both acutely understanding that those particular segments of life were better left in the past.

It turned out that meeting Juliana was a delightful surprise. She had Louie's humor and playful manner, and he could tell that, as he had once been as a young man, she just needed a little push to let herself free to enjoy life, live a little on the daring side. When Jack spoke of sailing, she held back, not quite committing, hedging with excuses for not going near the water. All it took was a flight on his de Havilland Beaver floatplane and she was as giddy as a schoolgirl when the plane skimmed the water on landing and takeoff. Her laughter was as infectious as Lizzy's had been whenever she sped in the Zephyr or the roundabout. He could hardly believe it when his niece squealed a "woo hoo!" and clapped with excitement to go sailing when they returned to Long Island.

It was a miserably cold morning on the Sound and the stratus clouds hung low in the gray sky but that hadn't kept Will from the task at hand—finally changing the oil on the de Havilland. Once again, he stood on the dock looking at the red, white, and black sleek lines of the plane as he held a steaming cup of coffee in his hands. Focusing on finishing the job seemed near impossible. With the old engine oil emptied and his greasy gloves tossed beside the float, he felt entirely uninspired to get back under the plane. The coffee break was unprecedented, maybe even a convenient excuse to re-visit the still unopened FedEx envelope now sitting on the coffee table. Lord knows, he had walked past it three times looking at it almost with fear only to promptly walk out the back door. Now here he stood and unless he finished working on the convenient transport to and from his home, it would remain out of commission in need of its replacement oil.

He walked toward the plane with resolve, took a sip of joe, then placed the mug upon the dock. The discarded gloves awaited him but, unfortunately for the plane, his curiosity over Al's correspondence was finally winning the battle.

He thought of Paris and the intimation that Lizzy would be there, maybe waiting for him. Something was set to happen in that romantic city that had once been party to the deaths of thousands five decades ago. His niece felt strongly that it was important he be there to witness whatever Robertsen family event that was to take place. Traveling there was certainly do-able, but he didn't want to revisit the Pletzl during the anniversary week of the Roundup. Will sighed, acknowledging to himself that it had been years since he paid a visit to the school he established in 1980 in his aunt's former home—The DeVries School for the Handicapped. Perhaps now was the time to do so.

If Lizzy was to be in Paris, would she realize his impetus for the school?

He suddenly turned on his heel from the plane and coffee and dashed down the dock toward the house, only to stop on a dime midway, running his hand through his hair. "Arggh!" He groaned, frustrated by his indecisiveness and innate need to learn about the woman who broke his heart. The echoing comments that Jack had made on Monday piqued him.

She never stopped loving you. I know this not because she told me but because of how she lived her life, the specific things she did with her life. ... He was a Jewish war orphan, surviving the Holocaust, and my grandparents traveled to London to bring him to America.

Were her actions in life similar to those he made in her memory, honoring that which was closest to her heart? Nah, she most likely became a self-absorbed society wife forgetting, or worse, disregarding that informed, caring woman she had been blossoming into in '42.

He paced for what felt like hours but was only two or three minutes, until he ran down the dock to the deck stairs, taking them two at a time until he flung open the back door to the cabin. Chest heaving and heart racing, his eyes settled upon the envelope and he sat before it, taking it into his hands.

"Do you want to see her again?" He asked himself. "Yes. I want to see her again. True home is where my heart has always been." A slight tremble to his fingers seemed to beat in unison to his heart rate as the blood rushed filling his mind with a memory so clear and real it was as though it was yesterday when it occurred. There was no fog of war in remembering that day.

Negotiated by Stalag Luft I's senior American and British officers, the camp had been abandoned by the Nazis instead of a forced one hundred mile march by its POW's. Liberation was near and a party comprised of officers had been dispatched to make contact with the advancing Russians. May 1st, 1945 saw almost eight thousand American airmen and fourteen hundred Britons on tenterhooks awaiting their evacuation and return home—return to life as they once knew it. Sweethearts, children, families, and jobs would be awaiting them.

One could hardly consider the wood-chip filled mattress a bed, but Will hunched over his bunk folding the torn, threadbare blanket neatly, careful not to bang his head on the bunk above him. Of all the small blessings that found their way into his captivity, he was most thankful that his crew hadn't been separated upon their arrival shortly after May 17, 1943. Following their capture, they had begun their "stay" in the South Compound and the Commandant had not separated McCarthy and him from the non-

commissioned fellas of their crew. Apparently, even in a POW camp, officers and enlisted men were separated and the hierarchy functioned just as it did in an airbase. There were chains of command and a hope that you had a good commanding officer to petition the reasonable Commandant on behalf of his men.

Even in May, Barth, Germany on the Baltic Sea was cold and the men of the PPL were thankful for the kitchen duty he had secured for them, along with the coveralls and wood shoes he demanded they needed. They ate better than most and at least had clothing other than what they crashed in or what the Red Cross was able to bring them in '44. After fifteen months in South Compound, it was more than any man could survive for the duration. He petitioned the Senior American Officer to transfer them to North 1 compound where they had running water and latrines. It only seemed fair, since they were among the first Americans to arrive at the, then, largely British camp. Small and big blessings and, as a Kriegie, you took what you can get when G-d sent them to you, and you were thankful for each and every one of them.

-What's the first thing you're going to do when you get outta this shit hole, Skipper? Rocco asked.

-Kiss the concrete stoop before entering my father's house.

No one but Al, also a Jew, knew it would have been a mezuzah he'd kiss if one had hung from the entrance door frame of his family home in Park Slope.

-Not me. I'm gonna take the subway up to Luigi's Restaurante on Arthur Avenue and blow my back pay on a table full of lasagna, ravioli, and brachiole. Followed by the best damn crème puffs this Bronx boy has ever had and topped off with a jug of Luigi's family recipe.

Will smiled, thinking of his mother's Dutch apple cake.

The clock above the microwave chimed the hour in time with the bittersweet recollection causing his heart to clench. In May of 1945, he hadn't known that his mother was dead, having passed in June of 1943 from a massive heart attacked following receipt of the War Department's Missing in Action telegram. Thank G-d Louie had been on a nine-month training exercise following the Guadalcanal bloodbath and was able to come home. Yes, that was a blessing, but it accompanied the misery of knowing that his beloved mother might have lived had he been the mustard in the cockpit everyone expected him to be.

His hand smoothed the tattered blanket. Home. It was the first thing he thought of when coming to, following the engineless crash, and it was the last thing he thought of every night when he laid his head upon his other rolled blanket, now also in tatters. There were no thoughts of Lizzy in the camp. She represented the guilt he had for his crew being there in the first place. His sole focus was on bringing his men through their captivity. Although time and again McCarthy attempted to reason with him that on that low altitude mission over the Ijmuiden and Haarlem Power Stations in Holland, he was doubtful any of the 451st returned home and not because of some girl. Intense flak tore through every Marauder, and the PPL couldn't withstand the barrage and the eventual equipment failure. The ship was tossed and shaken violently in the clouds from the impact of ack-ack. It wasn't because of his flying ability or his distraction that brought them down. They did the best they could under the worst of situations on only their second bombing mission out. Hell, they probably had been one of the few able to drop their bomb load over the target before going down. Plain and simple, the PPL just couldn't stand the heat and once the second engine blew, it was his skill that landed them all safely on a farm. Bringing her down was what he did best. Not to mention he was Lucky Bastard Martel.

Several of the men beside the coal stove coughed. Their bronchitis reverberated within the barrack that was usually filled with forty men, but now with liberation so near, many were in the communal rooms or on the football field where a game was taking place. Thankfully, the towering guard houses were now empty and they could open the shutters of the barrack for proper ventilation. Home was so close, but some of these men were in need of proper medical care before the Russians' arrival.

Will's men knew never to ask about going home to Lizzy. One drunken night in a pub in Rattlesden back in late April of '43 informed them all that the PPL had crashed and burned. They watched as he took his Zippo to the snapshot once taped above the altimeter. Rocco didn't need to ask if he was going to attempt to see his old flame when he got home. Truth though, now, standing in the middle of the barrack, realizing that home was so close, he

471

wanted to see her and it upset him. Over the course of two years, he had pushed her deep within the hidden recesses of his heart and mind, only to have her resurface when faced with the reality of actually going back to New York, to a house he had purchased for their life together. The war was over for him and he'd have to begin again, but she was his home. Only she had moved on without him, most likely making a home with someone else.

No. He would never see her again. Never seek her out and ever speak of her. Seeing her would tear open the wound.

Will held the FedEx envelope in his hand and toyed with the paper tab. He held his breath with its sudden tear, pulling it open to reveal a thick stack of white paper as well as a couple of newspaper clippings. Carefully, he removed the stack from the tight-fitting sleeve. The top letter was addressed from Gardner & Gardner, Attorneys at Law.

Dear Will,

It was great to talk with you last week. Glad to hear that you're considering coming east. After all these years, it'll be good to see you again and we can catch up in person. It hardly seems like fifty years since our time in Germany together. The dreams we had as young men and how you had helped me to realize mine seem like only yesterday. Consider this packet just another way of thanking you for putting me through law school all those years ago, although that can never be repaid. I dug deeper than you indicated and I think you'll be quite surprised by what you'll find here. This Elizabeth Robertsen is a remarkable woman. I thought I recognized the name, and it turns out that she's a major benefactor for the United Jewish Appeal Federation. Since 1951 her personal monetary donations to UJA exceed over eleven million dollars, spread out over the various divisions. Rachel knows her from the Women's Philanthropy Division. Her main focus is on children and family services. Funny thing, she and her husband donated at least a half a million dollars to that private organization you flew for out of Holland, bringing the displaced into Israel. The late John Robertsen, then Vice President at Robertsen Aviation, now Zephyr Avionics, donated a C-47 transport plane. Small world? Is that how you know her?

No charge for the extra detective work—this one's on me. I did find some curious facts about her family and Frederick Renner, but those reports are not included. Call it a gut feeling but I figure you knew about that already. If you want me to send them, just let me know. I'll FedEx them out to you, otherwise they'll end up in the circular file. Hard to believe it all. I thought that kind of stuff only happened in the movies.

When you get back to New York, you better get your ass up to Yonkers so that I can introduce you to the family. Let them meet the mensch who took this poor Jew out of the ghetto and helped me to make something of myself. Take care, my friend, and give my regards for the best of health to McCarthy. All the best,

Al

Will snorted a wry laugh. "Only in the movies? Yeah, right. Truth is stranger than fiction and Renner was a cowardly bastard."

The letter acted as further confirmation that Lizzy had become so much more than he had feared she would as a society wife in affluent Long Island, wasting her vitality attending dinner parties and playing bridge with a group of upper-crust snobbish friends. It was also confirmation of what Jack had said about how she lived her life. Will never expected humanitarian, philanthropist, and forty years of serving and providing for Jewish communities in both New York and Europe. *Was this for me or was it as she said in that fateful letter the night of their blissful, impassioned affair—atonement, reparation?*

He skimmed through the pages, noting several articles from the *Gold Coast Social Diary*. About the third page into the stack was a type-written dossier outlining the specific events of her life. It seemed odd to view Lizzy through this black and white myopic prism. The spirited ingénue he once knew was full of color and vibrancy. Words to describe her shouldn't be conveyed in a perfunctory Selectric typewriter courier font; she deserved flourished calligraphy in a palette made up of the many hues of her personality.

The pain and anger still remained as though it was Gordon's christening in 1949 all over again, and he was seeing her with her Robertsen family for the first time. Jack was right; he had yet to forgive her for leaving him twice, for choosing a comfortable, predictable life of society.

Name: Elizabeth Marie Renner
Birth: February 22, 1922
Place: Meercrest Estate, Glen Cove Long Island

Spouse: John Alfred Robertsen
Married: February 16, 1943
Place: The Little Wedding Chapel, Elkton, Maryland
Died: January 26, 1982

Will's eyes fixed on the wedding date and he grit his teeth. The muscles in his jaw clenched and moved from his rising anger at the insult of her having waiting only six weeks after his departure for Europe. The pressure upon his jaw caused his temple to throb and pulse.

Child: Annette Estelle Robertsen
Birth: July 21, 1943
Place: Lebanon Hospital, Bronx, New York

Child: Henri Robertsen
Birth: 1942, (Certificate of Adoption December 22, 1947)
Place: Haueman, Alsace, France

Child: Daniel Robertsen
Birth: November 12, 1948
Place: Nassau Hospital, Mineola, New York

The page beneath the family tree was a newspaper article featuring a photograph taken on December 19, 1942 at the Glen Cove Society's Holiday Ball at Meercrest. Although dressed beautifully, Lizzy looked wan and unhappy standing beside her sister Gloria. Gone was her normal effervescence that usually leapt from every snapshot he had ever seen or taken. It was so unlike her, especially since he knew she had loved the holidays. On the far side of the photographed group, John stood beside Ingrid with his arm circling her waist. The caption below read, *"Glen Cove's darlings, sweethearts since childhood, John Robertsen and Ingrid Renner are expected to announce their engagement any day. Aviation and railroad, a natural merger."*

Confused by the caption, he furrowed his brow. If Robertsen was engaged to Lizzy's elder sister, what happened? Why had Lizzy married him instead? He continued to scan through the pages, finding a facsimile of a legal document creating the non-profit charitable organization The Phoenix Foundation in 1975. A three-page list stapled behind it tallied every project, including The Long Island Holocaust Museum in Glen Cove. The Phoenix's newest project, slated for groundbreaking in six months, was the Liberty Senior Residence, 6 Rosebud Lane, Glen Cove. He had written that address hundreds of times—Meercrest. The heads of the foundation were Elizabeth Robertsen and Katherine Landry.

Another page turn brought an even more agonizing image to his eyes. The happy new Robertsen family stood beside one of Robertsen Aviation's P-47 fighter planes as John christened it with a bottle of champagne. Lizzy held their baby daughter in their arms and the caption read: *"July 21, 1944 Mr. and Mrs. John Robertsen, Vice President of Robertsen Aviation, christen a P-47 Thunderbolt named in honor of their daughter's first birthday: "Daddy's Baby Girl."*

Like a rushing wave of clarity, the jealousy Will held onto these five decades cleared in a startling awareness at the words "first birthday" and "daddy's baby girl." A snippet of conversation with Lizzy from long ago came rushing back:

-You better be careful, I might not give your heart back once you give it to me, he had said.

-Too late, daddy. It's yours. Like the song—I'm all yours. After all, I am painted on the side of your Marauder. It's the highest compliment when a skipper names his ship after his girl. It means true love. Forever love that will endure the high seas and rough waters side by side, even when distance separates us—me and you.

John wasn't that kind of skipper, not a pilot. He was a fisherman and would name a boat—not a plane. Was "daddy" meant to imply ...?

His heart hammered as he quickly flipped back to page three again. Robertsen and Lizzy married in February of 1943. Their first child was born at the end of July. *Prematurely?* Annette—named after his mother Anna? Estelle—my aunt? He ticked on his fingers, counting backward nine months. July 1943 ... October 1942. Lebanon Hospital was located in a Jewish community in the Bronx, far from Glen Cove. Elkton, Maryland, at that time, was the elopement capital of America. *Could it be? Was she ... Is that why Lizzy married Robertsen?*

He rapidly blinked; a sudden cold sweat broke upon his brow. Was Annette *his*? Was he *"the daddy"*?

Will lowered the papers and leaned back against the sofa, closing his eyes as his mind whirled. He felt it in his bones, that adorable little girl with chestnut ringlet curls was their child. Lizzy must have been pregnant and John protected her reputation and baby by marrying her in his absence. He was stunned. *I have a daughter.*

... and Lizzy never told me. My G-d.

He ran his hand over his face, stilling his trembling fingers over his mouth in utter shock, emotions vacillating between joy, anger, pain, and panic. These were the same emotions he experienced the minute the church doors opened in '49 and Lizzy walked through them with the sun backlighting her beauty like an ethereal vision.

He looked at the photograph of the baby in Lizzy's arms, his heart wrenching. "We have a daughter?"

Abruptly standing, he began to pace the length of the room, once large now seemingly so much smaller and suffocating. His hand shook almost as anxiously as his head with each thought of Lizzy's deceit and his disbelief. Aggrieved, he suddenly stopped, rubbing his pounding temples and trying to make sense of his speculations. "Maybe you're wrong, just jumping to conclusions. Maybe their daughter was premature."

Suddenly Paris didn't feel as though a passing thought or a place to fear. Just like his trip to the Pletzl in 1980, it was a place for answers and some sort of restoration, replacing death with life. He could have a daughter ... grandchildren, a life surrounded by family. His rancor was allayed by that fact alone.

He resumed his march across the floor as he speculated—and hoped—that his gut feeling was accurate. He thought how with less than two weeks away, it would give him just the right amount of time to think about exactly what he would say to Lizzy when he demanded explanations for *everything*. After all these years, he wanted to find peace: Why did she stop writing? Why did she marry Robertsen? Was it because she was pregnant? If Annette was their child then why did Lizzy never tell him? He ran his hand through his hair. "My G-d, all these years. I have a daughter."

Thirty-Nine

East of the Sun
July 4, 1992

Juliana stood windblown in the bright midday sun, grinning from ear to ear beside Jack at the helm of his sailboat, the *Liberty*. Her cheeks bore the same healthy tan as her exposed body between and beyond the white short shorts and a red bikini top. Her blood had surged with excitement just as when, three days before, she'd flown in her great-uncle's floatplane in Alaska. In a million years, she never expected to actually enjoy sailing, but her entire life had changed this month—thanks to one house, two men, and a stack of old love letters. In fact, she'd had such a good time this morning, her nervousness at imminently meeting Lizzy and her entire new family at Evermore had completely subsided. It seemed significant to be out on the *Liberty*, feeling untamed and free on the Fourth of July. She knew her father was looking down upon her proudly.

"Did you have a good time?" Jack asked as the sailboat slowed to a crawl, coming about toward Evermore's dock on Mill Neck Creek. The bow faced into the gentle breeze, and he found himself captivated by the movement of Juliana's blonde tresses when the sunlight spun golden flickers within each strand.

"Oh my G-d, I had a blast! When can we go out again?" She beamed, bouncing on her toes.

"Whenever you want."

"Tomorrow?"

"Sure. Does that mean you've decided to stay tonight at Evermore with me?" he nodded eagerly, urging her agreement. The Giants baseball cap he wore, mandatory apparel as his grandmother would surely be televising the

478

afternoon game against the St. Louis Cardinals, bobbed up and down accentuating his request.

Juliana wrapped an arm around his waist and gazed up at him with a playful twinkle in her eyes. She stood on her tiptoe to whisper in his ear. "Yes. I'll stay, but no monkey business." A little nibble to his earlobe followed.

"Keep doing that and I won't be responsible for my actions."

He steered the boat alongside the lengthy pier, leaving her side to grab the two dock lines before jumping up onto the dock. Having sailed solo hundreds of times, he'd grown accustomed to tethering the boat without a helper. One day, he'd teach her, but for now, he just wanted her to enjoy the experience of cruising the Long Island Sound on a day when the water was like glass and the wind was perfect.

It was a sublime day. Watching Juliana loosen up and take to boating was an enchanting experience, particularly when she felt comfortable enough to remove her life preserver. Seeing her smile and hearing her laughter float upon the salty air made his heart stir and now he was preparing to introduce her to the woman who began it all.

Within minutes, the boat was secured. After gathering their belongings, he helped Juliana step off, onto the pier, his eyes taking in her relaxed sun-kissed form. "Are you ready to meet everyone?"

"That's it? You're just going to leave the boat like this?"

"Sure. It's my grandmother's dock. It's safe, don't worry."

Jack looked down at her questioning brow. Taking one of her hands, he wove his fingers with hers as a slow smile spread upon his lips before bending to kiss her. Sweet and salty mouths met, and he could feel the warmth upon her lips. He pulled away and gave her a heart-filled look. "Let's go meet your family, Julie. They're waiting for you."

As they walked down the dock, she licked her bottom lip reveling in the lingering tingle he had deposited. There was something in that tender kiss, something she hadn't felt in the few they shared previously. As wonderful as all those prior kisses had been, including their first one in the sunroom at the Sea Otter Bed & Breakfast, this kiss stirred something deeper in her.

A breeze blew and the trees at the edge of the pier seemed to dance, bidding them welcome to safe ground. Everything felt crisp, as though a lens had come into focus. Gone was any lasting anger toward her mother. Somehow, somewhere, and at sometime along this journey, she had come to terms with Susan's abandonment. Sitting across from her uncle and searching his eyes, Juliana discerned the wounds buried in his heart and soul. In his words she heard his inability to forgive, the pain he carried in his broken heart. He was clearly a man who'd been abandoned for the second time by the one person he deeply loved. William Martel, a man she once considered so wholly unconnected to her modern life, had irrevocably altered her perspective on so many things—unbeknownst to him.

At the tree line, a tilted, weathered wooden sign read "Evermore" with child-like writing in black paint. Juliana heard music and laughter carrying on the breeze from beyond the shrubs and sand. Butterflies flapped wildly in her tummy as she followed Jack along the stone paver path through the woods at the back entrance of the estate.

"Nervous?" he asked.

"Nah, a walk in the park. Tell me again, how many cousins I have?"

"Plenty, but the generations are a bit skewed because Lizzy had three children before Lillian gave birth to your father and Aunt Kitty started her family a lot later. Aunt Annette, Lizzy's eldest child has three sons: Adam, Mitch, and Doug. Aunt Kitty also has three kids, two sons: Gary the physical therapist is single, and Sammy the cardiologist is married to Patty. Sammy and Patty have two boys: Stephen and Jake. Kitty's youngest is Jeanna but she isn't married. Wendy—"

"Jack, hold on, I'm not going to remember all this."

"Sure you will. It's not that tough. Wendy is Uncle Dan's daughter. She and Doug are the youngest of the entire clan. She's pregnant but try to overlook the fact that she's not married. Things happen, but everyone's excited about it. But, I have to warn you, if you call Lizzy a great-grandmother, she'll crucify you. It makes her feel about 90."

She laughed. "Good to know. I wouldn't want to piss her off on our first meeting. Annette's son, Doug, he's the flirt, right?"

"Yes. He has a thing for blondes so look out. I'm the oldest of the first cousins, followed by Adam. He's the quiet one who eats, sleeps, and breathes Robertsen Aviation. He's not rude or arrogant but merely reticent, so don't be put off by him. My grandmother says that still waters run deep, whatever the hell that means."

"It means he's just shy and intelligent, but underneath that placid exterior he's very passionate."

Jack snorted. "Yeah, he needs a wild woman to shake him up and get him out of the house."

"And what about Mitch and Jeanna?"

"Spitting personality images of what I assume my grandmother was like at their age. Wild and adventurous, total free spirits. Mitch is a surfer, married to Sunny for about a year. Jeanna's a typical redhead and is funny as all get out. She'll have you pissing in your pants with her imitation of Grandmother waterskiing."

"Lizzy water skis?"

"Hell yeah, but she wears this white bathing cap from the 1950s that makes her look like a Cone Head from *Saturday Night Live*! Jeanna imitates Jane Curtain's voice whenever she makes fun of Grandmother shouting 'Woo hoo' with an arm in the air. You'll have to ask her to do that."

"What about your dad and mom? Will they be here, too?"

"Absolutely! Do you really think they'd miss an opportunity to meet Lillian's granddaughter? It's bad enough they never met your dad. They're not about to miss out on meeting you, too."

It was the last thing he said before opening the wood picket gate leading them through Lizzy's garden. Fully blossomed hydrangeas of pink and lavender welcomed them. The scent of old Long Island and Evermore's herbs and roses mixed with the sea air and Juliana's coconut suntan oil.

"Do I look all right? Should I put a top on over my swimsuit?" she whispered.

"Are you kidding? You look beautiful. You're the most beautiful girl I've ever met."

"And you're full of shit."

Jack halted, stopping them both below an arched trellis covered by hot pink clematis. He dropped the overnight bag he held onto the grass then took Juliana into his arms, breathlessly holding her against his chest. "Are you fishing for a compliment, Julie?"

She grinned naughtily, watching a trickle of perspiration roll down his temple. "Perhaps. Perhaps I'm fishing for more than a compliment. You are quite a waterman after all, and I seem to be highly susceptible to your charms and skill at the helm."

Jack's playful smile descended to her lips for another kiss as his splayed palm glided down her bared spine. This lip lock was heart stopping; their probing tongues dueling in exquisite tandem. Jack's embrace engulfed her entire body, molding it, and consuming it into his. She felt like she was floating on air, yet grounded by the anchor of his obvious emotion. Simultaneous feelings of security and euphoria almost caused her to swoon with an unfamiliar certainty that she was exactly where she wanted to be and feeling confident about everything, even her worthiness to experience this type of bliss.

Jack's mouth had barely separated from hers when he whispered. "I love you."

She smiled coyly, nodding slightly, unable to articulate with words that she too felt something so much more than an attraction.

"C'mon," he said, their eyes locked, both happily grinning. In the distance, the Beach Boys sang "Fun, Fun, Fun." There was a party going on and, according to Jack, she was the guest of honor.

They giggled as they ran down the grassy path toward the lake where the annual family gathering was taking place. The scent of hot dogs and hamburgers cooking on the barbeque wafted toward them. As soon as they passed through the shrubs, they both stopped dead on a dime, hands clasped and mouths agape at the scene before them. On the grass, everyone was dancing and twisting to the music, singing along with Mike Love. In the center of the circle Lizzy and Louie laughed together as they contorted their bodies to the fun lyrics.

Juliana looked up at Jack's humored expression as she cried out, laughing. "My grandfather's here!"

Lizzy turned in their direction, letting out a squeal of delight.

She was a beautiful woman, exactly as her photographs conveyed, only with delicate laugh lines and a toned, tanned body. As though the passage of time hadn't aged either her appearance or her youthful spirit, she wore a red tennis skirt paired with a Grateful Dead t-shirt that read, "Giants, Steal Your

Base" across the front. In Juliana's opinion, she was the hippest 70 year-old she had ever seen.

Lizzy ran to Jack and Juliana with outstretched arms. "Oh. My. Gawd! You're adorable! Jackie, she's adorable! Welcome!"

Two arms encircled Juliana's slight form like a vice grip in a huge bear hug that wouldn't let go. Her wide eyes took in all the relatives, whose activities had abruptly ceased, gathering closer, watching them. She spotted Aunt Kitty wiping away brimming tears as a pregnant Wendy wrapped her arm around her, now familiar, great-aunt.

A very handsome, tall guy stood off to the left with his arms folded across his chest. He wore a quizzical expression and even in the chaos of Lizzy's greeting and the family kissing and hugging Jack, Juliana thought she recognized a similarity in manner and appearance between him and Uncle Will.

She felt overwhelmed by all the attention and the fierce hug. Looking over Lizzy's shoulder, she saw her best friend—her rock—emerge through the crowd: her grandfather bearing that comforting trademark smirk of his. She thought she saw tears in his eyes, too. Even Louise was present, walking behind him with a joyful countenance.

Lizzy set Juliana back. "Let me look at you. Your grandmother would *not* approve. You need some fattening up!" She laughed devilishly. "Well we're here now to pick up where she left off." She waved to Mr. Quizzical Expression. "Fill this little one a plate with a double cheeseburger and potato salad, Adam. Danny, make an egg cream for my great-niece."

Juliana chortled. "Hi, Aunt Lizzy."

Lizzy turned serious and thoughtful, placing the palm of her hand on her niece's cheek. Green eyes embracing blue, her words conveying the deep emotion in her heart. "Hello to you, dear girl. Welcome home. It's about damn time."

They smiled affectionately to each other until Louie stood beside them, pulling his granddaughter into his solid embrace. "Bet you didn't expect me here. Did you, my jewel?"

"How on earth?"

"Your grandfather telephoned me out of the blue. I love surprises, but this one knocked me for a loop!" Lizzy hooked her arm with Louie's and leaned into him. "I haven't seen or heard from my brother-in-law in forty-three years, and he hasn't changed one bit. Still a wolf, still a dreamboat, and still as charming as ever. He invited himself today, not that he needed an invitation to begin with. Evermore had always been open to him and my sister."

"Yeah, well that's a conversation for another day. Not today," he said.

"Then, we'll have to save that topic for Paris ... when we're *all* together." Lizzy winked at him.

"You're sure about that, huh?" Louie raised an eyebrow.

"You forget, brother dear, I'm an optimist." She leaned into his ear and whispered, "I know Will, and since he's not married, I'm sure he'll be there. Jack is certain of it, too. He may still be thinking about it, but in the end, he won't be able to resist his heart."

"Hmmm. You just may be right."

Louise came to stand beside the group, attempting not to intrude, but it was Juliana who broke the ice.

Besieged by all the affection, she courageously edged her way closer to her grandfather's friend. "Hi Louise. I'm really happy to see you here. I know we got off on the wrong foot, but I'd like to start over with my best foot forward."

"Oh, darlin'. I completely understand." Louise laughed. "Frankly, I should have presented myself a little better."

Juliana didn't know what possessed her but she reached out and hugged Louise. "Well, from what I understand, my grandfather is hard to resist. So don't think anything of it."

Lizzy held back the tears welling in her eyes. On this glorious day, healing was taking place. John would be so happy. Her eyes met Kitty's, the emotional chasm between them bridging ever so slightly as they smiled wistfully at each other. She wished Lillian could be here to witness this special reunion and be a part of what should have taken place a long time ago. Now, only one more person remained to bring back into the fold of her fractured yet loving family. According to Jack, Will had a lovely house—but needed to come home. She knew that he needed his daughter and his grandchildren. And, he needed *her*.

Jack tapped Juliana's shoulder and leaned down to her ear. "I'd like to introduce you to my parents."

Following yet more introductions of Jack to her grandfather and Louise, Juliana turned, recognizing Henri from the video in the museum. In person, she could really see the similarity between him and his son. The twinkle in their eyes and the confident stance they both possessed were quite endearing. He had a tangible warmth about him that made her feel right at home in this foreign setting of an actual family tallying far greater than a mere four people, now.

"Julie, this is my dad, Henri and my mom, Marion."

They hugged as though they had always known each other and when Henri spoke with such kindness and familiarity, she knew her life and her relationships had turned a corner.

"I owe your grandmother my life, Juliana. I can think of no one better suited than her granddaughter for my son to fall in love with. If your heart is anything like hers, well then, my son chose wisely."

She looked at Jack smiling sheepishly beside her, then back to his parents. "Boy, for a family that keeps its share of secrets, he sure didn't waste any time in telling you how he felt about me. Did he?"

Marion laughed. "Oh, I like her, Jackie. She's as funny as her grandfather."

"Cuter, too," Jack said.

Adam walked over to the foursome, holding out toward Juliana a plate piled with potato salad and a double hamburger. He stiffly said, "Hi. This is for you."

She took the ample offering. "Thanks! You must be Adam the rocket scientist I heard so much about."

He smiled tightly and shifted his weight a bit. Juliana was mesmerized by him and the resemblance to her great-uncle. "So does that make you smarter than a brain surgeon?"

His smile grew to a grin and it was then that she noticed that exact dimple and the presence of a small cleft in his chin. Annette approached them at that moment, beaming in the same fashion: dimples, perfect teeth, and a particular twinkle in her brown eyes. Again, Juliana couldn't help thinking about Uncle William.

****

Kitty's two-year-old grandson, Stephen, sat on Juliana's knee as she bounced her leg up and down playing horsey with him. His gleeful baby laughter rose above the conversation and amusement taking place at each wooden picnic table.

Juliana laughed along with him, holding his hands outward to keep him balanced. Lizzy watched her great niece from her position beside the old rickety barbeque—a cherished heirloom from the seventies that would not be replaced until it cooked its last burger. They had many gatherings on this lawn beside the lake; some beloved family members had died, and now others had come to take up their places in the empty seats. She smiled thoughtfully at how Jack admired Juliana from the opposite side of the picnic table. He held a dreamy look, one all men in love possessed when gazing upon their sweethearts. It had been a very long time since someone looked at her like that. John never did, but she deeply hoped that Will still would.

Without thought behind the action, the grandmother in her smoothed a hand down Adam's back as he stood beside her char grilling the remaining hot dogs. He was just like her Will, and therefore, he'd always held a special place in her heart.

"Is that it for the hot dogs?" she asked.

"Yup. Do you want me to grill the last few hamburgers?"

"No. Why don't you take them home to that bachelor pad of yours. Have Karen cook them up for you. She can make them into a meatloaf or something."

Adam snickered. "She broke up with me about three weeks ago."

"Impossible!"

"She did. She called me a bore because I wouldn't go mountain climbing with her."

"Oh, I'm so sorry, dear. Why didn't you tell me?"

"Because I knew what you'd say, Grandma."

"And what's that? You think you know me so well." She cocked an eyebrow.

"You'd tell me that I should have gone with her. That I should do a lot of things that I don't."

He was right. Lizzy sighed. "Listen to me." She turned her grandson to face her then reached up, cupping his cheeks flushed from the barbecue. "Listen to me, dear boy. The *right* girl will make you *feel* like climbing Mount Everest, and you will. The *right* girl will inspire you to do things you have never done before—for her, with her, because of her. Love does that, and you obviously didn't love Karen. She simply wasn't the *right* girl, but you can't bury yourself in work all the time or you'll never find *the one*."

"I thought I loved her."

"No, you didn't love her. You never looked at her like your cousin Jack is looking at Juliana, or like Mitch is looking at Sunny."

Adam glanced over to his free-spirited brother reclining on the cedar lounge chair. "Mitch is stoned, that's why he looks like that."

Lizzy playfully slapped his arm. "Oh you! The only elixir he's on is love. You'll know when you're in love—It'll bolt you from the blue and you'll look stoned, too."

"Dad never looked at Mom like that with that sick puppy dog expression."

She patted his cheek before turning to leave. "And that, my darling, is why she kicked his sorry ass to the curb."

Adam laughed. "Hey, that's my dad you're talking about."

"And thank G-d you inherited very little of his looks, personality, temperament, or doll dizzy ways. No dear boy, your DNA is just perfect. You get that from your mother's side."

She smiled brilliantly then departed, making a beeline straight for Juliana. They had a few things to discuss.

Lizzy bent and kissed her great nephew's cheek as she lifted him from Juliana's lap. "Sweet Julie, would you care to take a stroll to my tea garden with me?"

"Uh oh, she's going to pump you for information." Jack chuckled when his grandmother deposited Stephen into his arms, with her devilish grin.

Juliana beamed, reached across the table to Jack, and removed his Giants ball cap, promptly settling it upon her head. "Sure, I'd love to take a walk, Aunt Lizzy. I have something to give you. Something important that I brought with me." She reached below the bench, carefully withdrawing her backpack with its sacred contents.

"Oh, you shouldn't have bought me anything. Really, honey—your presence is my gift."

"It's not that kind of gift."

A hooked arm tucked within Juliana's one guided them away from the family. Several cousins jumped into the lake from the small dock beside them. Their adult shouts carried across the yard as though they were children. Aunt and niece chatted pleasantly until Juliana suddenly stopped at the garden gate, her hand gripping the wooden frame. She turned to look back at the family celebration.

Her eyes drank in the panorama before her, Jake, Stephen's brother, laughed, running through the gathered family as everyone talked and ate. Her cousin Mitch's wife sat on his lap with her arms wrapped around him. Henri and Marion danced—and Grandpa Louie and Louise were out there, too!—to an unfamiliar Doo Wop song as Uncle Danny placed his hand upon Wendy's tummy to feel his grandchild's movement within. All around Juliana was the dream she had always conjured—a big family, and in the center of it all sat one man looking frazzled by little Stephen fidgeting upon his lap.

Jack looked up and their eyes met through the crowd. They smiled affectionately at one another and her heart flipped. Yes, she had fallen for him. Yes, he was the *one*. Meeting him had been the real catalyst that completely changed her outlook for the future.

"What is it, Julie?"

"I have a family," she stated dreamily in reply to her great-aunt. "I've wanted this my whole life. I just can't believe that this is *my* family. I wish Dad could be here to be a part of it."

"Oh, he is honey, and so is my sister." Lizzy brushed the hair framing Juliana's face. "We're all so happy you're here."

"Me, too. I feel like I've finally found home."

"You have."

Lizzy wrapped her arm around Juliana's waist and held her close. Turning, they walked together, traversing a floral maze alternating from pergolas to trellises, stream to pond. When the stone pavers finally gave over to thick green grass, they arrived at her quiet refuge hidden from the cacophony of the world outside. A metal garden bistro set sat in the middle of the small clearing bordered by blossoming Sweet Williams. The wafting fragrance of honeysuckle and roses intermingling created a blissful aroma.

"Wow, this is beautiful, Aunt Lizzy. I feel like I'm in the Garden of Eden."

"It is paradise, isn't it? It's the one place where I feel completely and utterly at peace. No CNN and no telephone, just me and my thoughts and on Sundays with a newspaper or two. I have some of my best conversations here."

"Alone?"

Lizzy smiled softly, thinking how she had never been truly alone in this garden. "Alone with my memories."

She smiled thoughtfully. Like her annual dancing to her and Will's song, this garden was where heaven existed on those private, permissible moments of escape to 1942. Of late, it seemed that every day she found refuge here with her treasure box. Sunday visits to her tea garden had become daily ones and significantly, without any newspapers.

Juliana walked to a low-growing border planting of small, vibrant pink flowers and bent to inhale their fragrance. "They smell like cloves."

"Yes. I think of all the flowers in this area, the starry-flowered Sweet Williams are my favorite. I planted them because, in the language of flowers, they represent gallantry and your great-uncle was that. Those across from you are also from the Dianthus family. They're called First Love."

"So, is that your entire theme in this garden? A tribute of sorts?" *Sort of how I found the mantle in Primrose Cottage.*

"Yes. Every flower here means something. It's hard to find perennials to last the difficult northeast coastal winters but I painstakingly continue. Like that pitiful looking Gardenia." She sighed. "One day that baby is going to blossom for me."

"That's very optimistic of you."

"I'm determined to wear one in my hair." She motioned to the bistro set. "Let's sit and talk about you, sweetheart. Jack tells me that you work for *Allure* magazine and that you were considering writing an article about the romance between Will and me."

The women sat across from one another, when Juliana shifted uncomfortably. "I was but ... that's changed." She sighed. "Actually, the article was really an excuse to go and find you both so I could learn your story."

"Why was it so important for you to discover us?"

Juliana's eyes settled upon the effusive hot pink color of the Sweet William's displayed beyond where Lizzy sat. It wasn't that she was avoiding her aunt's gaze, but she couldn't help her mind roaming to the significance of the flower.

"Julie?"

"Right. Sorry. They're just so captivating. Passionate, really. The color is quite evocative and the white trim on each petal reminds me of a tender innocence which explodes into this burst of intense rapture."

Lizzy grinned. "That's exactly why I planted them."

"Well, that's why my curiosity was piqued by the photographs and the things I found in my great-uncle's footlocker. I felt that intense love between both of you from the moment I entered Primrose Cottage. I know it sounds weird, but it was as though the *house* wanted a happy ever after." She snorted. "I'm not too familiar with those. It's not as if I'm experienced in relationships. Heck, I never believed that I could be worthy of such a thing, or even, if intimate romance actually existed at all. But you two showed me that love ... deep, abiding love of true devotion can endure—even when apart. And now ..."

"And now?"

"I'm a believer. Absolutely. I'm willing to put myself out there."

"Because of my grandson."

Juliana blushed. "Yes, because of Jack. He's everything I wanted to find in a man. I have never before felt the way I do when I'm with him. He's different from the other guys I've dated, and he makes me feel as though I can do anything." Her voice grew more animated, more excited with each declaration of Jack's attributes. "He's kind and gentle, easy going, and patient. He took me sailing! We went to Alaska, and I flew in Uncle Will's floatplane! I went to Temple and afterward Jack and I cooked a meal together from one of the Dutch cookbooks at Primrose!"

"You went to Temple? With Jack?"

"Well, we stopped in together. I wanted to see what it was like. So we went to Temple Beth ... something ... not far from my house."

"Wow, that's unprecedented, Julie. Jack hasn't attended services or stepped foot in a synagogue since, probably his Bar Mitzvah."

"Well we went, and he seemed excited about it. He taught me about the Holy Ark and the Torah scrolls. I showed him the mezuzah at my house and the Kiddush cup. Did you know that my uncle was Jewish?"

Lizzy smiled. "Yes, I knew. It seems as though you affected Jack as much as he affected you. I do believe that my grandson is in love with you, you know."

"I know, and I think I'm in love with him, too. I just don't want to rush it."

"G-d willing, there won't be any need to rush your romance. Just don't wait too long, and be sure to speak your heart freely before something unexpected comes your way and it's too late."

"Is that what happened between you and Uncle Will? He told me that you stopped writing him. Was it your father who separated you?"

Lizzy's eyes drifted to the barren Gardenia bush. "No. Frederick didn't know that we still corresponded. He had nothing to do with our separation." She sighed and held Juliana's gaze. "You see, I was led to believe him dead."

"Because he was in a POW camp for two years?"

The palm of Lizzy's hand smoothed across her furrowed brow, sliding down to hover over her mouth. "I didn't know that he was a prisoner of war. That must have happened afterwards. After our correspondence ended. Oh dear. He never said so in ..."

Try as Lizzy might, she was having a difficult time concealing her emotions. Her eyes pricked with tears at the thought of his wartime experience and it near broke her heart to think of him in captivity, in such horrible conditions after all he had been through, all the unnecessary heartache that had preceded it.

Her thoughts trailed and silence ensued for what felt like many long minutes as she reeled in her distress. Finally, she forced a smile. "Well, so what's this gift you have for me?"

"Oh, I almost forgot!" Juliana reached into her backpack, removing the Tiffany blue box. "These are yours. Well actually, they were my uncles. You sent them to him; they're your letters. I would have given them to him directly, and I do think he would have been happy to have them again, but I figured you would want to give them to him personally. You know ... when you see him in Paris."

Lizzy's tentative fingers lifted the lid to reveal the stack neatly tied with the green bow. "Oh my. He saved these." Overwhelmed, her eyes completely filled with tears. Damn if this conversation wasn't getting the best of her resolve to not cry over the past and only look forward to the joy waiting for Ducky and her in the future. "Was, was this his bow?" *He was always such a romantic.*

"Yeah. That's just how I found them in the bottom of his military trunk along with all your photographs in the attic."

A small smile formed on Lizzy's lips when she slid the first letter out of the beribboned packet. She read the first page and chuckled lightly. "I remember writing this to him. I was utterly devastated thinking him indifferent to me after our first meeting at Meercrest's Memorial Day lawn party. He was quite a catch in his uniform, very gentlemanly, and I was a little too full of myself!"

"He's still quite a catch. He's very handsome and still a gentleman— single, too. Can I ask you something personal?"

Holding the letters up, Lizzy said, "Of course. You know most of it already. Go for it."

"Do you think it is better to have loved and lost, than to never have loved at all?"

"Well, that's a very black and white question. Of course, the regret I have is that we had to end at all, but we did, and I would never take away a single moment or memory that we made together or the memories I made with my husband, either. If Will and I had *never* loved, then my life would have developed into nothing, and who says that a new love can't take the place of an ended one or ..." She chuckled. "... or that a love *lost* can't rekindle again. I've always been an optimist and the one time I wasn't, I felt it backed me into a corner. I made the wrong decision when I doubted.

"You'll see as you mature, Julie, there are all kinds of love that come and go, grow and fade, but all for a purpose and at their rightful time. I truly, truly believe that my time with your great-uncle has come—now. So what did appear as a love lost, wasn't really lost at all. It just got waylaid until the best time."

"That's the optimist in you. I feel the same way and that's why I'm okay with my grandfather and Louise."

"I'm glad you see that. They seem happy and I know Lillian, of all people, wouldn't object to his finding a companion, someone to love and care for him. I hope I answered your question."

"You did." Juliana reached into her bag again and removed the plastic sleeve that held the charred remains of Lizzy's letter to William. She hesitantly held it back for a moment, unsure how to deliver it. "Um, there's also this. I found it at Primrose Cottage when I first moved in. I've never shown or ever mentioned this to Jack, and I'll continue to hold, what I assume happened, in confidence." She slid the letter toward Lizzy.

Lizzy hesitantly picked it up and began to read, pursing her lips together to keep from biting her lower one. Her entire body froze at the moment she recognized the burned letter. She vividly remembered that night and her heartache when she penned those words. Only a fragment remained, attesting to Will's desperate distraught and his decision to burn her sentiment, her good-bye. He had attempted to destroy the tangible proof of their incredible final night together, and in essence, all vestiges of their extraordinary seven months together.

A tear dropped, and then another. Her lips tightened, straining to contain the inner agony, imagining his pain once again. She swiped at her cheek. "I swore I wouldn't cry anymore, but I just can't help it. I'm sorry."

"It's okay. I understand. I'm the one who should be sorry. I didn't mean to upset you. It's just, this is the letter that began it all. It's why I had to find you."

Closing her eyes, Lizzy nodded. She took a deep breath. "It's the reason for my flower choices, the First Loves and the Sweet Williams—just as you realized. They remind me of that night following your father's christening. It was the last time I saw your uncle. Leaving him was the second hardest decision I ever had to make. Thank you for returning this to me, and thank you for not sharing it with Jack."

A delicate hand reached across to connect with Lizzy's own that remained resting upon the stack of letters. "I'll take that secret to the grave."

"I know you will, Julie. I'm indebted to you for bringing us all together and for healing our family, for unknowingly making us face our demons and share our secrets. We've kept them far too long."

Lizzy contemplated their clasped hands resting upon the letters, wishing she could impart every bit of wisdom and knowledge she had into the smooth youthful ones. Feeling suddenly older than usual she said, "Don't let Jack get away. He's such a good man."

"I have no intentions of letting him go now that I've found him—he's quite a dreamboat!"

They both broke out into a fit of laughter as Lizzy held the fragile letter to her heart, looking ahead to the future and counting down the days until she could see her Ducky.

Forty

Peace Brother!
July 14, 1992

T he Hotel Turenne was situated on the Right Bank in the historic and busy Marais section of Paris, just blocks from the famous Place des Voges. Narrow streets boasted fine eateries and local delis with the ethnic flavors of both Ashkenazi and, in the last twenty years, Sephardic Jews. The neighborhood bordered the Pletzl, that little section dominated by the Jewish community that had maintained its heritage even after WWII.

Since Will's last visit twelve years earlier, the area had seen many changes in the subtle movement toward "gentrification" and was now considered a growing area of affluence. Once considered poor, now its real estate was highly sought after.

He stood overlooking the small balcony of his hotel suite, scanning down at the busy streets of the Pletzl aglow with restaurant and shop lights. He could easily surmise that the old world and tradition would eventually come to blows with the inevitable encroachment of modernization where Jewish butchers and tailors would be replaced by perhaps a McDonalds or even an insulting Hugo Boss shop.

Will sipped his brandy, attempting to calm his nerves. Knowing that Lizzy was in this very hotel had caused him to hide in his room, requesting that room service deliver his dinner tonight. Unfortunately, his trademark rumination over the prior two weeks turned out to be a bad decision. It only fueled his anger. There was no logical mediation or quiet thoughtful study of the facts on the dossier. Worse yet, the de Havilland floatplane still sat oil-less at the dock and a small, newly discovered leak in the roof went entirely ignored. These past two weeks only seemed to infuriate him. Fuck, his blood pressure raised so high he had to go see his physician last Tuesday when the pulsing headache hadn't tempered in over three days. Six times he had made to pick up the telephone—he had Lizzy's number. Gardner had included it in the packet. Six times he yelled at the phone instead. "Damn you, Lizzy! You should have told me!" "What were you thinking?" "I've missed a lifetime!"

He placed the rocks glass on the edge of the balcony and stared out into the Parisian evening sky. The view was spectacular and just like he'd done in 1980, he wished he was here under other circumstances; not for a confrontation but for his enjoyment. They had, long ago, dreamed of traveling together to Paris, Rome, the gondola in Venice under the Bridge of Sighs where he would kiss her at sunset as the bells of St Mark's Campanile tolled—the promise of eternal love.

He wondered what the next few days would bring and who would contact him first: Jack, Juliana, or the woman herself. She had some explaining to do, and he surmised that was the reason for his trip here.

A knock on his door sounded, and he picked up his drink, piqued at who the hell would be visiting him at this hour. A sudden surge of fear coursed through him thinking it could be Lizzy.

"Coming."

Will looked through the door's peephole and his hand went to his heart. He took a step backward and sucked in a deep breath, closing his eyes. "Ho ... ly ... shit."

A turn of the knob and a swing to the door revealed his brother standing at the threshold, grinning like a Cheshire cat.

"Well, well, well. If it isn't Mr. I Ran Away From Life And Moved To Alaska himself."

"And if it isn't Mr. I'm The One Responsible For Causing My Brother To Run Away From Life."

"Can I come in?"

"Sure. You're probably here to collect your two dollars om 1942. I never figured you for a cheapskate, keeping a tally all these years. I refuse to pay interest but I'll pay for inflation, even though your Yankees still suck."

"They're playing better than your lame Dodgers who can't field for shit. 'Outfield of Dreams' my ass. Darryl Strawberry should have remained with the Mets."

Will walked to his wallet resting beside the television and removed a twenty, holding it out to Louie. "I expect change."

"And I expect you to listen to your older brother. I don't want your money. I want your forgiveness."

Will reluctantly pocketed the bill but said nothing after Lou turned away to walk to the bar service cart.

Louie poured himself a scotch then sat in one of the two armchairs. After placing the drink down on the end table, he wiped his brow and reached into his breast pocket. "Do you mind if I smoke?"

"Yes, I mind. It'll kill ya'. Give you lung cancer."

"So you *do* care."

Will stepped back and sat on the edge of the bed facing Louie. "I care. Just because we're estranged and no longer thick as thieves doesn't mean I don't love you. You're still my brother."

"Thanks for the flowers for Lillian and Gordon."

"You're welcome. I was sorry to hear of their untimely passing. I'm sorry for your loss."

"How did you know?"

"Al Gardner. Did you think my Army buddy wouldn't remain my lawyer after I left town?"

"I suppose I did. I didn't think you'd need a lawyer, let alone one who had only just passed the bar. Well, you've had the advantage then. Al never told us anything of you. Do you mind telling me where you've been since 1950?"

"All over the world really, putting my piloting skills to use, flying medical transport. It began in Holland actually, bringing the displaced to Israel, and then I settled in Tel Aviv, married briefly, then divorced, before I finally settled in Alaska. I'm technically retired but I still fly medical and organ transport for charity only."

"Israel and a marriage, huh? That's a surprise. You should have written— more than the tri-annual greeting card."

"I meant to write, even telephone, but the longer I put it off, the harder it became. Before I knew it, decades had slipped by." Will shrugged uncomfortably, forcing the confrontation to continue.

"Enough of that ... you have my ear, Lou. You know what I hold you accountable for. I don't think I need to state my case again, but I wonder what else you've kept secret these forty years."

Will watched his brother's gnarled, arthritic hand grip around the glass, then take a long draught. Clearly, this was hard for Louie. Apologies always were.

"I didn't know that she would be at the christening, but I did know she had married. My wife never explained to me why Lizzy married John, but I have my suspicions that only Lizzy can confirm. That's not my business. My business today is to heal the wound I inflicted upon you."

"I'm listening."

"Look, Will, my wife chose a path of silence concerning all things Renner and that included keeping the confidences of her sisters—even from me. But yes, I did know that Lizzy married John. They both came to the hospital after Lil gave birth to Gordon. You remember ... my girl had complications, lost a lot of blood, and was told that she couldn't have other children. John had dropped Lizzy off at the Methodist Hospital, and then left with their two little ones. It was only then that I found out Lizzy was married—to John no less. I had been summarily shunned from the baby ward. And remember? I hung out with you and Dad, crying on both your shoulders back in Flatbush. Turned out Lizzy put up quite a fight with the nurses and she managed to remain beside Lillian day and night till the immediate crisis was over."

Will nodded. "That was very Lizzy-like. She was very sensitive and devoted to her sisters. Get her mad—and she was a sight to behold."

"The three sisters remained close through the years, although Lil hardly saw them. They corresponded and spoke on the phone. As you know, my girl liked her life in Park Slope, and didn't really want to leave, stating that she had traveled enough during the war. But I knew the truth even if she didn't want to discuss it—the family was blacklisted, the name defiled, their legacy destroyed. She wanted to keep us far away from anything remotely connected to her father."

Will could relate to Lillian's running away and hiding out from the pain and the ugly truths, separating herself even from those she loved. He nodded. "What is it that you suspect about why Lizzy married Robertsen?"

"I suspect she found herself in a position in 1943 where she had only one choice before her and she took it."

"Annette?"

Louie's eyes widened, and he promptly replied, "I didn't say that."

"Surely you know something more. Unless, of course, you're determined to keep more secrets from me."

"I don't *know* anything. I only have my own supposition, which could be totally wrong. You seem to have some information of your own."

"Yes."

"Look, what I *do know* is that Lizzy wants to see you. I know that her family is as loving and warm and welcoming as you and I could have hoped for—hoped to be a part of. I know that all of her children are incredible individuals, and one in particular has a son who could be your twin. He's even a pilot."

"I have a grandson?"

"I'm not saying that, but if that *is* the case, then you have three grandsons, all good men.

Standing, Will ran his hand through his hair and walked to the balcony doors.

"I also know that what Pistol has done with her life was for *you*. She told me that she even started a foundation in your honor. She friggin' even built a Holocaust museum where she featured my Lillian's story of courage."

"I know about the foundation. And about the museum," Will said, turning his back to his brother. His eyes clouded with tears. G-d this hurt. All of it. He was too damn old to feel this pain after so long a time. He was too damn old to hold this grudge against Louie. Anger at both of them had traveled with him throughout his life and now he had to give it up. *Three grandsons?* Yes, he wanted peace, and he hoped that Paris was the place to find it. Moreover, he wanted a family with Lizzy and he needed his brother's well wishes, too.

"Lou, for years we had surmised about Grandfather and *Tante's* fate in this city, and I swore that I would never forget. To me, by not raising Gordon in the Jewish faith you betrayed that very notion, dishonoring their memory. I understood that you were married to a Christian, but to never even share your Judaism with Gordon and later Juliana, I felt was reprehensible, particularly after 1980 when I had written you confirming their murders in Auschwitz. Now here you sit confirming to me that the woman I loved did more for the preservation of our heritage than even you, my own blood— their blood. I have learned all she has done. Her commitment astounds me."

From behind him, he heard the clink of Louie's glass upon the end table. "War changed you Will but it also changed Lizzy and me. We three all emerged from the ashes—one seeking atonement, the other disbelieving in the presence of G-d, and you more grounded and rooted in faith. Her penitence spanned five decades. Mine only just began when I removed my mezuzah from its hiding place three weeks ago. Now I ask you, after asking G-d, please forgive me for the role I played in keeping secrets from you and for turning my back on our Judaism as an adult as well as not honoring the memory of our mother, Aunt Estella, and Grandfather."

Will turned to see his brother standing directly behind him. Gone was the cocky, hardboiled Marine with the shit-eating grin and standing in his place was an older, humbled man. So was he.

He sighed. "I forgive you," holding out his hand to shake, just as they did in Pennsylvania Station all those many years ago, Louie once again tugging on the extended arm to pull his brother into him. Embracing in a strong bear hug, both had unexpected, yet welcome, tears running down their faces.

"I love you, Vaporhead," Louie said.

"Soppy Jarhead," Will replied stepping back from their embrace. "I love you, too."

They laughed and Will tentatively asked, "How are you feeling? Juliana tells me that you had some difficulty ... memories and things."

"My little jewel is a worry wart. I'm fine. Lately I feel like a young bull again."

"Because of the new woman in your life? I understand that you two were discovered in a compromising position one morning."

"I told you once before, I do not kiss and tell, but apparently my granddaughter isn't above telling my secrets. Well, if you insist on knowing—Louise has a pair of knockers on her that put Raquel Welch to shame. Va-va-voom!"

"You're such a wolf."

"Yes I am, Brother, but once before a good woman put an end to my doll dizzy ways, and so has Louise. I care for her, and we're moving in together in the fall."

"At that old age home you're living in?"

"No, too many old flames living there. We're going to move up to Gordon's place on the Upper East Side. Juliana doesn't want it, so I told her that I'd trade her my remaining shares in DeVries Diamond for the condo. She likes Brooklyn and wants to stay there. I always knew she was a Brooklyn girl at heart."

"She *is* a jewel, Lou. You're a lucky man to have such a granddaughter. She's smart, too, but if I can only convince her to ditch the Yankees and start rooting for the Dodgers then I'll consider her brilliant."

"That will never happen! I was thinking of encouraging her to move down to Park Slope, out of Primrose Cottage now that you're coming home."

"I didn't say I was coming home."

Louie walked to the door, his masterful smirk back in place. "We'll see what Lizzy has to say about that. She's single, you know."

"I know."

"Do you also know that Pistol's a diehard Giants fan?"

Will chuckled. "She always was, and don't think you're going to try to butter me up toward her by talking baseball. I'm madder than blazes at Lizzy and have no intention of letting her off so easily, no matter what she's accomplished in her life."

"Yeah well, if I were you, I'd get over it. Don't spend too much time thinking about how you're going to handle this 'Annette' issue or you'll miss out on a good thing. The past is the past. You've got to look ahead, old man. I'll see you in the morning for brunch at ten. We have someplace important to be at two. Wear a suit and don't be late."

He left Will standing in the middle of his suite nodding his head. It was as though only yesterday his brother had said, "Write the girl." Smiling, he thought *I'll see her tomorrow.*

****

Lizzy's dinner with Henri, Marion, Annette, Jack, and Juliana was a complete gastronomic overindulgence, which lasted three hours followed by a walk along the Seine on the Rive Droite. Their return to the boutique hotel was after midnight, and although she was tired, the effects of jet lag hadn't kicked in yet. Not to mention, she was too wound up knowing that she'd be seeing and, hopefully, talking to Will tomorrow. Her long-awaited reunion would be forthcoming, and she struggled to conceal her anxiety to her family. Apart from Louie, only Jack and Juliana knew what lie ahead, and even they all thought she and Will were merely wartime sweethearts, separated for some unknown reason.

Further, her forty-year quest was about to end with the return of the ill-gotten Monet and Degas masterpieces to their rightful families. Furthermore, her personal commitment to locate and reinstate the Henry Avercamp was also about to come to fruition once she placed it into Louie's hands—with Will as witness to a small restoration of the DeVries/Martel legacy.

Chattering and laughing, the Robertsen family entered the empty lobby where only a solitary night clerk manned the front desk. Lizzy momentarily reflected how Louie and his lady were missed at dinner but she knew her brother-in-law had his own reunion to attend tonight, and she wondered how it had gone between the estranged brothers.

Lizzy kissed Annette's cheek. "Good night, darling. I'll see you tomorrow at eight for a morning run along the river?"

"Yes. If you insist. I can't believe I'm here ... in Paris ... with you, and I can't believe we found the rightful families of the paintings."

"It's going to be a beautiful ceremony. I'm sure of it. It's important that you're here, not just for the paintings, but for a lot of reasons. Thank you for joining us last minute."

Annette laughed. "Are you kidding? Where else would I be?—apart from the Social Security Office to change my name back to Robertsen? That bastard always promised to take me to Paris. Instead he took his twenty-five year old secretary. It seems fitting that I should visit after the divorce has been settled." She kissed Lizzy's cheek. "This is the best birthday gift you could have given me. I love you, Mom."

Her mother cupped a hand upon her daughter's cheek and jaw. "And I love you ... more than you could ever know."

"Thanks for letting me move back to Evermore. I promise I'll get on my feet, find my own place once the dust settles, and look for a job."

"Oh, sweetheart, stay as long as you like. It's your home, and Lord knows I love your company."

Still chattering, the family moved down the hall, stopping near the double-doored entrance of the cocktail lounge beside the elevator bank. They continued to say their good nights, kissing and making plans to meet for breakfast the next morning.

Will sat at the bar, nursing a brandy, only his profile visible to the noisy group. Feeling like a curmudgeon, he couldn't help the disapproval he felt at the rude Americans who obviously had no regard for either the hour or the other patrons.

Someone must have made a joke.

A devilish, familiar peal of laughter hearkened toward him, as if soaring on Zephyr's wings and piercing his soul.

His back stiffened as an anxious feeling overcame him. He was trapped, unable to leave the room. Unsure of whether to move or remain paralyzed in his seat, he hoped she hadn't seen him. As the only patron in the lounge, he knew he stuck out like a sore thumb. Even the bartender had disappeared into the kitchen. Attempting to shield himself, Will swiveled on his stool, looked down at his drink, and prayed that Lizzy would get onto the lift.

Nondescript piano music played low from the overhead sound system, failing to soothe his sudden nerves as he attempted to draw a deep breath. Although curious to see the beauty that stole his heart as a young man, he wasn't ready to see her. In truth, he was a little drunk—no, a lot drunk. Unexpectedly seeing Louie and clearing the air of forty years separation had left him raw. Fine French brandy was a most amenable friend tonight.

Everyone piled into the elevator with the exception of Lizzy. She stood ramrod, her attention diverted into the dimly lit lounge. Her heart stopped. The moment had arrived.

"Mom, are you coming up?" asked Henri.

"Um, no. You kids go ahead. I think I'll have a nightcap."

"I'll stay with you," said Jack.

"No, dear. You and Julie get a good night's sleep. We have a big day tomorrow." Her eyes drew back to the lone figure sitting at the bar. "I'd like to be alone tonight." She smiled wistfully when the elevator doors closed on her family.

For a moment, Lizzy stood at the entry to the lounge with her heart, now shocked back to life, hammering violently. She smoothed her hair.

Across the distance, she admired the contour of Will's fine physique. Even in the subdued lighting, she observed that he wore blue jeans and his strong expanse of broad shoulders were draped in an aqua polo shirt. The unfamiliar salt and pepper curls at his nape, brushing against his collar, as well as, the memorable angle of his jaw, which she had once kissed many times, captured her rapt attention. She felt both elated and dreadful, desperate to run to him while simultaneously fearful, wanting to bolt in the other direction.

Will didn't see her approach or hear her tentative footsteps over the plush red carpet. However, he *felt* her energy as she drew nearer. In anticipation, his lips formed a tense line and his hand clutched tighter around the rounded glass goblet. He stared at the amber liquor within.

Lizzy's delicate hand gently pressed upon his shoulder; the weight felt so comforting, as calming as coming home. He gazed up into the mirrored wall facing them. Between the colorful, half-filled bottles, their eyes locked in the reflection, and five long decades disappeared.

Lizzy was a vision, as exotic and captivating as he remembered. She was twenty again, and he, only twenty-one. Spellbound, he reveled in the sparkle of her green eyes and those familiar twisting plump, peachy lips when her breathy voice spoke the adored greeting he hadn't heard since truly, a young man.

"Hi Ducky."

Instinct propelled his hand to clasp hers upon his shoulder. Their two broken hearts sparked in a renewed connection; the fissure between them dissipated and began to meld into the one heart they shared.

He wanted to be mad, but his Pistol always had a way of rendering him illogical. Their eyes continued to envelop each other in wordless wonderment.

Will could see in the mirror how her lip trembled and then she bit it. That alone was nearly his undoing, and he closed his eyes, caught up in the softness of her fingers thread through with his. He fought the innate need to pull her into his arms.

It was too much to bear and just like that night in '49, he thought it an intoxicating dream or a drunken delusion. His eyes snapped open, and he twisted her fingers in his. His face darkened, his brow furrowing, the set of his lips forming into an angry thin line.

Lizzy saw the immediate change in his countenance, how he transformed from anxiety to relief, then almost portrayed his joy at seeing her, but this last evolution was the emotion she had dreaded—animosity. It was palpable when he swiveled on his stool to finally face her, only to abruptly release her hand as though it was tainted.

"*Mrs.* Robertsen," he said.

"I'm glad you came, Will. I knew you would. I knew you couldn't keep away forever." She resisted the urge to reach out to him again, to touch the errant lock of hair at his forehead. "You ... you look well."

"So do you. You haven't changed at all."

"I'm older. I hope wiser. Definitely tamer." With a slight tremble, her hand defied resistance and she smoothed the wave. "I've never seen your hair so long. It becomes you."

His pulse throbbed in his temples as the acrimonious words tumbled from his lips. "Why am I here?"

Lizzy looked around the empty room, her eyes settling on the front desk clerk through the open double doors. "I don't think this is the time or place, but we have to talk. There are things that I need to tell you. Important things that you need to know."

He rose to his full height, mere inches from her, towering over her in an attempt to intimidate as she gazed up with those captivating eyes of hers. They stood face to face for the first time in four decades. He looked down at her lovely chin raised in defiance. Many times before he had kissed that perfect chin, but he wouldn't do so tonight. Roughly, his hand clasped over her bicep and barely containing his resentment he said, "Well then let's go to my room to talk, shall we?"

"No … no … not tonight. Not like this. You need a clear head for the things we need to address and you've been drinking."

"Did you expect to find me sober, if you ever intended to find me at all? Besides you're well-trained in dealing with drunks."

"That was callous, Will." She removed his hand from her arm.

She could feel his warm breath flowing down upon her. She could smell the brandy as if she had drunk it herself. It took everything in her power not to embrace him to calm the storm brewing within him, so clearly evident in his darkening eyes and set of his jaw.

"No, I'll tell you what was callous, Lizzy. I was young and foolish to give you my trust and my heart. You dumped me when I needed you most, without even the courtesy of a letter. I wrote you for months and you never even replied. It was callous to let me worry about you in *that* house with *that* father of yours. What was callous was your marrying the very man you knew I was jealous of, as soon as I left for England. What was hatefully callous was your using me, years later, to satisfy a lonely housewife's craving, leaving me only a tear-stained letter, as if you had really cared. Yet you never came back, never contacted me. Dammit, Lizzy, you never tried to find me!"

She choked on her regrets. "Is that why you left? Because you wanted me to follow you? To find you? Oh, G-d. Will, I couldn't have done that."

Her hand reached out to touch him, but he stepped away lest they had a repeat of their torrid one night affair. That was all it had taken that night— her simple touch. He had practiced ad infinitum what he needed to say to her at *this* reunion, and he would not be swayed from his course.

Lizzy begged, "Please, Will. If you're insistent on discussing this tonight, then let's go to your room and not have this conversation out here. Please, let's discuss this rationally, soberly. I promise, I'll tell you everything about what happened. I told you then, I had thought you were dead. It wasn't my fault."

"Then whose fault was it, huh? Was it mine? Did I deserve to be treated that way? You were nothing but a spoiled debutante who lied and betrayed me. You ruined me for every woman after you."

He mumbled under his breath, abruptly moving away from her shocked expression. "What does it matter? It was fifty years ago. You can keep your secrets."

"Secrets?"

Will snapped at her, his eyes flashed, boring into hers. "Yes, secrets!"

Lizzy broke from his intense condemnation. Her voice lowered with anger. "You're drunk, and I refuse to air those secrets in the middle of a cocktail lounge. If you can sober up and want answers, then you will follow me to your room." She pivoted to walk away.

"How do you know what room I'm in?"

Halting in her tracks, she turned back, facing him with eyes blazing with fire and passion. She placed an indignant hand upon her hip and retorted. "Because I arranged for it! You're here as my guest. You're here because after all these years, I've never stopped loving you. And you came because you have never stopped loving me! *This* is our time, Will, and I'm tired of life slipping away before we can be together as we were always meant to be. I've waited too damn long for this opportunity!"

Turning back on her heel, Lizzy stormed to the elevator, clutching her purse. She pressed the up button non-stop in her frustration, fighting the tears and praying that he would have the sense to follow her.

The doors slid open, and she stepped into the empty lift.

As they began to close, Will thrust his fisted hand through the narrow opening, jolting her and the doors back open. He casually walked in as though he didn't have a care in the world and stood beside her, his arms folded across his chest.

"Fine, Mrs. Robertsen. We'll discuss this in my room, but I assure you the outcome will be entirely different than it was the last time I was alone with you."

"I have no doubt, William."

"William?" He chuckled sardonically. "What happened to Ducky?"

"Ducky didn't drink, and even if he did, he'd never talk to me like you just have. He was a gentleman."

"*Ducky* learned to drink after the Pistol shot him down, crashing and burning behind enemy lines. Two years in a POW camp introduced me to all sorts of ungentlemanly things I never did before. You talk about being older and wiser, well … you're not the only one."

They stood side-by-side only inches apart listening to the ding of the elevator as it climbed to reach the upper floor suites. Will's arms continued to posture defensively across his broad chest, and Lizzy stood straight, her arms, mimicking his in defiant obstinacy. The strain between them was palpable.

The elevator stopped on the third floor and the doors opened. Will and Lizzy further separated to make room for the bellman and his cart laden with dirty food trays from his midnight floor collection.

"*Bonsoir*," he said, intruding between them into the thick tension.

"Good evening," they replied simultaneously. Their eyes momentarily met one another's, then quickly diverted forward to the closing doors. The awkward verbal silence and annoying elevator music increased their anxiety.

Again, the elevator lurched and the doors opened onto the fourth floor. The noisy cart rattled out of the lift as the bellman departed with an *"Au revoir."*

Lizzy dropped her arms and began to clutch the purse draped over her shoulder, looking straight ahead at Will's reflection in the gold-toned elevator doors as they closed. His face was set in stone, so similar to their very first meeting at Meercrest after she ran him off the road. *Oh G-d, those muddy trousers. He was such a stick in the mud back then. He still is!*

A giggle bubbled up from her lips, quickly turning to a small laugh that she tried to suppress with pursed lips, failing miserably until she burst. Folding her arms over her middle, she howled with raucous belly laughter.

"What's so funny?" he stoically asked, further rankled that this meeting was not going as planned *at all*.

Lizzy didn't answer, just continued to torment him with that addictive sound she emitted. He couldn't help but to smirk at it. *Damn!* She wasn't even *trying* to break him, yet she was doing just that. He knew she would be the death of him, so he put into place that impenetrable vacant expression honed as a guest of the Luftwaffe in Germany. He was mad—yes, mad, and this woman who lied to him was not going to break his reserve! He stood up to fucking Nazis, for Christ sake! *But so, too, had she.*

The elevator lurched for the last time on the top floor and the doors slid open. With determined footsteps, Lizzy led the way down the hall to his room. He lingered, holding back with languid steps behind her, refusing to allow her the upper hand even in his progress toward their confrontation. This would be on his terms, not hers! *She'll wait for* me.

Lizzy could almost feel his burning stare at her derriere. He might have been older now but with a physique like his, she was sure that urge hadn't died, but *that* could not be foremost on her mind.

She neared the room then finally his long legs brought him to stand right behind her.

Will's arm reached around her waist to open the door, allowing her to enter before him so that he could once again inhale her fragrance, a scent he was unfamiliar with, but it beguiled him nonetheless. The latent wolf was becoming untamed from the brandy and her own intoxicant until he forced himself to focus on the source of his anger. He wanted answers about her daughter.

The stocked bar service in the sitting area caused Lizzy to walk across the room until she stood between Will and it, placing her purse on the glass top.

Noting her passive aggressive maneuver, a snicker escaped his lips and he instead went to the balcony, opening the doors. "It's warm in here."

"Is it? I think it's rather chilly."

"A drink will warm you then."

"No thank you. You've had enough for both of us."

Will sat down on the bed before her, his hungry eyes raking up her slender, fit form. Her long legs encased in sheer nylon vividly recalled the painted image on the PPL. He couldn't help the softening of his demeanor with a tender compliment. "You really look great, Lizzy."

"Thank you. I feel great. You look great, too."

"Thanks. I try to keep fit."

As quickly as they had reverted back to the Pistol and Ducky of affectionate admiration and innocent love, Lizzy's anxiety re-emerged for the conversation that lie ahead.

She paced before him, wringing her hands, and he could see her struggle, the furrowing of her brow, her halting footsteps, then the resumption of her constrained repetitive path. Finally she said, "It didn't happen the way you think it did. None of it. Not even my coming to you that rainy night."

"How was it then? I'm all ears. I'm not so old that my memory is shot."

"Hmm. Well you don't have the facts."

"Gee, there's a fuckin' surprise."

Lizzy stamped her foot and petulantly placed a hand on her hip. "Stop it, William!"

He swept his hand in invitation for her to continue. "Then enlighten me, Mrs. Robertsen."

"I don't know where to start." She began to pace again, twisting her fingers together. "After Christmas of '42, I never received a single one of your letters ... until two weeks ago when my sister Kitty gave them to me ... and you never received any of mine because she kept those as well."

"Kitty?"

"Yes, my sister. The one who had polio. Don't you remember? Kitty was in the wheelchair?"

"Of course I remember. I remember *everything*."

Lizzy stopped and turned to face him, impertinently accusing, "Apparently you don't because you forgot the part where I said, 'Until the end of life's story,' didn't you?"

"In case you forgot ... you married someone else."

She couldn't argue with that, but ignored it. "I only *just* listened to the Letter on a Record that you sent me from England. I didn't know. I never knew that you had proposed to me. I was never *given* the record. Had I known then, it would have changed everything! Kitty took all of our letters and even those to and from your mother and Louie."

"What are you saying?"

"I'm saying that if *you* had received *my* letters then you would have learned—"

Will abruptly stood, jolting her, and cutting off her sentence. He stormed to the balcony doors, running his hand through his hair, digesting her statement with his stunned silence. With that one explanation, everything he had come to assume had summarily been shot down. With startling awareness, he realized that his anger all these long, long years had been misdirected. *This cannot be.*

Finally, he took three forceful strides to her and suddenly grabbed her shoulders. "Say that again."

"It was Kitty. She took our letters. I've only just read them, Will. I have never cried so much, with so much regret, in my life."

"Why did she do that? Why did she deliberately separate us!"

"It's complicated."

Will shook her. "What's complicated? Tell me!"

"Stop it, Will. Give me a minute. This is difficult."

"You owe me answers, Lizzy!"

She couldn't help the sudden burst of tears that began. "She wanted me to marry John. She believed that if I thought you dead I would marry him ... and I did. It was a marriage of convenience but also of necessity for several reasons."

Will dropped his hold upon her and bowed his head with a deep expulsion of air, the smell of brandy nearly toppling her. "Because you were pregnant."

Lizzy's eyes widened as she took a step back, her hand flying to her heart in utter shock.

"You ... you knew?" she gasped.

All this time, her conscience had been tormented over keeping Annette a secret from him and here he says that he has known and stayed away. Stunned, her mouth gaped. "How? For how long?"

He stepped back from her further, his face darkening, his lip sneering. "That's irrelevant."

"It's not irrelevant, Will! How long have you known?"

"Not long enough! Jesus, Lizzy, I had a child! I'm a father! I'm a grandfather! Why didn't *you* tell me?"

"I did tell you in the letters and then I meant to following the christening ... but I couldn't ... I chickened out ... I was married."

"Oh and of course, John couldn't wait to get into your bed and assume my rightful role as father, lover, and husband! He wasn't about to let me steal you *both* from him—like he had done to me!"

In fury, Lizzy stepped back, recoiling from him. "How dare you! You will *never* disparage John. He saved your child!" She took another step back. "You're not the man I knew. The man I knew would be grateful that someone such as John Robertsen raised your little girl with love and tenderness, cared for her in your honor, following your *assumed* death as if she were his own. Cared for me! *He* gave us refuge and security when the world around us collapsed! He was there to pick up the pieces following my almost nervous breakdown—I thought you were dead, and I discovered who my father really was. He was there to wipe Annette's nose and sit up with her when she had the croup, holding her for hours in the steaming bathroom when I couldn't do anything for her! *He* was there!"

"I never had the chance to be!" Will shouted.

"And that was *not* my fault!"

"You loved him! Didn't you?"

"Yes, I loved John! He was my husband for forty years!"

Will's pitiful drunkenness and her rage in defense of that man plummeted down into his long-wounded, young heart. He lowered his voice. "But you were supposed to love only me."

Lizzy seethed but sighed; her heart was moved to pity, but not clemency—not with him being this drunk. Her voice softened, the tears now rolling freely down her cheeks as her voice trembled. "Oh, Will. I loved you differently. I loved you from my soul, in my blood, and with every breath I took. I lived my life as nobly as you expected me to and I did it all for you. I loved you through every action in my life."

Lizzy walked to the door that connected to the next room and removed her hotel key from her purse. She turned back to him. "For forty-three years I have regretted and fought with my guilt from not telling you about your daughter, but we will only continue this conversation when you're sober. And then you can apologize for your unkindness to John. I hope that you'll show me that you are still the man I always dreamed you were, not this stranger standing before me. I had hoped there was some Ducky left in you, but perhaps that was the foolish romantic in me. I have hoped and prayed that you would be able to understand and forgive."

A turn of the key opened the connecting door to her suite beside his, and she disappeared, pulling it tightly closed from the other side, but optimistically leaving it unlocked.

He fought the urge to go after her.

Forty-One

Long Ago and Far Away
July 15, 1992

I n the course of his life, Will had probably experienced worse nights, but not by a wide margin. Through the sleepless night, he had lain in the dark, staring at the ceiling, finding himself reaching upward several times, just to touch the adjoining wall that separated him from Lizzy. He was sure, as hotels went, her headboard was mirroring his on the other side, and he wondered if she was too angered not to do the same as he—lifting her delicate hand to press against the intervening wall during the night. Perhaps their palms had met.

He wondered how their argument had grown so out of control so fast and how did it end up that *he* was the one on the receiving end of her sharp tongue and raised voice. Where was *his* wrong doing? He had considered himself blameless ... up until the point where he insulted John ... the man who had raised his child as he knew he, himself, would have, with love.

Now, with the sun rising, Will watched from the balcony as the worn-with-age cobblestones of the Pletzl came to life awakening the surrounding community. It was a radiant morning, and he felt strangely liberated having gotten the anger off his chest that he had carried for so long. It hadn't been his intention to wound her, just tell her the damage she'd done, but the drink got the better of him, as evidenced by his splitting headache and the regrettable fact that she was on the opposite side of the wall, not in his room—not in his bed—not in his arms.

He'd have to examine the intense surge of hatred he was feeling toward Lizzy's sister, then further, acknowledge and accept that whatever was done was done. Unforgiveness was nasty business. He knew acutely how it could eat up a person, but today was not the day to address the woman who had betrayed them.

Making this right between Lizzy and himself was his sole mission for today. Hell, it would be his mission for the rest of his life. Wherever Louie was taking him this afternoon would have to wait. The love he had in his heart for Lizzy demanded that he hear her entire story until he'd heard it all and not condemn her for keeping Annette a secret from him. They couldn't go back in time, only forward. Jack, Juliana, and Louie were absolutely correct in that respect.

He sighed, thinking of Juliana and the thanks he owed her. She did what he never could find the guts to do. It had taken fifty years of pondering to finally decide to telephone, but his great-niece bravely acted on every clue she'd found in Primrose Cottage to track him and Lizzy down—to bring them together—in just a matter of weeks.

Will looked across the street below at an elderly shopkeeper opening his place of business. The man couldn't be more than a few years older than he was. Funny, he didn't consider himself elderly. The woman next door made him feel twenty-one again. Blue jeans and bare feet, navy t-shirt and a hip hairstyle were only the visual attestations to his youthfulness. Damn his heart raced like it had another forty years left in it—because of her. *Baby aspirin, my ass.*

A knock on his door alerted him that the moment had arrived. This morning would be the start of everything new and wonderful. Paris was the perfect place to begin. Lizzy said she still loved him and was correct in her assumption that he still loved her. They were both too old to agonize over what could have been. Now was their opportunity and by G-d he was going to grab it lest it slip away like the last time.

He opened the door to greet the same porter who had been in the elevator the night before only this time the cart was laden with fresh fare and hot coffee. The sweet scent of flowers wafted together with the welcome aroma of French breakfast cuisine.

"*Bonjour, Monsieur,*" he greeted, wheeling the cart to the center of the room.

"Yes it is." Will signed the room service bill and gave him an easy smile along with a generous tip. The door closed, and he looked over the ordered assortment after lifting the silver lid to reveal its contents below. His eyes then traveled to his and Lizzy's adjoining door, and he lowered the dish cover then pushed the cart toward his future.

A deep breath accompanied briefly closed eyes and the little shake of trepidation to his hand when he opened the unlocked door into her dimly lit room, just barely breached by the early morning light slipping through the balcony curtains. He left the cart in his room and stepped into hers, his heart hammering.

Will nearly chuckled hearing her deep rhythmic breath, bordering on snoring. Even *that* sounded melodious, so much like her laughter.

The subtle trespass of daybreak traced her cheek as she lay on her side facing him. Still stunning, still as glorious as the sun, she seemed to have defied the decades—her timeless beauty had never faded.

He paced the perimeter of the oversized bedstead, then back, until he gave into his long repressed, audacious compulsion as though he was returned to that precious period of 1942 and she was first his.

Before he knew what he was about, he sat down beside her. She barely stirred from his weight upon the mattress. Initially his hand was hesitant as it hovered over her cheek, only to be retracted, but eventually he gave into the impulse.

His palm tenderly caressed from temple to chin, tracing the delicate angles of her face. Lizzy's skin was soft and warm, exactly as he remembered. Once imprinted upon his soul its reality felt as though he'd come home.

His mind whirled at taking these liberties, but he knew Lizzy, he knew she would have no objections to his affections, even after their harsh words to one another—even after five decades.

His thumb ran lightly along her slightly open lips, reveling in their plumpness and his recollection of their twisting impishness. Will briefly closed his eyes at the sublime feeling of their malleable softness beneath his gentle stroke. *Awaken, sleeping beauty.*

Adorned by only a narrow satin lingerie strap, her bared shoulder enticed him, his hand hesitating only seconds before boldly cupping her delicate bone structure, then sliding down her arm. *Awaken, my love.*

So lost in his emotional exploration of this woman he had loved, lost, and would die loving again, he missed noticing the smile emerging upon her lips as he continued to feel and examine her fingers splayed upon the flat plane of her tummy.

Reaching Lizzy's hand, Will thread their fingers together. His gaze traveled to that serene, angelic face of hers, supposedly slumbering in peace.

Their eyes locked. Her tender smile and the brilliance of her green orbs held him transfixed, euphoric as though anything was possible.

He smiled back, his heart filled with peace.

Dreamily Lizzy asked, "Ducky, is that you?"

He chuckled. "Yes. It's me."

"It's about damn time."

"Of course I'd come to you and, yes, I'm entirely sober now." He brushed the hair from her forehead. "I brought us breakfast."

"Hmm." She turned and languidly stretched, breaking their entwined hands. Suddenly, she pulled the covers up over her face with a hasty thrust. "Out! Get out! You can't see me like this."

He laughed and tried to pull the covers down, but her grip upon the warm linen was unrelenting. "What are you talking about, Lizzy? Put down the sheet."

"No! Come back in five minutes!"

"I've seen you in the morning before. Stop this."

"I said get out!"

Will rose from the bed, laughing until he looked at his watch and finally said, "Five minutes, starting now," and departed the room with a deep chortle.

Lizzy flew from the bed, her satin negligee twisting between her legs in her haste. She made a beeline for the bathroom and stared into the mirror at the unsightly reflection. "Oh G-d! He saw you like this!" Her recently highlighted hair was wildly disheveled and her green eyes were reddened and puffy, having cried herself to sleep the night before. Quickly, she turned on the cold faucet and washed her face, brushed her teeth, and tore a stiff bristled brush through her hair. It seemed as though she had four hands, they worked so fast.

Nearly running to the balcony, as she shoved her arms into her satin robe, she pulled open the curtains then literally dove onto the bed. After grabbing the peachy colored lipstick off her nightstand, she applied it with one hand as the other straightened the sheets around her.

He knocked. "Are you ready?"

With a last second sweep of her arm across the nightstand, Lizzy pushed all the creams, book, keepsakes, and cookies into the open drawer, quickly shutting it before speaking as nonchalantly as she could muster, "Come in."

Will opened the door and pushed the breakfast cart through with a sheepish smile. "Room service."

She giggled. "There had better be coffee on that cart."

"Would I deny you your coffee, Pistol, especially since I'm already skating on thin ice?"

He stopped his progression beside the bed and stood looking down at the image she presented—one of perfect, alluring femininity. Speechless he smiled, heart swelling with emotion. Draped in champagne-colored satin, her golden-infused brown locks complemented the fabric color and hung against that sensuous curve of her neck that he adored. Her eyes sparkled and her flushed skin glowed.

Feeling exposed and insecure, she was embarrassed by his smoldering stare and smoothed her hand across her cheek, "I know ... I'm not the beauty I was at twenty."

Will sat close to her on the bed. Directly facing her, he extended one long finger, smoothing it down her cheek. "No, you're not. You're even more breathtaking."

Lizzy's eyes filled with tears and her lip trembled.

She whispered, "I'm sorry. Please forgive me."

"I do."

He leaned toward her, his hand threading into her thick locks but he faltered, unsure of his presumption until she nodded. He felt her hand reach out to rest upon his waist, her first intimate touch. Guiding her head to him, his heart skipped a beat.

Yearning mouths captured one another in a fragile kiss of forgiveness and re-acquaintance, as sweet and innocent as their first, so very long ago, on the carousel. The familiar softness was as natural and perfect as remembered, as beautiful and transcendent as their enduring love. Romantic excitement surged as though a new love was born, yet both knew this truly was the long awaited return to a love that still burned brightly. Heavenly.

Their mouths separated and she nearly cried, "Oh G-d. I've waited so long to do that."

With foreheads pressed together, their breath commingled. "Me, too. I dream about you so often. I never stopped loving you. I tried, but I couldn't."

"That's because you knew that I'd always be yours."

She kissed him again, as the joyful tears she'd been holding back streamed down her cheeks. Her lips clung to his in a searing collision, their embrace consuming and reassuring that they had finally found one another and weren't about to let go—ever.

Will dropped lingering kisses down her damp cheek, erasing her salty droplets, to finally bury himself at her neck. She heard his murmur from upon her shoulder. "Please don't leave me again," as he deposited another searing kiss to her throbbing pulse, sending tingles down her arm.

"Never. I'll never leave you. You have my solemn vow. We have a whole life ahead of us."

He lifted his head, gazing into her eyes. "Lizzy ... I love you."

"I love you, Will."

For several exquisite minutes, they held one another in silence until she broke their intensity with a giggle. "I really could use a cup of coffee."

Will's mouth took a last quick suckle before he rose to stand beside the cart. "I brought you something special with breakfast." He lifted the lid to reveal two crepes, and resting upon them were two gardenias.

Delighted she said, "You remembered."

"I told you last night, Lizzy. I remember everything about you. I even remember how your hair smelled when I secured that very first gardenia for you." He handed her the flower and brushed a cheek with his index finger when she inhaled the sweet scent of the delicate bloom. "Will you wear it for me? Maybe at dinner tonight?"

"Is that an invitation?"

"Yes. I'll buy you a fresh one for dinner tomorrow night ... and the next night."

She tucked the flower into her hair and beamed the smile that reached into his soul as only hers ever could.

Will poured two cups, handing her one prepared just the way she had once liked it.

It surprised her when he sat in the bed with his back against the headboard, crossing his bare feet upon the mattress. She giggled that mellifluous sound. "You still have perfect feet, I see."

"And you still laugh like a little devil."

As if the most natural action in the world, he draped his arm around her shoulders and pulled her into him. A peace washed over her. Gone was the anxiety or any modicum of fear of telling him the things she had kept hidden all these years. They sat leaning against each other, drinking their coffee, connected and feeling as though they had never been separated.

"Where have you been, Will?"

"Everywhere. I traveled a lot when I came home from the war. Then after our night in '49 I waited a year, hoping for your return. Dad died a few months later and when you didn't come back to me I left Brooklyn permanently. It was really hard to live in Primrose after all the plans you and I had made. Your leaving again destroyed me."

"Oh, baby, I'm sorry. I couldn't; believe me, I wanted to come back, but I couldn't. It took everything I had in me to stay away, stay focused on the children."

He kissed her forehead when she looked up to him. "It's in the past."

"Where did you go?"

"I left for Amsterdam. I needed to find out the status of my grandfather's house, which I found occupied by a family who refused to leave. I stayed and between fighting them in the Dutch courts, I began flying dozens of still-displaced Jews to Israel on a C-47." He looked down at her reaction when her posture instantly straightened.

"We donated a C-47!"

"So I've recently found out. And, yes, it was donated to the organization I flew for."

"Wow."

"Yeah, that's what I thought, too, when my lawyer informed me."

"So how long did you stay in Holland?"

"A few years until I decided to relocate to Israel. Later in '67, I flew in the Six-Day War. I left Israel after my divorce in '77 and moved to Alaska where I still live, flying medical transport and fishing whenever I can."

"Divorce. Oh. I wasn't sure if you had married. I mean, I'm sure you ... um ... it's not like I expected you wouldn't."

He tried hard to keep a straight face when he said, "What—are you kidding? I had them coming out of the woodwork. I didn't live like the fuddy duddy you used to claim I was. I was quite the roving bachelor before and after Sandra."

A sly glance down at her astonished expression tipped her off to his teasing.

"Oh you!"

Lizzy swatted his chest then settled back down into his arm and he kissed her forehead, relishing the petal softness of her skin below his lips. "Sandra and I were happy for a short while, but it couldn't last. When I couldn't give her all of myself, she surmised that I was in love with someone else."

"I see, but ... were you happy? Is your life happy, Will?"

"Yes. My life was and is happy, only now it's *complete* and at peace."

"I feel the same way." She took a deep breath, let out a faint sigh, and finally said, "My father was forcing me to marry George Gebhardt. In fact, on the day my pregnancy was confirmed, he proposed—and, of course, I declined, but Frederick was relentless. They had even chosen a wedding date for the early spring. That's one of the reasons I took John's offer of marriage in February."

She paused, taking a deep breath before continuing. "Will, it was just as you had suspected, both Frederick and Gebhardt were members of the Nazi Party. They had plans for John, too, with a marriage to my eldest sister. They were going to take over Robertsen Aviation for the Luftwaffe in America. When the FBI got closer in their investigation, Frederick hung himself at Greystone in a secret office dedicated to his Nazi activity. Actually, I discovered the office on the day of Annette's quickening and I telephoned the FBI about four weeks later—after I moved Kitty someplace safe. The room had files about your family, confirming their arrest, deportation, and then their ... murder."

"He knew of my family?"

"Yes." She swallowed, her eyes pooling with tears. "He may have been responsible for their death. I will never forgive myself; It's my fault."

"No, baby. You can't think that way. You can't carry that guilt. It wasn't your fault." He sighed. "I'm sorry you had to experience all of it without me. I wish I had known. When I returned home from the war, my father told me of Renner's demise. Apparently, it made all the papers, but he never told me that you had turned your father in. That was extremely brave of you."

"It never made the papers because I made the contact as an anonymous tip. John helped me through it, encouraging me to do so after we were settled. We were newly married when I made the call."

Lizzy snuggled closer. "Frederick and Ingrid knew you were Jewish, and then your letters stopped coming. As the baby showed, I became more desperate. At first, I just thought the mail had been delayed, but then I feared you dead. I wrote your parents but never received word from them either. I was so ill, I could hardly keep up appearances. I would have traveled but I was so sick all the time. As it was, I had a doctor in the Bronx and it wore me out to travel uptown to see him when I did. I was afraid for the baby if I had waited longer. John had offered a solution if I found myself alone. He did so to honor you and your sacrifice."

"I don't understand why Kitty took the letters."

"I do. She was afraid I would leave her, maybe she'd be sent away—she was afraid for her life and that of the baby. She was a desperate teenager who saw John as the only viable option, one where I could take her with me. To her, your fate was uncertain, your possible return, surely not imminent."

Will's arm squeezed around her, and he let out a deep sigh. What could he say to that?

"Have you been close to Kitty all these years?"

"Yes. Her betrayal of us, and hiding the secret all this time cuts me deeply, but I have done the same to you in keeping our daughter from you. Kitty hopes for your forgiveness, too. I have a letter from her to you, explaining everything."

Forgiveness ... the damage was done long ago. He had to look forward now, not back. He'd think on it.

"Tell me about our daughter, Annette."

"She was born July 21, 1943, and is as beautiful inside as she is out. I'm so proud of the woman she has become, but even as a child, she held your genuineness, your thoughtfulness. Sometimes, I would just watch the way she cared for Henri and Danny, as though she was a little mother, and I saw your gentleness in her. It resembled the kindness you once showed to Kitty. In some ways, Annette is the best of both of us. She's a wonderful mother of three sons. You're a grandfather, Will."

"Wow, Newly made a father and a grandfather. Paris restores my family. Amazing. You named her Annette—for my mother?"

"Yes, and her middle name is Estelle, in honor of your aunt."

"And Robertsen ... the man who protected my family. I'm thankful, more than I can express, for what he did in my stead."

He placed his coffee cup down on the nightstand and turning, collected hers to place beside his. Shifting his weight, their bodies touched in places that they hadn't in a long, long time. His strong frame hovered over hers as they moved to recline slightly upon the bed pillows.

"I'm sorry for having maligned John and insulting you. Will you forgive me?" his voice quiet and remorseful.

She nodded and touched his cheek.

"Lizzy, why did you not tell me about Annette that night you came to Primrose?"

"I meant to. That's why I went to your home—that and to just see you again. I didn't mean for what happened to happen and then afterwards, I realized that in telling you about her—I would end up destroying John who had given us so much. He was so sickly and the children gave him life. It would have been all over the newspapers, and following the scandal of my father, I just couldn't bear the thought of wounding everyone, especially the children. I recognize that you would have worked something out with us, but back then, in '49—it just seemed too unrealistic to hope for."

"I guess I understand. It's not like I gave you much opportunity to discuss anything that night."

Lizzy snorted, "What was it—six seconds before you had me undressed?"

"What can I say, you were quite an alluring vision, and ... I needed you." Their eyes drank in the other. "I needed you."

"So Annette doesn't know about me?"

"No, but she's here in Paris. It's my hope that we can tell her together."

His eyes fastened on hers, a crease of consternation suddenly marring his brow. "What will I say?"

A gentle smile formed on her lips. " 'Hi duckling' is a good place to start."

"Duckling?"

"Yes, that's what John and I called her—child of Ducky. He even christened a P-47 in honor of you on her first birthday, 'Daddy's Baby Girl'."

Will adjusted the flower in her hair, securing it further in her tendrils. He smiled, gazing deeply into her eyes that remained focused on his. "I knew about that. I saw a newspaper article a couple of weeks ago. I ... um have a confession to make."

Lizzy raised an eyebrow. "Bigger than mine?"

"I started to look for you about a month before Juliana and Jack showed up on my doorstep. I had my lawyer track you down and that's how I found out about Annette—and the foundation, and I knew then, that I had to see you again."

"You know ... about the foundation ... it was how I could show the world how much I love you—through my actions, even if I couldn't be standing beside you. I have loved you more deeply every day since 1942, channeling it into the foundation."

"I did the same, Lizzy. When I visited Paris in 1980 to find out more about my grandfather and aunt, I stayed awhile to establish a school for disabled students, to turn their home into a secondary school. It was my way of honoring what you felt most passionate about. It's called The DeVries School for the Handicapped where they meet the needs of children with both physical and learning disabilities. Some students live there so they need never feel isolated."

"You did that? In honor of Kitty?"

Will blushed. "Yeah. In honor of your love and devotion to your sister. It was for you."

She bit her lip to keep from grinning at his expression of love.

His hand slid down her silky form, gliding over the curves of her shapely figure. In spite of the pooled tears in his eyes and the choked up feeling in his throat, he teased seductively. "I'm going to have to kiss you to keep you from biting that lip of yours."

"Oh Ducky, don't you know by now?—that's the reason I do it."

Their kiss began as a needy crash of lips that burned with re-ignited desire, and sustained unrelenting fervor, capturing so much more than yielding flesh—youthful love, home, and peace—all within a single kiss.

****

Jack stretched in bed, raising his arms above his head and feeling quite satisfied. He had a great night's sleep. The best he'd had in a long while, even though actual "sleeping" only consisted of about three hours. He'd been to Paris many times. He'd slept in hundreds of hotel beds, and almost every city in every country had its special unique flavor of romance and allure, but never before had travel been so fulfilling since meeting Juliana.

The sun streamed across the tiny suite, and he could smell the hopefully still warm cup of coffee beside him, obviously procured as he slumbered. His ears perked when he heard from the bathroom the shower turn off, then a not-so perfect voice singing Fleetwood Mac's "Don't Stop." Suddenly, the song he had heard played, ad infinitum back in the States, wasn't annoying him. It held a different significance for him and Juliana, one that didn't represent an optimistic political presidential campaign. No, for them it represented the hopes of his grandmother, the romantic future he hoped to continue with Juliana, and the closure for two unknown families who had waited for the return of their priceless paintings. But he had also come to learn that looking back had been integral to everyone's journey. Yesterday may have been gone but addressing it through the letters and visiting Meercrest, Primrose Cottage, and synagogue had opened his heart to love. He was now able to see how exploration of the past can shape the future. Yes, to never forget was tantamount.

He sat up in bed and bent his leg, the blanket haphazardly draping across his naked torso. His girlfriend continued to sing, and he imagined the sway of her towel-clad hips as she looked into the steam-fogged window in the bathroom, most likely using a hairbrush as a microphone.

The door opened and Juliana stood at the threshold, smiling with playful intimation. She was a seductive vision with her wet blonde locks slicked back and the perfectly sized small towel wrapped around her, barely concealing her sex. "Good morning, babe," she cooed.

"Good morning, sex goddess."

"How do you like my singing?"

"Is that what you were doing? I thought you were strangling a cat in there."

"Ha. Ha. Ha. I thought you liked the way I sing. You didn't object last night when we danced to "At Last" before bedtime."

Narrow hips sauntered flirtatiously toward him and his arousal grew harder at the sight.

"Well, Julie you were naked and I was enamored by the feel of your soft body in my arms. I wasn't concentrating on your pitch, just your willingness for me to make love to you."

She sat beside him and curled into his arms, resting her head upon his shoulder. When her hand smoothed through his chest hair, it took great restraint by him not to roll her onto her back and make love to her again.

"Are you going to say what I know you really want to say?" he asked raising an eyebrow as he looked down at her, his arm tightening around her waist. She had come so close last night, but stopped herself not allowing the words to come. He wasn't pressuring her, he just wanted her to feel comfortable in releasing the sentiment, wanted her to be reassured that he welcomed her declaration.

"I will." She drew errant circles around his nipple and watched the goose flesh appear from her tickle. "I'll say it when the time is right. I'm not going to rush it, but you know what's in my heart. I'm just afraid that I'll say it and then everything will go to shit—even if we are in a city known for love."

"And lovers." He did roll her onto her back then, the wet towel between them cooling his heated flesh. "It won't go to shit, Julie. I won't let it. I'll fight for it because we definitely have something special."

"How do you know that? How can you be so sure?"

"Because it's the manifest love of our family legacy, lifelong love that brought us together. After all these decades the love between Lizzy and Will never died, and their reunion today will finally bring them the relationship they waited for."

"But that's them. How can you be sure that our destiny is the same?"

"Because I'm an optimist and because I've never felt this way before."

Juliana whispered. "I'm afraid."

He whispered back as his lips inched closer to hers. "Don't be. Let yourself go. I got you babe, and I always will."

"Always?"

"Yes, always."

She felt the thrill of his kiss as his lips descended and his tongue plundered hers with sweet intensity. There was no mistaking his feelings for her. His emotion was evident in his gentle caress of her leg, his desire fueled by tenderness as he slowly opened the knotted towel, pressing his hot body next to hers.

Yes, she loved him and even though the words wouldn't come, by G-d she could show him.

Forty-Two

It's Been a Long, Long Time
July 15, 1992

Three families, one from Germany, another that had settled in Brazil and the third, hailing from New York congregated within a private gallery of the Louvre. These rightful dignitaries attending this auspicious ceremony comprised of children, grandchildren, nephews and other extended relations of victims of so much more than material spoliation during the Shoah. Their shared, yet unique, experiences and journeys following the war formed a tangible bond between these former strangers. All were present to witness this much-anticipated restitution of looted paintings to their rightful owners, due entirely to one woman's personal mission.

Juliana stood in the center of the room, attentive to the distinct accents and gentle laughter that reverberated within the opulent Louis XV salon. Used exclusively for special events, the walls were lavishly adorned with gilt moldings that reached upward to high frescoed ceilings framing sparkling crystal chandeliers. The palpable energy of joy within this Eighteenth Century salon was the perfect atmosphere for these masterpieces as well as the memories of those whose heavenly crowns had come for them. Smiles and handshakes abounded as media crews captured every moment for worldwide telecast on the evening news. Reporters from the Associated Press availed themselves every opportunity to interview the first generation survivors who explained how they had waited fifty years for the return of their family's plundered paintings.

The priceless works of art soon garnered Juliana's attention, individually covered by fine linen, each perched upon a simple wooden easel. Roped off from the public's curious exploration, the three masterpieces stood adjacent to the presentation podium where six chairs flanked a Lucite lectern.

Her eyes drew to Lizzy and Annette standing near the velvet-encased security ropes. Looking every inch professional, both women exuded quiet, sophisticated affluence. It was obvious to anyone observing them that they were mother and daughter, but for Juliana who acutely watched them, she could swear that Annette's resemblance to William was uncanny—or maybe not so uncanny. Anxious to compare Annette to her uncle, due to the niggling suspicion in the back of her mind, Juliana couldn't stop her not-so-subtle glances in her cousin's direction. Having arrived early with Jack to assist in the final arrangements before Lizzy and all the others, she hadn't seen the man in question or her grandfather arrive yet.

Through the crowd, her survey met Lizzy's dazzling gleam and her great-aunt smiled, her fingers unconsciously touching the gardenia pinned to her pink Chanel suit. She looked different this afternoon. Even in spite of the speech she was about to make, she looked more at peace than she had since their initial meeting on the Fourth of July. She gave Lizzy a reassuring smile, remembering Jack's initial objection to his grandmother's insistence on personally addressing the assembly. He explained how he now understood that this was the final piece to his grandmother's redemption. The secrets of the past would no longer remain concealed from the public. The guilt she carried would finally be assuaged by this last act of reparation. He further conveyed that Lizzy felt released after fifty years of retribution for acts of hatred committed by another upon a nation of people.

"Where is your grandfather?" Jack whispered into Juliana's ear, breaking her stare upon her new family members. "They want to start the ceremony but can't until they get here."

"He'll be here. Maybe he had a hard time getting my uncle to come. Grandpa said that Uncle Will doesn't know what this is about."

"So they've made up? They spoke to each other and cleared the air?"

"Yes, Grandpa didn't go into detail but he said he got his money and that was that. When he smiled and winked at me, I knew everything was okay."

"His money?"

"Inside joke about baseball."

"So we did it— we've succeeded in half of our endeavor?"

She grinned. "Yeah, *we* did it. Let's hope the next reunion goes just as well."

Jack leaned down to her ear with a naughty smirk. "Did I tell you that you look incredible?" A deep breath preceded his next compliment. "And you smell heavenly."

Tilting her head, their eyes lovingly drank in each other. "I bet you say that to all the girls."

"Only to the one I love."

He looked striking, wearing a dark blue suit and light blue tie, which matched his dancing eyes perfectly. Her heart slammed against her chest almost as thunderously as the night before when they made love for the first time. Having committed her heart and soul, this morning, she was overcome with emotion and couldn't suppress the urge to finally confirm aloud what was in her heart. "I love you, too."

He cocked his head, reading her with a quizzical brow. "Do you mean that?"

"Yes, Jack Robertsen. I love you."

Their tender smiles and sparkling eyes communicated more than those little three words.

The heartfelt exchange concluded rather abruptly as Louie and Louise entered the crowded gallery filled with a cacophony of excitement. Uncle William walked tentatively behind them, clearly unsure of what this was about. It wasn't every day that one was invited to a private salon within the Louvre.

The debonair Martel brothers were both finely attired in business suits and silk ties, though the professional image they exuded faltered slightly when Juliana's grandfather smiled his cocky grin and winked at her, before leading Louise to Marion and Henri.

The crowd seemed to disappear, no longer of interest when her uncle entered the salon. Juliana watched as his gaze instantly found Lizzy at the far end of the long room. Their eyes locked. Everyone present, even the preeminent veiled paintings, became blank canvas beside the deep, rich palette she knew to be their undying love. She was witness to their reunion.

Will smiled tenderly at Lizzy and Juliana felt herself an interloper. She could feel the tangible emotion as the fissure between them united, and it brought tears to her eyes.

He touched the gardenia pinned to his lapel; it matched Lizzy's. When her great-aunt bit her lip, he responded with a chuckle as if they had been together forever. His smile grew, as did Lizzy's. Clearly, they were sharing a private secret involving the flower adornments over their hearts.

Juliana's focus settled upon that radiant smile of his—his dimple. The same smile as Annette's and her son Adam's—the spitting image of her great-uncle. It was then that her speculation was confirmed. No one needed to tell her that Aunt Annette was Lizzy and Will's daughter. She wondered if Annette would notice the resemblance. Did she know? If not, this day was about to get even more interesting.

The assembly silenced as though they, too, could feel the electrifying energy between Pistol and Ducky but in fact, it was in response to the French Minister of Culture taking his position at the microphone. Clearing his throat, he alerted everyone to the beginning of the formal service.

"Ladies and Gentlemen, welcome to this auspicious ceremony. We would like to commence so if our participants could please take your designated seats on the podium and if our esteemed audience would please be seated, we can begin."

Will took a seat in one of the white folding chairs that faced the podium, having no idea what this "special ceremony" was about, assuming it had something to do with Lizzy's foundation. His girl had been very cryptic this morning after Annette telephoned to beg out of going jogging. After hanging up the telephone, Lizzy had settled back in his arms, resting her head against his shoulder.

"I know you dislike surprises, but I have another one for you this afternoon. Will you wear your gardenia for me?"

Now, five hours later, he was stunned to see his brother stride to the podium and hold out his hand to assist Lizzy, though Will's eyes were momentarily diverted as her long slender legs gracefully surmounted the step up. Brother and sister-in-law sat side-by-side as the other participants took seats on the opposite side of the platform. Broad smiles were captured amidst the plenitude of cameras, flashbulbs popping. Lizzy sat closest to the lectern.

As the official carefully began withdrawing the concealing drapes over each of the paintings, Annette made her way through the crowd toward the virile aviator she recognized from the photograph Jack showed her at the museum. She took the empty seat beside him as the official solemnly completed his task.

Now exposed to the appreciative attendees, three long-lost masterpieces were revealed: a Degas, a Monet, and finally, an Avercamp. She watched the stunned expression appear on the handsome face of the man seated next to her.

Annette leaned to Will's ear, whispering, "Do you know that painting? The Avercamp?"

The sound of his daughter's voice and its particular Lizzy-like effervescence reached down into his soul where familiarity infused every cell of his body at the mere resonance. No one needed to point his child out to him. No one needed to make an introduction. He knew without a shadow of doubt that this stunning woman with chestnut curls was *his* little duckling, and he fought the overwhelming urge to take her into his arms and weep.

He tried not to let his voice tremble speaking his first words to his child. "I do know it. If memory serves, my family has an almost identical one in Brooklyn. I'm shocked to see one so similar here."

"The one in Brooklyn, it was inherited by your mother, right? One for you—the other to be given to your brother."

Will furrowed his brow, his eyes searching her face, drinking in the curve of her chin, the plane of her cheek, the sparkle in her green eyes. "How do ... how do you know this?"

"Because that's your brother's painting on the easel, confiscated by the Third Reich during the Vel d'Hiv Roundups fifty years ago tomorrow."

He looked to the Avercamp again and he wiped his brow. "My G-d. How ... did ..."

"My mother Elizabeth. She's tenacious. For years, she's been trying to get the painting back to your family but the French government wouldn't part with it. I only just recently came to learn the painting's history."

Although shocked by her statement, he couldn't help wondering if Lizzy had decided to tell Annette on her own about him. He leaned toward his daughter and whispered, "Do you know who I am?"

"Yes. You're Lou's brother, William, my mother's old flame."

Which still burns bright. "I am, and you must be Annette, her daughter."

She smiled and nodded, turning in her seat to shake his hand with hers, grasping it, and squeezing slightly, unknowingly initiating an acquaintance he had dreamed of almost incessantly these last two weeks.

An impish grin formed upon her lips. "Isn't my mother beautiful? As beautiful as you remember?"

Will looked to where his glorious Lizzy sat studying the paintings, her profile stunning in the afternoon sunlight streaming into the gallery. "More radiant than I remember."

"She's single."

Will laughed lightly. *No, she's not and she never will be again.* "That's good to hear because for fifty years, I haven't stop thinking about her."

Their conversation ended when the officiating dignitary adjusted the bendable arm of the microphone and then straightened his tie. He spoke, segmented, in first French and then English about the restoration of lives and legacy and the darkness that removed these treasures from victims of the Holocaust. He spoke of France's gratitude to The Phoenix Foundation for their coordination and diligent effort in locating the descendants of the rightful owners of these masterpieces, and he briefly spoke about the horrific events that transpired here in Paris five decades earlier. However, as usual, the government fell short in its much hoped for, anticipated apology for its complicity.

Will's fist tightened and he sought the peace needed in Lizzy's expression when their eyes met. The minister said, "Today's restitution ceremony is a result of one woman's tireless dedication. I would like to introduce Mrs. Elizabeth Robertsen, Co-Founder of The Phoenix Foundation."

She rose, smoothed her skirt, then shook the official's hand. Readying to make her address, her smile spellbound Will who waited in anticipation to hear her speak. He had no idea what she was about to say. He had had no idea about the painting, accepting that it had been lost forever after never hearing from the government following his claim submission in 1980 requesting its investigation and return.

Lizzy re-adjusted the microphone. "Thank you all for attending this long overdue occasion. I also would like to thank the French government for hosting the return of the Degas and the Monet. Although stolen from German citizens in 1941, the authentic provenance of these major artworks will be rectified today here at the magnificent Louvre Museum. My deep personal appreciation goes to the Ministers of Culture and Education who worked together to facilitate the return of the Avercamp to its rightful owners after its having hung in a regional museum in Dijon for over thirty years."

Will clung to every word Lizzy spoke with her perfect poise and a professional maturity he had never known her to possess. The woman he had always loved had grown into everything he hoped that she would and he loved her more because of it.

"Personally, the process of reuniting the paintings with their families has been quite a campaign for me, one filled with deep contrition and committed recompense. It is a journey, which began in the summer of 1942, continuing throughout the years as a labor of love, and culminating in this very moment.

"As a young woman, I was inspired by a dashing Army pilot whose love, goodness, and principles taught me that true happiness is found when we think and act for others, when we believe that we can positively affect lives for the good of mankind, and pursue forgiveness at every turn for injustice. Happiness is best found when we answer the call to protect the marginalized and stand up for human rights and dignity."

She swallowed and looked to him seated beside their daughter. A tender smile formed upon her lips as she gathered her strength from that poignant image. Will's wink and buoying nod gave her stalwart courage.

"What we didn't know then was that my father was the antithesis of those beliefs. It was only after my sweetheart flyer left to fight evil in Europe that I learned that the patriarch of my family was a member of the Third Reich, an American in name only. He was the recipient of both the Degas and Monet after they were stolen from your families. Papers found within his office attested to the fact that they were given to him as gifts for his anti-American acts and he had displayed them with bombastic pride at my family estate in New York. I did not come to learn of his affiliation with the Nazis until after his heinous financing helped to murder millions—including those of that young pilot's family following the Vel d'Hiv Roundup exactly fifty years ago tomorrow. Both he and his brother are in attendance today to finally receive their family's treasured heirloom—the Avercamp.

"The Avercamp was owned by his maternal Dutch family, the DeVrieses, for five generations, as I am sure the Degas and Monet were similarly cherished by the Hermann and Lentz families. Their return to you brings me an overwhelming sense of joy—one that words cannot sufficiently define. Their restitution represents another victory over an evil that sought to annihilate not just the human spirit, but the very attestation of their existence.

"As a result of the inspiration of that young man, William Martel, coupled with my never-ending love for him, The Phoenix Foundation was created in his honor—from the ashes a people will be reborn, their legacies restored, and their courageous stories, recorded and accurately told. Every dollar of its charitable contributions and restorative projects have been financed by my late father's immense fortune and will continue to do so, until and beyond the time that his very last penny is spent. To date, the foundation has spent over a quarter of a billion dollars in reparations, an amount that is meager in comparison to the loss."

Lizzy paused, again locking eyes with Will, resisting the urge to cry but it was for naught. Tears formed and her lip trembled. This forthright admission was so difficult, but his strength became hers, his calm giving her fortitude. She straightened her shoulders and raised her chin, ready to shed the massive weight, choosing to lean on his enduring love as her support.

"I stand before you and the Martel brothers, as well as some members of my family who have kept the secrets of my father's role in the Shoah, and I ... I publicly ask for your forgiveness. I humbly beseech you to not condemn me or my family for the sins of my father and to find it in your hearts to accept The Phoenix Foundation, its volunteers, and its financing as our public acknowledgement and sincere apology."

Will's heart clenched. He had never been so moved in all his life nor ever, so proud of someone. Without pause, amidst the applause and response from press and attendees, he immediately stood tall, towering over the seated audience. He walked through the chairs and advanced to the podium. His adoring smile told all present exactly how he felt.

Reaching for Lizzy's hand, he stepped onto the podium and folded his sweetheart into his arms, holding her in a tight embrace so that everyone could see the measure of *his* love and forgiveness.

****

Will felt like a king holding Lizzy's hand with a firm grip, reveling in the reality that she was walking beside him, not in a dream or a memory, but in the flesh. On the opposite side of him his daughter, the child born out of his and Lizzy's abiding love, tucked her arm into the crook of his as they all casually strolled side-by-side. Annette squeezed into him to avoid the crush of passersby on the narrow bridge as they crossed the Seine River to the Ile de la Cite. He grinned. His girls. These were his girls and his heart was so full of emotion that he felt he could weep with abundant joy at any given moment.

It was just the three of them on this outing. The others in the Robertsen and Martel families had made excuses following the restitution ceremony. Louie stayed behind at the Louvre to make arrangements for the transfer of the Avercamp back to the States, and Juliana and Jack had a familiar gleam in their eyes—one Will knew well every time he looked at Lizzy. Her eldest son, Henri, and his wife had previously visited this outing's destination, the Memorial of the Martyrs of Deportation, having traveled the year prior on their family trip back to the Alsace in preparation for Lillian Renner's Story of Courage. There were other memorials, places they would all, as a family, visit tomorrow on the Commemorative Anniversary of the Roundup.

No, this destination was meant just for Will's immediate family.

"Tell me more about you and my mother, Will. Was she as wild as that snapshot alludes? The one of her painted on your bomber?"

"That photograph really got around didn't it?" He chuckled and looked over at Lizzy and those twisting lips of hers. She looked resplendent in the sun, back dropped by the ancient white wall and rippling waters, and he couldn't disguise the deep affection in his tone. "She stopped my heart, Annette. She had an infectious *joie de vive*, but she didn't fool me. I knew there was a serious woman in there just waiting to blossom."

"Yes ... you did, Will," Lizzy said.

"Did she tell you that she went skydiving for her seventieth birthday? Jack took her up. In the 1970s, she also took flying lessons on the q.t, but I found the pilot's manual in her handbag."

Again, Will glanced at Lizzy, admiring the schoolgirl blush that spread upon her cheeks. He made no comment to that divulged secret but it told him so much about his girl. He further delighted that their daughter was shamelessly trying to promote their renewed romance, having no idea that it had been sealed with a kiss at 6:20 that morning.

"After my father died, Mom even trained for the New York City Marathon."

Impressed, he cocked his head. "Did you do it? Did you run?"

"Yes." She beamed. "I came in 75th in my age group. Four hours and 32 minutes."

"Do you still run?"

"Only a couple of miles in the morning, nothing like a marathon. I no longer have a need for that type of running. Been there, done that."

"Now she waterskis."

Lizzy continued to blush, embarrassed that Annette would so eagerly out the latent pistol-like ways she had tried to keep concealed from almost everyone. Good humored, though, she laughed and shook her head. "Would you stop, Annette. You're going to run him off, and I've only just found him again."

"Don't bet on it, Pistol. I'm not going anywhere—ever."

"I'm hardly that pistol any longer, Ducky. I spend my days gardening and at the museum now. Although, I am looking for a partner in crime, someone to travel the world with. Would you be interested?"

The twinkle in her eyes undid him, and he continued to search her face as they walked. Annette was seemingly all but forgotten outside of the lover's stare.

"A partner ... hmm ... absolutely. I always wanted to go to Rome. Would that interest you?"

"Venice, too?"

"Without a doubt, Venice, and kiss under the Bridge of Sighs. I once made a promise that I intend on keeping."

"Oh yes, that promise in Lakeland beside the swans that mate for life. I like a man who keeps his word." Lizzy's satisfied grin teased him. "I knew you would keep it ... eventually." Yes, she wasn't going anywhere without him—G-d willing—for the next twenty or so years.

"Florida?" Annette asked. "Did you stay at Rosebriar Manor?"

Will grinned naughtily at Lizzy, and she playfully smirked before stating in typical Will fashion. "Perhaps."

At the end of the bridge, the back of Notre Dame's steeple towered in the distance. The threesome's playful banter and talk of the future dissipated into somber silence. There was a solemnity in their approach, one that was more than apprehension to walk these hallowed grounds of the memorial. Below their footsteps was the crypt-like shrine to the 200,000 people deported from Vichy France to Nazi concentration camps between 1940 and '45.

Annette separated from Lizzy and Will when they arrived at the lush green park where the memorial invited visitors to reflection within the cultivated beauty. Gray stone walls surrounded two stairwells that descended to the narrow entrance to the tomb where a sacred gallery lie hidden from view. Within, urns of ashes from each camp as well as golden crystal-lined walls symbolized the call of remembrance to the victims. A singular flickering light on the stone floor represented an unknown deportee killed at the Neustadt camp.

Lizzy searched Will's face as he watched Annette smooth her hand over the rough wall, her countenance was thoughtful. Her affect seemed to be more than one who had worked at bringing the museum on Long Island to fruition or having an adoptive brother who survived the Holocaust. Her expression was profoundly moved and troubled, and Lizzy wondered if she felt an innate connection to those memorialized here.

A squeeze of his hand brought Will from the tender regard of the elegant daughter he didn't know. "I'll go to her. Maybe we can talk below that tree on the bench there," Lizzy quietly spoke.

"Lizzy ... I'm fearful about this. What if—"

"Me, too, but Annette is unlike any woman that I know." She touched his cheek. "Her heart is as pure as yours. She's all goodness, just like her father."

"What if she doesn't want me?"

"Nonsense."

His lips tenderly pecked hers and he furrowed his brow, speaking from his heart. "I love you. I ... I didn't thank you. Thank you for her. Thank you for doing what I couldn't—for protecting her, loving her, and raising her surrounded by my faith, giving her brothers and a father who would provide her the world."

"Oh, baby, you don't have to thank me. Your love gave her—and me—life."

She kissed him more fully before leaving him standing there awaiting his girls beside the river. He watched as Lizzy approached Annette then took her hand in hers and whispered something into her ear. He swallowed hard and prayed, hoping that his daughter would know him in her heart—and accept him without condemnation to either him or her mother. Moreover, he prayed for her forgiveness toward Lizzy at keeping such a secret from her.

Together the women walked arm in arm to him, the younger of the two giving him an easy smile. His heart hammered in anxiety. He smiled back and the three of them casually strolled to the stone bench beneath one of the island's ancient linden trees.

"The two of you look as though you have the weight of the world upon your shoulders," Annette observed. "It must be this memorial. I feel it, too."

"Please sit, Annette. Will and I have something important to share with you."

"Are you marrying my mother already?"

He looked to Lizzy and smirked. He didn't need to waste days, weeks, or months mulling that decision over. "Perhaps."

A breeze blew and Lizzy could hear the rustle of leaves above. Encouraged by their energy, she reached for Will's hand, tightly clasping it. "You never asked why my romance with my flyboy came to an end?"

"Well, I just figured that was your business. You never asked how I knew about Frank's cheating. Some things we keep private."

"And some things we shouldn't and what I have to say is something I should have told you many years ago, at the very least, when your father died."

Will remained silent, watching the changing expression on Annette's face, noting similarities to his mother's when trepidation furrowed her brow.

He squeezed Lizzy's hand. "Your mother thought I was dead during the war, and I thought she didn't want to wait for me when her letters suddenly stopped. You see, someone had deliberately taken our correspondence in their attempt and success to keep us apart."

"During that same time, your grandfather was pushing me to marry one of his Nazi thugs as I waited for a letter, word ... anything. Frederick and Ingrid knew Will was Jewish and I panicked."

"Feeling alone and frightened, John Robertsen came to her aid, offering what she believed was the only choice from the dilemma and dangerous position she found herself in."

Lizzy took a deep breath before stating with a tremble to her voice. "I ... was pregnant. With you. You weren't premature—in fact, you were a little late, born just over nine months after my visit to Florida."

Annette's face froze as she absorbed her mother's shocking declaration. "What? ... What are you saying, Mother? Are you telling me that Dad wasn't my father, and that Will *is*?" She leaned away from Lizzy, seeking clarity and a damn better explanation than "you weren't premature."

"No. John was your father in almost every way, but Will is your *birth* father. He gave you life, and John saved it—both out of intense love."

Annette looked up, her eyes switching from her mother to the man standing before her. She said nothing in reply. Her expressionless face failed in concealing the tumult coursing through her.

Attempting to maintain her equanimity, she silently rose, forcing Will and Lizzy's hands to separate when she walked between them to the stone wall at the river's edge. Her mind raced as she looked out at the water. The weight of her mother's declaration felt suffocating. She felt sick to her stomach as though having lived a lie.

Her parents watched her from behind, both unsure, both tentative on how—or if—they should react—go to her or patiently wait for her readiness or, worse, censure. They looked at each other and Lizzy gave up a slight, unsure shrug, shaking her head in uncertainty. Will gave her a reassuring smile and, once again, took her hand, squeezing it.

Together, they watched as Annette raised her arm and rested her palm upon the tree trunk beside her for support. She stood still until her body expended what they assumed was a deep sigh. They hoped it was resignation when she glanced over her shoulder at them, her lips a taut line.

Finally turning to view them face to face, her expression remained impassive as she walked toward them. She took their clasped hands into hers, leading them both back to the bench.

Lizzy sat beside Annette, but Will dropped to his knees before his daughter, speaking with fear in his heart. "I know you're shocked. I was, too. I didn't know either, Annette. Otherwise, I would have come to you years ago, but please, don't be angry with your mother. It saddens me that I've missed your life, but I forgive her and, in time, I will forgive the person who separated us all those years ago. But, more importantly, I hope you can forgive as well. Lizzy loved your father and breaking his heart was the last thing she wanted to do, but in hindsight, I should have married her before I left for England. I should have married her in Lakeland." His voice cracked slightly when his emotion bubbled to the surface, eyes meeting Lizzy's tear-filled pools. "But I was too chicken."

"But ... all these years. You said you never stopped thinking of her."

"That's true. She's my soul mate."

"And in hindsight, I should have tried to go to Will's parents when I found out that I was pregnant because the love I have for him could never have been substituted. I am sure, they would have cared for us."

"But, but you loved Dad, too, enough to keep me from knowing my birth father."

"Yes, but I loved him differently, as he loved me differently. However, he deserved my fidelity and commitment. He deserved every happiness. Apart from Will, John was the best of men. He married me to protect us both, as well as your aunt Kitty, and he undeniably loved you as Will would have."

Annette reached her hand out to Will, their fingers entwining becoming one as they both held tight to the other. Her heart raced, seeing the hopeful expression in his eyes. She didn't know what to think—what to believe. Her mind felt scrambled and overwhelmed, but what she did feel was that holding his hand felt right. She looked down at their clasped hands and smiled thoughtfully. A quiet calm pervaded her spirit and a sense of coming home like she had never before experienced. She adored her deceased father, but this man made her feel content and comfortable. His very presence felt grounding. He was a rock of strength, and the way her mother clung and looked to him for support both at the restitution ceremony and now, it was clear that she thought so as well—even after five decades of separation.

She sighed. This man before her was her flesh and blood, and she scanned his handsome face—the cleft chin, the small dimple, his brown eyes, and his quiet reserve. Why hadn't she noticed the resemblance to Adam before? It was there on that photograph all along. An amused smile formed. "Earlier, Mother called you Ducky. She used to call me Duckling."

Annette looked back and forth to their matching gardenias, now limp after the long day. "You're the reason she never stopped trying to make the gardenia bushes bloom at Evermore. The Avercamp ..."

In sudden realization, she turned to look over her shoulder at the memorial. "In addition to Henri, you're the reason we were all raised with the tenets of Judaism in our family. Your faith is my faith, your family history is my family history—the reason I never felt at home sitting in a church."

Lizzy cocked her head. "Really? Is that true? You never said."

"It's why I wanted to be married at Evermore not Trinity Church. Oftentimes, I thought of converting but Frank was such a jerk about it, I never pursued it. If only you had told me."

"There were many reasons why I didn't. I was afraid of hurting everyone, but in the end I did just that. I'm so sorry." Lizzy hung her head in shame. "I'm so, so, sorry. Please forgive me, darling."

Annette's eyes welled with unshed tears at seeing a lone teardrop fall from her mother's eye. "I can't be mad at you. I want to be, but I can't because I know, truly know, that everything you have done—or not done—was out of great love and honor. Seeing the two of you together, hearing your story, it is clear that you sacrificed your own heart's desires for us kids and Dad, and for that, I can think of no greater reason to forgive you."

Mother and daughter hugged as tears streamed, the weight lifted from Lizzy's burdened heart and mind, the final piece of atonement made.

Annette released her mother from their embrace and turned to Will, once again taking his hand in both of hers. Their eyes met. "Will, I'm so happy that you've come back to my mother, and I am delighted to learn that

I am a Martel as well as a Robertsen. Very few women throughout their lives are given the opportunity to have two loving fathers pick up where the other has left off in the course of 49 years. I can think of no better birthday gift."

Will bit his lip to keep it from trembling until she hugged him.

"My dearest, darling daughter," he cried, holding her tightly against the strong rhythm of his heart.

Forty-Three

Till The End of Time
Two months later
September 18, 1992

W ill opened his eyes to the most perfect sight in the world, Lizzy lying beside him as the rising morning sun turned the horizon of San Francisco Bay shades of pink and purple. Even the image of the Golden Gate Bridge in the distance paled in comparison to her slumbering in peaceful tranquility. Long lashes kissed her tanned flesh, and he resisted the urge to do the same, afraid to wake her as he watched her in awe. Two months ago, this image was only one he imagined in his dreams, but there was no mistaking this as reality. He never felt so alive in his life.

After flying them down on the Cessna the night before, they had arrived at the Fairmont Hotel and boldly loved one another with the balcony doors wide open to the moonlit city. He laid their admiring her and chuckling how Pistol insisted on trying position number 30 from the *Kama Sutra*. Amazed that, at their age, they were able to accomplish "the deck chair," he was sure that, after looking ahead in the book, number 32 would be the death of him. Lord knows they had to skip number 15 altogether, finding themselves sprawled naked on the floor and laughing hysterically at the absurdity of him attempting a back bend. Not even at thirty would he have been able to accomplish that. But he was game to try, and that in and of itself was monumental.

She smiled in her sleep, then dreamily said, "What's so funny?"

He deposited a gentle peck to both her closed eyes before dropping a kiss to her luscious lips. "I was thinking of number 30," he murmured, smoothing the palm of his hand down her nude, soft skin. Delighting in the feel of her, there was no longer the need to call upon the memory of her curves. She was here for real in all her glory, beside him, wanting him—forever.

"Hmm, that was amazing. You were amazing." Lizzy slid closer to him, her nipples brushing against his bare chest and she could feel his growing arousal against her apex.

"Number 31?" she asked.

"You're insatiable, my love."

"What time do we have to leave today? Do you think we can reach 34 by then?"

Will laughed. "I'm not twenty-one, but glad you think I have it in me. Perhaps if we leave at noon, we might make it to number 32."

They laid feeling their pounding hearts beat against the other's chest. Will brushed her cheek with the back of his fingertips, slowly sliding them down her neck in a tender caress. So consumed by emotion, he fought the urge to cry, his heart overcome with *this* unbelievable reality.

He whispered in the shadow of her near lips. "Do you remember the first time I made love to you?"

She nodded, smoothing her fingers over his brow.

"Every time feels like that time. I loved you so much as a young man that it etched into my soul for all eternity. But the love I feel for you now, Lizzy, is so much more than even that. It's so intense that I have no words, only intense feeling. I burn for you. I yearn for you. I'm consumed by you."

He watched as a trickle of tear rolled down her cheek, then he kissed it away, savoring the saltiness comingled with the sweetness of her joy. His kisses traveled to her chin.

Rolling her to her back, Will laid upon her completely as his lips found their way to hers. Their mouths made love to one another, giving and receiving, tongues stroking and petting in unhurried devotion, not dueling in fiery zeal. Their bodies melded in oneness sharing one breath in heated desire.

She opened her legs, encouraging his long, smooth entrance, needing to show him that she felt the same way. Crying out, "Oh Will!" when, with a thrust, he seated himself fully in her womanhood, she clung to him.

Stilling above her, his body recalled and mimicked that first innocent time when his heart thunderously pounded just as it did now.

"Don't stop," she said with a tremor to her lip. "I need you so."

There were no fancy positions, no number 31, just the purity of his flesh joining to hers, becoming one.

Lizzy wrapped her legs around his waist, pulling him into her, rocking with him with each probing entrance and retreat, with each descent and thrust. He made love to her with both tenderness and fierceness, his plunges building in intense emotional power reveling in the warmth of her essence with each glide.

"I love you!" he cried with tears, his heart bursting in unison with their joint climax as they held tightly to one another, determined to never separate.

Entirely spent, Will fell atop her with labored breathing upon the bend of her neck. "Sometimes ... it feels like a dream," he said.

"I know. I still can't believe it. I never thought I'd ever get to number five let alone 31."

He laughed and kissed her throbbing pulse, his fingers threading with hers.

"When are you going to get up the nerve to ask for my hand?" she panted.

"Is that what you want—right away?"

"Yes, silly. I didn't wait this long to be Mrs. Martel, only to shag about shamelessly. What sort of message is that sending to our grandchildren?"

"Who are you kidding? You love it."

"Yes, you're right. I do."

"I'll have to think on it. You know what they say, fools rush in."

Playfully, she slapped his shoulder, rolling him to her side. "Great. I'll be 95 before you make up your mind."

Tickling fingers along her torso sent her wriggling beside him. "I just may surprise you, Pistol. You know how I love surprises."

****

Exactly fifty years had passed since Lizzy and Will had written about their love of baseball and the hope to attend a game together when the war was over. But, after their separation, she had been sure that such a day would never come to fruition; yet here she sat in Candlestick Park, home to the San Francisco Giants baseball team, feeling utterly happy. It was a beautiful afternoon and the setting sun had no effect on warming the grandstands, as it fought with the wind for dominance and victory. Just like her dream of long ago, she wore a white, long-sleeved sweater with decorative red stars upon it. Will's silver pilot wings were pinned at her shoulder.

The fans in the stadium were going crazy with enthusiasm as one of the home team's players hit a double against their long-time former New York City rival, the Los Angeles Dodgers. They were his team, but she paid no attention to the field or the exciting play happening below them. The overhead music, the requisite traditional organ, the colorful electronic scoreboard, and the roar of the crowd went virtually ignored as she focused her attention solely on the man sitting beside her at the aisle. The man she waited a lifetime for—Will.

Her heart skipped a beat as she watched him from the corner of her eye. He looked twenty-one, again, wearing that blue LA ball cap of his, the long tendrils of hair peeking out below the fabric edge, his expressive eyes sparkling with excitement as his Dodger rounded first base.

The two of them had been inseparable for the last six weeks, never leaving one another's side following Paris. She blushed, then bit her lip recalling position number 32 from the *Kama Sutra*.

"You're staring at me. Watch the game," he said, popping a peanut into his mouth then dropping the shells into the open bag at his feet.

His strong hand fascinated her. "I like staring at you. I'm making up for all those days that I couldn't do so."

Will glanced over at her and smiled, tapping the visor of the black Giants cap she wore. "What's going through that mind of yours? Victory? Cause I gotta tell ya', my boys are kicking your team's butt all over the field."

"Ha! You forget, darling. I'm an optimist, but I am having such a good time I don't care if they lose!" She laughed.

Their eyes drank one another in with small smiles playing upon their mouths until she leaned over gifting him a tender lip lock. The taste of peanut was negligible as she enjoyed the overwhelming feel of his soft lip's tender caress.

He whispered, "You're so adorable."

She smirked. "I know."

"Are you happy?"

"You know I am. Are you?"

"So much so that I feel as though I've died and gone to heaven. The Dodgers and my girl on the same day—what more can a man ask for?"

"Adam, Mitch, and Doug sitting on the other side of you."

He smiled, looking forward to spending time alone with his grandsons. "We'll have the entire World Series together." He kissed her again, unable to stop doing so. "No, Pistol, today is strictly for you and me."

Lizzy could see that across the stadium "the wave" began. Thousands of cheering fans rose in sections from their seats with arms rising in a wave above their heads then back down, as they sat. The next section followed suit in the same manner. The wave was headed their way. "Get ready," she said with a mischievous gleam in her eye, so sure of his reaction.

"No way."

"Don't be such a fuddy duddy. Get ready. Here it comes."

"I'm not doing it."

"Do it!" she laughed, grabbing his hand, pulling him up with her when the wave arrived. They rose together, their clasped hands sweeping upward in the air above them. As though two kids, they laughed raucously.

Taking in her glorious smile, Will's heart pounded. Each moment they spent together left him spellbound and in awe at how Lizzy seemed to have defied aging. Making love to her every night was as though they were young and virile again. She made him feel that way, more alive than he had felt while living over five decades, finally now able to live that last unfulfilled life.

He watched her cheering beside him, chanting "Hey batter-batter," out at the green field below, the chilled wind giving a rosy blush to her cheeks. He loved her more today than he did in '42. Reaching into the inside pocket of his leather bomber jacket draped over the arm of his seat, he removed a box of Cracker Jacks. For what felt like long minutes, he held the cardboard in his hand, toying with it as she watched the game and he watched her. He was learning to be more spontaneous, trying not to analyze everything to death. No, he wasn't about to make the same mistakes he had made over the course of his life, but couldn't help his innate habits from surfacing.

"Are you sure about spending the next couple of months in Alaska?" he asked. "You love Long Island, especially in the fall, and with Wendy's baby coming and me and the boys flying back and forth between World Series games, wherever that is ..."

She smiled sweetly, but then furrowed her brow because this was a topic they had covered two weeks ago. "Yes, I'm sure. I told you—your home is my home, and I'm excited about living someplace new as we begin again with one another. While you're away for that week, I can get acclimated to your bachelor pad. Will, this is *our* time and Evermore just wouldn't feel right."

"But Sitka is so far away."

"Don't you remember, we decided to split the year between Alaska, the kids, and travel?"

"Yes. Of course I remember. I just want to be sure that it's what you *really* want. I'd go anywhere you want to, you know, even Evermore."

"I know that. Besides, Adam already has dibs on Evermore and with Annette now living in Primrose Cottage and Juliana and Jack installed down in Park Slope, I think our options are a little limited until we can find just the right place for us."

"There's always Rosebriar Manor."

She snorted a wry laugh. "The only way I'll visit there is to put it on the market. No thank you."

Nervously, he fidgeted with the box. "Do you still want to go to Venice in the spring."

"You know I do. What's with all these questions? You're not having second thoughts about us already, are you? Sheesh. Only this morning we were talking marriage. One rival ballgame and already you're thinking of ditching me."

"God no! Don't *ever* think that! Did I not make my intentions clear this morning?" He took a deep breath, releasing it in a long stream of air. With an outstretched hand, he gave her the box. "Here, have a Cracker Jack."

"That's your answer? 'Here, have a Cracker Jack?' I love that you remembered my dream and you're such a romantic, but we're not going to find answers in a box of caramel popcorn."

"I told you, baby. I remember everything. Now open it. Let's see what prize you've won."

She chatted away, tearing into the paper and prying upon the top. "They're nothing but cheap plastic toys now, maybe a comic or word game. Nothing like when we were kids. When I was a little girl, I once found a red metal ambulance and cherished that for years."

Digging her fingers in, the popcorn contents fell out when she reached deeper in search of the treasure. Once her index and thumb pinched the booty, she beamed. "I got it!" she exclaimed, pulling it from the bottom of the box to the surface.

Will suddenly stood, dropped his program to the floor, and knelt upon it beside her just as she removed the diamond engagement ring that had sat undelivered in Primrose Cottage.

A nervous sweat broke upon his brow when Lizzy's hand flew to her mouth. "Oh my, G-d!" She squealed, her fingers trembling as they held tightly to the ring.

On the video screen above the field, their image flashed with the words "50-Year Giant & Dodger Fans." Everyone in the stadium watched as the Dodger fan removed the pretty Giant fan's manicured fingers from her mouth, clasping them in his hand.

Will took the long awaited token of his love from her and slid it onto her left ring finger.

Lizzy's tears flowed down her cheeks, her glorious grin causing others in the stadium to also shed a tear.

"I asked you once before, but this time I hope to hear your answer, just those two words—the two words from you that would be music to my ears. Will you marry me, Lizzy? Will you be Mrs. Martel till the end of life's story? Will you *finally* be my wife and make both our dreams come true?"

Choked up, she nodded, blubbering "I will! Oh G-D, I will!"

He kissed his girl in the only way he knew how: with an earth-shattering kiss that actually stopped the game on the field as the players looked up at the flashing screen that read "Congratulations!" He held Lizzy tightly, and the crowd went wild when he dipped her back in her seat, his cap falling to the floor with hers, resting one atop the other.

Emerging from their passionate embrace, their ragged breath commingled as his lips hovered over hers. Her heart burst at the image of the man she loved, looking the happiest she had ever seen him.

She panted, "Where's your horseshoe? There should have been two prizes in the box."

"I don't need a horseshoe. You're my good luck charm. You always have been—my Pistol Packin' Lizzy."

Epilogue

That's My Home
<u>September 26, 1992</u>

P utting back the pieces of Annette's life after divorce had been easy. Losing her house, not so much so. Moving in with her mother had been a short-lived comfort, and discovering a father she never knew proved to be an overwhelming joy. However, the single most shocking adjustment was Juliana's gift of Primrose Cottage and the astonishing fact that she now had four million dollars sitting in a bank. Following her parents' announcement (at yet another family barbeque) that she, Annette, was William's heir, her cousin, with an open and loving heart, stood making her own announcement.

Sitting in the rooster-décor filled kitchen of her new home, she enjoyed the birdsong outside the window while savoring a cup of coffee. The sweet fragrance of the yellow roses climbing the wooden ledge, wafted in the slight breeze further lightening her spirit with peaceful contentment and happiness. The delicate heirloom blooms were something new to enjoy in this mysterious house that continued to reveal its details and secrets every day since her arrival three weeks ago. Only yesterday she had discovered back issues from the *Brooklyn Daily Eagle* neatly tied in brown paper. Found behind a secret door in the octagonal library, the newspapers dating between 1902 and 1915 were a historian's jackpot. The top paper detailed the sinking of the Titanic, and it now lay with all the others scattered on the floor awaiting her attention for a Saturday afternoon trip through time.

Annette felt something in this house. It seemed alive and she felt acutely in tune to it as though it was speaking to her soul. At times, she imagined the former occupants, the Guggenheim newlyweds experiencing the first blush of marriage and passion. Once, she thought she heard her mother's voice in one of the bedrooms, but apart from moving day with William, her mother had never been to Primrose Cottage. Although, come to think of it, there seemed to be a special gleam in both their eyes, and to the astonishment of Adam who stood by holding boxes, his grandmother unabashedly wept upon entering the house. Will comforted her against his strong chest, whispering "It's a tender memory."

Annette even thought she saw Juliana and Jack dancing in the living room one evening when she played a record in the old Zenith. She made a mental note to ask her nephew about that. It was as though the house held the memories made within it. None of it frightened her though. Built for the sole purpose of love and lovers, it gave her hope that true romance might once again come back to this house—to her. The magic of Primrose Cottage had already touched the Guggenheims, her parents, and Juliana throughout the ninety-one years of its existence. Apparently, 300 Bradford Road was erected for that purpose alone. Briefly, she wondered what her fate in this house would be.

Annette smiled wistfully at the October issue of *Allure* before her. Dear, sweet Juliana. How proud they all were of her. She did the impossible: unknowingly divulging every secret this family concealed and uniting them all in the process. Yes, happy ever afters did happen—no matter the age or circumstance. She began to read the slick magazine open to her cousin's first article,

True Romance
By Juliana Martel

Junior editors of fashion and style are rarely given an opportunity to write an op-ed piece about romance, particularly one that was back in the day when our grandmothers rarely kissed on the first date or had sex with her dreamboat sweetheart before marriage. So, it might surprise you that I've been asked to do so by my senior editor who can smell a good story a mile away.

I never believed in love, well the kind of love we read about in romance novels, especially those bodice rippers you see in the supermarket's aisle nine beside the bread. You know the type of love I'm talking about ... the kind that shifts the earth on its axis when he steps into the room, makes your heart flutter and your palms sweat the minute he speaks your name or gazes into your eyes. The kind that makes you do silly things you never thought you'd do—like sneak onto the Central Park Carousel without paying or take pilot lessons because he simply loves to fly.

But I'm here to tell you to not give up the dream—it exists. Take it from me. I've seen this kind of love and in the process came to find it for myself. I'm sailing the adventurous seas of romance, having taken a chance with the dashing grandson of the couple who opened my eyes and his.

You see, this couple's love spanned fifty years and they weren't even together. He was a Jewish, Army Air Corps Pilot from Brooklyn and she was the debutante daughter of a Nazi party member on Long Island. It was love at first sight in 1942 and ill-fated from the beginning.

My journey to uncovering their story began with a mysterious house and a stack of letters ...

A noise pulled Annette from her focused reading, and her ears perked up listening for its location. She stilled, removed her reading glasses, and rose from the kitchen table. There it was again, a scratching in fast swipes, then a long one, sounding like fingernails against wood.

"Hello?" she called out, expecting to see a ghost traverse the entry hall before her. Such were the happenings she came to expect at Primrose Cottage.

The wooden front door was open, allowing the crisp fall weather to cool the house. Beyond the screen security door, she could see the curbside maple tree blow in the breeze, a magical wave of falling yellow and orange leaves floated away.

The noise, coming from the front porch, happened again. "Hello? Is someone there?"

She peered out the screen to see a golden retriever puppy sitting before it. He panted wanting entry, as his paw scratched the old frame. "Oh, hello," she said, opening the door, walking past her grandmother's newly installed mezuzah nailed to the threshold. With bare feet she stepped onto the porch. "Aren't you a cute little fella?"

His happy, pink tongue slobbered her hand when she squatted, reaching out to pet his head. "Where did you come from? Are you lost? Where's your owner?"

As though she had asked for his hand, he attempted to give her his paw, obviously wanting affection. From the corner of her eye she saw a man running down Bradford Road, his dog leash empty, the look on his face, panicked.

Annette stood and waved to him, calling out, "I take it this friendly pup is yours?"

The humor in her voice, obviously calmed him when he stopped running. Flashing a winsome smile and a nod, he panted breathlessly, "Doolittle ... hasn't learned the word 'stop' yet." He laughed and it carried to Annette like a thunderbolt to her heart.

Devastatingly handsome, he had her full attention as he neared the house. With each step he took up the walkway, she drank in his long legs, NYU sweatshirt, and blond locks. With her pinky, she tucked a curly tendril behind her ear. "Doolittle?" she asked.

Out of breath, he stood at the bottom of the brick porch steps. "Yes, I named him after one of the greatest Army Air Forces commanders in World War Two."

Interesting ... and drop-dead gorgeous.

"I'm sorry about him. I hope he didn't disturb you." He offered, eyes raking over her.

"No problem at all. I was just reading, and about to settle into some old newspapers I found. I'm Annette Robertsen-Martel." She reached her hand out for a shake as the puppy came to stand between the two, looking up at them.

Chilled hands met warm ones with a literal electric spark, causing them to jolt back and laugh uneasily. "Nathan Lehman. Nice to meet you."

"Are you an aviation buff?"

"In a way. I'm a professor at New York University. I teach Modern U.S. History."

She smiled, unnecessarily tucking her hair for a second time.

With wagging tail, Doolittle ran down the steps to his owner and Nathan bent to pet him. "You're killing me, little guy." He gazed up at Annette.

There was something in his eyes that made her think there was interest on his part. The stammer in his voice confirmed it.

"Thanks. We ... um ... better get back."

"Of course. Your wife is probably wondering what's happened to you."

He snorted. "I doubt it. She's enjoying my Mercedes in Vero Beach with her boyfriend."

"Ah. I have one of those, too. Not a Mercedes, but an Ex." Glancing back into the house over her shoulder, she added. "But I'm better off without him. Everything happens for a reason, maybe as previously ordained."

He hooked the leash to the dog's collar and stood, pausing thoughtfully with a smile as though wanting to say something beyond, "Well. It was really great to meet you, Annette."

Ask him! Just ask him! She took a step down, reaching out to touch his arm as he turned to walk away. "I'm new to the neighborhood and wondering ... maybe ... would you like to meet for coffee sometime. This house, and my father have interesting histories that you might find fascinating. He was a pilot of a B-26 with the 8th & 9th Air Forces and met Jimmy Doolittle in 1942."

Nathan grinned. "A Marauder Man. Wow."

She could see that he was intrigued. "He was a POW, too. My other father, the one I grew up with, built P-47 Thunderbolts during the war."

"Really! Robertsen Aviation?"

"Yes. That's us."

He tilted his head, curiously asking, "Two fathers, you say?"

"It's a long story—a good one, but long."

"Now I'm intrigued. And the house—this is the Guggenheim honeymoon cottage isn't it?"

"Yes! It's perfectly preserved. My birth father bought it from the family in 1942. How do you know of it?"

He blushed, looking down at his tennis shoes, sheepishly replying. "My great-granduncle and aunt were Isidor and Ida Straus of Macy's and A&S fame. Our families all belonged to the same temple for generations."

She couldn't help grinning at that even though the headline of the newspaper she just found read that they had perished aboard the Titanic.

"You said your last name is Martel? As in the owners of DeVries Diamond House?"

"Yes. There's a fascinating story about the history behind the business here in America."

Nathan looked her straight on, his light blue eyes filled with a sincerity that made her heart flip. "I'd love to take you out for coffee," he said. "Your father sounds like my kind of guy, but for starters, I'd like to learn *your* story first."

"Great! How about we meet at that little deli on Cortelyou Road," she said, resisting the temptation to shamelessly flirt, not sure if she even remembered how.

"Is tomorrow too soon?" he asked.

"Not at all. How's ten—for breakfast? They have great bagels and lox."

"Sounds perfect."

Nathan descended the steps and continued down the street with Doolittle leading the way in eager excitement. He stopped, turned, and waved to her.

Annette sighed and waved back, feeling quite confident that she had met her long delayed happy ever after. "Yup. I'm now convinced—It's the house. It's enchanted."

Book Club Questions for Discussion

1. Imagine you have inherited an old house from an unknown, distant relative. Would your immediate reaction be to: Call a realtor and list it, sight unseen? Make a visit? Search out information on the relative before taking action? Would the "time-capsule" condition of Primrose Cottage intrigue or dissuade you?

2. The generation that participated in WWII has been anointed, in recent decades, as the "Greatest Generation." Those who survive are, mostly, approaching their 90s. When you encounter individuals of that generation, do you ever reflect on the events and sacrifices they have experienced? Do you wonder whether you, yourself, or more recent generations would respond similarly to the choices and challenges they faced?

3. Given what we know of the historical events of WWII today, and in light of our current information "ease of access," do you find it conceivable that Lizzy could have been so naïve and sheltered within her debutante lifestyle about the world around her?

4. To your knowledge, within your own family were there any "boycotts" of manufacturers or products based on their WWII actions or affiliations? Did your family express support of one company over another based on political sympathies? Are those preferences still consciously adhered to when you make a purchase?

5. Jack believes in looking only to the future, avoiding the disturbing, painful knowledge of his family's past. Yet in order to overcome the pain from her past, Juliana seeks out her roots to explore who she is. As the novel unfolds, their positions and outlooks change. Discuss the parallels.

6. Do you think Will suffered more deeply because of Lillian and Louie's silence about Lizzy marrying? Would his pain and anger have been lessened had they told him before 1949 when he saw her after so many years?

7. Both Juliana and Jack are faced with the reality that their grandparents are pursuing romantic relationships after the deaths of their respective spouses. Can you relate to their displeasure? Their concerns?

8. In any way, can you understand Kitty's deception and theft of the letters? And could you forgive her in that knowledge.

9. Given what Lizzy faced: her father's perceived role in the arrest of Will's family, Kitty's endangerment, a pregnancy with a half-Jewish baby, and an imminent forced marriage to Gebhardt, do you feel that she made the right decision to marry John?

10. Given her obligations and society itself, did Lizzy make the right decision in 1949?

11. Discuss the rationale and subsequent ramifications behind Lizzy's silence as it pertained to Annette.

12. Forgiveness and atonement are key elements in *A Moment Forever*. Do you feel that Lizzy, Louie, and Kitty were forgiven too easily for the secrets they held? Or can you embrace, as Will eventually did, that "They couldn't go back in time, only forward."

13. How extensive were the repercussions of Will's positive influence on young Lizzy and future generations?

14. Discuss how Will's war experience enhanced his religiosity and strong feelings as opposed to his brother's experience and turning from his faith.

15. Do you believe in soul mates? That love can span the test of time and that one moment in time can last forever?

Author Note

Thank you, friends for traveling with me back to 1942 and 1992! I have thoroughly enjoyed the learning process that came with writing *A Moment Forever*. As such I have compiled a novel website featuring a chapter blog that features articles and information discovered along the way. There, each chapter has corresponding information in addition to the end notes and glossary.

Creative liberty was taken in several instances, changing names of various locations. The most important to note is the Long Island Holocaust Museum. A fictitious name with a fictitious history, the novel's museum was loosely modeled both in its locale, appearance, and in its mission after the noteworthy Holocaust Memorial and Tolerance Center of Nassau County (HMTC) located on the former Pratt Estate, Welwyn Preserve in Glen Cove, Long Island. "HMTC was the first and only Holocaust museum and education center to serve the nearly 3 million people of Long Island." *ref: museum's official website*. Please visit their website to learn more about their incredible work and mission at tearing down the walls of intolerance and injustice.

Primrose Cottage, located at the fictitious address of 300 Bradford Road in Beverley Square West, Victorian Flatbush, Brooklyn is modeled in both its historical background and architectural design after an actual historical landmark. According to the Brooklyn Historical Society the house in question still exists today. It was named the Honeymoon Cottage built in 1901 for one of the daughters of the Guggenheim family.

Both Meercrest and Greystone were visually inspired by the residences of the late Captain Joseph Raphael DeLamar. The former, an estate named Pembroke was located in Glen Cove on the Gold Coast of Long Island and has since been demolished. All that remains is Lizzy's water tower. The latter, a townhome in the Murray Hill section of New York City was sold several times after 1923 and is now the Consulate General of the Republic of Poland.

Acknowledgements

There are many people who have traveled back in time with me in the creation of *A Moment Forever*, each one blessing it with their special talent, advice, and encouragement. The most special is my husband William. You have been my rock during the two-year process in bringing this novel to publication. You are my forever love, until the end of life's story. I couldn't have done this without you.

Thank you, my BFF, Sheryl for the tedious edits from the very beginning when it was born from just a tiny prologue, a plot bunny that had so much potential one morning over coffee. But your gifts and touch upon this story are deeper, a magnificent experience that I will cherish forever. You saw me through thick and thin at a time when life had challenges that threatened to derail me and this novel. Love you, kiddo. Kristi, your talent and commitment in the editing process has made AMF a stronger novel and helped me to tell the story that I needed to without distraction to the reader. Thank you for your tireless commitment. You are a true gem and a beautiful person. In appreciation to the lovely, generous ladies who assisted with their beta edits and insight when the novel humbly began as a forum read: Estee, Kari, and Jean. A special shout out to sweet Daniela, *A Moment Forever*'s greatest cheerleader who withstood the angst and tears, and loved the journey through it all. You bring joy with you wherever you go.

No acknowledgement page could be complete without thanking my Heavenly Father for inspiring me and teaching me through this story, and for my mother and father, heaven-sent angels on earth.

Lastly, I want to sincerely thank my dear friend and publishing partner at Vanity & Pride Press, award-winning novelist Pamela Lynne for all your support and encouragement to follow my dream.

About the Author

Cat Gardiner is a born and bred New York City girl who has fallen in love with the romance of an era known as the Greatest Generation. She and her husband love to explore the 1940s home front experience as living historians, wishing for a time machine to transport them back seventy years.

"I'm inspired by those everyday young adults who changed the fate of the world, and I write about them ... taking you on a romantic journey during WWII. My historical fiction novels always begin in my beloved Big Apple and surround the reader with the sights and sounds of a generation through Pinterest boards and music playlists."

She is the author of four Jane Austen-inspired contemporary novels. However, her greatest love is writing 20th Century Historical Fiction, WWII-era Romance. *A Moment Forever* is her debut novel in that genre.

A member of National League of American Pen Women and Romance Writers of America, Cat loves pulling out her vintage frocks to attend U.S.O dances, swing clubs, and re-enactment camps as part of her research for her WWII-era novels. It is her belief that everyone should have an understanding of The Forties Experience.

facebook.com/cat.t.gardiner
vanityandpridepress.com / twitter.com/VPPressNovels
cgardiner1940s.com / twitter.com/40sexperience

Other Novels
by Cat Gardiner

Lucky 13
Denial of Conscience
Villa Fortuna
Undercover

⁂

Other Historical Fiction Novels
by Vanity & Pride Press

Dearest Friends by Pamela Lynne
Sketching Character by Pamela Lynne

83756495R00338

Made in the USA
Columbia, SC
12 December 2017